mB X good

JOHN FARRIS

SON OF THE ENDLESS NIGHT

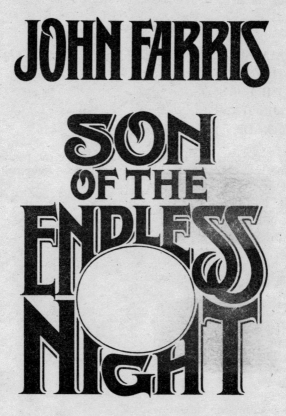

A TOM DOHERTY ASSOCIATES BOOK

SON OF THE ENDLESS NIGHT

Copyright © 1984 by John Farris

First TOR printing: April 1986

A TOR Book

Published by Tom Doherty Associates
49 West 24 Street
New York, N.Y. 10010

Cover art by John Melo

ISBN: 0-812-58266-7
CAN. ED.: 0-812-58267-5

Library of Congress Catalog Card Number: 84-22867

Printed in the United States

0 9 8 7 6 5 4 3 2 1

For my father
John Linder Farris
1909–1982
And my mother
Elinor Carter Farris
1905–1984

The spirit of evil peers from
a silver mask.

—Georg Trakl,

To the Silenced

Translated from the German
by Michael Hamburger

PART ONE

Polly

1

From the testimony of Donald Ray Stemmons before the winter grand jury, Haden County, Vermont, February 17, 1984 (*Twenty-six years of age. Occupation: part-time bartender. Winter address: 135 Barberry Lane, Sligo, Vermont. Tall. Bones sharp, like blades beneath the skin. The kind of face inevitably described as "Lincolnesque," but with an unkempt yellow beard and a complexion inflamed, made nearly ulcerous by sunflash on the great white glaring heaps and long whalebacks of the ski trails in the area. A nervous habit of stroking the end of his nose with a forefinger while being addressed by the state's attorney for Haden County*):

Mr. Cleves: What happened when you tried to open the terrace doors?

Mr. Stemmons: Nothing. Couldn't do it. Those doors're never used in the wintertime as far as I know. They were iced shut, and with the new snow, must have been three feet of drift piled up against them.

Mr. Cleves: Yet you could see, despite the snowdrifts, what was going on outside?

Mr. Stemmons: Pretty much. Had to wipe the panes with my shirtsleeve, and the others in the tavern, they were doing the same. I didn't do much looking, though, after I saw what was happening out there, and the girl screaming all the time. I just tried to force those doors apart. Finally gave up, busted one open with a barstool so I could get outside. But by that time I had a gut feeling I was probably too late to do any good.

Mr. Cleves: Why?

Mr. Stemmons: Well, the girl had stopped screaming by then. She was down again. Not moving at all. He must have hit her at least a couple of dozen times with that

3

crowbar, or tire iron I guess it was. When I got a look at her up close, so much blood on the snow I couldn't believe it. Well, she—it looked—looked like—somebody had shot and dressed a deer.

Mr. Cleves: Did you recognize the victim at that time?

Mr. Stemmons: No, sir. Nobody could've recognized her. That's how bad it was.

2

Twenty minutes south of Chadbury, with the snow having begun and daylight fading, Richard Devon played the brief tape he'd taken from his telephone answering machine.

Hi. This is Rich. I'm not in right now, but I expect to be back shortly and I do want to talk to you. When you hear the tone, please leave your name, the time you called, and a number where I can get back to you. Thanks for your cooperation. Remember now, wait for the tone before you leave your message.

The girl's voice: youthful, high-pitched, a whining sound, from strain or desperation.

Richard, it's Polly! You remember me, don't you? You told me I could call you if I ever needed anything. Well—they've been hurting me, Rich. I'm afraid they'll hurt me a lot worse if somebody doesn't stop them! You're the only one I could think of. I know I can trust you. Please come. Don't let them—

A sharp intake of breath, the click of the receiver at the other end going down. Rich's smoky, well-traveled Porsche sideslipped uneasily on a patch of hilltop glaze. He felt Karyn's warning hand on his right elbow. He glanced at her, looked at an upcoming bridge for more trouble spots, slowed down, and punched buttons on the tape deck until Polly's portion of the recording was repeated.

" . . . been hurting me . . ."

"I don't want to hear it again," Karyn said testily.

Rich ejected the tape. "What do you think?"

Karyn stretched, giving her backbone a couple of pops; it had been a long two hours from New Haven.

"What I've always thought. She's a little girl with an overactive imagination. Like those children in *The Crucible*, and . . ."

"Didn't it sound to you like she was cut off?"

" . . . and that's probably all that's the matter with her. Cut off? No."

Karyn frowned at the snow quickening from a darker sky, shuddered, pulled up the zipper of her maroon and silver down-filled jacket. The car heater had quit weeks ago. Rich finally had his Porsche, a dubious bargain, but no money for repairs.

"Getting worse out," she said. "Do you need to put the chains on?"

Rich shook his head. Karyn picked up the Fleetwood Mac cassette they'd been listening to before he surprised her with Polly, but she didn't play it again. She was troubled and still angry at his lack of timing, his insensitivity, his absorption in this problem child. For his sake she had suffered Polly once. She wouldn't do it again.

"I thought we were just going skiing."

"Chadbury's as good a place as any."

"That's bullshit, Rich." She was building up a head of steam. "When you're not straight with me it's terrible for the relationship. The truth is, you're still obsessed with that girl, and obviously you made a hit with her. So that stupid phone call is all the excuse you need—is it the first time she's called you? Since August?"

"Yes."

"I hope that's the truth."

"I'm worried about her, Karyn. And I want to get to the bottom of—"

"She's not your responsibility. Her father—"

"Keeps her locked up most of the time, and nobody does anything about it."

"Because she's—"

"Strange?"

"Weird is a better word."

"You spent time with Polly. How can you say that?"

"If you wanted to ruin my weekend, you could have left me back at school."

Rich held his tongue—no easy task for him—and watched the road, only tapping the steering wheel with the heel of one hand to indicate that he was irritated with her.

Karyn stared at him for several seconds longer, then looked deliberately away. They had left the Interstate at Braxton and taken a rural road into a more mountainous area, through hamlets deep in winter. Sky of gunmetal, a seam of light mildly pink, like a depleted vein, far to the west. They crossed a river that was plunged into the heart of winter like a tempered blade. Rich now needed head-lights and wipers. Karyn saw a grange hall, red snowplows standing beneath a bright light with a conical shield. Men in plaid mackinaws and earflap caps.

With the windshield glass becoming a mirror, she was aware of herself. Curls were the vogue again. Very nine-teenth century. Tresses. *Little Women.* She'd always been cheerfully faddish, but this wasn't a style that suited her. She felt cross about the mistake. The holiday she'd been looking forward to was off to a rotten start.

"Look, Rich—"

"I know she's half starved for attention. Oppressed by that old man of hers. She needs kindness. Friendship. But that's not all there is to it. If Polly's convinced she's in danger, I want to know why."

"You're being manipulated, Rich. Kids are *so* great at that. But what if it's something worse? She could very well be psychopathic—"

"Polly's twelve years old!"

Karyn's tone softened; she could speak with authority on this matter.

"Her age has nothing to do with it, luv. You should see some of the cases I've come across in the children's clinic at Mount Sinai. One little boy I remember tied his mother up with her panty hose while she was sleeping, then gouged holes in her with fingernail scissors. He had the sweetest brown eyes I ever saw. You couldn't turn your back on him for a second. He was ten."

Rich started to speak, smiled a little glumly, and said no more about Polly as they came within sight of the inn.

Karyn and Richard were graduate students at New Ha-ven. Karyn had decided on a career in child psychology and Rich, who had interned for a year on the *Register,* was becoming serious about journalism-as-literature; he greatly admired Halberstam and McPhee. His interest in Polly, Karyn suspected, was not totally altruistic. He sensed a story.

They had met at the beginning of their junior years, Karyn transferring from Smith after a desultory term abroad. Rich, on scholarship, was well known on campus: political, defiantly threadbare. He was a little short but nearly always on his toes, argumentative, a fast talker with quick hands batting away irrelevancies, too graceful in dialectic for his Southie accent, the spasms of coughing that marred his spiels—he'd been smoking himself to death since he was thirteen. He had street style but few manners. She liked his pale and slightly hooded eyes, the faint soft winning smile, a cynical way of biting his lip when he disagreed with you. He disagreed with Karyn often and earnestly as they became acquainted, and seemed not to know what to do about her tentative interest in him. Rich made approaches, he backed away.

Karyn had the kind of gloss that demanded attention, sass without meanness, and not much conceit. The Yalies flocked around, keeping her busy, but her attention always strayed back to Rich. She was at breakpoint with her most recent beau, bored with his rugby, his healthy hedonism, the smooth self-assured way he embraced her in bed. She craved rough edges, a relationship with something a little perilous in it.

Rich was a long time playing up to her, but when the time came he touched her boldly and with appreciation. The tense self-awareness that had always plagued her in sexual relations vanished. He was the first man she'd ever truly wanted to lie around naked with, for the sheer bumptious good-natured hell of it. Within a couple of weeks they were looking for digs to share. She weaned him from cigarettes and he taught her the art of plain speaking. She was less flighty with Rich, a quality old friends claimed to miss.

3

Chadbury was a T-shaped town, four blocks of graceful, gently sloping village green intercepting the narrow highway, or Post Road. The green was lined with churches, modest ramshackle inns, a couple of Vermont marble public buildings and some fine old Federal-style homes. The Post Road Inn overlooked the green from the crossbar of the T. It consisted of three buildings, unconnected, which dated from the late eighteenth century, several hilly acres with boxwood hedges almost as old, and a parking lot that was inadequate for the weekend ski crowd, many of whom had arrived in minibuses and campers.

"They've had a fire," Karyn said, as Rich concentrated on edging the Porsche into a narrow space between a van with dark bubble windows and a couple of snowbound boulders.

"Do I have room over there?"

"About three inches," Karyn said, rolling down the window to look out.

"Okay." Rich finished parking and turned off the engine. "What do you mean, a fire?"

"The rear wing. It's dark, and some of the top windows look boarded up."

Rich got out and Karyn followed him, sliding under the steering wheel. Snow was flying, obscuring their view of the inn. The buildings were each three stories, uneven in size, asymmetrical. The rear wing, uphill, was the largest, and had a pitched roof. It looked to Rich as if the west end of the roof had partially caved in.

"Something happened. I hope they're not overbooked."

Karyn gave him a dismal look and yanked luggage out of the back seat. Rich unclamped their skis from the rack and they trudged to the inn, skirting a Jeep that was blading the driveway down to a half-inch of hardpacked snow.

8

There were still fifteen minutes before the first seating in the dining room; the tavern at the rear of the main building was elbow-to-elbow, and a large group of ruddy drinkers in gorgeous sweaters had clustered near the log-jammed fireplace at the south end of the lobby.

"There's Benny and Elise," Karyn said, brightening for the first time in an hour. She waved a big hello to a blond girl wearing Eskimo boots and a tunic, and her boyfriend, who had long slicked-back hair and was smoking a pipe the size of a small saxophone.

"Go ahead," Rich told her. "I'll check in."

"Do you want a beer?"

"Badly," Rich said, with a grateful smile.

The assistant manager of the Post Road Inn was a plump girl who wore a single braid, thick as a ship's hawser, over one shoulder. According to the badge pinned to her yellow corduroy jumper, her name was Fran. She went quickly through the card file and pulled Rich's reservation.

"Got you right here. And you wanted number 21. On the back."

"As far away from the road as I can get."

Fran smiled. "You've been here before."

"The last week in August."

"Here you are, sir. How are you paying? Visa? Thank you, I'll just run off a copy of the charge for you."

"Looks like you have a full house."

"We're *stuffed.*"

Rich began filling out the registration blank. "When was the fire?"

"Six weeks ago. I thought the whole place would go up. But the fire department's just down the road, and half the town came running to pitch in."

"Much damage?"

"Confined to the top floor, but we can't use any of the building until repairs are made—I guess that won't be until late spring. And all the rooms smell of smoke."

"How did it start?"

"Nobody knows. Probably in the wiring. Luckily it was the middle of the afternoon, only a few people were in their rooms. Let's see, we'll have to give you the second seating for dinner, that's at eight fifteen."

"Fine. Is Mr. Windross here?"

Fran opened the door to a small office behind her. "Mr. Windross?"

She looked around at Rich. "He *was* here, about fifteen minutes ago. He may be in the kitchen. Was it something in particular you wanted to see him about?"

"Just thought I'd say hello. I'm a friend of his daughter's."

She selected a big brass key from a pigeonhole and turned with a smile. "Here you are, room 21. I didn't know Mr. Windross had a daughter."

Rich gave his lower lip a brief chewing. "Her name's Polly. She's about twelve. Blond. How long have you worked here?"

"Since the start of the winter season. Almost three months."

"And you haven't met Polly?"

Fran shook her head slightly, still smiling, but puzzled. Her manner became a little stiff, as if she suspected Rich was, for some obscure reason, putting her on.

"Mr. Windross lives alone. And he's never mentioned a daughter to me. Hope you enjoy your stay at the inn."

"So do I," Rich muttered.

Fran went to the other end of the reception counter to answer the phone and Rich turned, looking for Karyn, wishing she'd appear to give him a hand with the cumbersome ski gear. She was nowhere in sight—probably still wedging her way up to the inadequate bar in the tavern. He acknowledged greetings from a couple of acquaintances from New Haven, picked up bags, two pairs of boots and skis, awkwardly made his way up the narrow staircase to the second floor and then to his right down the dimly lighted hall to the end.

Their room had a low coffered ceiling, an uneven floor, a big featherbed that took up a third of the space, and a small private bathroom, not big enough for Karyn and himself at the same time, unless one of them was in the tub. The room was at the opposite end of the building from the tavern, so that the volume of sound from the jukebox would be received only in dull thumping waves should they wish to be asleep before midnight.

Rich dumped their gear and used the toilet, rinsed his face, raised his eyes to his image in the mirror.

He's never mentioned a daughter to me.

Rich felt a light chill across his shoulders; his mouth tightened cynically, a defensive reaction whenever he was confronted with the inexplicable or implausible. So Polly wasn't here? Then where had the frantic phone call come from? Boarding school?

". . . been hurting me, Rich . . ."

Who was hurting her, and how? Physical punishment, mental abuse?

The hurried phone call, the breathless pleading, now seemed, perhaps deliberately so, ambiguous. Nothing he could go to the police with. Still, he didn't want to believe that Karyn had her pegged correctly after all: a slightly askew twelve-year-old asimmer with prepubescent fantasies playing a not particularly nice joke on him. Emoting on the telephone. Kids played those phone games all the time. Maybe she'd had a friend listening in. The two of them falling apart from giggles after hanging up.

After giving it more thought, Rich rejected the idea that her father had placed Polly in a private school. She was simply too shy and introverted to survive in any kind of competitive environment. Also Windross had been extremely reluctant to let the girl out of his sight the couple of times Rich had persuaded him to let Polly go for an outing. As if he was afraid for her to go. Afraid of what might happen to her? Not exactly.

As if he couldn't be sure what she might do away from his watchful influence.

The lightly coiled feeling of apprehension had snuggled down at the base of Rich's neck.

He could buy only one version of the phone call: Polly had been under a severe strain and was desperate for his help. Nothing else made sense. He and Polly had formed a bond, that last week in August. She was enigmatic but not strange, as Karyn insisted. Hesitant from shyness but, when she came to know him better, talkative. Curious about him. Full of questions. Certainly not a budding witch. Only troubled—by what he never learned. And Polly was very lonely. It was this memory of her loneliness that pierced him now, gave him a renewed sense of mission. He was going to find Polly, and soon.

When Rich came out of the bath Karyn was standing in the doorway of their room holding a couple of frosty tankards of draft beer. Snow pelted the windows. Rich took an offered mug, drank deep, gave her a sudsy kiss. Karyn leaned against Rich instead of the door jamb, put her free arm around him.

"What's happening?" Rich asked her.

"Benny and Elise went to dinner. Barbra Streisand's making a movie at Mount Snow, and they had one of the chair lifts tied up most of the day. Wexler's here with that girl from *Vogue* magazine. The one who looks as if she masturbates with an icicle." Karyn pulled her eyes tight with her forefingers and pouted chillingly.

Rich laughed. "It's a whole hour until dinner. Let's take our clothes off."

"Down to the bare skin? Why should we get undressed?"

"Why do Boy Scouts rub sticks together in the woods?"

Karyn kissed him again, getting a lot of adroit body-work into the effort. Her eyes went out of focus. "I don't know if it's the snow or the beer or the damn drafty rooms they have up here or that big featherbed. I feel like I've been hostile, and I think we'd better make up."

4

With the vital closeness reinforced, their mood of intimacy lasted well past the dinner hour. They ate a lot: creamy deep-dish chicken pie, four kinds of vegetables, home-made hot breads and fruit cobblers; smiled for no reason, touched frequently. Rich talked about the glorious possi-bilities of a career in journalism ("You can write about anything. No subject is trivial. It isn't eloquence that matters as much as precision—the right thought, the right word at the right time"), his determination to break into *The New Yorker*, the almost scalding desire to be respected for his craft.

Karyn nodded, enthralled, and began to think again about marrying Rich. To hell with how her family would take the news. Plenty had already been said about the relationship, all of it negative—there was no chance her father would ever accustom himself to having a common Boston Irishman for his son-in-law. The hostilities would never cease, Rich not being the sort to accept their scorn lightly—but it was her life, God damn it; she wanted above all for it not to be dull. No one but Rich could please her body and engage her mind so well.

After dinner they were fitted into a table in the jammed tavern. Rich and Benny went at it; their social evenings together were one long argument. Benny Childs was dapper, blue-cheeked, in his second year at the Divinity School. He had his eye on a distinguished ministry at one of the affluent churches in New York City, a profitable sideline in glitzy weddings and the kinds of funerals where you needed ten cops on motorcycles to keep everything moving, and the authorship of self-help manuals for the spiritually bushwhacked (*God Wants You to Get Yours*). Rich respected Benny for his scholarship and enjoyed twigging him about his fondness for luxuries.

"My brother's knees," Rich claimed, "are permanently deformed from kneeling on concrete floors."

"Catholics have always confused physical discomfort with piety," Benny said. "Does it place you closer to God if you shave with cold water and observe Major Silences?"

"Abnegation sucks," someone said, as if proposing a debating topic.

Benny tittered. "I am never closer to Him, nor more profoundly aware of His blessings, than when I uncork a bottle of Pol Roger '71 in the company of a few close friends." He contented himself with what was left of the tepid beer in his mug and hugged the buxom Elise. "Except maybe when I am only a few joyful strokes away from—"

"Ben-jamin." Elise was stern but unblushing. And delicious in an overblown way, with slanty Siamese-blue eyes and a head plump with tight gold whorls. Lately she had begun to wear braces on her teeth, a child's full set that gave her a startling smile, like the maw of a meatgrinder. She placed her mouth close to Benny's ear and laid down the rap about his deportment among their friends, then nibbled that ear as a postscript.

Benny looked up and around with an exhalation of pure

bliss and discovered an overworked barmaid at his elbow. "Do it again," he said to her. "Whose turn is it? Mine?"

"How about blessing us with some Pol Roger '71," Karyn suggested.

"If only I could! But my last bottle left me both nearer to God and so broke I had to sell the crowns from my wisdom teeth." Benny puffed on his oversized Meerschaum pipe and focused on Rich again.

"You never have much to say about Conor. Did he ever tell you why he left the priesthood? Loss of faith?"

"I doubt it. He still practices, and all the kids are in parochial school, which is no small expense. I think it was a loss of perspective. Too much of God, not enough of the world he lived in. He had dreams, he said, of being handcuffed under water."

"All part of the psychoneuroticism of a doomed religion. I'm not saying there aren't good men to be found in the priesthood, but—"

"Excuse me," Rich said, getting up. Benny looked startled, as if he was afraid he had offended.

Karyn said, "It's his kidneys, I think."

Rich glanced at her, smiling abstractedly. "No. I saw Windross over there by the bar. I want to ask him about Polly." And he was gone before Karyn could nail him with a look of icy displeasure.

"Who's Polly?" Elise asked.

"Don't get me started."

Rich caught up to the owner-manager of the inn as he was leaving the tavern. Windross, an expatriate from the Bronx, was one of those morose-looking men who seem unweaned from their mothers even when they are past the age of fifty. He was short and wide and covered his nearly bare, oblong scalp with a few long strands of hair, which did nothing but emphasize its bareness, a babyish vulnerability.

"Excuse me, Mr. Windross?"

Windross looked warily at him, as if expecting a complaint.

"I'm Richard Devon. I was here in August."

"Glad you came back," Windross said with a cursory smile. "We must be doing something right."

"Don't you remember me? I spent some time with Polly."

Windross was jostled, and sidestepped uneasily toward the door. He peered again at Rich. He was a toothsucker, working away at some obstruction or cavity at the back of his mouth. In the yellow light of the tavern he looked seriously jaundiced and not at all delighted by Rich's presence.

"Yes, I do remember you. Polly's friend."

"How is Polly?"

Windross hunched his shoulders. "Prettier every day," he said, somehow not sounding like a proud father.

"I'd like to see her. Has she gone to bed yet?"

There was a high sheen of perspiration on the man's head. He brushed at the moisture with his fingertips, then dived into a pocket of his sagging tweed jacket for a wadded handkerchief. "No. I don't know. What I mean is, Polly's not here anymore." He made sucking noises; his hands worked to explain, as if he'd suddenly been stricken dumb.

"Not here?" Rich prompted.

Windross shook his head, and got his voice back. "This was no place for her—a young girl. No mother. I'm too busy all the time. You see how it is."

"Sure. Where is she?"

"With my sister—living in Canada."

"Oh, Canada."

"That's right. Sorry. I know she'd like to say hello. You hit it off with her real well. Polly liked you."

"She's okay, isn't she?"

"Fine. Polly's fine."

"I was sorry to hear about the fire."

"It could've been worse. Fortunately it didn't put me out of business."

"Was anyone hurt?"

"No, of course not!" Windross said indignantly. "There were only a few guests in the wing at the time. And it was mostly smoke. We had the fire out in ten minutes." He clutched at Rich's sleeve, as if begging an indulgence. He smiled heartily, but there was an odor about him, a sourness. He looked very worried despite the smile. Maybe, Rich thought, the insurance hadn't covered the damages.

Or maybe the state wanted him to put in a sprinkler system he couldn't afford. It was a short season, after all, and even the young moneyed ski crowd wasn't enough to guarantee a profit in a depressed economy.

"Listen, I don't have time to talk now. You see how busy, right? But if there's any extra little thing I can do to make your stay pleasant—" He let go of Rich's sleeve, made a fist, punched the boy's arm lightly, intimately. "How's the room? The room's comfortable?"

"Yes."

"Good." He punched again. "See you around, Rich. Nice meeting you again."

Rich made room for another couple trying to squeeze inside the tavern and watched Windross as he crossed the lobby. The man moved lamely, hipsprung, dragging his left foot a little, wearing out the leather on the inside of the expensive molded shoe he wore.

Karyn came up behind Rich, touched his shoulder. Rich jumped.

"What's the matter?"

"Nothing. I was just thinking."

"So what's the latest on Polly?" Her expression said, *Try to imagine how little I care.*

"She isn't here, he told me."

"Oh," Karyn said, and she looked down for a few moments, lips pursed. "Are you satisfied?"

Rich forced a smile. "Guess I'll have to be."

"All the smoke in there is killing my sinuses. Let's go play in the nice clean snow."

"Freeze your tookus."

"We'll thaw out in a hot tub. Do you know what I've been thinking about all evening? How nice it would be to have a baby with you. My sister told me once that she knew the exact moment when she conceived. That must be the best thing that can ever happen—to have great sex, and know at the same time you've made a baby."

"What brought this on?" Rich said, only half pretending to be alarmed.

"Just that crazy thing called love, I guess."

5

He should have slept soundly all night, deep in the four-poster featherbed with a good weight of comforter on top, hip to cozy hip with Karyn. No reason for him to wake up suddenly feeling as chilled and wet as if he'd been swimming in a frigid sea. He shuddered hard enough to disturb Karyn, who stirred and groaned. At the moment he opened his eyes something seemed to pass over the bed: shadowy, yet with weight and menace, like a low-flying bird of prey. Rich caught his breath and sat up slowly, not wanting to awaken Karyn. The chill lingered; his teeth chattered. He looked toward the windows.

There was in the room a mild draft that caused the floor-length diaphanous curtains to swell and tremble, an obscure light that stippled the ceiling with patterns of frost. Apparently the snowfall had stopped. It was quiet in the inn, except for a far-off drunken male voice trying to carry a tune. Presently the drunk gave up. Rich clenched his teeth and blotted his moist face with the edge of the sheet. He looked at his watch. It was five minutes to two. He felt an insistent pressure in his bladder he thought he should do something about. Six beers usually meant at least two trips to the bathroom during the night.

It was awkward trying to creep out of the featherbed and Karyn, disturbed once more, turned over on her left side, groping for him. With her other hand she had a good grip on Moses the Squirrel, who'd had priority as a bed companion since Karyn was ten years old. Rich barely tolerated Moses the Squirrel, whose once-opulent tail was a stub and whose body was lumpy from too many launderings. But he still had both of his white felt front teeth, and an indomitable grin.

"WheregoingRich?"

"John. Go back to sleep."

"Umm. Okay." Karyn sighed. He sat on the side of the

bed for a couple of minutes longer; when he heard her breathing slowly and deeply he got up and moved across the creaking floorboards.

Just enough light came into the room to create a small eye-catching luster on the thin band of metal that encircled one of the bedposts. The dark fluted posts were shaped like Indian clubs: narrow at the top, wider where they joined the frame. The band was almost at eye level or he wouldn't have noticed.

Rich studied it curiously. It hadn't been there when he went to bed, he was certain of that. When he touched it he found it was a chain. He traced the minute links to the circle clasp, explored further until he came to a heart-shaped locket that was just a little larger than his thumbnail.

Karyn owned nothing like it—but even as he was trying to fashion a rational explanation, a surge of delirium caused him to grip the bedpost hard with both hands. He trembled, he was weak at the knees. Never mind how it could have gotten there, *he knew what it was*.

His fingers were blundering and stiff; he needed several minutes to remove the locket from the bedpost. Karyn slumbered on obliviously beneath the comforter, breathing between parted lips, making little liquid sounds as if she were a child learning to blow spitbubbles.

Rich went into the bathroom, closed the door, relieved himself copiously, and then sat on the high rim of the tub holding the locket in his right fist. He breathed deeply but erratically, controlling first panic, then a giddy exhilaration, almost a coke high that twinkled brilliantly through the cells of his body.

The locket was fourteen-carat gold, the chain gold-filled. Together they had cost a little more than twenty-six dollars at the Cambridge Jewelry Store in Chadbury, engraving three fifty extra. A not inconsiderable sum for a guy on a limited budget, but he'd wanted to do something special to show her that someone really cared. And she had come close to tears when he gave it to her.

To my friend Polly, from Rich.

He opened the locket. His picture was there, too, crudely cut, probably with fingernail scissors, from a Polaroid snapshot. It had been Karyn's camera, he remembered. The three of them had taken a picnic lunch to a shady overlook high in the Green Mountains. Polly had asked to keep a couple of the pictures.

And defaced this one. Or so he thought, until he looked closer.

A number had been scratched, perhaps with a pin, across his face.

It didn't mean anything to Rich, not right away. He was still trying to logically assess the finding of the locket, asking all the right questions of himself.

If it wasn't there before we went to bed—and it wasn't— how did it get into the room?

—Somebody brought it into the room, walking slowly across the creaky floor, and fastened it to the bedpost, then went out again, quietly shutting the door.

Good explanation. Was I that sound asleep?

—What do you think, Devon?

I think the door was bolted when I went to bed. I think it's still bolted. Isn't that what I think?

—Go look. If the hall door is bolted on the inside, that means nobody could've opened it from the outside. And if the door didn't open, nobody walked in. Therefore you didn't find the locket. You're not sitting here wide awake on the edge of the bathtub staring at it, with your balls all shriveled up and your head starting to ache.

Rich got up, put the locket on the green glass shelf above the wash basin, ran water, doused his face. The shaking had started again.

He returned to the bedroom, checked the bolt on the door. In place. He wanted just to forget about it, dump the locket on the top of the George II dresser, and go back to bed.

But he couldn't. Polly was at the inn after all, and somehow she'd managed to let him know. And there was trouble. Trouble of such dimension he couldn't begin to conceive of it.

He only knew he had to find out where she was.

Rich dressed quietly and took his Eddie Bauer parka with him. The locket went into his wallet. He walked downstairs to the lobby.

There was a night clerk behind the reception desk, yawning through the pages of the Christmas issue of *Penthouse*. College kid, tall, with acne that rose from his shirt collar to the roots of his hair. Weren't they using sex hormones now to treat the really bad cases? The doctors around Chadbury probably still advocated plenty of soap and water and less self-abuse. The kid looked up grinning at Rich's approach, swiveled the magazine around for Rich to have a look at the centerfold, a dusky young woman with pinkish hair and slave bracelets.

"You think it's true what they do?"

"Come again?"

"If you look at one of these photographs close enough—you know, with a magnifying glass—instead of seeing tits and beaver you just see a lot of little colored dots."

"Takes all the magic out of it."

"Guy I know used to work in the printing plant where they run these off. He said they rearrange the dots, so they spell out subliminal suggestions. Like *Get horny* and *Don't you want to fuck me?* Stuff like that. You can't really see it with the naked eye, but the subconscious gets the message."

"I'll bet it does. Can you tell me where room 331 is?"

"I'm just filling in tonight, don't really know my way around the place myself. Three thirty-one? Wait a minute." He looked under the counter, pulled out a couple of floor plans, laminated in yellowed plastic. "Let's have a look. Uh-huh. Can't anybody be in that room. It's in the burned wing."

Rich chewed his lip in annoyance. "I guess Jerry gave me the wrong room number. I guess he wants to drink all the booze himself."

"What's going on? A party?"

"Yeah. Well, I don't feel much like it anyway. Not if I'm going to be on the slopes by sunup."

"Wish I had your ambition. G'night."

Rich went upstairs slowly, taking the locket from his wallet. He opened it again and looked at the number gouged into the Polaroid photo. Three thirty-one. He had thought it could only be a room number, but perhaps it meant something else. Or nothing at all.

He walked part way down the hall toward the room where Karyn slept, then stopped and just stood there, feeling out of bounds, vaguely intimidated by the shut doors on either side, as if his sleeplessness were illicit. He didn't want to go back to bed, despite the late hour; but he didn't know what else to do with himself. The tavern had long since closed for the night, no hope of getting a beer even if he had wanted one very badly. If there were any parties going on in the inn, the participants were unusually subdued.

Rich let the locket dangle and twist slowly on its chain, gathering light from the small glass tulip of the overhead fixture, dispersing it in moody flashes like a temperamental projector; charmed, he saw Polly emerge in hoarded fragments, her attitudes and self-conscious poses: she had been too pale for late summer, almost unexposed to the sun, long hair like spider's silk winding down and around her face from the force of the wind on an open hillside until it became like a woven mask with only a blue signet showing through—her flattering, enamored eye.

If there was something to investigate here, he thought, jumpy from dissatisfaction, then he was doing a piss-poor job of it.

He went back downstairs. The temporary night clerk was deep into his *Penthouse* magazine, eyes inches from the pulchritudinous photos as he absently fingered one of his terrific collection of zits. He glanced up. Rich rubbed his own jaw and tried to look as if he were in pain.

"Toothache coming on. I must have left the Demerol in my car."

Outside, the familiar vault of sky looked rigged with prehistoric points of starfire, lights focused on an immense unused stage set, the earthly fall of fresh snow; he felt himself shaping drama as he crunched along. Zero air froze the hair in his nostrils and burned his sore lips. Rich pulled up the hood of his parka and tightened the drawstrings, fumbled for his sheepskin-lined gloves. He struck off down a lighted but unshoveled walk that took him away from the parking lot and toward the burned-out wing of the inn.

There were a few muzzy lights on the property, shielded by conical tin. He saw and encountered no one. The snoring sound of a snowmobile came out of the hills beyond the inn, then faded to a waspish buzz. A tractor-trailer went whining by on the Post Road. Then it was so quiet he was startled by the sounds of his boots squelching through the granular snow cover.

Someone had backed a car close to the entrance of the
burned wing, which was fronted by a pipe-frame canopy
skeleton. The car was a long old tail fin Caddy, the
battleship of motor cars, king of the road in the late 1950s.
This one was solidly black in color but without luster, the
original finish having worn down in most places almost to
the primer coat. Rich, always interested in classic and
near-classic cars, paused to look it over. Vermont plates.
He observed the wear and tear of a quarter century of use:
pitted and rusted chrome, missing radio antenna, a jigsaw
piece of taillight gone, slovenly interior. But the snow tires
appeared to be new, judging from the depth and sharpness
of the tracks they had made in the snow. Whoever owned
the Cadillac Fleetwood apparently cared nothing for show:
but he was a careful driver. There was no evidence on the
body of the car of major miscalculations, just a few minor
pings and dents.

There was also a small wordless bumper sticker, nothing
on it but the stylized fish that symbolized the Christian
faith: ⊂⟩. This one was reflectorized.

The hood of the Cadillac was still warm from the heat of
the engine. Between the car and the entrance to the building there were numerous bootprints, male and female, in
the snow. Rich counted six different ribbed patterns. They
had arrived as a group not more than fifteen minutes ago
and had gone directly inside, not pausing to kill time on
the steps or wait for others. It had been a businesslike and
orderly procession.

One set of footprints came up from the main wing of the
inn. Whoever he was, he had a short wide foot and, Rich
judged, an impaired stride: there was a tendency to drag
his left foot.

Windross.

Rich went up to the double doors. A sign had been
posted beside them. CLOSED DUE TO FIRE. DANGER. NO TRES-
PASSING. There was a chain and a big laminated padlock
that hung open. Many panes of glass in the doors had been
replaced with crudely cut squares of plywood. The doors
weren't tightly closed. Rich walked in, making a minimum
of noise.

A battery-operated emergency light mounted on a wall
of the foyer provided a strong glare that threw his shadow

in disarray across the wide staircase. Rich's teeth were chattering again, from tension and excitement, a sense of something important about to be revealed. The building was as cold as a meat locker, but a taint of old smoke remained indelibly in the air. The wallpaper beside the stairs looked dingy, as if a black cloud had come boiling down from above. Along a hallway icicles hung from the pipe that ran beneath the ceiling, and there were huge blips and blisters of ice all over the warped pegged boards of the foyer, residue from the streaming hoses the firefighters had run up the stairs.

Rich thought he heard voices, but they were far away, no louder than bees around a hive. Coming from behind one of the closed doors on the first floor? Or were they upstairs, closer to where the fire had originated?

Rich crossed the foyer, his shadow jerking and stabbing upward into darkness; there were no emergency lights up there. He bent down and examined the soiled runner on the steps, found traces of snow from the boots of the visitors. He followed these traces a step at a time until he was nearly out of light, facing blackness, the smoke odor more distinct and irritating. Now he heard the voices a little more clearly.

They were reciting something. Men, women, men, women, then all joining in together: their words remained indistinguishable, but the voices had a kind of religious cadence that distressed him because this was no church, and there shouldn't have been anyone around at two in the morning.

Wherever they were, he knew he wouldn't be able to locate them. He was now at the top of the stairs on the second floor with the glow of the emergency light beneath him just strong enough to show the way up to the third and topmost floor. But with the windows at the ends of the hall shuttered tight, he would be blind in the dark before he'd gone more than a dozen feet in either direction.

Then the child cried out.

It was a thin wail of pain or terror that stilled the muttering voices and caused a dark-tasting liquid to heave up into Rich's throat, nearly choking him. With his nerves tingling sharply he gagged against the sleeve of his parka, then spat on the floor. He swallowed hard, straining to hear again, hear anything, shivering in the cold of the partially burned building, feeling in danger, in mortal terror himself.

There was, quite unexpectedly, a light at the far end of the hall to his left, a vivid snakelike glow in the stinking dark. As he stared, he saw it move. The crook of light seemed to float through the air two or three feet above the floor before coming to an abrupt stop.

It was not quite the worst thing he might have seen, after the voices and the outcry that had silenced the voices for now; a dangling riddled corpse or something large, hairy, and shuffling would have been worse. But it was enough to send Rich into a near-panic: he whirled and headed for the stairs, for the safety of the open air. And just as he was about to hit the stairs running, a rigid fold in the hall carpet, standing almost as high as a curb, tripped him. He did a flailing somersault and came down hard on his left shoulder, a fall that wrenched his neck and knocked most of the wind out of him.

As he lay there momentarily helpless the thing came shooting at him from out of the dark and seemed to describe a 180-degree turn in the air above his head; it landed beyond his feet with arched back and stiffened tail and a playful squall of excitement. He saw a big nondescript cat wearing a luminous night collar that had caught the meager light from below. The cat stared at him with big peridot eyes, waiting, as if it had felled an enormous mouse and was now disappointed that the sport couldn't continue.

Once, during the pandemonium of Bladderball Day, Rich had been accidentally kicked by someone in the mob of stoned ecstatic Yale students, kicked hard in the diaphragm and half paralyzed for several minutes, just barely aware of his surroundings. His friends never missed him and he was left in the rapidly emptying streets outside Phelps Gate to fend for himself. He felt almost as bad now as he had then, and there was a complication: now he was scared, scared half out of his mind as he struggled for breath.

Because he'd heard them coming. They were close, and he couldn't move.

Whoever they were, whatever they were doing in the

building at this time of night, he knew he didn't want them to find him lying there dazed from the fall and unable to explain his presence. He forced himself to his knees, and looked up.

Footsteps. The beam of a flashlight grazed the wall not far from his head. They were at the top of the third-floor stairs, starting down. But they had paused. Someone was in a state of grief verging on hysteria. Man or woman, it was difficult to tell. The others tried to calm their grief-stricken companion. The diversion gave Rich the few extra seconds he needed to recover sufficiently to get down to the first floor.

The cat shot past him when he reached the doors, sprinted off across the snow as he went outside. The door groaned when Rich opened it, but he didn't care. He knew they had to be right behind him, would see him no matter how quickly he walked away. Running was out of the question. He wanted, above all, not to be seen. But he had only a few more seconds.

There was boxwood nearby, packed with snow, a hedge about five feet high that closely bordered the building. Rich jumped from the steps into the dark space between the building and the hedge, backed up until he was snagged on ice-covered twigs. He crouched there, shuddering, facing the entrance to the building a few feet away.

Two women came out first, followed by two men. They all looked middle-aged. Slightly careworn, or saddened; otherwise nothing noteworthy about any of them. They wore dark clothing: boots, long coats, hats. Rich saw a Bible-thick book in a gloved hand, a red ribbon dangling from it, the gilt letters or symbols on the cover nearly worn away from long years of devout usage.

They all turned, waiting, a couple of them with out-stretched hands, for another to emerge.

It was Windross. He was virtually carried from the building, his left foot dragging. Perhaps he could no longer walk unaided. From his expression he looked as if he'd been cruelly tortured. He coughed and wept in spasms. A third woman, dramatically taller than the others, spoke urgently to Windross but in a voice pitched so low Rich couldn't overhear much of what she said. There was something about not giving in, no matter what he, Windross, saw. About strength of purpose, and the value of endurance, of repetition. The woman had widely spaced and intensely dark eyes and a fascinating scar low across one cheek that seemed to underscore an attitude of command.

". . . bring him with us," she was saying to her companion, a large stoop-shouldered man who supported the distraught Windross.

"I want Polly!" Windross screamed, fighting the hands that held him.

The dark-eyed woman spoke to him again, her mouth next to his ear, her eyes staring off into the darkness. The others waited, watching, faces seriously uniform; before each face condensing breath hung, mysteriously alight, forms cloudlike yet palpable, as if their souls had been let out for an airing.

After half a minute of listening to her Windross moaned suddenly and seemed to fall into a faint, his head lolling. The woman straightened and studied him, betraying neither compassion nor annoyance; then she glanced at the stoop-shouldered man and indicated the Cadillac with a motion of her head.

Others assisted and they carried Windross away. The dark-eyed woman stayed behind, rooted, not watching, lifting her own face slowly to the stars; she sighed and in that moment seemed vulnerable, sorely tried.

Rich couldn't take his eyes off her, and perhaps that was a mistake. She must have sensed his scrutiny. Her head snapped down and for several moments she stared right at him.

The motor of the Cadillac rumbled and the exhaust belched. Rich, his hindquarters already freezing, turned to a lump of ice inside the parka, even though he couldn't be sure the woman was able to distinguish anything at all there in the dark behind the hedge. Someone called to her; she glanced away but didn't move. *She knew.* But apparently she couldn't decide what to do about Rich. They waited together, in suspense.

Snow tires spun, slewed, found purchase. Another call, insistent.

"*Inez.*"

She made up her mind then; and without another look at the place where he had attempted to hide she went down the steps in a girlish hurry, popped into the front seat beside the slumping Windross, and was driven away.

Rich waited two minutes, then rose slowly with a gloved hand clamped to his wry neck. He grimaced at the pain, pushed his way out from behind the hedge. The Cadillac was not in sight.

Silence was a blessing; stars shown with the timid luster of banished gods. He scooped a handful of snow for his dry mouth. Liquefying, it burned his tongue but tasted wonderful. He looked up at the doors of the closed building and, dreading the night and the impulse that had brought him up here in the first place, knew he must go back inside.

6

Karyn woke up coverless in their bed, shivering.

One of the windows in the room had been raised; the shutters stood wide open. Cold air poured in and the thin curtains billowed.

She slid off the bed naked and went sleepily to the window, teeth chattering. The window wouldn't budge when she tried to close it. Frozen in place, she thought. But who had opened it, and where was Rich?

The icy wind wrapped yards and yards of the voluminous curtains around her; she was all goosebumps and the material clung to her roughened skin as if it were highly charged; fine hair on the back of her neck and along her backbone sizzled. She gave up struggling with the window and concentrated on freeing herself. But she couldn't move her hands quickly enough inside the developing cocoon. She plucked and fretted but she was in a daze, her head hot and bothered; the material had little density but seemed to be in humming motion, vibrating at a frequency like that of a bee's wings. Karyn's futile efforts to free herself were exhausting. She just couldn't wake up and make the few decisive strokes necessary to break out.

A light, somewhere. Flashing distantly, isolated, but with a sense of something enormous behind it, weight and momentum like an oncoming train. The felt momentum set her heart to pounding. The curtains had slumped across her nose and mouth, almost sealing them. Her arms were pinned against her breasts, her bare legs were bound together. She needed to pee. Urgently.

"Help," she said meekly, feeling ridiculous in this situation.

The light was coming closer, swaying in air, throwing off rings of color that moved with the liquid blurred speed of circular saws spinning in opposite directions, cutting away the dark. Somebody was there, behind the light, and she was bare-assed, on view to unknown eyes.

"G-get me out of—"

It was the flame of a candle upheld in an old pewter holder. The flame illuminated in trembling light the inclined head of the blond child, who wore a flannel nightgown in a faded peach color. Her narrow blue-veined feet were bare. She walked on the balls of her feet, pickily, like a goat. She had pulled her hair starkly away from her face, which as it was wrenched from darkness looked spoiled by trouble.

"Polly!"

To Karyn's dismay urine dribbled between her closed thighs. She groaned.

Polly was amused. She extended the candle almost to arm's length to see Karyn better. Polly's eyes were wide, although most of the topaz blue had faded from them, leaving thin ice. She moved again, sideways, fairly dancing from excitement. Then she stood on tiptoe, rising to Karyn's height. Woman to woman. There were two small flaming spots on her cheekbones. The irregular edges of her teeth gleamed between parted arched lips.

It was a rapacious mouth she exhibited, and Karyn's skin tightened barrenly as if from the contraction of scar tissue.

"Polly, be c-careful with—"

"Rich wants to be with me," the girl said.

Her voice sounded thin and remote, but that might have been due to the faintness Karyn was experiencing as blood drained from her head toward her groin. She was suffocating in the clinging curtains, couldn't feel the floor with her feet. And the cocoon was becoming opaque, filling with a cloudlike whiteness.

"Please help me!"

Polly danced again, sidestepped trippingly, the candle waggling closer to Karyn's beclouded face. She sang, wordlessly, under her breath. "La-la, la-la, la-la!" Then she stopped and gave her tied-back hair a toss and said with smug good cheer, "Rich is coming."

"Oh God *yes* where is he?"

"He's going to play with my mouse."

Karyn bit her lip in a frenzy; she was finding it more difficult to draw a sustaining breath. The candle flame seemed only an inch away from the highly flammable curtain.

"P-play with—" She had bit her lip more severely than she thought; she tasted blood, and a fine mist of it sprayed the curtain over her mouth. "I d-don't know what you—" Her own blood on her tongue, naked humiliation, the girl's smirking antics and side glances, unexpectedly aroused Karyn.

"You hateful little bitch! Put that candle down and help me get out of here right now!"

Polly was taken aback; she stiffened, and her tongue pecked uncertainly at the corners of her mouth. Then she recovered and smiled slowly, condescendingly.

Just as slowly, with her free hand, she began to raise her nightgown, gathering it in folds until she had lifted it to the level of her ribcage, exposing her naiad's lucent belly and a jotting of floss over the flagrant pubes.

"This is my mouse," she said slyly.

Karyn simply stared through the thickening cocoon, feeling faint with disgust and fear.

"Do you want to see something else?"

Polly's face looked spoiled again, darkly sinful, her hot little mouth working ecstatically. With a grand gesture she jerked the nightgown above her pretty virginal breasts, which trembled like pale fruit on a bough. But it wasn't her breasts she was showing off.

Just below the breastbone, centered between the shapely nippled mounds, was a ballooning membrane. It pulsed ominously, glowing like a live coal, and betrayed life within its opaque skin. Karyn had a glimpse of something coiled and resting, like an unborn serpent. But feathery, with sharp angles, spurs, tiny hideous eyes that fastened savagely on Karyn.

"Rich will be with me!" the girl said, her downcast eyes worshipful. The glow from the distressing membrane flushed balefully across her face. *"Forever."*

Karyn shrieked.

Polly let the hem of the nightgown fall to her feet. To Karyn's failing eyes and assaulted consciousness she seemed less substantial, a glowing image in a mist. But the candle flame stood inches high and steady as a blade. The stench of melted candlewax filled Karyn's nostrils.

Polly curtsied, her head bowing almost to the floor. Then she arose and there was no expression in her face as, almost imperceptibly, she advanced the candle toward Karyn's body. A small blackrimmed hole opened in the material. Terrified, Karyn threw herself back toward the open window. She felt the curtains rip and tear free of the rod. But she wasn't in time; the icy draft from the window sucked at the candle flame and turned it into an explosion: she was hurled like an incendiary moth through the window space into blackness.

7

In the burned wing of the inn Rich found his way blocked by temporary walls of unpainted, three-quarter-inch plywood at the top of the third-floor stairs. Workmen had installed a door in each wall and equipped them with stout hasps and padlocks.

If anyone was behind either of the doors, he or she was securely locked in and probably even colder than he was.

He thumped the walls a few times, hearing dismal echoes, and called to her.

"Polly! It's Rich!"

Until a coughing fit overcame him he listened intently,

unsure of how well his voice would carry. He could see almost nothing. The emergency light in the foyer cast only a faint outer-planet glow at this level. No lights, no heat. If Polly *was* up here she couldn't make it through the night. *I want Polly!* Windross had pleaded, but in retrospect it wasn't possible to interpret his plea. Did it mean they had left her behind? Surely her own father wouldn't permit Polly to spend even five minutes alone in a place like this: dark, reeking, dangerous.

But there was the fact of the locket, and the cat. He'd had only a couple of glimpses, but Rich was certain the cat was Katrinka, Polly's pet. The big head, the stubby body were familiar. If Katrinka was here, then—but undoubtedly the cat had the run of the inn; she might have followed Windross here to this rendezvous with his strange consortium.

No matter what the story, Rich felt he wasn't going to learn any more tonight. His head and neck hurt. Time to go back to bed, lie there sleepless until he decided what to do next.

He trudged back to the main wing of the inn. The night clerk was away from the desk, the lobby deserted. Rich went upstairs and let himself into his and Karyn's room.

The bed was empty, the covers in a wild tangle on the floor. He thought he smelled smoke, but it might have been just an olfactory illusion; he had breathed deeply of cold clean air on his way back but still felt polluted by the atmosphere of the burned-out wing.

"Karyn?"

No reply. Rich pulled off his gloves and parka, tossed them in a chair—she would fuss about that in the morning, he knew—picked up and straightened the comforter and top sheet on the bed. The radiator hissed. The bathroom door was closed. Karyn was taking a long time in there. He went to the door and rapped softly.

He heard her inside, breathing in a rasping, last-ditch sort of way. Thoroughly alarmed, he shouldered the door open.

Karyn was huddled naked on the floor beside the tub. She had Moses the Squirrel clenched tightly in one hand. There was a stink of vomit. Some of her regurgitated dinner had caked on her bare legs and feet. She looked up at him with a sagging jaw, eyes like stones in aspic.

"What's the matter?" he said stupidly. "Are you sick?"

"Help," Karyn pleaded, trying listlessly to rise. She fell back down with a moan, an elbow ringing against the tub. Rich sponged her off hastily, picked her up, and carried her to the bed. She was cold and flaccid. Her lower lip looked bitten; it was flecked with blood. She moaned again. He tucked her in and chafed her hands and wrists.

"Rich. Where were you? Why did you leave me?"

"I went for a walk. Christ's sake, what happened? Did somebody get in the room? Did he—"

Karyn shook her head emphatically. A strange light came into her eyes; she laughed in a way that shocked him, broke it off gagging. But there was nothing left in her stomach; only a little yellow froth came to her lips. She looked at him again, eyes rolling pathetically.

"There was nobody. Nobody like you mean. I want to go home. Now. I can't stay here anymore." Karyn lunged up suddenly, locking arms around him. She began to cry. Her breath was bad from vomiting. She shook and sobbed, pulling Rich down on top of her, using him as a shield.

"Awful—*awful*."

"Karyn, what is it?"

"I burned. I burned."

"What are you talking about?"

"I woke up. The window was open. I got out of bed to close it. The curtains began to wrap around me. Around and around until—I couldn't move. Then—they caught fire. I burned, it was *horrible*."

Rich glanced at the windows. Both were closed, the curtains smoothly in place. He cradled Karyn, stroking her calmingly.

"Nothing but a bad dream, one of those—"

"No! It was real, *happening* to me! I know the difference, I know when I'm having a nightmare!"

"You're not burned. There's nothing wrong with you except you got scared and puked."

"Yes, I'm scared. I'm terrified! I want you to get me out of here. Promise, Rich, *promise!*"

"There's nothing to be afraid of. It was just your mother again."

She'd had these dreams before, since childhood. When Karyn was seven her mother had been burned in a kitchen accident, literally going up in flames before the eyes of the petrified child. Quick action by the Vale family houseman had minimized the damage, and subsequent scarring, but the trauma still lay deep in Karyn's psyche.

"No! It was nothing *like* those dreams." She fought him then; irrationally, bitterly. "Go away! You're no help. You don't understand."

"Just explain—"

"I can't explain. But it was real. All of it."

"You were wrapped in those curtains? Listen, Kare, the comforter was on the floor when I came in, you must have got tangled up while you were sleeping and fell off the bed."

Karyn didn't answer him. Her tears dried up. "I feel like I want to barf again. But nothing comes up. Could I have a drink of water? And bring me Moses."

Rich brought her a glass of water, icy from the tap, and the toy squirrel, which he held disdainfully by the stub of its tail. He returned to the bathroom. She'd left a mess in the tub. It nauseated him, cleaning up after someone who had been sick, but there was no one else to do it. He held his breath, rinsed, and swabbed.

When he looked in on Karyn again, she'd pulled on a nightshirt and was so still he hoped she'd fallen asleep. He undressed and crept into bed beside her.

"Rich?"

"Uh-huh."

"I hate this fucking place. I hate you for bringing me back."

He'd had enough for one night, so he snapped, "You're being childish."

She turned her back to him. "If you won't take me home, I'll take the bus."

"It's three A.M."

"Something bad's going to happen, Rich. I feel it. I didn't tell you everything."

She sounded so forlorn he snuggled close to her, re-arranging the flannel nightshirt, uncovering her below the waist. His penis stiffened a little between soft yielding cheeks. He placed a finger down there beside it, feeling the long narrow stroke of hair that grew from the tip of her backbone to the opening of the vulva, like a chastely tucked-in tail interrupted only by the tense eyelet of her anus. He rubbed her gently there with the hardened glans, not really capable of making love again, knowing she didn't want to either; but Karyn didn't resist him. He kissed a brown mole on her shoulder blade.

"Tell me now."

"No. I can't. I don't think I can tell anybody *ever*."

He put an arm around her waist. "Okay like this?"

She sniffed. "Yes."

He moved his hand up between her breasts, and found Moses the Squirrel.

"I love you, Karyn. Whatever happened, I'm sorry."

"I'm sorry I said I hate you. But I went through *hell*, Rich. That's the only way to describe it."

"Okay, okay, it's over. I'm here. Try to go to sleep now."

It was twenty minutes or more before the tension began to leave her body. When she slept at last she slept badly, jerking, calling for her father, elbows prodding Rich. He got up once and went to the windows, where a thin draft of cold air came through the shutters. There was a damp spot at the edge of the carpet. He touched it with a finger, sniffed. It was urine. He looked carefully at the curtains. Except for a small round hole someone must have burned there with a carelessly held cigarette, he discovered nothing. But Karyn's panic had left him wide awake. He could still smell the vomit he'd cleaned up. He wanted a cigarette badly.

At four thirty he dressed again, went downstairs, found a machine, bought a pack of Kents, and sat smoking with a sense of greed and guilt in a solitary corner of the lobby, listening to a cabinet clock tick and chime, thinking, his mind exploring dead ends and implausibilities until it became light enough to see the spires along the Chadbury green emerge and glow pinkly in the winter's dawn.

8

Karyn was up and dressed for the slopes when he returned to their room.

"I don't want to have breakfast here," she said, recoiling slightly from his kiss. Her lower lip looked swollen; there was a spot of dried blood she hadn't been able to wash off.

"I'm back on the straight weed," he admitted.

She grimaced in disapproval but didn't say anything. They drove to Hermitage Mountain as the sun rose above the black glistening treeline along the road, ate sparingly on a glass-enclosed terrace of the Davos Chalet Lodge at the base of the mountain, only a hundred yards from the major ski lifts.

Rich's cigarette hack had returned and he could barely turn his head. A big dose of aspirin diminished the pain, allowing for improved mobility. Still, he had a problem. Karyn had been skiing almost since she could walk and had tackled expert trails all over the country. Rich had worked at the sport for most of his college years and felt competent, but he only managed to keep up with Karyn when she took pity on him. With his neck in poor shape he was afraid of winding up in traction before the day was over. He explained his problem and they compromised on a couple of reasonably difficult intermediate slopes on the lower mountain.

Some of his soreness disappeared with strenuous exercise and the sweat he worked up, and by late morning Rich was feeling better. The day was cloudless, the temperature rose to twenty degrees. Karyn still was in no mood for conversation as she tried to get the most out of trails that were basically child's play for her.

By the time they took a break at the snack bar outside the ski shop the area was saturated; the wait for each of the chair lifts was nearly half an hour. While Rich stood in line for hot chocolate Karyn chatted with a couple of former classmates from Brearly, and came back to him looking as if she'd shaken off the effects of her recent nightmare.

"Tam and Brooksie said we might be able to get a room here! Some of the crowd they were coming up with canceled at the last minute."

"You want to stay here?"

"*Yes.* Anywhere but the inn. Please, Rich, see what you can do."

Rich learned that the management of the Davos Chalet had covered an overbooking problem with the rooms allotted to the no-shows. The reservations clerk hinted that something might be found for them tomorrow if he'd check back later in the day. Rich was a little thin in the wallet and didn't feel like parting with another twenty bucks to ensure the clerk's cooperation. They had a perfectly good room already; he couldn't see the sense in catering to Karyn's newly developed aversion to the Post Road Inn.

When he returned to the ski area Karyn was, as usual, with a group. One of them stood as tall as Frankenstein in his blocky ski boots, but the blueprints had been better for this kid: he had a broad flawless good-humored face with the frosty radiance of a new penny, flaring to red along the taut bonelines. Women were staring at him. Karyn had an arm fondly linked with his, and seemed amused by everything he had to say. Rich was pleased to see the dragonfly quickness and beauty of her eyes and was jealous that someone else had effected this restoration of her soaring spirits.

"Everybody, this is Rich. Rich, that's Popper and that's Jerrill and that's Kristy. And this big guy here is Trux Landall."

"Hiya."

"Hiya."

Rich sipped his cooling chocolate and followed the gossipy conversation without contributing to it until Karyn's friends went off looking for new mountains to conquer.

"You didn't have much to say," Karyn chided him.

"I'm not from Preppie Land. I don't know the code words. *Trucks?*"

"T,R,U,X, Trux. I dated him when I was a freshman at Smith."

"And he was on leave of absence from the right hand of Zeus."

"Amherst '82."

"Was it serious?" Rich asked idly.

"I thought I was in love."

"I don't blame you. He's a hunk. What does he do now?"

"Harvard Law."

"Brainy too."

"Don't be snide. And don't be defensive. He's not competition."

"That's what you think. His kind has always been competition for me." He was dressed like they were. He had a good haircut. But he gave off the wrong emanations. They all knew each other, blindly, like ants from the same nest.

"Oh, here we go. Amazing that you didn't say anything about street riots with the blacks or your police record for breaking into parking meters."

"I was only thirteen, they gave me probation. And my brother beat the flaming Jesus out of me. You know what I'm talking about."

"I know you get that withdrawn resentful look whenever you're around someone like Trux."

"And Bates and Kyle and Justin. They'll never have to play their way into the big leagues." A term his old Irish grandmother had used, scathingly, came to his lips. "Hoipoloi." He relished it silently. *Hoi-poloi*. Maybe he could corner the T-shirt concession.

"You don't loaf through Harvard Law. When Trux was seventeen he sailed six thousand miles on a fifty-six-foot ketch with his uncle. They placed fifth in some kind of ocean-to-ocean race. Trux was washed overboard twice, once by a fifty-foot wave. Of course he was wearing a safety harness. Have you ever seen a fifty-foot wave?"

"I don't swim and I don't sail. I get queasy when the shower doesn't drain fast enough."

"Trux has broken a few bones free-soloing. He has this scar running up the back of one thigh—"

"How far up?"

"Never mind. He's someone you might like to know, if you'd give him half a chance. You're afflicted with reverse snobbery."

" 'Afflicted'?" The word made him feel curiously diseased, a dread pariah. "I need a smoke," Rich muttered, looking around for a place to buy a pack of Kents. But the queue at the snack stand was long.

"Did we get a room?" Karyn asked him.

"Uh, no. Maybe tomorrow; that is if I want to bribe—"

"Rich, I am not staying at the inn again tonight!" She almost stamped her foot, but she was wearing ski boots. He had another, rare glimpse of the prima donna she must have been around the age of twelve. He was perversely infatuated; he wanted to kick her butt.

"What is it about the place that—look, just because you had a bad—"

"Dream. No it wasn't! I told you that! Why do you have to fight with me? Why can't you just say, 'Yes, Karyn, I *know* you're upset, *yes* I'll try to help you, we'll stay somewhere else tonight.' " She subsided dispiritedly, touched her swollen lip, looking aggrieved and angry.

Rich put a hand on her shoulder and she twisted from under it, retaliated with an ungentle open-handed shove that put some distance between them. Her head went down; her eyes were lost in deep shadow as if she were wearing a domino mask. Rich fretted and stopped thinking momentarily.

"Karyn, I want to show you something."

He screwed his Styrofoam cup of chocolate into the snow, unzipped a jacket pocket, and took out the locket and gold chain. He held it in the palm of his hand. Karyn glanced at it, then looked rigidly away, staring at the undulating shadows of the chair lift moving up the mountain.

"Do you know what it is?"

He thought she wasn't going to answer him. His fingers, ungloved, had turned lumpish and were smoldering from the cold. He was awkward trying to prize the locket open so that he could show Karyn the numbers scratched across his face. Light from the gleaming surface was reflected streakily to Karyn's cheek, the orbit of an eye. Unmasked, her pupils dark and delectably hot in the surfeit of light and space around them, she flinched and said in a low voice, "I know. Put it away."

"It's the locket I gave Polly in August. I found it in our room last night." Something jumped in Karyn's cheek, a dimple appeared like a shuddering question mark, which only encouraged his enthusiasm for the mystery. "I don't know how it got there, but I think she's trying to tell me—Kare, I'm convinced they're keeping her prisoner in—"

He was unprepared for the swift change in Karyn's mood. With a long belligerent backhand she swatted the locket from his outstretched palm. It lay in the snow as if decapitated, the head of a small blind snake.

"Get that thing away from me!"

"Karyn, what're you—"

"I told you before, I don't want to hear any more about that loony girl! I don't know what's got into you, I don't know why you're so obsessed, but I'm telling you, Rich, there's something wrong in that place and I'll never go back! And if you can't forget about Polly then you better just forget about me!"

"Stop shouting, for Christ's sake," he said furiously.

Karyn, with a pained sullen mouth and eyes brimming like watery stars through a torrent of her condensed breath, made a fist, a shocking declaration; he paused, reconsidering a move toward her. Their voices might have carried for a mile in the crisp almost windless air, which now seemed negatively charged, as if in the aftermath of a sinister loudspeaker announcement. Nearly everyone around the snack stand and lift shed was looking at them.

"Karyn—" His eyes slid from her uncompromising face to the vast frame of the sky around her head, of a blue so intense it easily took on some of the toning of the royal purple ear warmer she wore. He shrugged defensively.

"I'm staying here with Brooksie and Tam," she said, pitching her voice to a more intimate level, trying to exclude eavesdroppers. "They'll take me in tonight. I want you to go back to the inn, pack my things, and bring them to me. Otherwise I don't want to see you until you've promised you won't have any more to do with that sick, psychotic—"

His voice strained by resentment, Rich said, "Hey, what gives you the right to say she's—"

Karyn's head jerked, cutting him off. She said through her teeth, "Oh, I don't know *what* she is, something evil and vile and disgusting and nobody, *nobody* is going to make me go through another night like I had last night! I wasn't dreaming. You'd just better accept that and drop this whole thing about Polly. Drop it, Rich, drop it!"

The hell I will. But he didn't say it.

They glared at each other, standoffish, for several heartbeats. Then Karyn lowered her bronze goggles as she turned full face into the sun.

"I'm going up again, to the Rocket." It was a steep run, a twisting cascade through subalpine forest; Rich couldn't hack it and felt demeaned by the oblique contempt her choice implied. "I'll see you when you're ready to start thinking about me for a change."

Karyn claimed her skis and poles from the ski corral and glided effortlessly across packed-down snow to the T-bar, where the wait was shorter. Rich retrieved the locket from where it had fallen, trying to do so by making an insouciant stab into the snow, but he miscalculated; hampered by the weight and stiffness of his Nordica boots, he almost pitched nose-first into a trash basket. Nearby a girl, seeing through him, tittered; he wouldn't look at her, but his spirits caved in with a lurch.

When he raised his head with a carefully bland stare he found that everyone had gone back to their own business. There was no one to intimidate, to turn away with what remained of his righteous anger. He heard the cries of children on the beginner's slope, whoops of holiday laughter elsewhere. Motionless, he fizzled in the sun. Her preppie friends would pass the word, that's what really rankled, more than her irrational attack on the defenseless Polly. *Karyn had a fight with what's-his-name.* Their casual malice. *What does she see in him?* The knowing smiles, the little clannish headshakes. Rich wanted to lash out, memorialize his anger by smashing a ski or throwing a pole to the pitched roof of the lift shed. Better yet, he could pin one of those specimens of social butterfly to a wall with that same pointed pole, see how long it took him to wither and wilt. *Hi, I'm Trux. I was born goddam rich and you weren't.*

Rich's stomach contained sour heat, like a burning skunk cabbage. Conor had often left him feeling this way, tentative and exhausted, after they wrestled. Expert feinting to get him off balance, break his wind, utterly confuse and frustrate him. Then *wham*, on the mat and helpless, Conor so much bigger and not half working at it, applying just enough pain to get him crying. Inside arm bar. Head scissors. Side chancery. *You'll never be fast enough, kid.* The old sick feelings of inadequacy. A million miles from Mulrooney Street to Big Eli, a million more yet to go. Without Karyn? He gave up his pretense of indifference and searched for her. She was still waiting on line; Rich was jolted, alarmed by how magnificent she looked in tight racing pants, her hair bound up inside the headband for fast downhill runs. *Have you ever seen a fifty-foot wave, Rich?* No, he wouldn't concede this fight so easily. He had other things to do. He damn well could find something to do with the rest of his day.

9

What he did was drive back to the Post Road Inn to pack Karyn's clothes and toiletries. Sun-glazed somnolence of midafternoon, everything he touched aromatic of her. He felt grouchy and mean-spirited, thinking of her graceful christies in deep churning powder as the blue shadows of waning day enclosed the mountainside. He smoked a last bent cigarette from the pack he'd bought the night before. Then he lay down on the bed, the gold locket chain around his right fist. He stared at the slightly battered locket, opened it, closed it. He had no insights. He felt more confused than ever.

Before long he was yawning, unable to keep his eyes open. Two hours' sleep, all that exercise. The spacious bed felt wonderful. The inn was quiet as a pharaoh's tomb.

No way, he reflected drowsily, anyone could have entered their room and left the locket on the bedpost. But he wanted, demanded, a rational explanation.

Then he had one.

Suddenly wide awake, Rich sat up and lunged off the bed, padded in his socks to the door. There he bent down and discovered an eighth of an inch of space between the bottom of the door and the floorboards. Enough space to push through an unfolded *New York Times* on those days when the ads weren't running heavy; more than enough to slide the locket into the room.

That much was solved. So how had it gotten to the bedpost?

They had made love; he had fallen asleep; Karyn, by habit, had gone to the bathroom to douche. So she found the locket, looked inside, fastened it to the bedpost where he would be sure to see it. She had recognized the locket, all right, when he showed it to her up at the mountain. Just enough fuel to really touch her off. A strategic mistake on his part, knowing how she felt about Polly.

Rich parted the curtains at the window, raised the window and opened the shutters all the way, looked out at the burned wing of the inn. White boards with wintered ivy clinging, barn-red shutters, only a little smoke damage showing from this angle. A good-sized hole in the roof, temporarily patched over and tarped to prevent further damage from the elements. Windross should have had crews at work restoring the place before the winter season ended. Maybe there was a hangup with the insurance. . . . Rich yawned, cracked his jaws, shut the window and turned back to the bed. He dived into it and fell asleep face down.

The telephone woke him up. Third or fourth ring. It was nearly dark outside. He knew it was Karyn calling. He struggled across the bed on his elbows and grabbed the receiver. His neck had stiffened in sleep. He rolled over carefully onto his back.

"Rich, I'm sorry."

"Me too."

"What're you doing?"

"I was asleep."

"Oh. What about my clothes?"

"All packed."

"Listen, I got us a great room at the Davos Chalet. With a sauna." There was a mischievous lilt in her voice. "Ac-tually, it's the honeymoon suite."

Rich winced. "Yeah, well. I'll still have to pay for two nights here."

"I don't care. I'll help pay. I know you think I'm acting—" She sounded exasperated, but more with herself than with him. In a more gentle tone Karyn continued, "Just try to be patient with me."

"Okay. Don't worry."

"I want you to meet me somewhere at eight thirty."

"Eight thirty? So where are you now?"

"Some little town." Karyn turned away from the phone, made a muffled inquiry, came back on. "Brewster Center. They have this fabulous antique shop Tam knew about; rooms and rooms full of goodies . . . oh, thanks." Her words became a little slurred; she was trying to talk with her mouth full. "And I found the most b-ful—present for an'versary—"

"Whose anniversary? What are you eating?"

"Walnut fudge." Karyn swallowed. "Delicious. My parents. Their thirtieth wedding anniversary."

"Are we going? When?"

"Of course. Black tie. Twenty-eighth of January. Oh, about tonight. It's a restaurant a few miles north of Londonderry called the Frog Prince. Supposed to be great. All the food is prepared on wood-burning stoves. Reservations are very hard to get. We've got a big table."

"Did you ski all afternoon?"

"Almost. My wrist started hurting. I strained it again, I think, trying to dodge a couple of kiwis who wouldn't give track. How's your neck?"

"Stiff. I need a hot bath."

"Sauna's better for it. Why don't you go right on over to the Chalet? We're already checked in. Don't worry about what it costs, I still haven't cashed my birthday check from Aunt Bets."

"I'm paying, Karyn. We have this understanding, don't we? I'll put the bill on my Visa card and worry about it for the next ten months."

"Thanks for doing this for me, Rich. Now get moving."

"What's the rush?"

"I just don't like for you to be in that room, that's all."

An operator came on the line and wanted Karyn to deposit more change for another three minutes; she said a hasty good-bye to Rich instead.

After he hung up Rich went into the bathroom and ran smoking water in the tub. In the bedroom, while the tub slowly filled, he set out clothes for the evening: a tan and rust ski sweater Karyn had given him for Christmas and a pair of olive wool slacks. Skiers were returning to the inn from the slopes; car doors popped in the parking lot, voices called back and forth. Through the window he saw a few bright stars in an indigo sky.

Something else caught his attention as he was about to turn away and pull the curtains together; a light shining from a high window of the burned wing.

At first he thought it was a chance reflection, the last rays of the setting sun striking metal or glass. He lingered, eyes on the light, but it didn't vanish; instead it became stronger as the short dusk deepened into full night. The light was coming from a third-floor room on the west end of the wing. All of those rooms had French doors instead of windows, and little balconies that were more ornamental than useful. The doors were shuttered, but apparently the shutters were missing a few slats.

The light was steady; certainly not a flashlight, probably not even candlelight. Yet the rest of the wing remained dark.

Rich was aware of a thickening in his throat, a faster pulse. He pulled the curtains together, went back to the bathroom and turned off the water. He picked up his parka on his way out and checked for the car keys as he jogged downstairs to the lobby, where a fire fed noisily on pine logs and the after-ski crowd had begun to tank up and thaw out.

He ran all the way to the parking lot, slipping a couple of times on patches of ice. He opened the trunk of the Porsche and took out his flashlight. As he was about to close the lid he saw a big screwdriver with a blue plastic handle and took that as well. He had forgotten his gloves, and his fingers began to sting from the cold. He put them in his pockets. His breath was a fogbank. He made his way quickly uphill to the burned wing and found the entrance doors securely padlocked.

Rich backed off and stood craning to see the gleam of light he had noticed from his room. But there was no easy way up to the third floor; a climb from ground level was out of the question.

The least difficult route, he decided, was over the roof and down to the balcony, a drop of about eight feet. He looked over his shoulder at the main wing of the inn some forty yards downhill; lighted windows like little lanterns hung from the bare branches of intervening trees. A ladder, something—but a frontal approach was out of the question, someone was sure to notice him. He wondered where Windross was, what had happened to the man since he had been driven away in the old Cadillac.

Rich prowled around to the rear of the burned wing. The snow was deeper here, and he wasn't wearing boots. His feet were turning numb, and so was the end of his nose. The cold was almost palpable, a series of thin glass walls surrounding him, entombing him. Each movement shattered a wall invisibly, noiselessly, but another slid instantly into place. Behind him was a hill, then a higher hill, and the rising moon. He shivered, stamped his feet, looked up at the building. The fire damage was worse on this side. A twisted length of tarpaulin, torn by wind, hung down from the roof. Probably it was anchored to something up there, but he couldn't be sure. Nor could he reach it—the end of the tarp was a good ten feet above his head.

Jogging in place from impatience and the effects of the extreme cold, Rich looked around with his flashlight. He saw a pile of boards nearby, crusted with snow. Fat nailheads stuck up through the snow. He hauled one of the heavy planks off the pile and upended it, staggered by the weight, leaned it against the wall of the building a couple of feet from the dangling tarp. The board, a two-by-twelve, was about ten feet long. It had no bend in it. Dime-size nailheads stuck out an inch, two inches, some of them well enough placed to afford tenuous footholds. It wasn't much of a ladder, though, and it would be very dangerous if he should slip.

But there was no other way to go, and in two or three minutes he would be too thoroughly chilled to make the attempt. The necessity to climb, to scale the roof and let himself down the other side to the small balcony, went unquestioned. Rich had made up his mind that Polly was there, in that room, and he was going to get to her. After the frustration and humiliation he'd been through, he had to know what had been going on at the inn, fathom the matter of Polly's anxiety and her pleas—direct and indirect— for his help.

Reaching the dangle of tarp required delicate balance on the leaning board. His fingers rapidly were losing feeling. He leaned out and grabbed a double handful of the stiff tarp, tugged hard, decided it would take his weight, and began an awkward climb, hand over hand the last few feet to the old copper rain gutter. Hauling himself up over the gutter to the slant roof was an exercise in desperation. On his stomach, he clawed at more of the frozen tarp for purchase, until his fingernails were torn. It was too cold for blood to flow immediately. There was nothing he could do about his feet, they slipped and slid wildly on the roof, which was covered with ice, then layers of frozen and fresh snow.

When he reached the level where the roof had burned through it was easier: cinder blocks which had been placed there to hold the tarp down had been frozen as if welded to the roof—nothing could dislodge them. Rich picked his way easily over the scattered blocks to the flat ridge line of the roof and crouched there, looking down at the balcony, his chest heaving as he breathed.

The balcony seemed a small target, barely three feet by six, missable if he should lose his footing at the crucial instant he launched himself.

He took the screwdriver from his pocket and used it to hack handholds in the expanse of sloping ice below. When he could reach no farther he began a cautious backward descent on his stomach, negotiating the last few feet down by driving the screwdriver into the hard snow cover and anchoring it as if it were a piton.

Rich made it to the gutter and, with feet planted firmly, turned himself until his back was against the slant of the roof, knees bent, feet braced somewhat awkwardly at the gutter's edge. Again he was gasping for breath. He sighted down between his knees, bent his back, pushed off with his hands and then his feet and dropped over the side.

Half a foot of snow on the floor of the balcony took up most of the shock of his landing, but still the pain in his half-frozen feet was unmerciful. The balcony cracked like a shot and for a terrifying few moments seemed to sway: he thought it might let go and drop him another thirty feet in a jagged tumble of wood and old rusted iron.

Rich waited, on hands and knees, not daring to move. The cold air he sucked in through his mouth seared the lining of his throat, but he couldn't seem to get enough to fill his lungs.

"*Who's that?*"

So he'd been right, and the effort to get to her was worthwhile!

Rich stood shakily and leaned against the shutters over the French doors; he called to her.

"Polly, it's Rich!"

She cried out joyfully, saying his name again and again. Rich laughed and flexed his fingers, trying to get the circulation going. He blew his breath futilely into cupped hands.

"Honey, come on, let me in, it's freezing out here."

"*I can't.*"

There was a loose slat in one of the shutters near his head; Rich pried at it, cursing, and pulled it loose. Peered into the room.

She was standing a few feet from the bed, anticipation and frustration in the pale narrow oval of her face. She was taller than he remembered. But she'd be twelve and a half now, verging on puberty, shooting up. She wore a gray tweed skirt, a crewneck Nordic sweater, red knee-high socks. It was a large square room they had her in, untouched by the fire and smoke. He wondered how that could be, but he was overjoyed by the sight of Polly, at last, and not disposed to dwell on the pristine condition of the walls, covered with a silver and buff paper, a faded woodland scene, or the coffered ceiling. The room was plainly furnished. A single bed of stout maple, a round table by the bed, a lamp and a miniature TV on the table. On the bed a pillow and a patchwork quilt, some dolls and stuffed animals, teen magazines strewn at one end and falling to the floor. A small radio played so softly he almost didn't hear it.

Polly tried to take another step closer to him, but couldn't move her left foot. There was a metal ring padded with tape around her ankle, a chain attached to it. The chain, perhaps seven feet long, was padlocked to the bed.

With a cry of despair Polly bent almost double, soft blond hair falling in a wave to her knees.

"*Rich, I can't!*"

He had dropped the screwdriver before jumping, and now had to scrabble in the snow of the balcony to locate it. The shutters had been nailed together with a piece of angle iron. He found the screwdriver, dug it into the soft wood, frantically pried at the piece of iron until he could force the shutters apart.

The French doors weren't locked. Rich stepped up into the room and, stopped by a sudden hard wrench of caution, took the time to close the shutters again. In case anyone happened to look up there and see the light shining from the room. And came to investigate. Despite his anger he was afraid of that. Cautious and afraid, not yet knowing what the two of them were up against.

Then he had Polly in his arms, his fingertips already throbbing, about to become excruciatingly painful. He could feel her bones through the sweater, the faint fluff of her hair against one cold red cheek.

"What's going on? Why did they chain you to the bed? For God's sake—is your father responsible for this?"

"Yes!"

Rich guided her to the bed. Polly hid her face against him, as if she were overcome with embarrassment by her circumstances; the tears flowed on and on. There was a tray of food, largely untouched, on the table, a tang of childish urine from a chamberpot. Rich went down on one knee to look at the padlock that held the chain to the bed. Forget it. Nor could he move the bed. The clubbed maple feet had been bolted to the floor.

He rose in indignation, one hand on the girl, who had curled into a nest of well-worn animals and *Tiger Beat* magazines. He had just begun to thaw out but he noticed that the room was warm and dry, despite the fact that the rest of the hotel wing was as dark and coldly unpleasant as a catacomb.

There were spots of excited color on Polly's cheek-bones; her eyes glowed despite the tears.

"I knew you'd come!"

"Why did he do this?"

Polly straightened on the bed so abruptly he could hear the pop of vertebrae. "Because he thinks I did it—I set the fire! But I didn't! I almost started a fire a few years ago but this time wasn't my fault, Rich; honest. It wasn't, and I told him that! Nobody listens to me! They say I'm a little bitch and w-won't—they just won't—"

Polly began to heave and claw at his slick parka, desperate for his understanding. He unzipped the parka and pulled her closer to him, kissed her cheek, her forehead, the tip of an ear. She licked her lips frantically, like a sick animal; the humid swipe of her tongue tickled his nostrils. Her forearms shivered from the effort of holding fast to him.

"They were here last night—they're hurting me, Rich-ard!"

"Hurting you? How?"

"They beat me. Last night *he* beat me."

"Your father?"

Horrified, he stared at her. Their faces were inches apart. Perhaps it was too warm in the room, almost hot—Rich couldn't tell yet, he hadn't been inside long enough—but there was perspiration in the hollows of Polly's eyes, a few strands of hair were pasted to the angle of her jaw. Her ears, he thought, were too pale, bloodless to their tips.

"Don't you believe me, Rich?"

"But—why—!"

"To get all the mischief out of me! That's what they say! And they say—they say I'm evil, I'm going to do someone real harm if they don't get all of the evil out of me! There's this word they use—I don't remember—*scurtch*—"

"Scourge?"

"Yes! But I just can't take any more, why do they want to hurt me? I hurt so bad, Rich!"

"What have they—what do they do it with, Polly?"

"A big leather belt." The memory of it caused more

pain; Polly's head came up, she leaned back, biting her underlip. "With metal things on it, that's what really hurts."

"Studs?"

Polly nodded.

"Want to see?" she asked, timidly.

"I—yes, I'd better have a look."

Polly rocked for a few moments on the bed, gaining some sort of terrible mind-momentum; then, quickly, her hands went to a knee-high stocking. She rolled it down almost to the ankle. Then she turned on her right haunch and elbow to reveal more fully the back of the calf of her long leg, which was streaked red and purple, livid and swollen from multiple lashings.

"Oh, Polly."

"But there's worse."

"Worse?" he repeated, stunned, unable to believe the damage he'd already seen.

Polly shifted position again, undid the side snap of her skirt, unzippered it. She rolled over on her stomach, tensing, pressing her face into the patchwork quilt and flannel sheets.

"Look."

Hesitantly he took hold of the loosened skirt; she raised up a little from the bed and he pulled the skirt down around her knees. She wore white cotton underpants. They seemed not to have been changed for a while. He was not prepared for the rounding maturity, the fullness of her buttocks.

"You can take them off," Polly said after a few moments. Her voice was muffled, neutral. "So you can see better."

Rich worked the underpants down carefully. They stuck to Polly. She flinched and hissed and hammered on the bed with her fists. There was an unclean, unhealthy odor, of stored corruption. The studded belt had cut and stippled gruesomely, the cuts had bled in ragged diagonals; it was dark blood he'd seen soiling the cotton. Infection that he smelled.

He dressed her, trembling, his vision dimmed by outrage, from the blood surging in his head.

"I'll get you out of here. This is—he's not—nobody can treat you this way. I'll have your father put in jail."

"Don't leave me, Rich!"

He hugged Polly to dispel any notion of abandonment, his mind still dwelling on the terrible welts, the violated young body. It was the same as rape. He was curiously, tenderly aroused in contrast to a much stronger emotion: his almost unbearable desire to repeatedly smash Windross's mealy face with his fists.

"Rich, I love you so much! Nobody else has ever cared. I don't know why. I'm not a bad person. Believe me!"

"I know you're not, honey." He cradled the girl, murmuring to her. "How did you get the locket to my room, if you're chained—"

"Rich, I can't breathe! You're holding me too tight."

"I'm sorry."

He sat Polly back, against a big bear with one black felt eye missing. Polly's knees were spread wide, bony and charming; the fingers of one hand interlaced with his. The chain that imprisoned her dragged heavily across the calf of his right leg.

"What locket? Oh, the one you gave—I honestly don't know what happened to it. I had to take it off to wash, I put it right there on the table—a week ago—and—how did you find it?"

"Somebody put it in my room last night. They scratched the number of this room across my picture."

Polly caught her breath, eyes rounding.

"How weird."

"Maybe it was one of those people who came here with your father."

She frowned. "I don't understand."

"I don't either. But one of them may be looking for a way to help you. How many are there?"

"Six. Usually. Sometimes more."

"How long have you been here, Polly?"

"I dunno for sure. But I saw another show of *Dallas* last night, and that's the second time *Dallas* has been on."

"And how many times have they come since you've been here?"

"Uh—" She counted silently. "Five."

"Could you identify—do you think you'd recognize all of them again, outside this room?"

Polly nodded emphatically, a momentary hard glint of vengeance in her faded blue eyes.

"Do you think they might come back again tonight?"

"No," she said, "it's never two nights in a row." She hunched her shoulders, as she must have done hearing them outside the door. Desperately trying to will some sort of defense against their implacable cruelty. He'd heard of incidents like this, read about the self-righteous child abusers. *Well, she was acting bad, I had to hold her hand down on the stove so she'd learn to mind.* Or shove her into scalding bathwater, or break her ribs with a broom handle. *Got to teach the children a lesson while they are young enough. Whip the sin out of them good and early, before they can turn on you. Because we are all born as sinners. It's all right there, in your Bible and mine!*

Polly began to squirm, trying to find a reclining position that didn't bother her.

"Doesn't matter," Rich said. "When they come again, you won't be here—no, don't." Rich stayed her hand; she'd been about to rub her lacerated bottom.

"But it itches," Polly complained, her chin crimped, her mouth turned down at the corners. "It hurts."

Unexpectedly his eyes brimmed with tears. He leaned forward to kiss Polly, to one side of her compressed lips. Then full on her softening mouth. His tears flowed. He was so sorry for her. Thank God and sweet Mary she hadn't broken mentally. A very tough kid in her own way. She was suffering: anxious and frightened. But she seemed fully capable still, not half crazed or inclined to hysteria.

"I'm going for the cops. We'll take you to the hospital right away, Pol, and have those cuts treated."

Enraptured by his show of concern, with her fingertips she spread his tears over his cheeks and then her own. Content in his arms, she closed her eyes. Her face, momentarily steadied, was tranquil, the nostrils flaring slightly as she breathed, breathed him.

"You're crying for me. Oh, Rich. You don't know how I prayed. 'Please get my message, Rich. Please hear me.' "

"You'll have to tell me how you managed that."

Polly's eyelids popped open; she was startled. She stared

up at him, and smiled. Her two front teeth were longer than the rest, subtly out of line, and raked against each other. Nothing you'd want to try to straighten out, make too perfect.

"I will. But get me out of here first. I just can't wait any longer—now that I know you're here, I'll go crazy waiting!"

The problem, Rich decided, was getting himself out. He cased the room, squeezing his aching hands together, limping a little from the stabbing needles in his toes. He didn't think he could manage to reverse the circuitous way over the roof. And as he remembered, the hall was boarded up, the door in the new wall padlocked. Now that he could take the time to think about it, he realized he was almost as much of a prisoner in the room as Polly.

10

At the Frog Prince restaurant near Londonderry, Karyn waited until eight thirty-five before she made her first attempt to locate Rich.

She put in a call to the Davos Chalet, but if he was already in the room then he must be using the sauna, and couldn't hear the phone ring. Nor did he answer the phone at the Post Road Inn, and to Karyn's annoyance she was told that Rich hadn't checked out. Giving him the benefit of the doubt, she decided he must be en route but was having trouble locating the restaurant, a converted farmhouse in an area where almost all of the roads qualified as back roads, many of them not well marked.

She returned to the table, which dominated a side porch with fogged-up storm windows, fabric-covered walls, a small Victorian fireplace, and sprays of hothouse flowers in cloisonné vases. The group, nine in all, was on a third bottle of Cru Beaujolais prior to dining. She knew five of them—Tam and Brooksie and their boy friends, and Trux Landall, who was there with a tough-looking but emaciated Belgian youth who had spent his last two years immersed in the Amsterdam drug scene. He knew a lot about getting stoned; at least it was all he cared to talk about.

"Real cocaine, totally pure, does not give a rush," he explained. "That is a common misconception, even in this country, where coke is such a status symbol. The rush, the flash, the assault on the brain is nothing but a speed high. Nearly all coke sold in America, perhaps ninety-nine per cent, is very heavily cut with some sort of 'garbage'—isn't that the right word? Debased by amphetamines, caffeine, just anything to jolt the heart and electrocute the senses. The 'right stuff' is pink flake from Peru, blue diamond from Bolivia; they provide a totally different sensation. A glow, a spreading sensual warmth that is totally beneficial. One feels, how should I describe—"

"Mellow," Tam volunteered.

"Yes, *mellow*. Uplifted. Blessed. Filled with all of the most noble sentiments and aspirations of mankind."

"Wow."

"Where can we get some?" Brooksie asked.

"Ah, well." The Belgian spread his hands. "That is the difficult part."

Tam's boyfriend, whose name was Larry, said, "There's a guy over in Sligo my brother's done business with. He has a growhouse. I'll call Clubber and get his number."

"Freebasing's different, isn't it?" Trux asked his friend. "You don't get the bad side effects with freebasing."

"Unless you call cremation a side effect," somebody commented.

They all laughed, except Karyn, who looked unaccountably grim as she reached for her nearly empty wine goblet.

Trux poured more of the Beaujolais for her. "How's it going?"

She forced a smile. "Oh, great, you know."

"Rich couldn't make it?"

"I'm sure he's on the way. This isn't such an easy place to find. You have to know somebody who's been here."

Trux gave her right hand a reassuring squeeze. "Good seeing you again, Karyn. We had fun, didn't we? How did we lose track of each other?"

"People come and people go. As I recall, you went after Penelope Wycherly."

"But you weren't in love with me."

"Yes, I was: for about nine minutes once on a rainy afternoon when you called me collect from Paris and tried to read a poem by Mallarmé in that awful French of yours."

"I must have been shitfaced; I don't even remember doing it now."

"For the first and only time in our relationship, you were doing something madly inconsequential, inspired by the mood of the moment. Now I suppose you're back on your preordained course, busting your ass at the Yaaadd. How do you like it?"

"I like it better than being flayed alive, but not much. The law school is still dominated by the old ballbreakers. The Socratic method. They humble you fast. That kind of classroom demagoguery makes hopeless sycophants out of some promising legal minds. Then they break what's left of your desire on the wheel of the appellate case method. Two goddam years left. I think I could learn just as much law from correspondence courses. Most of us figure, what the hell. It's not the degree that matters, it's the university. Thank God for notepools."

His hand had stayed where it was, lightly cupping hers. For a few seconds she had wished ruefully he would remove it; Brooksie was not looking at her exactly, but she had the finely honed awareness of a court gossip: her nose seemed pointedly to sense liaison. Oh, well. Seeing a trim familiar scar on Trux's hand, like a landmark on a now-blurred emotional map, Karyn was reminded, not uncomfortably, of what they had been to each other. He took care of his nails. No biting. No nerves, despite the rigors of learning by the Socratic method. She was glad Trux was there and she wasn't just sitting around getting more and more on edge because Rich had screwed up, or whatever. Momentarily she permitted a remorseful vision of the Porsche overturned somewhere, Rich sprawled unconscious beside an icy road, flares that turned snow pink and blood jet black, police; but then she dismissed it with a little hard practical flick of a mental whiskbroom. He was a good and careful driver, he'd show up, and she was in a mood to forgive him regardless. The wine was excellent and she was among friends. She wondered if Trux was fucking the blond Belgian, boy but decided no, dope and boys had never been his milieu, she would have heard something. The Belgian was just one of those strays whom he occasionally befriended, out of intellectual curiosity.

"Ouch."

She withdrew her right hand, protectively, encircling the wrist with the fingers of her left hand. Trux looked down at her.

"What's the matter?"

"I strained my wrist skiing." One of his fingers had accidentally prodded a sore spot.

"Let me see."

Trux held her forearm gently, the hand palm up, and carefully felt the tendons of her wrist with his fingertips.

"Does that hurt?"

"Right there. Oh!"

"Tendonitis. It'll be sore for a couple of weeks. Soak your wrist in a Jacuzzi and wrap it tight. Ski left handed for a few days."

"That would be like trying to fly with one wing."

"You can do it. I'll teach you."

He inclined his head in a dignified manner and kissed the inside of her wrist, and Karyn felt the tingle she was intended to feel.

Larry said to Trux, "Before you eat that, I can tell you the roulade of rabbit with basil they serve here is better."

"Having had both," Trux said softly, "I disagree."

"Screw you," Karyn said spiritedly, enjoying the attention, and she downed the rest of the wine in her goblet.

It was a quarter past nine before she gave Rich another thought, and that thought was a guilty one: she was having a wonderful time, they all were, his tardy arrival would be an intrusion of a sort, and he would not be in a very good mood for having wandered around the mountains of southern Vermont for at least an hour and a half trying to find them. And they weren't *his* friends, they were hers, always a point of contention with Rich. Maybe he'd just decided at the last minute not to come. Well, she could handle that, for now.

And tomorrow she'd really let him hear about it.

11

Rich needed to do a considerable amount of poking around the third floor with his flashlight before he discovered a potential exit from the burned wing. By the time he found it he was filthy; his nostrils and throat were clogged with soot.

He returned coughing to the room where Polly sat on the very edge of the bed, facing the door, wavering with the delicacy of an angelfish inhabiting a pool of magical light and warmth; he brought from the hall outside cold and painful currents.

"There's a big hole in the floor of one of the rooms down the hall," he explained to her. "I can use one of those bedsheets, tie it to something, let myself down to the second floor. The stairs aren't blocked on two. The front doors are chained, I'll have to break a window down below to get out."

"How long will you be gone?"

"Maybe an hour. Don't worry."

"You promise you'll come back!"

"Honey, you know I will."

He leaned on a bedpost, considering the effort that would have to be made; their eyes met but he was preoccupied, and this lack of attention caused her to quail, succumbing to the tortures of abandonment.

"Rich, what's going to happen to me? Where will I go?"

"I don't know yet. Let's just get you out of here first." His fingers lifted a shock of hair from one shoulder, slipped through it to the faintly throbbing indentation of temple. "You've been brave so far. Just a little longer."

Polly accepted the commendation with a little wince and fluttery release of breath, then sank down into herself, hands overlapping, chain rattling. She reached for the bedraggled bear behind her, pulled him slowly into her lap.

"For me," he said.

"Just hurry, that's all. Hurry!"

12

Dinner at the Frog Prince restaurant, beginning with Belon oysters and finishing with a well-aged Chèvre and perfect, ruby-red strawberries offered up, after some unimaginably complex transit from a warmer, more fertile place, at six dollars the serving, lasted until eleven o'clock. Karyn had lost track of the quantity of wine consumed by the group, but she suspected they'd all had at least a bottle apiece, except for the Belgian boy. He drank sparingly and disdained food except for samples of Trux's sweetbreads and oysters in lemon and green pepper sauce. But on three occasions he had crumbled something, probably gorilla biscuits, into a glass of 7-Up that he held between his knees under the table.

There was considerable talk about rounding up some high-grade cannabis to end the fun on a protracted mellow note. They divided into groups in the bracing night air outside the restaurant and went off jammed into two cars to seek out the local grower Larry's brother had recommended.

Karyn found herself in the back seat of an anthracite gray BMW sports coupe with Trux and the Belgian boy, who was slit-eyed and nodding. Trux was in the middle and presently he began to kiss her. She liked it, reminding herself that he was just a good friend of long standing, no disloyalty to Rich intended. And it certainly would go no further. She didn't want any real heat generated, and Trux seemed aware of her wishes without having to grope for a rebuff.

The Vermont grower, who had a long scraggly beard and a long ponytail, lived with his girl friend in a shacky farmhouse down a back road to East Jesus, a local euphemism for nowhere. His home was less comfortable and well-appointed than his growhouse, which had double walls of corrugated, galvanized steel with nine inches of insulating material between them, a sloping translucent roof twelve feet high made of heavy gauge Filon that admitted the full spectrum of light favorable to the sturdy growth of his plants, an underroof of latticework barbed wire, reinforced steel doors with hidden latches, and a security system that featured a Uzi machine gun, which he carried with him everywhere. The inner walls of the growhouse were lined with aluminum foil for maximum reflection of the thousand-watt metal halide grow lights he'd installed. From the outside the growhouse was virtually unapproachable: the dog kennel surrounded it.

The group's resident authority, newly alert in this jurisdiction, sampled the Vermont grower's sinsemilla and Afghani and was highly complimentary.

"Basically it's the compost," the grower explained. "A friend of mine has a vegetarian restaurant over in Saxtons River. He gives me all the garbage I need. I've been experimenting with some hybrids and getting good results. This plant here is a cross between a male indica from northern India—that's one of the best black hashes going— and a female sativa from Peru."

Karyn smothered tiny yawns and clung to Trux, because she was a little wobbly under the hot lights and feeling dismal pangs of the illicit. She had a minimal interest in dope, and the stubby tough-looking weapon scared her. Their host seemed low-key, but his fingers drummed metallically against the Uzi's magazine. The sluggish eyes of the pregnant girl seemed to reflect a mind weighted in permafrost. Karyn wondered how the baby would turn out. Holding on to Trux wasn't easy, she kept sliding off his full-length sealskin coat ("If it keeps my ass warm," he'd said matter-of-factly, "screw the baby seals.") He had to use both hands to prop her up. The lights all had enormous vivid halos to her eyes. She wondered if she was going to pass out, despite the pungent atmosphere.

Their host offered a few samples of his wares, including a crude brick of Manali hash that was dark and flaky and had a faint bluish-green luminescence. Karyn nibbled cautiously. Larry and the Belgian conversed in low voices and struck a bargain for some hash and a few bags of cannabis.

Then they were off again on the deserted, neatly plowed roads, car filling with strong sweet smoke. A scarcity of houses, the hills crowding in, all smoothly sheeted rumps and shoulders and domes, her marijuana-stoked thoughts turned whimsical: they seemed to be scudding nervily through a dense stalled parade of white elephants. Around the next careening bend—wide feet in the road, lowering pink eyes. Albino anger. A single elephant could crush them like a pea. At the circus when she was eight or nine, she had seen a woman in scarlet satin briefs grasped at the waist and lifted, horizontally, unconcerned, in the beaky embrace of an enormous old duffer who had then, to drumrolls, raised himself on his baggy back legs to a height of nearly fifteen feet. Karyn, focusing on that distant spotlight, the fixed frail smile of courage, the woman's Eurasian face cradled in one hand, her elbow braced on thin air, prickled at the remembered sound of nervous jerky applause rippling through the darkened arena. The spot dwindled but her emotions surged, leaving her perversely thrilled, sexually sensitized, in a vast untenanted cavern. Her heart churned. She was grateful for Trux's undemanding embrace, his reassuring familiarity.

But thoughts of Rich occupied the corners of her mind. Center stage there was something forceful in the charged darkness, an act readying; now the sizzling blue pencil of the spotlight would nudge it into antic life. Ta-daaa! *Ladeez and gentlemen! . . . Presenting none other than. . .* POLLY!! WINDROSS!! in her nightclothes, with that lethal candle, jigging to a faulty tune, her face alight with the same druggy luminescence Karyn had seen on the surface of the Manali hash brick. An evil twinkle rimming her eyes like stuck-on sequins. Twinkle once, twinkle twice—and the child was fully and flamboyantly naked, although she didn't have enough body yet to justify the trampy insolence. But it was not her slim figure Polly was showing off, it was her nemesis-twin, miniaturized, flimsy but shocking inside the rheumy sac that bulged out from beneath her breastbone. Rich! That room at the inn: was he fool enough to spend another night there after she'd told him—? But she hadn't told Rich nearly enough, she hadn't dared speak of the monster's hostile, saurian eyes. Eyes that burned through to the soul like bits of fiery metal.

As soon as they reached the Davos Chalet, Karyn insisted on seeing if Rich was there. Trux accompanied her. She raced. Rich wasn't in the honeymoon suite. Her luggage hadn't arrived, either. Trux looked at the round bed with a polar bear skin throw, sleek cedar walls, a mustard-yellow shag carpet, all of it reflected by a mirrored ceiling.

"Nice," he said, suppressing a smirk.

"Damn it, I don't have anything to wear! What is Rich *doing* to me?"

Karyn cut short a rant and headed for the bathroom. When she came out, unsteadily, only slightly revived by applications of cold cloths to her forehead and the back of her neck, Trux was sitting on the bed. He'd taken off his sealskin coat and casually draped it over a loveseat.

He took Karyn gently by the left wrist and guided her to the bed beside him.

"Time to cut loose from the crowd," he suggested.

She looked at him through an alcoholic haze. She knew her head was lolling, just a little wobbly, and she made a serious effort to keep it straight. Trux looked back at her. Then, instead of trying to be seductive, which she had anticipated as his next move, he mussed his hair, crossed his eyes, and made a stupid, bucktoothed, lovesick face for her, like Jerry Lewis in the old comedies. He stammered in a high insipid falsetto.

"Wha, wha, well, here we are. Gosh, I've never been alone with a girl before."

Karyn got the giggles, which turned into sobs. Trux dropped the comedy impression.

"He's not coming tonight, Karyn. Isn't that obvious?"

"But he will!" Tears trickled down her face.

"No he won't. Now, look. Don't cry. I can't make love to you when you're all soppy like that."

"I don't want you to make love to me, Trux," she said in an unsteady voice, her tongue getting treacherously in the way.

She trembled as she spoke, knees knocking. He put an arm around her, a gentle, unforced gesture.

"I just want Rich!" Karyn bawled.

"I know, I know," Trux said soothingly.

"I love him!"

He held her more tightly, and tickled the lobe of an ear with a flicking thumb.

"Of course you do. And you're hurt because he didn't

show up at the restaurant tonight. Are you two having big problems? That fight this morning—"

"Problems? Everybody has problems. I mean, what the h-h-hell."

"Shh."

Trux's hand covered her feverish forehead. He smoothed back her hair, which smelled of the cannabis they'd shared in the car. Karyn had never enjoyed being petted, like a dog; but his touch was, at this down point of her day, almost heavenly.

"Want to tell me about it?"

She'd always found it easy to do what Trux wanted. Her friends at school, when she was a freshman and didn't know chicken shit from chicken salad, had said that Trux led her around by the nose; but they were envious. Their relationship had always been affirmative, pleasant, unfussed. Even sex hadn't seriously complicated her first campus affair, although she wasn't much of a lover then. She was better now. He probably knew that. Trux knew almost everything about her, without having to ask. She needed his help, admit it or not. She could trust him.

"There's this girl," Karyn began timidly. "Her name is Polly Windross."

13

Police headquarters in Chadbury occupied two small rooms in the basement of the city hall. A hand-lettered sign Scotch-taped to the inside of the frosted glass in the door listed emergency numbers to call after ten o'clock. It was five minutes to ten and a woman in her late thirties was about to lock up for the night when Rich walked in. She had a pleasant oval face, coarse brown hair streaky with gray that was pulled into a businesslike knot at the back of her head, and spreading hips emphasized by the width and sag of her black gunbelt. She wore a tatty blue vest over her uniform shirt.

"Help you?" she asked, eyes lingering coolly on his face, which was smudged with charcoal. She put a finger on a cassette player without looking at it and ejected the classical guitar tape she'd been listening to.

"I want to report a case of child abuse."

The officer nodded slightly and sat down in a swivel chair behind her desk. She reached for a blank complaint form.

"Your name?"

"Richard Devon."

"D-E-V-O-N? Are you local?"

"No, I'm from New Haven. I'm staying at the Post Road Inn."

"And the name of the child involved?"

"Polly Windross."

She looked up with a quick frown, then made the notation. "And the nature of the abuse?"

Rich took a deep breath to give himself a few moments to deal with his irritation at her deliberate pace.

"They've got her chained to a bed in—"

"Whoa. Who is *they*?"

"Her father. Some other people. Polly doesn't know who the hell they are. Some kind of loony religious fanatics. They read the Bible and beat her with a belt. Her backside's a mess. I just want to get her out of there as fast as—"

"Where is the girl now?"

"In a room of the burned-out wing of the inn. Room 331."

"The burned wing? How long has she been there?"

"About two weeks. She's lost track of time." Rich began to pace, unable to suppress his nervous energy.

"And she's chained to a bed?"

"Yes. We'll need bolt cutters to get her loose. And call a doctor; there are a lot of cuts. Some of them are infected."

"Hold on," the officer said. She swiveled around to pick up the receiver of a telephone behind her. She cradled it on her shoulder and began to dial.

"Who are you calling?"

"My uncle." The woman finished dialing, looked around at him, her chair squeaking. "He's the chief of police." She glanced up at the clock on the wall, and again at Rich.

"I'm Stefanie. Help yourself to coffee if you want. I was about to throw it out."

Rich sniffed the air. The coffee smelled burned. "No thanks."

"Jim? Stefanie. Got a problem." She told him about it, listened, clicking a fingernail against a front tooth. "So did I; someplace in Canada, wasn't it? Uh-huh. Hold on." She looked at Rich. "How long have you known Polly Windross?"

"I met her last August."

"And you're sure it's her?"

"Positive."

Stefanie repeated this information to her uncle. Listened. "Two weeks," she said. She listened for another few seconds. "Okay, meet you there."

Stefanie hung up and got to her feet, reaching for a key ring on the desk in front of her. To Rich she said, "Did you walk down from the inn?"

"Ran."

"Ride with me, then; I'll just take a second to lock up."

They waited for the chief of police, whose last name was Melka, in the village police car in the driveway in front of the inn. The heater was malfunctioning and Rich, inactive, began to shudder uncontrollably. Stefanie seemed not to notice the cold, nor his discomfort. She spent the five minutes they waited filling him in on her background in law enforcement. Presently a pair of headlights showed behind them.

The chief got out of his own car, crunched down the drive, and rapped on Stefanie's window. She lowered it. Chief Melka was wearing a camouflage parka with the hood tightly drawn around his face, which was as red as a cooked salmon. He had a wild tangle of eyebrows and a blackberrylike growth in the middle of one of them. He looked in at Rich.

"This the complainant?"

"Richard Devon," Stefanie said.

"How long ago did you see the girl?" Melka asked Rich.

"T-twenty minutes."

"And she's where?"

"The b-burned-out wing."

"Cold enough for you? Come on inside, let's get Windross and see what we can make of this."

Rich and Stefanie followed Melka into the inn. The night clerk was the boy with the zits and the fondness for artificially ripened centerfold girls.

"We want to see Mr. Windross."

"I think he's gone to bed already."

"Wake him up."

"Yes, sir."

The clerk called Windross's quarters while Chief Melka leaned on the counter and stared at Rich.

"Where did you say you were from?"

"New Haven."

"College student?"

"Yale."

"Been up this way before, you said?"

"I met Polly here last summer."

"Windross has only had this place for a little over a year. Bought it from Shields and Blanche Ripley. They just got too old. We used to see his little girl around town. Pretty, but it's been three, four months. She kept to herself. Didn't go to the local school. Something about her health. She had a tutor, I understand."

"There's never been anything wrong with Polly's health. Her father—"

"Can't you get him?" Melka snapped at the clerk, who was so startled he almost dropped the phone.

"Ringing."

Rich said, "I'd like to get back to Polly if I—"

"We'll all go together," Melka said, gesturing for him to stay put.

He turned and took the receiver of the phone as the clerk held it out to him. "Mr. Windross? Sorry it's so late. This is Chief Jim Melka. I hope you can give us some help with a complaint that's been received. Yes, it does involve you personally. And your daughter Polly."

Melka stood listening to a series of squawks from Windross, gazing at a point a little distance from Rich's left ear; his eyes appeared to go out of focus. With his free hand he took out a Chapstick and basted winter-raw lips. Then he cut the innkeeper off in midsentence.

"The information we have is that right now she is chained to a bed—yes, *chained,* that's exactly what I said, and I'd appreciate it if you didn't interrupt me again—to a bed in one of the rooms in the burned-out wing . . ."

"Three thirty-one," Stefanie told him.

"Room 331. I want to go up there right now and check that out. Yes, sir, it is a serious allegation." The chief's black eyes flicked to Rich as if to emphasize this point. Rich felt a fulminating anger at the fat innkeeper, who was stalling while Polly sat alone and frightened in that dismal place. "Sir, I want you to be out here in the lobby in just one minute, or I'll come after you. Do you understand that? Okay."

Melka hung up, checked his watch, and shook his head slowly. They walked away from the reception desk, out of hearing of the clerk.

"I think," he said, "of all the felonies I've had to deal with in twenty years, baby rape and other forms of child abuse are the worst. And we seem to have our fair share up here. Must be the long winters. What kind of shape is the girl in, Richard?"

"From what I saw, she's bound to have scars."

Melka whistled cheerlessly through his teeth. "I'm glad you took the trouble to report it. Just up here for the skiing, hell, you might have figured it wasn't worth getting involved."

"Polly's a friend."

Windross reached the lobby in something under a minute, having pulled on wrinkled trousers, unlaced boots, and a fleece-lined corduroy coat. His face had the pocked, sickly, melted-down appearance of a lump of suet in a bird feeder. His mouth trembled.

"But Polly's not here! God is my witness! She's staying with my sister in Canada!" The innkeeper's eyes jumped to Rich, like a spark jumping a gap. He was caught up short, lurching. "You! Why do you want to make trouble? What are you trying to do to me? What have I ever done to you? I don't even know you!"

Stefanie had her notebook and pen out. "Where in Canada? What's your sister's name? Her phone number?"

"Phone, phone—there is no phone! It's just a little

village, smaller even than Chadbury! St. Janvier, in Quebec.''

"Mr. Windross," Melka said, "we're going to go up now and have a look at room 331."

"All right! Go ahead! There's nothing to see!"

Windross lunged toward Rich, hands raised but not too menacingly, as if he were trying to capture a rare bird before it could fly away. Stefanie moved in anyway, smoothly, putting a strong arm on Windross to keep them from colliding; Rich was in no mood to back off.

"What is it you're saying? What lies have you been telling about me? You had no business snooping around my inn!"

"It's a good thing I did," Rich said grimly. He caught a whiff of the man's breath. Windross had been doing some serious drinking before the telephone roused him.

"Come on," Melka said. "And Mr. Windross, you watch yourself, or there may be an assault and battery charge in addition to the allegation."

"*What* allegation?" The innkeeper's voice broke; his lips moved ineffectually.

"Mr. Devon has alleged child abuse."

"God is my witness! There's no child abuse! How could there be, even if I was that kind of father? I'm telling you . . . she's the apple of my eye."

Windross began to sob uncontrollably, kneading his face with his hands. The outburst of emotion stopped them like a shockwave. Melka grimaced at the spectacle. He took hold of a plump arm and directed the sodden, weeping man to the door.

"Mr. Windross, I want you to get hold of yourself."

Windross dragged his left foot, continuing to weep and moan. From sheer terror, Rich thought, with no trace of pity. Because soon, with witnesses looking on, he was going to have to face the daughter he had treated so unconscionably. The question was why: what had warped their relationship? But Rich wasn't very interested, as Karyn might have been, in the psychopathology of Windross. He only wanted to get Polly away from her father, forever.

14

They drove in the police car to the entrance of the burned-out wing. Melka took bolt cutters from the trunk of the car while Windross fumbled through the keys on his ring, looking for one that would let him in.

Melka glanced at the chain and laminated padlock and said to Rich, "How did you get in here? Break a window?"

"I went around to the back, improvised a ladder, then climbed up and over the roof." Rich pointed to the third-floor balcony where he'd landed. "That's the room she's in."

"Hah!" Windross said nervously, a little blast of frosted air hanging over his brows as he loosened the chain. He shook his bare hands, not liking the touch of the cold metal. "I'm telling you, Chief, there's not a word of truth in this. It's some kind of a—a crazy college stunt. I'll show you! Then we'll see who has charges to make. My lawyers—"

"Let's go," Melka said, motioning him inside with the big blue steel electric torch he held in his left hand.

As they were walking slowly up the stairs the policeman flashed his light around, taking in the damage. Rich was behind him, Stefanie following.

"How did you know where to find the girl?" Melka asked.

Rich explained about the locket in his room, the light he'd seen. Except for a bad wheeze as he climbed the stairs Windross was silent; he seemed engrossed in Rich's explanation. But he hadn't looked at Rich since they'd left the lobby of the inn.

Once the door in the temporary wall on the third floor was open, Rich pushed impatiently past Windross and, with light glancing off the smoke-darkened walls ahead of him, raced to room 331.

"Polly, it's Rich!"

The door, which he had opened without much effort earlier, now was stuck tight. Rich pounded on it, rammed a shoulder against the thick panels, pain stabbing through his sore neck.

"Locked," a plodding Windross said behind him. The innkeeper was subdued, breathing hard, his expression glum. He seemed to be tuned to some internal disturbance, perhaps monitoring an insubstantial heartbeat.

"It's not locked," Rich protested. "It can't be. Polly can't move more than a few feet away from the bed."

"I have a key," Windross said. "Light, please."

Stefanie angled the beam of her flashlight over his shoulder while he searched the key ring again. Their mingled breath formed a sizable cloud in the glare.

Melka was casting around the hall. "Lot of footprints." To Rich he said, "Some of them yours?"

"Yes. I was looking for a way out." Rich glanced at the door to 331, wondering why Polly hadn't answered him. She couldn't have gone to sleep. He knocked again. "Polly. It's okay, don't be scared. I'm back."

Windross located the passkey and slowly looked up at Rich, his eyes glistening, a glowering look of hate on his heavily shadowed face.

"You have no idea," he said quietly, "of the trouble you've caused me. How much harm you may have done."

"Just open the door," Rich said, but now it was he who was afraid.

"Gladly." Windross inserted the key in the lock, worked it for several seconds before the bolt slid back. Then he stepped aside, continuing to back up until he was in the middle of the hallway. He bowed his head.

Rich opened the door, and encountered blackness.

Something electric hit him at the base of his neck, a shock that dropped his jaw. He breathed the stale sour residue of greasy smoke. A little soot sprinkled down from the charred jamb above his head. The room was cold and empty, like all the other rooms on the floor. He turned clumsily, bumping Stefanie, stared at the smudged brass numbers on the outside of the door for verification. *331*. He looked down, at the footprints he'd left earlier on the filthy hall carpet. Then he groped for the flashlight in Stefanie's hand, took it from her, threw the beam inside.

No furniture. A tarnished ceiling fixture, wreckage of drapes over the French doors to the balcony.

Rich turned again, encountering Melka's skeptical stare.

"I—this—it wasn't like *this!* The room was clean and warm. And there was a bed"—he aimed the flashlight again—"*there,* next to the wall. With a table beside the bed. One of those little Sony TV's on it. A tray of food—but she hadn't eaten much. And there was a—a patchwork quilt on the bed. Orange and blue. Flannel sheets. Polly was wearing a tweed skirt and a ski sweater. This—this isn't the room, then, I must be—"

"Next door," Melka rumbled. "Mr. Windross?"

Windross sighed and obligingly unlocked another room for them. It was in much the same condition as 331: gutted, blackened, barren. A few other doors along the hall were unlocked at random. Windross stood waiting, hands deep in the pockets of his corduroy coat, chin on his chest as if he had fallen asleep, while Rich darted from room to room.

Belatedly he remembered something important. "Come here," he shouted to Melka. "I'll show you how I got out. I used one of the sheets from Polly's bed!"

He led them to the room with the hole chopped in the floor. Rich's face was flaming, but the rest of him was prickly cold. The new shock barely made an impression physically, just kicked his heartbeat higher for a few seconds.

There was no trace of the flannel bedsheet. His footprints in soot lay all around the jagged hole in the floor. It was like a devastated wishing well, as if in a fairy tale that had no happy ending.

"Do you have an explanation?" Melka said to Rich, his tone not exactly unfriendly. But he wasn't pleased with the way it was going.

"No." Rich slumped against the wall outside the room, breathing noisily through his mouth. "I was—here, you can see that. Those—are my footprints. But I didn't jump. I knotted a bedsheet, I swear—"

Melka nodded patiently.

"I—I just don't understand—what they could've done with Polly."

He roused himself and borrowed Stefanie's flashlight again. He brushed past Windross, who raised his head and stared at him. Darkness and ill will bled from the landlord like ink from a cuttlefish.

"Now where are you going?" Melka asked sharply.

"I'll find something to explain this! Wait."

He reentered room 331, the beam of the flashlight traveling from corner to empty corner. Melka's own flashlight doubled the gliding parabolas, spreading thin Rich's headless shadow on the dark brown walls. Windross began to complain, his voice rising. Rich continued to turn randomly, his ragged breathing becoming sobs as he gave in to despair, and the fear that he was going mad.

Suddenly he sickened, began to choke and gag. He stumbled out into the hall, spewing vomit, and fell to his knees.

"Oh my God, what's the matter?" Stefanie asked.

Rich looked up at her through watery eyes. "That odor! Don't you smell it?"

"What odor?" Stefanie went to the doorway, leaned in, sniffed audibly.

"Rotten—putrid—like decaying flesh." Rich heaved again, bringing up a trickle of vile liquid.

"He's a lunatic," Windross said to Melka, waving his hands for emphasis. "Can't you understand that? I've cooperated—now why don't you do something about *him*, punish him! He had no right to disturb me this way, make accusations, destroy my peace of mind!"

Rich lunged up, blindly intent on tearing Windross's head from his shoulders. Melka smacked him hard on the back of the skull with an open hand before Rich could touch the innkeeper. Rich went sprawling. Melka turned the beam of the electric torch full on his face, immobilizing him.

"Calm down, Richard, before you let yourself in for a whopping lawsuit."

"Me!"

"I don't want to sue him, what does *he* have? I just want him to get out of my inn! Leave me alone!"

Melka offered a hand to Rich and pulled him to his feet. "Did I hurt you?"

Rich rubbed the back of his head resentfully. He was black all over and sticky from vomit; he couldn't stop gasping from the charnel odor that had filled his nostrils.

But the blow had helped to restore his equilibrium, his dogged faith that he would be able to prove what he knew was true. Polly had to be here—somewhere. All he needed was more time. He would search every room.

"I didn't smell anything," Stefanie said, with a glance at Rich and a shrug to indicate she might be sorry.

"Oh, hell, let's get out of here," Melka told them.

"Wait—there are dozens of rooms we haven't—"

"Richard, let me say this to you very sincerely: I'm about thirty seconds away from riding you down to the jail and letting you study this matter, this obsession you've got on your mind, in a holding cell for the next day or so."

"But I'm telling you the—"

"Boy, I really do think you have a problem of some kind. What it is, I couldn't hazard a guess. I do recommend that you sort it out far away from my jurisdiction. Now, Mr. Windross has requested that you pack up and go. Do that. Stefanie will stay with you until you're ready. Don't come back."

Richard leveled a finger at Windross. "He knows—believe me, he knows everything! He's *hiding* Polly. Ask him!"

Windross looked astounded and aggrieved. Melka tapped Rich on the point of his right shoulder with the barrel of his electric torch. Rich realized, despite his agitation, that he was about to plunge through very thin ice. He shut up.

"I want to lock up," Windross said. "Is that all?"

"Unless you'd care to file a formal complaint against Mr. Devon."

"I only want to forget about the whole thing," the innkeeper said wearily, with a last, seemingly incurious look at Rich before Stefanie took him away.

Stefanie allowed Rich time to shower. While he was in the bathroom she made an illegal but thorough search for controlled substances, found none.

In the steaming shower Rich scrubbed himself furiously to keep from going numb all over; he fought a lassitude that threatened to become a blackout. By concentrating on Polly, the reality of her touch, her tears, he fanned his anger to a consistent glow, and kept his bearings; the thin potential of a resolve to return, and find her.

After his shower he dressed; his hands were almost as

useless as rocks, and he still trembled. He was unable to draw a decent breath without reviving the sickening odor that had staggered him in room 331: every cell of his body seemed saturated with it. Dimly he recognized hysteria. The disgusting slashes on Polly's body had smelled, faintly, of corruption: anxiety had exaggerated this shock into an olfactory horror.

"Time to move on," Stefanie advised him.

"Sure," Rich said bitterly.

Outside he paused to look at the deserted wing. A dark cloud was transiting the moon. In his mind it took the shape of a panther's head, turning; its baleful yellow eye blotted reason. He coughed and gasped and, with his tender face feeling numb again, got into his Porsche.

Everything about the interior was distantly, unimportantly familiar to him: the worn leather covering on the steering wheel, the sheepskin seat covers, the old St. Christopher medal dangling from the rearview mirror. Yet he couldn't remember how to operate the machine. He rolled up the window, traceries of frost on the glass. Stefanie's watchful face was dimmed as if by extreme old age. Everything was waxworks now. No sound. In this void he fumbled for keys. The rough edge of the ignition key elicited a mechanical response. Key in the ignition, turn; press the accelerator. The engine started. The booming, flatulent sound of exhaust returned him a little nearer to reality, though he still seemed mysteriously divided into two people, one of whom was dreaming the other. As he put the car into gear and backed away from the motionless Stefanie, Rich felt himself slipping back into the ruined wing of the inn, roaming the blackened rooms, his movements slowed by the horror of Polly's inexplicable absence.

But she had been there. *Been there!* The familiar, faded blue eyes. The lips he had kissed. *No mistake.* Her fingers clutching his arm. He heard her crying for him now, a scalding lament, as he drove slowly away from the inn, defeated, lamed by some ungodly magic. *Don't leave me, Rich!* Her voice sounded so real, he was wild to look back—but it was all he could do to hold the road, he was in tears himself.

(You're not crazy)
he assured himself. *(Whoever they are*

> *they pulled one on*
> *you.*

Windross in on it. Took Polly out of there, changed the appearance of the room somehow. But they can't hide her forever:

> *forever:)*

On the outskirts of Talbot, a college town seven miles down the road, he was attracted by a roadside tavern sign shimmering blue in the night. A stiff drink. Yes. Snap out of it. There were a few cars in the steep parking lot. He pulled up in front of the door and went in.

It was a popular watering hole, but late for crowds. All the odors and trappings were reassuring. *(I'm not crazy. Think this through. God's sake find an answer.)* There was a collection of barflies beneath the TV at one end of the bar; a couple of women negotiating the dangerous curves of forty with their horns blaring; a scattering of quieter, younger couples around the big room. He bought cigarettes from a machine, settled in an empty corner booth as far from the bar as possible. There was an octagonal window just above his head, facing the Post Road. The lone waitress working the tables wore jeans and boots, a paisley neckerchief. He ordered Jameson's. His hands trembled so he kept them out of sight, beneath the table. A fierce headache had set in.

For the first time in hours Rich thought about Karyn and, guiltily, he remembered their dinner date. What was the name of the fucking place where they were to have met? That he couldn't remember. Londonderry, she'd said. He looked at his watch. After eleven. Londonderry was a good half hour to the north. The restaurant would be closed by now. No use trying to call, even if he could think of the name. He would just sit here awhile, try to pull himself together, achieve a mental groove that would enable him to think this thing through.

Rich drank the first whiskey in a couple of gulps. Bad form, but he wanted quick results. He seldom drank liquor, having profited from the examples of his father and several close relatives, who had been laid to rest with devastated livers while a few prime years remained. But just as he sometimes needed pot, there were hardship occasions that called for whiskey. He motioned to the waitress and ordered a double.

15

"You mustn't interfere," the woman said softly.

For a few seconds Rich wasn't sure anyone had spoken to him; his head, bagged in a rarefied substance not unlike cotton candy, lolled above the nearly empty tumbler on the table in front of him. He had been studying the intricate sparkly tangle of the design in the Formica tabletop, likening it to the best work of Jackson Pollock. An amazing discovery, in a nowhere bar in the wilds of Vermont.

He looked up, mouth agape. Holding his head in this new position unbalanced him, and he nearly toppled sideways in the booth. He clutched the edge of the table, blinking, trying to bring her into focus. The barroom was on the move, whirling slowly, tilting like an unstable carousel. ZZ Top on the jukebox. "Gimme All Your Lovin." He licked his lips. They were dry from cigarettes and the several potent whiskeys he'd knocked back in less than an hour. He was barely aware of the other customers in the bar. He felt detached from humanity, like a tired cuckoo sprung from a rundown clock.

She came a little closer to the booth, stood just beyond arm's reach. She was tall and severely dressed, in black or midnight blue. Sweater, skirt, boots. Her only ornaments were diamonds in the lobes of her ears and a shiny sickle scar low on one cheek.

"What did you say? Who are you?"

"My name is Inez Cordway. We almost met last night. I decided at the last moment it would serve no useful purpose. That, I believe, was a mistake."

He touched his own cheek, sketching with a fingertip the mirror image of her scar. She nodded.

"Yes. That was me. With Windross."

"*Mother of God.*"

She replied with a cool, tolerant smile. "You've had quite a time for yourself tonight."

"Tell me about it." Anger brought Rich to near sobriety for a few seconds. He started to get up. "You. You must know where Polly is!"

She stopped him with only the slightest of movements, a tilt of the head which in turn revealed a glimpse of something unnerving in her eyes; her gaze could be as strict and unforgiving as an adder's bite.

"It isn't just Polly anymore," Inez Cordway said.

Rich slumped on the bench seat, breathing hard, all but choking on backed-up fumes of alcohol. The corner they occupied seemed withdrawn from the rest of the barroom, at the wrong end of a telescope and bathed in St. Elmo's fire. His ears, his forehead, smarted. His fingernails glowed on the tabletop. His eyes, straining, lost focus; the woman faded from substance to angular shadow. But her voice was dismally clear.

"The child is fully possessed by a demon. Perhaps more than one demon. That isn't certain yet. The rites have only just begun. It could be weeks before we know exactly what we're dealing with."

The raw taste of whiskey spurted into Rich's throat; he clapped a hand to his mouth. Some of the liquid trickled through his fingers.

"You've had too much to drink," she said dispassionately. "But getting drunk is certainly not the worst thing that could have happened to you tonight."

Unexpectedly Rich began to cry, low against his chest, in frustration and fury.

"What the hell do you mean—*it isn't Polly*? I saw her—I talked to her!"

"Yes, I know. In room 331 of the inn."

"When I went back she wasn't there! What did you do with—"

"Listen to me." She leaned a little closer; the movement revealed, suddenly and unpleasantly, too much of her face to him. He was aware of a high-style gleam of gold encasing several teeth, her dark eyes astringent as cloves.

"Polly was *never* there. She has not been at the Post Road Inn for more than five weeks."

"You don't know what you're saying!" He felt his heart knocking; he mustered a threat. "But I'm going to find out what this is all about."

"Let me assure you of one thing. Polly—the host Polly—is in a safe place. She is loved, protected, peaceable—for the time being. We have a chance to redeem the child—safeguard her immortal soul. But I say again: you must not interfere."

"Interfere with *what*?"

She drew back; she achieved magisterial height.

"The exorcism."

Rich tried, too quickly, to get up; he was blocked by the edge of the table and sat down again. Faintness, heaviness; his brain half-stunned, lying at the edge of a vast darkness like an animal hit in the road.

"I want to see Polly!"

"You will do her, and all of us, a very great favor if you forget about her. You can't help."

"If Polly isn't—wasn't—at the inn, what were all of you doing there last night?"

"Strict obedience to the ritual requires a visit to the site of the possession, if it is known."

"Possessed? How do you know she's—God damn it, who *are* you?"

"I've told you my name. I have spent much of my life dealing with Satan. Oh, I am very sure. That's why I've come to tell you to leave us alone. It's obvious that you're much too susceptible to Polly. The demon knows that, and is already using you. This could become extremely dangerous. Please believe what I'm saying. You should go home at once."

Inez Cordway turned and, in the mists of his vision, was quickly under way, a dreadnaught on a dark outgoing tide. Her departure was so abrupt, it seemed a conjuring trick in reverse. One moment she was standing over him, formidably knowledgeable about things that refreshed the terrors of his youth; the next she was gone.

The barroom was still in motion, but not as disconcertingly as before. Rich levered himself up and out of the booth, swayed, willed himself to stand erect, fished a thin wad of bills from his pocket, and threw down on the table what he thought was a twenty. Then he went after the woman.

16

The black Cadillac was pulling out of the parking lot onto the access road when Rich emerged from the tavern. The flash of cold air in his lungs revived him, as if someone had taken a point-blank shot at him. Adrenaline followed, giving him a false sense of sobriety, but his reflexes were sluggish. He banged a hip painfully against another car getting to his Porsche. Behind the wheel he turned his head frantically, trying to keep the old Cadillac in sight while he started and encouraged the balky engine.

By the time he had backed out of the inclined parking lot, Inez Cordway had disappeared eastbound along the road to Talbot.

Rich gunned the Porsche to fifty. Only about half a minute had gone by; he knew he would catch up to her in a matter of seconds. The Porsche shot over a hill and around a tight curve. No traffic in either direction. Just ahead he saw a blinking red traffic light: a four-way intersection. Rich groaned in frustration as he down-shifted to a crawl.

He could see perhaps half a mile up the road he was traveling, to the lights of the village. His vision was a little swarmy but his view of the road was unobstructed; and he could see well enough to distinguish the unique high tail-lights of the Caddy, if she had gone into Talbot. The only moving vehicle in that direction was a pickup truck with a snowplow attachment; it was coming toward him.

Two choices.

Rich made an instant decision and twisted the wheel to the left, sped north along narrow twisting blacktop, past rock walls nearly buried in snowbanks, isolated homes and woodlots that crowded the road. He was half sick from momentum and the whiskey he'd drunk, cold and sweating at the same time. He pushed his speed to the limit of recklessness, where any little problem would mean trouble: there was always unexpected ice on the best-plowed roads, wildlife, a slow-moving car with dim lights hogging the centerline.

Just as he decided he'd made a wrong guess, and was starting to slow down, Rich came over the crest of a hill to an unmarked, unlighted intersection, and the end of the road he was on. Snow from several plowings formed a six-foot-high wall around the thick trunks of birch trees. If he hadn't already had his foot on the brake he would have smashed head-on with undiminished speed into the snow and the trees. Instead, braking too hard, he spun around twice into the intersection and hit the snowbank broadside. The well-packed snow provided enough of a cushion to keep the Porsche from crashing into the trees.

Rich got out, overcome by a rush of nausea, and vomited raw undigested whiskey, aggravating his already-sore stomach muscles. Then, too weak to stand or even lean against a tree, he sank down into the snow.

Several seconds passed before he was aware of the rough chuckle of the Cadillac's idling engine.

When he lifted his head he saw the car less than a hundred yards away down the left-hand fork of the road. Her foot was on the brake; the taillights glowed. It was about all he could see of the Cadillac, taillights and parking lights. The car was approximately in the middle of the road. He wondered if she'd been waiting there for him, waiting for the expected accident.

Rich got to his feet and started toward the Cadillac, walking unsteadily, breath coming hard. He couldn't manage a straight line but he didn't lose his balance; he kept going doggedly.

Tires squealed on the road as the brakes were slow to release. Then the Cadillac lurched and drove forward.

"Wait!" Rich yelled, breaking into a jog.

She didn't wait. Perhaps she'd only wanted to know that he wasn't seriously hurt. The Cadillac went around a bend, she was still driving with parking lights only. The taillights flashed briefly through a stand of trees and then disappeared. Rich came to a limping halt, swearing tiredly.

As far as he could tell when he returned to it, the Porsche wasn't badly damaged. But both rear tires were hubcap-deep in snow and he couldn't drive it away. Wishing endlessly for cigarettes, he sat behind the wheel for nearly forty minutes, the erratic heater putting out just enough warmth to keep him from freezing, until a couple of high school boys in a hardtop Jeep Renegade came along and gave him a lift into Talbot.

"Do either of you know where Inez Cordway lives?"

Rich repeated the name; the boys looked at each other and shook their heads. He described her.

"Nobody I know," the Jeep driver said. "How about you, Ted?"

"No, I don't recall I've ever seen her."

Rich also described the fifties Cadillac, wishing he could remember the license number.

"Sounds like old Bob Thurlow would like to get his hands on that one," Ted commented.

"He must have a couple dozen old wrecks he's restoring."

"But you haven't seen Inez Cordway's car on the roads around here?" Rich asked the driver.

"No, and I'd remember a Cadillac that old. Nobody lives near us has got one, that's for sure."

17

Rich spent sixteen dollars of his thinning cash reserve to take a taxi to the Davos Chalet at Hermitage Mountain. He stopped at the desk for the room number of the honeymoon suite and carried his bags and Karyn's upstairs, not bothering to call first. It was twenty after one in the morning. He was so exhausted he almost fell asleep standing up in the elevator.

He was halfway down the brightly lighted hall before he noticed a couple necking in a doorway, and almost on top of them when he realized the girl was Karyn. Her back was to him. Trux Landall held her tightly, one hand between her shoulder blades and the other, roving slowly and possessively, on her ass.

"Oh, shit," Rich said.

They looked at him. Karyn's lips were still parted, plump and contact-reddened, her eyes steamily wistful from the long-held kiss. She backed inside the suite and Trux took a step out into the hall. He was dressed nearly head to foot in shimmering dark sealskin. One hand pulled the coat together as if to conceal what must have felt to him like a monster hard-on.

Rich dropped one bag and heaved the other, Karyn's tan SportSac, at Trux's head. The tall boy ducked without effort, and frowned.

"Take it easy, guy."

"Get the fuck out of here!" Rich shouted.

"I was just going."

Rich tried to kick him in his bulging groin. Trux backed away pacifically, but raised his hands just in case. Rich picked up another bag, his green duffel, and swung it by the leather strap.

"Rich, stop it!" Karyn pleaded.

He glared at her, dumped the bag, which was awkward to use offensively, and swarmed in on Trux, both fists going, kicking and slugging, street technique that had won many fights against bigger boys. But he was sluggish and a little awkward, and Trux parried without suffering any damage. He glanced helplessly at Karyn while keeping Rich at arm's length.

"I don't want any part of this, Karyn."

"Rich!"

She caught at an arm; he muscled her aside. Trux had time to take aim and nail him below the breastbone with a short right hand.

Rich sat down hard, mouth ajar; he rolled over whimpering for air.

"Sorry, Karyn," Trux said.

"Oh, God, he can be impossible when he gets like this!"

Rich was hazily aware of another door open down the hall, indistinct faces. More witnesses to his downfall. He got to his knees, discovered pride alone wasn't enough to get him back in the fight and stayed there massaging the spot where he'd been jabbed, knowing that he would topple if he tried to stand. Air leaked into his lungs. He gasped, looked up and around at Karyn's face. She was crying.

"Get you—for this," he said, to nobody in particular.

Trux said, in parting, "I was only saying good-night."

"Didn't she give you enough—inside?"

Karyn, her face reddening, gathered up the luggage Rich had thrown around the hall and carried it into the suite. She banged the door but opened it again in a fury, not caring who was listening.

"God damn you, where've you been all night? Couldn't you call? I was worried sick!"

"Accident," Rich said. With a wall behind him he stood. But he couldn't straighten all the way, or get his feet to work. Trux was blithely on his way to the elevators, turning with a good-bye wave to Karyn. She didn't notice.

"*Oh, no!* Where? What happened?"

"Car—ran off the road."

Karyn put an arm around him. "Wrecked? Oh, well. Come on."

Petulant, he resisted. "Was tricky Trux fucking you?"

"Rich, grow up! Trux was just keeping me company. You weren't here when I got back, I didn't want to be by myself. Now will you please get inside?"

He needed her help at this point, and grudgingly permitted it. His feet shuffled. She sat him down on the bed, which was mussed but not unmade. Rich lay back, wincing. Another time, he could have taken Trux. Flash but no guts, he knew the type. Got him with a sucker punch.

"Kill the bastard," he said vaguely.

Karyn made a tough tight face to control her tears. "Just shut up! It was a good-night kiss. Okay, a little heavy. I used to go with him, for God's sake! Trux is a friend."

Rich rolled his eyes in disbelief. "So just tell me the truth. Did you fuck him tonight?"

"No, I did not."

After a while Rich said generously, "Okay, I believe you."

"I don't give a shit if you believe me or not! I'm sick of the way you're acting. I don't know what's got into you.

All I want is to be happy. I want to feel good about us, Rich. Can't you make it a little easier?''

He was silent, eyes half closed, face with that taut, famished look of extreme fatigue.

Karyn got up sniffling, went to the bathroom for a tissue, came back and sat down closer to him. His hand moved tentatively, touched her cold fingers. Karyn gave him no encouragement, but she didn't move her hand away.

''Sorry.''

''Is the Porsche hopeless?''

''I don't think so.''

''About Trux. I guess—if you hadn't come along—maybe we would have come back in here. I don't know for sure. But no matter what we did, it wouldn't have meant—''

''Sure, sure. I don't want to talk about it anymore. Or him. I need to sleep, Karyn. Honest to God, I'm really tired.''

After a few moments Karyn curled up beside him, touched his face softly. Rich kissed the palm of her hand.

''You left the lights on,'' he complained.

''Oh—I don't want to go to sleep in the dark.''

''Why not?''

''There are things—that just can't be there with the lights on,'' Karyn said, trembling a little as she snuggled closer, her eyes wide, her face bleak.

18

Karyn did her best to get him out of bed at sunrise, but Rich protested bitterly that he was too tired and said that he hurt all over. Finally she gave him a conciliatory kiss, covered him up again and went down to the slopes by herself.

About nine o'clock, with the sun cutting like a laser across his face, Rich gave up trying to sleep any longer and crept into the bathroom, which was equipped with an oversized shower with numerous jet-spray nozzles, a Jacuzzi, heat lamps, and a sauna. He sweated for twenty minutes in the sauna, took a needle shower that was so cold it made his back teeth ache. With his blood flowing briskly he felt physical improvement, but the heavy depression that had settled in the moment he was up remained with him. He had dreamed, off and on, of the blackened room, the missing Polly, the gold-lined teeth of Inez Cordway, her pearly scar and presumptuous warning to him.

They were hiding the girl, brutally beating her, and they thought they could get away with it! Rich wasn't intimidated. But he had no clear idea of what to do next, only the intuition that he must move quickly, for Polly's sake.

Coffee on the sun-warmed cafeteria terrace lifted his mood a notch. He was ready for a big breakfast, which he packed away while keeping an eye on the runouts at the base of the mountain for Karyn. Saw her, a couple of times, near the chair lifts. Trux wasn't with her, or he might have been compelled to go out there and finish what he'd bungled the night before.

Rich poured more coffee and saw Benny Childs making his way toward the table, hobbling with the aid of a cane.

"What happened?"

"Strained my knee yesterday. No more skiing. I heard you and Karyn were staying up here now. Wish I could afford it."

Benny eased down into a chair, keeping his left leg, which was bulky with wrappings beneath his trousers, straight. He reached for a honey nut muffin on a plate, and was short. Rich handed him the plate.

"Yeah. The honeymoon suite. Coffee?"

"Thanks. The honeymoon suite? Are congratulations in order?"

"Premature. The suite was all that was available, and I can't afford it either. But Karyn couldn't move out of the inn fast enough."

"Oh, really?" He saw that Rich wasn't going to explain why. Benny held his coffee mug in two hands, smiling over the rim. "How is everything with you two?"

"What have you heard?"

"There was a tiff. No blows were exchanged."

"We made up."

"Good. Are you about to hit the slopes?"

"No. I left my car in a snowdrift last night. I need to start thinking about hauling it out."

"Tow truck required?"

"I don't think so. It's right by the side of the road."

"I'll loan you my Saab. There's about ten feet of heavy-duty tow cable in the trunk."

"That ought to do! Thanks, Benny."

"I'll just ride along with you. Nothing else to do this morning but read a dull book on the Gnostics."

On the way to Talbot, Benny told a couple of scatalogical jokes in an attempt to get Rich to lighten up; he was dour behind the wheel, head jutted forward, jaw clenched. Rich laughed perfunctorily, as if he'd missed the punch lines.

After a couple of silent miles Benny sighed and said, "I miss your company."

"What's that?"

"The brilliant dialectics, the cynical wit. Nothing offending you lately? The stewheads in Washington? The terrible state of the economy?

"Sorry, Benny."

Benny watched a hobbling dog by the side of the road, its left leg twisted backwards from the knee down. The sight depressed him. "You're sure everything's okay with you and Karyn?"

"Yeah. I wasn't thinking about her."

"So what's on your mind?"

"Benny, what kind of people believe in the devil?"

"Ahhh," Benny said, warming to a discourse, his mood improving. "Your kind of people, to begin with. The last I heard the devil hadn't gone the way of Mass in Latin, St. Catherine's feast day or fish on Fridays. The devil is still a part of the articles of faith, the essential dogma."

"Yes, but does he exist?"

"My personal view, or the rationalist policy line at Yale?"

"What do you believe?"

"If you ask me do I think there is a power opposite and equal to God, no, I don't. God is the only uncreated being, who always was and always shall be. God created the angels, and to the angels He gave free will. Some of them abused this freedom; by so doing they became His enemies and, indirectly, enemies of thee and me. So there are devils, small *d*, probably a slew of them; and their leader is called Satan. But he is the opposite of the Archangel Michael, not of God.''

"But there's never been any proof that devils, or Satan, exist."

Benny tenderly rubbed his swollen knee, which he couldn't properly straighten in the cramped front seat. "Proving a negative is no cinch. St. Paul thought Satan was God of this world, and the New Testament is filled with the appearances of demons. Jesus exorcised them, probably with the showmanship of one of our modern evangelists. Satan, next to Christ, is the best-known figure in Christian lore. I'd say that belief in demons is consistent with the rationality of Scripture, Christian tradition, and the common belief of mankind throughout history. Also, and this may be of great importance, such belief is not in conflict with anything which science has demonstrated to be true."

"Assuming demons exist, what are they like? How could any of them possess a human being? Have you ever witnessed an exorcism?"

"I've seen an attempt, by a southern fundamentalist preacher I thought was more crazed than the poor lout he was trying to exorcise. Traditionally demons are represented as hideous inversions of the animal world—grotesque symbols which the mind of man can grasp. But we are, after all, talking about fallen angels. Creatures who exist on a higher plane of the natural order. Logically they have no form. They are a rarefied state of intellectual energy, or vibrations. If they want human form, and they must, they have to seize it."

"Why do they want human form?" Rich asked.

"Because they're afflicted with a kind of spiritual cannibalism, to borrow a fine phrase from C. S. Lewis. They prey on each other, and on easier targets: us poor humanoids. They have an imperishable hunger for human souls. No other motive than hunger. It's a pure, or impure desire if you will, to ravish and dominate, to be strongest. Of course that's a paradox. They can only despise God, never equal Him. They are merely shadows made by His immortal light."

Rich located his car without difficulty and, using Benny's sturdy Saab as a tow truck, pulled the Porsche out of the snowbank. It looked lopsided from the snow and ice clinging like barnacles to the right side. He used a rubber mallet to knock off the clumps of snow and clean out the obstructed fender wells; where the snow was harder than frozen, it resisted his hammering as if petrified. When he had cleaned it up he saw that the Porsche had some new dents, but the frame looked all right. He'd been luckier than he had a right to be, chasing around unfamiliar roads at high speeds at night.

Having worked up a good sweat and a jogger's heartbeat, Rich dumped the vinyl-covered tow cable back into the trunk of the Saab. Benny got in behind the wheel.

"Can you drive okay?" Rich asked him.

"I only have to use my right foot. No problem."

"Thanks for the help, Benny."

"Why don't we all get together tonight? Elise and I will drive up to the Chalet. Nine, nine thirty?"

"Fine."

Benny said, but not as if it were an afterthought, "Why the interest in devils, Rich?"

Rich hesitated, tempted to spill everything about Polly, her father, and the mysterious Inez Cordway. But he realized there would be too many gaps in whatever explanation he might make now; Benny inevitably would have questions that couldn't be answered. Benny waited, with the sly smile of one expecting an entertaining answer, but Rich only shrugged.

"Something I was reading. A paperback on demonology I picked up. I think it's all bullshit. I was just interested in hearing the theological point of view."

"Demons have been demythologized by most of our prestigious scholars. Entire books on Christianity have been written, by Hans Küng and others, that don't even refer to Satan. On the other hand, the worse things get, the more we hear about him. The charismatic movement is stronger than ever. We all want to blame something or someone for the pain and suffering in life, and our God is not Yahweh. So we give credence to evil personified: the Jews invented the devil to justify a spiritual crisis, their failure to achieve the nationalism they felt was theirs by divine right. That can be a tricky problem. If there are demons, which I believe, and we develop, let's say, an obsessive and unhealthy interest in them, they have a way of responding to our expectations and our needs.'' Benny started the car and put it into gear. ''Elise will be wondering what happened to me. What are you doing the rest of the day?''

''I'm not sure. I may be attending an exorcism.''

Benny laughed. ''Matinee or evening? Tell me all about it tonight.''

19

In Talbot Rich did the obvious first, consulting the area telephone directory, but there was no listing for Inez Cordway, or anyone named Cordway. She was not on the computer at the Green Mountain Power office. Nor was she a registered voter.

He bought a road map of the county at the college bookstore and spent half an hour in a coffee shop smoking and studying the roads in the vicinity of the T-cross where he'd come a cropper while in pursuit of the woman. There was no guarantee that she actually lived in the immediate neighborhood; she might purposely have been leading him nowhere. The boys who had come along in the Jeep obviously didn't know Inez Cordway—at least he hadn't detected any Yankee reluctance to furnish information about locals to a stranger. He'd never gotten a close look at the license number of the Cadillac, so there was no way to tap the files at the state motor vehicle bureau. He had to start somewhere, no matter how much time it took.

Rich thought about Windross. His skin still itched from the rash of frustration and humiliation he'd suffered in the burned-out wing of the Post Road Inn. He had decided it was useless to try to get information from Windross, who had everything to hide at this point; any attempt to do so would land him in the Chadbury jail, possibly initiating a legal hassle he could do without. Nor would that help Polly.

When he emerged from the coffee shop the sun was vanishing in a thick overcast and a biting wind was on the rise, scouring the village with loose particles of snow. More snow seemed to be on the way from the west. He retraced the route to the T-cross and began systematically to explore all the back roads within a ten-mile radius. There were a lot of them, and many houses set well back in the countryside, marked only by the roadside presence of frequently anonymous mailboxes. Numerous driveways were impassable to his low-slung Porsche. He had to leave the car as close to the side of the road as he could and slog on foot to the doorways.

No. No. Don't know her. Never heard of any Cordways. Not around here. Sorry.

Deep snow on the ground, flurries in the air, dreary woodlots, the tang of woodsmoke on the wind, the skies by three o'clock almost to treetop level and blackening. Because of the numbing cold there were no loose dogs in these backwoods. His only blessing. More pallid faces and suspicious appraisals behind steamed-up storm windows, faces gathered around a wood-burning stove in an isolated general store. Postmasters and mistresses shaking their heads.

And finally:

"I did hear of some Cordways over to Ripington Four Corners. But come to think of it, they spelled it with a *u* and an *e* on the end. Courdewaye. That help you?"

Seventeen miles to Ripington Four Corners. Snow coming down in the early dusk. The post office again, a white frame structure across from the Congregational Church. They'd closed for the day. There was a light on in the mailroom in back, a hunched figure moving deliberately behind the opaque glass in the door. By insistent knocking Rich raised a clerk, a rheumy octogenarian wearing a soiled blue government-issue apron. He let Rich in only after a careful examination of Rich's *Register* press credentials.

"Courdewayes? Yes, sir. Courdewayes lived here for, I'd say a hundred and fifty years."

"Inez Cordway," Rich said eagerly. "Do you know where I can find her?"

"*Lived* here, is what I said. Haven't been any Courdewayes around for, oh, it's been since right after the war."

"Which war?"

"War Two," the old man said, lighting a tacky-looking briar pipe.

Rich carefully described Inez Cordway. The clerk listened with an occasional solemn nod, blue smoke around his head.

"About what age would you say?"

"Mid-forties."

"Uh-huh. Sounds to me like Matt Courdewaye's youngest, Leslie. But nobody could be that well-preserved. She was twenty-two, twenty-three years old when the war ended. So we're talking about a woman of sixty-some, if she was alive."

"What do you mean?"

"That's a question mark. You see, Leslie ran off with a war hero, name of Dunstan, Major Michael Dunstan, right after he returned home from the European theater. That was, I recollect, in the fall of 1945. She took him away from his wife and three small children, and off they went. There was a mighty big scandal. Her family, they were the last of the Courdewayes, disowned Leslie; then bad luck just seemed to happen to all of them. Matt was run over in the road that winter, and his wife died of cancer Maundy Thursday of the following year. The others, Leslie's brothers and sisters, moved away one after the other. And you might guess Leslie and her war hero didn't live happily ever after. He was gone off in the head from the fightin'; battle fatigue they called it. Treated her badly, couldn't hold a steady job. They hopped around the country, wound up south of the border. Down Mexico way. Things really went to pot there. If you know what I mean."

"Not really."

"*Pot*. Isn't that what you young people call it? Mary-ju-wanna."

"Oh—sure."

"Leslie and Michael fell in with a bad group of people in Mexico. All of them goin' to hell in a handbasket. Crazed by narcotics and orgies. Seems that Leslie had a couple of children along the way, but she wasn't much of a mother. A case of total neglect. And her husband's mental condition went from bad to worse. She must have been unbalanced herself. What I hear happened, she took his service revolver and shot him and both of the youngsters in the head, then poured gasoline over them and set them all on fire.''

"Good Lord."

"Nothin' heard from Leslie since. I expect she died down there in some hovel, sellin' her body to live, needles every day. That's the end of her sad story, but I guess there's a point to it. Can't be Leslie Courdewaye you're lookin' for."

"No, I'm sure it isn't. But it may be some other member of the family—you said several of them moved away."

"Far as I know, none of the Courdewayes have been back for even a single day."

"Where did they live?"

"Cutler Road. You turn right at the fire station, about two and three-quarter miles on to the house. Brick. Three big chimneys. House sits back from the road below a knoll so that about all you can see, winter or summer, is the tops of the chimneys."

"Is the house abandoned?"

The old clerk snorted. "Fine property like that? The Gannaways bought it in '49. New York people. His son uses the house now, every summer and sometimes durin' the holidays."

"But the house is empty now."

A nod. "Avery Myatt looks after the place. He'd have told me if he was expectin' them to come up from the city."

"Well—I guess I have the wrong Courdewayes."

"Appears to be."

Rich got back into his snow-covered Porsche and followed the postal clerk's directions to the house that Courdewayes had built and lived in for generations. Even though he'd been warned about the low visibility of the homestead, he nearly missed the chimneys in the deepening dark and heavy snow.

He was forced to continue on for another quarter of a mile before finding a place to turn around; then he returned at a crawl behind a bulky snowplow. The driveway of the Courdewaye place angled uphill through a rock wall and a wooden gate locked open by drifts. The drive was steep but packed down; it looked as if several cars had driven in or out during the afternoon, one as recently as ten minutes ago: the treadmarks were only a little blurred by the new fall of snow.

Rich idled in front of the driveway, cautious, for no reason he could readily define, about following any recent arrivals to the house. The story he'd heard from the gossipy clerk had stuck in his mind.

She took his service revolver and shot him and both of the youngsters in the head.

Logically there could be no connection between the benighted Leslie Courdewaye and the woman who had confronted him in the bar last night, but his daylong search for her had left him tired and on edge. What if he had finally tracked her down? Her warning to him had been explicit: *Don't interfere.* He didn't believe Inez Cordway's bullshit explanation of Polly's travail, not for a moment, but obviously the woman was deadly serious, possibly demented and therefore a danger to both Polly and himself. And of course there were others potentially as dangerous: Cordway's followers. Rich knew he had no reason to go to the police at this point—assuming she was in the house—but it wouldn't pay to recklessly show up at the front door demanding to see her.

He needed to find a place for his Porsche where it wouldn't block someone's driveway or be half-buried by the plows on the state road. After hunting for a quarter of an hour he parked the car close to the side wall of a gas station–market that had closed. It was at least half a mile from the Courdewaye house and there was nowhere to walk but in the slippery road. Fortunately only a few cars came along.

Most of the drivers stopped to offer him a ride. One did not, and he was forced to leap into the snow above his knees at the side of the road to keep from being hit. The car was a late-model Oldsmobile, with several passengers. He thought at least two of them looked back. He was wearing a knit seaman's cap pulled low over his ears, and the lower part of his face was muffled in a wool scarf, but not knowing who they might be, he kept his face averted.

Rich barely noticed the cold, the difficult footing. He was awash in adrenaline, having convinced himself that, with every step, he was getting closer to Polly Windross. The coincidence of names, the evidence of activity at a house that normally was closed in winter: this had to be Inez Cordway's—and Polly's—hideaway.

His suspicions were heightened as he approached the house along the rutted drive. A few mullioned windows were faintly alight, two chimneys were smoking, and several cars, including the Olds that had missed him by inches on the road, were pulled up in front. The Courdewaye house was atypical for the region: it was an expensive brick-and-slate reproduction of an eighteenth-century English manor, large enough to have twenty rooms. There were walled gardens, the outlines of which were barely discernible in snow, a frozen pond behind the house, huge birches and copper beeches in stately clumps on the grounds.

Two detached buildings mimicked the style of the main house. One was a guest cottage, the other a garage.

No concealment was possible, but in the snow and the dark he doubted if anyone watching casually from the windows of the house could see him coming. Nevertheless he followed the left-hand bend of the drive toward the garage and away from the front door.

When he reached the garage he brushed snow from a pane of glass in the door and peered inside between cupped hands. When his eyes adjusted to the blackness he could make out the fifties-fantasy, rocketlike tail assembly of the old Cadillac.

This confirmation of the end of his quest left Rich feeling more grim than elated. The hard part was about to begin, and he was less sure of himself than he had been earlier. The house had looked formidable, barring easy entry, and it was obvious that Inez Cordway had a lot of company.

"As long as you're here," the woman said behind him, "you may as well come in and have supper with us."

20

Rich whirled in shock. Inez Cordway was standing only a few feet from him, the wind whipping her long dark skirt and the loose cowl of the cable-knit coat sweater she was wearing. Just to her right stood a large dog with the narrow frame and curved back of a wolfhound, although in coloring he was either dark brown or black. In spite of a coat as thick as a woolly mammoth's the dog was shuddering. Its slanted yellow eyes, fixed on Rich, were pale but alight, like burning tallow.

"I—I've been—"

"You have spent most of your day looking for me," she said resignedly. "Yes, I know all about that. You're a tenacious sort. That's to your credit. But you don't listen very well. Perhaps you should have trusted my judgment."

"Is Polly here?" Rich demanded.

"Yes. She is."

"Well—s-show her to me."

"Suppose you come inside. We can't talk if we're freezing. Hugo!"

The shaggy hound turned eagerly back to the house. Inez Cordway waited until Rich fell into step behind her. Her hands were in the pockets of the coat sweater. Despite the wind and the snow Rich smelled her pungent, tropical perfume.

"Miserable weather," she said, with a faint pucker of distaste. "One becomes accustomed to it, if one must. I was born in this house. But it's been many years since I lived in Vermont."

"You don't live here now?"

"Mexico."

His misgivings crystallized as dread, sharp as bits of glass flooding the chambers of the heart.

"Then you're—"

"I *was* Leslie Courdewaye. That was a lifetime ago."

94

He thought he saw a smile within the cowl, a saturnine gleam of gold. "What have you heard about me in town?"

"The postal clerk—"

"Jud Sweeny. That old fool. But they're all fools here. I assure you, I never shot my husband. We were devoted to each other, to the life we found in Paracuaro."

"What about your ch-children, are they—"

"They died years ago, of natural causes. Do you never run out of questions?" But she said it good-humoredly.

Rich's teeth were chattering; he felt frail in the full bore of the storm, a cage of bones.

"Wh-why did you c-come back to Vermont?"

"I was chosen," she said cryptically, as they reached a side door of the brick house, a small porch roofed in copper, latticework covered in creeper vine on two sides. From inside the house Rich heard voices, a burst of male laughter, and music: something symphonic, a riotous tarantella from a popular opera, but his brain was as numb as his face, he couldn't recall which opera. The quivering dog edged in between them and disappeared through a pet port before Inez could open the door.

"It ssss-sounds like a celebration," Rich said.

"Not at all. We have nothing to celebrate. Nor do we have a reason to mourn. Yet."

Inside there was, unexpectedly, candlelight, the lovely aroma of a feast in the making that had Rich's mouth watering in seconds. They had entered the house by way of a small mudroom off the kitchen. The dog shoved his way through a swinging door and Rich had a glimpse of bright copper and stainless steel, island work areas surfaced in hard maple, cooks and maids hard at work in an amiable clatter and wisps of steam. He saw a golden roast pig with a baked apple in its mouth, fruit pies lined up to cool. His apprehension was vulnerable to this homely bustle. No danger here.

Inez Cordway sat down on a bench to pull off her boots. The dog was sent out of the kitchen and whined at her; she rubbed behind his ears and looked up helplessly at Rich.

"Could you give me a hand?"

Rich helped her off with the boots. She stood unexpectedly short in her black-stocking-covered feet. Rich stamped off most of the snow from his own boots.

"This way. Hugo, stay."

Rich followed her up a short flight of steps to the butler's pantry, where an elderly man in a pinstriped vest was decanting wine, again by candlelight.

"Doesn't the electricity work?"

"Of course it works. I like candles."

The long dining room table was set for sixteen guests. The china looked old and expensive, the tablecloth was aged ivory lace, an immense feat of hand needlework. Inez paused to finger the material.

"Spanish," she said to Rich. "From the royal household of Aragon in the sixteenth century."

"When can I see Polly?"

Inez tilted her head, darkly disapproving of his impatience. The scar low on her right cheek was an ever-present ghostly smile.

"Polly is sleeping. She needs her rest. The ordeal has nearly worn her out. She's just a child, you know."

"Ordeal? God, you don't mean she's been beaten again!"

"Beaten?" Inez said, as if the conversation had taken a turn she couldn't follow.

"She was cut!" Hostility flared in Rich's face as he stared at the woman. Her self-righteous attitude—*she needs her rest*. But Inez had been with Polly; if she hadn't actually administered the whipping herself, she was just as guilty as the rest of them. "The cuts bled—they were infected. Did you get her a doctor?"

Inez took a step toward Rich, thrusting her face close to his.

"You must not be confused." Her tone was low, firm. Rich's face reddened more, but he felt a tingle of fear. "What you think you saw, heard, *touched*, in fact did not exist. It was only an illusion. The real Polly Windross is here. And I assure you, no one has beaten her."

The surge of blood to Rich's head was making him dizzy and ill. He had to sort out her words one at a time hoping to make sense of them. He thought of Polly and decided Inez was either lying or insane.

"Show her to me!"

"You may not give me orders in my house."

She touched him lightly, stiff fingers against his breastbone; the weight of her authority, irresistible, seemed

centered there. Rich leaned against a high-backed chair.
He licked his parched lips. The clear image he had of
Polly in her bondage melted at the edges, blurred as if the
flame of a candle had burned through the center of his
vision. His tongue was numb with cold, uncertainty. Her
gaze was unrelenting, pinning him in place like a moth on
the crimson velvet of the chair.

"I—I'm sorry. . . . I can't . . . I j-just don't know what
to make of all this."

Inez became less rigid; she stood back, her eyes softening, little crinkles at the corners.

"Of course not. You came for enlightenment. And you
will have it, at the proper time."

"I only want to help Polly," Rich insisted.

Inez swelled with a sigh and turned away. "I doubt that
you can." She hesitated, then took him by the elbow.
"Come with me anyway. Meet the others. Have something to drink, and relax. Then we can decide."

Rich accompanied her from the dining room, down a
hall past a graceful spiral staircase to the den, where the
music was, and a leaping fire that illuminated some vaguely
familiar faces. Inez smiled grandly at their entrance, presenting him.

"I would like for all of you to meet Richard Devon."

A sudden silence that, for some reason, unnerved him.
He received curious, if not penetrating, glances. Then
Rich made the rounds with Inez, shaking hands. He remembered only a few of the names he heard. Jim Seaclare.
Andrew Tyding. Rose Benidorm. But his nerves were
anesthetized by their ordinariness: some of them, he was
sure, had been a part of the exorcism conducted in the
burned-out wing of the inn. The friends of Inez Cordway
were in their forties and fifties. No one was conspicuously
fat or thin, handsome or ugly. The men were a little gray,
the women plumping up at the chinline. Everyone had a
drink and some of the guests had a nice glow on. He was
properly greeted, then largely forgotten.

Rich was offered a glass of red wine by a maid who was
wearing a little starched cap and a black and white uniform
with a lot of frills. Inez had left him momentarily to chat
with another couple. The wine was dry and too redolent of
earth, not fruit, a disappointing bouquet. A cabinet clock

against the wall opposite him was chiming: it was seven thirty. Already. He felt a poignant wrench, a sense of dislocation at the disappearance of the day. Rich stared into the flames of the hearth, just now able to control the chills that had racked him, feeling the warmth of the house beginning to seep into his bones. The glow of two dozen tapers placed around the paneled room was easy on his smarting eyes.

He drank more of the wine and was gratified by a lessening of the tension that had crowded him all day. There was a full-length portrait of a man and a seated woman in a gold frame above the marble mantel. The family resemblance was obvious but Inez said, as she glided up to him in stockinged feet and slipped a hand inside his elbow, "My mother and father."

"I thought this house belonged to another family now."

A grimace of distaste crumpled the scar and gave a fleeting impression of lizardly old age, belied by the petal smoothness of the rest of her face.

"They aren't here in winter. I removed a few things from storage when I arrived. So that the house would always be as I've remembered it." She looked at him, tightening her grip subtly; her hip brushed against his and Rich felt a pleasant sexual charge. "Do you like my father's house?"

"Yes."

"I'll show you more of it later. Are you feeling better about me now, Richard?"

"Yes," he said, but couldn't return her smile.

"You weren't injured last night, were you? You shouldn't have tried to drive in your condition."

"You—you just came in, and—"

"Caught you by surprise. I suppose I *was* too abrupt. One of my failings. But you'd begun to distress me greatly. After all, it's Polly's well-being that concerns us. Now that I've come to know you better, I see that I may have misjudged you, Richard. You could be useful. I want you to stay here tonight."

She'd caught Rich by surprise again, but before he could say anything Inez was on the move, sallying to another group, breaking into their conversation with a gesture and a remark that brought laughter.

Rich hunched his shoulders, looked at the half inch of wine left in his glass, finished it. The fire burned hotly. His mind settled into neutral. He felt a little tired. Seven thirty. Karyn was going to be mad as hell at him.

He looked around guiltily, wondering about a telephone. Good idea to let her know where he was. He didn't see a phone in the den.

The maid was nearby, with a tray of fresh drinks. He approached her.

"Telephone? Yes, I'll show you. Would you care for another glass of wine?"

"Thanks." Rich helped himself.

The maid picked up a candelabrum and led the way. Rich followed her across the marble floor of the entrance foyer and through a dimly lighted formal living room to the family room at the other end of the house and, at last, a telephone. But there was no dial tone, just a sparkly resonance.

Lines down somewhere, he thought. He hung up and then tried again, with the same result. Annoyed, he held the receiver to his ear, sipping wine with the other hand.

"Richard?"

The voice, loud in his ear, startled him. Someone on an extension phone in the house, he thought.

"Yes—who's that?"

No reply. He listened for several seconds, hearing again only the faint resonance of an inoperative phone line.

"Is anybody there?"

"It's Windross."

"*Windross!* Where are you?"

He heard the familiar wheezing breath, and a kind of dry sob in the man's throat.

"*For God's sake—for the sake of your soul—get out! Run! Before they—*"

"Richard," Inez said quietly from the doorway, "what's the matter?"

With the receiver of the phone half lowered, Rich turned a stricken face toward her.

21

Right after dinner, as was his habit, Avery Myatt fell asleep in the La-Z-Boy lounger in front of his TV while watching *Family Feud* on the cable. His spinster daughter Min finished the dishes in the kitchen and then limped, all three hundred pounds of her, with a crumpled bag of Meow Mix to the cat's bowl by the back door, which was rattling in the wind. Earlier on the six o'clock local news they'd been predicting six inches of snow before morning.

"Here, Figgy. Figgy, Figgy, come and get it!"

The elderly housecat was way ahead of her, slinking past one stumplike and arthritic ankle to get to his dinner. Min rationed the stuff severely, determined to get another three meals out of the nearly empty bag; the price of cat food, like everything else these days, was in the sky.

She was surprised to hear her father up and around in the den, clearing his throat, rattling the newspaper, changing channels on the TV before *Family Feud* was over. Just as the Delano family from Ukiah, California, was charging into the lead on points, thanks to their sharp little daughter-in-law, who'd be so much prettier if she just got rid of those harlequin-style glasses. The rest of the Delanos, God bless their hearts, they were dumb as fence posts in every category. Min shuffled to the breakfast counter and peered over it at her father. Usually he napped through until about ten o'clock, had a snack, watched the late news, and then went to bed.

"I wasn't through watching that," she admonished him from the kitchen.

"Didn't know you were watching, Min. You must have eyes in the back of your head."

"Well, I was mostly *listening*, while I did the dishes. Do you want another couple of Di-Gels?" She assumed it was his stomach that had prematurely awakened him. For dinner she'd fixed one of his favorite meals: fried pork chops, mashed potatoes with cream gravy, biscuits, and chocolate cream pie, and he'd eaten more than the doctor said was good for him. But whenever she tried to cut him down on food he turned grumpy and picked on her, making remarks about her own eating habits when everybody knew it was a glandular problem she had.

Myatt came into the kitchen. He had a half-shut eye like an ogre in a kid's picture book, florid stubbly chins, and a noisy catarrh that traveled through walls and sometimes kept his daughter awake nights. He pulled the Mylar-covered back door open and spat thickly outside into the snow. The cat arched its thin back as cold air swept in, lashed out complainingly with its tail.

"What's bothering you, Dad?"

"I don't know that anything is."

"Well, you never get up like this, right after supper."

Myatt used a toothpick and stood blankly in front of the old winter coats hung from pegs opposite the back door.

"I was thinking it might be a good idea if I run over to the Gannaway place."

"Why?"

"It's been three or four days. I ought to make sure everything's tight."

"They don't pay you enough to get you out on a night like this."

"They pay me a hundred dollars a month. That's like finding money in the street."

"Comes to maybe thirty cents an hour, the time you put in over there. You fuss over their house and let this one go."

Myatt reached for his plaid wool jacket, the pockets fat with leather gloves. "What have I let go?"

"If you don't know already, I'm not going to tell you. But you know."

"Roof's tight and dry. I put in the new copper water pipe end of October. Why do you make me play guessing games with you, Min?"

"Just go into my bathroom sometime, and see the condition of the linoleum around the toilet."

"Oh."

"Oh. Yes. This isn't the first time I've had to mention it. But I hope it'll be the last."

"What has you so mean lately?"

"I could use a new hip joint, for one thing. But we'll never have the money."

Myatt pulled on his galoshes and went outside to the garage. He drove his Isuzu shortbed, equipped with oversized snow tires and extra quartz-halogen headlights, the mile and a half south to Cutler Road. Even in his well-equipped truck he didn't feel secure in this pelting snow, and he proceeded slowly. He met no one else along the way, and wondered about the nervous impulse that had got him up and out here this late when it would have been more convenient to drop by in the morning. The old Courdewaye house was so well built it was, in Myatt's opinion, well-nigh indestructible: he'd bet its walls against a bulldozer anytime. It had survived worse blows than this halfhearted blizzard and would continue to do so, as long as the owners allowed him to stay on top of all the little maintenance chores. He maintained the thermostat at sixty-four degrees in winter, high enough to protect the furniture and the plumbing. They could afford the cost, even with gas so expensive.

But sometimes, when least expected, things went wrong. Mentally he went over his checklist: doors, shutters, toilets, wellhouse pump, hot water heaters . . .

Avery Myatt was distressed to see, as he neared the driveway, that the gate was open and bogged down in snowdrift. There was a good latch on the gate, and he'd checked it on his last visit. Kids, maybe. He fretted about vandalism. Too much trouble to dig the gate free and close it tonight. First thing tomorrow; he'd give Lars Tucker's middle boy three dollars to help him, save on the shoveling, save the old ticker too.

Even with snow tires chewing away, the drive was almost impassable; he'd have to plow again. Myatt's Isuzu crawled around the wooded knoll, and the powerful headlights illuminated the dark house: first the roof and tall chimneys, then the third floor, and as the truck dropped lower with the curve of the drive, the lights swept across the ivy-framed front entrance. The windows were intact downstairs, he observed—no shutters torn away. Everything was as it should be, at five minutes past eight in the evening.

Still—

He parked opposite the front door, unsnapped his key ring from his belt, and stepped down from the cab of his truck. He had only to take a few steps to reach the door, but the wind had a weight and velocity that astonished him; driven before it as if caught in a floodtide, he was banged painfully against the fender of his truck. Breathless, he turned his back on the unrelenting wind. He hunched over the fender to keep from being blown away. The shriek of the wind was like nothing he remembered hearing in his lifetime, and he'd been through seventy-two Vermont winters.

A sudden unreasonable panic rose in his breast; he felt his heart swell enormously, like a bullfrog's throat. *I'm going to die,* he thought. The snow was in his ears, his nose, his mouth, an avalanche of snow—swept off the roof?—smothering him.

Broadside to his truck, clinging for his life, he reached for the side mirror mounting and grasped it. The blizzard that had broken loose upon his arrival continued unabated. He turned his head inchwise toward the house. Above the scream of the wind he'd heard something else.

Music.

For a few moments, through the horizontal flash of snow, he had a glimpse of the windows glowingly alight, the figures of men and women inside the den, a fire on the hearth, the serene, vaguely aristocratic faces of Courdewayes above the mantel, faces he hadn't laid eyes on in more than forty years.

Then it was all blotted out by more driving snow, and the front door swung open, open to blackness and the eyes of some kind of thing hovering a good four feet above the stoop, sharp red eyes a handsbreadth apart in a wedge-shaped head. The eyes had enough of a glow to illuminate an upthrust hairy snout and long outcurved incisors. The beast was too big for a dog and not big enough for a bear, the wrong size anyway: petite in the hindquarters, powerful, like a gorilla, across the shoulders, all of the body covered with a wild matted coat. He could smell it across the surging wind, knew it had smelled him, too, in all of his fear.

Myatt clawed his way to the door of the cab as the storm

tried to tear him away from his truck and send him bowling across the dooryard to the maw of the beast on the stoop; and the music played on. His heart, he knew, couldn't take it. Already he imagined the heart of him thin as the membrane of an egg, and under such evil pressure a blowout was inevitable. But a heart attack was preferable to the jaws of the thing that had come out into the snow, more than curious: its attitude was one of menace.

Myatt pulled his legs inside and slammed the door and ground the starter, geared down when the engine roared. The wheels spun, the truck shuddered and sideslipped. Desperately he turned on all the lights but could see nothing except the heavy streaking snow all around his truck.

Blind as he was, Myatt drove, somehow staying to the drive and not blundering into deep drifts. He knew that if he got stuck he would stay there until the gas ran out and he froze to death; he would *not* open the door, he would not get out of the truck and try to make it to the road on foot. The beast filled his mind, eclipsing reason. Its sheer ugliness, glimpsed in the violent purity of the storm, was paralyzing.

Then—a miracle to Myatt—he was around the knoll, past the open gate and on his way home, the worst of the blizzard behind him: looking back he could see only the red bleed of his taillights along the road.

The faces. The music. The beast. His own face was hot; sweat dripped from beneath his earflap cap. His heart would last out, he thought cautiously. This time. Thing was, he'd made a bad move going out on such a night after a heavy meal that he hadn't even begun to digest. It was causing him considerable pain now, that big gutful, and obviously it had affected his nerves, even his mind. The sudden ferocity of the storm had scared him, made him imagine all sorts of things. A kind of mirage. Extremes of weather could do that to a man.

By daylight he would investigate, but there would be nothing. No need to call the law: the story would get around, he'd never hear the end. The music was still in Avery Myatt's head, but fading now. Fading further with each slowing beat of his overstressed heart.

22

"Dinner is served."

Rich had just helped himself to another glass of wine. His fifth or sixth glass, he'd lost track. Odd that he hadn't cared for the taste of it earlier in the evening. Now he couldn't get enough: the most delicious, aromatic claret he had ever drunk, although Inez claimed it wasn't anything special in price or cachet, certainly not the equal of some of the noble French wines that Karyn's obnoxiously knowledgeable father had served on Rich's infrequent visits to the Vale house in Rye. Ordinarily any quantity of the grape gave Rich a bad head—stuffiness, a vague ache behind the eyes, blood pounding at the temples—and a slowly deepening feeling of melancholia. But this claret was having just the opposite effect. He was sober, alert, charged with energy but not restless, a little impatient to get on with the business that had brought him here. But in control of himself, certain of his ability—with Inez skillfully guiding him—to relieve Polly of her burden, which was more than any child should have to bear.

But Polly was asleep; the time wasn't ripe. It was time now to relax with his new friends, the most congenial group of people he'd met in a long time. Rich was not shy, and in the last hour or so he'd really warmed to the company, overcoming his earlier reservations about them. They loved his anecdotes about growing up in south Boston, life in a strict Catholic household, his amusing imbroglios with the Paulist fathers at St. Malachy's, none of whom had thought he'd make it to Yale.

Even Windross proved to be not such a bad sort, after he'd come downstairs for a glass of wine and apologized for his childish attempt at a joke over the telephone. Rich was assured of Windross's devotion to Polly. He was a good father after all. Within a few minutes he excused

105

himself to return to an upstairs bedroom and his vigil beside the sleeping child.

Rich solemnly shook the innkeeper's hand and vowed that before the night was over he, Rich, would see to it that Polly was at peace. That brought tears to the man's eyes; he overflowed with gratitude.

"I don't know how we would have managed without you."

"Just don't worry," Rich said.

Since retrieving him from the den, Inez hadn't left Rich's side. He had grown accustomed to, dependent on, the sweet-sour fragrance of her perfume, the nearness of her firm body, the heat of her breath when she whispered companionably in his ear. When he looked at Inez he imagined her naked and waiting for him in bed, but of course this treat would have to wait for a while, too, though he was already aroused, a hefty swelling evident in his groin. He defended himself in advance. Nothing wrong with his desiring Inez. It was suitable revenge on Karyn, who was turning out to be—not to his surprise—a whore, eager to fuck with Trux Landall or any other stud who showed an interest. Wouldn't she like to know that every woman in the den coveted *him* right now: they showed it in their deliberate, lingering glances where he was hard and eternally powerful.

But Rich belonged, heart and soul, to Inez. Her body he judged to be exceptional, but her scar was the biggest turn-on of all; he had contrived a couple of times to brush his fingers across it, which made her eyes flash and shine, prompted the pointed tip of her tongue to caress a full and lusciously red lower lip. He was imbued with her musk, flattered by her close attention and intimate laughter, teased by what Inez no doubt felt was her superior sexuality. She was older, more experienced; nevertheless Rich was confident that before the night had ended he would teach her a few things—have her whimpering, crawling, obeisant beneath the angled altar of his unfailing cock.

"Dinner is served."

And high time, he was starved: he could have cheerfully, gluttonously torn his way through a raw carcass, swilled hot blood in place of the invigorating wine that had so sharpened his senses. Inez gracefully linked an arm with his; her fingertips were on the pulse in his wrist. The sensual flaring of her nostrils assured Rich that she was aware of all of his appetites, and shared them.

Inez seated him at one end of the long table in the dining room, facing her. Three serving girls and the tall butler paraded, loading the table with choice meats and fowl. Chubby-cheeked pork, pheasant with feathers intact and steaming, venison marinated in onions and rich gravy. While they dined and drank two more courses of wine Inez smiled often at Rich through the steady flames of the centerpiece tapers. There was no other source of light; the room was lively with their vast shadows.

The conversation improved, if anything. Inez holding forth. She had a fund of wicked, amusing stories. Rich found himself red in the face and gasping for breath as she described, in exquisite detail, the disciplining of her late children. Arnold, age ten at death, Mary, age eight. Dressing them, head to toe, in musty woolens, forcing them to remain rigid for hours in the hellish Mexican sun until they collapsed from heatstroke in pools of their own sweat. Then, to reverse the effects of dehydration, bloating them with water from a hose until, standing naked and clinging to each other in the bathtub, they were ankle-deep in urine.

"Tell about the scorpions!" Rose Benidorm squealed, her chin flesh aquiver with excitement.

Inez looked slyly around the table, building anticipation.

"Well, the children were *very* frightened of scorpions," she began.

Rich giggled ecstatically.

"We would put two or three of the big black ones on ice until they were sluggish, near death. Then the children would sit in their little chairs, and I would sit in my chair between them, and turn on the music, and we'd play—"

"Hot potato!"

They all regarded Rich fondly for a moment, then gave their attention back to Inez.

"It sometimes took three or four minutes, frantically passing a scorpion from hot hand to hot hand, before the scorpion was revived enough to sting."

Inez paused, and held out her own hands, palms toward the dinner guests. "I played perfectly fair with them. Sometimes the scorpion even stung *me*."

"Why did you kill Arnold and Mary?" Rich asked, after the howls of merriment had died down.

"Well, darling," Inez said, tidily disposing of a piece of crackling pork skin, then wiping her lips on a snowy napkin, "Mary was not of sound mind, and poor Arnold—he became so consumptive he *longed* for the embrace of his Master."

"You did it with gasoline?"

"Yes, Richard," Inez said, as if she had become slightly bored with talking about her children. "Gasoline makes the hottest fire." Inez looked at her other guests. "Have we all eaten well?"

Groans of satisfaction, extravagant compliments to the hostess filled the dining room.

"Gee, I'm having a good time," Rich said.

Inez gazed indulgently at him.

"More wine?"

"No, thanks. I just couldn't drink any more."

"Well, I hope you realize that the rest of the evening won't be all fun and games. There is a highly serious matter to be taken care of."

"I know."

"How do you feel about it, Richard?"

"I'm ready."

"Are you? Truly?"

"Yes."

Inez sat back with a sigh, picked up a crystal handbell, and summoned the maids, who cleared the table. As the remains of the huge meal were borne away they all heard Windross singing in a breathless, hoarse voice, "Scarborough Fair," the stanzas punctuated by excited bursts of girlish laughter. "Dad-dy! Dad-dy!" Windross came panting into the dining room carrying Polly on his shoulders.

"*Here* she is!" Inez cried dotingly. Windross brought his daughter close to the table and bent over awkwardly. Polly's thin arms were around his neck. She leaned toward Inez to give her a peck on the cheek.

"Did you have a good nap?"

"Yes, Inez."

"Slide down from there now, and come sit with me."

Windross eased his daughter off his shoulders, and Inez reached out to take the girl into her lap. Windross stood by sweating, red in the face; he glanced at Rich with a plaintive smile. Rich was sitting erect in his chair, tingling with pleasure and excitement at the sight of Polly. She was wearing a ruffled white dress that buttoned to the throat, high white stockings and white patent shoes. Her hair was brushed to a gleam the pale lemon of the candle flames, and parted on the left. Her complexion was almost bloodless, but there were marks of discoloration beneath her eyes.

Inez whispered something inaudible in the girl's ear, and Polly listened intently. Inez turned a dark eye toward Rich, and Polly looked up too.

"Do you know who that is sitting down there at the other end of the table? You got all dressed up for him tonight, didn't you?"

Polly nodded, smiling shyly.

"Yes. Hi, Rich."

"Hi, Polly. How are you?"

Polly dimpled and seemed to blush. She turned her face to Inez, looking for support.

"Well, go on, tell him," Inez said, giving the girl a bit of an affectionate dandle.

Polly looked at Rich again, the corners of her mouth curling. "They say I'm—full of the devil."

Shrieks and caws of laughter around the table. Jim Seaclare bellowed so loud he blew down a couple of tapers in front of him, extinguishing the flames, darkening the room a little more. A grinning maid peeked in at the swinging door to the butler's pantry.

Rich enjoyed the joke more than anyone. He pointed an accusing finger at Windross.

"You put her up to that!"

Windross shrugged and gestured innocently. He was sweating more profusely, and mopped his streaming forehead on his shirtsleeve.

When they all had settled down enough to pay attention to her, Inez raised a commanding hand. Silently the guests slid back their chairs and stood, stepped closer to the walls and as far away from the table as they could get. Their faces fell into shadow.

Rich remained seated.

"Is it now?" Polly said uncertainly, almost whispering to Inez.

"We have to leave that up to Rich."

Rich gave a purposeful nod, but he was a little tense now that the ordeal was to begin.

"Richard, do you have the courage to accept your obligation in relieving Polly of the earthly burden she has carried so faithfully?"

"Yes, I do."

"Polly—"

"Inez," the girl whimpered, face pressed against Inez's bosom, "I'm afraid."

"It'll be all right, Polly," Rich said, his voice unexpectedly loud and profound to his ears in the stillness of the dining room.

Inez gestured to the sideboard, and the waiting butler poured red wine into a silver goblet, which he brought to the table.

Seeing it, Polly made a drab face.

"I don't like the taste. Very much."

"It's special. Good for your nerves, dear."

"All right." Polly turned in Inez's lap and grasped the goblet, swallowed hard before drinking, swallowed again with a little shudder, and lowered the goblet, leaving a plum-dark scimitar on her upper lip, an upside-down replica of the scar that graced the cheek of Inez Cordway.

Polly's eyes, seen through the heat dance of candle flame, met Rich's.

At this mating Inez got slowly out of the chair, leaving Polly to sit by herself facing Rich.

Polly rested the heavy goblet on the edge of the table in front of her.

"I love you, Rich," she said, her eyes half-lidded.

He took a deep breath. "I love you, too, Polly."

"And don't you love my pretty white dress," she said, tears forming, dropping from the corners of her eyes.

"You look just beautiful, Polly."

The girl picked up the goblet and tilted it toward her. A few drops of wine splashed on the crewelwork of the bodice, darkening it. She put the goblet back on the table and gave it a deliberate little push to one side. Stood.

The drops of darkness on her white dress grew larger.

There was a barely suppressed, orgiastic sigh from those watching in shadow, and Rich's heart constricted. He rose slowly from his chair, eyes on the dress now more swiftly changing from white to jet black. A tremor went through him; he felt severely weakened. He gripped the edge of the dining table for support.

Polly's blue eyes had paled to glass; she stared at a point above his head, and deep within those bottomless wells of glass a secret redness shone.

The shadows around them also deepened as blackness spread in hurried fingers the length of her dress. A candle went out with a puff of smoke; another. Polly's dress, her hair, moved as if a strong wind had disturbed them; but the dining room was stifling, close, the air turned fetid from the combined breaths of the onlookers.

Polly's lips now parted, stretching over her white, charmingly uneven teeth. She was trembling; the charge in each of them was communicated the length of the table. Polly cried out in tongues, words distinct but unfamiliar becoming a meaningless snaffle of sound. And blood trickled from the corners of her mouth.

Rich groaned, unable to look away. She commenced some snapping, contorted movements of her body, like an eccentric dancer with feet nailed to the floor. Now her dress was all black. The bending, the jerking, the whiplash motions of her blond hair continued frenziedly. Her eyes had a ruby brilliance, but no pupils.

"Time, Richard," Inez reminded him from the shadows.

Rich was dumbstruck at this critical moment, unable to move or even to catch his breath as he stared in torment at the transformed Polly.

Polly, whose face was now alight from the hot eyeless glow, from socketed furnaces, began flamelessly to burn: smoke wisped from her gesturing hands, from all of her exposed skin, which had deeply reddened and even begun to char. She was screaming, a searing noise almost too high-pitched for his ears to catch.

"No!" But his throat was so thick from the horror he could scarcely manage an effective outcry.

Inez appeared at his side, gripping him.

"Quickly now. He is ready. Accept Him and free Polly."

"Who?"

"*You* know, Richard," Inez said, faintly impatient but still able to smile. He turned his head slowly, glimpsing a shade of himself in the mirror surfaces of her dark and comforting eyes.

He nodded. "But—"

Inez cut him off with a chuckling sound. Her scar seemed to be writhing slowly on her cheek. "So simple. *Must* we go over it again? Think, Richard. Embrace Polly with all of your love. Call her, and she'll come to you."

"What—happen—then?"

"Then union will be consummated. Oh, Richard. Now I *know* I gave you too much to drink. I promise you the supreme moment of your life: ecstasy. What is it you have always dreaded? What frightens you most about life? The danger of being overlooked. Of being just another face among billions. Well, Richard. *This* moment is what you have lived for. You will be unique among men. And what must you do to achieve uniqueness? Join with Polly. Join with Him."

"Don't know—if I—"

All the circulation in his arm below the clamp of her hand had stopped; and the numbness spread, as the black of night had spread over Polly's chaste dress. Now she was of the grave, though still recognizable.

"Of course you can do it," Inez said, all encouragement. Her breath in his face was exciting but had a rankness; faintly nauseating.

"Just call her. Hmm? Do it now. She's really in agony there, and we've all had a very long evening. I know I have."

In her grip he had no choice but to turn and look at suffering Polly.

"I . . . love . . . you . . . Polly," Inez whispered.

"I love you, Polly," Rich repeated. His nausea was worse.

"Come to me, and I will keep and hold you always."

Rich said that too. Polly, heedless, writhed and screamed in a most dreadful manner.

"Louder," Inez prompted.

"Come to me, and I—"

"Lou-der!"

"COME TO ME AND I—I WILL—WILL KEEP YOU ALWAYS!"

"There!" Inez said, pleased with him. She let him go and stepped back, out of his line of sight.

At the other end of the table the black dress flew up, smoking, over Polly's head, and she was lifted by the force of it, by a flapping surge that carried her above the long table. The dress flew into tatters, into streaming pennants that, to Rich's eyes, became husky wings moving slowly in the humid air, crackling with a kind of St. Elmo's fire. The crackle of discharged electricity traveled corner to corner in the dining room, bringing out the lurid faces against the walls.

And another face appeared where Polly's had been, as the thing in the air continued to hover, part bird, part bat, part of something else from the dim beginnings of earth, seen lurching through grimy skies by the light of erupting volcanos. Mad darting eyes as red as pared flesh, a hundred sharp teeth in a beak that belonged on a crocodile, the breast of it leathery but teated like a woman's, it craned to gaze at Rich and rowed the air with sharp-framed wings.

"I know," Inez said, her voice somehow clear and strong inside his head as the monster continued to expand and shape itself in grisly ways, "that this is the hard part. But it will be over in a few seconds."

Rich screamed and screamed again, stopping only to vomit.

And while he was at his most helpless, with his stomach inside out and his bowels voiding, the creature flew down to claim him as a sacred wail rose like the wind and all of the remaining candles atop the table puffed out from the violence of winged passage.

Rich felt an instant of intense heat, a pain in his solar plexus as if he'd been struck by the tip of a horny beak. And then a renewed numbness, a sensation of drifting away from all that had terrified and oppressed him moments before. From dismal charnel dark into darkness that was different, somehow soothing, a coursing vein of warmth that carried him

to his wedding bed.

In a chamber of ivory purity, tall candles all around.
Polly was there.

Naked on satin sheets, except for a chaplet of flowers in her hair.

Cornflower blue to match her eyes.

She'd been given a touch of makeup; artificial, whorish excitement high on the cheekbones. Her lower lip was caught between her teeth as she pleaded sexual transport. Panting, little nubby chest rising and falling.

Rich was hunched over her, kneeling, hands on her shoulders. Polly moved her pillowed hips without art. Her ribcage was frail and as luminous as a paper lantern. Polly's simple, anointed vulva, pure as porcelain, had a deeply fired rosiness where she enclosed his snake-veined cock. He seemed gross and exaggerated where she was most exquisite. He dealt her full and vigorous strokes; each breath she released was like a scream of ghosts.

When he became fully conscious of what he was doing to the girl Rich tried, in horror, to withdraw. It was wrong—this was never what he'd wanted, or intended. She was only twelve years old. But Polly reacted to his hesitation and reluctance with a bitch's frenzy, one slim hand encircling him just above the ponderous balls, another going to his cock to hold him inside her. She had only to grasp him like that, signaling desire, and he came, nearly blowing apart from the strain of having so long withheld. She jumped as if gunshot at each lavish spasm, back arching, head tossing, weary flowers tumbling about her small ears.

A sigh in his own ear, the neat tip of tongue inserted, full kisses of joy which he could not return. He steamed in his shame, still immersed in the child's fenny cunt. She lay tangled in his bright tree of semen. Some saliva had fallen from her mouth. It trickled like silver between the muffin mounds of breasts down to her navel. Polly licked her stone-pale lips, eyelids aflutter, pulse in her throat growing faint by wavering candlelight: flames without bodies, eyes without souls. He watched fascinatedly until the pulse ceased altogether. Her grip relaxed, fingers sliding away.

A last dim caress; she breathed deeply and then seemed not to breathe at all.

After another minute Rich was able slowly to disengage. There was a little pleased smile on Polly's sleeping face. With his weight off her she turned contentedly onto her right side, drew her knees up a little, placed her hands beneath one cheek.

Rich drew a sheet over the girl and got unsteadily to his feet, still hard as if he'd never ejaculated. He looked around in surprise at Inez, who was wearing a nightgown of thin material and leaning with a big yawn against a wall of the chamber.

"I thought you'd never finish with her," she said, mildly complaining. Her own healthy body barely masked, pudenda thick and hairy as a bear's paw below her belly, pearly breasts on the rise like hangmen's moons. "It's so late, Rich. Stopped snowing, though. You'd better get dressed."

"What—are you doing here?"

"Waiting for you. Time to shut the lights and everybody go to their reward. But you can't, not yet. You've had your treat; now there are things to do."

"What do you mean?"

Inez gave a small shrug and bounced a breast idly on the back of her wrist. "I'm not privileged to know. Whatever you do from now on will be in *his* service, of course."

"Of course," Rich said, echoing her dully. "I need a shower."

"Take one. But don't be long."

When he came out of the adjoining bathroom with a towel decorously around his waist the aspect of the chamber had changed; Inez had extinguished all candles in the room except for one, which kept watch over the waxen child in the bed.

Rich stared at Polly as he dressed. It seemed to him that she wasn't breathing, but he was fuzzy-minded and exhausted. Dead in the groin for one thing, as if he'd experienced ten orgasms instead of one. Impaling the child, killing her. The bed in which he'd raped Polly seemed to have taken on the dimensions of a rather spacious coffin. Deep satin and her composed, upturned face. He walked slowly toward the coffin, but Inez blocked his way.

"No time for fond farewells."

"Is she—?"

"Polly will always live in your memory, Richard."

He swallowed hard, remotely saddened, and accepted the inevitable with a nod. He thought he was going to cry, but his eyes only smarted. Inez held out his seaman's cap and muffler and warm coat to him. Rich didn't look at Polly's face again but followed Inez from the chamber and then down the stairs to the fóyer of the Courdewaye house. Inez snuffed candles as they descended, the dark following them down.

Rich opened the front door and looked out on huge undulate whiteness, a nascent moon, thin shadows of bare trees. The wolfhound was sitting on the front stoop in a cloud of freezing breath. It turned its elegant head toward Rich, like a debutante trying nearsightedly to make out the face of her next dancing partner. The dog had hanging black folds at the corner of its mouth, and a long leer.

" 'Night, Rich," Inez said, dancing barefoot on the cold doorstep. She kissed his cheek. "It went well, don't you think?"

"I suppose so. Will I see you again?"

"We just don't know these things, do we?"

She clucked to the dog, who turned and trotted inside. Rich saw the door close, Inez's parting smile, the low-down scimitar of scar on her cheek, a brief flashing redness where her eyes had been, a kind of strobe effect. Then he walked down the shoveled steps to unmarked snow and began his trudge back to the gas station–market where he had left his Porsche some time ago.

23

Karyn was fed up with Rich, and didn't care who knew it. She had kept her angry mood on simmer long past the dinner hour, not talking to anyone about it, even Benny and Elise. Ordinarily when she was among friends she could persuade herself to have a good time no matter what was weighing on her mind; tonight, despite a cheerful boisterous crowd in the tavern of the Davos Chalet and a group called Sons and Lovers who played good old-fashioned ass-kicking rock, Karyn couldn't purge herself, nor keep her disaffection from her eyes.

"He'll show up," Elise said encouragingly.

Karyn was looking at Trux Landall's broad back. He was at a nearby table sitting very close to a toothy blonde whose face was so violently sunburned she looked radioactive. Karyn felt doubly abandoned. Trux had seen her and smiled but hadn't come over despite the fact that Rich wasn't there. So what was he trying to prove, were they friends or not, and never mind that little scuffle he'd had with Rich.

"Reeshard said he would be here," Benny volunteered with a smeary grin. Benny was in one of his infrequent moods where he wanted to drink himself under the table as quickly as possible.

"Said? Did *you* see Rich today, Benny?"

Benny nodded. "Breakfast." He tilted his glass again. Elise cautioned him with a baring of her metalized teeth.

"Better make it last. You're not going to get another one."

"Elise is being mean to me," Benny whined.

"I don't go to bed with drunks."

"Quit it, you two," Karyn said urgently. "Benny? Benny?"

"At your service."

"What did you and Rich talk about this morning? I mean, did he give you any idea—"

"Helped him pull his car out of a snowbank."

"Fine, what time was that?"

"Late morning. I forget."

"Well, did he tell you what he was going to do the rest of the day?"

"No."

"What did you talk about?"

Benny shrugged, trying to recall. "Devils."

"Devils? Be serious," Elise said, giving him an elbow where his stomach mounded over the beltline.

" 'S true. Reeshard was in a very serious frame of mind this morning.''

"What about devils?" Karyn asked.

"Reeshard said he'd been reading a book on demonology, which subject he had reasonable doubts about—I believe 'bullshit' was the word he used to describe his reaction. But at the same time—something was bothering him. He wanted to know—what I thought.''

"What do you think?" Elise said.

Benny got the giggles. "We're all a bunch of horny little devils, aren't we?"

Elise shot Karyn a despairing look as Benny's head nodded toward his chest.

"Benny," Karyn said insistently, "Rich must have said *something* about where he was going. Can't you tell me?"

"Oh . . . uh, he was just pissing around, I'm sure.''

"What does that mean?"

Benny raised his head and leaned toward Karyn. He took off his misted glasses and wiped the lenses on Elise's sweater, put the glasses back on and stared at Karyn with eyes of mild turquoise.

"Said he was off to attend an exorcism. And I said, 'Matinee or evening?' '' Benny chuckled and felt around on the table for his drink, which Elise pushed out of his reach with the back of one hand.

"Meant what I said, love.''

Benny fetched a spiritless sigh. "Just because I—messed up last night. Can't give me a break, can you?"

"Don't tell the world all your troubles, Benjamin.''

Somebody across the table said, "What happened last night, Benny?"

Benny screwed up his mouth and nodded, pondering a reply. His forehead creased heavily. He rubbed it and broke into another fit of giggles. "I came too soon," he whispered.

"Benny, shut up," Elise said, furious with him.

"Again," Benny concluded, meekly.

"Nobody's interested, Benny!"

"Welcome to the club," someone else said.

"Well, *you* never come at all," Benny said archly to Elise, whose face, turned to him, had a ghastly emptiness, like a vampire's hollow tooth.

"Let him have another drink," one of the girls suggested to Elise.

Benny slumped defenselessly in his chair, and the conversation dwindled as the rock band returned from a break. Karyn looked at her watch. It was a quarter after twelve. She needed to go to the john, but it was across the dance floor, which was again chockful of wriggling bodies. She looked at Trux's table and found that he had turned in his chair to look at her. He smiled and this time gave her the high sign. The blonde he'd been with was on the dance floor, hair whirling around her shockingly rosy face, her jugs bouncing almost as high as her chin.

" 'Scuse me," Karyn said to her table, and she got to her feet.

Trux met her halfway and ran interference for her across the dance floor. Karyn emerged on the far side gasping for air. Trux turned her toward the door with a hand on her elbow.

"Hi."

"Hi. There are some subjects we aren't going to discuss tonight." And she pressed two fingers gently against his lips to insist on the ban.

"Agreed. What do you want to do?"

"What else can you do in Vermont after midnight? But I don't want to do that. Has it stopped snowing?"

"I think so."

Karyn left him to visit the bathroom. When she came back she slipped a hand into his, and they walked across the lobby.

"Let's grab our coats and boots and go out," Karyn suggested. "The smoke in the tavern was awful. My eyes are still burning."

They stopped first at a room belonging to a friend of Trux's, where he had left his coat and a shaggy gray wineskin filled with burgundy. Trux uncapped the *bota*, expertly aimed a stream at his mouth almost at arm's length, and drank without spilling a drop on his white alpinist's sweater. Then he held the wineskin for Karyn, the nipple an inch away from her parted lips.

"I need to learn how to do that," she said, infatuated by the strong red stream of wine, a sense of primitive communion; drink and be merry.

"Simple. I'll show you. Outside."

Near the lodge they tramped through the fresh snow toward the double chair lift. Trux carried the wineskin by its strap, and his left arm was around Karyn's shoulders. There were still a few flakes of snow in the air but the storm had passed, leaving a pure and windless space, a partial sky that trembled with titanic violence so distant it barely met the eye. Karyn felt good again, good enough to laugh at some silly thing he said. It was always fun with Trux; was she making a serious mistake about Rich? His odd obsessions, his disappearances the last couple of days had her in knots. She wouldn't stand for this kind of treatment anymore. Maybe it would be better to move out, date other men for a while, put some distance between herself and Rich until she was sure of what she wanted.

She explained all of her misgivings and half-realized convictions to Trux.

"Sometimes you let yourself get tied up when it's not really what you want at all," he concluded.

"It isn't that I don't love Rich. I know I love him."

"Doesn't mean that it's good for you."

"Rich and I need to have a long talk. I've made up my mind."

"Well, if you decide to cool it with Rich for a while, I'd like for you to come up to Cambridge some weekend."

"Hey, that would be fun!"

"How about some more wine?"

"Sure. Let me hold the *bota* this time. I can wash this jacket."

Karyn dribbled everywhere, but most of the burgundy made it to her mouth. She licked her lips and wiped her chin with a forefinger, laughing again, breathing freely for the first time in several hours.

They walked on, staggering a little in the heavy powder, leaning on each other, alone, unobserved except by the driver of the Porsche that had come uphill to the Davos Chalet and pulled into the east parking lot.

24

To the eyes of the possessor, the world to which he had newly returned was a hated place.

It was true that this was a world soaked in blood from the slaughters of tens of centuries, a world in which, every day, men of free will condemned themselves to hell through acts of greed, treachery, sadism, enslavement, and murder, most often and conveniently in the name of a greater good, in the name of gods from El and Ishtar to Baal and Yahweh. But there could never be enough spilled blood and rotting bones to satisfy the possessor's lust, nor enough souls to fling to his darkness. He was insatiable.

Tonight his desires were modest enough: he had communicated them to the possessed, stifling every returning qualm until resistance was so faint it didn't matter anymore.

Richard.

"I see them."

The possessed saw, in fact, with an animal's flawless eyes. Toy figures in the moonlight, black against the glittering snow, crossing beneath the terminal pylon of the double chair lift. Pausing, face to face. Their hands on each other. And with an animal's heightened powers the possessed felt the electricity between the man and the woman, a sensual communication. His rutting instinct was aroused, and his hatred for the rival. He responded with the jealousy of a man, the slavering appetite of the possessor.

"But I can't—"

The resistance was quickly suppressed.

She is faithless. They were words in an ancient tongue, harsh, nearly vowelless sounds reverberating in the captive mind. *Quite a little liar. But is that all she is?*

"Liar. Bitch. Whore. Slut." Each word seared the tongue and lips like nodules of phosphorus, firing up his blood. The animal body twitched expectantly, the instinctive hunter was in command.

What do you want to do, Richard?

The answer was wordless, yet as powerful as an orgasm.

You might have quite a time with him. I mean, it might not go well. He's much bigger than you. And strong. We don't want anything to happen to you, to defeat our purpose.

"I know"

Think of what else you might do. It's Karyn you really want to hurt, isn't it?

Karyn and Trux, close together on the slope, almost but not quite merging with the black column of the chair lift support, motionless, faces together now. Kissing passionately. The eye of the animal was huge, unwinking. He saw how he could slip noiselessly through all the snow, and take them by surprise. He thought of Karyn's long and playful kisses, her adventuring tongue, the loins that entranced another. His hand went to the door handle of the Porsche.

No. Wait. Not yet.

Rich's hand relaxed. He closed the car door.

"When?"

You'll know.

25

Because of the wine they'd had to drink, more than she could handle ordinarily, it didn't seem cold to Karyn at all. Karyn and Trux had talked for a long time, walking slowly, never getting out of sight of the chalet. Kissing him, coming to grips without undue ardor, was sweet, and being cherished in this way was necessary at crucial turns of her self-examinations. After a while she felt astonished and mildly elated, empowered by starlight; the landscape, so absolutely composed of black and white, demanded of her a resolution: quick, bracing decisions. By the time they said good-night at the entrance to the hotel Karyn knew she was not going to live with Rich anymore—beginning now, tonight, even if he had returned while she was out walking with Trux. Odd how a relationship could turn around so drastically in just a couple of days. But it must have been on her mind for a much longer time; she hadn't wanted to face the drudgery, and the pain, of the separation. Trux had pointed out to her that it wasn't necessarily the end. Once she was freed of the often-tedious interconnections of a long-running affair, had taken months or even a year to think about what he meant to her, she might then decide to resume with Rich. In the meantime, if he was truly right for her, he would understand.

It was nearly closing time, but after leaving Trux she went briskly into the tavern, hoping to find Rich. The band had quit for the night, leaving behind their unconnected amps and tiers of soiled, played-out drums. Her friends had left; there were only two couples hanging on and a solitary boy nodding at the bar. The air was depressingly stale and she began to feel the wine she had consumed outside flaring in her blood, sending waves of mist to the brain.

The rawboned, bearded bartender was reaching up to hang clean glasses in the overhead rack. He smiled a little tiredly at her approach.

"You could manage a quick one."

"Just looking for somebody."

The boy who was nodding off roused himself and said with an attempt to be charming, "And I've been looking for you—all my life." What appeal he might have had he spoiled by farting. Karyn ignored him.

To the bartender she said, "He would have come in during the last hour or so. About this tall, blond, short hair, a little like Paul Newman in his prime. Boston accent."

"No, I don't think I saw him."

"Oh, well, okay."

"Can't fix you anything?"

"I've had enough," Karyn said.

The drunk boy slid off his barstool to his knees and leaned his head against the bar, crooning softly to himself. Karyn started to walk around him. Behind her there was a quick tapping on the glass of the terrace doors.

"Karyn!"

Rich's muffled voice, calling her.

"That him?" the bartender asked, as Karyn turned.

At first she couldn't tell. He was just a dim figure out there on the terrace, and the doors were half-glazed with ice, blocked by frozen snowdrifts, which further obscured her view.

He rapped on the glass and beckoned.

"Karyn!"

When she didn't respond he turned his head impatiently, breath a cloud made incandescent by the moon. She saw the familiar shape of his chin. It was Rich, all right.

She hurried to the doors and tried to open one. They weren't locked, but she couldn't budge them.

"Froze shut," the bearded bartender advised her. "Won't get those doors open till spring."

Rich had backed off about ten feet, where he stood awaiting her, arms folded across his chest. Why was he acting like that? Karyn gestured helplessly.

"I can't get the doors open, Rich! Come around through the lobby."

But he continued to stand there, staring. Or so she thought, because she couldn't see his face, or eyes. Was he drunk? He appeared steady on his feet. She looked at the bartender.

"Is there another way I can get outside?"

"The hallway between the bathrooms, that door's not locked."

"Rich, I'm coming out," she called to him, and left the tavern.

"Okay, people," the bartender said to the others. "Time for me to lock up." He came around from behind the bar and looked in exasperation at the boy who was kneeling and embracing his barstool, snoring raggedly. "Anybody know him?" he asked. They didn't. He reached down and shook the boy, not getting much of a response.

Donald Ray Stemmons was standing there combing his beard with his fingers and trying to figure a way to get the husky kid on his feet and out of the tavern—he would be somebody else's problem then—when he heard the first scream from the terrace.

26

"Rich," Karyn said, "what's the matter with you? Where'd you disappear to all day?"

She approached him across the open rectangular terrace, boots scuffing through the new layer of snow, beneath which the footing was rugged with ice. The management of the chalet made no attempt to keep the terrace clear in winter. The soles of her boots were ribbed but still she stumbled and went down on one knee, hurting herself. He didn't make a move to help her up, didn't speak. She flushed from anger, looking up at him.

"I hurt my knee, Rich." It sounded more plaintive than Karyn had intended, as if, perversely, she desired to be babied. Still he wouldn't move. His behavior was so strange that she got up slowly by herself, keeping most of her weight on the other leg. She hopped a couple of steps in Rich's direction. Anger was replaced by concern, and the first feathery touch of fear.

"Hey, are you all right? What happened today? *Talk* to me, God damn it!"

Karyn hobbled closer. His head was down, covered with that wool watch cap he liked to wear in bitter weather. He said something to her, but so softly she couldn't understand. Her irritation was freighted with guilt. Now she had forgotten her spunky resolve to end the relationship, cast him out. Her heart was frantic. She was nearly overwhelmed by a cold, dismal sense of loss that rapidly turned to dread.

Karyn jostled against and then embraced him.

"Oh, Rich, what—"

He lifted his head, just a little. Their eyes were inches apart, and Karyn realized with a shock that bonded her tongue to the roof of her mouth that it couldn't be Rich she was holding.

She screamed and had taken a long step back when he swung the notched iron bar of the jack from his car.

It caught her at the diminished end of its arc but still with enough force to cave in the cheekbone below her right eye; blood gushed instantly from her nose into her throat.

Karyn staggered and fell down into the snow, in a sitting position. She raised fingertips delicately to her misshapen face. Vision in the right eye had dimmed. She felt no pain, just a monstrous numbness, but was aware she had been grievously hurt.

And he bent over her ceremoniously with that length of iron, sizing her up for a more devastating blow.

''Zarach','' he said, and swung.

Karyn threw up both arms and one of them took the blow; her right elbow was demolished. This time pain rocketed up through the top of her head, nearly blacking out the brain. But all she could think about were his red eyes, her powerless desire to escape the condemnation she saw there.

Her throat was full of blood. She coughed up a gout of it as she got to her feet, the injured arm dangling. She screamed in his face, spotting him with her blood. He concentratedly flicked a heavy drop from his eyelashes and stepped away in the next movement of his strange, vicious dance: he took her measure and swung from the sky.

This blow shattered all the knuckles of her other hand, raised to protect her face. It dislodged an eye, which lay on her cheek like a large pip squeezed from an orange. He rested, panting; Karyn wandered away from him, then turned back, inexplicably, completing her own movement of the dance. She was pounded, high on the already broken arm, and fell. She did not think about dying; instead she was suffocated by feelings of betrayal and grief. And crazed from pain. She rose, she screamed, he battered her in silent response. With each great arc of his iron more stars fell, precious light dribbled from her downcast eye.

The terrible noise of her skull cracking in half deafened Karyn, but, unmercifully, she couldn't lose consciousness even then. She fell one last time and, with a sense that all was lost, lay on her back in quickening convulsions while his iron bar flailed. Her frontal lobes were clenched like the fists of a newborn on her divided forehead. She sank slowly and with no further sensation of anxiety into a blanket of snow that steamed with her blood.

Her unbroken eye never closed, and she studied him faintly through blow after blow. Seeking Rich, but never finding him.

Then the last of the light sped from her eye into the outer dark; his own eyes, all that remained of a desolated universe, opened wide. They were red giants toward which her body, quieted, was attracted in a nightmare orbit.

Who? Karyn thought, as she died. And never knew the answer.

PART TWO

Zarach'

27

Several hours before the death of Karyn Vale in Haden County, Vermont, a professional wrestler named Irish Bob O'Hooligan, six feet four and 245 pounds, teamed with his partner, the Matamoros badass Chico Panache, to trounce the good guys in a preliminary to the main event at the high school gymnasium in Dempster, Massachusetts. The bout lasted fourteen minutes and ended in a lively free-for-all, where the main objective was to whip the crowd into a lather and survive in good enough shape to wrestle again the next night. At some point, while he was applying a persuasive but illegal reverse deathlock to the handsome kid who called himself Reno Studaway, he'd taken an accidental shot to the kidneys from the boot of Reno's partner, and he suspected it would have him chewing aspirin and pissing blood for the better part of two days.

Afterward Irish Bob and Chico split the winners' purse, two hundred fifty dollars, and each contributed ten percent to their manager, the former World Wrestling Alliance heavyweight champ Buddy Dilworth. Buddy had promised them an eventual shot at the New England states tag team championship if they continued their villainous crowd-pleasing ways in the small-time rings where they earned a decent living.

The pain in his kidneys persisted through a hot shower, and Irish Bob considered adding to his high medical expenses by seeking out the family doctor in the morning. On reflection he decided not to bother. He was only thirty-seven, but his doctor had already advised him on three occasions to get out of wrestling. The poundings had taken their toll in places that didn't show: tendons, joints, and soft irreplaceable organs. Some men could go on and on in the ring, and some couldn't. He knew he was already heading downhill, but he could still fake it. As if he had a choice. Three kids at home, these days he wasn't about to find something that compensated for the nightly traumas and the heavy travel. Close to thirty-six thousand last year before expenses. And it was largely a cash business, no W-2 forms. A lot of charity promotions. *Half for me and half for thee, and fuck the IRS*.

Jackie Bailiff, who had kicked him too enthusiastically from outside the ring ropes, apologized to Irish Bob in the showers. Jackie had a purpling lump over one eye from having been slammed repeatedly face-first against a turnbuckle by Chico, who sometimes got carried away when he went into his berserk-greaser routine. All in a night's work, anyway. It was a fraternity of large individuals, further swollen by boisterous egos, the touching vanity of the very ignorant. There were always minor offenses to sulk about, personality clashes; but the sincere feud was a rarity. They saved their calculated outrage and blood lust for the promotional spots in front of the TV cameras on studio wrestling days. Real pain added to the sleaze glamour of their routines.

For the truly talented and charismatic the bucks could mount up. But Irish Bob was realistic about his career. He would never wrestle anywhere but near the bottom of the card at a class hall like Boston Garden or the Hartford Civic Center, even if by some freak of chance he got there before a knee gave out for good or the headaches became such a problem he was forced to quit. He preferred sticking to Dilworth's New England circuit, which seldom required him to work more than a hundred miles from home.

Dempster, Massachusetts. The temperature down around six or seven degrees, snow starting to fly in the quick-moving storm that had passed through western New England several hours ago. Irish Bob dressed quickly in the high school locker room, wishing he had time to take advantage of the diathermy machine in the trainer's room. The kids here still had terrific facilities despite the ravages of Proposition Two and a Half, which had cut funds for public school athletic programs all over the state. And left him without his other job, as assistant wrestling coach at the high school in Joshua, where he lived. The school board had figured one wrestling coach was enough, and they could also do without his services teaching remedial English to dull-witted freshmen. Ten thousand a year down the tubes. But he was still wearing the handsome wool Joshua Jaguars athletic jacket, leather piping down the sleeves, patches on the elbows. Someday, maybe, he would go back to coaching full-time. Too bad the good Lord had not seen fit to gift him with even one kid who had straight teeth.

Trying to ignore the pain in his lower back, he let himself out of a side door in the gym, yowls and catcalls echoing behind him. Two women wrestlers were on; the card had another twenty minutes to run. With no reluctance Conor Devon left Irish Bob O'Hooligan behind and headed for the center of his life.

Gina was waiting for him in the Ford station wagon; she had the engine and the lights on. Couldn't be much mistake about who he was but she made sure before springing the locks to let him in, and even then she cradled in her lap the Colt Python revolver, which she had learned to fire with exceptional accuracy, until he settled himself beside her and the doors were locked again.

"Hi, babe."

He kissed her and handed over the cash. She was a snub-nosed strawberry blonde whose name had been Travitano before he married her. The coloring of northern Italy, the short-waisted, big-breasted figure of the south. In the back seat someone was snoring from the effects of a lingering head cold.

"Who did you bring?"

"Dean. He didn't have any homework for Monday and he wanted to spend some time with his daddy. Better at least wake him up and say hello."

He did better than that; he reached back and picked up the sleeping ten-year-old and lifted him over the seat. Dean yawned and blinked away cobwebs.

"How did you do?"

"The bad guys won, I'm happy to say."

Dean snickered. "You're not a bad guy."

"Who am I?"

"You're my dad. Where're you going tomorrow?"

"Albany, New York."

"Okay." Dean snuggled closer and shut his eyes as Gina backed out of the parking space and drove away from the gym. In the lights from a passing car she looked tired; smudges under her eyes. The boutique in Joshua which she operated with a friend had had a dismal Christmas season and some of their accounts were sixty days behind; Gina and her partner Kay Finlay had met with their accountant that afternoon trying to decide if they should call it quits. Gina loved the shop and had invested five years in it; he hoped they could save it.

"What did DiFalco say?"

"We'll run the sale to the end of the month. If there's enough cash then we can hold on till spring. It's a *good* spring line, but we'll need to advertise. Radio, the papers."

"How much would that cost?"

"Four thousand, I figure."

He sighed. "Maybe we could—"

"Uh-uh, no way! We agreed in the beginning. One Pearl Place had to earn its own way. We don't touch personal savings, Conor. No sense throwing good money after bad in this economy."

She was still silent for a couple of miles, until they were traveling northbound on 495 toward home. It was snowing harder; the windshield wipers were going. Gina had put on her glasses, but still she didn't see well at night, and the Interstate was slippery.

"Want me to drive, honey?"

"No, no, I'm all right. I was just thinking. Do you know how many small businesses failed in this country last year? More than twenty-seven thousand."

"Things have to get better," Conor said.

"I forgot to ask. You okay?"

"I'm not the horse I used to be," Conor admitted. He was hurting from the weight of the sleeping boy in his lap, but didn't want to move him. Times likes these were too precious. He lightly stroked Dean's blond head. Reddish blond like his mother. The same tough, intelligent eyes, lips that had a tendency to flake and peel no matter what the weather.

Hillary, Dean, and Charles, who was the youngest of the Devon clan at eight. They'd come along with surprising regularity the first years of their marriage. No telling how many there'd be now if the fourth one hadn't been stillborn; the doctors had advised Gina to have her tubes tied. Not bad for an ex-priest, he thought. He was making out all right in the world, though he still remembered vividly the shock of renouncing his vows, the feelings of impotence and abandonment. No worldly goods other than those he could pack into a very small suitcase. No idea of what to do with himself. So in six months, still without prospects, he was married, to the first girl who was nice to him. Although Gina claimed to have had her eye on him since they were fifth-graders at St. Ignatius. A likely story, but Conor knew how lucky he was. Not many women could have stayed the course, through his fits of depression, his neuroses and drinking bouts. Spiritually she was the toughest woman he'd ever known, including his own mother, who had been through three husbands and a leg amputation before a stroke got her.

Grateful not to have to make the forty-five-minute drive himself, Conor dozed until they pulled into the driveway of their home in Revere Park, the best area of Joshua. The house, a Williamsburg Colonial with four bedrooms and a den which he'd turned into a gym, was set on a knoll above the street. The long slope of the drive was the only drawback: in winter both family cars had to be equipped with chains to make it. Gina maneuvered past the babysitter's Honda and put the wagon in the garage.

Conor carried Dean into the house and up the back steps to the boys' room, took his time tucking him into the upper bunk; he hoped Dean would wake up again and want to come down to the kitchen for hot chocolate and a chat despite the late hour. But only Charles woke up, and requested a drink of water. Conor got it for him, paused to chew four aspirin, kissed his youngest good-night, and went downstairs.

Gina was fixing his post-match meal: six scrambled eggs, fried Polish sausage, biscuits. Black coffee in a mug with a shot of Bushmill's on the side. He settled carefully onto a padded stool at the breakfast bar, and when she put a heaping plate in front of him he ignored the food momentarily, preferring to put an arm around her waist and hold her close.

"Your beard needs a trim."

"I know."

Smoke from the fat sausages was faintly visible, greasing the air around them; Gina opened the back door a finger's width. Cold air snaked in.

"I'd better take a look at that stove vent fan in the morning. Hasn't been working right for a week."

Conor had his shot and half a mug of coffee before tackling his meal. Gina sat next to him, elbows on the counter, chin on her clasped hands, and watched him eat. He sneaked a look at her, hoping for what he saw so seldom nowadays: the calm of a madonna, her spade-shaped face bridal-serene. Instead he saw new lines, obscure agitation, fitful shadows in her eyes.

"Worried about the boutique?"

"If it goes under, well. Women just don't shop for clothes like they used to. Who can afford it? I'll find something else to do. It isn't as if we've been depending on the income."

"How are we fixed?"

"All bills are current. There's eleven hundred in checking, seven thousand in the government securities fund, stocks are worth sixteen six, and SCM just split two for one. The utilities are still yielding a little better than twelve percent."

"That's good news," Conor said, smiling at her acquired expertise.

"Do you know where I think I could make a fortune? Retailing?"

"Where?"

"At the new mall that's going up in Lowell."

"Rentals are steep, aren't they?"

"The builders were six months behind schedule going into winter, and they only have seventy percent occupancy so far; I hear they're willing to make concessions."

"Move One Pearl Place to Lowell?"

"If we stay solvent I'm sure we could swing a loan."

"You're talking about twenty miles a day, each way. And you'd be staying open most nights until nine, nine thirty. Have to hire more help."

"I worked it out today on the Apple. I really haven't been using my time to best advantage, Conor."

He had to smile again. "Is that so?" She was seldom in

bed before midnight, up for early Mass every morning at Blessed Sacrament Church. Car pools, scouts, midget hockey, committees, good works, a full-time job with a struggling business that hadn't paid her a salary for over a year, an infirm mother to visit twice a week in Mattapan. Gina still did all of the cooking and some of the cleaning in their thirty-two-hundred-square-foot house. And they tried to have two date nights a month: bowling with friends, dinner out, a Bruins game at the Garden where she invariably yelled herself hoarse.

"Really. I'll show you later." She reached out to flick a crumb of egg from his beard.

Conor poured another shot of Bushmill's for himself, looked inquiringly at Gina. She shook her head and put more sugar in her coffee instead, then with a spoon fished out one of the saturated cubes and sucked thoughtfully on it.

"I think we could gross nearly a hundred thousand a year the first year. Of course we have to pay a percentage of the profits to the mall. But it would be worth it. Our location's hurting us now; we can't build up enough steady customers. What do you think?"

"I think you should have been twins."

She kissed him and whirled off her stool. "I need to do a little sewing before bed, can I get you something else?"

"I'm just fine, honey."

Conor cleaned up after himself, rinsing the dishes first in the stainless steel sink, enjoying the modest domestic chore. He put everything into the dishwasher, which already was half filled with the dishes from dinner; the thrifty Gina only ran the Kitchenaid when it had a full load. He looked briefly at the bottle of Bushmill's on the breakfast counter, decided against smuggling it upstairs to bed. A long time ago, to get him to cut down, she'd made a firm rule: "The only thing I want to smell on your breath in bed is my pussy."

The thought made him smile and put heat in his groin; he left the Irish alone and went upstairs.

Gina, in a pale blue floor-length Dior nightgown, was seated in the alcove off the master bedroom putting a patch on some purple leotards for Hillary, using the old black Singer that had been in her family for fifty years. Conor undressed and went morosely into the bathroom, stood over the toilet and was relieved to see only traces of red in his urine. His lower back still hurt, a hard lump of pain as if he were growing an unneeded bone down there. He pulled on a sleep shirt with IRISH BOB and his caricature—which made him look a lot like Yosemite Sam in the Bugs Bunny cartoons—on the back, turned on the TV for the CNN news, and crept gratefully into bed, which was already nicely warmed by the electric blanket. Gina thought of everything. Spoiled him, in fact.

The Celtics were big winners, the Bruins had tied at St. Louis. Conor yawned. "Don't keep that up all night," he called to Gina.

"I'll be right there."

Tonight, for a change, she did make it to bed before he fell asleep. He had her out of the nightgown in half a second.

"Oh," Gina said, lying back in an Odalisque pose, her eyes shapely with sexual intrigue, "what's the matter, didn't you get enough exercise throwing those big gay studs out of the ring?"

"They just kept bouncing back."

With her thick wedding ring she rubbed the underside of his bullish glans. His fingers dabbled in her buttery breasts, plucking at the little tightwads of her nipples. They kissed and kissed. Her hair shaky over his cheeks, her tongue warm as a bath. How he loved the gingery curl and deep-down grain of cunt, the flex and tug of insistent muscle drawing him in like a baby's famished mouth. The speed of her blood. The touch of blunt toes on his shin-bones, climbing. The little bulge of a blue vein on one thigh. Her laugh. Her greed.

(You're fucking mefuckingmefucking   me
No don't put it in yet.)

Gina looked stealthily back over one shoulder.

"Maybe I'd just better lock the door first, Dean's been walking in his sleep again."

She took care of the door and the lights and snuggled back into bed, fawning over him, lips avidly apart as if she were silently caroling.

*   *   *

(Can you get bigger? Bigger? What do you want me to do to make it bigger?

Lick me.

Oh I want to lick you. And then what do you want me to do?

Get on top.

Would you love it if I got on top?

Really love it.)

She took several delicious minutes sucking, then working his cock fully into her, and by then he was nicely separated from his wits. She fucked him slowly and all he had to do was hold on, feeling the muscles at work in her small ass, which had not lost any firmness after ten years and four babies. When she began to moan softly with each long, released breath he placed a wettened finger carefully in her anus, stretching her but not painfully. Her own fingers winnowed through the abundant hair on his chest, tugged at his wiry beard when she came in scalded gasps. He came a little after, like a fountain flowing miles-high and condensing into soft cloud.

She cuddled then beside him, and they went to sleep secure in each other, the TV still on and murmuring, casting rainbow shadows across their glazed faces. Married folks. The sex familiar, always nice and sometimes still terrific.

The next thing Conor heard was the telephone.

When he opened his eyes at the third loud ring the room was dark. Gina had gotten up at some point after lovemaking, probably to sit on the toilet and read her missal before putting her nightgown back on and turning off the TV. She was lying on her side at the far edge of the king-size bed. He got up on one elbow, was stabbed in the back, grimaced, and reached over her to grope for the phone. The luminous clock face showed the time: three thirty-five A.M. Gina suddenly rose up in front of him. "'S okay, I'll get it."

Conor groaned crankily and lay down again.

"Hello? Yes—yes. Well, he's asleep now, could you tell me—"

Conor had been half afraid it was bad news about her

mother, but apparently the call was for him, which caused no anxiety. It wasn't an unusual occurrence. Some inconsiderate wrestling buff who'd found out his home number despite the alias he used and wanted beerily to challenge Irish Bob to a no-holds-barred fight behind the challenger's favorite tavern. He tuned out the interruption and was sinking gently back into sleep when he heard Gina cry out.

"What? Are you sure? *Richard* Devon?"

Conor was up again, a hand on Gina's shoulder. She was rigid, holding the receiver of the phone in both hands.

"Yes. Yes. Oh, my God. I don't *believe* it! Not Richard!"

"Gina—" Conor said, a lump dark and hot as coal tar rising in his throat. His back ached fiercely.

She turned to him. In the mild light, frozen halogen from a distant street lamp, her face was frightened. Worse, to him, the light her mind gave back in the bedroom dark was as shocking as a scream. Wordlessly she held out the receiver to Conor and, as soon as he took it from her, reached for her rosary, which was always close to hand on the bedside table.

"This is Conor Devon," Conor said, feeling Gina's breath coming to the side of his neck like a fog. Tremulous, dimly outraged, sensing that the life they had so meticulously made and cherished so deeply was now threatened by forces beyond his control, he cleared his throat harshly and continued, "What about my brother?"

28

Haden County, Vermont, bounded by the Connecticut River on the east and, roughly, by the Green Mountains on the west, has a population of 35,000 permanent residents. The Appalachian Trail bisects the northwest corner of Haden County, and several of the most popular ski areas in the eastern United States lie within its borders. Some famous old inns in quiet little villages attract large numbers of both summer and winter vacationers, and at peak times of the year the county's population nearly doubles with transients, many of them from the nearby metropolitan areas of Boston and New York. Major crimes are still a rarity in Haden County, but in recent years misdemeanors have quadrupled; the freedom to acquire and abuse drugs has become a much-discussed problem. Murders, most frequently involving local drug merchants, have been committed here, six in the last four years. And murderers have been prosecuted in Haden County, in the superior and district courts.

But the killing of Karyn Vale was unusual, partly because of its sensational nature and partly because it involved nonresidents, vacationing college students from Yale University. And Karyn's father was a stockbroker, president of a large firm his grandfather had begun: the family was wealthy, they had impeccable social credentials and close friends in high places both at home and abroad. The murder, consequently, commanded major space in the newspapers and on the network news programs within twenty-four hours.

Before much news had leaked out of Haden County, however, before the TV people began to arrive to do their preliminary reports on the courthouse steps or in front of the Davos Chalet Lodge where the murder took place, Conor Devon drove into Chadbury shortly before sunrise on the twenty-first of January, a Saturday, and received directions to the state police unit from a couple of telephone company linemen working to repair an ice-damaged cable on the Post Road.

The state police unit was surrounded by cyclone fencing. It was a low concrete building with narrow dark-toned windows inset on a diagonal and communications gear all over the roof. There was a helicopter on a pad in a cleared area to one side of the fenced parking lot, and a hell of a lot of cars pulled up in front. Conor found space for the ten-year-old Lincoln he cherished because of the leg room it afforded and went into the building.

He asked the officer on the desk for Captain Moorman, referring to a scrap of paper he took from his pocket. The captain, he was told, was busy; they were all busy this morning. The telephone console was lit up, with nearly a dozen lines in use, and the phone kept ringing.

Conor was directed to a seat in the lobby and offered coffee, which he accepted. The coffee was old and the shell plastic chair, a bright orange that didn't go well with the pastel blue walls, wasn't accommodating to his bulk. He stood, his back against a cold concrete-block wall beside a framed portrait of the governor, a man with silver-tipped sideburns and a canny smile, flanked by towering flags of the state and country.

Conor picked up a wrinkled old supermarket tabloid to stare at well-tended faces he had seen around, before bedtime, in early afternoon, the TV on while he doggedly worked at his Soloflex conditioning machine in the converted den at home. Fixed by the almost nuclear glare of photoflash, they seemed curiously poignant fossils, condemned to stratification in endless back numbers of the *National Enquirer*. He lived himself at the very fringe of their kind of celebrity, miles from the severing arc, a gimp-kneed dinosaur bellowing in the pits of stagnant towns, answered by catcalls and the bloodyminded insults of savage strangers. He shuddered from knowledge of the speed at which they were all being hurried to extinction, his stomach hollow, a hellish rumble of gases within. Painful. Threatening. He thought of his brother. His mind froze then out of gear at the concurrent thought of murder; of Karyn, dead, somewhere.

A couple of kids in their early twenties came from inside the building through sliding glass doors. Pretty girl with a flippantly upturned nose and dark, tangled tresses, a lanky boy with shoulders narrow as a goat's and crinkled carroty hair. Both looked as if they had spent a sleepless night under interrogation. Conor's scalp prickled. Witnesses. They had seen. The girl had a cold, red-rimmed nostrils. She paused to light a filtertip cigarette while the boy jittered, perhaps from coffee nerves, a starey, aimless look of exhaustion in his eyes.

She spat out smoke and complained that the cigarette had no taste. "Shid."

"Come on, let's get out of here," the boy muttered.

"Do you think we'll have to come back today?"

"I don't know, Caitlin."

"Whad's a grand jury do? Is id like a trial? Shid. Thad could take *months*." She flung a hand wide, to indicate the immensity of a span of time to which she, not a criminal, had been unfairly sentenced. "I have to be back on campus *tomorrow nide*."

The boy shrugged.

"I wish I hadn't seen anything," Caitlin said wanly, using nasal spray. She looked at Conor, standing wild and red and disheveled against the wall, looking quickly away when their eyes met. He had wanted at that instant to take a step forward, speak to her—*is it true, what my brother did*? But something about him—his size, the desperation in his face—had disturbed her.

"I wish to God I could forget what *I* saw," the boy replied. He held the outside door open and the girl went out with a leggy stride. She flipped the unsmoked cigarette into a snowbank and shrugged into a classy fur jacket.

The sliding glass doors behind Conor whooshed apart again.

"Mr. Devon?"

Lady cop. Yellow-bordered green stripes on her khaki sleeve. Elfin blond haircut, Valkyrie bust, a raspy complexion; but pretty despite the flaws. She was tall enough in her boots almost to look him in the eye.

"I'm Sergeant Wilde. Would you come this way, please?"

"Could you tell me—"

"Captain Moorman will be able to answer your questions; I just came on." She smiled, waiting. Conor went first. She told him to turn left inside the doors. All the way to the end, past doors of blond simulated oak to an end office with venetian blinds closed, a glare of fluorescence overhead. Nearly the whole ceiling.

"Did you have a long drive?"

"It's about a hundred and twenty-five miles, I guess."

"Coffee?"

"No thanks. Where's—"

"Captain Moorman will be right with you," she said, smiling again; and she went out, closing the door behind her.

Conor stood in the middle of the room, clenching and unclenching his hands. Two metal chairs in front of a small desk, a computer terminal, screen and modem on the desktop. Green blotter pad, manila file folders, telephone.

There'd been no name on the door. Most of the keys on the telephone console were alight. He thought about picking up the receiver, eavesdropping at random; his itch to be informed was nearly unendurable. *What the hell is going on?* He went to the windows instead, opened the blinds, looked out. The day was clear, the sun a perfect orb, milky orange through a screen of tall evergreens along the road. It was five minutes after eight by his watch.

The door opened and Captain Moorman came in. He was barely the acceptable height for policemen in this country. Conor could have put him in his hip pocket and had room left for a couple of cub scouts. Moorman was about forty-five, with a weekend skier's bronze-toned face, a neat dark mustache, and not much hair on his head, like the nap left on a worn-out teddy bear.

Conor turned from the windows, tears flowing freely. The captain was taken aback.

"Mr. Devon?"

"*Yes.*"

"Are you all right?"

"What do you think?" Conor said, his face screwing up. He reached for a handkerchief. He cried easily when frustrated or unhappy, and didn't care who saw him. Weeping also inflamed his face, which always made him look dangerous and unpredictable.

"Under the circumstances I—I'm very sorry. Would you like to sit down?"

"No. I want to hear about my brother."

"Of course." Moorman took a photocopied report from a slim black leather case under one arm, referred to it quickly.

"I can tell you at the moment that your brother is under arrest, suspicion of murder. The victim—"

"I know all that already. But *why* did he do it? What made him—what in sweet Jesus' name—" Conor sobbed and paused to blow his nose. "None of this makes any sense. Rich is my half brother, actually; we had the same father. But *I* was like his father. Even though I was in seminary part of the time while he was growing up. He just isn't—he couldn't—my God, she's such a sweet girl! *Why?*"

"I'm afraid Richard hasn't been very clear about his

motives. He was in an agitated, nearly incoherent state when we took him into custody several hours ago.''

"Incoherent?"

"He appeared incapable of fully understanding what had taken place. When he spoke, according to the arresting officers, at times his words were foreign, a language they didn't understand.''

"What did he say when his rights were read to him?"

"He indicated comprehension.''

"Well, then, he must know what he did!"

"Not necessarily. Forty-five minutes had elasped. His rights were read to him a second time on his arrival here. He knew that he was under arrest. He asked that we contact you, and provided the telephone number.''

"Was he drunk?"

"That hasn't been established. It was the opinion of the officers who were the first to arrive at the scene that he didn't exhibit common symptoms of alcohol or narcotic intoxication. We'll have to wait for the lab report. Your brother agreed to give us a blood sample.''

"What *did* he do, Captain? I mean, how—''

Moorman consulted his report again. "Five witnesses saw him repeatedly bludgeon Karyn Vale with a tire tool, which we believe is from the trunk of his own car. This happened on a terrace outside the tavern at the Davos Chalet Lodge on Hermitage Mountain, at approximately two o'clock this morning. The victim had no opportunity to defend herself or run away. Richard allegedly struck her more than twenty times. The victim was pronounced dead on arrival at the E.R. of Good Shepherd Hospital in Braxton. An autopsy will be conducted to determine the exact nature of—''

"Where do you have Richard?"

"He's in the county jail, under sedation.''

"Can I see him now?"

"No. After two o'clock this afternoon. In the meantime you could be helpful—''

"How?"

"We'd like to know more about your brother. He's a graduate student at Yale, works for the school's publicity office, and has a part-time job with the New Haven *Register*. That much we've learned from the cards he carries in his wallet. But you may be able to tell me something that will—let's say, shed more light on his motivations. Does he have a history of mental instability?''

Conor hesitated. ''Hold it. I don't want to go into this. I don't think I want to discuss Rich with anyone until after I've seen him, and talked to a lawyer.''

''I appreciate that,'' Moorman said. ''Because both you and your brother are from out of state, you may want some assistance in choosing an attorney. Why don't you drop by the public defender's office when they open this morning, and see what they recommend.''

''Thank you,'' Conor said numbly. ''What will he be charged with, first-degree murder? Is there a death penalty in this state?''

''It's up to the grand jury to indict. Death penalty? No. First-degree murder carries a sentence of thirty-five or forty years to life.''

''What about bail?''

''Unlikely, under the circumstances. The nature of the crime, no local ties, and so forth. If you want to petition, the superior court judge for Haden County is Sam Bracken. But get legal help first.''

''I will. Do Karyn's parents—''

''They've just been notified. It took some time to locate them. They were vacationing in Barbados.''

''I—I think I want to call them. But I don't know how to get in touch—''

''I can't help you there, Mr. Devon.''

''What a tragedy. He really loved that girl. I just—it can't be. Because. Something. *Something* must have got into him, not his fault, it just couldn't have been Rich.''

Moorman looked queerly at him. ''What do you mean?''

''Maybe somebody slipped something into his drink. PCP. One of those drugs that makes you crazy. Rich wasn't a doper himself. I swear to that. He spent two and a half days with us at Christmas, I think I know the kid well enough. Who were the witnesses? Who saw it happen? Is it okay if I talk—''

''I don't know how advisable that would be. But we can't stop you. We're still interrogating two of the eyewitnesses. All of them were employed by or vacationing at the Davos Chalet. Will you be staying in Chadbury?''

"Yes. I don't know where. I just got here."

"After you've checked in, please let us know where we can find you."

"All right."

"You look familiar to me. I know I've seen you before."

"I'm a professional wrestler. Irish Bob O'Hooligan."

"That's it. My father never misses the wrestling on cable. Again let me say how sorry I am. We'll try to help you if it's at all possible. Ask Sergeant Wilde for the address of the public defender's office. Third door on the right on your way out."

29

"Gina?"

Conor was crying again; he'd had trouble making out the numbers on the stainless steel studs of the pay phone. "They won't let me see him until two o'clock. He's probably sleeping now; he was sedated. The police said he was incoherent. Didn't seem to know where he was or what he'd done. Can you imagine that? Maybe Rich doesn't realize yet that he killed Karyn. I'll have to tell him."

"Oh, Conor!" She was struggling against tears herself. "What are you going to do now?"

"I checked into a place in Chadbury called the Waites Inn. I'm in room 16. I want to talk to some of the kids who saw it happen. There's a girl named Caitlin—then I—I just don't know, I have a list of lawyers to choose from. Criminal lawyers. Rich has to have a lawyer right away, I don't think the public defender can handle this."

"If he didn't know what he was doing, then can't he plead—"

"Temporary insanity? I think so. There's no telling what got into him. Rich was a tough kid, but always a fair fighter. That's the way I taught him. And he'd cut off his hand before he would hit somebody with a rock or a club. Gina, there's no reason; just no reason on earth for him to—until they tell me otherwise, I'm assuming he was drugged.''

Gina broke down. "Oh, Mary. Mother of mercy. I want to be there with you, Conor.''

"I know. I need you too. Just pray for him, Gina. If anything's going to help now, it's prayer.''

"I will. I'm praying hard. I love you. Take care of yourself. Call me after you've seen him. That poor girl. *Rich adored her!* Conor, what's it going to cost? I mean, lawyers? Can we manage?''

"I can't think about that right now, Gina,'' he said, with a hint of irritation. He wiped his swarming eyes.

"I shouldn't have brought it up. Rich comes first, we have to help Rich. There's enough equity in the house, I'm sure no matter what we'll be able to handle it. Listen, I've got to pick Charley-chuck up at hockey and drop Hillary at jazz ballet.''

"I'll call you later at the shop. Try not to worry.''

30

It was one thirty in the afternoon before Caitlin Miller woke up in the overheated room at the chalet which she had shared on this skiing holiday with her cousin from Biloxi, Mississippi. The pleasant holiday that had gone so disastrously wrong: a microsecond after she sat up in bed the memory was back, tormenting her like a scene from a tacky slice-and-dice horror movie she was condemned to go on watching with the mind's eye forever. She couldn't breathe very well and she had a thumping headache. She held her stuffy head and groaned pathetically.

Crystal came out of the bathroom still beaded with water from her shower, a slight varnish of freckles across the backs of her shoulders; otherwise her skin was as fresh and slightly pinked as the inside of a cut strawberry. Lashes wet, heavy, gorgeous. Limpid brown eyes. Hair in hazy tendrils peeked from beneath her shower cap.

"How do you feel, hon?" Crystal asked in a drawl that sounded like a candied pear tasted. Caitlin, who talked and giggled through her nose and regretted it, had long wished she could sound like her cousin. Languid and laid-back and ripely flirtatious. You allllllll. But you had to be born there, hock-deep in hominy grits. A way down south in de land o'cotton.

"I feel like shid."

"Me, too, kind of." But Crystal's eyes had too much sparkle for Caitlin to take her seriously.

"I just wand to ged oud of this place."

"They said we could leave, right after we signed the depositions." Crystal laid a thoughtful finger against one temple. "Whatever *they* are." There was dreamy, bashful Crystal, whom the boys went after in yapping packs, and then there was Crystal the premed student at Rutgers, fours across the board in all the hard subjects Caitlin found unendurable at her own college. Chem. Biology. Physics. *Ughhhh*.

Crystal sat down on the bed beside Caitlin, hands on her knees.

"Want to get somethin' to eat?"

"No. Why is id so fucking hod in here?"

"I woke up with the shivers and shakes, so I turned the thermostat way up. Well, I'm hungry. Kind of." She looked appealingly at Caitlin. "What say we get dressed and go down-stair? Some company, sure, touch of sun, little lovin' cup of hot chocolate on the terrace, maybe."

"If we can avoid the boys. Because then all we'll be able to talk aboud is—" Caitlin drew a forefinger across her throat, choking realistically.

Crystal looked mildly at her.

"What you got to do now is, just put it out of your mind. I did."

"Id could have been any one of us," Caitlin said, with a look of doom, clenching her lower lip between her teeth.

"Noooo, Lord! He wasn't *that* kind of crazy. I mean, I think all he had in mind was to do in his girl friend. Who knows what she did to deserve it."

"Deserve id! Her head was splid open and her brains were oozing all down her face. Her bones were so crushed—"

"Shhh! It was a crime of passion, it's over and done, he'll get what's comin' to him. No way we can bring that girl back by agonizin' over her. Now the way you get it out of your mind is, you meditate."

"Shid. I cand meditate."

"Anyone can."

"You can do all sords of things I cand do. I'm so jealous."

"Why jealous? Lookit how you can ski those slopes. Lord, I am so spaz on skis it's ridiculous. Come on, let me teach you how to meditate. Won't take but a few minutes. You'll feel so much better. That's got the Crystal Kinsman guarantee behind it."

Caitlin grinned crookedly. "Love to listen to you talk."

"Just unclasp your hands and uncross your knees there and sit back. Relax."

"You honestly liked Warren? Did I do good for you this time, Crys?"

"You did fine. Now listen here to what I'm gonna tell you. First of all do you know what a chakra is?"

"They ged between my teeth when I ead them."

"I swear, you just won't be serious for one—"

The telephone rang. Caitlin tensed and frowned at it.

"Led's don't answer thad."

"Why not? Probably your folks or mine. Heard about the murder, wantin' to know are we all right." She reached past Caitlin and answered on the second ring. Listened.

"Yes, I am. Yes. Yes, we are. Who did you say?" Her eyes shadowed briefly. "I see. Yes, sir. I am real sorry about that. How can we help? Well, we were just now doin' our best to try to forget—"

Caitlin pulled the covers over her head and sank down in the bed with a muted cry of despair. Crystal listened, talked, listened.

"Who was thad?" Caitlin demanded in a muffled voice after Crystal hung up.

"Said his name was Conor Devon. He's the brother of that boy. Wanted to know if we could see him for a few minutes."

"Don't tell me. Don't tell me you promised—!"

"Poor man. He was all but in tears on the telephone. This is such a tragedy, Caitlin. Her family. His. Nobody understands a thing about how or why it happened. I think since God saw fit to put us there in that tavern last night, we have a duty to help as much as we possibly can.''

''I'm nod gedding oud of this bed until id's time to go back to Mount Holyoke!''

''Don't be that way.''

''There was nod *one square inch* of her body thad wasn't—''

''Stop that. Get dressed, now.''

''You mean he's coming over here? To the chalet?''

''He's down-stair a-waitin' on us right now, hon.''

Caitlin was dead still for several seconds; then she threw off the covers and went bounding starkers toward the bathroom.

''I'm going to be sick!''

She slammed the door. Crystal looked back and raised her voice slightly.

''Caitlin, do you want to wear that cute pumpkin-colored jump suit, or just a wool skirt and a blouse?''

31

Conor learned immediately that it was Crystal Kinsman of Biloxi, Mississippi, whom he could relate to. The other girl, Caitlin, who sat slumped in her chair on the hotel's second-story sun deck, was ill and sulky and unfriendly. She drank two bloody marys through a straw, shaded her eyes with one hand, and stared at Conor as if he were somehow responsible for what Rich had done. Crystal cut a Monte Cristo sandwich into small golden bites and ate steadily while she answered Conor's questions.

''We were havin' a nightcap with our dates when she came into the bar.''

Conor looked at his notes. ''The boys are Warren Hasper and Jeff Pepperdine?''

''Yes, sir. Warren was my date, and Caitlin here has been goin' with Jeff for about a year.''

"He's a senior at Williams," Caitlin volunteered, moodily stirring her drink.

"Anyhow, she came into the tavern and I couldn't help noticin' her even though it's not the brightest in there, because she was just so attractive and didn't have anybody with her, you know? And the bartender, I don't know his name—"

"Donald Ray Stemmons," Conor said.

"—Asked her did she want a quick one, because they were fixin' to close. And she said, 'No, I'm just lookin' for someone.' Then she must have described her boyfriend to Mr. Stemmons, but her back was turned, I couldn't hear what she was sayin'. Okay. Mr. Stemmons shook his head. About that time, this drunk ol' boy who was at the bar sort of slipped off his stool and sat there, real comical, on the floor. Then—" Crystal took a deep breath, licked her lips tidily and glanced off at the skiers on the mountain. "Then your brother, he knocked on the glass of the terrace doors, to get his girl's attention."

Caitlin grimaced and shuddered, slumped down a little more in her chair and touched a sore pimple at the root of her *retroussé* nose.

Conor said, "Rich knocked on the doors, from outside on the terrace. Could you see his face?"

"No, sir, couldn't make him out. He was just a dark shape there against the glass. And he called to her."

"How close was Karyn to him?"

"Oh—she must have been a good fifteen feet away. She didn't seem to know him at first, or recognize his voice. She kind of hesitated, then when he called again—his voice was muffled, like he had a scarf over his mouth—she went straight to the doors and gave a couple good yanks to try and open them. But they were frozen shut."

"And Rich was standing right outside all this time?"

"Yes, maybe two or three feet away from the doors. But she still couldn't get them open, so—she told him to come on in, round by way of the lobby. He wouldn't budge. Then she asked the bartender was there another way outside, and he told her, and she left. Mr. Stemmons came out from behind the bar, said he had to lock up; next thing I know the girl screamed."

"I don't know why we have to tell this again," Caitlin

complained. "I don't even wand to think aboud whad happened next."

"It's very important," Conor said, "that I know *exactly* what happened."

Crystal took time to break a Hershey bar in half and stir the pieces into a cup of steaming hot chocolate. Caitlin watched this in exasperation and envy.

"After that, it was kind of confused for all of us," Crystal explained. "Because, that first scream, we all just knew it was somethin' awful. We looked around, but there wasn't much to be seen. It was just shadows."

"All I saw was him," Caitlin put in. "You couldn't see *her* because he'd already knocked her down; I guess he was standing ride on top of her. Then he bent over her, or maybe he kneeled in the snow and raised his hand, and the bartender, he goes, 'Shid!' Like that. He was closer to the terrace and we were across the room. He could tell your brother had something in his hand and was aboud to hid her again."

Conor rubbed his aching head and had a long swallow of the beer he'd been working on.

"But," Crystal said, "she screamed again before he could hit her a second time. And all of us, we'd been kind of frozen for a few seconds after that first one, we just jumped up and all ran to the doors. Pushin', shovin', it was a madhouse. And one scream after another. She got up a couple of times, Lord knows how she managed, she was tottering, goin' around in circles in the snow tryin' to hold her head up while he took a rest, or whatever. Then *whack,* he'd knock her down again with what he had in his hand. Finally she didn't move. We were screamin', too, I tell you, bangin' against the doors. He didn't pay attention, didn't even look our way. Kept flailin' away with his club or tire tool or whatever it was—"

"Id was a big iron bar," Caitlin said. Tension haunted her, like an indistinct blue shape lying just beneath the skin. "I saw id ride after. He'd dropped id. And id was all stuck up with her blood and skin and brains." She coughed harshly and turned her pretty, bony face away from them. Conor gazed at Crystal with sad reddened eyes.

"I know," Crystal said sympathetically, "that this is a terrible thing for you to have to listen to."

"How did Rich act afterwards?"

"I couldn't tell you. I never went near him. You see, Mr. Stemmons shoved us all out of the way and broke down the doors with a barstool and went boundin' out there in the snow, the boys right behind him. They were real brave to do that because for all anybody knew your brother could've had a knife or a gun too. I went the other way, to the telephone, and called the police. By the time I got back to the tavern, it was all over. A few other people had come to find out what was goin' on. It turned into *bedlam*. But I admit, I couldn't make myself go any closer. She was down in the snow, just a dark shape, face up, I think, but like she'd fallen off a twenty-story building. Your brother, well, they had him surrounded, three husky guys, Warren and Jeff and the bartender. And Caitlin was right there too."

"I—" Her voice betrayed a tendency to croak; she cleared her throat with an effort. "I tried to help the girl, but ride away I could tell id wasn't any use. She was pulp. Just pulp. When I was fifteen we were coming home from a football game, convoys of cars, paper streamers and all thad, the lead car god into a head-on with a big truck and, you know, there were six kids in thad car and probably three of them were killed instantly. Just as soon as you see them, scaddered around on the road, you can tell there's no hope."

"How was Rich acting?" Conor asked Caitlin. But she had retreated from thinking of the dead, unlucky at highway roulette; she was sullen in contemplation of her own vulnerability, and wouldn't speak.

"Crazy, Warren says," Crystal volunteered.

"Crazy?"

"Oh, talkin' to himself. Sayin' she was a hoor and deserved to die, she'd suck anybody's see-oh-see-kay, if you'll pardon me, and other filthy stuff like that. Well, those were the words you could understand. Other times it was like he was talkin' in a foreign language, or just plain gibberish. They had a pretty good hold on him but every once in a while he'd try to make a move in her direction. Say, 'Come on, Karyn. Get up.' Like he was real annoyed she was lyin' there like that. 'Let's go to bed.' I mean, that's *crazy*, after what he'd done to her. I wish I could spare your feelings, Conor.''

Conor sat with his face in his hands. "Go on.''

"Then the cops came, they made good time although I couldn't tell you just how long it was. Mr. Stemmons opened the bar for us, thank the Lord. They questioned us there, then took us all down to the station till about—what time did you get back this mornin', Caitlin?''

"I don't remember.'' She sniffed and looked hard at Conor. "Your brother knows whad he did. He was just pudding on an *act*. Now he'll probably ged away with id. Thad's why I'm so—disgusted. *No* punishment is good enough for him, bud''—she began to gulp and cry—''bud everybody's going to say, 'Oh, well, he didn't know whad he was doing. *Poor guy*.' Shid. Fuck. Piss.''

"I don't suppose,'' Crystal said, ignoring her cousin, "you have any notion how he could do such a terrible thing?''

"I only know he loved Karyn very much.''

"Have you seen him yet?''

"No.'' Conor looked at his watch. "I'm driving over to Chadbury now.''

Caitlin said, "I'm going to call and see if they have those depositions ready to sign.'' She got up nervily, throwing a cape around her shoulders, and left the table without a word or a glance at Conor.

"She's not usually so rude,'' Crystal explained. "It's just what she went through. Nothin' compared to what you must be goin' through. For what it's worth, I'm sorry as can be. I can tell you were close to your brother.''

"I'd better go. Thanks for talking to me, Crystal. Take care of yourself.''

Crystal polished off the last neat square of her Monte Cristo and looked up at him. In the delicate, faintly rosed complexion that fried foods and love of chocolate couldn't corrupt, in the shape of a wishful smile like that of a child completing prayers, there was tenderness and a purity of feeling that so touched him he was just able to bear it. With a wisp of a handshake they parted.

32

Before he left the lodge, Conor tried to get a close look at the terrace, but the Crime Scene Search Unit had barricaded it. Not much could be observed from inside the tavern; the broken doors were boarded up. Donald Ray Stemmons, he learned, wouldn't be back at work until the following night. Conor wanted a whiskey but denied himself. He got into his Lincoln and drove down to Chadbury to visit Rich.

The jail was in a wing of the county courthouse. Conor was relieved of almost everything he had on him, including loose change and a roll of breath mints. They let him wear the crucifix on a thin gold chain around his neck and allowed him to keep his pocket breviary.

Then he was shown into the small visiting room, which was starkly empty except for a pair of five-foot-long benches bolted to the floor and facing each other. There was no partition between the benches. The door was steel, with a small observation window in it. The ceiling light was recessed, with a heavy wire grill covering, and the two dirty windows had similar grills over them. The floor was scuffed asphalt tile in a mind-drubbing shade of grayish tan. There was nothing to look at while he waited for his brother to be brought to him except for a sign on one wall that forbade smoking. He soon found that the room was a place of subtle torture, the architectural equivalent of a hair shirt. Conor had been perspiring all day despite the January weather, and he smelled himself. The skin beneath his beard flamed and itched. His back was too painful after all the driving he'd done to allow him to sit. He paced slowly and tried to read Scripture while waiting, but the evangelical reverberations, instead of pacifying, resulted in an excess of thought, like a blood blister that jammed the brain, bringing on a headache hot as a geyser.

Finally the doors opened, and with a loud rattling of

keys and bolts a guard escorted Rich in and locked the door behind him.

The brothers stood six feet apart, not speaking for a few moments. Conor was too shocked to say anything. Rich wore a wrinkled khaki prison jumpsuit and a cotton sweat jacket with a monkish hood tightly enclosing his face, which was as pale as a marble cameo, dense with ordeal. His feet were bare except for a pair of cheap corduroy slippers. His teeth chattered audibly. His nose had been running; there were dried scales of snot on his upper lip. He needed a shave. He looked shrunken without his shoes. His lips were blue, his eyes starkly mystified; the sight of his brother, vivid in the flesh, sweltering in his anxiety, might temporarily have blinded him.

"C-Conor."

"Oh, kid, God love you!"

They embraced. Rich sobbed, the sob rattling up as if through an abandoned well of the spirit. Exhalations of sorrow were so withering they panicked Conor, reminding him of why he was no longer a priest.

"Karyn's dead."

It could have been a question; Conor simply nodded, not trusting his own voice.

"But I, I don't know how it happened! I was there, only it really—wasn't—like—being there."

"What do you mean?" Conor frowned and held his brother at arm's length, taking in the wrecked demeanor, the eyes with a kind of sickly fervor, yet so innocent of intellect, of redemptive thought.

"That's the truth!" Rich blurted. "I told the doctor. I didn't tell him anything else. He wouldn't have believed me." Emotion sparked briefly in his face as if from a live wire. They studied each other. Conor bit his tongue to still the painful gripe in his guts. "You don't believe me either." He clutched Conor's hands with his own.

The touch was peculiarly unpleasant, as if Rich's hands had no skin, were lumps of dead flesh. And the nails were dark red, still packed—*God, how could it be?*—with Karyn's blood and tissue. Conor fought his own gorge; his blood was cold; at that moment he loathed Rich with a savagery that snapped the boy to attention, caused his eyes to flare in frightened recognition.

Shame flooded through Conor, sweeping away the destructive emotion, the betrayal of their brotherhood. "I'm going to get you out of here, Rich. I'll get you a damned good lawyer, and a priest."

Rich turned his face aside. "That won't do any good," he said coldly. From moment to moment it was like talking to totally different people. "I killed Karyn. Don't you think I deserve to die?" He glanced at Conor, away again, a sudden chilling evasiveness, eyes leaping wide in demented enchantment, his mouth twisted, meanly amused.

Conor fought that smile, shaking Rich, reordering his expression as if his face were that of a craftily lifelike doll.

"No, Rich! You don't mean that. What happened wasn't your fault. You must have been drugged. *Look at you*. It's still in your system. That will come out in court. No jury—"

Rich's laughter was an ear-splitting bray. Conor almost dropped him.

He glimpsed an amorphous face at the observation port in the door, a suspicious ballooning eye that reminded him, irrationally, of a childhood concept of God as the Omnipresent, the All-Seeing, like the eye of the giant squid in the movie *Twenty Thousand Leagues Under the Sea*. After a few moments the face floated blurrily away, leaving Conor feeling coldly oppressed.

"Rich! Rich! Get hold of yourself!"

The boy had been mumbling under his breath, words Conor found unfamiliar, heathenish. Rich looked up, startled at the sharp intrusion of his brother's voice. He fell mute, his face going slack. The eyes grew heavy-lidded, the complexion even paler than it had been. Then, after a long suspenseful period of time, as Conor felt himself drawn irresistibly toward the darkness and the depths where his brother had disappeared, Rich came back to life. It was like a half-drowned face rising gradually to the light of day.

"Drugged? Probably. I only wish . . . that could be all there is to it. But it's worse, Conor." He hissed the word again. "*Worssse*." Then he sat down on one of the benches, hands knotted between his knees. "And you're the only one—who can help me now."

"I'll do everything that's in my power, kid. And with God's help I know we can—"

Rich turned aside the suggestion with a cutting gesture of one hand, a grimace of disdain. Now he looked more like himself. Muscles bunched randomly in his face, like little knots of worms beneath the skin. The flashes of other personas had ended. Certain drugs did that, Conor knew. He'd seen a lot of drugs, both as a kid in his Boston neighborhood and as a priest. He knew first-hand of the schizoid effects that LSD, angel dust, and even cocaine could have on otherwise normal kids. Whoever had done this to Rich, hell was too good for them! He felt a little tingle along his spine, a current in his bones. He sat down opposite his brother, leaned toward him.

Rich looked back at the door. For now they were unobserved. "How much time do we have?" he asked quietly.

"I don't know. A few minutes more. But I'll be back."

"And *he'll* be back," Rich retorted. He shuddered, but he wasn't cold. His pores had opened, his face rained perspiration. Drops of it glistened on the backs of his hands. He spoke urgently, in a near-whisper. "Find them for me, Conor. Windross. Polly. Well—I think Polly must be dead too. Listen to the tape in my car, the tape from the Record A Call. That's how it all began, with Polly." He spoke faster, not pausing to breathe; he seemed to be under enormous internal pressure.

Conor, although he could barely make sense of what Rich was saying, suffered for him. They edged closer toward each other until their heads, confessional, were almost touching.

"And Inez! Inez Cordway. That's what she calls herself now, but her name used to be *Courdewaye*." He spelled it and nodded, licking at the wet salt on his lips. "Inez knows the truth. She's real. I know she's real. The others—I'm not sure. Anyway, find Inez. She can tell you everything that happened to me. But if she offers you wine—for God's sake, Conor! *Don't drink.*" Conor leaned back; Rich's tone had made him feel light-headed with horror. Rich's eyes leaped to his, looked away. "*I was only trying to help Polly!* There's so much I can't remember. I don't think *he* wants me to." Rich's complexion was suffused with a dusky red, he gasped for breath.

"I can't follow—who are you—"

"No, Conor! Just listen. *Remember*. He's not here right now. But I know he'll be back, and then—I don't know what he'll have me doing next. I dreamt—dreamt I was a fly, hanging upside down from the ceiling of my cell. I *think* it was only a dream. *Are you listening?* The Courdewaye house, Ripington Four Corners. Ask anybody in town, they'll tell you—how to find the place. All I remember—it was snowing. Hard. I just can't—now it's a blur, most of the time."

Rich had stiffened again. His eyes squeezed shut, receding behind closed lids as if they were being drawn into a vacuum; depths closed over him, volumes of darkness, and he started to topple sideways. Conor grabbed him.

Rich's head revolved eerily: he might have been trying to follow something in rapid flight around the room. But his eyes remained tightly closed. "Look out, look out!" he cried. "What is it? Some kind of horrible—"

He was jolted, as if struck powerfully in the solar plexus. Then for fifteen or twenty seconds he appeared catatonic, unbreathing. Down there in the deeps where God was. Or something unmade by God, uniquely hideous. Conor's senses reeled, he almost couldn't catch his own breath. "Dear Lord, save him," he prayed.

"I f-feel sick, Conor," Rich complained, drawing breath, still unmoving.

"*Dear Lord*," Conor said again. It was the voice of a child he had heard.

Rich's face swam to the light; a sear of pain bloomed there. His eyes opened, he stared at his big brother. "It flew at me, Conor! Make it go away." His face convulsed, he was determined, the little tough guy, not to weep. But there was a stink of urine in the air. He had wet himself, all down one leg. "He's got me. He's in me, Conor! He killed Karyn. Made me hit her. And hit her, and *hit* her—until she *died*."

"What are you saying?" Conor straightened the angle of his brother's lolling head. He saw something disappear from the secluded eyes, like a scuttling bug when the lights go on. The swift shadowy departure of an unknown vileness caused Conor to tremble. But Rich's expression remained earnestly childlike.

"The dee-monn!"

"Mother of Heaven. Are you trying to tell me—you're *possessed*?"

Rich screamed hysterically, rocking on the bench.

Conor smacked him across the face with a hard palm. The hood fell from around Rich's head. His gaze seemed wildly fragmented, broken into shards of light. His voice changed again.

"Pol-Polly. Tried to help Polly. But she died too. That was—after *he* took me. Poor Polly. Poor Richard!" He jumped to his feet, hands grabbing for Conor's face, his beard. "You're a priest, Conor. You can help me, can't you? *Get him out of me!* Before he makes me do something terrible again!"

The door opened. The guard came in, hickory swinging from a leather thong around his wrist.

"What's going on?"

Conor looked up powerlessly, holding Rich at bay by his wrists.

"It's an attack of some kind. He's sick. *Don't do that!*" The guard had drawn back his club.

"Can you handle him?"

"Yes. Yes." Conor lowered Rich back to the bench. The boy sat there in a pathetic huddle, shuddering, one side of his face scarlet and beginning to puff up from the impact of Conor's hand. A single tear inched down the assaulted cheek.

"He should be in a hospital, not a jail," the outraged Conor said.

The guard looked carefully at the big man, his club still half raised.

"I have to take him back now, fella."

"Put him in a cell? Look at him!"

"There's nothing *I* can do." The guard squared his shoulders and said in a tone of pious cruelty, "You forget what he's in here for? They said the girl didn't even have a face when he got through."

"Shut up," Conor told him, quietly enough, but veins were standing out thunderously on his forehead.

The guard, keeping the bench between himself and Conor, reached down and pulled Rich to his feet; he handcuffed

him one-handedly with the deftness of a stage magician
locking up an assistant. Conor couldn't bear to watch.

"Pissed in your pants, did you?" the guard said disgustedly. "Let's go."

"Remember," the boy whispered. "*Windross. Courdewaye*. Help me."

Rich went scuffling along with the guard, his head
down, feet tripping up; he lurched into a wall and struck
an elbow, cried out in pain. His cry freed Conor from
his paralysis and he tried to follow, but was turned back
at a barred and armored door.

"I'll get help, Rich!" But he saw only the prisoner's
back, the shape of shoulder blades beneath the prison
jumpsuit, sharply winged from the stress of having his
hands locked behind his back. Conor couldn't be sure the
boy had heard him as he was led down a flight of echoing
iron steps.

33

Conor's visit to the Franciscan father who was the lone
priest of the small parish in Chadbury was unrewarding.
First Father Gregus had to be roused from his nap by the
rectory housekeeper, a Swiss-German woman who spoke
English almost incomprehensibly and resented Conor's ig-
norance of their routine: the hours during which the priest
was available to parishioners were clearly posted on the
rectory door. Conor pleaded an emergency and was received in a tiny study lightless except for the blue flames
in a stove.

Father Gregus, in brown robe and sandals, was elderly,
hard of hearing, only a year away from retirement. He had
heard about the murder, and was repulsed by it. His throat
clearings, varying in tone, duration and profundity, were
like another language by which he conveyed a lack of
sympathy. Nonetheless he would do his duty as long as
there was a Catholic soul in jeopardy. He offered, after a

promise to visit Rich, to hear Conor's confession. Conor declined, preferring to spend his time in prayer at the altar in the sanctuary.

Alone, on his knees, he experienced a terrible weakness; his prayers were blocked, his mind simply wouldn't function. In this country chapel he felt the consequences of his disavowal as if the shadow of the angel of the Annunciation that stood near the chancel door had fallen across his back with the weight of stone itself. Faced with the Lord's sublime agony, he heard his brother's voice.

Courdewaye. Windross. Polly. Find them, Conor!

He drove back to the state police building and asked for Captain Moorman, who had gone home for the day. Conor spoke to him on the telephone.

"Did you see your brother?"

"I don't know *who* I saw! There was so little resemblance— One thing, I know he doesn't belong in a jail cell. He's obviously a very sick man. Hallucinating. He needs medical attention. Can't he be moved to a hospital?"

"Facilities are limited here. Only the state mental hospital has a ward equipped to deal with homicidal patients. But a psychiatric exam would be required, and that's out of my hands."

"Who was the doctor who saw him this morning?"

"Harbison? About all he can do is keep your brother tranquilized."

"It's better than nothing," Conor muttered.

"Have you seen a lawyer yet?"

"I haven't had time. What happened to Rich's car?"

"The Porsche? We impounded it."

"I'd like to have a look."

"Why?"

"There's something in the car Rich wants me to have. A tape cassette. He said it was from his telephone answering machine."

"Why does he want you to have it?"

"Something to do with a girl named Polly. Rich wants me to find out where she is now."

Moorman thought it over. "All articles in the car were collected, along with his clothes from the suite at the Davos Chalet. They were checked in to the police property department. I can't release them to you, but—I could arrange for you to listen to that tape tomorrow. Of course I'll want to hear what's on it myself.''

"Thank you.''

"Is Polly another girl friend of his?''

"I never heard the name before. But Rich kept referring to some people he may have met up here. Inez. Windross. And Polly. He said they knew what really happened to him.''

"What did he mean by that?''

"I don't know, Captain. He said he was trying to help Polly, whoever she is. They were both at a place called the Courdewaye House, in Ripington Four Corners. Does that mean anything to you.

"Ripington Four Corners is about twenty miles north of here. I don't know offhand of any Courdewaye House—is it an inn?''

"I have no idea. But whatever it is, after talking to Rich I'm convinced something happened to him there that had a—a drastic effect on his behavior, and probably led to the killing of Karyn.''

"If you're referring to drugs, no. The blood screen turned up some alcohol, but in a quantity well below the level legally established for drunkenness.''

Conor couldn't think of anything else to say. At the other end of the phone, in the policeman's house, a dog barked, kids quarreled, there was a television going. His throat thickened with a need for his own nest, for the familiar jumble of domesticity. *Drugs? No.* It was a blow, a loss of hope. Had Rich simply gone insane, for no apparent reason? What about a brain tumor? He refused to think about the third possibility Rich had insisted upon.

Dee-monn!

The word was a bombshell inside the brain. It cast a chilling unholy light that made Conor blanch.

He's got me! He's in me, Conor! He killed Karyn!

"Hello?''

"Oh—I'm sorry. Thanks for your time, Captain Moorman. When can I see you tomorrow to listen to that tape?''

"Nine o'clock would be okay.''

34

Conor drove back to the Waites Inn. It was just before six, the cocktail hour ending; a dinner bell called the boisterous ski crowd into the dining room. They were like a splendid fellowship he could no more think of joining than if he were a troll from a cave. He smelled Yankee pot roast and baked bread and was famished, but the act of eating represented an ordeal he had to prepare himself for. He collected a whiskey at the small bar in a parlor corner of the lobby where cigarette smoke still hung spectrally in the air. He sat on a long couch that faced the fireplace to drink it. He knew he should call Gina, but had no idea of what to say to her.

"Mr. Devon?"

Conor looked around reluctantly. He saw a man of about thirty, wearing a collegiate-looking brown tweed suit, blue shirt with a button-down collar, rep tie. His hair was brown, razor cut, mildly bouffant, and he wore a shaggier, lighter mustache that threatened to overwhelm his upper lip. The woman with him was close to the same age. Pretty, with a kind of frivolous space between her upper front teeth that relieved some of the ponderousness of thick eyebrows. They had the smiles of Jesus freaks, or yellow journalists.

Conor wanted to be rude, but merely shrugged, and turned his face back to the low fire. A log broke; sparks flew like meteors into the black space of the upper hearth. The young man came around one end of the Naugahyde couch and offered his hand.

"Adam Kurland. This is my associate Lindsay Potter."

"Hello," Conor said without warmth, putting some effort into the handshake. The young man didn't flinch. He had bigger bones and more muscle than Conor had taken in at first glance. He decided to stop being a bastard, relaxed his grip, and nodded pleasantly to the woman. "Reporters?"

"Lawyers," Kurland said, offering his business card. Embossed. Two colors, dark blue and gold. It had a certain dignified presence between Conor's fingers, establishing—no questions asked—reliability and value. "Kurland Bates Harpold, in Braxton. Do you know Vermont?"

"I've wrestled here a few times, in Burlington and Rutland."

"Oh," Lindsay Potter said with a not overdone lifting of her heavy eyebrows, "are you a professional?"

"That's right. I use the name Irish Bob O'Hooligan." He should have business cards of his own printed. *Bonecracking and divers entertainments.*

She nodded, but clearly the name didn't mean anything to her. Conor liked her. She had a long neck and a tomboy stance; wise pixie eyes, hazel, but shading to a brass yellow by firelight. The bones of her wrists, the lobes of her ears incurable plebeian, blue collar, "triple decker." Conor's habitat, and he had known many like her. Born with the intellectual vitality to escape her Dorchester neighborhood, the inevitable stifling marriage, too many kids. Some still became nuns. This one had gone to a good college, upgraded the accent; but nobody had taught her yet how to wear clothes. Suit of a conservative cut, too brownish for her complexion. The wrong lipstick. She wasn't diminished by her choices, they just made her more interesting in a haphazard way.

"Braxton's the third largest city in Vermont," Kurland told him. "It's about sixteen miles down the road from here, on the Connecticut River."

"What do you want?" Conor said uninterestedly.

Kurland didn't hesitate. "I want to defend your brother."

Conor took a deep breath and settled a little more snugly into the couch, ignoring the twinges of pain from the region of his kidneys. He raised his glass, gazed through it at the now-amber fire and drank.

"You're young to be heading your own law firm."

"That was my grandfather and my father. But I'm the only Kurland with the firm right now. I'm thirty-two. My practice is limited to criminal law."

"Dope dealers? Rapists?"

"I've also defended three alleged murderers in the past two years. Two of them went free, the other is incarcerated at the state mental hospital."

"This case may be out of your league, Mr. Kurland. Do you know who Karyn was? Her family, I mean?"

His question didn't faze the lawyer. "I've found out quite a lot about the Vales since eight thirty this morning." He glanced at the dining room, where the first course was being served. "Have you had dinner, Mr. Devon?"

"Not yet."

"Linds and I know a good steak house in Talbot. Morecambe's. Have you eaten there?"

"No."

"Please be our guest. I'd like to convince you I'm the best man in the state of Vermont to defend your brother. I'm assuming you don't have counsel yet."

"I just got here." Conor looked at Kurland, who was serious and well composed except for a habit of rotating the expansion-band watch on his wrist, as if gearing himself up for another round of smooth salesmanship. And at young Lindsay, who smiled gently and seemed to commiserate with Conor in his dilemma.

Even if he didn't hire Kurland, he thought, he might get some free advice as to what he should do, whom he should see about Rich's mental condition. Conor heaved himself up off the couch and went with them.

Morecambe's was a glorified tap room with rough-hewn paneling, no windows, and not even enough light to read a menu by. But there was no menu. You chose your own steak from a butcher's case, took baked or fried or wild rice trimmings, put your own salad together from the variety of crisp offerings on crushed ice at the back of the long room. They all drank whiskeys while waiting for their steaks.

"Convince me," Conor said.

"I was third in my class at Georgetown Law Center. I took every course in criminal law they offered. That doesn't make me a trial lawyer, of course. You're born with the talent, you polish it in the rough and tumble of a courtroom. I had the advantage of growing up watching my father in court. He was one of the best criminal lawyers in New England. Anyone will be glad to vouch for that."

"And how long have you been at it?"

"Going on eight years."

"How about you, Lindsay? Are you a lawyer?"

"Yes. Boston U. I've been with Adam—I mean, Kurland Bates Harpold—for four years." There was a big candle in the middle of their table. She was seated opposite Conor. Her eyes, like a soothsayer's, gathered light while much of her face lay in flickering shadow. He was becoming addicted to those eyes. They were as potent as Chinese mustard.

"Why do you want to defend Rich?" Conor asked Adam. "*Can* he be defended?"

"Of course. Before I explain how and why I'd like to defend him, I want you to know there is a possible alternative to a trial. Considering the violent nature of the crime, Richard undoubtedly will be indicted for first-degree murder. If convicted, there is no mandatory sentence, only a minimum sentence of at least thirty-five years; the judge who does the sentencing can stiffen that considerably. But once your brother is indicted, we may be able to plea-bargain. Do you know what that is?"

"I'm not sure."

"We would agree to enter a guilty plea in exchange for a reduction of the charge, from first- to second-degree murder, which in Vermont is worth ten-to-life, with a possibility of parole after six years and eight months."

"That doesn't sound so bad," Conor said hopefully. "He's just a kid now. Six, seven years—he'll only be thirty when—"

"Unfortunately, as I see it, we're not likely to get far with a plea-bargain maneuver. The state's attorney probably will not be willing, in spite of the cost to his office, to let go of a first, especially when there's bound to be a lot of publicity attending the murder. And there's another factor. Vermont has a commendable system that elects lay judges to assist presiding judges in our superior courts; they're allowed to rule in questions of fact and sentencing in criminal proceedings. And the 'side judges,' as they're called, have been influential in discouraging plea bargains in capital cases."

"So—what can you do for Rich?"

"From what I've learned about the case so far, the only logical plea is temporary insanity. Just to be careful we would keep the case out of superior court. There are no side judges in district court who might complicate matters. I'm confident I can win acquittal for Richard in district court."

"How can you be so sure?"

"For one thing, I know I'll be up against Gary Cleves for the state. Gary does a competent job. He works hard. But the simple truth is, I'm better than Gary in a courtroom, particularly when insanity is the issue."

Lindsay nodded her approval, having made a face when Gary Cleves was mentioned. Conor now openly admired Lindsay, was pleased that she let him know she noticed. He liked the way she drank whiskey, without a chaser. She listened well, and obviously felt no need to promote herself or second everything that Adam Kurland was saying. So far Conor liked everything about her. Conor was developing, after a day of tension, pain, and bewilderment, a ravening need for the attractive Lindsay. It happened to him sometimes, with this much impact: immediate arousal, longing. But he never did anything about the women who stimulated him. He wouldn't do anything about Lindsay Potter either, although he dearly wished he could.

"Anyway," Adam continued, "I want the case not only because I believe your brother was innocent of premeditation, but because I think we're in danger of losing the insanity plea in capital cases. Many states have already amended their statutes to disallow it. Part of the backlash from Hinckley. But I think it's a valid and necessary plea. There *are* mentally ill people who commit crimes because they are unable to control their actions, but probably no more than two percent of all the criminals who are brought to trial. Use of the defense in no way represents an abuse of our legal system. Your brother's case may well be a textbook example of NGRI."

"Rich wouldn't have to go to prison?" Conor said, a little stunned by the implications after a day of heartache.

"We know he was totally incoherent following the fatal assault. At least five witnesses will corroborate that. I believe I can prove that at the time of the assault Rich was acting under psychotic compulsion. Yes, he wanted to punish her, that was his motivation. But once it was done, according to what I've heard, he wasn't aware he'd even hurt her very badly.''

"Do you think Rich is insane now?"

Adam spread his hands. "I haven't talked to him. You have."

"He's certainly disturbed. Unbalanced, maybe. I don't know what to tell you. He's not the Rich I know."

Adam leaned forward confidently. "I would push for an immediate psychiatric examination. Tomorrow wouldn't be too soon.''

"Why do you say he wanted to punish Karyn?"

"There are witnesses at the Davos Chalet who saw her playing around with another guy up there.''

Conor finished his whiskey and immediately lusted after another. Lindsay read his desire and signaled the waitress. He smiled at Lindsay. She looked directly into his eyes. It bothered Conor, and inflamed him as well.

"That's hard to believe, about Karyn."

"His name, believe it or not, is Trux Landall."

"A hunk," Lindsay murmured, tying small knots in the cocktail straw that had come with Adam's whiskey sour.

"Karyn dated Trux and probably had an affair with him when she was a freshman at Smith. Then he showed up in Vermont, and Rich tangled with him night before last; caught Trux kissing and feeling her up in the hall outside their room. He tried to punch Trux out, but came off second-best.''

Conor looked at him in admiration. "How did you find that out?"

"Let's give credit where credit is due," Lindsay proposed.

Adam flashed a smile at her and held up her right hand above her head; Lindsay made a triumphant fist. "Lindsay's a damned good investigator. Obviously Rich couldn't tolerate the competition. Something snapped."

"Crime of passion? It's so hard to believe. Sure, Rich loved Karyn. But I can't see him going berserk just because there was another guy."

"Berserk is the only way to describe his behavior. And we know the results.''

"Yeah," Conor said glumly.

Another whiskey arrived for him, and one for Lindsay. She sipped along with him. A jukebox was playing "Misty Blue." They all got off the subject of Rich for a while. Adam entertained with anecdotes about his grandfather, a shrewd country lawyer in the tradition of Daniel Webster. The steaks came. Conor ate his and wished he had two. There was more whiskey, throughout the meal; Lindsay just kept it coming and, incredibly, as far as Conor could tell, she matched him drink for drink.

After a while her face was all he saw. The high cheekbones, the precious part between her teeth. He knew just how her lips would feel, enclosing the end of his cock. Sheer ravishment. There were times, after he'd wrestled night after night for weeks, only the occasional Sunday off, when he'd find himself standing exhausted in the middle of a ring in some town he couldn't remember the name of, sweating, bleeding, bruised, and look around for a long moment. And think, *None of this makes sense*. He felt the same disorientation now. He was about to choose a set of lawyers, crucial to Rich's future, mostly because he wanted to see Lindsay Potter again tomorrow after an empty tonight, and because there was a pornographic vision inside his head of how her pussy and naked breasts would look in his bed.

"I don't have much money," Conor said, knowing his tongue was thick. "People think, well, he's a wrestler. But we're the poorest paid group in pro sports. I risk a hernia or a ruptured disk every night for maybe a couple hundred bucks and change."

"The fee isn't that important to me," Kurland said. "I'd want five thousand dollars as a retainer, the rest on contingency."

"Five thousand. Well, I think—I ought to talk to my wife."

"I understand. Why don't I give you a call in the morning?"

"Okay."

They shook on it, hands across the table. Conor, clumsy, upset a stemmed water glass, drenching Lindsay's lap.

She took it just fine, telling him not to worry. He was so embarrassed he started to cry. Couldn't help himself. But

Lindsay understood that he was an emotional man. He felt very secure in her understanding.

After she had dried off they walked him out to the car, Kurland's white Seville, although Conor made a sincere effort to stay on his feet all the way, without help from anybody. In the back seat, lulled by instant warmth and the new-car smell, he sprawled out and was asleep in two minutes, snoring.

Lindsay found something soft and pleasing on the excellent car radio and snuggled against Adam.

"Poor son of a bitch," she said.

"Conor? Why?"

"Today's probably the worst day of his life. He doesn't have an inkling the real shit storm is yet to come."

"Tomorrow he may wake up and fire us."

"No he won't. He's loyal to his friends. And we're already the best friends he's ever had."

Adam squeezed her knee. "I hope so. Going to be a tough one, Linds."

"I'm a little scared of it." She laughed uncertainly. "Make that a *lot* scared. How are we going to come up with the big zeros we need to mount a decent defense? I don't think Conor has any money to speak of."

"First thing tomorrow we'll put a lock on publication rights."

"What are they worth?"

"Who knows? Conor's profession makes him interesting. The girl was lovely. We'll contact a good agent in Manhattan. Better set up a press conference for noon on Monday."

"Office, or courthouse?"

"Courthouse," Adam said. "After I've talked with our new client. Give Maggie Renquist a call, see when she can get up here from Hartford to run some psychological tests." He whistled a few shrill and tuneless notes, softly, his way of announcing a possibly outrageous notion. "If we're quick, we just may be able to get Devon declared incompetent to stand trial."

Lindsay smiled, skeptically. "Pross will demand their own shrink, as soon as we file. Probably Ingersoll. He hasn't sided with a defendant in years. Remember that poor asshole who was found sitting on his dead mother's head masturbating? Ingersoll considered that neurotic, not psychotic behavior.''

''Ah, that's what makes it all so interesting,'' Adam concluded, fingers flexing on the steering wheel. He was a fast, assured driver. There was a little smile on his face as he peered ahead into the darkness peeling away on both sides of the high beams as they hurtled back down the road to Chadbury.

35

Conor was awakened, with a splitting head, at five minutes to eight the next morning. It was Gina on the phone.

''Why didn't you call me last night?'' she demanded, a little shrill from worry.

''I was—I had a long conference with Rich's lawyers.''

''Oh? Who are *they*?''

''His name is Kurland. Distinguished Vermont legal family, or something. Her name is Lindsay, Lindsay—I forget what.'' A nutcracker had laid open his skull. His brain felt shriveled and rancid.

''Her?''

''They work together.''

''What's it going to cost? Rich's defense.''

''Haven't worked it out yet.''

''Get a contract.''

''I will.''

''I want to read it before you sign.'' Gina had once taken night courses in law at BU, while she was carrying Charley-chuck and thoroughly bored by yet another period of gestation. ''Did you see Rich?''

''Yeah. Poor kid. He—his mind—'' The only word that would come to him was *chaos*. ''Rich isn't making a lot of sense, Gina.''

''I wish I could get out there. Maybe if he talked to me for a little while, it would help.''

Conor didn't think so; and he didn't want Gina seeing

Rich the way he was right now. He asked her how the kids had taken the news.

"Oh, you know how kids act when something so enormous has happened. They can't find a way to talk about it, let it out. They get too loud and exaggerate every little grievance; their emotions are like shadows under the skin. I hope you remembered to cancel Albany last night."

"I called Dilworth. He made the arrangements. I think Kurowski subbed for me. I told him he'd better find another body for Worcester on Tuesday."

"Conor, is something else wrong? I can always tell by the tone of your voice."

"I'm hung over."

"I expected that," Gina said, with a lack of delicacy that approached shrewishness. "I mean, what did Rich tell you? Did he have much to say?"

"Not much. He said—" Conor, at this hour, found himself unable to adequately convey the gist of what he'd heard from Rich's lips; the effort to concentrate was rewarded with physical pain, a spasm in the already tense muscles of the back of his neck beneath the cranium. The pain brought tears to his eyes. "It's all hazy in my mind," he mumbled, trying to beg off.

"*Talk* to me, Conor."

"Gina, I don't know—some nonsense—he's got this weird idea that he's possessed."

He heard a sharp intake of breath, and then she said something fervent and rapid in Italian that he couldn't sort out. Switching to English, Gina exclaimed, "Holy Mary! Where did he get a notion like that?"

"I don't know."

She made a tremulous, keening sound, unusual for Gina, although it reminded him of mourners at an Irish wake. "I'm getting goosebumps. I don't *like* this, Conor."

"But it's nothing. The kid didn't know what he was saying. Karyn is dead and he can't remember what happened and he's groping for answers. Like the rest of us."

"Are you sure?"

"Gina, I just got up. I'm not sure of my own name. I'll see Rich again this morning, talk to others who might know more. Last night I heard that an old boyfriend of

Karyn's had been hanging around. Rich got jealous; you know."

"So? He might give the guy a knuckle sandwich if he was provoked. But he wouldn't touch a hair on Karyn's head, just because of jealousy." Her tone changed again. She sounded weary, fatalistic. "Conor, maybe you'd better—just to be safe—when you visit Rich again, take the local father with you. And—and holy water."

"Gina, stop it."

She was silent for a few seconds. He heard her sigh. "But there's no rational explanation for what he did. Is there? All I'm asking, be careful."

"Rich isn't dangerous."

"But the Evil One is! And you were a priest. You know how that's always worried me."

He had to laugh. "You mean since I've already fallen, I'm more easily tempted?" Conor shifted the angle of the receiver against his ear and caught sight of himself in a mirror opposite the foot of the bed. His spontaneous laughter became a deep, unconvincing chuckle. *Father, forgive me, I have sinned; last night I lusted after a woman not my wife.*

"Don't make fun. I miss you! I couldn't sleep. None of the kids wanted any breakfast. I made walnut waffles. It's so gloomy around here! We're all seeing Monsignor Raines after Mass. I hope he'll be able to put things in a little better perspective for them."

"I know he will. I should talk to them myself. Next time I call. Let's make it six sharp tonight."

"They'll be waiting. Where will you be if I need you in a hurry?"

"Try the state police in Chadbury. If I'm not there they'll get a message to me."

"Have they been helpful?"

"Yes, but I have to remind myself whose side they're on. The main thing, I think what we all want to know, is why Rich did it."

36

Richard, it's Polly! You remember me, don't you? You told me I could call you if I ever needed anything. Well—they've been hurting me, Rich. I'm afraid they'll hurt me a lot worse if somebody doesn't stop them!

Captain Moorman played the Record A Call tape twice, sitting back in cool appraisal of Conor's reactions. Conor only shook his head.

"I don't know what it's about. I don't know who the girl is."

After rewinding the tape the policeman took the cassette from the machine on his desk and replaced it in a small clasp envelope, which went into an accordion folder with Richard Devon's other personal effects.

Moorman then confided, "We do. Her name is Polly Windross. She's twelve years old. Her father is Henry Windross. He owns and manages the Post Road Inn, where Rich and Karyn stayed when they came up here for the skiing three days ago."

With a little start of excitement that caused his hangover headache to come snarling back to life like a large bad dog he'd been trying to tiptoe around, Conor said, "*Windross.* That's one of the names Rich mentioned."

Moorman sat on a corner of his desk to load up his pipe. The tobacco was dark, strong, and very smelly. To Conor, in the throes of recuperation, it was as bad as the odor of gangrene released from a pocket of his abused, corrupt body.

"The Chadbury chief of police is Jim Melka. He had some interesting information about your brother." Conor waited, edging toward the windows where the fragile morning lay under wraps, as yet untouched by sun. Moorman got his pipe going. "It seems that Rich appeared at the police station shortly before ten o'clock last Thursday night. He was dirty; his clothes were smudged and his hands blackened by charcoal. Also, according to the officer on duty, Stefanie Van Zant, he was very upset and wanted to lodge a complaint of child abuse.''

"Polly Windross was the abused child? Then Rich must have seen her.''

"Your brother claimed to have visited Polly in a room of the burned-out wing of the inn. He said she was chained to a bed in that room, and showed signs of having been whipped, presumably by her father and some religious fanatics he'd fallen in with. Officer Van Zant called Melka, who met them at the inn. They spoke to Mr. Windross, who flatly denied the allegations. He told them that his daughter was living with his sister in a remote village in Quebec.''

"Why would he tell such an obvious lie?''

"Did he? Polly definitely was *not* in room 331 of the burned-out wing, nor any other room, contrary to Rich's claim. The room was empty; not a stick of furniture. Melka was mad as hell. He was ready to lock Rich up. The only thing that stopped him—Rich seemed so convinced. So appalled not to find her there. If he was acting, Melka told me, then it was a great job of acting. And Rich stuck to his story, even though there was no point.''

"There *must* be a point. The girl called Rich. She was afraid of being hurt. It all ties in with what Rich told the chief of police.''

"But we can't be certain that's the voice of Polly Windross on the tape,'' Moorman pointed out.

"Her own father ought to know! Can't you get him over here?''

"I will," Moorman said, his expression a little cold.

"I don't think that girl's in Canada.''

"Jim is following up on that, but he hasn't heard anything from the local authorities up there.''

Conor tugged at his beard in frustration. "Getting back to Rich's story—''

"It was plausible," Moorman allowed. "He convinced two experienced police officers that an emergency existed. There was nothing abnormal about his behavior. But I'm sure there are mental disorders that even trained psychologists find difficult to diagnose at first sight. Some psychopathic personalities are the most sincere and convincing people you'd ever want to meet. That Bundy fellow, convicted of killing those sorority girls in Florida. I'm not saying Rich *is* a psychopath, you understand.''

"I know he isn't. In spite of what he—of what happened to Karyn.'' Conor gazed at Moorman, wondering how much he should confide in him. "But Rich said two things to me yesterday that may be significant. Before he told me to listen to the Record A Call tape, he said, 'I think Polly must be dead too.' ''

"Was he implying that he killed her?''

"No. No, I didn't have that impression. He was trying to tell me something really awful took place in that house in Ripington Four Corners.''

"The Courdewaye house?''

"You found it?''

"Yes. Hasn't belonged to the Courdewaye family for years. And nobody's been there since the Christmas holidays, according to the caretaker.''

Conor winced. "*Rich was there*, I'm sure of it. This is like a—a pattern, very disturbing, because—''

"What else did he say about the girl?'' Moorman tapped his front teeth with the pipe stem. "Maybe we should get a warrant and really look that house over.''

"Yes, I think you should.''

"You were going to tell me something else that could be significant—?''

"You may as well know. Rich told me he was possessed.''

Moorman took in some smoke the wrong way and coughed. "What does that mean, possessed?''

"Rich is Catholic. In the Church it means only one thing. Preternatural manifestation: diabolical possession of a human being by the devil, or demons from hell.''

"That's a fairly common mental aberration, isn't it? If you're brought up believing in such things.''

"I'm talking about an inhuman spirit of unspeakable evil exercising the power to invade a physical body and manipulate the captive individual according to the demon's will. It's rare. Damned rare. But the Church acknowledges the reality of demonic possession. There is an office in the Vatican devoted to investigating major cases of possession.''

"Do you believe in it yourself?''

"I was a priest," Conor told him, and the policeman's eyebrows went up a little. "Demonology is an academic subject in seminaries and the pontifical universities in Rome. What I believe is what I was taught. And I was taught that the devil is real, that none of us, even the most holy of men, are ever safe from trespass by the Evil One and his legions. Let me tell you this. Rich was clearly trying to help that girl. He thinks she may be dead now. It doesn't take a great leap of logic to hypothesize that Polly and her father were mixed up with a demonic cult; they abound. And the girl became an unwilling victim. These people must be very skillful at covering their tracks; nevertheless they *are* out there, they do exist. I'd have a long talk with Henry Windross, because something is very wrong at that inn he owns, and also at the Courdewaye house, no matter what the caretaker says. He could be lying."

It became clear to Conor that Moorman wasn't listening very hard anymore. There was a patient smile on his face, showing signs of wear.

"Everyone is lying but Rich," the policeman murmured. "Rich is the innocent one. Is that how you see it?"

"I see you're not going to take any of this very seriously."

"I'm not licensed to practice psychiatry or interpret the effects of theology on a disordered mind. I'll continue to follow up on any facts pertinent to the investigation of the murder of Karyn Vale, which is what I'm paid to do." He reached behind Conor and picked up the receiver of the telephone. "See if you can get Henry Windross for me. He's the owner of the Post Road Inn."

Conor stood by the windows cracking his knuckles, loud angry popping sounds. Then he walked slowly to the door.

Moorman watched him. "I hope for everyone's sake another body isn't going to turn up before this is over. By the way, have you talked to any trial lawyers?"

"Adam Kurland. We're both seeing Rich again this morning."

"Uh-huh," Moorman said, nodding. Not exactly a recommendation of the young lawyer, but he didn't seem to disapprove. He smiled at Conor, bemused. "How long were you a priest?"

"Three years."

"Why did you quit?"

He'd been asked the question often, ingenuously, as if there could be a single answer for him to dispense like the packaged philosophy in a fortune cookie, to satisfy someone's transient interest. The more involved the explanations were, the hazier his motives seemed. But this time the perfect answer occurred to Conor.

"When I went from theory to practice I found I just couldn't do it. For the same reason I could never be a cop."

37

In the late afternoon of the twenty-fourth of January, three days after Karyn's death, Thomas Horatio Harkrider made himself comfortable on a Regency sofa in the living room of the Vale home in Rye, New York, and looked closely at the faces of the girl's parents: faces still warmly radiant from the tropical sun, festive, at odds with the grief that had distorted each like the weight and pull of an invisible noose around the throat. He was Martin and she was Louise. Her tan was spoiled by the crinkly white of old scar tissue at the base of her throat, on the backs of her hands and arms. Burn scars. She took her suffering straight, without, Harkrider presumed, pills or booze to stifle the rockets of pain firing several times a minute into the heart: the glass of sherry in her left hand had been untouched since a maid had poured it for her. She looked steadily at Harkrider, a little too keenly, as if she found him lacking in substance, a glamorous phantom who was bound to disappoint her.

Martin Vale paced in short erratic bursts of energy, eyes and hands never still. He'd been in his youth a floor trader on Wall Street, and the habits, accentuated in times of stress, were ineradicable. He was of average height and had wide shoulders and a sumptuously full head of hair, dark except for two white waves from each temple spilling back over the ears. His jaw was firm, his eyes small as a sparrow's, giving off gleams of rage with each darting turn of his head.

"It was premeditated murder," he declared to Harkrider.

"How do you know that?"

"They'd been arguing—fighting in public. Karyn wanted to break up with Rich and everyone knew it."

Louise Vale said, with a small confirming nod, "Only a week ago she told me on the phone that she wasn't as happy as she ought to be. Wanted to be. She had a lot of doubts about that boy."

"Were they engaged?"

"No, not officially," Vale said. He needed a cigarette; he slapped at his pockets and then went charging off to a lacquered table and a silver case, scooping it up without breaking stride.

"Was Karyn your only child?"

Louise answered him. "There's Norma. My oldest. She's flying in from Kansas City tonight with Frank. That's her husband." She pressed a wadded linen handkerchief to her mouth, anticipating the hardship of a reunion under such terrible circumstances. The first joints of two of her fingers on the right hand were missing, possibly a consequence of the same fire that had left so many visible scars.

Tommie Harkrider lifted the crystal tumbler of bourbon and spring water from his stomach and sipped. He was an inelegant figure against the muted lemony stripes of the antique sofa. He had the lines of a beached whale. His shoes lacked gloss, his shiny suit he might have purchased second-hand from a subway conductor. His wife trimmed his snowy mane, when she could get him to stay in one place long enough. He had a nose like a baked potato wrapped in crinkly red foil, white eyebrows like limp parachutes, the generous mouth and self-infatuated, introspective eyes of a parkbench philosopher. He was one of the three best criminal lawyers in America, and opulent surroundings, great fortunes, and social prominence didn't impress him. His own income was close to two million a year.

"I made a call to the state's attorney's office in Haden County before I came out here today. Of course they won't have much to say until an indictment is handed down, but that indictment, based on my limited knowledge of the crime and the alleged state of the relationship of Karyn and Richard Devon, is almost certain to be murder in the first degree. The victim's death was the result of a clear-cut intention on the part of the accused to cause that death.'' His voice seemed loud in the spacious living room, oratorial, although he made no effort to project beyond a normal conversational tone. But it was a very quiet house today.

"Can they go for the death penalty?" Martin Vale asked. He juggled cigarette, lighter, and silver case as he circled in front of the bow window that overlooked a wintry wooded point of land and the white-capped gray surface of Long Island Sound.

"Not in Vermont. Evidence of premeditation, of cold-blooded planning on the part of Richard Devon, could enhance the possibility of a life sentence without parole, although traditionally Vermont judges haven't come down that hard on convicted murderers. A more realistic projection would be forty-to-life, with the possibility of parole after about fifteen years. I think a plea bargain, reducing the crime to second-degree murder in exchange for a plea of guilty, is probably out of the question. But it's premature to think about sentencing. The prosecutor will have his hands full merely winning a conviction.''

"What?" Vale said. He was suddenly, forbiddingly still; even the smoke from his first hungry puff on the cigarette was motionless in the air. The telephone rang, a faint, musical chiming; neither of the Vales looked at it. All calls were being taken by a relative in another part of the house.

"Devon's attorney will go for and, if he's any good, ought to win acquittal on the grounds that Devon was insane at the time he committed the murder. NGRI, not guilty by reason of insanity.''

Louise Vale sat up a little straighter opposite Harkrider. Her shining face was still composed, but there was something unsettling, even ghastly, in the way her right hand clenched the handkerchief, that crippled squeezing to hold back a storm of sorrow and outrage.

"And then what will happen to him?" she asked.

"He'll be remanded to a state institution for the criminally insane and treated; eventually, in all probability, he will be released. According to a report issued a few years ago by the New York State Department of Mental Hygiene, which criticized the uses of the insanity plea, persons found not guilty by reason of insanity were confined, on the average, for 238 days post-trial.'' Harkrider awaited the inevitable reaction, preferring to say nothing about those individuals who are never deemed releasable.

''Eight months!'' Martin Vale crossed the room and leaned on the back of his wife' s chair; she, not taking her eyes from Harkrider, rolled her head slowly and despairingly between the knuckles of his gripping hands.

''It isn't fair—it isn't *fair*.''

The lawyer grimaced in sympathy. ''Nevertheless, the insanity plea is a legitimate tool for the defense, and they will use it; and its use does not always represent a miscarriage of justice. Proving insanity is not a simple task in a court of law. No two psychiatrists have ever agreed upon a precise definition of mental illness.'' He nipped again at his bourbon. ''We can't dismiss the possibility that in fact Devon *is* mentally ill.''

''Or faking it; you have to know Richard to know what I mean.'' Harkrider raised an eyebrow but didn't comment further. Vale continued, ''You'll never convince *me* he's crazy, but what sort of cynical self-serving bastard would represent him in the first place? There is no doubt that Richard murdered my daughter; for God's sake, Karyn's blood was on his hands, and a half-dozen witnesses saw it!''

Louise gasped, almost inaudibly; her husband looked down at her. Tormented, he backed away, taking the cigarette from his mouth and staring at it as if he were tempted to grind it out in his palm as an act of contrition.

''The boy is factually guilty of the crime, and will be so charged. As for us self-serving bastards, all criminal lawyers defend guilty clients, or it would be a mighty long time between clients; the sad truth is there are few innocent defendants in our courtrooms. The strength of the Anglo-American legal system is founded on the bedrock of inalienable rights: the right to a trial by jury, and the right of anyone accused of a crime to have an adequate defense.''

"Would you defend him?" Louise said softly, with only a hint of accusation in her voice.

"I haven't been asked to defend Richard Devon; I haven't been asked anything yet, except my opinions, which I freely give to you."

"Tommie," Martin Vale said, "I want you to represent my daughter. I want the dead to have all the rights of the living. I don't want her forgotten, like that poor girl over in Scarsdale was forgotten while her killer was getting off with a tap on the wrist."

Harkrider nodded; he knew the case referred to, which also had involved two students at Yale. "*The People* v. *Richard Devon* will be in the hands of the state's attorney for Haden County, Vermont. Unless I'm specifically invited to assist the prosecution in building its case, an unlikely occurrence, there is nothing I can do."

"Then represent us. *Help us*. You're the best, Tommie. And I want him punished. I want Richard to get everything he has coming to him under the law. If it's a question of money—"

"It's always a question of money. I'm not thinking of my fee. I doubt that many people outside of the legal profession have any idea of how expensive it is to prepare for a trial in a capital case, particularly when an insanity plea is contemplated. The trial can last for months. Exhaustive investigations are essential, expert testimony must be paid for. The cost to Haden County alone will surely be more than the entire budget for the prosecutor's office for the next five years. But if adequate funds are not made available, the prosecution is likely to lose the case."

"Then how can we help?"

"I can talk to the state's attorney. A young man named Cleves. I know nothing about him personally, but I assume he has ambition and not nearly enough experience to cope with the demands about to be made on him. I shall point out to him how well his career will be served by a conviction, and how ignominious it would be to lose yet another murderer to the insanity plea. I believe he can be persuaded that the work my staff is prepared to do will only enhance the quality of his pretrial preparations, and I will convey my earnest desire not to usurp his limelight. By the time we have finished our talk I'm confident the two of us will have achieved a high comfort level.'' Harkrider chuckled quietly and drained the rest of the drink in his glass, a signal that their time was up.

"When can you start?" Martin Vale asked him.

"I'll just have a look at my calendar, make some adjustments. And I'll be in Haden County the first of next week.''

They accompanied him to the front door. Harkrider's limousine was waiting in the drive. It was a long silver and midnight blue Cadillac with a boomerang antenna mounted on the trunk lid, windows like the spectacles of the blind. Tommie Harkrider had been nineteen and a half minutes with the Vales. They had reacted just as he had intended, providing him with a legitimate means of entrée. He had no great interest in the outcome of the Devon murder case, but it was a case he had been seeking for many years. All of the elements, including the small-town setting of the upcoming trial, were ideal. Justice, with his invaluable assistance, not only would be done but would be exalted if his modest proposals were accepted. And he was confident they would be. He was, in addition to being a master of the big game, the hotly publicized trial, expert at directing the media to achieve his purposes.

"God bless you,'' Louise Vale murmured, already totally won over.

Thomas Horatio Harkrider vigorously embraced both of the grieving parents, taller by a head than either of them, his white hair flowing with the wind, a serene smile on his face as they sobbed helplessly in his arms.

38

After twice driving past the house in which generations of Courdewayes had lived, and seeing very little of it from the road, Conor decided against looking up Avery Myatt, the caretaker, and trying to persuade Myatt to open the house for him. He had no official status, for one thing, and no rational reason for wanting to get inside. Rich's half-delirious assertions that something terrifying had happened to him there did not justify an intrusion into the house, even if it was presently unoccupied. But Conor was determined to gain entry, by force if necessary, although he knew that would leave him open to charges of housebreaking.

The elderly postal clerk in Ripington Four Corners had helped Conor to make up his mind, after the clerk had taken a long look at the photo of Rich that Conor carried in his wallet.

I remember him. Come in just before the storm hit, it was Thursday last. Had a lot of questions about the Courdewayes—Leslie in particular. Long gone from here, I told him. Say he's your brother? You don't look much alike.

We're half brothers, actually.

That a fact? How is it you're lookin' for him? Is he missin'?

No. I know where he is.

Conor found a parking place for his Lincoln in front of a combination gas station and grocery about half a mile from the house. He bought a Diet Pepsi to slake his thirst and walked back along the side of the road, where the snow had receded from saltings and was frozen in sharp sculpted tiers; he found the footing treacherous. The sun on his brow dazzled him to the point of headache.

Snow had been shoveled away from the gate across the drive, and there was a new brass padlock in place. After waiting until there was no traffic on the road Conor climbed over the gate and walked through snow that came to his boot tops down to the brick manor house in the cove. The drive had not been used for several days. Beneath a blue sky the house held its own darkness, a look of perpetual night. The chimneys cold. The windows glazed with frost. Conor found wading through snowdrifts tough on his knees and paused to wipe his streaming forehead and blow his nose. There were some black birds in a barren tree near him, sitting still as stones, voiceless. He pushed on.

The front door of the house, as he had expected, was locked. He looked in through a narrow window to one side of the door, unable to make out much of the entrance hall or the large rooms on either side. He trudged around the house, stopping again and again to peer through double thicknesses of glass at the interior, seeing only the trembling light of day in mirrors, his own faraway reflection within cupped hands, staring lonesomely at the polished sumptuous rooms, at a dining table with place settings for sixteen.

The side door was locked. He reached the back door: up two steps, little flared copper roof above with pointy bridgework of icicles, trellis sides that held bitter green leaves embedded in ice. The height of a hill directly behind the house probably kept the winter sun off the porch all day. In the bottom of the door there was a big porthole, an iris of rubber through which family pets could come and go.

There were sharply defined pawprints in the snow outside the door: big ones. Dog. The snow had a thick crust; judging from the depth of the prints, the animal weighed well over a hundred pounds. That gave Conor pause.

He looked back over his shoulder and saw, a dozen feet from the bottom of the steps, a still-steaming hole in the snow stained a bright dogpiss yellow around the rim.

If there was a dog in the house, Conor reasoned, despite the unmarked driveway and the absence of vehicles someone must be in residence.

He hesitated, then knocked boldly at the door.

"Anyone home? Hello!"

Conor waited, all ears, for a response, shifting from one foot to another, exhaling mightily, vapor freezing and adding to the fringe of ice already clinging to the red whiskers around his mouth.

From behind the door he heard a whimpering sound.

Dog, all right. No mistaking it. He glanced down at the gray rubber iris in the pet port and backed off uneasily. But the animal had neither growled nor barked at him, as any reasonably alert watchdog should have done the moment he came near the door. Maybe this one was, despite his presumed size, uncommonly timid, or sick. Conor knocked again, more gently.

"Hello!"

Again there was no answer, except for a mild scratching, as of claws, against the inside of the door. A helpless sort of sound. Still it managed to stir the hairs on the back of his neck because he couldn't *see* the dog, he had only these hints of its presence less than three feet away.

Conor approached the door and knelt down beside the pet port. He put his gloved hands cautiously on the rubber iris and opened it, ready to snatch his hands away if a suddenly snarling dog thrust its head out at him. But nothing happened. He widened the aperture and peered inside.

Momentarily he heard clicking sounds, as if the animal was walking rapidly away across a hard surface. Then silence. Conor saw, through the opening, an expanse of kitchen floor paved with tile, the satiny sheen of side-by-side stainless steel refrigerators. He heard the hum of their motors. A quiet slow drip of water from a faucet. A cabinet clock distantly chiming the half hour. He couldn't distinguish the clicking sounds any longer. But he smelled the lingering rankness of the dog that had been there: damp, not very clean fur. There were little pools of melted snow on the mudroom floor just inside the door.

Conor grimaced and straightened, reaching for the doorknob to help himself up.

The knob turned in his hand. The door opened.

The unexpected release of the latch excited and appalled him. He chewed at the ice in his beard, staring at the narrow space between the door and the jamb.

Then he opened the door and walked in.

"Your back door was open! Is anybody home?"

He waited for an answer, an invitation, not wanting to startle anyone—not wanting surprises himself. A shotgun, for instance, in the hands of the caretaker.

"Mr. Myatt? You here? Name's Conor Devon, I'd like · to talk to to you, please sir!"

Another half a minute passed. He now wondered if, after all, he was hailing an empty house. Empty except for the bashful mutt. He observed a few more traces of the animal, little bits of melting ice, a trail leading out of the mudroom and up a short flight of steps to what looked like a butler's pantry. Conor's eyes adjusted to the level of the light inside. As long as I'm in, he thought, no harm in having a look around. His conscience was clear. The back door had been left unlocked.

Carelessly . . . perhaps.

He stamped his feet on a hemp mat near the door to clear the snow from his boots, and used his handkerchief to dry them. Unmannerly to mess up the floors, even if their dog already had made tracks. He pulled off his gloves and stuffed them into the pockets of his storm coat. Then he walked up the steps to the butler's pantry. An uncovered window on the north wall, glass-front cabinets on three sides, a built-in silver safe, chafing dishes and serving pieces laid out on the counters. A can of silver polish, a buffing machine; someone recently had been hard at work, the smell of polish was still in the air. His reflection flowed from one portly tureen to another as he went through a swinging door into the dining room.

"Mr. Myatt?"

Conor stood quietly with a hand on the velvet-covered back of a chair, listening. He looked at the chandelier above the dining room table. An ugly and obviously valuable piece. It appeared to shiver and swing slightly as he stared at it, but his eyes were still running from the cold outside—the movement he sensed might have been illusory.

Or it might have been someone with a heavy tread crossing the floor of the room upstairs.

Conor raised his eyes again, sniffing, rubbing his leaky nose with the back of one hand. The dining room had a tray ceiling, painted white, with deep carved moldings all around, every inch an intaglio. When he focused on the artwork he made out tiny figures: mythological beasts, from graceful unicorns and winged horses to squat epicene satyrs, entwined with nymphs and shepherd boys who played lutes and other simple musical instruments while simultaneously gratifying the females of all species with their enormous erections.

Conor grinned disdainfully, wondering why anyone would want a display like that where they took their meals.

He heard a cork popping from a bottle, and turned convulsively to the far doorway. Then he moved fast, almost running, the floorboards creaking under his weight. He left the dining room and crossed a small entryway with a door to the outside on his left, another door at the foot of a spiral staircase, and a third at the front of the house.

This door was standing half open, revealing plush dove gray carpeting and walls paneled in solid cherry, the hot

gleam of gas log flames reflected from the polished paneling. A cozy den. He barged right in.

"Hey!"

In this house Conor seemed always to be entering rooms
that someone—or something—had just left. He felt frustrated and annoyed. What was the point of playing games
with him? After a moment's hesitation he crossed the den
on a diagonal to another door inset between bookshelves
and yanked it open. He looked across the broad marble of
the entrance hall to another, larger, shadowy staircase. He
opened his mouth to call again, and knew he would be
ignored.

He shut the den door, almost slamming it, and turned to
face the hearth, the yellow fire behind tinted glass. There
was a grouping of love seats and armchairs around the
hearth, brass firetools on the rough-cut gray stone. A silver
tray on a hatch-cover coffee table held an opened bottle of
red wine, the cork, and two glasses filled to within an inch
of their brims.

Two glasses?

He raised his eyes to the portrait over the mantel.

She was dressed all in black, a Spanish riding costume:
bolero jacket, long skirt, boots with four-inch heels, one of
those flatcrowned hats with a wide brim. She had a riding
crop in one fist, which was planted on her left hip. A
tourmaline the size of a robin's egg was prominent on one
finger. The other hand, empty, was extended palm up as if
in welcome, offering the gift of the wine on the table
below. *Won't you join me?* She had a cocksure smile, with
a hearty, desperado gleam of gold on one tooth, and a
scarred cheek. Her vitality was conveyed by the style of
the painting: thick strokes, broad slashes of the palette
knife. By firelight the paint seemed scarcely to have dried:
there was a touch of wetness on the lips, unexpected
highlights in the pupils of her eyes.

"Inez?" he said, half aloud, knowing this had to be the
woman whom Rich had talked about.

*Cordway. That's what she calls herself now. But her
name used to be Courdewaye. . . . She's real. I know
she's real. The others—I'm not sure.*

Remembering his brother's words, Conor found it suddenly difficult to swallow. His throat was very dry. Parched.

He cast a longing glance at the bottle of wine, looked up again at the woman in the portrait. She didn't look threatening or intimidating to Conor. Mischievous was the word . . . a merciless tease.

If this was her house—and it had to be—then she was around. He was sure of it now. And he was going to talk to her, if it took the whole damned day before she got tired of her cute disappearing games and was ready to meet him face to face.

Conor dropped onto a love seat and unzipped his storm coat. There were magazines on one end of the big coffee table. *Architectural Digest. Town and Country.* Nothing he could take an interest in. He sat back and stared at the poured wine, then reached for the bottle and looked at the label. The wine was a Spanish claret. He inhaled at the lip of the bottle. A little sharp and earthy, but maybe the wine in the glasses had been allowed to breathe long enough. He licked his chapped lips, put the bottle down, smiled slightly, took up a belled glass and studied the woman in the portrait.

"With pleasure," he said sardonically, and took a sip. Good. In fact, very—

If she offers you wine—for God's sake, Conor! Don't drink!

A little of the wine went down the wrong way and Conor choked; he put the glass down before any of the wine spilled, pulled out his handkerchief and coughed explosively into it, leaving stains as his face got redder and redder. But at least he had spared the expensive carpet.

As soon as he had himself under control he heard the whimpering dog again.

Conor lunged to his feet and went to the door that opened onto the entrance hall. The whimpering was louder. He started slowly across the marble floor, looking at doors, all of them closed, looking up at the top of the curved staircase.

He saw a gleam of animal eyes next to a baluster in the shadowy upper hall.

Conor stopped and whistled softly.

There was no movement, only a tawny hint of the animal's body as Conor's eyes adjusted. The eyes of the animal were steady and, he felt, somewhat sorrowful as they gazed down at him.

"Here, pal. What's the matter? I won't hurt you."

The whimpering had trailed off; now it was barely audible. Conor went up the steps slowly, keeping his eyes on the shape huddled down in the dimness upstairs.

He was only a few feet away when he saw that it wasn't the dog he had expected. It was a child's stuffed toy, a big-eyed replica of Bambi, so familiar from the Disney movie he had seen more than once with his children. The toy was about a foot and a half high, with large ears, a plush tan body, and the nubby beginning of antlers. His daughter Hillary, now pushing impatiently toward thirteen and a semblance of adulthood, had her own Bambi, stored on a closet shelf in her room with other childish treasures she had only provisionally parted with.

Conor picked up the toy and ran his thumb across the nap, put it down where he had found it, let out a long breath, and looked around irritably for some sign of the dog he'd heard.

All the doors but one along the upstairs hall were closed. This door was at the end of the hall to his right, and at the front of the house. Diffused daylight painted the wall opposite the door; a soft radiance with a hint of rainbow. He went that way and looked into the room.

It had been a child's playroom or nursery; now there was no furniture, only candy-striped wallpaper, a mural on one wall of the Little Engine That Could, dancing bears and squirrels in appliqué on another wall. All the walls were nicked and scarred, grubby in places from childish hands. There was a window seat and curtains half parted on a tarnished brass rod.

The room was cold; far colder than the rest of the house. As he zipped up his coat he became aware of a raw powerful odor. The room was flooding with it.

Not dog odor—

Gasoline.

Conor looked around slowly, beginning to shiver but not from cold. He felt unsteady on his feet; he was wrenched by emotion, by sorrow and fear. This childish room was not a happy place. He began to back toward the door, his stomach tightening into a hard knot, pressing upward into

his diaphragm, which made breathing more difficult. . . .
And the fumes were bad, stifling. He wiped his hazy eyes.

Something lay on the floor near the window seat. He
was sure that the floor had been empty when he walked in,
but there it was, a square white card. . . .

Never mind.

Yet he couldn't, despite his strong desire to get out of
the room, ignore the card, any more than he could ignore a
letter in a mailbox. Conor put his wadded handkerchief
over his nose, the fumes almost strong enough now to
knock him over, and crossed the room to the window,
where he bent down to pick up the

stiff piece of cardboard, which was like
yes, exactly, the backing on a Polaroid snapshot, and
dry slithering sounds on the wall near him but he didn't
look up because he had already turned the photo over in his
hand and seen
the gasoline searing his eyes, making them water
seen
what—
what?
Oh Jesus Mary and Joseph what was *this*?

Now Conor raised his eyes from the photo and, still
stunned, took in the merry bears in vests and porkpie hats
and their friends the squirrels all topsy-turvy and rearranged in a big hot blare of sun into letters on the wall,
spelling out a word of

drowning in gasoline, must get away from
fast!
word of warning:
BEWARE!
said the chubby little animals,

as the sun went out, its light receding in a red threatening storm through which Conor stumbled with a numbed
mind to reach the hall. The door slammed shut right after
him, almost nipping off his fingers on the left hand, which
had been poised on the jamb an instant before.

His eyes flowing, his lashes sticky as pinkeye, Conor
retreated almost blindly toward the staircase, nostrils still

clogged with the gasoline odor, maybe the whole house would explode in a flash, *get out,* the Polaroid snapshot was bent double in his fist.

Who were they?

Top of the stairs. He reached for the railing.

And as he did so, Conor heard a snarl at his feet. Then there was a fighting surge of animal fur and hooves and hot breath between his legs; he was upended. He crashed against the railing and nearly broke through it, tumbled and rolled down the stairs pursued by nipping teeth; they came very close to his balls. The snarl, the raging thing all over him, claws—no, *antlers*—prodding, digging, trying to rip him apart, only the tearproof, down-filled storm coat keeping the antlers away from his flesh. He saw a large mean eye and a long velvet snout, the tawny hide, the two of them crashing down the stairs toward solid marble. It was Bambi, and Bambi was trying to kill him!

Conor hit the floor on his back hard enough to knock the wind out of him, and just before his eyes filmed over blackly he saw the improbable, full-sized beast looming above him with splayed legs and lowered head and magnificent rack, all the meat and muscle behind those pointed tips that hovered inches from his face and throat.

At the instant of catching his breath he lost consciousness, for no more than a few seconds. When he opened his eyes again it still hurt him to breathe and he was clawing at the air in front of him, but Bambi had vanished. He no longer smelled the shocking odor of gasoline.

Conor raised his head, and pain speared through it upward from the back of his neck; his conscious mind was a pulpy churning mass of terror. He was sick to his stomach. He found that getting up on the marble floor was as treacherous as if the floor were made of ice. He leaned against the balustrade and dimly saw the damage he had done crashing down the stairs; he looked around in shock.

The child's toy he had stumbled over was lying on the floor nearby, regarding him with a reproachful pasted-on eye. One leg was torn, and stuffing leaked from the seam.

Conor, struck by the absurdity of what he had done, and imagined, started to laugh, but had to clap a hand over his mouth and lock his throat to keep from vomiting.

Madness.

The shortest route to the open air was by way of the front door and Conor tried it, but there was a multitude of locks and he couldn't get out. He had to retrace his steps, limping, to the kitchen. He averted his eyes from the portrait on the wall of the den, the silver tray with wine glasses; he was deaf to the measured, tranquil tick of the cabinet clock.

As he left the house the nausea passed. He went to his knees and packed snow where his face was flaming. The cold had a beneficial effect on his pulse rate, it refreshed his blood. He quickly put some distance between himself and the house. The tracks he had made, the damage—he'd be lucky if he wasn't arrested. But his mind was more on his feeling of shame, and unease. He'd let himself be spooked, no doubt of it. Was someone—the woman in the portrait—watching from a window now, laughing at him?

Halfway to the gate at the top of the knoll he made himself stop and take a long look at the Courdewaye house.

He couldn't stop shivering. His hands were freezing, his throat was raw from cold.

Now, he thought, prepared to be stern with himself, *what actually happened?* How much of it was nerves, and how much real?

He fished in a side pocket of his storm coat and felt the crumpled Polaroid photo there. So that was real. And he didn't have to take another look to remember what the camera had recorded.

There were two children in the photo he had taken from the former playroom. A boy and a girl—or at least she appeared to be a girl. Her hair was longer, she was more delicately shaped. But when a child is abused, perhaps only a few weeks from death by starvation, that child tends to appear on the delicate side. The children were eight, maybe ten years of age, and each wore white pajama bottoms, or—Conor had another thought—the kind of simple white cotton trousers everyone seemed to be wearing in those parts of rural Mexico which he and Gina had passed through on their honeymoon. That made sense, because he remembered the kids also were wearing sandals. Above the waist they looked skeletal: prominent ribcages and pale drained faces. Their sunken eyes seemed utterly exhausted, bereft of light, like the faces one saw in the photos of the Nazi death camp survivors. They were sitting down, looking directly into the camera, and they were joined together, quasi-Siamese style, by a length of frayed rope knotted at their throats.

All this was bad enough, God knows, the horror of their situation, the tortured emptiness of expression. But there was more in the photograph that made it uniquely chilling and awful, details that, combined with others Conor had seen, smelled, and sensed in the Courdewaye house, completed a tapestry of evil. The woman's hand, for instance. Placed in a proprietary way atop the boy's head, fingers not digging in exactly, but gripping the shorn bony round head as if she were about to pluck it and cast it into the shimmering sea in the distant background, a sea the precise blue-green color of the stone in the silver ring so prominent on one of her fingers.

Conor had seen that same ring on the hand that held the riding crop in the portrait in the den.

The thickness of red wine in his throat: the vapors turned to gasoline.

For God's sake Conor don't drink!

The cartoon animals on the wall. His fall down the stairs. The aches and bruises he now felt. What was real and what was not? *Bambi*. He choked on laughter. So he'd gone a little berserk, let himself be frightened. By what or whom he didn't know. He was sure of only one thing: He didn't have much of an imagination, no, not nearly enough to dream up something as revolting and despicable as the yoked children—and the gasoline can that was just visible between the long shadows of cacti in the background of the Polaroid photograph.

With his eyes still on the house, which was in deeper shadow now as the afternoon faded into dusk, Conor took the photo from his pocket and straightened it out. He looked at it with reluctance and loathing and nearly fainted.

It was all still there: the woman's hand, the terrace near the sea in that distant sunny place. The shadows. The implicit evil.

Only now there were three children instead of two.

They were *his* children. Hillary. Dean. Charley-chuck.

With a strangled cry of profanity, Conor dropped the

photo and began smashing it into the snow with the heel of his boot.

The sun was setting behind his back, momentarily lighting up every window down below: a brazen, formidable glow. His eyes were blinded again, he couldn't look any longer.

Now whom could he tell, whom could he bring, whom could he convince as he himself was convinced that Rich was right about this house, about the evil that had lain in wait for him there?

Shaking, distraught, Conor reached down to retrieve the photo.

The image had faded nearly to nothingness. Only a pale blur of color remained, about where the woman's hand had been.

Conor ripped the stiff white square into several pieces, and scattered them.

He wondered what he would find, what would be waiting for him this time if he dared go back into the house.

But he knew he would never go back into the Courdewaye house. No power was sufficient to compel him to do so.

He would have to find another means to help his brother.

Helpless, devastatingly alone, Conor turned away.

39

Officer Michael O'Donnell, of the Casterbridge Police Department, received the call about the body by the railroad tracks south of Hungerford Avenue at eight twenty-three P.M. He'd been on his way to take his meal break at the New Daisy Diner on Route 9. Disgruntled by the timing of the call, he turned on the blue lights, swung his car around, and proceeded to the scene.

The temperature in the Berkshire Hills of western Massachusetts was near zero, with the wind chill factor bringing it to 28 below. Hungerford Avenue was an industrial eyesore little visited at night. The street was asphalt patch-ing over century-old cobblestones, sectioned by railroad spur lines. On the north side of the street were factory outlets, old Quonset huts and vacant lots enclosed by rusted chain link fencing. South of the main line, the roadbed of which was in such poor shape that the daily freights could make only twenty-five miles an hour through this part of town, there was an embankment and a creek, an unimportant tributary of the Queetoosuc River. Ten inches of snow lay everywhere, with a surface glaze as hard and brilliant as ceramic tile.

Near the Sixth Street crossing he was flagged by two men wearing parkas and ski masks, which were almost obligatory in this weather. Still, he didn't like not having faces to look at. O'Donnell slowed half a block away, unbuttoned the strap over his Police Special and considered calling for backup. Instead he flashed the side-mounted spot on them, and on a jacked-up truck with a front tire off. He used the loudspeaker.

"Hands where I can see them," he ordered the two men, his voice echoing metallically from the walls on his right. They obeyed.

O'Donnell got out of the patrol car, gun in hand at his side, cocked and locked, flashlight with the long steel barrel in the other hand, and walked toward the two men.

"Hey, Mike," one of them said. "Is that you?"

"Right."

"I'm Jack Surrey. This is my brother-in-law Pete Contardi from Woonsocket."

O'Donnell holstered the revolver. He knew Surrey from the Knights of Pythias.

"Don't blame you for being cautious," Contardi said. The air between the three of them was filled by a thick luminous cloud of breath. O'Donnell's exposed nose was tingling.

"What happened to you guys?" he asked, looking at the truck.

"Flat," Surrey told him. "No spare. I figured Angelo's Gulf down on Brookman was still open and I could bum a tire from him. Started walking east along the tracks and that's when I noticed it."

"You found a body?"

"What it is, I think. Better have a look."

O'Donnell went with the two men toward Fifth Street, which was a dead-end at the tracks. About fifty yards from the crossing where they had left the truck Contardi directed the policeman to shine his light down the slope; his own flashlight's beam was weaker. The beam from the six-cell torch was reflected from the solid ice of the creek bed and from bushes half-submerged in sculpted drifts of polished snow. Irregular, reddish black droppings were splattered on the hard surface of the embankment from the edge of the tracks to the creek bank.

Something curiously out of place was sprawled in among the bare thickets. Like a big shapeless meal sack. But the longer O'Donnell looked, the more it resembled human remains in a camel's hair topcoat. Nothing human was visible in the light they cast upon it: no legs or feet or arms. No head. Nevertheless there were bumps and bulges within the material that suggested human form.

O'Donnell crushed the hardpacked snow with the heel of a boot, making steps to get him down there; otherwise he'd slide on his ass like a greased pig twenty feet to the ice of the creek. He asked Jack Surrey to have a look along the tracks on down toward Fifth Street. Then he descended slowly, digging in at the heels, swaying to keep his balance, a gloved hand shielding his face to keep the wind that had risen from biting his exposed skin. Contardi followed him.

"Those spots on the snow look like blood."

"Could be," the policeman grunted, trying to save his breath. They reached the bottom. It was a camel's hair coat, all right, and there was a good reason why no feet or legs were visible. They'd been chopped off.

O'Donnell looked up at the tracks. The freights fairly crawled through here, a blind man could get out of the way of one. But this poor bastard hadn't made it. O'Donnell parted stiff branches and isolated the head of the victim in the beam of light. Battered, misshapen head, the bones jumbled with swollen brain tissue under the nearly bald pate. A mass of brain like a hemorrhoid protruded from one ear cavity. His own mother might not recognize him. But both arms were still joined to the body. He was wearing suede gloves that were almost new. Not someone you'd expect to find in this neighborhood. One hand clutched a brown bag full of—O'Donnell reached down and prodded with a gloved finger—broken glass. Despite his stuffy nose he smelled the fumes given off through a tear in the paper. Scotch whiskey.

The policeman straightened and constructed a rough scenario. At some time during the last three hours, since darkness had set in, the deceased had left one of the three bars along Hungerford Avenue and, carrying a large bottle of whiskey with him in the sack, had attempted to cross the railroad tracks. It was not a good place to cross, so probably he was unfamiliar with the area. All right. A passing train had struck and killed him. How he could have been so intoxicated as to miss the approach of the train, while not so drunk he could still walk, was a mystery O'Donnell had no desire to figure out. Or maybe he was just a happy lush with a thing for trains, liked to get right up close and admire them as they rumbled by. Got too close this time, had one swig too many from the paper bag and keeled over under the wheels. Not much blood. Too cold, and from the appearance of his head he had died instantly.

There was always a third possibility. Suicide. O'Donnell had seen the bodies of people who had taken their lives in stranger ways than this. The simple act of stringing oneself up probably took a hell of a lot of guts and determination; more, he imagined, than plunging half stoned under a moving train.

Oh, well. Someone had to be notified he wouldn't be coming home.

O'Donnell was lucky; he uncovered the victim's wallet on his first try, probing the inside pocket of a tweed jacket. He flipped the wallet open to the driver's license.

"Somebody local?" Contardi inquired.

"Nope. Vermont. Chadbury, Vermont. Must be a car around here someplace, belongs to him."

"Hey!" Jack Surrey called down from the railroad tracks. They both looked at him, shifting the angles of their flashlights. He was holding, by the bend of the knee, a rigid length of leg, still neatly dressed, the black leather mold shoe in place. "What do I do with this?"

"Just put it down there," O'Donnell said disgustedly. "And don't handle any more loose parts you happen to find."

40

Conor Devon parked his grimy Lincoln in the driveway beside the kitchen door and went into his house. Dinner was over; he'd told them not to wait for him. He smelled lasagna, slightly scorched. On the winterized back porch they used as a rumpus room the television was on, although it was a school night and TV was forbidden between six thirty and eight thirty, homework hours. The immortal Archie Bunker, secure in rerun heaven, was ranting at his son-in-law.

"Gina?"

"Here," she said wanly, from the porch.

He walked through the kitchen and found her on the tartan plaid sofa with her legs, encased in red leg warmers, propped up on the coffee table. Like every other casual piece of furniture in the house the table was constructed of slabs of rock maple, neo-Colonial in style, glossily finished and sturdy enough to be considered childproof. Gina's head was sideways on a pillow in an attitude of dejection, her eyes on the TV. She had a wine glass in one hand, some watered-down Chianti in the glass. Conor was startled, and a little concerned; Gina almost never flaked out this way, at least not before eleven at night.

"Hi, honey." He sat down beside her. She smiled, a slow sad curving of her mouth, and slid her head from the pillow to the beefy crook of his arm.

"Thought you'd never get here."

"How are the kids?"

"They're in their rooms. I had to separate them after supper, they were driving me crazy with their squabbling. It's just nerves, I guess. All the stories about the murder in the *Globe*, and on TV. No way they can avoid it. And it's their *uncle Rich*. They're so uptight, I don't think it would be any worse for them if you and I were getting a divorce. You know the way Hillary is when she's depressed."

201

Conor nodded. Hillary was the family melancholic, after his side of the family. Even before puberty she was subject to disconsolate spells that had them worried. He would see her lying abed for no good reason at unlikely times of the day, her face a study in bleakness just this side of torment, twining her long hair around her fingers like a spent princess.

"Just keep Hillary busy, that's what she needs. I'll talk to the kids in a few minutes; I need to unwind."

"Fix you a drink? The lasagna was good and I saved some, but the oven temperature was too high—I don't know how that happened—and it's sort of ruined. I'm sorry." She wiped at an eye with the back of one hand. Her mascara had been rubbed into the little creases beside the eye; it looked like a tire tread. "There's still some Sunday roast, if you want a sandwich."

"I, I don't know—sure. I'll eat something. Just a glass of ale, though, skip the hard stuff."

Gina drank the rest of her Chianti and got up. Her hair needed combing; in the unflattering light that flickered from the TV screen her face seemed puffy. Gina saw him looking too long at her and, hunching her shoulders self-critically, explained, "I got my friend, and I just haven't much felt like making an effort today. But I'll make myself pretty for you later."

He murmured something reassuring. "Love you," Gina murmured back, and went into the kitchen. Charley-chuck, who was eight and a half but the size of a twelve-year-old, came soundlessly onto the porch, carrying a pet gerbil in one commodious pocket of his sweat jacket. Conor had no affection for the ratlike animals, but they couldn't have a dog or cat in the household because both he and Gina were allergic to the dander. The gerbils and hamsters, ordinarily confined to two tiers of lucite cages in the boys' room, had been a compromise to satisfy the children's hunger for something furry to love.

"Hi, Dad." The boy came close enough to kiss him, then retreated, one hand stroking the gerbil's darting head.

"Hi. Who have you got there?"

"Pandora. She hasn't been feeling too good. I got an eighty-nine in math today."

"That's terrific. My math scores for four years didn't

add up that high.'' He looked more closely at a big adhesive square on the boy's brindled cheek. "How did you get that—hockey?"

"This kid on the Rangers was high-sticking. But we beat 'em six–zip."

"When do you play again?"

"Friday, at five-thirty."

"Afternoon, I hope."

"No, morning."

Conor groaned, and rubbed his son's red head. "I'll do my best to be there."

"Are you going to be home for a while?"

"I think so. Two or three days anyway."

Gina came back with a foaming glass of Bass ale for Conor. She looked sharply at their son.

"Hey, ten minutes to eight already, did I hear the bath running?"

"No," the boy said, with a shadowy stubbornness. "I wanted to talk to Dad."

Conor said placatingly, "Go on and take your bath. I'll be up soon."

When they were alone, Gina sat on the edge of the low coffee table in front of him, knees almost touching the tops of his shins, her tilted oval face stylized in satiny shadow like a religious carving; downcast madonna, woodenly worshipful, hair lightened to a withering incandescence by the backlighting of the TV: the worm in her wood, presentiment of bitter old age, death: he felt his heart aging in his chest.

She said, "I saw that lawyer on the six o'clock news."

"Adam Kurland."

"He's young. He's awfully young. Smooth. He looks as if he doesn't like getting his hair mussed, you know what I mean? Wouldn't Rich be better off with someone like F. Lee Bailey?"

Conor considered the publicized face, front-page for years. Jet pilot barrister, his foxy battle stripes, the huckster knowingness. Conor cringed. "How could we afford Lee Bailey? Besides, Adam and Rich got along. It's hard to tell, but I think Rich trusts him. That's important."

"So—" She made a small gesture of resignation with

her hands. "You and Rich have made up your minds already. How is Rich acting now?"

"Well—he's better. He's on tranquilizers. He had some lunch today, hasn't shown much interest in food lately."

"Not acting crazy?"

"What's crazy? Rich looks and behaves like someone who is very disturbed and has to be sedated. He sits and smokes, not calm, just immobilized; the opposite effect, half the time, is motion, constant motion. He walks around the room, very self-absorbed, but a little frantic, like a mouse trundling through a maze. When you talk to him you can't be sure he's listening. His most coherent remarks are about things that happened to him five, ten years ago. Then he's very animated, fast-talking. He goes on about his mother as if she were still alive. *How's mother taking it?* Once he opened and started picking through Adam's briefcase. Every piece of paper. He'd look at each one and then put it back. His face was so *dreary*. It was as if he—he had misplaced his citizenship in the human race. Even though watching him is so awful, tears my guts out, Adam says I still have to be alert to the possibility that some of it is put-on."

Gina, having slowly assimilated hearsay evidence of Rich's disorientation, if not dementia, found this sudden contradiction—or accusation—hard to deal with.

"He's faking? But—you'd know better. Wouldn't you?"

Conor shrugged his heavy shoulders. "I try to look at him that way, as something cunning, lying, inhuman. I just can't conceive of it. There's nothing much left to believe, except for the possibility of illness, a brain tumor; but sad and tragic as those things are it's what I want to believe. It'll take a psychiatrist, probably several of them, to arrive at a diagnosis. Adam's hired one. Rich is undergoing psychological evaluation tests later this week."

"That ought to prove something. Has he said any more to you about—being possessed?"

Conor had rehearsed the lie all day; it came out casually enough. "No."

The lie was for her own peace of mind; but virtue tasted gallish on his tongue.

"Thank God!" She looked momentarily stunned by

relief. "But maybe it's something he doesn't want to talk about in front of the lawyer."

"I wouldn't worry. He's just a—a very sick kid." Conor put his glass of ale down and leaned forward to hold her for a few moments. "We'll all get through this. We'll get through it, babe."

"What about Rich? What are *his* chances?"

"I was hoping he wouldn't have to stand trial. Adam isn't so sure. There are periods of apparent stability. Rich is aware of his predicament; he knows why he's in jail, knows that Karyn is dead. But he clams up whenever she's mentioned. Is he capable of assisting in his own defense? Right now that's an open question."

Something stirred at the outside edge of his vision and Conor, turning his head slightly, saw his daughter appear in silhouette in the doorway, shoulders drooping. For a few moments she just watched them, uncertain of her welcome. Then she straightened and said jauntily, "Can anybody get in on this?"

Conor smiled and extended an arm to Hillary, who joined the communal embrace, scrunching up more to her father than to Gina. She was wearing a bulky sweater with a shawl collar over leotards, her favorite around-the-house costume. Conor's hand rested on a subtly outcurving hip. Hips were something new, and the beginning of a bustline. But Hillary's face retained the roundness of childhood—a glow of ethereal purity about the violet eyes, the skin lucent as tracing paper, untouched by makeup; Gina wouldn't permit it yet.

"Mom tell you about all the phone calls?" Hillary said to her father. She glanced at Gina. "I forgot, Uncle Vito called while you were in the bathroom. Said if it's money, not to worry. That's what he told me to tell you."

"Hillary," Gina said, softly exasperated, "you have a lot to learn about your uncle Vito. Let me take the phone calls, huh?"

As if avoiding a snub Hillary shot her gaze to the TV, taking in Archie Bunker's beetling asperity. "Is that bigot supposed to be funny?" she said. She stood *sur la pointe* and leaned on her father's shoulder, morally lofty.

"Laughter has always been the best antidote to bigotry."

"I just wish he wasn't so—so Irish." Hillary seemed to

be saying, I wish *I* weren't. Conor released his casual hold
on her. She came down on her heels and gave him a quick
kiss on the forehead. "I said my rosary. I tried to pray for
Rich." She paused for a couple of seconds, breath
suspensefully held. "It was a wipeout. I couldn't."

"Hillary—" Conor began, looking, with a bellyful of
remorse, at her, at his child about to emerge into a world
of adults who killed—treacherously—those whom they were
rumored to love. He saw her as enraged, and deeply
frightened. Whom could she trust? He held out his hand;
her slender fingers were lost as she grasped it, conciliatorily.
But her strength told of deep panic. She broke free.

"Gotta run; gotta call Debbie." She skipped away from
them and vanished, all legs and butt going out the door.

"She's okay," Gina said, but knocked wood; and they
exchanged quick worried glances. Despite her absence
their daughter's essential nature, her fragility, seemed to
vibrate on the porch like crystal threatened ultrasonically.

"Up one minute, down the next."

"It's her age, mostly, Dr. Wersheba says. Any really
bad sinking spells, well, they can treat it pharmacologi-
cally as long as we own up to the need for treatment."

Conor swallowed tensely, thinking of the possibility of
his daughter being swept away by some of the same
morbid currents that had engulfed Rich.

"She just can't take much stress," Gina reflected. "Some
people are built that way."

"Not everybody's as tough as we are," Conor replied,
with a smile he had almost to bite in half to keep from
crying.

Gina got up swiftly. "I'll have that sandwich done in a
minute. Another ale?"

"Okay." Conor got up, too, glass in hand, not wanting
to sit alone on the darkened porch. The storm windows
rattled in spates of wind. Archie Bunker had given way to
the Jeffersons. *Movin' on up . . . We finally got a piece of
the pie.* He turned the TV off.

"How many calls altogether?"

"I'm not sure; there's a list by the phone upstairs in the
bedroom. Everybody said, well, if you have the chance, if
you want to talk, da-da, da-da, da-da. Milt Kramer; Lou

Kopsinis you ought to give a ring to. Are you going back to work soon?''

Conor rubbed his semicauliflowered ear, the left one. ''I'll call Dilworth. I think Chico and I are supposed to go nontitle against the Incredible Orlandos Thursday night in Pawtucket.''

''Win or lose?''

''We'll stomp the liverwurst out of them. Until it's time to play dead.'' Conor yawned, already bored by the prospect.

After she fixed the jumbo sandwich, rare roast beef and half a tomato sliced thin on sourdough bread, Gina excused herself to take a shower and wash her hair. Conor took a couple of big bites, which he had trouble swallowing, then carried the sandwich plate and a bottle of ale upstairs. He looked in on the boys. Charley was slowly getting ready for bed and explaining to Dean, authoritatively, the merits of a wingman the Bruins had just acquired from Winnipeg. There were times when Charles, the tummyless athlete, seemed dominant in the relationship with his intense, bookish older brother. But sometimes he would dissolve in childish tears at some minor outrage, as when his brother and sister teamed up against him in a taunting contest; or sometimes he would go off to amuse himself blissfully in the tub with his collection of exotic starships and windup swimming porpoises.

In his own room Conor sat down at a desk in one corner and scanned the list of names and phone numbers Gina had prepared for him in her neat backhand. He pulled the phone toward him and took from a shirt pocket an address book bound in pigskin, which had been worn to a dark and buttery thinness. Some of the names in the book went back twenty years. The tattered pages were ascrawl with updates on the whereabouts of friends, mostly from seminary, whom he'd tried to keep in touch with. Conor already had made several credit card calls that afternoon, the most distant to Rome. There was a fresh notation in ink beside the number of the Institute of Religious Works which he had contacted in the Holy See. He pondered it red-eyed for many moments, listening to the gushing sounds of the shower in the next room and to Hillary down the hall laughing on another line—''Gross, just *gross*, Debbie—''

heavily aware of the ball of venomous snakes he might be about to cast into the midst of all their lives. Then he made his last call of the day, half-wishing it would go unanswered.

41

"I had to call all the way to Rome to find out you were in Boston," Conor said.

Monsignor Paul Joseph Garen looked up from the airmail edition of *Osservatore Romano* he had been reading through granny specs and smiled in welcome and astonishment.

"Conor! What a pleasure after all these years." He rose to his full height, which brought the top of his head to the level of the knot in Conor's tie, to give Conor a double handclasp. In this sanctum of gustatory tradition, with English bucolic paintings on the paneled walls and antique crystal chandeliers, luncheon was a social ritual presided over by druids in cutaways. Several businessmen in dark suits had looked up in muted disbelief at Conor's passage to the cleric's table, which afforded an alcove view of the wide icebound Charles. With his size, his tangled pimento red beard, his houndstooth check jacket, he was like a cymbal clash introduced into a Bach fugue.

"You're even more imposing than I remember," Garen continued. "Of course I've only seen photos of you with the beard."

"Part of my brawling image," Conor said with a laugh that was too hearty. He was nervous and it showed.

"Oh, yes. You're still wrestling? I thought you had become a teacher and a coach."

"That too; but the job didn't last."

"Sit down, sit down. Well, we have some catching up to do."

"I've never been here before," Conor said lamely, taking an upholstered chair opposite Garen.

"Nor have I; but the archbishop is a member, and His

Eminence was kind enough to make arrangements. I believe he always enjoys this table.'' They both looked, as if on signal, out the wide window, blinking amiably in the mildly torrid light. Through a rent in stratified gray levels of cloud a golden radiance floated above the grim river like an incubating summer's day. Conor was stuck for words until the captain arrived to solicit drink orders.

"Conor?"

"Beer, I think."

"Domestic, or—imported?" the captain inquired with a faintly sarcastic smile.

"Narragansett," Conor growled, and picked at a wart growing on the base knuckle of his left thumb.

"A Campari and soda for me," Garen added. He took off his little tricky folding glasses and slipped them into an inside jacket pocket beside a calculator. The jacket lining, Conor noted, was a majestic purple. Silk. The rest of the suit was comparably beautiful in the quality of its cloth, the distinctive tailoring that was the hallmark of Rome's House of Gammarelli. He felt a deep momentary yearning, like a man who has been off smokes for twenty years but still can't resist looking at the displays in a tobacconist's window. So Paul was a monsignor at thirty-seven, and still youthful, though his widow's peak was more pronounced and there was a sprinkling of gray in the neatly trimmed, wren-brown hair around his ears. His complexion was ruddy; he dwelled amid hotbeds of fiscal crisis. From a class of stumblebums and turnabouts Paul Joseph Garen had emerged an unqualified success.

In their days as seminarians in upstate New York, even if one had doubts, deeply concealed, about one's own adequacy and prospects, none of Paul's classmates had doubted that someday he would be, at the least, a bishop. Rome had always been his goal; he had been discovered by a Vatican talent scout early in his career and had just completed his tenth year at the Holy See. He led an astutely well-managed life within the labyrinth of curial bureaucracy. He was well-connected with other rising young administrators in various Vatican offices. He was skillful in nuance, as sensitive to critical tolerance as a high-wire artist, fiscally progressive without being considered a wheeler-dealer. His skills were needed at IRW; he was a financial genius, specializing in real estate, and already the ranking member of the bishop's staff. Following the Sindona frauds and embezzlements, Garen had proposed some ingenious maneuvers which substantially reduced the seventy-million-dollar loss the Church had suffered; his tax strategies involving Vatican properties in several countries had straightened out a serious cash flow problem. Had he been for hire, he could have started out at two hundred thousand a year at his choice of any of the prestigious investment banking houses of Europe and England.

"Are you here on vacation?" Conor asked.

"In Boston? In the merry month of January? No, I've been participating in some rather involved negotiations on behalf of the archdiocese." He rubbed a weary eye. "I dislike dealing with bankers; they're such high-minded whores. But we may go on for as long as another six weeks. Even that won't be time enough for all I'd like to do, everyone I'd like to see."

"I appreciate your taking time to have lunch with me," Conor said quickly.

"Not at all, Mousy."

The nickname they'd tagged him with at seminary, largely forgotten by Conor through the years, startled him. Garen grinned delightedly.

"That just popped into my head. Remarkable, the names we had for each other. Let's see, I was—"

"The Kingsnake."

Garen nodded, his ruddy color deepening. "Rather a wasteful extravagance on God's part, considering my vocation."

"I don't think there was one of us who didn't win a few bucks betting on you Saturday nights at Ed and Irma's."

"I have to admit, after all these years, that I rather relished my celebrity. Do you suppose they're still holding long-shlong contests there? Ed and Irma's Bar and Grill. Ah, shuffleboard. Those greasy onions and overdone hamburgers. Draft beer. I assume Ed and Irma are still going strong, even though Archangel Michael has closed its doors forever."

Garen looked at the table for a few moments, contemplative, wistful, perhaps saddened. Conor picked at his wart, which bled. The drinks came, restoring their mutual spirits.

"To your health, Conor. Let's see. You're living close by?"

"In Joshua. About eleven miles south of Lowell."

"How is that area? Still economically depressed?"

"No, the microchip revolution saved us. I guess I'd still be living in Dorchester, if the blacks don't have it all by now; both my wife and I grew up in Southie. But even the parochial schools are in trouble in this town; public schools, the worst. We have a good life in Joshua; we both keep our noses to the grindstone, but it's worth it."

"Four children?"

"No, three. Two boys and a girl." Conor reached immediately for the photos he kept next to his wallet, passed the folder to Garen.

The monsignor held up each child's face to close scrutiny. "This one is most like you."

"That's Charley," Conor said. After a few cold swallows of beer he was finally beginning to feel at ease.

Garen turned to a Polaroid snap of Gina, taken after Mass the previous Easter.

"And your wife. A lovely *signora*."

"Thank you."

Garen handed back the photos and sipped his Campari, regarding Conor with the beamish distant fondness of a wealthy uncle preparing to turn aside a touch. A slender finger along his nose, gently tapping, was a forewarning of chastisement.

"I think married life agrees with you," Garen said.

"Yes, it does." Conor cleared his throat, fiddled with the knot of his tie. "I was wondering, Paul—you don't hold it against me? That I walked. I had to."

"I have no doubt of it." The finger was still, the clever gray eyes half closed. "We are not all meant to settle the questions of our identities in the service of our Lord Jesus Christ. You were wise, Conor. And lucky, it appears. Victor is continually on the outs with his archbishop. His drinking, if anything, is worse. James was murdered, for a few dollars, in a halfway house in New Orleans. He was a known consort of pubescent homosexuals. Andrew"—Garen frowned, striving to remember—"I've lost track of Andrew. You know about Glen."

"Killed himself."

"And Walter—he married, but I understand he was unable to have sex with his wife. They're now divorced. A heavy toll. More than thirteen thousand men left the priesthood in the six-year period following the Second Vatican Council."

"John Paul's taking a tougher stance."

"Yes. 'It is a matter of keeping one's word to Christ and the Church.' But the petitions for release from vows keep coming in, and every year fewer young men hear the call to the priesthood. Wojtyla is a brilliant man, a brave man, but the wrong man for these times. He dispenses dogma to the indifferent while the survival of the Church is in the balance. His acts of crushing Lefèbvre and silencing the radical theologians perhaps only leaves us more defenseless in the sociopolitical tides that are rising above our heads. The future of the Church is being written in the blood of civil war in Latin America; in Wojtyla's Poland. I doubt that spiritual force alone is enough to resist these tides; nor is a childlike faith in eschatology. The Church lives through the will of its people, not through blind obedience to archaic orthodoxy. If this truth of a living Church is denied, the sun of the third millennia may well rise on a bleak landscape, a world in shambles, bereft of comfort or hope. Ah, well. I've made you squirm and I didn't mean to. I find you, Conor, after God knows what turmoil, a settled, useful, and devoted man. I'm delighted. Maybe you can tell me something I've wondered about all these years. Is all that dreadful punishment you wrestlers dish out to each other for real?"

Conor said with a slight smile, "Call your neighborhood book and try to get down on some action, even a well-promoted title fight, and they'll laugh at you. That says something about how the game is played. Basically we're in the amusement business, like Barnum and Bailey's clowns. On the other hand, I don't often have to exaggerate how I feel when somebody even bigger and nastier than I am is trying to twist my arm out of its socket. Showmanship exacts a price, if you're any good at it."

"It's a living?"

"It's a living."

"Splendid. So you're happy at home, well-adjusted on the job, you go to Mass regularly, your children are beautiful. They are. Quite beautiful. I can't suppress a slight tickle of curiosity as to why you went to so much trouble to look me up after all this time."

"A week ago my half brother, whose name is Richard, beat his girl friend to death in Chadbury, Vermont. It's been in the papers. Her funeral was on the TV news two nights ago. Rich used a tire iron and left very few bones in her head and body unbroken. On three separate occasions since he's been in jail he's told me that he is possessed by a demon from hell. And the demon made him kill Karyn."

Monsignor Garen looked Conor full in the face for nearly half a minute. His own face, so perfectly poised between dismay and disbelief, seemed in analysis to have no expression. The glass of Campari he had raised halfway to his lips was forgotten. A gull surged near the window, vanished with a luminous downbeat of wings that disturbed the pupils of the watcher's eyes like drops of rain on still water. He let out his breath and the bell of thin crystal in his hand took on a momentary pall, the bitter red liquid quivered delicately.

"What a pisser," he said.

"I don't know what to do, Paul."

"Nor do I. Suppose we order some lunch, then we'll talk about it again."

42

While Conor and the monsignor were making their choices from the luncheon menu of the Storrow Club, Dr. Margaret Renquist met Richard Devon in a stuffy interview room at the district courthouse in Chadbury. He had been in jail for one day less than a week and was still being sedated, a dosage of Thorazine she thought appropriate; the tranquilizer would not interfere with his taking of the standardized intelligence tests she had brought with her, and should not significantly affect his test scores.

Renquist was a heavyweight handsome woman in her fifties, and she liked a lot of pearls with her pinstriped business suit and frilly mayonnaise-colored blouse. Her hair was an almost iridescent shade of red, like the choice plumage of a fighting cock. She used rimless glasses for close work, popping them on and off the bridge of her nose as adroitly as a jeweler with his loupe. The glasses were fixed to a lapel of her jacket by a gold chain.

Her eyes came to grips right away. His were shy and tired, light-sensitive, irritated. "I could use a smoke," Rich muttered, looking at Adam Kurland.

"Dear, I'm a lifelong asthmatic, but if you must. I want you to be comfortable."

"Well—" Rich figuratively backed off from the un-opened pack of Marlboros the lawyer had produced, and looked around at the straight wooden chair he was sup-posed to sit in. Renquist was already seated, opposite the empty chair at a small scarred table. He stifled a yawn and licked his dry lips, a boyish, deprived mannerism. He sat down slowly and tried to find something to do with his hands. There were two manila folders on the table, a ball-point pen, a notepad to Renquist's right, a clear plastic carafe of water that was three-quarters full, white Styrofoam cups. Finally Rich leaned on an elbow and partially shielded his face from the strong slant of light coming through venetian blinds. His eyes, vaguely silvered, the pupils large, were bluntly motionless. Adam stood against a wall with his arms folded, watching him.

"Did we wake you?" the psychologist said indulgently, in response to his lassitude.

Rich yawned again, nodded. "There's not much to do. I sleep mostly in the daytime."

"And not at night?"

"He doesn't let me sleep at night," Rich said, in a voice so low and unemphatic she had to lean urgently over the table to catch the last syllables.

Adam stirred restlessly.

"*Who* doesn't?" Renquist asked, with her squinting, aggressive smile. "Is there someone in the cell with you?"

The lawyer, knowing better, shook his head. Rich seemed

not to have heard the question; then his head turned queerly, neck stretching: a smile broke out. It was not a happy smile. The facial muscles were abominably strained and his eyes danced in a kind of delirium. But almost as soon as the smile appeared, it switched off; his lips closed in a bleak line. He said nothing. They all waited, hearing a droning voice explaining a point of law in another room, courthouse echoes. A clangorous old elevator gate. Spiffy heel taps on marble. Finally Renquist acknowledged the impasse by squaring her shoulders and uncapping her gold Cross pen.

"You're Richard Devon. Do you have a middle name?"

"Padraic," Rich said promptly, adding, with a shading of admonition, "but I never liked being called Paddy."

"Richard Padraic Devon. Age?"

"Twenty-two."

"Do you know your social security number?"

After a moment's hesitation he reeled it off, then looked up at Adam. "Is my brother coming?"

"No, not today, Rich. He's in Boston."

Rich accepted this news with a solemnity that bordered on sorrow. "What day is it?"

"Thursday."

"I see."

"Richard," the psychologist said, reclaiming his attention, "when you're sleeping, how do you sleep?"

"On my back."

"I mean do you sleep well, or restlessly? Do you wake up frequently?"

"Yes, I do."

"Are you bothered by nightmares?"

Rich stared at her, then through her, with almost blinding intensity. Then he suddenly dropped his gaze, reached out carefully, and opened one of the folders on the table. He looked at the Stanford-Binet tests.

"This is going to be a waste of time. I can tell you my IQ is 136, which isn't bad."

"We'll get to those."

"If they're necessary."

"They're very necessary."

"If you say. I can't tell the difference anymore."

"About what, Richard?"

''What's a nightmare, and what isn't. When I'm awake and when I'm asleep. Am I supposed to be crazy?''

''That's a word I never use.''

His appeal having been tabled, Rich was attracted by the sound of Adam coughing lightly into his fist. ''Something's happened,'' he said to the lawyer, ''that you don't want to tell me about. Is it Conor? He's okay, isn't he?''

''Sure, Rich. Why wouldn't he be?''

''Threats have been made. He's not liked.''

''Conor isn't?'' Adam said, raising his chin and fingering a patch of razor burn on his throat. He glanced at Renquist, who sat twiddling with her glasses, casting fleet little ellipses saturated with rainbow color on the wall opposite the windows. Her eyes were so tightly screwed up in concentration only pinpoints of pupils showed.

''Who made the threats?'' the lawyer asked.

Rich shook off the question with a doleful twitch of the head. ''But it's his daughter. Hillary. She's the one who has the weakness; there could be trouble. Maybe I shouldn't ask Conor to visit me anymore. Still—I have to let him know. Karyn was buried this week, wasn't she?''

''That's right.''

His grief, cold and compressed, flashed by with the stealth of a comet in funerary space. ''Karyn's dead and gone. Polly's not so gone, though; I'm telling you now there's going to be *big* trouble.''

Renquist wrote something on her notepad, looked up with a hard jutting meaningless smile. She reached for a cup and the carafe of water, momentarily taking her eyes off Rich.

''Better not touch that.''

She stayed her hand. ''Why not?''

''You can't drink anyway. It's frozen solid.''

The psychologist, as if taking a dare, jauntily picked up the carafe; but she dropped it quickly, wrist unhinged by the weight. The carafe made a hard clunking sound on the tabletop, rolled in a clumsy half circle.

''Was I right? Frozen.''

Her smile broadened, but she seemed numbed by this phenomenon. ''It wasn't frozen earlier. How did you know?''

"I know a lot of things," Rich said curtly. "None of them good. I try to know everything—what I don't know can hurt me." His eyes whipped to the lawyer. "What *did* happen, that you're trying to keep from me?"

"I don't think it has any bearing on your case," Adam said. "The police were interested in talking to him, I know that much. The innkeeper—Windross—he was found three nights ago beside some railroad tracks in Massachusetts. Run over by a freight train."

"Goddam!" Rich said explosively, momentarily agog with implications. Then the news seemed to fade from his mind. He sat in a slump, worriedly, and took a deep breath. Before long his motor began to race. His lips jittered, and then he said, spilling the words out, "What it is—there's no dead or alive. Only there or not there. See? Sometimes the lines are crossed. I don't know how it happens. Or we ask for it. Point of entry: the solar plexus, or else from the left, at the base of the brain, where the neck and spine are joined. I'll be punished for talking so much, I know it, but I— Take my word for this. The human race is in worse trouble than ever. He's been waiting and waiting. *Time*, shit. Time means nothing to him."

"*Him* again?" Renquist said brightly, tapping her pen on the notepad.

"Yeah," Rich said, leaning a little toward her, elbows on the table.

"Can you tell me his name?"

"He doesn't want me to. This early."

"Why is it too early?"

"I don't make the plans or set down the rules," Rich said firmly. "My tongue is tied."

"Is it?"

"Want to see?"

"If you want to show me."

Rich opened his mouth a little and, modestly, stuck out the tip of his tongue.

"Looks all right to me," the psychologist said.

His mouth widened. Another half inch of furry tongue protruded.

"There *is* some coating. You're not digesting your food properly, which is certainly understandable."

"Ah, ahhhh," Rich went, head back, jabbing a finger toward his glottis. The gristly rings of his windpipe were apparent beneath the stubbled skin of his throat.

"Now, Richard."

"*Ooookkkk!*"

"I am looking. There are no knots in your tongue. So you can tell me." The psychologist took off her glasses and smiled expectantly at Rich's distended face; his complexion had deepened from crimson to plum. Saliva wormed down his chin. "It won't go any farther than this room," she assured him.

There was a loud popgun sound; Adam flinched as something gleaming white shot like a projectile from Rich's mouth.

Maggie Renquist's head jerked, she uttered a cry of pain and consternation, clapping both hands to her face.

And in the next instant, in the blink of an eye, Rich did an amazing thing: a backflip from a sitting position, winding up prone on the floor behind the chair, face down, arms rigidly at his sides.

Adam was dazed by this feat, he couldn't believe what he'd seen. Renquist gasped several times; he turned his attention to her.

"What happened, Maggie?"

"My God—I don't know!" she exclaimed. "Something struck me here, in the face."

"Let me see."

Renquist lowered her trembling hands, and stared at Rich on the floor. "How did he get *there*?" She was feeling all round the bloody thing that protruded more than half an inch from her right cheek.

"I don't know, he just, uh, fell out of the chair or something, no, don't touch that, let me look."

On examination Adam saw that the object had the appearance of a front tooth, including the long exposed roots. The cutting edge was firmly embedded in the rouged flesh of Maggie Renquist's cheek. But he couldn't bring himself to trust his conclusions, so outlandish and improbable.

"Well, what it looks like, a, a *tooth*." His voice cracked immaturely, hadn't done that since he was fifteen.

She was standing, scraping her chair back, eyes on Rich. "Never mind, I'm all right. Let's see about Richard."

He was catatonic, unbending. Moving him was like lifting the lid of a stone sarcophagus. Together, custodial, they laid Rich on his back. His eyes had rolled far up in his head. But his mouth was still open, and beyond the tranced rim they could see his tongue. Withdrawn like a moody serpent, but he hadn't swallowed it. His color was pale, not cyanotic, though Adam, hurrying, couldn't detect breath or pulse. The lawyer was having palpitations. It was obvious that Rich's upper right front tooth was cleanly missing from the burgundy socket.

"Get help," Renquist said sensibly. She staggered to her feet, wheezing. She touched her impaled, throbbing cheek and stared at the lying-down boy—motionless, but not dead, listening, like a seedbed, for rain.

She smiled as Adam beat it out the door, then began a slow retreat until she was standing in flecked slices of light, her back almost against the venetian blinds, a little drop of blood coursing down her cheek from the wound. The many ruffles of her blouse fluttered like gills as her chest expanded hugely with the effort she was making to breathe. There seemed something vain and malevolent about his stasis, this state of ungrace. She sensed a presence, something reciprocally watching *her,* the impress of a calculating third eye secreted in flesh. With one hand she groped for her heart. Maggie Renquist was having an asthma attack. Smile still big and blasé, but her eyes squinching shut from the oncoming pain and her lifelong fear of asphyxiation.

43

Conor, his throat scratchy from doing so much talking, took up his fork again during a pause to prod listlessly through the remains of the lobster salad he had ordered for lunch. Evidence of vigorous appetite surprised him. He hadn't been conscious of eating more than a few bites. His beer glass was almost empty again, there remained suds and a small half moon of gold in the thimble-sized bottom. He craved another but was uneasy about reordering. He hadn't kept count, but perhaps Monsignor Garen had counted for him.

Garen had been content with a green salad and a plate of chilled gazpacho; for the most part he had been a listening presence, studiously hunched, seldom raising his eyes from his meal even when he had questions to ask. Outside the window a flock of gulls broke apart with a noiseless big bang, creating an instant flurried universe before Conor's brooding eye: how often had God been provoked to say, *Once more, and let's get it right this time.*

The tickle in Conor's throat set him to coughing dryly; he sipped from his water glass.

"So," he said, "it's like a kind of—shadowy double-shuffling going on. I see Rich, and then I don't see him. There's somebody else he seems to be listening to, trying to please. Or appease. And then a peculiar, baleful light steals into his eyes and I know I'm seeing—the one who isn't Rich. The sensation is—more than eerie. It's terrifying."

"Um-hmm, um-hmm." Garen raised his napkin to his lips, placed it crumpled beside his plate, touched reflectively the small flashing crucifix worn outside his vest. "I know it must have occurred to you that what you've described may be a classic case of dual, or multiple, personality. In recent years psychiatry has come to recognize that these cases are far more common than once was thought possible."

"Psychiatry," Conor said with scant admiration, "is still an infant science. If there's any science involved at all. A couple of hundred years ago Rich simply would have been tried and executed for witchcraft."

"Joan of Arc is alive and medium well," Garen murmured, with a smile that revealed more gold than his crucifix could have contained; the body of Christ packed into one broad molar. The sight made Conor feel a little dizzy from chagrin.

Garen, misreading his distress, said instantly, with a thin knitting of brows, "I'm sorry. That was a bumper sticker I saw on the street a day or two ago. Insensitive of me, it just slipped out.''

Conor chuckled belatedly. ''But what I was trying to say—''

''Oh, yes, yes. This is the age of the empirical readout. No behavior is so bizarre it cannot be expressed binarily. Our devils are all emotional, due to faulty linkages in the id.''

''But that's not where you and I come from.''

''The devil exists, we have no doubts about *that,* on papal authority. And the devil would persecute us all, out of envy and malice for the imperfection of not being God himself. *His* name is legion. Humankind would be in a sorry state indeed if we did not have the love of the Father to protect us from these treacherous and corrupting spirits.''

''What I don't understand is how someone like Rich could be afflicted.''

''Is your brother a good Catholic?''

''So-so. But he's not against the Church, like so many kids these days.''

''Would you like coffee, Conor?''

''No, thank you.''

The monsignor checked his watch. ''I'll have to be returning to the conference table in a few minutes.'' He summoned their waiter with a raised finger.

Conor said, ''It's really been very kind of you to hear me out.''

''Not at all. I'm deeply sympathetic, it's a terrible ordeal for you and your family. I must say I feel most of your evidence for possession is circumstantial. An equally impressive case for, say, paranoid schizophrenia could be made. Of course I'm no expert. You should bear in mind that authenticated cases of demonic possession are great rarities, thank the good Lord. Thousands of claims are investigated each year; only a fraction require intervention by an exorcist.''

''I truly believe this is a claim that should be investigated.''

''Conor, I shall take the matter under prayerful advisement. And if I can help—''

The bill was presented; Garen turned abruptly to sign it.

"Will you talk to an exorcist?" Conor persisted, aware of being like a large ugly bleating child.

"But I don't know any," Garen said, sounding mildly exasperated. He pressed a fist to his mouth, perhaps repeating the spicy gazpacho. "The Church is not unlike the CIA in that respect. Of course we have priests with those rare abilities demanded of exorcists, scholars of the *Mysterium Iniquitatis;* but their work is secretive, their investigations dangerous. One may not know who they are unless one demonstrates a need to know. And I'm aware that there is a strict protocol to be observed, beginning on the diocesan level. Evidentiary requirements. It can take a great deal of time, Conor."

In the vestibule of the Storrow Club the monsignor gripped Conor's hands with enthusiasm, in sight of escape from what had been a glum luncheon; whorish bankers would be a relief after Conor's recitation of woe.

"God bless. My love to your wife and fine children. Expect to hear from me."

He took the elevator, turning inside to face Conor squarely, his smile cheery and correct; he made the sign of benediction as the sliding door closed him out.

Abandonment: Conor's heart dropped with the invisibly plummeting elevator. *I am no longer a priest.* Done. For a year or more after renouncing his vocation he had suffered vexing spells of numbness in his extremities—fingers, toes, once the whole of his left leg. Again facing his limitations and the remainder of a bleak afternoon, Conor went into the men's room and stood rockily in a stall for several minutes, nearly convulsed, aware that he had introduced too much noontime richness to his touchy digestive system. He belched, swallowing air freighted with the odor from urinal antiseptic cakes to drive out even worse air; farted dismally and at length. In a few hours he would wrestle; a week of neglect of his conditioning routines had made him vulnerable. He was injury-prone anyway. One bad fall could end his second-rate career. Hospitalization. No money coming in. All up to him, children's survival, Rich in jail, what good was he to anyone? Gray metal walls of the loo a sepulchre of guilt. Throw it up or piss it out. He settled for pissing. Clouded yellow, not healthy, kidneys again. The outpouring seemed to empty his head as well as his bladder. His brain wizening, dying speeded up beyond the limits of normal daily cell attrition. Less smart than he had been at this exact time yesterday. Tomorrow was a block of granite he would have to chip his way into. Time pressing in on him, *hurry,* mortality the shadow of a cliff on the nape of his neck. With the solid stream of urine reduced to a dribble, he shook his penis to clear out the last drops. *Expect to hear from me.* But Paul had been right: where was his proof to engage the attention of the professionally skeptical? He was no less certain of his conclusions, and prolonged waiting would be torment— for him, especially for Rich. He must act. Surely there were books on the subject of demonic possession, even the Boston Public Library would have them. Accessible to all.

44

Late Wednesday night, the first Wednesday in February, Lindsay Potter drove in from New Haven and parked her chocolate-colored Mazda, streaked with salt from the winterized roads, beside Adam's Cadillac in a roofed, radiantly heated alcove that adjoined the converted barn they shared five miles from the hub of Braxton, Vermont. The Connecticut River lay a quarter of a mile downhill in scalding moonlight, past rock walls and orchards that took up the bulk of the fifteen-acre property. She pulled from the back seat her luggage and a big attaché case that contained her Brother typewriter, two cassette recorders, and nearly a gross of miniature cassettes, and went up a flight of steps in the scintillating cold to a large cleared deck. She let herself into the shadow-filled barn, twenty-six feet from hardwood floor to stained roofbeams, all open area except for sleeping pallets on galleries that could be enclosed by means of sliding walnut panels on tracks. The lighting was very subdued, half of the living quarters and the office in darkness. It was a showplace but chilly inside: a bitch to heat, never mind the expense. They kept the thermostat low in winter and relied on amenities for warmth; hot tub, fireplace, electric blankets at night.

A phone rang, twice; an answering machine gobbled up the incoming call. A single high spotlight isolated a portion of the hot tub deck to one side of the native-stone fireplace wall; she could hear water bubbling minerally, and through the rise of steam saw Adam immersed to his chest, head cradled on a waterproof pillow. There was music, dialed low; Crystal Gayle, heartrending, her voice a shade too glamorous and expert for the country material.

"Hey, I'm home," Lindsay called, and he started, looking around puzzledly. "Linds?" "Yeah, expecting your mother?" "C'mere." "In a minute, I need a drink." She dropped her baggage on a section of sofa and pulled off her lowtop boots, hopskipping but not pausing in her beeline progress to the island kitchen. "You dead?" "I'm *dead,* lover." Her exhausted eyes scanning across the rack of bottles above the bar, "Ginginnygin, what did you do with the goddam gin?" "Refrigerator." "Oh, yeah, sure," padding with straight narrow feet to the restaurant-size stainless steel refrigerator. She pulled out the bottle of cool Tanqueray's and rummaged for a Bitter Lemon, put both on a maple block and selected a tall glass, paused to take off her cardigan sweater, her blouse and bra, dropped them on the floor, shuddered and puckered, made her drink, added circles of clear ice from a dispenser, tasted, smacked her lips, unsnapped her skirt and dropped it, too, shuddered until her bones rattled, walked in her soot-colored panty hose to the mists of the hot tub, handed down her drink for him to hold and, still wearing the pantyhose, stepped down blissfully into roiling water and sat beside him, a hand dangling on his damp hot shoulder. They kissed. His hands slid slowly down her naked ribcage to the waistband of the panty hose and he peeled them off her, tossed them sopping onto the stone ledge above them. She fished for his penis and held it and said, "You know something? I think I'm just too damned tired."

Adam smiled wisely and tilted the glass at her lips. "You'll recover."

Lindsay drank and scratched the tingle of his mustache against her cheek. She said sternly, "Listen, dollface. This is a bad habit you're getting into, falling asleep in the hot tub. One of these nights I'll come home really late and have to rake your bones off the bottom.''

"Oh, I wasn't asleep. Just dozing. I haven't been in that long anyway, feel me.''

"I am feeling you.''

"The rest of me.''

"If you get any softer I could make candles out of you. Just don't stay in much longer.''

The phone rang again, a droplet of sound in the big space around them. The second ring was pinched off.

Adam said, "So what do we know about Richard Devon we didn't know a week ago?''

"He's never been hospitalized or treated on an outpatient basis for any kind of mental instability. He was a hotheaded kid, fought a lot. Sort of a runt. The usual feelings of inferiority because of his size. Some minor trouble with the law; two arrests, charges dismissed.''

"One for the prosecution,'' Adam said, not sounding intimidated. "He's not mad, he's bad. She jilted him and he couldn't take it. Premeditation. Teach her a big lesson. If I can't have her, nobody can.''

"We're left with five witnesses who will swear he was in a state of lunacy more compelling than hydrophobia when he murdered Karyn, plus there's the testimony of arresting officers and the noted police surgeon Dr. Arthur K. Harbison, all of which isn't worth a free pass to the Miss Nude Octogenarian Pageant at the old ladies' home, and—''

Lindsay paused for breath; Adam had gone down laughing in the tub; bubbles exploded above the dark wavering circle of his hair. She grinned, waited until he reappeared, choking, then concluded, "and we'll have the testimony of as many friendly clinicians as we can afford. Speaking of funds, I'm going around with two bucks in my wallet.''

"It's reasonably definite the county will give us the same amount of money we had to defend DuBois.''

"Seventy-seven thousand? That was a twelve-day trial! It'll take weeks just to select a jury this time, not to mention—''

"Okay, okay. I was in Montpelier all afternoon seeing what the state machinery can crank out for us. I should get a call from Spru Norfleet the first of next week. Spru has always liked me.''

"Yes, she and your father"—a new light appeared in Lindsay's eyes: competitive, bitchy. "I hope you didn't give her the impression you were going to crawl in the sack with her, little lovey-dovey camping trip some weekend in August.''

"She's already several years beyond my definition of middle age, and anyway it would be kind of incestuous.''

There was an absence of guile, of studied frankness; Lindsay gazed complacently at him, then began delicately to comb his drenched mustache with a long fingernail.

"Speaking of greasy machinery," Adam said, "I had lunch with Gary Cleves yesterday.''

"How *is* Crusader Rabbit?''

"Smug about something, other than what he refers to as his 'locked case.' Gary quoted *Powell* v. *Texas* to me and had one martini over his limit. He was that confident I was going to lose my nerve and try to plea-bargain even before the indictment comes down.''

Lindsay licked the last tart drops from her glass and said with a pat, malicious smile, "Gary's so reactionary it's made him stupid. Doesn't he know some of the folk around here still believe in witches? Deep down inside, oh yes, they believe. And the more I think about it, the more I'm sure we can sell irresistible impulse and diminished capacity to any jury he cares to impanel.''

Adam cautioned, "But the pretrial publicity will hurt us. That's Gary's ace.''

Lindsay held out the glass and, catching her lower lip with her teeth, said coaxingly, "Fix me another?''

"Sure.''

Adam lifted himself up out of the tub and reached for a long striped terrycloth robe. Lindsay's eyes flitted, like sunstruck hornets. She admired his ass, his trim ankles. On the way to the kitchen he stopped to turn up the gas log fire on the hearth: they both disliked wood smoke indoors, which eventually saturated all furniture and drapes with a sour ashy odor. He made the gin and bitter, then opened a cabinet and laid an orange exercise mat at an angle in front of the fire, broke out bottles of unguents and oils and mild balm, took off his robe, and waited, kneeling, for Lindsay to emerge from the tub and dry off.

They shared the fresh drink and then she lay down on her stomach, nude.

He massaged her, using the Shiatsu method of pressure on problem areas, beginning with the cold papery feet, so tense to probing fingers she twitched and yowled. Bones there like thinly buried arrowheads, knives of blue flint, balls of the toes in grapy bunches, the heels tough, each with a rind of flaking callus. He had been a gymnast and had taken up cross-country skiing. He loved the human body, musculature. He sang the names of the muscles to Lindsay like a romantic pushcart vendor, a wafted litany, *latisssimussss, trapezzziussss,* as he worked, steadily and ardently, toward her heart, his hands leaving her newly enlivened body only to pour another dollop of oil. Without interrupting his rhythm he reached down occasionally to strop himself, maintaining an iron hardness, drops of his own clarified essence mingling with the sweet sesame oil. By the time he had begun to loosen her shoulders, which were like a carapace beneath the skin, he was astride her spread radiant hips, with each firm, strenuous movement forward his penis nosing against the base of her spine.

Lindsay, head turned to one side on the orange mat, face stupefied like that of a vixen in poppies, groaned at his power, demanding more. He turned her neatly, positioning himself between her knees; her belly was sopping, clear perspiration, not much hair on her body, little shieldlike smudge barely containing the febrile pout of labia: the head of his cock dallied on the surface of all this briny sensuality, bobbing, teasing. And something tainted, fierce and whorish, rose swiftly through her familiar depths to lunge; her mouth was twisted. *Fuck me, fuck me. I'll kill you if you don't give it to me now!*

They recuperated, in matching velour wraps with hoods that made them look like mismatched sparring partners, side by side at the range. They made biscuits and omelets in small square frying pans, the omelets thinly crisped on the outside, stuffed with diced mushrooms and black olives, a teaspoon of chili sauce each. Hot black coffee and food and an earful of Stevie Nicks; they sat munching companionably on stools at the breakfast bar.

"Do you think that was Conor trying to get you earlier?" Lindsay said.

"I doubt it. He's cut down to half a dozen calls a day. The last time I heard from him was this afternoon; he traced me to Spru's office in the capital. He's coming up tomorrow for the day, to see Rich. He told me he was more than ever convinced that Rich isn't crazy. He's not ruling out a tumor, but he said, 'I know what to do. I know how to get to the bottom of this.' "

Lindsay spooned thick wild honey onto a biscuit half, licked a dribble of the honey from her slender thumb. "Bottom of what?"

"Rich's behavior, I suppose. I couldn't get him to elaborate, he was using an outdoor phone on the New England Thruway, big trucks zooming by, it was hard to make him out. I guess he was going someplace to wrestle. Did you dig up the reasons why he left the priesthood?"

"No. Why, was I supposed to?"

"I thought somebody might have mentioned it."

"I heard the usual gossip, passed off as inside stuff. I know Conor had what might be described as an ambulatory nervous breakdown after he separated from the Church; he was boozing too much but he never joined A.A. —marriage and the love of a good woman redeemed him. A trite story, but one I never get tired of."

"He sure was tossing down the Cutty Sark the night we took him to Morecambe's."

"He had six. So did I."

"You've got more peat bog in your stomach than the average Irishman. I just have this doubtful feeling about Conor. He's big and he can be fierce and he has worse body hair than the abominable snowman, but underneath he's a frail reed, and he'll break. Soon. Give him another week at the most."

"I'll put ten bucks on Conor. For the honor of my people, even though I'm only Irish by adoption."

"Done." They hooked little fingers together to seal the wager.

Lindsay, still rosy from her exertions, humid in the hollows of her face and throat, leaned to her left to give him a kiss. She said, "I found out Rich has no history of epilepsy. But you couldn't have used that anyway."

"Uh-uh. Still, I'm convinced it was an epileptic fit he had. I've seen them before. He jackknifed out of his chair, and he was rigid on the floor."

"For how long?"

"Six or seven minutes."

"You should have insisted on an EEG *immediately*."

"Insisted? I screamed myself hoarse. That fuckoff Harbison was hours getting around to Rich, and then all he did was flash a light in his eyes and give him aspirin." Adam shook his head in awe and displeasure at what he had to put up with. "Right away I petitioned Southern District to get Rich out of jail and into the hospital for at least a two-day stay, but Bracken turned me down on the grounds that there wasn't demonstrable need—like a collapsed lung—and security couldn't be guaranteed. Harbison said it was just a fainting spell. How do you like that? *Harbison.* I've seen more brains in birdcrap. *He* wasn't there. I was. I don't know who looked worse, Richard or Maggie Renquist. Her asthma, you know. And something had her really scared."

"I think," Lindsay said dryly, "I'd be a little shaky too if someone spat a tooth at me hard enough to put an eye out. She was lucky that didn't happen. How the hell do you suppose Rich managed it? Was it a pivot tooth? Could he have done it on purpose?"

"I have *no* explanation. It's one of those Fortean occurrences. Like little green toads raining down from a clear sky."

"Get serious."

"The facts are, Rich is minus a front tooth, which I have in a Tic-Tac box in my office, and it took three stitches to close the hole in Maggie's cheek. She'll be scarred. I've wasted far too much time thinking about it already, and I'm not going to think about his goddam tooth anymore. Rich is crazy as they come, and I know I can prove it in court."

"Hey." What she could see of Adam's face, like the moon's last quarter contained by the cowl, looked sleepily saintlike about the brow; but his mouth was humanly troubled, unassured. He was trying to turn his fork into a pretzel. She nuzzled against him, seeking bones within all that velour, the hard definite shape of him. "Needless to say, Maggie wants no more to do with our client."

He put the fork down. "Not at all. She's tough. And fascinated with Rich. I don't think Maggie's ever seen one quite like him before. After this, uh, cooling-off period, she'll meet with Rich again in a couple of days and give him the prescribed tests."

Lindsay poured more decaffeinated coffee for them and was starting to clean up when the door chimes pealed. She glanced at Adam, who leaned across the counter and activated the watchdog TV camera focused on the area around the front door; a flaring black and white picture appeared on one of the four nine-inch monitors of their security system.

They saw, at a downward angle from a height of seven feet, a lone man, hatless, big, wearing a dark overcoat and flowing muffler, stamping his feet on the welcome mat. He had poetically untamed hair, pale blond or white, tumbled around his face, and a prominent nose. After a couple of moments he looked sideways at the lens of the camera, holding his face up confidently for a full inspection by the occupants, signaling amiability and good will with short bursts of condensed breath. His head at this distorted angle was huge, spheroid; his feet might have been on another planet.

"My God," Lindsay said over Adam's shoulder, clutching him, "do you know who that looks like? It looks like— couldn't be—my God!"

"It's him," Adam said, so startled his chin quivered, a childhood thing which, like hiccups and nervous rashes, is never quite outgrown. Adam pushed a button. "Hello?"

The familiar face creased, a lupine smile. "Do I have the honor," the radioed voice said, "of addressing Mr. Adam Kurland?"

"Yes, I'm Adam."

"Please excuse my intrusion at this hour; I telephoned several times and then took a chance I'd find you still awake, a night owl like myself. I'm Tommie Harkrider. May I come in?"

Adam had already given Lindsay a nudge and she was flying up a short flight of steps to the foyer landing and the door. Adam released the latch with a silent buzzer just as she got there and Harkrider, turning, nodding to her out of a luminous thin fog, stepped inside.

"You must be Lindsay Potter."

She shook her right hand free of the heavy sleeve and offered it, peering past him outdoors. "Is that your car? Is someone else with you? Wouldn't they like to come in?"

"No, no, it's my chauffeur. Bernie will be quite comfortable with the engine running, and he has movies on video disc for entertainment. I can't be long, I must be back in the city for a breakfast meeting, but I didn't want to miss this initial opportunity to meet Adam and yourself."

They walked side by side toward Adam, who had come halfway from the kitchen with a taut quizzical smile and just a hint of wariness. Harkrider struggled a little clumsily to unwrap the yards of muffler, which Lindsay took for him, as well as his shapeless alpaca coat with its dated velvet lapels.

"Mr. Kurland."

"A pleasure, sir."

Harkrider looked around him in admiration.

"Marvelous what one can do with these old barns. Is it your design?"

"I took it over from a friend who ran into trouble at the bank. May I offer you a drink?"

"Thank you, sir; two ounces of Drambuie, if I may presume."

"We have Drambuie," Lindsay said, pleased, and she hastened to the bar to pour it for him.

Adam, his coffee mug in one hand, escorted the bigger man, who walked nippingly, as if he had very bad feet, to a conversation area framed in blunt low-backed sofas upholstered in blazing blue sailcloth; he turned on a podshaped lamp suspended from a chromed fishpole that was anchored in a block of Carrera marble. Harkrider lowered himself by degrees until he was satisfied that his piece of the sectional sofa wasn't going to slide out from under him.

He smiled, a gentle interrogative smile that still had something of the cagey old wolf in it, and looked more closely at Adam.

"I have the impression we've met before."

"Yes, we have, at Virginia Beach three summers ago.

The National Institute for Trial Advocacy seminars. I thought your dissection of Arnold Sondheim on cross was, uh—" Adam hesitated, having almost said *brilliant;* not wanting to appear to fawn, he substituted: "very illuminating and helpful."

Harkrider nodded meditatively. "Oh, yes. Sondheim. One of my favorite whipping boys, although of course I intend no serious disrespect to an esteemed scholar in the law of evidence. But the adversarial process, to my mind, is not a forum of discovering 'truths,' as he would have it. As trial lawyers we are engaged in settling disputes, and a well-run trial is a mechanism of almost exquisite balances and counterbalances, which can be reduced to junk by unnecessary and inept cross-examinations. The cross in our legal system is a tool for the wise and restrained litigator, but most of our young lawyers feel that their credibility is on the line if they say 'no questions.' The thing to remember is that their witness is going to hurt you a lot more often than he'll help you."

Lindsay came with a liqueur glass for their visitor and sat down wide-eyed beside Adam, slippered feet tucked beneath her.

"When is your book on juries coming out?" she asked Harkrider. "It seems as if I've been hearing about it for years."

The old barrister chuckled. "From a series of short addresses and essays it seems to have grown into a magnum opus; but I'm happy to say the last section has just gone to the printer's, and I fondly hope my labors are over—although I never seem to run out of cogent thoughts about that monster we have built and rebuilt in our courtrooms for some thousand years. As soon as the book is off the press, I would be pleased to send copies to you."

Adam and Lindsay murmured their thanks. After a short interval, during which Tommie Harkrider sampled the dark liqueur and looked around as if he had forgotten how he came to be there, he said abruptly to Adam, "You've grasped a tiger by the tail. I'll be most interested in observing how you handle Mr. Devon's defense."

"There's only one defense. I'm sure it isn't just coincidence that you happen to be driving around southern Vermont today, Mr. Harkrider."

"Please; it's just plain old Tommie, if you will."

"Well, Tommie, it does come as a relief to find out I haven't been replaced."

Harkrider laughed delightedly. "I can see you and I are going to achieve a high comfort level, Adam. No, I represent the family of Karyn Vale. I felt I should pay my respects to the prosecutor of Haden County and offer what help and advice I can, although Mr. Cleves doesn't need any help. I have no doubt, from what I've heard today, that you're a very competent young lawyer. But the prosecutor will convict, despite your best efforts. I don't think even I could get your client off."

Adam took this prophecy, or admonition, like a dose of castor oil, getting a little turgid around the mouth before remembering to smile. "According to existing statutes of the state of Vermont—you may not be that familiar with them—Richard Devon is not guilty by all legally accepted tests of the disease process known as insanity. M'Naghten, Durham, American Law Institute, irresistible impulse."

"More and more it's an unpopular view, a disputed verdict; and there is no doubt that the liberal picture of insanity has resulted in its fair share of courtroom abuses."

"Well, we're not moralists, Tommie, not required to be, and the legal system doesn't reward innovative trial lawyers."

"Nevertheless, popular views can become law, under certain conditions. Today the reactionary view on insanity is much easier to sell to juries than it once was, because people have had a bellyful of letting murderers go free. From all appearances *Vermont* v. *Devon* will be a classic case, closely watched; as you know, there is already a rather baleful glare of publicity. I think you may want to read up on *California* v. *Cromer*. The defense had everything in its favor, just as you feel you have. A woman killed her child; it was a crime conceived by an unquestionably disturbed mind. Cromer had been hospitalized for mental illness, and she was under continuous treatment for a number of years, with no periods of remission. Yet the jury found the fact of her illness not exculpating, and she was convicted of the murder."

"I don't know the case," Adam admitted.

"It's appropriate to my contention that we have come to a critical juncture in modern jurisprudence. Our standards for insanity are no standards at all. It's the main reason why I'm deeply interested in the conduct of this forthcoming trial: I sense an opportunity, through exhaustive examination of the issues, to establish a workable alternative to the 'mad or bad' criteria, a clinical picture of insanity which will quite clearly separate the degree of responsibility and the degree of punishability."

Lindsay, sitting there tired but fascinated, had an insight into the forces that had made Harkrider a great litigator. His pull was powerful, nervewracking. She felt as if she were under the influence of a full moon that had overstayed, refusing to wane.

Adam said carefully, "I'm not sure I follow you."

"What I advocate is a two-stage trial. In the first stage the jury will be asked to decide if the defendant did in fact bring about the death of Karyn Vale, regardless of his mental disability. In the second stage, the jury will decide, according to the severity of that disability, if the punishment for the crime should be subordinate to the treatment and possible rehabilitation of the defendant, with the protection of the public as the main consideration in reaching their decision."

"Changes similar to your two-stage trial have been proposed in the past."

"They have," Harkrider agreed.

"The result is, the absence of mens rea is no longer accepted as a negation of intention; therefore the insanity defense is effectively abolished. Which certainly makes the prosecutor's job easier, if not the jury's. Have you talked to Gary Cleves about this?"

"He has provided an attentive ear."

"I'll bet. I wonder if a two-stage trial is possible under Vermont law?"

"I've researched that. The latitude exists in the statutes of many states, not only Vermont's. But the decision to conduct such a trial rests with the presiding judge."

Lindsay said, "And the counsel for the defense."

"Your cooperation would be essential."

"What it amounts to is a relinquishing of my client's

rights under existing laws. He would walk into the courtroom a guilty man, with nothing left to do but decide how
to dispose of him. I don't want to be known as the
criminal lawyer who surrendered his client to a lab experiment and then congratulated him on his pioneering status
as he went off to serve a forty-to-life.''

Adam spoke softly, without sarcasm, running a hand
through his uncombed hair; Lindsay noticed how thin it
was without the camouflage afforded by blow-drying. The
brackets around his mouth were prematurely deepened by
the placement of the overhead lamp. Lindsay looked at her
hands—they were ivory yellow in this light, the slight
sordidness of faded suntan—and at nails with chipped
polish she had no time to repair. Tommie Harkrider twirled
the toy-sized sparkling liqueur glass between his thumb
and forefinger, musing, legs crossed, a disreputable old
shoe dancing. He seemed unrebuked, cheerfully full of
himself, dangerous in his status. Although he had been
there scarcely fifteen minutes, his bulky presence had
evolved into something permanent; their lives henceforth
would be furnished with that something, unwished-for but
difficult to remove, like a dark unplayable grand piano
willed by a distant relative.

''Your assumption is understandably hasty,'' Harkrider
said, pushing a finger slowly through the air as if repulsing
a creeping tension between them. ''I think you'll agree the
proposal is worthy of further consideration, if only because
it provides a viable alternative to almost certain defeat. In
terms of what is best for your client, and your own pres-
tige, a harsh rejection by a jury of the liberal insanity
picture will, at this point in time, because of the scrutiny
this case inevitably must bear, have far-reaching consequences. *It will open the floodgates for reform!* Will Adam
Kurland be praised for his foresightedness and courage or
will he be largely forgotten? I can't answer that question—
we've only just met. Now, I didn't come here tonight to
sell you a bill of goods—it's just one hired gunslinger
sitting down for a chat with another. What I've hoped to
accomplish is to stretch your angle of vision a little bit.
The matter under advisement will take time; it will require
earnest study by all the parties involved. But I am *deeply*
convinced that, one way or another, Adam Kurland is

destined to be involved in legal history before *Vermont* v. *Devon* reaches its conclusion.''

A beeper attached to his belt went off; Tommie Harkrider rose promptly, struggling just a little to balance himself on his feet. ''That's a call waiting for me in the limo; but I need to be on the road anyway. I'd be very pleased if the three of us could have lunch one day in the city. I don't fly myself, but I'll send the firm's plane for you, save you some time. I know how busy you'll be for the next few weeks.''

''Thank you,'' Adam and Lindsay said, almost in unison; they glanced at each other self-consciously, and Lindsay went to retrieve the old lawyer's coat and muffler.

''My all-time favorite actor,'' Harkrider said to Adam as they walked to the door, ''is Spencer Tracy. He's before your time—Spence died along about '67, '68—but you may have caught him on the late show in something with Kate, or—''

''Inherit the Wind.''

''One of his best roles. He *was* Clarence Darrow, and you want to know something? Spence could have made one of the finest criminal lawyers who ever drew breath. Can't say that about many of the great ones. Brando? Bogart? Nah. But Spence—I represented him in some little matter once, forget now what it was. I said to him one day, 'Spence, what's acting?' He thought about it for a few seconds, pushing his lower lip out, seen him do it a thousand times, and then he came back with 'Acting is standing there, and listening as if your life depended on it.' That's an apt description of the successful trial lawyer. But how many have the God-given ability? You remind me a little of Spence, not in looks, but in the way you handle yourself. I feel good about our little tête-à-tête— because I *know* you've been listening. I like what you do with your hands as well. I mean, you don't use 'em much when you talk. Hardest damn thing in the world to learn, whether you're an actor or a lawyer addressing a jury. What to do with the hands. Good-night!—'Bye, honey.''

He clapped Adam on the shoulder, hunched down to buss Lindsay's cheek, mouth reeking with that brownish salt reminder of old cigars, and took himself across the deck with eager little steps. The door closed, their heads turned, their eyes met; Lindsay, feeling a little flimsy as if in the aftermath of a huge slow-moving storm, said, "You ought to see your face."

Adam laughed dourly, his only comment.

"He must mean business," Lindsay said. She was a little walleyed from fatigue.

"Why now?" Adam mulled. "Why me? Well, it won't work. I can't be intimidated. So it's going to be Harkrider—I knew something like this was inevitable. Martin Vale, all his muscle, we couldn't expect him to do nothing. He wants blood."

"Did you have the feeling that Tommie was going to burp, and up would come bits of Gary Cleves?"

The space around them, which had seemed queerly dilated to accommodate the majesty of their midnight visitor, vibrated from implications. Adam fixed them each a nightcap, sticking to gin. Gimlets. He juiced fresh limes. By then a snaky flow of adrenaline had him aloft like a Japanese kite, from which vantage point he surveyed new terrain of challenge and confrontation—the ones for which he had been dutifully preparing, and which surely would define his life thereafter. He wanted to talk and Linds wanted to sleep, but with the vacant resolve and footsore goodwill of a door-to-door hawker of religious pamphlets, she listened to his opinions. Trial research, law of evidence, a shadow jury: by the time he had finished she felt hollow, a cavern of insomnia in which she nodded, lashes fluttering like bats, but grateful, as if they already had tried the case, and won hands-down.

But no amount of discussion, or the pooled experiences of their young lives, could have prepared them for what the morning would bring.

45

At ten A.M. Conor Devon was waiting for them on the courthouse steps wearing his familiar ratty plaid topcoat and red earmuffs. The unclouded sky foretold a cold but tranquil day; his eyes, of a like shade of blue, held more troublesome weather: a burning, a tumult. He grasped Adam's hand and glanced unsmilingly at Lindsay and said, "I stopped by Captain Moorman's office this morning. Something you ought to know. On the fourteenth of January, that's three weeks ago, Polly Windross left St. Janvier in Quebec. Her aunt put her on a bus for Montreal. Her father was supposed to meet her there. But the last anyone saw of Polly, except for Rich, was when she got off that bus at the terminal in Montreal. And now as you know her father is dead, run over by a train."

Adam looked thoughtfully at the big man and then put a hand on his elbow to indicate they should proceed inside. Conor walked up the remaining steps between the two lawyers.

Adam said, "It's never been clear to me why you believe there's a connection between Polly Windross and her father and the murder Rich is being held for. Have you been keeping something from us, Conor?"

Conor opened the brassbound courthouse doors for them. "There *is* a connection, but I haven't been able to prove it. Today I think I can."

Lindsay said, "Well, shouldn't you tell us what's on your mind before we go in to see Rich?"

"I want you to hear the story from Rich, in his own words."

In an antechamber of the interview room where Richard Devon had met with the psychologist Maggie Renquist a week ago they took off their coats and the two lawyers opened their briefcases to inspection. Conor had with him a sealed carton of cigarettes, filtertip Kents, for Rich, and a gold crucifix six inches long. The guard held the crucifix suspiciously in the palm of his hand for a few moments. There were no sharp edges. It weighed only ounces and would have made a poor weapon. He allowed Conor to pocket it.

They served themselves at a Mr. Coffee machine and filed into the interview room while the guard telephoned the jail. Conor went directly to the single window and adjusted the blinds to let more light in. The glass, which contained a webbing of wire, was covered with little chiseled fans of frost; there was a heavy grill fastened to the outside of the window. He kept his broad back to them, uncommunicatively, while Adam told him about the visit from Tommie Harkrider. Lindsay put a fresh minicassette into her Dictamite and tested to make sure it was recording.

Conor replied, "What they want to do is take away your means to defend Rich?"

"That's how it shapes up. Needless to say I have no intention—"

"Maybe there's a better defense. Because as I've been telling you all along, my brother isn't insane."

Adam said, with weary forbearance, "If there's any other possible line of defense, I haven't heard—"

The door to the interview room opened and Rich was escorted in, wearing one of the wrinkled cotton jumpsuits and a jail sweat shirt with a hood, which lay bunched at the back of his neck. He was beginning to need a haircut. He had not shaved this morning. He looked patchy and transient, an habitué of breadlines. There was a puckered Band-Aid on one cheek the color of the jumpsuit. His eyes were flat and mild, his lips seemed glued together in a complex way; he had an air of half-amused disenchantment. His hands were at his sides, asymmetrical, one palm in, one palm out, as if they had nothing to do with the rest of his body. He stood near the center of the room with his head hung shy of the light, not speaking until the door closed again, looking surreptitiously toward Conor, who was slow to turn away from the window.

"Hi, Conor. Haven't seen you for a while." There was no recrimination in his voice; it was just an acknowledgement, an acceptance of things as they had to be.

"Well, I need to earn a living, kid," Conor said a little gruffly; something hard to swallow in his throat.

"Sure." Rich, still motionless, passed his eyes over Adam and Lindsay, who smiled; his lips reacted, as if he had borrowed the smile and was returning it as unusable. Lastly he noticed the carton of cigarettes on the table. "Are those for me?"

Conor had turned; he was staring hard at Rich, his own eyes rimmed in liquid red. He was so tragic in appearance that Adam was alarmed.

In his movement toward his brother Conor had created a field of tension which Adam felt as something inward, hard and low like a threatening appendix, and he glanced at Lindsay for confirmation of his misgiving. Maybe it hadn't been such a good idea, bringing Conor up here, until they had taken him firmly aside and grilled him to learn what was on his mind.

But all Conor said was "Help yourself to the cigarettes, Rich."

"I wouldn't mind having one myself," Lindsay proposed. She was a sometime smoker who could quit at will; Adam hadn't seen her light up in weeks.

Rich nodded, and Lindsay broke open the carton, took two cigarettes out of a pack, handed one to him. Adam decided he might as well smoke, too, and produced his Dunhill lighter. Conor stood on the outside of this ritual, brooding, spellbound.

"Tastes good," Rich said, nodding gratefully. He inhaled again, let the blue smoke sift out through his nostrils. He sat in a straight chair and crossed one leg over the other. The soiled slipper fell off. His toenails were blue. He raised his eyes to Conor again. Something about the light, inimical, struck across his pupils, canceling them.

"Rich," Conor said. "You asked me to help you. And I, I've done my level best. I saw Captain Moorman again this morning. Windross is dead, there's no trace of Inez Cordway. And Polly Windross seems to have disappeared. You may have been the last one to see her."

Rich, admitting nothing, took a stout drag on his cigarette, head lowering, chin tucked in, until his forehead and blond hairline were brazen in the flat stroke of sun; his gaze, foreshortened, was that of a blind man.

"What we need to know—what you have to tell us now, so we can continue to try to help you and get you out of here—is everything that happened the night you saw Polly. Rich—do you remember now?"

Lindsay sat down near Rich and to his left, the little tape recorder unobtrusive in one hand; with the other she smoked. Adam stood where he could observe both Rich and Conor. He still felt painfully apprehensive, but didn't know why.

"I remember." As if roughened by the cigarette, Rich's voice sounded gutteral.

Conor said, quietly, "Tell us."

Rich's head shot up; his eyes, wide open, seemed to pull in the light at a terrible velocity; then the light was reversed in a glare of alien ardor as his mouth savored self-satisfaction; his voice was a feeding animal's growl at being disturbed.

"I sodomized the piglet. Babyshit and blood and come were dribbling from her scrumptious pink asshole. I shot off in her face, you should have seen her lap it up. And then I broke her cherry, I fucked her till she fainted."

Lindsay's hand had paused, halfway to her lips, her face so burdened with shock and surprise the weight seemed to make her nod involuntarily; she blinked haplessly when Rich's head jerked toward her. His mouth, which was open, showed the gap where one front tooth had been. The incompleteness looked bestial.

He spoke again from deep in his throat while ice crept under her scalp and froze all her joints; his lips and tongue didn't move. "Ask Conor about lust; ask him about sodomy. He jerked off just last night, alone in a motel, thinking about your slick little cunt. He came in his sock, and cried afterwards."

"You're not my brother!"

The head jerked again, the eyes narrowed drastically. He had kicked off the other slipper and both feet were on the floor, clenched like claws, the toenails scraping and screeching. His hands were poised on his knees, cigarette smoldering between two fingers.

"Stay where you are. Don't touch me, spoiled priest! Keep your hands in your pockets. Leave. Don't come again. I don't need you for *anything*."

Conor began to move with a certain light-footed grace,

as if he were in the wrestling ring, left hand in the pocket of his jacket, right hand free and raised and ready to grapple; he moved not toward Rich but around him, tenaciously intent on the mussed blond head, and when he encountered Adam in his way the lawyer backed off without having to be told.

Rich turned a little in the chair with each step Conor took, keeping him fully in view. His brow creased, his mouth settled in an uneasy crimp.

"Hey, what's wrong, Conor?" he said in a more recognizable voice, his tone nasal and whining. His hands fidgeted. "Can't you take a little joke? Of course it's me: Rich. Why are you acting like this? You're not going to hurt me, are you?" The whining was more pronounced; he cringed. "I haven't done anything to you. Don't you know I love you, Conor?"

Conor, still pacing, motioned for Lindsay to get out of her chair, which she did with alacrity, banging a knee against the underside of the table. She hobbled backward into Adam, who grasped her and said, "Conor, listen, I think—"

Conor, staring Rich down, said fiercely, "In the name of our Lord Jesus Christ—"

"*Shut up you bag of shit!* You're going to die of cancer, let me be the first to tell you; you won't live to see Charley-chuck graduate high school!"

With a move that was almost too quick for the eyes of the lawyers to follow, Conor reached out and plucked Rich from the seat of the chair and flung him face-first against the farthest wall. From his coat pocket he withdrew the crucifix. The room was charged with violence; light flashed hotly from the gold in Conor's hand. He pounced on Rich, who had rebounded and collapsed full-length, and was trying, stunned, to rise. He held the crucifix inches from the back of the boy's head.

"Demon, Serpent, Foul Tyrant, I show you the cross of our most precious Lord! God, the Father of us all commands thee! Obey Him! Reveal thyself, speak your name, filthy spirit, despised of heaven! Imp of Satan: the Father, the Son, and the Holy Spirit abjure you, begone!"

One of Lindsay's vivid memories was of a disaster witnessed, when she was ten years old, at a fair in the state of New Hampshire, on a September weekend of early russet and flame orange in the trees, of thunderheads and rumblings in the languorous middle distance. Above the fairgrounds, where all motion was intensified, mad and elliptical, the sky was like a very old dome of Lucite, abraded with so many tiny scratches that the power of the invisible sun gave it a prickly radiance. The air itself was sultry and down to earth, unmoving; fine dust floated at the ankles like marsh gas, partially obscuring the black-snake cables that everywhere nerved the metal bodies of jolting, swaying, high-flying machines. She had wandered, agog, with an older brother named Robert who also was adopted, and who ached to be rid of her so he could fling himself into the pandemonium of a ride worth bragging about afterwards. With a cakey dryness about the lips, the sweetness of cotton candy filming her teeth, numb to cacophony and in her element, little Linds saw out of the corner of her eye a switched-on filament of stilted brilliance in the no-color sky, heard mobbed shrieks out of tenor with the cries of thrillseekers. She saw a loaded ferris wheel fall down like clumsy jackstraws. This happened with a veiled slowness, as if it was the ultimate excitement the day would offer, a logical progression of imploding reality, even as her mind shied ever so delicately away from the hard truth of catastrophe. Robert had scooped her up and run away with her before reality could be turned rightside-out again, but thereafter Lindsay dwelled on those fantastical moments in dreams—that measured stroke of doom, the disjointed ferris wheel; the fated falling bodies.

This time, in a fifteen-by-fifteen chamber in which there was no room to run, the stroke of doom again had no sound, though she went immediately deaf as if both eardrums had collapsed; rather she felt it inside of her, the raging scream, whatever it was, like a knife blade scraping interminably against living bone.

A number of grotesque, absurd, and terrifying things happened, perhaps simultaneously, while reality imploded all around them.

Rich seemed to vault high in the air, as if from a flexible floor, and, airborne, formed himself into a strict ball like a gymnast, head tucked against his knees, hands grasping his ankles; his eyes, like those of a fetus, were serenely sealed, his face looked untroubled by the trauma of birth. He went ricocheting with maniacal speed all around the room, floor to wall to ceiling and back again. Conor tried to catch him, as if he were a mammoth medicine ball. Conor was knocked flat and his nose, broken, spurted blood.

The venetian blind over the window flew riffling at the vertical, perhaps gravitationally attracted to the eccentrically orbiting body. Then the slats began separating with snickering, whispery sounds; swift sabers of metal whirled over their heads. Adam tackled Lindsay and dragged her down, but not before she was slashed across the forehead.

The carton of cigarettes on the table exploded. Lighted filtertips joined the rustling paper debris from their briefcases and there were puffs of flame; smoke spread throughout the room.

And Rich kept bouncing, bounding along, his flesh turning an ugly purplish red from impact, his skull knocking hard against every surface.

As Conor struggled to hold his crucifix upright it began to soften and melt in his hand, searing the flesh.

Conor crawled to the door on hands and knees as if he were going through a field deep in mud. He flung the door open, and the hurricane in the room ceased instantly. Rich went sprawling to the floor a foot from the corner where Adam and Lindsay were huddled; he was bleeding copiously from his nose, ears, mouth, and anus. His jumpsuit was ripped in a dozen places. He had welts all over his exposed flesh. He looked dead.

Lindsay pried herself loose from Adam and climbed over the inert Rich, scuffed through bent slats of venetian blinds and still-smoldering cigarettes and litter of paper on the floor, blinked earnestly trying to see through the blood pouring down her forehead and matting her eyelashes, and hauled herself out the door with a solemn series of groans.

She ran through the antechamber, past the startled guards there; they called to her but she couldn't hear. The high heel of a snowboot broke off and she nearly tumbled down the broad marble steps but clung to a polished brass railing and kept going, eyes saucy and dim from blood, to the doors across the shadowy lobby, out into the bright, pink-toned, eerily silent morning. There she pitched headfirst into a snowbank and rolled tormentedly, striping the snow red, putting out the blaze of pain on her forehead with deep cold. She felt hands on her body trying to lift, to comfort her, but she knew they were the wrong hands.

Then at last the hands were Adam's and she yielded to him, daring to sit up, to look him in the face.

He was pale but unvanquished, the brown eyes shocked but mercifully sane. He spoke to her; she heard something finally, but not his voice: it was a sudden electronic burp of police siren, piercing. Past his shoulder she saw state policemen, running into the courthouse, their guns drawn. Why? She stared imploringly at Adam and moved her own numb lips, ran a hand over her wet freezing face, and passed out in his arms.

46

Hillary Devon, on the telephone with her Blessed Sacrament classmate Beth LeMaster, said, "Look, Beth, it's the same formula, you just have to analyze the problem, break it down so you know what information is given. You know the *rate*. You know the *percentage*. So you let m represent the base. Five over one hundred equals thirteen over m. Multiply. Get it?"

"When you explain it to me I do, but then I can't remember how on tests. Oh, Goddd. I *loathe* pre-algebra."

"We both have first period free in the morning, I'll show you then. It's really very simple."

"It's all simple for you, Hillary," Beth said, not sounding sarcastic exactly; it was more of an airy, slighting tone that got on Hillary's nerves quite easily. *What you're good at doesn't count.*

They had been friends, on and off, since first grade, and were currently going through more or less a togetherness phase, being, but not by preference, in the same car pool. Beth could go cold and picky and say without warning something meant to be unforgivable. She was like that; a born manipulator. Hillary hung in there partly because their mothers were close. Also Beth's brother Dan was fourteen, and a dream, and Hillary didn't have much excuse for hanging around him unless she was visiting Beth.

Beth yawned, signaling a change of subject. She said, "What do you think of the new father?"

"For a Jesuit he's not hard to take. Do you think he really told Barb and Conni that joke about Superman flying over the nudist colony?"

"Sure. What's wrong with that?"

"Well—it's dirty, isn't it?"

Beth whooped. "You mean you didn't *get* it?"

"I know what a hard-on is," Hillary said defensively.

"But have you seen one?" Beth said, with a little snigger that Hillary found disgusting.

No, and you haven't either, she wanted to say, but she wasn't so sure. Beth was thirteen and a half. She had menstruated. She was a woman already. Hillary felt poignantly remorseful over her own ambiguous status. It was her turn to change the subject. She said, "Samantha and I couldn't get our locker open today. It was like somebody changed the combination on us. Mr. Eccles will have to drill the old lock out. Samantha threw a *fit.* All of her best glossies were inside and she had an appointment in Boston this afternoon with that woman from the New York agency, the one who discovered Brooke Shields."

"Oh, Samantha. I can't understand why everybody thinks she's so *beautiful.* If her eyes were any farther apart they'd be behind her ears."

Looking up, Hillary saw Dean passing by her bedroom door. She called to him.

"If you're going to the kitchen, would you bring me an apple?"

"Why?"

"Because I cleared the supper dishes for you tonight. Because I'm *hungry,* and I want an apple. Do you need ninety-nine perfect reasons to do somebody a favor, dummy?"

"Shine. I don't do favors for anybody who calls me dummy."

"I'm sorry, I apologizzzze! Please, Dean? Bring me an apple."

Beth said in her ear, "Who's your new friend?"

"That was Dean I was talking to."

"No, I mean the girl you walked home with from jazz ballet. Does she live on your street?"

"What girl? I didn't walk home, I walked a couple of blocks over to the IGA on the square and Mom picked me up in front a few minutes later. Nobody was with me."

"You were on Sorenson Street about four thirty, right?"

"Yes, but—"

"So Judy McRudd saw you. Is it some kind of big secret? I just asked you who the other girl was. Judy didn't know her."

"Beth, I told you. I was by myself."

"Be that way. Judy says she was blond; long blond hair, a little taller than you. She was wearing a red tam and a light green cape with a dark green border like the girls at McMorrow Academy have. So who is she, is all I want to know. Is she in your class?"

After a few moments of utter blankness Hillary said, "There are a lot of blond girls in my class. But I know I was by myself today, and I only walked as far as the supermarket. Maybe Judy saw somebody she *thought* was me."

"Okayyy," Beth said, like it couldn't matter less to her, but Hillary's cheeks burned slightly, almost as if she were guilty of something, the subject of ribald teenage gossip tonight all over Joshua. Why, when she was being totally truthful, should she be made to feel like a liar? She wished Beth's mother would come along and bellow at her for being on the phone too long.

"Look, Beth, it's a long nickel and I've got six chapters of *David Copperfield* to finish before my reading enrichment quiz tomorrow."

"Hillareeee, I don't know how you can stand all those *boring* books."

"I just like to read. Good-night, Beth."

After she hung up, Hillary stayed on her back in the center of her bed, feet elegantly elevated, studying hints of toes through the holes in her athletic socks. The aerator in her twenty-gallon fish tank purled soothingly, but her mind was in discord. She definitely had *not* been within twenty feet of any blond girl in a pale green cape today on Sorensen Street, period. Just like Beth to find the most insignificant little thing to nag about, make it seem mysterious—oh, what the hell. Let it go. It had been her most heartfelt New Year's resolution, *I will not let Beth LeMaster get the best of me in nineteen eighty—*

Dean, again passing by her door, lobbed a gleaming McIntosh the size of a softball; it struck her on the tender inside of one thigh.

Hillary collapsed in a tangle of legs. "Oww, *Dean*, why don't you watch what you're doing?"

"No brains, no pain," Dean said enigmatically, vanishing in the direction of his and Charley-chuck's room at the other end of the hall.

Hillary located the apple, which had rolled off the bed. She was about to crunch into it when she noticed that Dean—thoughtlessly as usual—hadn't washed the apple after taking it from the refrigerator; there were traces of milky dried insecticide around the stem. Ugh. Supposedly the spray was harmless to humans only minutes after it was first applied, but Hillary believed in being careful. She took the apple into her bathroom, ran cold water over it, and dried it thoroughly with a hand towel. Then she decided to take her shower and get ready for bed first; she would eat the apple while she zipped cozily through the remaining pages of *Copperfield*.

She put the apple on the end of the shelf above the pink porcelain sink, turned on the shower, and adjusted the temperature of the water. She pulled off her hockey jersey and black leotards and the gym shorts she had been wearing over the leotards, pinned her hair up hummingly, and sealed it against moisture with a pleated plastic cap. She got out a fresh figured bath sheet, left it folded on top of the covered commode, slid back the fluted opaque glass shower door, stepped over the side of the tub into the steamy downpour from the showerhead. For nearly ten minutes Hillary soaked and rubbed herself all over with the slidey softening bar of lilac-fragrant soap, making loops of quick-melting lather around her nipples, which in their recent burgeoning had become endlessly fascinating to her. She had a real cleft now between her breasts into which, when she pushed her shoulders forward, the soap half disappeared.

Down *there,* so far, nothing much seemed to be happening; a certain hippiness had overtaken her, and when she went to the toilet lately she had noticed a rusty fuzziness she could almost scrape off with her fingernail. She had learned that she could, by passing her bar of soap back and forth dreamily between tightened thighs, rub up a dense, tickly thicket of sensation, which left her feeling big-headed and drowsy and fumbly. Sometimes she cleaned herself too long that way and had to pull back, panicked, from the brink of something that felt imperative but *wrong;* then she would be miserable and cross, unable to be so easily rid of that insinuating thickety wrongness in her loins. Those were the nights when she couldn't go to sleep until she lay on her side with a pillow clenched between her legs, rocking gently, easing down from the pinnacle upon which she had nearly stranded herself.

Once she had rinsed, Hillary shut off the water and slid the door back. Through the mist that filled the bathroom something dark flickered; she barely saw it but was bothered. She reached for the bath sheet and pressed it, still folded, against her face and then her breasts.

As she was blotting downward she turned her head slightly toward the fogged mirror, and noticed, on the shelf, the brown wizened core of the apple she had placed there. It seemed to be acrawl with flies. As she was trying to make sense of this, one of the flies, big and soft and greenish, struck her buzzingly above her left nipple; she let out a little shrill cry of consternation and disgust. Instead of winging away, the fly seemed to disintegrate into a pulpy mess. The wings fell off. It slithered over the nipple and left a nauseating track on her skin, making her twitch involuntarily; what was left plopped onto the bath mat. Other flies took off from the remains of the apple and circled in the thinning mist, coming close to her head. Hillary flung the bath sheet about—flies in February? They had never had flies like this in the house at *any* season. Several of the flies, struck, fell into the tub, the treaded bottom of which was still covered with a foam of soapsuds. Hillary dropped the towel and turned on the shower full force; these flies also began to disintegrate. She grabbed the wash cloth and cleaned her tingling breast, snatched off the showercap and went running naked, half-dried, into her bedroom, banging the bathroom door closed behind her. For several moments she stood panting, electric, directionless, staring at herself in the mirror on the back of the closet door. Then, face reddening, she flung herself at the dresser, pulled out underpants and pajamas, put them on.

She opened the bathroom door again, slowly, and peered inside. No flies. The apple core was still there. She reached in and snatched it off the shelf, went running down the hall to the boys' room, opened their door, burst out crying, and flung the core at Dean's head.

"You think you're so damn funny, Dean! There are flies all over my bathroom!"

The apple core missed him widely and skidded off a poster advertising *Return of the Jedi*, landing on top of the hamsters' cage. The animals leaped and skittered, falling back in a palpitating huddle behind their water bottle.

Charley looked up in amazement from the handle of the hockey stick he was wrapping with tape.

"What's the matter with *you*?" Dean said.

"You know what! *You know!* You snuck in while I was taking my shower, invaded my privacy, took the apple I was saving, and left that rotten p-piece of garbage, and it drew *flies*!"

"No, I didn't," he said, growing hostile in the face of these absurd, unanswerable accusations.

"You're a damn liar!"

"I've been here all the time! Ask Charley-chuck."

"You're *both* big liars. I'm gonna tell Mom, I'm sick and tired of the way you treat me all the time, you think because I'm a girl you can get away with it." She stamped her bare foot as Charley's face creased in a befuddled grin. "It wasn't funny, it wasn't!"

"Stop this."

Their father's voice, so unexpected—he had returned home unnoticed by them only minutes ago—snuffed the argument. All eyes went to him, Hillary's still weeping.

Conor stood in the doorway, taking up almost all of the space, staring feverishly at them through slits where the flesh around his own eyes, dark as plums, hadn't quite swollen shut. His nose, also huge across the bridge, was taped. The edges of the tape lapped down unevenly over his cheekbones. Together with the bulges he had for eyes he seemed to be wearing some sort of complicated, profane mask, unspeakably dismaying in its crude symbolism, imbued with a pagan love of death. His left hand had been so thoroughly wrapped in stapled, flesh-colored hospital bandage that only the blunt fingertips showed. Conor held the hand, rather awkwardly, unsupported across his chest. In all the years he had earned his living as a professional wrestler he had never shown himself at home looking so thoroughly ravaged.

Hillary, with a galloping, thundering heart that dragged her attention behind it, glimpsed past him, where his side wasn't touching the door jamb, her mother's face, rinsed of color, flattened by a fright so vast she seemed only just recovered from the throes of a scream no one had heard. The level of blood in Hillary's body fell to her knees, leaving her head an unsupportable stone weight. Darkness; the miasma of deep melancholy she knew so well. She saw, as if from the distance of the moon, to the precious center of her life, now visited by purposeless corruption: the browning of an apple, the bath full of windy overblown flies. Jarred loose from her senses, she touched a cold breast moving in time to her immense heartbeat; she clasped a hand over her widened mouth so as not to let death in. The pupils of her eyes turned chalky. She gagged on hysteria and fell thrashing to the floor.

47

At six fifteen in the morning it was still pitch dark when Father James Merlo drove a Honda Accord into the parking lot of the Arcadia Winter Sports Center on Route 38 just north of the Joshua city limits. Even at that hour there were approximately three dozen other cars and recreational vehicles in the lot, grouped near the entrance to the fabricated steel building.

He got out of his stubby rental car, a surprisingly long-legged black man who wore a navy pea coat over boot-cut corduroys and a turtleneck sweater. He walked into the ice arena, which was reverberating with the sounds of a youth league hockey game in progress on one of the full-size rinks. The other rink was occupied exclusively by figure skaters who looked, even the youngest, to be dashingly adept, with the self-bewitched grace of cygnets coasting in a doze on mirrored surfaces. In contrast to the boisterous hockey players the skaters worked in a chilled, almost ethereal silence except for terse comments by coaches who were videotaping the sessions and the hiss, as of ripping silk, of blades on milk-toned ice.

Lingering for a few moments, Merlo admired the form of a young blond boy with a glossy thatch of hair; he seemed unbound by the demands of gravity as he careened through splits and backspins for which the priest had no names. He had never tried skating himself; it was all his parents could do to keep him in sneakers when he was growing up.

He paused at the snack stand to buy hot chocolate and a day-old cinnamon doughnut, munched his breakfast as he entered the arena where helmeted small fry were spanking the boards and sprawling ungracefully in pursuit of the puck. A referee swooped in with whistle shrilling to stop the action. There was a tier of green-painted bleachers on one side of the arena rising almost to the struts beneath the corrugated roof; Merlo looked up at little knots of spectators, all of them presumably family, at two more teams sitting edgily in a forest of upstanding hockey sticks, waiting for this game to end so they could have their turn on the ice. The fathers and mothers were doing an admirable job of demonstrating spirit and enthusiasm, considering most of them had probably been up at four thirty to get their kids here.

The priest spotted his man, who was sitting alone, with little difficulty: that beard was like a flag of provocation in the slightly fogged gloom of the upper stands. Merlo licked a residue of cinnamon and sugar from his fingertips, took a couple of swallows of the watery beverage, which tasted only vaguely of chocolate, and proceeded up into the bleachers three steps at a time.

"Conor Devon?"

Conor looked up questioningly, then flicked his eyes back to the ice, where a tall boy suddenly sprinted away from the snarled face-off with the puck teetering at the end of his stick; he headed for the opposing team's goal.

"All right, all the way!" he shouted. "Take your time, Charley-chuck, fake him out of there!" Conor half rose from his seat, ignoring Merlo, who also had turned his head to watch the action. Charley approached the goal from the left side, hesitated, then made as if to cut sharply to his right, causing the goalie to shift his balance too far in the direction of the anticipated thrust. The goalie fell down. Charley put on the brakes, wobbled, sighted open net, and fired the puck from a distance of fifteen feet. It went in.

"Yeah!" Conor cheered hoarsely. Merlo looked up at the little scoreboard where the tally had registered. Blackhawks 7, Maple Leafs 2, third period.

"That your boy?"

Conor glanced at the priest again, nodding. His eyes, so badly blackened two weeks ago, now looked almost normal, except for streaks of apple green and dingy yellow in the fleshy orbits. His nose, healed, was back to human proportions. His left hand, showing patches of shiny new skin, was still partially wrapped in an elastic bandage that allowed him to stretch and flex the muscles while protecting the unhealed portion of his palm and thumb, where skin grafts had been necessary.

Merlo held out his own hand. "I'm Father Merlo."

He didn't mind Conor's surprise—he had expected it. Nor did he mind the hesitation before Conor reached across his body to shake the offered hand.

"You're an exorcist?"

"Uh-huh. You look a little disappointed. Who were you expecting, Max von Sydow?"

"I—I didn't know what—who to expect."

Conor tried to size up Merlo in the nimbus of light from the ice rink. His skin was the color of eggplant. His cheeks were lean, unshaven, with a two-day growth of beard. His eyes had a slight sardonic tilt to them, a hint of the Orient in the tautness of the lids. His face still had the luster, the ease, the complacency of a favored young man. But his hair had been condensed, as if by conflagration, to an ashy skullcap. His ears pressed very close to naked runneled skin; his high and thickly boned forehead looked like a battering ram.

Merlo said patiently, "Do you want me to sit down, or did you just decide you don't need me anymore? That's okay; no hard feelings. I'll go get myself some sleep. Haven't had any for the last sixty hours."

"I—yes; I need you. I'm sorry. I didn't expect anyone to show up here, at this time of the morning. Please sit down, Father."

"Thanks." The priest nodded toward Conor's left hand. "Looks like that was a pretty bad burn."

"It's getting better now."

"Your boy there is a hard skater. What's his name—Charley? I guess athletics run in your family. Monsignor Garen said you were a pro wrestler. I can believe it; you've got *some* size on you, my man. I spent a year in the NBA myself, with the Bullets. I did my college at St. Peter's, third leading scorer in the history of the school. But I was a step too slow for the pros. Couldn't get my shots off, some jig the size of King Kong was always there to stuff the ball in my ear or steal it for a layup. And the *moves* they can put on you; the in-your-face disgrace shots: a very humbling experience. Earl the Pearl; Dr. J."

He seemed to be talking, not in a vaguely self-conscious, getting-acquainted manner but from a sense of release, wordiness being his way of repositioning his psychic furniture after a long stay in some nether realm of the lost and afflicted. Also he seemed, in the slack way he occupied the narrow bleacher plank, his knees cocked high and spread, boot heels propped against the green plank below, nomadic and perilously tired. "What else would you like to know about me? I was born and raised in the South Ward in Newark, when that was a good neighborhood to be from. My father worked for the Port Authority and my mother is a cosmetician. I was a grunt in Vietnam early on, back about '66, and that's where I began to do some serious thinking about my religion, trying to decide if I might be of some use to the Church. Well, after seminary I was assigned to Holy Rosary parish on 153rd Street in the south Bronx. That parish for some reason is a hotbed of witchcraft, voodoo, and the whole occult bag; we were always getting calls to untangle somebody from Satan. Some days it got so bad I thought I was back in Saigon. My experiences at Holy Rosary got me drafted by the Apostolic Penitentiary. For the last few years I've studied ancient languages. I've also been involved in close to a hundred exorcisms; the most recent ended six hours ago.''

''Around here?'' Conor said incredulously.

''In Providence, Rhode Island. An infestation, not a possession. Demons. Scuzzy little varmints without much status in the Kingdom, and no willpower. I threw the Book at them and they lit out like bats flocking home to a cave at sunrise.''

The priest hitched around and looked Conor in the eye. ''I hear you've got a worse problem.''

''I—I think so.''

''Before you explain,'' Merlo said, ''I should tell you I came up here this morning as a favor to a friend of a friend. I'm a priest of Rome and I don't have official status in any diocese; this is my day off, so to speak.''

''What does it matter?'' Conor said with an edge of exasperation. ''I need help, and the Church—''

''The Church, as we both know, is run by canon law; and in my line of work we follow even stricter rules of procedure or live to regret our lapses. I may not be able to give you much more than advice. With that in mind, do you want to tell me what happened? I prefer to ask questions as we go along, if that's okay.''

Conor began with his first meeting with Rich in the Haden County jail, his brother's desperate appeals to him to find Henry Windross and Polly and the mysterious Inez Cordway.

''Exactly how did Richard implicate these people in his supposed situation?''

''He didn't make that very clear to me. He said he had been trying to help Polly, but she died. Those are almost his exact words.''

''None of them have turned up since the night of the murder?''

''Windross was struck and killed by a train a few days later. Polly, according to the police, disappeared even before Rich claimed to have seen her in that room in the Post Road Inn. She's still officially listed as missing.''

"Have you been inside the house in—where was it?''

"Ripington Four Corners. Yeah, I went to the house. I got inside. To this day I don't know if anybody else was there. I didn't see a soul. The house appeared to be occupied but—not by anybody I'd want to meet if I had a choice. I guess I'm not making myself very clear. Some things happened that—spooked me.''

Conor explained about the wine, the mysterious whimpering animal, the sun-filled but sinister playroom, the odor of gasoline, the dreadful photograph.

"I don't know, maybe I was too keyed up and suggestible because of Rich's warning, and I—I didn't have any business being there. I know for sure I wouldn't go back into that house unless somebody held a gun to my head.''

"Okay, go on,'' Merlo said gravely after a long pause. His fingertips were pressed against his high forehead, hands shutting out the glare from the rink below, the fatly padded little boys huffing and tripping and lunging at each other as they neared the conclusion of their game. Whistle. Offsides.

Conor, gazing intently at the ice as if he were trying to interpret the skaters' ghostly hieroglyphs inscribed there, told what he had heard about Rich's first meeting with the clinical psychologist: the missile tooth, the apparent seizure. He paused again, wondering if the priest would have a comment; instead he appeared to have fallen asleep.

"Father Merlo?''

"I'm listening.''

Conor came to the near-disastrous morning thirteen days ago, events which in his recklessness he had provoked.

"*What* did he say about Polly?'' the priest asked sharply, raising his head when Conor was reluctant to try to repeat some of the language which had come from Rich's mouth. "I need to know the exact wording, if you remember it.''

"No, I don't. It was vile, I can tell you that much. But Lindsay Potter recorded everything that was said on her Dictamite, and Adam made copies.''

"Nothing happened to that tape? That's fortunate. I'd like to listen to it. What did you do next?''

Below them a sturdy boy, guilty of an infraction, whirled

on the misty ice, grinning like a gargoyle: his two front teeth were missing. Conor continued, his distress growing. The cloud of light before his eyes was like a formless apprehension leaked from his skull; his eyes watered pityingly, for the sake of his brother's soul, which he feared was, already, beyond redemption.

When he told of holding the cross behind Rich's head, Merlo said immediately, dismayed, "Where did you learn that little trick?"

"I read a book on demonology."

"And you couldn't wait to try out all the handy hints for banishing evil spirits. Easy as getting pizza stains out of your shirt."

"I had to be sure Rich was telling the truth," Conor said, annoyed and defensive. "And I didn't think the Church was going to give me any help."

"So now you know, and it was more than you bargained for."

"If I'd just had some idea of what was going to happen—"

"Okay, slowly. In detail."

"I held the cross behind his head. There was a sound like—I can't describe it very well—like solid rock splitting apart. A low, grinding, groaning that hurt my ears. It felt as if the little bones there were being ground to splinters and pushed into my brain. It was intensely painful, and I couldn't hear well for three days after."

"Where did the sound come from?"

"It came from Rich. He was on the floor on his hands and knees. Then he wasn't: he swelled up. I don't mean he turned into a balloon, but there was definite swelling all over his body until he literally floated three or four inches off the floor. All the time this groaning, wrenching, breaking noise came from him. You'll hear it. Then he—he suddenly popped into the air, rotated, compressed himself into a ball like a circus tumbler, and began to shoot around the room. I mean *fast*, from the wall to the floor to another wall, and then the ceiling. I tried to catch him, but it was like getting in the way of an avalanche. The impact busted my nose and loosened some teeth, and I had bruises all over my chest. There were other things going on at the same time. Slats from the venetian blinds whirling around, lighted cigarettes in the air—"

"Is that how you burned your hand?"

"No. The cross partially melted. It was eighteen-karat gold."

"Very impressive," Merlo said, with a bleak little whistle. "Want to tell me how you got out of there alive? You're lucky to *be* alive, by the way."

"I crawled to the door and opened it. Then everything just stopped."

"Uh-huh. What kind of shape is your brother in?"

"They put him in the hospital for eight days. He had a contused liver, a cracked rib, a sprained neck, a dislocated shoulder, more bruises than anyone could count, and spasms in the lower back. But other than the rib no bones were broken. It's hard to believe he's not in a body cast. If you'd seen—"

"I've seen a lot of human bodies fly through the air. How soon after the incident did he regain consciousness?"

"Three hours."

"How was he acting?"

"Like a child waking up after a long fever. He didn't remember anything from the time they unlocked the door of his cell to take him upstairs."

"And what did the authorities make of all this?"

"They assumed—and we decided not to contradict them—that Rich had simply gone berserk and caused all the damage. He's in a padded isolation cell now, the only one in the jail. The lights are on twenty-four hours a day. They won't take him out of there without putting a straitjacket on first, and they won't even unlock the door until a shotgun is trained on him."

"No more manifestations have occurred?"

"None."

"Just three witnesses. You. The two lawyers. Were there other injuries?"

"Lindsay was slashed across the forehead, near the hairline. Sixteen stitches."

A buzzer sounded; the disheveled skaters grouped according to their colors at opposite ends of the rink to cheer the opposition, then filed off the ice. Charley-chuck was looking for Conor in the bleachers. Conor stood and waved and the boy pumped his stick up and down victoriously; he had scored two of his team's seven goals. His hair, with his black helmet removed, was plastered to his forehead and looked as drenched as if he had been bathing. His cheekbones were white pennies in a dusky-rose face. He gulped orange juice from a paper cup a teammate handed him.

Conor looked down at Father Merlo. "I have to leave; Charley needs to shower and get ready for school. What are you going to do?"

Merlo said with a slight grin, "Retire." A blight of unhappiness occluded Conor's gaze. "Don't mind me," the priest said. "I'm always saying that. Actually I would like to see your brother."

"When?" Conor asked, not troubling to conceal his relief.

"Today, if it can be arranged. The fact that he's in jail presents problems. We should talk to the lawyers first. When can you be ready to leave for—what's the name of that town again?"

"Chadbury. It's about two hours from here. You said you hadn't slept for a while."

"If you don't mind doing the driving, I'll catch a nap on the way."

48

Adam Kurland said, as soon as the visitors were settled in his corner office on the fourth floor of the Deerhorn Valley State Bank building in Braxton, "I think I should make it clear before we get into any discussions about Rich that I don't buy Conor's conviction that his brother is possessed by the devil. I was raised a Unitarian, and I'm not so sure there *is* any such thing as the devil."

He was sitting on one side of his worktable, an oval of mermaid-green onyx bound in rococo bronze. It was almost the size of a snooker table and looked as if it weighed as much as the bank's vault. All the furnishings in the large rectangular office were similarly old and eccentric-looking, two centuries worth of family hand-me-downs, but someone had coordinated all this eclecticism beautifully. The walls, paneled in squares of ornamental tin, and the cast-plaster ceiling had been painted a uniform butter-scotch shade. The centered windows that overlooked the green were uncovered; the morning sunlight seemed blown-in, concussive in its brilliance.

Adam reached behind him and picked up a letter. "Maggie Renquist evaluated the first set of psychological tests Rich did for her when he got out of the hospital, and she's heard the tape Linds made two weeks ago. Based on his test responses she feels he's a classic paranoid schiz, capable of wildly divergent types of behavior. One of the personalities is the proverbial 'lost soul': weak, confused, unable to integrate his primal urges with the demands society has made on him. The other is a maniacal bully, given to outbursts of hostility and rage, which is how he solves *his* conflicts. He's very strong and agile, as we know, and contemptuous of human life and dignity. Rich calls him 'the demon.' Rightly so. It was a demonic impulse that resulted in Karyn's death. Titanic, unstoppable. But there are *no* significant religious implications, despite Rich's Catholic upbringing."

Father Merlo, who sat on a sleigh-shaped couch against one wall, an Egg McMuffin in a Styrofoam container in his lap, nodded amiably and glanced at Lindsay Potter, who was standing near the windows. She wore a tweed suit with an apricot blouse and a neat white rectangle of bandage high on her forehead. The direct light of the sun gave her averted face a look of scoured austerity.

Aware of his scrutiny, she said in a quiet voice, "I haven't been able to explain to myself—or to anyone else—what I saw; so I'll stay out of this."

Adam folded and refolded the psychologist's letter, lips pressed together in disapproval of her lack of support. A cabinet clock chimed: ten thirty.

"Maybe he is schizophrenic," Merlo said to Adam. "He could be a lot of things. Psychology's not my field. Neither is comparative theology. I'm trained to deal with certain phenomena I've found to be authentic, and at

Conor's request I'm here to meet with his brother. Under certain conditions. Otherwise I won't see him at all."

"What are those conditions?" Lindsay asked.

Merlo took a bite from his Egg McMuffin. "Nobody sees him but Conor and myself. I can protect the two of us well enough, but when there's a crowd it gets complicated. I don't want any prison guards hanging around with guns. *No guns*. I'll talk to Rich in a cell if that's the best we can do, but it's not necessary for the sake of security. While I'm with him I'll be in control."

"He's sedated," Adam interjected.

"He was sedated last time, when he went stunting around that room you were in. I use a different kind of tranquilizer: the Word of God."

"I don't think his body could survive that kind of stress again," Conor said vehemently.

"I can't promise there won't be a manifestation."

"I talked to Maggie Renquist about the—the violent physical activity," Adam said, turning his expansion-band watch around and around on his wrist. He stared assuredly at Conor, who had begun to prowl around the perimeter of a badly worn Persian carpet. "Maggie feels that, although Linds and I are trained observers, there is a *lot* of latitude between what we thought we saw and what actually occurred. None of us have been able to agree on exactly what happened; true? Okay, I'm certainly not an expert on what highly stressful situations can do to a person's mind, so I'm willing to accept Maggie's hypothesis. Her term for the phenomenon is interreactive hysteria."

"Bullshit," Conor exclaimed. "How do you explain the venetian blind flying apart? The cigarettes? *This*." He thrust up his bandaged hand. "Do you know what the melting point of gold is? I do: I looked it up. One thousand and sixty-three degrees *Centigrade*."

Adam sighed. "I don't want to be pulled back into an old argument, but it's worth pointing out that three of us had lit up, it's not a large room, and there was smoke aplenty in the air. As for the blinds, Rich could easily have torn them down. The cross was twisted out of shape, granted. Not inconceivable that someone of your great strength could have done it, unconsciously, under enormous provocation. The burns may have been self-induced, and I can explain that. I've given it considerable thought. Persons who have suffered for years from extreme pain, nerve problems or migraine headaches, learn to control that pain through biofeedback training, first by directing heat to the palms of their hands. I'm willing to believe that your hand was burned through some super-feedback complication, again brought on by stress that had a psycho-religious orientation. Now, I'm more than satisfied with Maggie's appraisal of Rich's mental state and feel that it's something we can begin to build upon for acquittal, NGRI, and I'm afraid I don't think Father Merlo's conclusions will be helpful toward that end."

"I want Rich to see him," Conor insisted. "I want to save his life—but I've become more concerned about his soul."

Adam spread his hands, a gesture that managed to be both accommodating and arrogant.

"Right. I just wanted you to know my position."

Lindsay said unexpectedly, "I was nearly deaf for three days. So was Conor. That terrible noise—how could it have come from a human throat?"

"Come *on*, Linds, you agreed with me—"

"Adam, I don't think I've agreed to anything," she replied, but not heatedly. Finding his face studiously closed, as if suddenly he had begun to solve difficult trigonometric equations in his head, Lindsay turned instead to Father Merlo, revealing, in a shy lifting of one hand toward her face—which was all but unseeable in the light that drowned her—the beginning of signing, a nervous entrancement with the power he represented, although he was not wearing a Roman collar and more closely resembled a once-sprightly Harlem Globetrotter than a priest. She was fallen away (he would have guessed), but not beyond the needs her religion had formerly served.

Merlo washed down more of his breakfast with a chocolate shake from a container with Ronald McDonald's vaguely malevolent face on it. "Let's hear the tape," he suggested.

Adam played one of the copies he had made on a reel-to-reel Nagra recorder. For the most part the priest listened silently. When the voice that sounded nothing like Richard Devon's said *"Ask Conor about lust; ask him about sodomy,"* Lindsay Potter turned her face away from the men in the room and Conor stood with his burned hand clenched and pressed against his lower lip, his cheeks scarlet from humiliation. But no one except Adam looked at him.

"Can't you take a little joke? Of course it's me: Rich."

As they listened, the power of the morning sun was slowly dimmed by clouds; their interconnected shadows on the butterscotch walls, once strong as char, faded to mere transparencies, negative images that powerlessly haunted each other. And then pandemonium, as on the tape Conor uprooted Rich from his chair and pasted him like an effigy against a wall of the interview room.

"Demon Serpent, Foul Tyrant, I show you the cross of our most precious Lord!"

"Turn it down!" Lindsay begged, still looking away from them, the reflection of her face trapped at one low edge of a glass-covered collection of powdery lepidoptera; she seemed pinned there herself, nervy and alive on mildewed black velvet. The sound began that she had dreaded: Low, cracking, groaning, a weight of pain like poured lead swiftly hardening in the volute chambers of the ear.

Merlo sat up straight on the couch.

"Let me hear that again! Can you play it fast-forward?"

"Sure," Adam said, reversing the tape, stopping it. He made the adjustment. The sound came to them again after moments of shrill babble.

"ZAAAARRRAAACHHHHHHHHHHHHH! ROHHHMMMMMMMMMM! BRAAAGHHHHHHHH!"

Four seconds, and it was over.

Adam stopped the tape again and looked dourly at the priest, aware that something would be made of this.

Merlo had laced his long fingers behind his head; the exposed palms, pale with their backing of purple-toned licorice, expressed a potency the hands of a Caucasian priest could never have. He scanned the ceiling, obedient to some inner alert. With the light of the sun withheld, the big office seemed colder than it was.

"It almost sounded like a voice to me," Conor suggested after a few moments.

"It was a voice," Merlo assured him, with a casual lack of emphasis, his own voice curiously soft and soothing, as if he had been thinking of a lullaby. But his posture was rigid, his brow sternly knit. "An old, old language which I know by sight but hardly know by ear, because I imagine only the long-dead or the unenfranchised still speak it."

Adam sighed in exasperation.

"What did the voice say?" Lindsay asked, with a tepid shudder.

"I'll have to study the tape," the priest answered; but they all felt he already knew.

49

"Hilllarrrrryyyyy!"

Hillary Devon, home in her bed with a cold and fever, drowsy from the medicine she'd been taking, thought she heard her name called: the sound blended poignantly with the receding daydream that had occupied her semiconscious mind, a vision of herself in an old-fashioned white dress in a summery field stippled with yellow flowers not unlike those on the wallpaper in her room. She was on an outing with her father, who was thinner and was allowing her to shave off his beard. So much more handsome that way. She sat up slowly, feeling an ache, a chill.

Maybe the television was all she had heard. It had been on all morning, for company. Soaps. Troubled faces and desperate passions, lingering closeups of actors who had bad complexions under their heavy makeup. The fish in her tank goggled at her and swam over blue gravel, through miniature sunken temples. Her mind felt as distant from her body as the lightweight shadows of the swimmers on the wall behind her study desk were distant from the watery chuckling tank. She rubbed a sore spot on one breast where a button on her pajamas had pressed too hard. It couldn't have been her mother, who was at work, or one of the boys, who were in school—weren't they? She blinked at the dashed red LED numerals on the clock radio. Ten after one. No, the boys were still in school, she had the house to herself, and so nobody had called from downstairs. Outside, then.

"Hillllarrrryyyy."

Definitely she was being hailed from outside. A girl's voice, but not one she recognized.

Hillary looked toward the windows. Beyond sheer figured curtains over blinds pulled all the way up she saw a dull gray day. That neutral, impoverished look of winter's bottom of the barrel. But snow had been promised by nightfall. She pushed the heavy covers aside and reached for a bottle of nasal spray, slid her feet over the side of the bed, creating static electricity. While she was jetting spray into each held-back nostril, her feet felt around for her slippers. When she had them on she got up and scuffed to the windows, coughing into a tissue, her throat acrid. She looked out through the curtains.

A car drove by on Carroll Street, slush spewing from the rear wheels. A girl was standing on the other side of the street, in front of the Capalettis'. She didn't seem to be waiting for anyone: she was looking directly at Hillary's bedroom windows. She could have been anywhere from twelve to fifteen. She wore a light green cape with darker border, a red tam, a red scarf, red snowboots. She held her hands inside the cape. Hillary was a little too far away to see her face clearly, but she was certain she didn't know the girl.

"Hillary?"

It was odd; she heard the girl, not as if they were a hundred and fifty feet apart with two thicknesses of glass between them, but clearly, conversationally. Hillary was receptive to every nuance of tone. The girl was glad, so glad, that Hillary had come to the window to acknowledge her. She had been waiting a very long time out there. Obviously she *must* know this girl. But where had they met? And what did she want? So puzzling.

Hillary desperately wanted to be able to think with more precision. Her brain was as dull as the sky of lightless lead. But she did recall fragments of the phone conversation she'd had with Beth LeMaster about the girl whom she supposedly had walked with from Erickson's dance studio to the IGA a couple of weeks ago. Beth had had a description: this was *that* girl, wearing the identical outfit.

No, but I was alone. Or was I?

Curiouser and curiouser. She couldn't trust her own memory anymore.

Go down and let her in.

That much was distinct in Hillary's mind, it was almost like a command. She *must* go downstairs *immediately* and—

But they had a strict rule at the Devons'. Her mother would be furious, unforgiving, if she violated it; would never trust her again. The rule was this: if for any reason she, Hillary, had to be alone in the house, even for a few minutes, she was never to open the door to anyone except a member of the immediate family. No exceptions. Not even if it was a policeman on their doorstep. Policemen's uniforms, Gina had told her, were not difficult for the wrong people to obtain.

The wrong people.

Hillary was aware of a biting knot of concern pulling tightly under the heart, and worse, she felt an almost painful tucking-in, a shrinkage below the navel, the way she always felt when one of the pediatricians had to see her without panties on and she knew his fingers would soon touch her in secret places.

"Hillllarrryyyyy."

She sounded so cold, lonely and despairing. In need of friendship.

Hillary peered out again. The girl was still standing there, motionless, breath steaming, lifting one booted foot slowly, then the other. A girl of about her own age, who was dying for someone to talk to. Maybe she had no parents, or—or else she had just moved to the neighborhood and hated her school. Hillary knew what it was like to be an outsider, at the mercy of cliques and snobs. She held her own but was far from the most popular girl at Blessed Sacrament. Tried too hard, sometimes, to be liked, which was always fatal. Hillary felt a tender sense of responsibility for the girl who waited, hopefully, for some gesture of kindness.

A Roto-Rooter truck went by fast, heading up the hill; the girl stepped hurriedly back from the curb. She took an ungloved hand from beneath the cape and appeared to wave, meekly, as if she knew what thoughts were going through Hillary's mind.

I'm okay, she might have been saying. *I'm just like you. We'll be great friends. Just give me a chance.*

Hillary was tired of her illness, now in its third day, bored with lying abed, sick of the television dramas and inane game shows and the long dragging minutes spent alone. She turned from the windows and picked up her robe from the foot of the bed. She was so lost in anticipation of meeting the girl across the street that her revenant reflection springing from the mirror on the partially opened closet door startled her. She hesitated, an icy spray of caution dispelling some of the mists in which her brain was wrapped. She was reminded of The Rule.

Hillary, please hurry.

Just this one time. Her mother wouldn't know.

"Coming," Hillary murmured, as if the summons inside her head had been as insistent as a knock at the stout front door.

She left her room and went slowly down the carpeted stairs to the center hall of the Colonial house. It was darker downstairs, because the drapes in the living and dining rooms, on each side of the center hall, had been closed almost all the way to conserve heat. But the polished hardwood floor of the hall lifted light toward her feet as she reached the bottom of the steps; the light came through narrow windows on either side of the front door, windows covered only with opaque pleated curtains on little brass rods. More misgivings, as she turned to the door; they were prompted by the expression on her mother's face that morning while she reminded Hillary, again, that it was necessary for her to stay in her room unless she needed something from the kitchen, and to keep all doors double-locked.

Don't answer the phone. When I call—

You'll let the phone ring twice, then hang up and call right back. Mother, I know. I know.

A kiss on Hillary's dry hot forehead, a stitch of guilt at one corner of Gina's mouth. *I just hate leaving you alone, even for part of the day, when you're sick.*

Oh, I'll be fine. Don't worry.

The front door was solid rock maple and had two locks, one just above the curved brass door handle with its thumb-pedal latch release. The first lock was not a very strong one, with only an oval-shaped bolt throw on the inside. The other, eight inches higher, was a massive Medeco dead-bolt arrangement. In the center of the door, at an eye-height Hillary could reach by going up a little on her toes, there was a peephole that gave a fisheye view of the front stoop and the steps leading down to the street. Fourteen steps in all, bordered by azalea bushes now winter-wrapped in burlap sacking, and two levels of terrace surfaced in old porous snow, crossed and recrossed by the tracks of small birds and animals.

Through the peephole Hillary saw the girl coming, confidently, up the steps toward the front door. Hillary could see her more clearly now. She was smiling. She was pretty, with a thin face and good cheekbones, but she was very pale, almost translucent in her pallor, as if she hadn't been well herself lately.

"Hi, Hillary."

The girl was still twenty feet away, climbing the steps in her red, red boots, so the clarity of her greeting was remarkable, as if the words had originated in Hillary's own mind.

Hillary was warmed by a resurgence of fever, shaken by tremors; she yearned for her bed, the covers piled high, the room closed and half dark and secure. She didn't *want* any company, nor did she want to talk to—

But her left hand, as she watched the blond girl approach, crept to the dead-bolt lock on the door.

She knew she had definitely decided to turn and go back upstairs, *running* if necessary, and not let the girl in, even for one minute, to find out her name and where she lived—*Oh, you just moved into the neighborhood? Listen, I've got a bad cold, so if you'll excuse me*—but her hand seemed unaware of her resolve, it had grasped the round knob that lifted the bolt, the stranger's smile was bigger and assured, she waved again as if she could see Hillary's eye pressed to the optical eyepiece in the door, she was nearly on the stoop, four steps more.

And there was a black cloud forming in Hillary's head.

The phone rang. Twice.

Hillary heard it, but faintly, as the blackness flowed down from her brain like a shadow mind at work, a strict guiding intelligence with a formality of purpose terrifying and unavoidable. The blackness crept along her spinal column; she felt a resonance that made her *so* drowsy. Her left hand worked the dead bolt; the lock opened with a snap.

The telephone rang again, as her hand dropped to the other lock on the door.

Oh, mother—!

She turned her head away from the door, fighting a lack of will.

"Open the door, Hillary. My name is Polly. And I want to come in."

It was a quiet, cool command. Allowing for no disobedience.

But the phone ringing. Ringing.

The other lock, though simpler, was hard to work with one hand. She needed to push against the door just a little, in the right place, so the bolt throw would turn cleanly. But she was looking toward the back of the house, where the telephone was mounted on a wall of the breakfast room.

"You can get that, Hillary, after you let me in.

"I'm waiting. Just have a look. I'm right here on the other side of the door.

"Let's be friends, Hillary. You need my friendship. And I need you."

Five rings. Six. Her mother probably thought she had fallen asleep. Oh, please don't hang up, I'm—

"You can call her back, Hillary!"

Hillary sobbed. "Oh, Goddd!"

She felt, from the other side of the door, a bolt of displeasure. The blackness like a cat nuzzling at the base of her spine, numbing all her nerves with a downward spread of entrenched claws. Claiming what remained of her will.

"GOD!" Hillary screamed, and found release. She tumbled backwards from the door, got to her feet, went flying down the center hall to the back of the house, the breakfast room with its hanging plants and striped yellow wallpaper. She felt as if something was pursuing her, the uncurling lash of a black whip; she seized the receiver of the telephone with both hands.

The whip touched her spine, lightly. Withdrew.

"Mother!"

"Hillary? Yes, what is it, what's wrong?"

Tears coursed down her cheeks. She had to pause to get her breath.

"Wrong—I—nothing. There was somebody at the door. A girl. But I didn't let her in."

It was beyond her powers to explain the creeping terror, the sensation of being gently pushed against her instincts to do something that would have devastating consequences for herself, for the family.

"Mom, when are you coming home?"

"Right now; I called to tell you. Hillary, are you sure you're okay? What did the girl want?"

"I don't know. I never saw her before! She must be somebody new in the neighborhood, maybe they moved into the Stoltes' house."

"I don't think anybody's bought it yet. Are you downstairs?"

"Yes."

"Well, go back to bed and I'll be there in twenty—"

Hillary gasped.

"What happened?"

"I don't know; nothing. I guess I'm just jumpy." But she thought she had heard a kind of popping noise, a brittle sound of breaking upstairs. She knew she was about to cry, from nerves, and wanted to get off the phone first. " 'Bye, mom, I'm okay, honest. I'll see you. I love you."

" 'Bye, honey. Twenty minutes."

Hurry.

With this unspoken plea Hillary replaced the receiver. She had lost one slipper in her flight down the hall to the breakfast room. Her bare foot was cold. She could barely make out the slipper lying on the floor of the center hall, halfway to the front door. There was no more light coming in through the narrow windows that bracketed the door. It was black as midnight out there on the stoop. She felt that she would never get as far as the stairs.

The doorbell rang, nearly jolting her out of her skin.

Near the phone on the wall was a very old woodcut, a Renaissance version of madonna and child, framed in gold. She snatched it down from the wall and held it against her breast, went up the back stairs, two at a time, gasping.

The door to her room was closed. She hadn't closed it.

Hillary put a hand on the brass knob, still clutching the semisacred woodcut. The knob was so unexpectedly cold her moist hand almost froze tight to it. She lost a little skin when she jerked it away.

"Oh God and Mary and all the saints please protect me!"

There was a sound on the other side of the door, a gurgling noise she couldn't identify. Then in a moment of horrified insight she realized what must be happening. Putting her hand into a pocket of her robe, she turned the doorknob through the pocket and entered her room.

On one corner of her study desk, where a lamp burned, the water of her twenty-gallon tank and her collection of fish were pouring through a hole in the glass, flooding the carpet. There were no cracks or jagged edges: the hole was perfectly round, about four inches in diameter. The edges of the hole were so smooth it appeared not to have been cut by any sort of instrument; rather the glass seemed simply to have dissolved, or dematerialized, where the water rushed through.

50

Conor and Father Merlo took adjoining rooms at the Holiday Inn on Interstate 91 at the Greenleaf Avenue interchange. Adam Kurland had insisted on accompanying them to the jail and being present during the priest's interview with "my client"; Merlo told him plainly that he expected unpleasantness. Adam said that both the police and the prosecutor's office now objected to Rich having visitors, and would undoubtedly refuse to let Conor and the priest meet with Rich alone.

Merlo said, "Find out if they can let us have a room without windows or furniture. A small stool is all I need."

In his room at the Holiday Inn the priest bathed, shaved, changed into his size forty-six long black mohair suit and a Roman collar and spent an hour in solitary meditation and prayer, while in the other room Conor fidgeted and Kurland, sitting on the edge of the bed, made telephone calls. Lindsay Potter had not asked to be included.

Father Merlo tapped on the connecting door when he was ready. He was not smiling. He had a black bag in one hand. Conor did not have to be told what was in it.

"I'm going to bless the two of you now; we don't want a repetition of what happened the last time you met with Richard."

He said a short prayer, anointed them with holy oil, and made the sign of the cross over each man's head. Conor's head was deeply bowed, and he added his own prayers half aloud. Adam, looking discomfited in a sporty plaid suit, gazed sidelong out the windows and kept quiet.

"What do you think will happen?" Conor asked the priest.

"He should be provoked when he sees me."

"Do you mean Rich?" Adam asked.

"No. That's not who I mean."

"Will you exorcise him today?" Conor said.

Merlo laid a hand briefly on his shoulder, but there was a weight of sympathy in his hand, and sorrow in his eyes, which caused Conor's heart to falter.

"The first thing I have to be sure of is that there's a need for either a lesser or major exorcism—the Roman ritual—before one can be authorized. The Church wants indisputable proof of possession. And preparing for a major exorcism is like preparing for a war—there are formal necessities, such as a black fast, and no exorcist works alone if he wants to survive the experience. For now I'm only after information."

"We're running late," Adam announced, looking at his watch.

Adam drove them in his car the fifteen miles to the county courthouse in Chadbury. There he conferred, alone, with the officer in charge of the jail, Steve Wendkos, a tubby man with a balding head and an astonishing mustache, so much uncontrolled hair it looked like an explosion of copper filaments beneath his nose. The jailer emerged from his office and shook hands with the priest, gazing up at him in mild astonishment.

Steve said, "Prisoner's been behaving himself the last

couple of days, sits on his bunk and talks to himself mostly. But I think one or two of us should be in there with you, Father. This man here''—he nodded to Conor—''is, I've been given to understand, a professional wrestler, but even he took a beating when the prisoner went on that rampage. They doubled his dose of tranquilizer; still, you never know.''

''He'll be in his straitjacket, won't he?'' Merlo replied. ''I don't think we'll have any trouble. I tend to have a calming effect on them anyway.''

''I can believe it. Well, okay, then—Duke!''

A dinky young man with a cast in one eye and a grudging manner took the visitors down a flight of iron steps into the basement, past a huffing boiler and down a corridor where gray paint was peeling off the walls in parchmentlike scrolls. Unshielded bulbs overhead provided illumination. Their footsteps echoed. Adam was whistling nervously through his teeth. Away from the boiler and the steam pipes it was drearily cold.

''Killed a rat down here the other day, size of a cocker spaniel,'' Duke smirked. If he hadn't been in uniform Conor easily could have imagined him in a shabby pool hall plotting supermarket robberies with equally unpromising confederates. They stopped at a metal door painted dark red. Duke unlocked it and turned on the single light, a hundred-watt bulb screwed into a porcelain socket on a wooden beam. It left areas of darkness in all four corners of the room. Just as well. The room was dank, the floor unswept. A single window high on one wall was black with filth, covered with a grill. Iron pipes, bitter-orange with rust, crisscrossed beneath the ceiling. The top of Father Merlo's head nearly brushed them as he walked in and looked around. Adam coughed gloomily into a handkerchief.

The priest placed his bag on the single stool in the room and opened it. He took out a purple silk stole, kissed it, and draped it around his neck. Then he sank into a meditative state that was almost like a trance. Duke waited with them, fiddling with the worn strap on his holster, which housed a very large revolver, until two more of the jailers brought Rich into the room.

His guards stood watchfully on either side of the prisoner, out of range of his feet should he decide to kick at them.

In the dingy straitjacket Rich looked lopsided, harrowingly deformed. In a straitjacket everyone appears crazed. Rich more so: or perhaps, Conor thought, he was influenced by preconceptions of his brother's condition that so long had preyed on his mind. Rich's pallid face, a little slack from opiates, was calm enough, even when his eyes took in the priest standing tall as a ship's varnished mast between Adam and Conor.

"Hello, Conor. Hello, Adam. Who's this?"

"I'm Father Merlo, son."

Rich's mouth twisted slightly; his tone was rougher. "I don't need a priest. I especially don't need a nigger priest who licks the cunts of menstruating nuns."

"Watch your mouth!" Duke snarled, and the other two guards raised their batons, but Merlo held up a hand.

"It's okay," he said, sounding disinterested to the point of boredom.

Duke said over his shoulder, looking as if he yearned to blast away at Rich with his Colt Trooper, "Ten minutes, Father, that's what Steve said. But that's all the time you're gonna want to spend with this guy."

He left the room still glaring at Rich; the other guards followed, and the door was closed and locked from the outside.

Rich looked around at the door, then back at his visitors. He smiled, preoccupied. "I'm going to take this thing off," he said.

He began to bend and twist and jerk so frantically and strenuously that Conor took a step toward him. Merlo held him back. His own face was impassive as he watched Rich's fierce struggle with the cruel binding garment. Adam, who had been checking out the tape recorder in his hand, stopped to watch with his mouth open.

In less than thirty seconds the straitjacket lay on the floor, unbuckled but not visibly ripped, and Rich was flexing his cramped arms.

"Better," he said. He raised his eyes to the priest. There was bitter hatred in them. His voice deepened. "What do you want?"

"I want to know who you are."

Deeper still; a rumbling. "What is your need to know?"

"I would do the will of God."

An odor saturated the room like brown fog. It was the odor of untreated wounds and charred flesh, of black vomit and cesspools and mass open graves. Of a world totally corrupt, ravaged and dead as it hurtled one last time around the sun. Conor threw his hands to his face; Adam was staggered and nauseated.

Father Merlo swiftly took from his black bag white surgical masks steeped in holy water.

"Breathe through these," he instructed them. Meanwhile he kept his eyes on the figure of Richard Devon, who flexed his hand and arm muscles but didn't move otherwise.

"Will you introduce yourself?" the priest said firmly. "We only have a few minutes, and I want to make the most of them."

"You will *die*, nigger! You will be torn to pieces on the first day of the Great Violence called Armageddon. You will see your blood stain the cobblestones in front of that shithouse St. Peter's! And we will drink your blood and brains from the vessel of your broken skull!"

Father Merlo sighed almost inaudibly and produced a wooden cross.

Something black and vile and unnameable began to ooze up out of the concrete floor as if it were as porous as a sponge. A pipe overhead burst and they were spewed with a yellow, puslike substance. Adam sucked wind violently, a loud scalded sound.

"Nothing can happen to you," the priest said calmingly, and then to the figure of Rich, "I command you to speak in the name of the Most Holy! What is your name? Who are you? Where have you come from?"

The skin of Richard's face was transformed as if he were an apple baking in an oven. The crusty blackened skin began to split and burst open. His eyes, twice normal size, stood well out of their sockets. His hair rose sizzling on end. And all the time he smiled, revealing black gums.

Adam slipped on the floor and fell down. He moved disconnectedly, as if hipshot, unable to get up again. He stared beseechingly at Merlo.

"You can't be hurt. He only wants to take your mind

away from you. Resist. This is *not* the hour of his greatest strength." He turned his full attention back to the entity that was deforming the head (bones bulging soft as tallow beneath the skin) and the body of Richard Devon. Rich's chest swelled until his jail jumper ripped at the seams. With his crotch exposed, Rich began pissing, the wimpled head of his penis lashing about like a one-eyed snake extruded from the russet basket of his groin. Piss steamed in acid clouds when it hit the cold floor. He farted enormously, wild organ chords blaspheming.

Father Merlo looked displeased.

"In the name of my Lord Jesus Christ," he said, each word precise as a pistol shot in the farting din, "I command you to speak your name!"

The farting stopped, and the shit began to fly, pouring out of the possessed body. Then came the answering voice, cold as winter thunder:

"I AM ZARACH' BAL-TAGH!"

There was a simultaneous whinny of voices in the room, an excited chorus from a distant fenland lit by purple lightning, beaten to dust by the little hooves of the lesser Unearthly.

"BAL! BAL! BAAAAAAAL!"

Outside the locked steel door Duke and the other jailers stood at ease and smoked and kept their ears open. But they never heard a thing.

"And who is Zarach' Bal-Tagh?" the priest demanded. He knew already, but it was submission he was after now; he had the information he'd been seeking.

"BROTHER OF LUCIFER—ENEMY OF GOD!"

In the eyes of the possessed, empty as wormholes in wood, sparks glowed; dark twists of smoke spiraled toward the priest.

Merlo said, indicating Conor beside him, "What do you want with this man's brother?"

"I DIDN'T WANT HIM. HE WANTED ME. NOW SHALL YOU *ALL* HAVE ME!"

"What do you mean?" Merlo said grimly.

"YOUR CORRUPT AND MISERABLE WORLD HAS NEED OF A REDEEMER—ISN'T THAT WHAT YOU PREACH?"

"No one of us is so sick or troubled that he needs you. Go back where you came from, Evil One."

"I SHALL RETURN WHEN I CHOOSE—WITH ALL OF MY EAGER FOLLOWERS. WITH SOULS BEYOND COUNTING. THIS PUTRID HUNK OF MEAT IS ONLY THE BEGINNING."

"Richard was—he is—a good man. How did you trick him?"

"HIS OWN LUST BETRAYED HIM. AS EACH MAN'S SINS CREATE A LOVE OF ME."

Even as he spoke the taskmaster who called himself Zarach' increased the speed and intensity of his psychic attack on Adam Kurland, who of the three interrogators had the least strength to resist him. Adam was convulsed, his sickened, strained mind drowning in offal. Merlo decided he'd better end this quickly.

From his bag he withdrew an aspergillum, filled with holy water.

"I'll be back," he promised the possessor. "For Richard's soul—brother of Lucifer."

Laughter flew in his face like a black bird with sparkling talons.

"IF YOU WANT THIS HUMAN, YOU WILL HAVE TO TAKE HIM FROM ME. IF YOU HAVE THE STRENGTH TO OPPOSE ME!"

The priest began deliberately to sprinkle the room and everyone in it with holy water. Crystalline purging drops charged with the power of undaunted love. Tears of Christ. They rained blurringly upon the possessed and there came a wild shriek, not of pain but of outrage.

Rich collapsed suddenly, in a dense scrabbling heap, his face pressed against the shit-covered floor. He groveled there briefly and then sat up, as if jerked from behind by a hand on his hair; his horrible defiled face began shrinking toward normality but still ran livid and mad with veins. There was brown froth at the corners of his mouth: he regurgitated some of the shit he had been made to eat. Conor crossed himself fervently twice, three times, to reinforce the priest's efforts to establish dominion over the inhuman spirit. Rich toppled then, and lay still. The ripe goo and heaps of sinister excrement dematerialized within moments. There were no further sounds except for Adam Kurland's panicked breathing. He lay on the floor in a fetal position, grinning vacantly, a grin that looked as if it were sewn to the bulging angles of his jaws. His eyes rolled so anxiously that Conor imagined he could hear them clicking in his head like pinballs. But his own mind was still jerking and balking, unable to fully assimilate the horrors he had thought himself prepared for; he was desperate to get out of that basement room.

He hauled Adam to his feet and found him lightly constructed, of rubber bands and scant padding. His Unitarian God, largely an intellectual exercise, had proved faithless under fire. Adam's entire life was a pragmatic structure, reason and clear thinking his sword and shield. His mind now would hold or not hold, like a car with old worn brakes parked on a steep incline. Seconds counted, no time to be gentle. Conor hit him in the face with a hand like a chopping board. A tooth chipped, blood flew from Adam's lower lip. There. Some spark of anger deep in his haunted eyes, a stiffening of the body. Conor glanced at Merlo, who nodded.

"There's nothing more I can do," the priest said regretfully. "Let's get out of here. And when Adam comes around, we have to talk."

51

Adam's nerve had been severely tested but not broken; his mind, trampled by cloven hooves, was not disabled. In the hours of the afternoon he recovered slowly, like a man with a totally unfamiliar type of hangover, his vision uncharacteristically misty at the edges. He recovered alone, finding both solace and a renewed will to survive in punishing physical activity. Until dusk he skied cross-country, covering twenty-three miles beneath a burnished overcast. When he returned to the remodeled barn, lungs weighted by fatigue, eyes hollowed, all the lingering boyishness had been seared from his face.

Conor, Lindsay, and Merlo were waiting for him. He looked at them as if they were foreign to him, said few words, went to shower and change his clothes. Lindsay had made Irish stew in a big iron pot, and soda bread. She took a drink, a stiff martini, into the bathroom for Adam and returned leading him by the hand. They settled down in front of the fireplace. Adam gazed into the blue and yellow flames of the gas log fire for a long time. Then he raised his eyes to the priest.

"Have you ever seen anything like that before?"

Merlo shrugged. "Well, I've seen much worse, but usually during the Roman ritual, when the—disturbances can go on day and night, sometimes for weeks."

"How can you stand it?" Adam said tonelessly, drinking so fast he seemed to be sloshing solid gin down his throat. Lindsay put a hand casually on his wrist.

"For one thing, I'm conditioned through my faith in God to withstand whatever the inhuman spirit, the guiding intelligence behind these assaults, can devise. And I know that, in the end, ninety percent of the time God will win."

"What about the other ten percent?" Conor asked, with a touchingly slurred voice. He was humped at one end of a blue sofa, working on another Irish and soda, one of many with which, during an endless afternoon, he had soothed his own nerves and blotted the ugly eruptions, like running sores in the mind, that remained of a sixth of a morning hour spent skidding helplessly part way to hell. He had tunnel vision, and poor depth perception; faces swung blandly in and out of his orbit, the fire either roared hotly right between his eyes or receded to the dimness of a star scratched on a windowpane, but he was following the conversation perfectly well, with a deadly ineradicable spot of fear on his heart.

"The possessed body," Father Merlo explained with a tired but still compassionate smile, "is unequal to the strain placed on it, the tug of war between God and devil. And—nobody wins." His own drink, a schooner of beer, had turned warm in his hand. He had reached the point where he couldn't lift the heavy mug from the arm of the sofa. And he was facing a long ride to Boston, a much longer flight to Rome, driven hammer-and-tongs by the sense of urgency that now possessed him as fully as Richard Devon lay possessed in his jail cell.

"Could that happen to Rich?" Lindsay said. She was

not drinking; she had agreed to see to it that the priest made his flight, which was scheduled to depart at ten thirty. She wore a headband to cover the bandage on her forehead, which made a bump like an unrealized but anxious thought.

"Yes. This is the first time I've come face to face with a devil who has the power, the status in the Kingdom, of Zarach'. It's almost unprecedented. The guiding entities behind demonic possessions always like to keep their identities secret. So I can be sure of one thing already: this is not a typical case of possession—in my experience, it's unique. I don't know yet what it means. But Zarach' Bal-Tagh was telling the truth about his place in the hierarchy of the Fallen. Before the world began, his brother, called Lucifer, was next to God in his majesty. But Lucifer wasn't content to be less than perfect. He wanted to possess all that God possessed: to rule, absolutely, the heavens. For this sin of covetousness he and Zarach' and the host of angels who also coveted God's powers were banished, or so we believe, from God's house.

"But they were not chastised in their banishment, nor did they beg God's forgiveness. They swore eternal hatred for their creator. Lucifer became Satan, which means 'the Father of Lies.' And the name Zarach' Bal-Tagh means, in the Palaic dialect of the Hittite language, 'the Son of the Endless Night.' "

"Hell itself," Conor murmured, drooping despite himself, his glass in one hand sinking below the level of his spread knees with a little tinkle of ice.

Father Merlo got up to walk off a strong urge to sleep. Not yet; perhaps on the flight to Rome. He felt that he was not yet out of range of the danger he had stirred up earlier. He rubbed his bald forehead with the heel of one hand.

"Not exactly. The Endless Night is that shadow of God under which the Fallen Angels perpetually dwell. The darkness from which comes all of their hatred, their evil, their disruptive energy. Hell for us, maybe: but it is *their* element. In the Endless Night all the negative energy of the universe is concentrated. Don't be misled because these spirits are described as 'fallen.' They have inconceivable powers. They're immortal; they don't obey physical laws. They possess all the arcane and mystical secrets of existence. They work ceaselessly for the destruction of mankind. In other words, you don't mess with them unless you know what you're doing. Are you listening, Conor?''

"Listening," the ex-priest mumbled. "Too tricky for us. The in-your-face-disgrace shot."

"Right," Merlo said, with a brisk handclap. Adam looked up, startled, and rattled the ice in his empty glass. He got up and went to the bar to make himself another drink.

"If they're so powerful," Lindsay ventured, "how have we all managed to survive this long?"

"Men have a covenant with God; and that covenant serves to protect them as long as they honor Him, and obey His laws."

Adam rejoined them with a refilled glass, slouching down beside Lindsay, his lower lip swollen, a deep, nearly black bruise along the jawline where Conor had belted him. He looked harassed and anguished. He said, "What I saw this afternoon will stay in my mind until I die. All right. Let's say I'm willing now to accept that Rich is under the influence of something, someone supernatural." He drew a heavy breath; another. "A spirit. The spirit has—dehumanized him, and may have directly caused the death of Karyn Vale. The question is, how do we save Richard?"

"There's no simple answer," Merlo told him. "The problem of Rich's possession is compounded by his being in jail, and by the nature of his possessor. Zarach' is very powerful. I'd have to do some extensive research into old manuscripts, but I know he's been seldom heard from during the past two thousand years. Yet he always seems to make an appearance just before periods of great upheaval, of world catastrophe."

"He said something about Armageddon," Conor reported; he seemed to be chewing the words through suet. His eyes, as he tipped his head to drink, revealed beneath the drooping lids bloodknots of pain.

"Armageddon," Adam said, but only as if it were his turn to keep the conversation going. His jaw muscles were bunched, on the side where it didn't hurt. Fear kept coming back to him unexpectedly, floodtides. He wondered, quite simply, if he would ever be a man again, having so ignominiously failed himself this morning. His tongue had stuck to the roof of his mouth. He had leaked in his pants. He shivered from self-doubt; only Lindsay felt it.

"The end of modern civilization," Merlo explained. "Which we supposedly face along about the stroke of midnight, December 31, 1999. I'm afraid I don't take that timetable seriously, or predictions of global disasters by so-called psychics. Doomsaying is a thriving cottage industry. A great many people are convinced that God is about to exact a terrible vengeance, through nuclear war or some natural calamity like the shifting of the poles of the earth. In their fear, unfortunately, they neglect God all the more. The Dark Ones are easily attracted by a mood of negativism. There's been a tremendous revival of belief in the occult, in Satanism. It's almost safer to play with high explosives. The Church, with the shooting of John Paul II, has reached a point of real peril. The appearances of Zarach' can't be coincidental. Simple possession may not be all he has in mind. That's why I have to return to Rome tonight, to talk to my superiors."

"You can't go," Conor cried, lunging to his feet. "What about Rich?"

"Conor, ridding your brother of Zarach' would require exorcism by the most experienced and holy men of the Church. I can tell you that the rites would last for weeks, even months. It would be an incredible ordeal, particularly for your brother. If we could do it. But we can't. He's in jail."

"Without possibility of bail," Adam said.

"There is nothing the Church can do to help Rich until—unless—he's acquitted."

"But he won't go to trial before May at the earliest," Lindsay pointed out.

"Well, speed it up!" Conor bellowed.

"We need time to prepare," Adam said crossly.

"Maybe *we* need a new lawyer."

Father Merlo walked over to Conor, put an arm across his shoulders and turned him, rather effortlessly, around, forestalling a confrontation. He talked to him quietly, and Conor nodded.

"Even if Rich gets off on an insanity plea, he'll be

committed to an institution. What good can you do him there, Father?''

''I doubt that we'd be granted permission to do anything. Our only hope would be to have him transferred to a Catholic institution, like St. Elizabeth's in Washington, then have him furloughed in our care; but there would be legal problems.''

''Conor,'' Adam said, ''I'm doing the very best I can. I'm sure we'll win. The best strategy is to deflect the focus of the jurors from the facts of the case to the complexities of Rich's behavior. The eyewitnesses will be very important, but I also need psychiatric opinions—expert testimony.''

''You wouldn't need it if a jury saw what we saw today!''

Adam whistled a few notes that descended, derisively, down the scale, ending with a flat exhalation. ''Unfortunately no one in this country has been allowed to plead demonic possession in a murder trial. I wouldn't care to be the first defense attorney to propose it.''

Lindsay got up and walked to the stove in the kitchen, stirred the stew with a wooden spoon, opened the oven door. The odor of freshly baked bread flowed along with her as she returned to them.

''If anyone's hungry,'' she said unhopefully, ''we can eat now.''

Adam was gazing at the fire with a composed, ironic smile. Conor, without Merlo's long arm to anchor him, merely drifted, a few feet here, a few feet there, like a vast and empty hulk on a windblown reef. Out of it.

Merlo spoke when the others failed to: ''Your stew smells wonderful. I'd love to have some.''

Lindsay brightened. ''Father, you've made my day.'' She whirled toward the butcher-block table, where place settings surrounded an arrangement of dried flowers in a Greek bowl, caught her lower lip between her teeth, hesitated. She smiled, a little cutely, over one shoulder. Her heart was hammering. ''You could make it even better.''

''How, Lindsay?''

''Bless this house before you leave.''

52

Crystal Kinsman and her cousin Caitlin met in New York Friday evening to have dinner and see a show, a Neil Simon comedy. Caitlin had taken the train into the city from Springfield, Massachusetts and Crystal drove her Ford Tempo over from New Brunswick to meet her. The plan was for Caitlin to return to Rutgers with Crystal and spend the weekend. There was to be a basketball game and a dance; Crystal had lined up dates for them.

After she stepped off the train at Grand Central and they fell into each other's arms with squeals of delight, and admired each other's outfits, Caitlin's smile faded. She said, "I'm worried sick about Jeff. He's been in the infirmary up at Williams for three days now."

"Why, what's wrong with him, hon?"

"I don't know for sure; he's running a high fever they can't knock down. I tried to call, but they wouldn't let me talk to him. That's how sick he is."

Crystal had met Jeff Pepperdine for the first time on that ill-fated ski holiday in Vermont, and she had found him likable, droll, and self-deprecating, unusual for a redhead. Usually they were pushy as all get-out.

"That's a real shame. But you know he's gonna be okay. Don't let it go and spoil your weekend."

They ate at the Four Seasons, a treat paid for by Crystal's uncle Roy, who had come up from Yazoo City and made a name for himself in the advertising game. Crystal, at least, found the Simon comedy a scream, the best thing he'd done in years. At the intermissions Caitlin went through half a pack of cigarettes, although too much smoking already had aggravated a fever blister that was almost as difficult to cover up as a cockroach on her lip, and she couldn't seem to keep her mind on their conversation.

Crystal gave her reassuring pats and was solicitous about the funk into which she had descended. Crystal herself had a good philosophy of life, which seemed composed of homilies from the lips of Miss America contestants but which nevertheless stood her in good stead: almost nothing could get her down. Caitlin just had this dark streak of fatalism and nothing could be done about it. She was convinced that Jeff had died while she was grudgingly laughing in the crowded, stifling theater, and she felt terrible about it. But she wouldn't go to the telephone after the play ended and purge her fears by calling the college: or perhaps she was genuinely afraid of having those fears confirmed.

Crystal retrieved her Ford from the municipal garage on Eighth Avenue where they'd left it. The city was free of snow but there was a bone-chilling wind; the constellated lights of the city were sharp against a sky black as a sorcerer's curse. There were always too many bums on Eighth, and the tenements of the far west side reminded Crystal of dungeons. She gladly partook of the delights which the city offered but never lingered after dark, and she *never* caught the bus to Jersey.

Crystal drove downtown on Ninth to the Lincoln Tunnel and they crossed beneath the Hudson River, traffic running moderate as far as the New Jersey Turnpike, which they picked up in Secaucus. Caitlin rummaged and found a tape of her current favorite group and popped it into the cassette player, but even the music didn't cheer her up for long. She smoked two more cigarettes as they traveled south along the boring stretch of turnpike from Newark Airport to the Raritan River.

"It was that murder," Caitlin complained. "See, I've just never been able to get it off my mind. I have such terrible nightmares, Crystal, you can't imagine. Sometimes it's *me*, and not her, that's getting killed." Crystal shivered sympathetically but Caitlin went on without taking notice. "You don't know how it's affected my *life*. I meet a new boy and I think he's really darling, but I don't want to be alone with him. Oh, no! Not for one second."

"Aw, you'll get over this."

"Maybe I should see a shrink," Caitlin said morosely. She looked around, as if expecting one to come cruising by in a mini-van. They were passing through flat terrain decorated with skeletal castles of oil refineries, robed in light and hissing flame high into the night sky. "Would you look at that?"

"Look at what?" Crystal said, her eyes flicking to Caitlin's face. But she rarely took her eyes off the road, and she kept two steady hands on the wheel. Five miles over the posted speed limit was as daring as she got. She knew better than to let Caitlin drive, funk or no funk. Caitlin lit out as if her pussy was on fire.

"It's not a cop," Caitlin said disdainfully. "They wouldn't be interested in *you.* It's an old Cadillac. Older than we are. You almost never see those any more. It must be what, a '58, '59?" She was peering, a trifle nearsightedly, past Crystal's shoulder. "Cousin Bertie Armitage had one like that, three summers ago in Pass Christian."

"Oh, yeah, I remember." Crystal turned her head for a quick look. The turnpike had four southbound lanes, framed by two asphalt-paved breakdown lanes, all of it enclosed by steel guardrails. She saw the Caddy in question, two lanes to her left, cruising slowly abreast of her own car. It looked to be a genteel wreck, although it isn't easy judging the condition of black cars at night. But the ludicrous tail fins were obvious, as was the heavy grill and chrome front bumper with its bulletlike projections.

A ripsnorting tractor-trailer came down the lane between them, and the small Tempo rocked in its wake. When the big truck had passed and Crystal looked again, she couldn't see the Cadillac. Perhaps it had fallen behind them.

Four miles north of the toll booths at exit 11 and the interchanges with U.S. 9 and the Garden State Parkway, traffic began to thicken suddenly, a bright stew of braking lights coming to a boil across all lanes. A huge overhead sign warned of an accident ahead; the speed limit had been reduced to twenty miles an hour.

"It's always *something,*" Crystal sighed, trying to discern what had happened. But they weren't close enough yet to the scene; she didn't see any state police cars or emergency vehicles. "We get off at exit 9, then it's only a few minutes more to the campus."

Caitlin yawned and sulkily bit a thumbnail.

Crystal remained in the second lane from the right. As they edged closer to the toll booth plaza and the Amboy

Avenue overpass, flames could be seen, and thick roiling smoke.

"It's on the overpass," Caitlin said. She rolled down the window on her side; a moving van, crusted with dirt, was directly in front of them, obscuring her view. Caitlin leaned out.

"Holy shit!" Now they could hear sirens.

"What is it, Cait?"

"I can't tell—it might be—I think it's a big gasoline tanker burning on the overpass."

"Oh-oh," Crystal said, feeling uneasy. "Wonder if it'll explode?"

"No. I don't think so. They wouldn't let any cars through beneath the overpass, would they? But we're moving. The cops are routing all traffic into the two left lanes; see if you can get over now."

Crystal shuddered. "Sure is getting cold in here."

"Oh, sorry." Her cousin rolled the window up.

Crystal turned on her left-turn indicator, hoping she could move to the far left lanes immediately, although the cars and trucks were creeping along almost bumper to bumper. She didn't like fires of any kind, and this one on the overpass (she had a glimpse of it now as the moving van pulled ahead, opening a thirty-foot gap between them) was huge: flames shooting high into the air.

The poor driver, she thought, and shuddered again.

They continued to move, but slowly. Glancing into the side-mounted mirror, Crystal saw an opening and attempted to pull over, but a car from the far left lane suddenly appeared to fill the space. It was the trampy black Cadillac they had noticed earlier south of Newark Airport.

"Damn!" Crystal said, veering back into her own lane, where she was penned between the van and a flatbed truck hauling big wooden spools of cables. The old Cadillac was only a few feet away on her left and she looked out the window at it, noting the poor condition of the paint job.

A woman was driving. She turned her face toward Crystal and smiled briefly. Kind of a Latin-looking woman, pale, with dark eyes well-mounted on superb cheekbones, and what looked like a long curved scar that lay low on one cheek.

It was the smile that most annoyed Crystal. "May you

get four flat tires and have to walk barefoot to Perth Amboy," Crystal muttered, as dreadful a curse as she had ever imagined. She didn't like the woman much, although she had no very compelling reason for the instant antipathy she felt; her car Crystal liked even less, it was too much of a hearse.

Caitlin had pulled out another cigarette, and she flicked her lighter. Three hundred yards ahead the blackened hulk of the overturned gasoline carrier could be seen lying almost on top of the overpass railing. It still burned furiously although high-pressure streams of water had been aimed at the wreck from chartreuse pumper trucks fore and aft. Water cascading off the bridge had turned to enormous icicles that hung down almost to the turnpike roadway. There were a lot of flares, policemen in slickers with bullhorns.

"What's trouble, hon?"

"Can't get my goddam lighter to work," Caitlin grumbled, holding her cigarette steady and at a tilt between compressed lips.

Something pricked Crystal to look out her side window again.

The driver of the black Cadillac now had a passenger, whose face was turned toward Crystal. They were no more than six feet apart, and Crystal could see her perfectly. Crystal's hair felt as if it were frying. She gasped.

It was a young woman's face, but wildly disordered, as if every underlying bone had been broken. Within the open mouth there were only slivers and stumps of white teeth. One eye was like a harvest moon with an off-center bloodspot for a pupil. The other eye socket was empty and oozing blood. Only her luxurious dark hair seemed untouched by carnage.

Crystal Kinsman knew who she was: had admired the thickness and flow of Karyn Vale's hair moments before the girl had walked out onto the hushed snowy terrace at the Davos Chalet Lodge and died so horribly.

From the burning hulk of the oil tanker a fireball shot up into the air. Two hundred feet above the packed lanes of traffic on the southbound Jersey Turnpike the fireball lost momentum, arced over slowly and then, picking up speed again, rocketed downward.

As Crystal screamed once more at the bad news of the apparition seated next to them, the black Cadillac became as insubstantial as a shadow: the windshield of her own car had turned golden, then fiery with light. At the approach of the big fireball Caitlin screamed too.

The fireball struck the center of the windshield, vaporizing much of the glass on contact, then blew apart inside the car, becoming a million incendiary droplets each as bright as a tiny sun.

The girls glowed luminously within this gaseous envelope and almost instantly shimmered down into little piles of ash and remnants of bone. The fire, if it could be called that, cooled down in less than a second and vanished as if sucked into a vacuum. The gas tank of the Tempo, untouched, failed to explode. Almost everything inside the car was made of synthetic materials: these were completely vaporized or fused into grotesque lumps of matter.

By the time would-be rescuers reached the car there was nothing to extinguish, and only wisps of pale smoke indicated where the girls had been sitting.

Within a few minutes Crystal had been identified with the assistance of the New Jersey Motor Vehicle Department as one of the unfortunate occupants. Caitlin's luggage, untouched, was in the Tempo's trunk; in one of her bags there was a letter addressed to her from Jeff Pepperdine, dated the thirteenth of February.

At exactly three A.M. in the infirmary on the campus of Williams College in Williamstown, Massachusetts, Jeff Pepperdine, hospitalized for treatment of a fever of unknown origin, went into massive convulsions and was dead on the floor beside his bed before a doctor could be summoned to help him.

53

On the last day of February Adam Kurland ran into the state's attorney for Haden County, Gary Cleves, at the courthouse. Cleves was a small slender man with a dark and well-shaped beard. He had oversized teeth and not enough lip to cover them completely; the resulting toothiness gave him, falsely, an endearing look. But Gary, despite his slight build, fancied himself a tough customer. He had a black belt in karate and carried a pistol everywhere he went, hinting darkly of ex-convicts, whom he'd dispatched to prison in the past, on the loose with axes to grind. He was one of those men who can't hold even a casual conversation unless he has linked himself physically with the one to whom he is talking: shoulder to shoulder, arm in arm, confidentiality his watchword. But never making eye contact: Gary was always too busy looking out for potential enemies or eavesdroppers. Without any form of greeting Gary took Adam by his elbow and guided him to an unfrequented corner of the lobby. All he said, while gazing raptly over Adam's left shoulder, was "Had your breakfast yet?"

"No."

"Coffee and Danish at the German's? My treat." When Adam hesitated, Gary gave him a little nudge in the ribs. "We need to have a talk."

"I don't think we need to discuss the case anymore before it goes to trial, Gary."

"We don't? I've been hearing rumors that you've considered withdrawing as defense counsel."

"Oh, that's bullshit."

But Gary Cleves had the hook in him; beaming, he trolled Adam on down the street to the popular café, where they sat in the prosecutor's favorite booth. It was a single on one side with high wooden armrests and backs, almost as solidly enclosed as a confessional. Adam determinedly made small talk, to which Gary replied in monosyllables, with little punctuating nods, until he had drunk half a mug of coffee and was ready to proceed.

"You haven't been spending much time with your client," he said to Adam, giving him a little reproving tap on the wrist. Gary's hand was furred thick as a glove to the half moons of his fingernails. "I'd almost say you're avoiding him. Nobody's been around to see him this week except that little priest from Pius the Twelfth Parish, and I hear your client scared the piss out of the good father. Want to tell me what's going on?"

"I don't follow you, Gary."

"Father Gregus has been saying that Richard Devon is possessed by the devil."

Adam rubbed his eyes, which were smarting from the brilliance of the sun on the misty window which the booth framed.

"Father Gregus is close to senile. They're retiring him this year. But he had no business going to see Rich without checking with me first."

"I suppose he just wanted to offer some spiritual guidance; your client's a Catholic, isn't he? But I have to tell you, Adam, I think it's a cheap ploy; and where can you go with it?"

"Go with what?"

Beneath the table their knees touched; Gary hunched forward on his elbows. He looked sideways, sharply, waiting until a waitress behind the counter turned her back on them.

"Demonic possession."

"I don't know what you're talking about," Adam said firmly.

With his head down Gary nodded, as if he were willing to wait for Adam to change his tune. Adam outlasted him. Gary said, "You'll plead him not guilty this week, of course."

"Of course."

"And you'll be filing Notice of Defense of Mental Disease or Defect."

"Gary, you'll know what I intend to file *when* I file."

The prosecutor shrugged and sat back. "Sure. Take your time. It doesn't make any difference to me. I'm just trying to be helpful, Adam. After all, we sleep in the same bed around here."

Adam tried not to laugh. "You've never had a gift for metaphor, Gary."

"You know what I mean. Take some good advice and have your client go easy with this devil-made-me-do-it stuff."

"I'm not responsible for everything Devon says." It was a dumb thing to admit. At this stage of events he knew he should be. Gary resisted the opportunity to chide him further. He was served a hot raspberry Danish with a heap of butter melting on it. Adam got indigestion just looking at it. His stomach wasn't good lately. He was sleeping poorly. He wished he had his father to talk to.

Gary dug into the pastry with a spoon. "Your client is sane, and you know it. I'm sincere when I say I don't want to see you hurt too badly by this trial, Adam. But you will be if you're not careful—and honest with yourself about your prospects. By the way, that was a real tragedy, what happened to those two girls down there on the Jersey Turnpike."

"Yeah."

"And that other witness dying the way he did. Tragic—a tragic coincidence. Three eyewitnesses gone, the same night."

"But there are two other eyewitnesses. Donald Ray Stemmons. Warren Hasper. And there are the state cops who were the first on the scene, Granger and Raff. It isn't only witnesses who are going to win this case for me, Gary."

"As a matter of fact, the witnesses will lose it for you. I know what you're going to try. It worked with Brodkey, but this ain't the same ballgame. There is no way you are going to sell Devon as the emotionally overwrought victim of a blighted love affair who went berserk when he found out she was cheating on him. Adam, it wasn't just one shot from a Saturday night special. He clubbed Karyn Vale to death, and he took his sweet time doing it. And to this day he hasn't shown a drop of remorse for the poor girl. The jailers say he's cold as ice. A born killer. He *bothers* them, and they've had some tough guys in their lockup. Bikers. Canuck loggers."

"He's pretty damn scared himself."

"Ha," Gary said, without mirth, looking closely at someone who had just walked in the door of the café. Satisfied that he wasn't about to be assaulted, he glanced at Adam. "You've got a weak case, counselor. Your weakest link is Devon himself. The jury's going to hate him before the trial is two days old. Attila the Hun wouldn't have liked him. I think you hate him yourself—something happens around your eyes when I mention him. Don't think I'm not aware of that. I don't miss much."

"I know you don't, Gary," Adam said patiently.

"Fact is, if you don't want to withdraw, which would be my sincere recommendation, I can offer you an alternative that's bound to be a plus for your career."

"What do you have in mind?"

"A two-stage trial."

"That's what I thought you had in mind. Have you been seeing a lot of Tommie Harkrider lately?"

Gary missed the barb. "He was up here a while back. I've talked to him on the phone several times since. He represents Karyn Vale's family."

"I know. And lately he's advocated two-stage trials in insanity pleas."

"I like the idea myself," Gary said, as if he was the franchise holder for the state of Vermont. "The insanity plea has become a cancer in the belly of the legal system. We—I mean, you and I and the state—have a chance to do something meaningful about that. *Vermont* v. *Devon* could be more than just another murder trial, Adam. It could be a landmark case. Don't you feel that's more important than getting Devon the works on a first-degree conviction. Or a free ride for a couple of years in the state hospital?"

"A two-stage trial would be an experiment, and I'd be doing my client a disservice even to consider it. As for the insanity plea, both of us have been down this road a few times, Gary, and neither of us knows what the jury is likely to do. At this point I'm sure of two things: Rich was not in control of himself when he killed Karyn Vale, and he remains in desperate need of—professional help. I have an obligation to see that he gets the help he needs, as quickly as possible." Adam glanced down at the table, as if to recalculate the odds from the cards the prosecutor had dealt him, then looked up quickly, catching Gary's eye. Gary winced, slightly pained by a threat of genuine intimacy. "Look, Gary, we've had some brawls in court but you have to admit I've always played it straight with you."

"Almost always," the prosecutor said, with a hint of petulance.

"Maybe we can cut a deal here and now."

"I won't plea-bargain."

"I'm willing to go along with the idea of a two-stage trial subject to an appropriate ruling from the bench."

"Now you're being sensible, Adam."

"In return I want my client sprung. Reasonable bail and appropriate custody."

"Whose custody?"

"Private sanitarium of our choice."

"Ha. Not a chance. He's too fucking dangerous."

"What if I can guarantee security?"

"Under the circumstances I wouldn't even let him go to max lock at the hospital. Out of the question. Ask me anything else."

"Richard Devon needs attention *now*, Gary. Isn't that obvious from what's been going on?"

"It's obvious he's a cold-blooded killer. If you want more psychiatrists to look at him, fine. Your option. But he has to be examined at the jail."

Adam stood and put a quarter on the table to pay for the coffee he hadn't touched. "See you in court, Gary."

"Wait a minute, Adam; we didn't even begin to discuss this."

"No discussion. You know what I want. Call me by five o'clock today, Gary."

Adam walked back to the courthouse through crunching snow, head lowered to keep the raw wind off his face. He hadn't looked at the prosecutor again as he was leaving, but he felt no confidence that his ultimatum would be met. It was worth Gary's job to let Rich out now, and he knew it. Another petition for bail consideration would be worthless, even if the Catholic Church would back the application.

Gary Cleves, he thought, had been right about one thing. The jury, any jury, would hate Richard Devon. Adam didn't hate his client—he was merely scared shitless of him, and dreaded being in the same room with him. But today he had to see him.

The prisoner was brought into the interview room by the pint-size Duke and two other guards. Adam asked them all to stay. He sat as far from his client as possible.

The prisoner was in a straitjacket again. He sat slackly in a chair, chin down, eyes coldly insolent. Adam looked into those eyes and saw nothing of Rich. The prisoner smiled at him. His voice, at least, was almost familiar.

"You can't get me out of here, can you?"

"No."

"Why don't you just drop the case, Adam?"

"Is that what you want me to do?"

"I need a lawyer. You're as good as any."

"Why do you need a lawyer? I'm no help to you unless you want to be helped. What is it you really want? For Richard Devon to spend the rest of his life behind bars? How will that satisfy you?"

The prisoner didn't reply. His smile pricked Adam's nerves. Adam's hands were clammy. Perspiration trickled down the back of his neck.

"What makes you so goddamned pleased with yourself today?" Adam said in exasperation.

"There's going to be a death in the family," the prisoner told him. He went on smiling.

54

Donald Ray Stemmons, the twenty-six-year-old bartender whose mountaineer's blond beard was stained around the mouth by chewing tobacco, worked the six P.M.-to-closing shift in the tavern of the Davos Chalet Lodge, which left his days free for women and other sport.

The first week in March, following several big snow-storms, brought the most beneficent weather they'd had for skiing all season. It also brought out the crowds. Accommodations were jammed, skiers were tripping over each other, and service was bad almost everywhere. The youthful employees at the various lodges and restaurants were all overworked, exhausted, and snappish from long weeks of burning their candles at both ends. Stemmons had given serious thought to walking out on his own job unless the management of the Davos Chalet hired another bartender to help him. He was temporarily without a female companion; the nineteen-year-old Finnish chambermaid he'd been screwing on other people's unmade beds had linked up with a group of ski bums who had migrated north to Smuggler's Notch. But early in this week of aggravating nights in the smoke-fouled tavern and days of fierce joyous release on the most difficult trails Hermitage Mountain had to offer, he'd had his first glimpse of the woman whom he found so tantalizing, and so difficult to make contact with.

She was in the sunup line of the cafeteria at Galeatry Lodge, three quarters of a mile down the mountain from Davos Chalet. No one was with her. For breakfast she was having grapefruit, coffee, and a box of 40% Bran Flakes. She was strikingly tall and dressed all in black, ski clothing that modeled to perfection the figure of a showgirl or a very expensive hooker. Her skin was stained the even dark shade of wild honey. Even from where he stood it was obvious she was no kid: she might be as old as forty. Stemmons had always favored older women for sexual liaisons, which was one reason he was immediately attracted to her. The other reason was—perhaps—the little savage arc of scar low on her left cheek, near her mouth, as if a sensual kiss by a tormented lover had slipped, and bitten deep. The gash of love. She had the ease, the contented expression of money, status, accomplishment.

Out of his league, of course. But then she turned at the register and looked his way. Her eyes were obsidian, they jumped out of her face at him like knives and he felt that curious lift and sizzle of nerves along the spinal column, the sensation of destinies commingled.

Once he had selected his own breakfast Stemmons took his time looking around the big noisy cafeteria to see where she was seated. He was surprised, and disgruntled, not to find her anywhere in the room. A very fast eater. He wondered if she could ski.

She was a superb skier, as he found out early in the

week. She was just ahead of him again, this time on the double chair lift; he followed her to High Hazard Two and probably could have caught up to her at the lip of the descent except for a problem with a binding that cost him several minutes. He could only watch as, unaccompanied, she swooped through sets of beautifully precise turns, the technique of an old master like Stein Erickson, leaving a shimmering snow wake in the halcyon air. Later that same day he had a glimpse of her from the heights of a chair lift pier; this time she was on the Devil's Pigtail, a fleet inky shadow, lost to her hips in the spuming powder, so lazily graceful as she laid into her turns that he ached to be there, complementing with his own crisp style her fluid descent, her airy excellence.

Suddenly he was spotting her everywhere on the slopes, but always she was maddeningly distant; he began to keep a mental diary of all of his glimpses of her, trying to figure out a pattern to her day so that he might intercept her. But she had no routine, she was consistent only in her elusiveness. One night, while he was hard at work pumping beer, he looked up to see her face in the glaring doorway of the tavern, turned toward him. He thought he saw her smile, and for a few moments it seemed as if she might come in, but then beer foamed over his wrist and when he looked for her again she wasn't there. He felt a sense of loss that had him in profane bad humor the rest of the night.

The week went by too quickly, and on Friday morning he didn't see her at all. Disappointed, he gave up his by now habitual scanning of the trails as he rose and fell, rose and fell, while the sun circled blindingly in flawless blue. Stemmons skied to classical music, a cassette player clipped to his jacket, small headphones clamped beneath his knit cap. For the lilting turns and cloud-filled plateaus of the High Hazards he liked Tchaikovsky or Mozart; Beethoven and Wagner suited the thundering express of the Rocket. Brahms soothed the lengthy jolting returns up the mountain.

The setting sun found him on the double chair lift rising once more to the summit where the several trails began and diverged, lacing down all sides of the mountain. Most of the ski crowd had packed it in for the day, and only a few of the chairs were occupied. The lift would cease operating, except for the ski patrol, at sunset. Probably ten minutes away. He would take the last long glide down in purpling dusk, through coves and tunnels formed from snowladen birches, the last rays of the sun flashing across his bronze goggles.

When he arrived at the lift ramp nearly four thousand feet above the darkened valley he lingered for a couple of minutes until the lift quit, waiting for the handful of skiers who had come up behind him to push off. Then he slid down the ramp and struck off down a packed, somewhat corny vale toward the most difficult of the mountain's runs, the Devil's Pigtail. It was marked with a sign that featured an impish caricature of a porker looking back over one shoulder at his corkscrew tail. WARNING: FOR EXPERT SKIERS ONLY. The horned pig was pointing to the left, to a cove still golden with the long light of the sun.

And he saw her, poised against a flushed violet sky, goggles raised on her high forehead. She heard his skis rattling down the trail and looked around inquiringly. He held his breath, sure that she was going to disappear before he could sideslip down to where she waited. But she smiled, and made no move. Stemmons couldn't believe his luck had turned at last.

"Hi," he said, coasting past her and executing a little jump-turn that placed him facing her and directly in front of the precipitous trail.

"Hello." Dimples, and those great, somewhat mocking eyes, and that alluring scar. She was wearing a pink joke button on her black partially zipped windbreaker. In white lettering it said THERE ARE MANY WAYS TO SAY I LOVE YOU. FUCKING IS THE FASTEST. Her smile widened when she caught him gawking at it. A rising wind spilled snow from the tip of a looming evergreen. Particles glittered, with a charged, fabulous light, in her hair, across the top of her forehead.

"I've been watching you ski this week," Stemmons told her. "You're good."

"I'm very good," she said, gently correcting him. "So are you. You're Donald Stemmons, aren't you?"

"That's right."

"And you were on the U.S. ski team two years ago?"

"No. Wish I could say I was. My best shot was a little too slow."

"Planning to try again?"

"I just ski for fun now. You up here on vacation?"

"You might call it a working vacation."

"Oh." He wasn't quite sure what to make of that. "How long will you be around?"

"Well, that depends."

"Maybe we could have dinner."

"That depends as well."

"On what?"

"Men have to earn me, Donald," she said, even more gently than before, and with a slight wistfulness, as if she had already decided he couldn't measure up.

He might have guessed. A hooker. So much for his luck. He had a trade-off coming at the Hickory Pit, steaks for two, but no money to pay for ass, even this choice piece.

"No," she said, more boldly. "I'm not a whore."

"Well, uh—"

"Dinner's on me. Provided."

"What?"

"We race to the bottom."

"And if I win, dinner's on you?"

"That's right."

"What if I lose?" He couldn't help smiling.

She cocked her head, considering the other side of the wager. "Dinner's still on me. But you do the dishes."

"At your place?"

"At my place."

"Sounds good to me. But in all fairness, you ought to have a head start." He nodded toward the trail. "I've been skiing up here since December."

"That's very generous of you, Donald. How much of a head start will you give me?"

"Fifteen seconds?"

"Oh, you *must* be fast. This'll be exciting. Well, it looks as if we're about to lose the light. Ready?"

Stemmons dug in his poles and jumped a full turn, sidestepped out of her way. She brushed past him lightly without another word and swooped on down the trail, which already was becoming a little vague in the declining light. He waited, counting half aloud as she described a series of balletic turns that carried her beyond a thick patch of woods and out of sight. She was moving very fast and he bit his tongue in his desire to overhaul her, but was faithful to the count. At fifteen he jabbed his poles deep and lifted off, hurtled through isolated stands of birches and around a broad mogul, establishing an instant almost effortless rhythm across slopes still mildly streaked with sun.

It occurred to Stemmons, belatedly, that he hadn't learned her name. He knew the trail so well he could have skied it by moonlight, and he knew where she would make the mistakes that would enable him to catch up. He just hoped she wouldn't spill. That would take the fun out of it.

When he cleared the woods and turned sharply right for the second stage of the now steeply plunging trail he didn't see her anywhere below him: the trail, in a thin reddish glow, was starkly empty, and he could see almost three hundred yards ahead. He pulled up quickly, astonished, looked past some big rocks and darkly banded trees, afraid that she had overshot this turn and gone pinwheeling into a shadowy pileup.

His spurted breath, frozen, drifted briskly away on the wind. He heard, but couldn't see, some distant ski patrollers. He cupped his gloved hands to his mouth to call out to her. But what was her name?

He wondered then if she had skied just to the woods and decided not to go on. She might be hiding in there, with that smile. Having decided, capriciously, that he wasn't worth her time after all. Nothing but a tease. Suddenly he was angry. The cunt. He regretted all the time he'd spent speculating about her, the rush of lust he'd experienced a minute ago, gazing into her wide-set eyes, dark as old brandy, subtly fuming. *There are many ways to say I love you. . . .*

Well, go fuck yourself tonight, lady. I don't want to play anymore.

Stemmons pushed off again, slicing down a narrow chute that was a little too icy for his liking, growing more dangerous as night came on and the temperature dropped. He made a left-hand turn and came out onto a narrow plateau, almost flat and devoid of growth, crusty moguls projecting from the ridgeback above him.

That's when he saw her again, far down the trail, a dim

figure in the dusk. She was standing with hands on hips, her ski poles at angles of forty-five degrees, looking back the way she had come. Looking for him. Head held at a taunting angle.

He couldn't believe, despite the start he'd given her, his brief reconnoitering pause above, that she had covered so much of the trail so quickly. He hesitated for only a moment, then thrust himself forward savagely and went into a racing crouch as he hurtled on rattling skis down the troughlike trail.

The woman crouched, too, though she was still facing him. She jabbed her poles into the snow and lunged forward. *Uphill*.

She was skiing uphill, flying toward him with the same reckless speed he had achieved.

For several seconds Stemmons's mind simply refused to believe what his eyes recorded. It was a physical impossibility. Yet here she came, all in black, the pink joke button glowing on one breast like a diminutive, romantic sun, eyes hidden behind dark goggles, the pale lip of scar somehow frightfully vivid despite the distance between them. At this velocity they would collide in seconds, nowhere to go but off the trail into rock after rock after rock. *Men have to earn me, Donald.* Her hair wisping like smoke, coiling in the air above her lowered head, her whole body now shimmering blackly, becoming amorphous even as her speed increased, and there was no stopping on this stiletto of ice-slick trail: nothing could stop him now short of a deliberate spill. He had seen racing friends rent from anus to navel by such spills, the bloody broken edges of ribcage and collarbones poking through pulverized flesh.

Donald Stemmons screamed; his skis left the track just as they met, soaringly, head-on. But it was not a fleshly woman he encountered, it was a whirling, seething, dense black cloud, a deeper blackness than anything he'd ever seen, even his own mother's shroud. The cloud drew him in and spun him around at breakneck speed, tearing the breath from his lungs and the skis from his boots before he was hurled nearly sixty feet down one side of the trail. In a splashing sunset moment he came down headfirst onto a thinly iced boulder with such force that every vertebra of his spinal column was crushed, his skull fragmented, his eyeballs ejected from their sockets. Most of his brains were pounded down into his mouth and throat.

Even before Donald Ray Stemmons died, the black cloud had begun to dissipate above the slick white surface of the Devil's Pigtail; streaks of it wafted toward the heights of flame-tipped trees and vanished, in pure thin darkening air, high above the summit of Hermitage Mountain.

55

For the entire week preceding the arraignment of Richard Devon, scheduled for the ninth of March, the prisoner's attitude and behavior were much improved. He spoke politely to his jailers, although no more than he had to. He asked for reading material and passed most of his time in his cell quietly absorbed in *War and Peace* and a life of Tolstoi. On two occasions he was allowed to watch television with other prisoners, although he had to wear his straitjacket.

Without restraint but with guards present he also had the opportunity to exercise. His appetite was good. He met once with Maggie Renquist and an associate of hers. He was cooperative but revealed nothing of his feelings when asked direct questions about the murder. Adam also met with the prisoner the day before the arraignment; he didn't know whether he was talking to the possessor or to the possessed.

On March 9 the prisoner, wearing a neat gray suit, figured blue tie, and black loafers with tassels, was taken in handcuffs to the courtroom of Judge Ralph D. McComb, where he stood silent and self-absorbed while his lawyer spoke for him, entering a plea of not guilty to the charge of first-degree murder.

Lindsay Potter saw him for the first time since the ordeal in the interview room almost a month before. As

Adam was speaking, the prisoner turned his head to look at her; there was something boyish but cruel in the set of the mouth, a look of boredom in the eyes. This one look inspired in her such feelings of hopelessness, despair, and fear for her life that she had all she could do to keep from weeping. The surge of emotions passed, but she was left with a sense of bleakness that was worse than any depression she'd ever known.

"Rich is gone, isn't he?" she said afterwards to Adam. "It's as if this other—thing—just moved in, packed all of Rich up in a small suitcase, and stored him in the attic."

"Did you notice the way McComb kept looking at him? Nobody is more plodding, pedantic, and unimaginative than Ralph. But five minutes after they brought Rich into the courtroom he was so nervous I thought he was going to swallow his teeth. He must be happy he isn't presiding."

"You know what it all adds up to."

"Rich seems without conscience, totally indifferent. If he's like this when the trial begins I don't know how I'll be able to sell an insanity plea to the jury, with or without expert testimony."

"Then we have to try to sell the truth: it isn't Rich, it's—"

"Establishing 'truth' is incidental to the process of law," Adam reminded her. "A courtroom is a place to reach a decision through the adversarial system, which is not the same thing as separating the true from the false. I'm not a philosopher. I'm a trial lawyer. Forget it, Lindsay. There's not much I can do."

"Are you quitting?"

His hands shook and he spilled coffee on his sleeve. He scowled.

"I hate that word, Linds."

"If you can't—or won't—defend him properly, you might as well turn the case over to the public defender."

"No, I—we can always get delays. Keep working, and hope we don't lose any more of our key witnesses. You know I can't build a case for NGRI with depositions. I need the people on the stand, telling the jury what Rich was like when he killed Karyn."

"Adam, I just don't think you have a case for NGRI. But in spite of your objections, I know it may be possible to plead demonic possession."

"How? Look what happened in the Arne Cheyenne Johnson case."

"I read the transcript. I don't know who was more inept, the presiding judge or counsel for the defense."

"Sure, it was a botched trial, but what matters is, the judge refused to allow the defense attorney to present his argument, let alone call priests or other key witnesses. So Johnson's lawyer switched to a plea of self-defense on behalf of another. Which I hardly think will work in Rich's case."

"But demonic possession pleas have been successful in England. I've sent for transcripts of two of those trials. They should be here in a few days. At least look them over, Adam."

He studied her skeptically, and with concern. "You're really serious about this."

"*Yes*. Believe me, it's not what I want to do. I want to just turn my back on the case, forget I ever saw Richard Devon. And try to get over being as scared as I am. But I can't, Adam. I also want to be able to respect myself for the rest of my life."

"I don't want to be the first Kurland to disgrace himself before the bar of the state of Vermont."

"You're much too good a lawyer. All you need are the means, a way to make it work."

Adam made sure his hands were steady before he lifted his coffee cup again.

"I'll read those transcripts," he said. "Doesn't mean I'm committing myself, Lindsay." But she looked so grateful and newly determined that he had the feeling he had.

"I'll try to get hold of Father Merlo today, find out when he's coming back. And he needs to know about Donald Ray Stemmons."

"Why?"

"Oh, Adam. All those deaths." Lindsay started a shrug that turned into a shudder, then made herself look him in the eye. "You don't really believe they were accidents, do you? *I* don't. We need him here; we need his guidance and his prayers. Because—it could happen to us. Couldn't it?"

56

On an uncommonly mild end-of-winter day in Rome, Father James Merlo met with his immediate superior, the chief investigator for the office that dealt with exorcisms and the claims of demonic possession that were referred almost daily to the Vatican by priests around the world, and the cardinal in charge of the tribunal known as the Apostolic Penitentiary, in the cardinal's study high above the San Demaso courtyard. Luncheon was served. The windows were open to a vista of Renaissance domes and rooftops and cream yellow clouds, and the breeze was refreshing, with only a hint of the monoxide miasma that usually enshrouded the Eternal City.

Bernardo Luis Cardinal Cosme, an elderly man poignant in his longevity, had decorated his study with some very old works of religious art, and one framed drawing from a recent issue of *The New Yorker*. It showed a rather startled middle-aged man who had opened his apartment door to a hooded, black-robed specter with a scythe over one shoulder. The caption read, "Relax. I've come for your toaster."

Father Merlo found the cartoon an intriguing touch of levity in these rooms where the monstrous and the diabolical were frequent topics of conversation. All forms of sorcery, including black masses said by renegade priests of the Church, were investigated by the Apostolic Penitentiary. Merlo liked to think he hadn't lost his own sense of humor in a job that could be overpowering, and he related better to the soft-spoken Cosme than to Monsignor Daviano, who seemed to have been compressed to a fiercely glowing cinderbrick by the demands of his calling, his duel of long standing with Satan and the knighthood of hell.

Father Merlo was bothered by conjunctivitis in one eye, a result of many long days spent with fragile old manuscripts and registers behind a locked oak door deep within *L'Archivio Segreto Vaticano*, the secret archives where the lore of demonology was kept. The condition was treatable with drops, and for the last few days, while his report on the phenomenon of Zarach' Bal-Tagh was being studied by Cosme and others entitled to know, he had used his leisure time for a few rounds of golf at the exclusive Aquasanta Club in Rome, for a visit to the opera, for meditation. The strategy of one of mankind's most devoted enemies was clearer, but as yet Merlo had no counter to Zarach's first bold move.

His Eminence withheld his comments until after they had eaten, preferring to dwell at length on a recent visit to his Andalusian birthplace. Monsignor Daviano ate too quickly, a piece of broiled fish with a lemon butter seasoning, and fueled his chronic indigestion. He had to excuse himself to go to the bathroom. When he returned, looking pale above jowls black with beard shadow, the discussion was opened.

"It is obvious," said the husky-voiced monsignor in English, "that the choice of the possessed, Richard Devon, was not made at random. It may have been carefully arranged, a most unusual circumstance. To date Zarach', except when forced to behave otherwise, has been almost discreet in his possession. He is acting as a caretaker, not with the usual ruthless disregard for the body he inhabits. Therefore he must want Richard Devon to endure, for some larger purpose."

"He wants to go to trial," Merlo said.

"Yes. Exactly. He is looking for a public trial of sensational origins. A forum guaranteed to provide a maximum of publicity when he—indulges in the reign of terror for which he has been noted through the ages."

Cardinal Cosme brushed bread crumbs from the front of his wool soutane. "I also reached this conclusion, and have informed Wojtyla of what we are facing. Needless to say, His Holiness is most concerned and would welcome some encouraging answers. How can we become more involved at this point?"

"Eminence," Merlo said, "I'm afraid it's next to impossible. There's a murder charge, it's a secular matter until after the trial. Which of course would be too late, no matter what verdict the jury returned. But I don't believe

Zarach' will let the trial develop any way except *his* way. None of us can afford the consequences.''

Cosme studied him soberly. "Are we helpless against this monster?"

"Frustrated for now; but not without the means of confronting Zarach' head-on.''

"Explain."

"We need a combination of legal *and* spiritual help. I think we have to call on Sundial.''

57

Trooper Norm Granger drove across the plank bridge with the other state police car a few yards behind him, only the parking lights showing, and stopped where both vehicles would be out of the line of sight of anyone coming along Marsham Road. He got out of his car, not bothering to zip up his lined leather jacket: it was a mild night for this time of the year, temperature in the high twenties. He walked back to the second police car, handcuffs clinking on his belt.

Pete Raff had rolled the window down. The radio was quiet; Monday night, their tour had been predictably slow for a couple of hours. Pete looked at the small country house beneath the moon a hundred and fifty feet away, the pronged radiance of a TV antenna strapped to the side chimney, the humble front porch that seemed as if it was about to collapse from the weight of cords of firewood stacked under its roof. He took out his Marlboros.

"This where she lives?" he asked Norm.

"Yeah," Norm said. He was a big sweet-tempered man who smiled often, even in his sleep. He was thirty-four. He'd been a good double-A ballplayer for a while in his youth, but couldn't hit well enough in the bigs to compensate for a lack of speed and a tendency to throw the ball away. Now he was balding, though it wasn't that noticeable yet, and he had developed a paunch. He was devoted to the simple pleasures of life: wife, kids, dogs, sporting guns, six-packs. Occasionally he had a little piece of ass on the side. He could have had a lot more, because women liked the way he smiled at them, but Norm was a little lazy, and a certain amount of effort was required in setting up liaisons.

"No lights," Pete said. "And I don't see a car."

"Probably in that shed. She's here. I told her I thought I could get by tonight."

"What's her name?"

"You know something? I never did ask."

Pete lighted his cigarette and sat back. Nine years younger than Norm, he was blond and thin and sallow, and no woman had ever dashed off her phone number for him after a couple of minutes of chitchat in the supermarket checkout line. Norm was sure-handed, easy. He caught them like moths beating senselessly around a bright light, treated them capably and gently, breathed new life into their bored lives, always left them feeling better about themselves.

Norm Granger had only one rule: no matter how tempted he might be, he never saw the same woman twice.

"Okay, partner, I'll cover for you."

"Thanks, Pete. Owe you one." Norm gave his gunbelt a hitch and tucked in his gut a little, as far as it would go these days, and crunched up the rutted drive to the house. The moon was bright enough on glazed snow; he didn't need his flashlight.

Wind chimes tittered on the porch as he walked to the door. There was a noise of tiny feet, scuttlings in the woodpile. He took off his hat and tucked it under one arm. There was a slit between curtains over one front window; he made out the flickering borealis of a color TV screen. He opened the storm door, polyethylene in a skinny aluminum frame, and knocked. Now he could hear the television, the sort of music that accompanied chase sequences on cop shows. He waited, but there was no response to his knock. And as he waited, he felt he was being watched.

Norm turned his head with care. A dozen feet behind him, at the foot of the steps to the sagging porch, stood a large dog. It had a winter's coat thick as a haymow, a sloping narrow head. Some kind of wolfhound. Russian.

Irish. After the first skipped heartbeat Norm realized the dog wasn't going to bother him. They either came for you right away, or they didn't.

While he was looking down at the wolfhound, the door of the house opened.

"Oh! I did hear a knock."

The dog bounded up the steps, and Norm stepped aside for him. The dog slipped through the opening and brushed the woman out of the way in passing.

"Hugo!" She scolded. "What's your hurry?" She looked at Norm, eyebrows slightly raised, a smile beginning. "You're a man of your word," she said. "Come in."

"Thanks." Norm walked into the house and looked around. From the shabby exterior he hadn't been expecting much, the usual clutter of worthless furniture, worn carpeting, water stains on the wallpaper. Cramped dark rooms. Instead he found himself in an expensively decorated hacienda. Bright Mexican tile on the floor, a corner hearth with a gas log fire, white walls, unframed canvases filled with bold blue skies and peasant marketplaces, the sturdy furniture upholstered in stripes of red and orange and gold, ceramic and copper bowls and vases in small niches and on tabletops, flowers and green plants everywhere. Over one ear she wore a red flower in her severely braided dark hair. Hibiscus. He had seen a lot of them in Arizona and Florida during spring training. Her mouth was like the flower; his fingers curled slightly as he smiled.

The wolfhound had taken over half of a sofa and lay shivering with his nose toward the blue-toned fire. The woman turned off the television and closed the cabinet doors. Dark old wood, handcarved. He watched her as she went immediately to the bar, where tapers burned in a candleholder, folk art in the form of a speckled dove. "I was having a little wine, would you care for some? Or how about a beer? Dos Equis." "Dos Equis would be fine; haven't tasted any since I was in Tucson with the Tribe. You have a nice place here." "It was an extravagance. But one gets so homesick," "Homesick for where?" "Paracuaro. Mexico." "Oh, that's where you were born?" "More of an adopted home, really. I'm a native of Vermont." "Well, I never would have guessed that. You look—more Spanish, know what I mean?'' And so they went, back and forth, the catcher and the moth.

She smiled and preened as if he'd rubbed her vanity in all the right places and brought him his beer in a tall glass. She was *mucha mujer*, Norm thought, warming to the spirit of his surroundings. Well into her prime, but not having to fight too many holding actions yet. Hips in taut silk without a trace of an untidy bulge, flat bare stomach that didn't ripple or pooch when she walked, breasts high for her age, and the nipples well defined beneath the black silk shirt she wore knotted at the breastbone.

She liked to stand close. He barely had elbowroom to sip his beer.

''Are you off duty now?'' she asked.

''Meal break.''

''I can't imagine what it's like, being a policeman.''

''Dull, most of the time. Some traffic accidents, stolen cars, a few holdups.''

''Murders,'' she said, with a thrilled flaring of her nostrils.

''Two, three times a year. We had a nasty one in January. At the Davos Chalet Lodge. Raff and I were the first ones on the scene. This kid beat his girl to death because she was fooling around.''

''Ah,'' the woman said, catching her lower lip between her teeth. ''Was he insane?''

''In my opinion. I never have seen a body that looked as bad as that girl's. But you don't want to hear about that.''

''No,'' she said, with a sigh and a shudder. She put a hand on his, the hand that was holding the beer glass. She wore a lot of rings. Topaz, tourmalines in silver. She drank from his glass, and a little beer trickled from one corner of her mouth; it left a glistening track across the low curved scar on her right cheek. He leaned toward her and kissed away the moisture, and she shuddered again.

The next time he kissed her, his hand went to the flower in her hair, and crushed it. He never did get to finish his beer.

She wanted him with his clothes off but his gunbelt on. Norm carried the most gun he was allowed, the Smith and Wesson Highway Patrolman with the six-inch barrel. Loaded, it weighed about four pounds. It had custom-made, finger-groove walnut grips. It was the first time he'd had sex with a woman with a gun strapped on, but she seemed to get quite a kick out of fondling the butt of the gun with one hand while she rang his dangle-down bells with the other. She came three times while Norm was coming once.

The experience fairly knocked her out. She whimpered and whined, and the dog whined, too, as if he had been aroused by the human rutting. Norm didn't know what he'd do if the dog came over and stuck his nose in. Sometimes you just had to draw the line.

"Oh, lover, lover," she moaned, when at last her hands slipped from his body and lay still at her sides.

Norm smiled down at her, but the truth was he hadn't enjoyed himself as much as he should have. He had made love despite some kind of stomach gripe that was now causing cramps.

"Was I good for you?" she asked.

"Uh, just fine, honey." He pulled away from her and sat up, holding his stomach.

"You're not leaving so soon!"

"I got to use the bathroom, if it's okay."

"Surely." She raised up, breasts bobbing, and pointed the way. "Through the beaded curtain there. The bedroom."

"Thanks—" He hesitated, as if he was about to say her name, but realized he still didn't know it and felt awkward about asking at this point. Then Norm let out a little gasp as pain lanced through his gut.

He got to his feet. The dog looked around at him, quickly, with a little malicious jab of its nose. Norm sensed the wolfhound did not like him. He walked a few steps, loaded down with the black gunbelt and holster, paused to unbuckle it, let it drop in the seat of a basket chair with a serape across the back and pushed on, through the doorway, down a short hall to the bedroom, which was just as nicely furnished as the rest of the house.

The cramps were coming bad now. It was all he could do to hold himself upright as he walked. He made it into the Mexican-style john. Tiled sunken tub, Jacuzzi, bright skylight. A hanging basket filled with bristling cacti. The toilet was a big expensive job with gold fixtures, a padded red seat. Hibiscus again. Her luscious, lewd mouth. He plopped himself down and sat holding his gut, nauseated, frozen by cramps. It was very quiet in the house. He heard nothing but his own grunting and groaning.

It took him several minutes to pass whatever had been affecting him, but the cramps went away almost immediately. Norm cleaned himself, wetting tissue to do a thorough job, then reached behind for the gold lever to flush.

The roar of the toilet was unexpectedly loud; he felt a cool wet blast of air on his tender buttocks, and suction that clamped him tightly to the soft seat.

It was so unexpected it scared him a little, that violent churning, as if there was a whirlpool just below his hanging balls. He tried to get up, and found to his dismay that he was stuck fast, as if glued to the seat.

"What the hell—"

He put both hands down and pushed hard, twisting his torso, trying to wrench himself free as if his buttocks were the cork in a wine bottle, but all of his strength wasn't enough to pop him loose. In fact he felt a pain of compression; he was being drawn millimeters farther down into the oval hole in the seat by the unbelievable suction. And there was a strong downward pull on his genitals as well. They hurt—God, how they hurt!

Frantically, he tried reaching behind him, jiggling the handle to shut off the flow of water. It did no good. He was being sucked into the toilet through an opening barely eleven inches wide. Terrible pain racked the bones of his hips and pelvis. His knees were jammed together. His feet could no longer touch the floor. The toilet roared like a cyclone.

Norm did the only thing left for him to do: he screamed for help.

Pete Raff had left the window down a few inches so the smoke of his several cigarettes could flow out into the night. He was munching potato chips from a bag and fantasizing about what was going on inside the modest house. He knew from other officers that the women who picked up cops liked to be handcuffed; they liked to be swatted lightly on their behinds with the long black batons; they panted for authoritative abuse.

The scream he heard jarred him; it was all wrong. It was

the woman who should be screaming at this point, not Norm Granger.

Pete jumped out of the car and ran up to the house, carrying his flashlight.

The wood piled on the porch smelled of dry rot, as if it had been undisturbed for years. The floorboards sagged. There was a screen door, the screenwire torn and rusted, hanging down in veils. The scarred front door was secured with a hasp and padlock. It had not been opened tonight; Pete could see that at a glance.

But inside the house Norm Granger was screaming in horror.

With his skin breaking out in lumps Pete gave a couple of lusty kicks to the door, then whirled to a window and broke open the old shutters. He hammered at panes of glass with the butt end of his flashlight, felt frantically for the corroded latch inside but couldn't budge it. He gave up and reached for a chunk of wood to clean out the rest of the window. He stepped over the sill and into the parlor of the house, boots crunching on fallen glass. He pulled his revolver and cocked it.

The room was colder than the night outside. The floor was covered with cheesy linoleum. The plaster walls were streaked with brown water stains. The only furnishings were a dumpy sofa with enough holes in it for a mouse hotel, and a three-legged wooden chair sitting akilter against one wall.

He saw Norm's gunbelt and holster draped across the seat of the chair, his uniform shirt and pants folded on top of a radiator. He heard Norm screaming in a strangled, nearly breathless way.

Pete followed his light to the back of the house, to a door leaning off one hinge. He heard a toilet running, and only the faintest sounds now from Norm Granger. But there were some loud groaning and snapping sounds, like a birch woods at sunrise after an ice storm. He passed through a small bedroom and located the bathroom with his flashlight.

He saw feet, ankles, legs; he saw hands and wrists and arms, all standing straight up out of an old wooden toilet seat, like a strangely provocative piece of living sculpture. The fingers and toes moved. But the centerpiece of the arrangement, jammed in between the white and hairy appendages, was Norm Granger's swollen, blood-darkened face. His lips were pursed around a tremendous tongue. His eyes, reacting to the light, opened a little, then closed. The toilet was roaring like a geyser, making sucking noises as Norm's bones continued to compress and snap. He slipped farther down into the toilet bowl.

"Yahhhhh!" Pete Raff said; he turned so violently from this scene that he banged his face against the door jamb and saw stars. He also dropped his flashlight, which winked off. Tears of pain sprinkled from his eyes as, in the terrifying dark, he groped to pick up the flashlight.

The popping, gurgling sounds of compaction and flushing continued. Pete raised his flashlight in both shaking hands and turned it on again. The wide beam lit up the whole bathroom. He couldn't avoid seeing what was happening in the toilet; the slow withdrawal of fingers, the last of Norm's long toes, the nail just growing back on the left big toe where he'd dropped the refrigerator he'd been helping his brother-in-law to move. Then there was a last, loud sucking and everything disappeared. The toilet quieted gradually, but by then Pete couldn't hear it anyway, could hear nothing except for the overstressed hammering of his heart.

He approached the toilet by inches. Getting there took most of the rest of his life.

He looked down into the blood-flecked rusty bowl, at the water slowly clearing from a pinkish brew.

A large bubble traveled through the pipe and the water belched at him; he jerked back, the roots of his hair icicles. When he looked down again, there was an eyeball floating in the slowly churning water, roots dangling like the tendrils of a jellyfish. Pete stared at it.

"Oh, Pete," he heard his mother say clearly from the other side of the hallway, "are you going to stay in there all night?"

He turned his head slowly and replied in a boyish voice, "No, Mama. I'm all through with my bath."

"Did you wash your ears?"

"Yes."

"Did you wash your peepee?"

"Yes."

"Be sure you scrub the ring out of the tub. Your father will be home in a little while, and he'll want to take a bath too."

"I did already."

"I thought I heard King at the back door a few minutes ago. Would you go down and let him in? I need to finish this sewing."

"Okay, Mama."

"Put your slippers on first."

"They're on already!"

"Well, you know I have to keep reminding you," his mother said mildly.

Pete took his cap gun with him to let King in. It looked just like a real gun. If a burglar saw it, he would run. Pete was six and he wasn't afraid of burglars. But he liked having the gun with him all the same.

King wasn't on the back porch when he looked out. But he saw fresh paw prints in the snow, going away from the house. To that part of the yard where they dug the vegetable garden every spring, where now the moon was brightest.

There he saw the dog leaping and cavorting, throwing up clouds of snow. But this long-legged animal didn't look much like King, who was a stocky mongrel with cropped ears. He was lanky and shaggy and almost the size of a pony; he had a long pointed nose. And someone was riding on his back, gripping a solid handful of his tawny coat. Fascinated, little Pete pressed his face close to the cold glass pane of the back door, holding his breath now so he wouldn't fog the glass.

The rider on the dog's back was a lady with long dark hair, and as he watched, it occurred to him that she was naked. She was having an exciting time. He could hear faint yips of laughter as the hound carried her dashingly from one corner of the yard to another; he soared with her over the snow-heaped stone barbecue. He was both a prince of dogs and a clown; he made Pete giggle, but there was an element of uneasiness in his mirth, foreboding.

He attempted to deny these feelings by raising the cap gun to the glass. "Bang!" he said. "Bang!" The hairy hound continued, untiringly, to leap from one snowburst to another, which were illuminated like fireworks by the brimstone of his eyes.

The woman became aware of Pete, as his fascination
with her nudity, her large breasts like hardboiled eggs with
the dark yolk showing through, became both an itch and a
guilt. He couldn't bear her scrutiny, her dark intimidating
eyes, as she deliberately directed the dog closer to the back
door. He slipped down below the level of the glass, and
sat with his back to the door.

He would have to tell his mother about the eye in the
toilet. Sometime.

He had flushed and flushed, but the eye just wouldn't go
down to stay.

She wouldn't believe it wasn't his fault the eye was
there in the first place.

With his lower lip stuck out and his cheeks burning,
Pete played with the gun in his lap. It seemed large to him,
heavier, unfamiliar. He ran a small finger across the ramp
front sight, down over the precise shocking hole in the
blued muzzle, underneath the six-inch barrel to the trigger
guard. He touched the nose of a jacketed hollow-point .38
round in the large cylinder. It was the exact size of the
head of his peepee.

Through the wood of the door he felt the heavy blows of
the dog's paw. He felt fear.

"You can't come in! Not till I'm ready."

There was room for him, too, on the dog's back, he
knew that. But if he climbed up there and went riding with
the naked woman, who could tell if they would ever bring
him home again.

Pete shivered and shivered. He knew that no one would
believe anything he said from now on, just because Norm
had to have a piece of ass.

With a forefinger he prodded the trigger of the revolver.
It resisted him.

His mother's voice called down the stairs, jolting him.
He'd heard that tone before. It meant—it meant—

He was in big trouble!

"Where did that eye in the toilet come from, Peter
Raff? I wouldn't want to be you when your father gets
home."

Wham! Wham! The hound with the long nose wanted
him to come out. But Pete didn't have to see him up close
to know that he had long teeth and claws.

"What I'd like to know," Captain Moorman was saying sternly, "is how you could just stand there, Raff, and let poor old Norm flush himself down the toilet. Are you listening to me? You'd better come up with an answer."

"Oh, shit," Pete mumbled, realizing he was a goner. Nobody loved him anymore. He would just crawl under his bed and stay there. In the morning maybe everything would be all right again.

He'd never liked the dark. He hated the dark. He wanted light and more light. Terrible things never seemed to happen when the sun was shining.

His finger prodded the trigger of the gun again. Wishfully, belligerently.

The dawn came up full in Pete Raff's face, it was hail and farewell and flags waving in a redhot breeze, the whistling microdot of a meteor arriving from outer space, circling one pinched, astonished eye while the brain, seething with the stricken power of a collapsed wasps' nest, gave off its final flashes of memory and regret, a strident note of music from a martial horn.

58

Hillary began to feel unwell during her third-period social studies class. Cramps had her white-knuckled and hunched over her desk when Mr. Rauscher noticed and dropped by to ask her quietly if she wanted to be excused to go to the infirmary. Hillary could only nod.

He gave the rest of the class a pop quiz, which earned Hillary some dirty looks as she went out the door with the teacher's arm around her. On the fourth floor the school nurse, Mrs. Groveman, took over and had Hillary lie down on the couch. She drew the shades over the windows. Hillary couldn't straighten her legs.

"Do you think you might throw up?" Mrs. Groveman asked her. She positioned a wastebasket with a garbage can liner near the couch.

"Don't know," Hillary said.

"You're not menstruating yet, are you, Hillary?"

"No'm."

"This could be it," the nurse said cheerfully. "Do you want to go home?"

"Yes'm."

"Let me get a cold cloth for your head, and I'll just call your mother."

Groveman wrung out a cloth at the washbasin and covered Hillary's eyes and forehead with it: Hillary's hands were clenched over her belly, and she hissed at a particularly prolonged pain, a couple of tears squeezing from beneath her pressed-down lids. Groveman produced a thermometer and cautioned her not to bite down. "I'll just be gone a few minutes," she said.

"Okay."

The last cramp had been the worst, but there weren't any more. Hillary straightened carefully on the couch and breathed easier. She felt wan and sleepy, barely aware of the slender tube between her lips, the silvery bulb nestled under her tongue. Mrs. Groveman had returned, silently; at least Hillary thought she heard the school nurse moving around in the room. The cloth, no longer cool, was plucked from her face. Hillary sighed, took the thermometer out of her mouth, and opened her eyes.

"Hello, Hillary," Polly Windross said, leaning over her with a smile.

Hillary almost leaped off the couch. Her eyes were goggled. A smattering of freckles darkened against the drained pallor of her skin.

Polly's blond hair fanned down across one cheek, and curled up like a pretend-mustache under her pert nose. She was wearing her familiar red tam, the light green cape with the dark green border. She held the washcloth in her left hand. Her right hand was out of sight beneath the cape.

"What's the matter? You're so jumpy. It's only me." Polly dropped the washcloth in the wastebasket and held out her hand, a sweeping imperious gesture. "Come on. We have to get going."

"Mrs. Grovemannnnn . . ." Hillary croaked; she had almost no voice. She edged backward on the leatherette couch, away from Polly's languidly beckoning fingers, the plaid skirt of her jumper riding up around her hips. She looked yearningly at the door to the infirmary, which was closed. The room was dark in contrast to the brilliant yellow rectangles of the shades over the windows.

"Oh, you can be such a baby," Polly said, a little wise twist to her child's shapely mouth. "I told you. It's time to go."

"Where?"

"Outside. All our friends are waiting."

"Who's . . . waiting?"

"Our *friends*, Hillary. Come see."

Hillary couldn't move. She was rigid from panic, backed up against a wall. Polly just stared at her, a touch of sharpness in the blue eyes. Tiny lights there, too, that played all around the pupils; Hillary felt something that might have been her own faint shadow enlarging on the wall behind her, becoming black and muscular, strong enough to give her a little push and stand her, unwillingly, alongside Polly, who strode off toward the windows in red boots, not a backward glance as Hillary was propelled, tentative and stumbling, a couple of steps behind her. Whenever she tried to resist, the flourishing blackness rubbed against her persuasively like a very thin, eager dog, pushing her forward. She had to keep moving despite the stoned awkward weight of her feet, the sensation of being pleasantly paralyzed at the base of her spine, the nape of her neck.

Polly reached down to release one of the window shades. It rolled up quick as a blink. The sky outside was gray with faint blooms of cloud. Hillary heard through the window a clamor, an uproar. Polly stepped aside.

"There they are."

Hillary took the last two steps to the window. She looked down at the asphalt play yard of Blessed Sacrament School, which also served as a parking lot for the church. A black iron picket fence surrounded the school and the rectory. No one was in the yard, but the street beyond was filled with young people. Dozens of them, shuffling through a kind of pathetic dance. Some played crude, homemade musical instruments that whined and whanged and twittered. Either they wore motley costumes and makeup (the touches of fresh blood were ingenious) or else, astonishingly, they were naked. Hillary saw shaved scarred heads, missing ears; others were more dismayingly deformed. They had the snouts of crocodiles, or squib arms like thalidomide cherubs.

Hillary felt a shudder which was quieted by the spreading numbness down her back. She looked slowly around at Polly.

"Is it Halloween already?"

"You poor dummy."

"Don't make me go," she sobbed. "I don't want anything to do with *them*."

"Too bad. Your father can't learn to leave well enough alone. He's a troublemaker. So you're going with us to teach him a lesson. And that's all there is to it."

Behind Hillary the window was unlocked and began to slide up. She heard it but was afraid to look back, to take her hot blurred eyes off Polly.

"No. No."

"There you go again. Listen, *baby*, you'll like it—once you get there. Hear them? They're having *fun*."

But Hillary heard only cries of torment, of degradation and woe. She was flooded with a fierce Irish rage.

"I won't go!"

"Oh yes you will!"

Polly's other hand shot out from beneath her cape. There was no flesh on it. Sharp, fire-cured bone struck Hillary in the forehead, a ringing slap as Polly's cape billowed in a gust of wind from the open window, obscuring her face. Hillary felt the low sill strike the backs of her thighs, felt herself curving outward into the air. Her upflung hands reached for something, anything, to hold onto. A scream of pure demented pleasure arose from the throats of the lostlings who paraded obscenely in the street. Above their cries she heard a man's voice call out urgently to her. Hilllary, poised in space, willed herself not to fall. But her feet slipped and she was diving backwards, head down; she had a streaky blurred impression of the sooty stones of the school building and the thick gray sky. Then a violent light exploded behind her eyes and she knew nothing more.

59

By two o'clock in the afternoon of the twelfth of March heavy fog rolling in from Boston Harbor had forced the closing of Logan International Airport to all traffic for the second time that day. The captains of inbound aircraft, including Alitalia's flight 60 from Rome, which was then 125 miles northeast of Boston over the Atlantic and descending for the final leg of its approach, were notified of a potentially long delay and given their options. The Alitalia jet, a Boeing 747, could be diverted to the nearest field large enough to handle the jumbos, which was Bradley International in Windsor Locks, Connecticut. But there was a fifty-fifty chance the wind would change and sweep away most of the fog in a matter of minutes. The captain estimated his fuel reserves at a comfortable two hours of flying time and reported his desire to hold for a favorable break in the weather. He was assigned a pattern some forty miles north of Logan at twelve thousand feet.

The captain then informed his passengers, among them Father James Merlo, of the delay. Merlo had been napping in a bulkhead seat of the no-smoking section in coach, where he had a little more room for his long legs. He half heard the news that the long flight was still far from over, grunted, rearranged the nest of little pillows that kept slipping away from beneath his head, and went back to sleep.

In the international terminal building Conor Devon saw a blinking green message on a TV screen that said ***All flights delayed by fog*** Consult airlines for further information*** Conor spoke to a slender Neapolitan girl with a short haircut, who told him that flight 60 was holding and they hoped it would be able to land soon.

He bought a bag of peanuts, checked the time, and made a credit card call to One Pearl Place boutique. Kay Finlay answered the phone.

"Oh, Conor, she isn't here. The school called about eleven thirty, quarter to twelve, something to do with Hillary. Gina went down there right away."

"What about Hillary? Is she sick?"

"There was an accident of some kind. But they said she's going to be all right."

"Thanks, Kay."

The word *accident* filled his mind big as a blimp. Conor hung up, leafed through his telephone book for the number of the principal's office and placed the call.

"Irene Wimbledon."

"Mrs. Wimbledon, it's Conor Devon. I just heard Hillary was in an accident."

"Oh—oh, but she's perfectly all right, Mr. Devon. Nothing to worry about. She twisted her knee going down the stairs between classes. The nurse put an icebag on it, and by the time your wife arrived the swelling was almost gone."

"Is Gina there?"

"No, they left about half an hour ago. Mrs. Devon was taking Hillary to lunch, and then I believe they were going to do some shopping."

"Well, she must be okay if Gina was taking her shopping."

"Oh, yes. She may have a slight limp for a couple of days."

"That's a relief. How are the boys?"

"The boys are fine, Mr. Devon. A credit to the school. I do have another call waiting, so if you'll excuse me—"

"Sure." Conor hung up and checked the time on one of the monitors. Two eighteen. No change in the weather that he could see. If Father Merlo had to deplane in Connecticut, then he would meet the priest there and drive him to Vermont. No sense waiting for him to be bussed all the way back to Boston. But as long as there was a chance Logan would reopen, he had to wait.

He settled down in a seat that was too small for him, opened his bag of peanuts, and munched as he leafed through a tattered copy of a wrestling fan magazine someone had abandoned on an adjacent seat. He looked at mediocre black and white "action" photos of men whom he knew almost as intimately as his own wife. He failed to find his own scowling face anywhere and cast the magazine aside. Thoughts of Hillary came to mind and he smiled, loving her. He had no inkling that he had not reached the Blessed Sacrament School at all, and that the voice on the telephone, so plausible and reassuring, had not been that of the principal.

60

Gina had arrived at the school a few minutes past noon, and found a parking place on the street beside the rectory. It was lunchtime, and the asphalt schoolyard was crowded with children running around shrilly and aimlessly, many of them in shirtsleeves despite the thirty-degree temperature.

As Gina crossed the yard, passing the grotto of the Virgin beside the rectory, she searched quickly through the mob of playing children but didn't see Dean or Charles. But all of the grades had hobby options during the free period following lunch; the boys were probably inside with computers or small animals.

Up a flight of steps and through double doors past the kindergarten, closed for the day. The lay principal, Irene Wimbledon, was waiting for her in the school offices opposite the first-floor auditorium. She was a small, plump, pigeonlike woman who nodded and becked and smiled; unlikely as it seemed at first glance she was a tough administrator who had survived five years under a hard-driving, bad-tempered parish priest who disliked all women but the Virgin Mary, to whom he was favorably disposed on the basis of her references.

"Where is she?" Gina cried, out of breath. "Is she hurt badly? What happened?"

Wimbledon laid a firm, soothing hand on Gina's arm. "Hillary had a very narrow escape from what surely would have been a fatal fall; she has some bumps and bruises, but she's not seriously hurt. She *is* badly frightened by the experience. Father Toomey is with her now in the sanctuary. I know you're anxious to see her, but please come into my office for a few moments.''

Gina allowed herself to be led past a row of glass-fronted cubicles into a room of rosewood paneling and beige carpeting. Mrs. Wimbledon closed the door and they sat down together in facing leather chairs that bristled with metal studs.

"I've called Dr. Wersheba. Unfortunately he's in surgery at St. Anthony's, but another doctor will come as soon as possible."

"Why does she need a doctor?" Gina said; her face felt as if she were wearing a hard coat of glue and she could scarcely move her lips. But the rest of her was shaking.

"Hillary is in a—highly agitated condition. I don't think I should sugarcoat it for you—she's hysterical and must be sedated, then examined. There is a possibility that she was assaulted.''

"Here? In the *school*?"

"I'm afraid so.''

"I'll take her to the hospital myself!''

"I doubt that Hillary will go with you. She won't leave the sanctuary. She feels it's the only place that is safe for her right now.''

"Well, what happened?"

"We know that she suffered abdominal cramps during her third-period class. Mr. Rauscher accompanied her upstairs to the infirmary, where Mrs. Groveman had her lie on the couch. Mrs. Groveman left Hillary alone for a few minutes to come down to the office to call you. The line was busy at first. When third period ended, Mr. Rauscher went back upstairs to see how Hillary was. As soon as he opened the infirmary door he saw Hillary standing very near a window which, we assume, she opened herself. She was pressed against the sill, leaning backwards, and Mr. Rauscher says she had a look of utter terror on her face.''

"Did she—have her uniform on?"

Wimbledon nodded. "She was fully dressed. Mr. Rauscher had only a moment to take in everything. A sixth sense told him she was about to fall—or jump—from the window. You know Mr. Rauscher, don't you? He was an outstanding athlete in college, and has very quick reactions for someone of his size and strength. He got to Hillary just as she fell and managed to catch her by one leg and pull her back into the room. It was a close call.''

Gina sat staring at the principal with tears streaming down her face.

"Why do you think—someone raped her?"

"But I didn't say *rape*, I said *assaulted*. The condition of her face—well, you have to see for yourself.''

"Wait—wait just a minute.'' Gina dug into her big purse for a tissue, pushing aside the Colt Python revolver she was licensed to carry. She wiped her cheeks and looked at her eyes in a compact mirror; she decided they weren't too streaky. She nodded. "Okay, I'm ready.''

Gina could hear her daughter as soon as she opened the side door to the sanctuary. Hillary's voice was fiercely high-pitched.

"BLESSED ART THOU AMONG WOMEN AND BLESSED IS THE FRUIT OF THY WOMB JESUS!"

Hillary was crouched low in the first pew on the left-hand side of the sanctuary. The Jesuit recently assigned to Blessed Sacrament, whose name was Toomey, sat beside her. The lights above the altar had been turned on.

"HOLY MARY MOTHER OF GOD . . .''

She gasped for breath; her body trembled in an agony of complex emotion. She had a rosary in one fist.

"PRAY FOR US SINNERS NOW AND AT THE HOUR OF OUR DEATH AMEN!"

Gina ran across the sanctuary. Hillary and the priest heard her coming. Hillary looked up wildly and then cringed, as if she refused to recognize her mother. Her face was wet, from perspiration or tears. There was a bony handprint on her forehead. It looked hot as a sunburn.

Gina, shocked, stopped short of the pew and put her hands to her mouth. Father Toomey, a reedy young man, stood up, scratching perplexedly at a fuzzy receding hairline.

"Mrs. Devon?"

"I CAN'T TALK TO YOU! I HAVE TO PRAY!"

Gina had never seen such sick and tortured eyes. Feeling a seductive desire to faint, Gina braced herself instead. Hillary turned her head, looking at the statue on one side of the altar. A gray Lenten shroud had been partially torn away, perhaps by Hillary, revealing an enameled Virgin with opulent skin tones and shapely sorrowing eyes.

"HOLY MARY MOTHER OF GOD . . ." The silvery beads rattled in her unsteady hands.

"What happened to Hillary's face?" Gina demanded of the priest.

"We don't know."

"We don't know," Mrs. Wimbledon repeated, appeasingly, behind her. Gina turned.

"Can't you get a doctor here?"

" . . . NOW AND AT THE HOUR OF OUR DEATH AMEN!"

Gina kneeled in front of her daughter.

"Hillary."

Hillary stopped her litany and panted; her eyes rolled in her head, ecstatically.

"Go away. Go away. I only want to talk to the Blessed Mother." She had bitten her tongue and there was blood on her lower lip. She looked up at the tall Jesuit; so did Gina. His smile seemed heartless, under the circumstances, but he was merely nervous. "*She* hears me, doesn't she? *She'll* protect me! *She* won't let them have me!"

"Won't let who have you?" Gina said. She tried with motherly firmness to take hold of her daughter's cold rosary-chained hands. Hillary rose screaming to her feet, jerking away from Gina.

"NOOOOOO!"

She scrambled bumpingly over the front of the pew and ran up to the altar, where she prostrated herself before the shrouded crucified Christ on the wall. As Gina was getting slowly to her feet a narthex door opened with a sound of cavernous thunder. She looked up the long aisle at a shadowy figure carrying what looked like a physician's bag in one hand.

"Hellloo! It's Dr. Richards."

"Oh, thank God," Gina murmured. She raised her voice. "This way, Doctor!"

Hillary was groveling and shrieking again. Gina held her stomach, feeling her daughter as a long-forgotten weight there, fetal but serene. It amplified her horror; she felt sickly from grief.

The doctor walked loose-jointedly down the center aisle. He wore a pin-striped gray suit and large rose-tinted glasses. He couldn't have been any older than Father Toomey. He very nearly lacked features: sketchy pimpled nose, thin pale eyebrows. By contrast his eyes were too intensely black and seemed to skitter like buttons around the inside surfaces of the curved and tinted lenses. Gina was reminded of certain Muppets, but this one wasn't cuddly or endearing; she felt repelled by Richards, by what she instinctively felt was an essentially frigid nature. Still, he was a doctor.

He glanced at Hillary, who was on her knees and elbows now, swaying, shrill. He looked at the adults.

"What seems to be the trouble here?"

Gina explained. "It's my daughter. Someone must have attacked her. She acts like she doesn't even know me. Can you do something?"

"What's her name?"

"Hillary Devon."

The doctor nodded and opened his bag. He took out a packaged disposable syringe and a small sealed bottle.

"First we'd better calm her down."

"What's that?"

"Tranquilizer. I'll need some help—you'll have to distract Hillary for a few seconds. And she'll be hard to hold. Be sure you get a good grip on her."

He went to his bag again for a small bottle of alcohol and a sterile package of cotton, which he handed to Wimbledon.

"I'll want you to swab down a spot just above the elbow, as soon as Mrs. Devon has Hillary under control. The one thing we don't want to do is frighten her more than she's frightened already."

"I'll help hold her," Father Toomey said.

"Oh, no, Father; I think that's just too many of us crowding around her. But if you could bring a pitcher of cold water it would be helpful."

"I'll get it from the school cafeteria."

Richards looked thoughtfully at the priest as he walked to the side door of the sanctuary; then he smiled at the women, tightlipped, as if it hurt his asshole to smile. They went up to the tiled and carpeted altar together, where Hillary was praying at the top of her voice.

"What's that in her hand?" the doctor said, pausing as he was about to bend over the distraught girl.

"It's her rosary," Gina said. Every time she looked at the doctor's face he appeared subtly different to her, as if it were an image on the surface of water and not flesh she was seeing. Nerves, she thought.

"You'll have to take it from her." His tone was a little sharp, and Gina frowned. Richards backed off a step and smiled; his hardshell eyes ran aimlessly around the inside of his glasses. "She might hurt herself, or one of us, with it," he explained. "Put out an eye. You just don't know what can happen when they're like this. So—would you mind—?"

"Yes, Doctor." Gina kneeled once more beside her daughter. Hillary yelled at this intrusion and tried to crawl away from her.

"Honey, honey . . . it's *mom*. Everything's going to be all right. Nobody's going to hurt you."

Hillary was motionless for several moments, and rigid, her head down. Then she toppled over into her mother's lap and Gina deftly removed the rosary from her right hand. She placed it in a pocket of her jacket while continuing to stroke her daughter's face. Hillary's eyes had closed. She felt very hot, especially where the imprint of a small hand, skeletal in its thinness, lay across her forehead. Her body twitched and she moaned.

"Could you just push her sleeve up, Mrs. Devon?" Hillary was wearing a short-sleeved light blue blouse with her plaid school jumper. "There, that's fine." Richards looked at the principal. "Now, then, if you'll wipe her arm down with the alcohol . . . ready, Mrs. Devon?"

Hillary's eyelids fluttered; Gina put an arm around her and held both hands at the wrist. The doctor popped in the needle of the syringe. Hillary gasped and arched her back, but in seconds it was done.

"The tranquilizer will be a few minutes taking effect. Just keep talking to her, Mrs. Devon, while I look her over."

"Doctor, her forehead—"

"Yes, she was hit very hard. A bruise on her leg here, but it looks like an old one. Let me have a look at the back of her head. Uh-huh. She may have a concussion. Something raised a heck of a lump. . . . Hillary. Hillary! Open your eyes, please."

Hillary responded slowly. She looked dazed. She was trying to speak, or to pray, but the words were unintelligible. Her lips were cracked and swollen.

Richards had taken a penlight from his bag, and he flicked it on.

"Look right here at me, Hillary. You're a very pretty girl, you know that? By the way, I'm Dr. Richards, but everybody has called me 'Pud' all my life. Kind of a funny name, isn't it? You can laugh if you want to."

Hillary didn't laugh. She stared dully at him, still twitching spasmodically, while he shone his light first into one eye, then the other.

"Pupils are equal and reactive. That's a good sign, but we'll want some skull shots regardless. I wonder if one of you good ladies would call an ambulance?" Gina looked scared; he put a hand reassuringly on her shoulder. "I don't want Hillary to be moved any more than necessary; it's only a precaution, Mrs. Devon."

"All of our phones have been out of order," Wimbledon said.

"Could you try again?"

"Surely." The principal looked at Gina. "There's a pay phone at the Exxon station. It's just two blocks . . . in case I don't get through."

Gina nodded. "All right. I'll try from there."

Hillary, holding her hand, said in a toneless voice, "Mom."

At the point of tears, Gina kissed her daughter. "I won't be gone long. The doctor will stay with you."

"She'll be just fine, Mrs. Devon. The tranquilizer's starting to work now."

Gina followed Mrs. Wimbledon out the side door and ran for her Ford station wagon in the street. She felt, as she got in behind the wheel and reached into the wrong pocket for her car keys, finding Hillary's rosary instead, that this was a mistake, that she ought to remain with her daughter, although it would take her less than five minutes to make the call and return. It was a very bad time for the school's telephones to be out of order.

She hesitated, breathing hard, a hand on the ignition key, thinking of how helpless Hillary had looked lying on her back on the carpeted floor of the altar, her eyes so glassy. *Get the ambulance*. She turned the engine over and pulled screechingly away from the curb, flung the Ford around corners, and pulled up on the apron of the Exxon station, leaving the motor running and the door open. Gina had committed a lot of local phone numbers to memory, among them police, fire department, and volunteer ambulance service. She dialed and spoke to them. *Hurry*. Then back into the Ford, roaring into reverse, she returned to the school. No time to park. Gina zoomed in through the open gates and cut across the asphalt play yard to the rear door of the sanctuary, ran inside and found the altar, the entire church empty.

Gina screamed Hillary's name.

"Mrs. Devon?"

She turned to find Father Toomey standing in the chancel doorway.

"Where is she?"

The priest looked startled. "Hillary? Dr. Richards took her with him in his car. He said he didn't think he should wait for the ambulance, and you could meet him at—"

"Did you see him leave? What kind of car is he driving?"

"A—one of those Japanese imports. Toyota, I think. Four-door, dark blue."

"Which way did he go?"

"East on Oxendine."

As Gina hurried down the steps to her station wagon she heard the sound of the ambulance on its way. She was sick with dread. He *wouldn't touch her while she had the rosary in her hand. Why? Where is he taking my daughter?*

61

Oxendine was a wide residential street as far as the Watkins Mill Shopping Center, a four-corner sprawl of discount stores, fast-food outlets, and a supermarket, where the major intersection was with Massachusetts 38, here named Chopick Pond Road. The shopping center was three quarters of a mile from Blessed Sacrament parish, and the wrong way to go if one was en route to St. Anthony's Hospital.

Gina covered the distance to the shopping center at sixty miles an hour, eyes flicking to each side road for some sign of the car Richards was driving.

A block before the shopping center Oxendine became three lanes in each direction, with one lane for left turns only onto Route 38. It was a three-stage light in each direction, and the wait could be long: there was always a lot of traffic north and southbound. About three dozen cars had come to a stop in front of her, waiting on the red; one of them, third in line for a left turn, was a dark blue Toyota.

Gina stopped sharply in the left lane, the seventh car back. Leaving the engine running, she got out of the station wagon and ran to the Toyota along the raised snow-encrusted median strip, past several startled drivers. The wind whipped her hair into her eyes.

The blond man with the rose-colored glasses and the acne-stippled nose didn't look at her when she pounded on the driver's window of the Toyota. All of the windows of the sedan were rather darkly tinted; his youthful face behind glass was as pale and indistinct as a fish belly-up in a murky tank, and Gina couldn't see into the back seat. She tried the door; it was locked.

"Where's Hillary?" she screamed.

The green arrow flashed on the traffic signal ahead. The man who called himself Dr. Richards was oblivious of Gina, his hands motionless on the wheel, his eyes fixed straight ahead. He appeared to be sealed in a capsule without atmosphere, without life, as if breathing was no longer one of his requirements.

She looked around in desperation for something with which to break the glass of the window. The two cars in front of the Toyota began to move.

Richards turned suddenly and stared at her. His pudgy lips were pursed in a soulless kiss of contempt; the steel-framed lenses of his glasses glowed redly. Gina saw, momentarily, images of her daughter in those heated lenses, her eyes closed as if in eternal sleep, her hair in flames.

Gina knew then exactly what she was faced with, had

been subconsciously trying to prepare herself for since the night Conor had returned from Chadbury with his nose broken and Hillary had fallen into an unexplained fit: she now had two choices, a split second to decide. She could surrender her daughter and go mad; or, on this windy suburban corner, under a sunless sky, she could fight.

Richards's face turned back toward the windshield, one hand slipping an inch on the wheel as he prepared to drive away. Gina reached into her purse, pulled out the Colt Python revolver, and, unconsciously assuming the two-handed grip and stance she'd been taught on the firing range of the Joshua Police Department, shot him in the head.

The .357 magnum slug took out a small piece of the window; the impact of bullet against bone knocked his head forward and down against the steering wheel. The left front windshield exploded in bloody crumbs of glass, his brains were on the dashboard and the hood of the car. Gina, jolted back one step by the recoil of the revolver, went suddenly deaf from shock. The day turned even grayer. Her field of vision narrowed to include only the nickel-plated revolver in her two hands, the dead man slumped over the wheel of the Toyota, the briny sparkle of pulverized glass. The red red flooding inside the Toyota.

On the other side of the divider strip a man in a delivery van had stopped to gawk at her; at least a dozen other people had seen her draw the revolver and fire into the Toyota, but she didn't know they were there. She was alone in the world with a man whom she had killed.

Then she was totally alone, because Richards straightened himself slowly behind the wheel, his shattered head erect, and drove away without a backward glance, making a left turn onto Chopick Pond Road.

Gina, finding this no more difficult to believe than the fact that she had killed him in the first place, ran after the Toyota, gun in hand, and was nearly struck down by a gasoline tanker as she crossed the highway. The Toyota pulled steadily away from her. She looked up at the astonished face of the tanker's driver, then turned and ran whimpering back to her station wagon.

She had left the engine running. It had died. She couldn't

restart it as she kept her eyes on the blue Toyota, which was almost out of sight northbound.

"NO NO NO NO!"

Gina picked up the revolver from beside her on the seat and jumped out of the station wagon; she ran across Oxendine Road, dodging oncoming traffic, to the parking lot of Grand Union. Looking for a car, any car, to take up the chase. She was nearly hit in the stomach by a shopping cart as she crossed from one yellow-striped aisle to another.

"Can't you watch where you're—Gina!"

Gina pushed herself up off the front end of the cart laden with shopping bags and tossed her hair from her eyes; she looked at the face of an acquaintance from Blessed Sacrament parish, Louise Briggens. They had served on committees together. Louise was inclined to be high-handed. She had six kids and a butt like the beam of a tugboat.

"Hello, Louise."

"What—what are you doing with that gun?" Louise said, her artificially blond eyebrows arching nearly to the top of her forehead.

"Louise, is this your car?"

"No, mine's the Cutlass Supreme over there. Gina, are you—"

"I need to borrow your car, Louise. Mine won't start, and he's getting away. Give me the keys to your car."

"THE KEYS TO MY—"

Gina leveled the revolver at her.

"I don't have time to argue with you, Louise. My daughter has been kidnapped and he's still able to drive, I don't know how, I shot him in the head. That means he's not human; you see what I'm up against? And there's no one to help me." She had begun to whine; she got her voice under control and squared her shoulders. "Are the keys in your purse? Give me your purse, Louise. *I'm going to get my daughter back and I swear before God I'll shoot you, too, if you don't do what I tell you.*"

Louise Briggens's eyebrows waggled up and down, like birds born in cages trying vainly to fly; she trembled and made gagging sounds and, abruptly, vomited all over a head of cauliflower at the top of one of her grocery sacks.

While the woman was thus distracted Gina snatched her

drawstring purse from her right wrist and ran with it to the
cream-colored Cutlass Supreme which Louise thoughtfully
had pointed out before she became so ill. Gina found the
keys and tossed the purse aside, unlocked the Cutlass, and
climbed in. Louise had fallen to her knees beside her
shopping cart; she was being gaudily hysterical. Gina paid
no attention to her. There was a film of perspiration on her
upper lip, emphasizing the pale growth of hair she had
there. Her eyes behind her driving glasses were bleak, but
the red could rise in them, terrifyingly, in an instant, as
Louise Briggens had observed.

Gina put her revolver down again where it would be
handy and backed out of the space, went zipping across
the parking lot to the Route 38 exit on the other side of the
building, heedless of lane markings. The car radio was on,
blasting FM rock from four speakers. Iron Maiden. Black
Sabbath. Death Freak. Louise Briggens revealed as a secret heavy-metal addict. The shrill music suited Gina's
sense of urgency, the doom in her mood.

Gina paid no attention to the flow of traffic against her,
just leaned on the horn and let fly across three lanes and
the bumpy median.

She was up to sixty in a matter of seconds, weaving
perilously in and out past slow movers in the nearly-new
car as the road curved uphill away from the commercial
area and the land became semirural, a mix of small orchards, shabby roadside businesses and woodlots, housing
developments of one or two streets carved into the hill-
sides. It was four miles to Chopick Pond, no major inter-
sections along the way. Gina called aloud to the patron
saints of both sides of the family, and stood on it.

62

The bullet that Gina had fired into the head of Richards
had scarcely been slowed by thicknesses of skull and the
plump package of brain tissue in between. It had been
deflected twice, first by bone and then by the steering

wheel, deforming each time until it resembled a chunk of metallic mushroom. The enlarged slug passed through the thin plastic shield of the instrument panel just to the left of the odometer and the 40 KPH marking and then through the firewall, ending up in the fuel pump, where it began to cause trouble almost immediately for the partly brainless driver. But Richards needed neither brain nor central nervous system to continue to function until he had fulfilled the purpose for which he had been created: he needed only hands and feet, which could be guided rather easily by the controlling entity.

The blue Toyota was another matter. Unlike the body of Richards, it was not a realistic and highly detailed materialization. Its riddled fuel pump spurted gas prodigiously; the car began to labor and smoke and slow down short of the intended rendezvous on the isolated east shore of Chopick Pond. Richards was made to pull the car off Route 38 immediately. But by then Gina had caught up and was right behind it, honking her horn, her view obscured by the billowing smoke coming from beneath the hood of the Toyota as both cars bumped along a narrow unpaved lane with walls of dirty snow on either side.

The lane meandered for two and a half miles down to the icebound shore of the pond with only a few summer cottages and one structure of any size along the way: a rambling wooden building constructed by enthusiastic but amateur carpenters with no sense of proportion. There was a snow-clogged parking lot in front of it, a stone gateway. This was the summer retreat of the Right Way Gospel and True Testimony Pentecostal Church. An imposing but somewhat road-weary green tractor-trailer truck was parked sideways behind the gate, its cab tilted forward over the front axle. A lanky mechanic wearing an arc-welder's mask and wielding a blue-tongued torch failed to look up as the two cars passed by on the lonely lane; but other eyes observed them.

63

"Buddy Buck," Zipporah said, pausing to take a peek through the curtained porthole above the bunk which she shared with her lover, "I believe that car went by us just now was on fire!"

"Zipporah," Buddy Buck Mayhew groaned, "what difference does it make at a time like this? Now you gone and lost the stroke."

"Well, I'm sorry; but I think it's our Christian duty to help our neighbors when they're in trouble."

"We don't have no neighbors up here, Zipporah. We just borrowed the church parking lot long enough for Sedalia to fix them rods."

"Jesus said—"

"Zipporah, now don't talk to me about Jesus when I'm fixin' to come. It makes me feel nasty."

"All right," she murmured, subdued. Her trim little bottom had ceased to waggle in ecstasy; Buddy Buck paused and said imploringly, "Ain't I doin' you no good, honey?"

"Well, you were, but then you touched me with your fingers and, you know, your fingers are always s'cold lately. Toes too. That's a real turn-off."

"I can't help it if my fingers get cold. We are for sure in a cold climate."

"I don't know why we had to come all the way up here to Massachusetts this time the year. I just can't get used to all the snow and the *ice*. And my throat's been sore for a week, no lie. I'm afraid I'll lose my voice. I wish we could just forget about it and go on back to Alabama. We were doin' s'good down home."

"Forget it? For*get* it? Honey, I realize it's colder 'n polar bear poop, but you got to remember one thing: the devil don't sleep and he don't hibernate neither. And he

336

ain't gonna *hide* way up here from Buddy Buck Mayhew.
God's Warrior on Wheels. Hallelujah!''

''Couldn't we just a gone coast to coast through
Louisianner and Texas?''

''This is the ideal place to start our First Annual Interstate Crusade. The devil come over to this country on the
Mayflower with the Pilgrims, and he ain't left yet. Didn't
you never read about the Salem witch trials?''

''Oh, yes, believe I did. That all happened around
here?'' Zipporah shivered dramatically.

''Sure it did. I may have done a little time at the
crossbar hotel before I come to be washed in the Blood of
the Lamb, but that don't mean I'm ignorant. I know
there's plenty of souls to be saved in Massachusetts, if we
can just get 'em to come outdoors. Besides, if folks don't
see me they ain't gonna want to listen to me on the radio.
And if I don't have no national radio exposure, I'll spend
the rest of my life tryin' to get more'n forty miles from
Sylacauga.''

''Why Buddy Buck, you just shrunk down to a nubbin.''

He said disconsolately, ''You know I like it without a
lot of conversation, Zipporah.''

''I'm sorry. Why don't we rest awhile. We already done
it twice before breakfast.''

''No, it's too cold to lay around. I'll put some clothes
on and give Sedalia a hand with them repairs. We got to
be at the Motorama Top Wheels and Deals lot no later 'n
four thirty.''

''It just don't seem right to me to be preachin' the
gospel while all around us they is sellin' used cars at the
same time.''

''All of Cousin Bob Pike's used cars got good warran-
ties on 'em, and besides we're gonna be seen *live* on TV
during the commercial interruptions. You know how many
people still watch them *Starsky and Hutch* reruns in these
parts? It's what they call in show business a big media
break. Praise God.''

Zipporah had stepped down from the low bunk in the
little stateroom of their Peterbilt trailer, her fair skin all
goosebumps, her big brown eyes wide with a kind of
apprehension. Her hands were joined supportively under
stupendous breasts, which, should she choose to stand

naked beneath a high-noon sun, would cast enough shade
to cover all of her lower body and a couple of dogs
snoozing at her feet.

"Buck, you know what?"

"I know," he said affectionately, "if Dolly Parton
could get a good look at you standin' sideways she'd just
waller right down into a big puddle a envy."

"No, no. I *heard* somethin', way off yonder. Like a
dynamite explosion. You didn't hear that?"

"How could I, when I'm partial deaf in my right ear?"
He gave her a generous pat on the rump as he reached for
his long underwear.

64

The blue Toyota was burning fiercely under the hood when
it finally jolted off the road and sank up to the front
bumper at the edge of a meadow brimming with crusty snow.

Gina slammed her borrowed Cutlass to a stop a few
yards away and got out, the revolver in her hand.

She saw the door on the driver's side of the burning car
open and the figure of Richards back out from behind the
wheel. His shattered head was beclouded with dark smoke.
He opened the rear door, jerkily, and reached inside with
both arms. He reappeared holding the unconscious form of
Hillary.

"Stop! Put her down!"

Richards, holding Hillary slack and lengthwise at the
level of his stomach, turned toward her. Gina saw him
better, and wished she hadn't. He had no forehead, only a
fist-sized pit in the cranium from his eyebrows to his
temples. The rose-tinted glasses hung to one side from a
single temple bar, an intact ear. So much blood had poured
down his face—and continued to hang from the jawline in
cooling strings and gobbets—that his head suggested a
jellyfish bobbling in a hazy sea. An eye incapable of focus
jiggled in that red mass. The other eye had disappeared.

Richards turned around and around, floundering in the deep snow, as if trying to get his bearings, as if he were homing in on a supernatural signal of some kind. Gina appraised all this horror with lunatic coolness, her mind on the Toyota, which she was afraid would explode, drenching the walking dead man and her daughter in flames.

But perhaps Hillary, too, was dead: she seemed so drained and lifeless.

"Hillary!" Gina screamed, her voice echoing, rebounding from the hard gray pavement of the sky, the frozen lake and deserted woods that enclosed them.

Gina thought she saw the child's eyelids and pale lashes flutter. It was enough for her.

She plunged through the packed snow at the side of the road, not knowing what she could do, how she could stop this. But not to move, now, was to be frozen eternally, eclipsed by the evil that was trying to steal the girl. She raised the shiny revolver, but couldn't fire. What impression would another bullet make? In her anxiety she might hit Hillary.

He was walking away now, across the meadow, taking big strides, sinking down into drifts, rising up again with a surreal buoyancy, bearing Hillary on across the open meadow toward a hillock above the pond, a big stone barnlike structure surrounded by black trees that looked like worn-out paintbrushes standing bristles-up against the sky.

Gina, shorter by inches, had real problems wading after him through a winter's depth of snow. She was, very quickly, short of breath, no competition for the unbreathing thing that was putting distance between them, despite the weight he carried. There were scrappy birds in the air above the line of trees, the barn roof; Gina heard their raucous cries as expressions of triumph, of giddy welcome.

Fifty yards behind her the Toyota exploded with a dull *whump;* the day brightened momentarily and she felt a sear of heat against the back of her neck. She struggled on.

"OH, GOD! HELP ME!"

The shrieks of the wheeling birds intensified; some of them were flying out over the meadow. They looked larger, and threatening. Gina felt faint from exertion, from terror. She was losing ground rapidly. She had the feeling that if she lost sight of Hillary now she would never see her again.

He could move without his brains; but could he go anywhere with both knees shot out from under him?

Gina came to a stop beside a barkless frozen mass of windfall and leveled her revolver, using a jutting branch as a benchrest.

He was twenty yards directly ahead of her, moving slightly uphill. She fretted about a possible ricochet from a rock just beneath the snow, then shut her mind to thoughts of failure and aimed carefully, concentrating on squeezing the trigger slowly and evenly. She had been a good pupil, the best shot in her class. *Don't jerk it, don't. . .*

Gina fired. Missed.

Fired again. And missed. The difficulty of a moving target was new to her.

Trembling, dismayed, she broke down her stance, lowered the revolver, then started over.

Shot him in the left leg behind the knee.

The high-velocity slug nearly tore his lower leg off. He sprawled forward and Hillary was dumped, face down, in the snow.

Gina ran as fast as she could, tears of cold streaming from her eyes. The tears partially obscured her glimpses of a woman, dressed all in dark clothing, who stood motionless on the hill near the barn with her hair streaming long, like a black banner in the wind. Her eyes held all the darkness of a terrifying eternity.

This ominous figure, and the hue and cry of birds roosting in the leafless trees, flying up like bits of paper from a hot chimney, distracted Gina. Streaks of blood on the snow in front of her. The dead man clawing with both hands, trying to reach Hillary. His loathsome, acquisitive hand falling on an exposed thigh. With her lips bared to the gums in a grimace Gina fell to her knees beside her daughter, pulling Hillary away from his clutches. Hillary was breathing. Out of breath herself, Gina sat down for a few precious moments. She felt as if she were being watched, from behind, with curiosity and mounting displeasure. She didn't turn her head. She concentrated on praying for the strength to get Hillary away from there. Her prayers were curtly interrupted, washed from her mind by a black tide of hate.

She is ours now.

"No!" Now Gina turned, finger on the trigger of her revolver.

This time she saw nothing but the flocks of dark birds knitting themselves, wing to wing, into a huge shroud in the trees. Suddenly the dead man's hand was on her ankle, groping, tugging at the soaked suede boot. She kicked violently, pushed herself to her feet and pocketed the revolver. She needed both hands for Hillary. The snow was stained all around them where the dead man crawled laboriously, and eerily without sound. Where had that hostile voice come from? The back of her neck felt frozen, not from the cold but from dread.

Gina, somehow, lifted Hillary. Once she could have sat her in the palm of her outstretched hand. Gina bawled. Her daughter was across her shoulders, bulky; she had a grip on her arms and legs. Fireman's carry, which she had learned in a paramedic course. She had carried a full-grown man across the gym and back. Applause. No snow then. No added weight of fear. The car seemingly a life-time's journey across the meadow, and no way to go except back the way she had come. The snow broken down some, a path of sorts to follow. Otherwise impossible.

Give her to us.

"FUCK YOU!" Gina howled, and choked on tears. She looked quickly back to where the woman had been standing by the barn, almost unbalanced herself. The woman had reappeared, and now she had a companion. A young nubile blond girl in a green cap. A hand of bone absently caressing one cheek. Others like them—nominally human, but each with his own appalling disfiguration of evil—seemed to be emerging, more or less boldly, in the gloom of the woodlot.

Gina paused, unzipped her jacket, tore open her shirt to expose the little gold cross between her breasts. Then she staggered on weary legs down the incline, Hillary riding uneasily on her stooped shoulders and bent back.

"I'm going to make it going to make it going—"

Behind her, screams. It gave her an unexpected jolt of confidence, she almost laughed at their childish outpouring of pique.

Thank God she had been to confession only two nights

ago. She was strong in her faith and without sin, she was not weak where they could get at her.

Only Hillary remained vulnerable.

A shadow appeared ahead of them on the snow, faint at first. She heard the whirring frenzy of small wings.

"Yea though I walk through the valley . . . of the shadow of death I will . . . fear no evil. . . ."

But she couldn't move quickly enough, the fuming large shadow was everywhere. Gina had a glimpse of the almost incandescent handprint on Hillary's forehead, looked past her face in dismay and amazement and saw them coming, a flickering mass of quick little birds, a dusky cloud of wings. The birds whirled in all around her, beaky and screeching, and then Hillary was gone, snatched from Gina's shoulders; they flew with her as if she were as weightless as a bit of string toward the hilltop, the barn, the cheering haunters.

All of this Gina witnessed with diminishing sharpness of mind before she staggered a final time and toppled sideways into the snow.

65

"My Lorddd! If I hadn't seen it with my own eyes, I wouldn't be near believin' it! Hey! Don't close your eyes again. You got to get up, you'll freeze to death lyin' here like this. Wake up!"

Gina was dimly aware of being spoken to, of the impact of a firm little hand against one cold raw cheek. She flinched away from an anticipated second blow, and brought the face in front of her slowly into focus. Pretty. If her eyes hadn't been spaced a little too close together, her small white teeth too far apart, she would have been a knockout. Her face was framed by a fur-lined parka. The tip of her pert nose was red. Even with this diabolical touch she didn't look anything like Satan, or one of his kind. Her eyes were as unsullied as rainwater.

Gina tried to speak. "Who . . . you?"

"I'm Zipporah Honeycutt, and I seen what happened to that little girl you was carryin'. It was like a big old black tornado cloud just whipped her up the hill to where those others was waitin'. Who was she?"

"Hillary. My. . . daughter." Gina tried to get up, and fell forward against Zipporah's large bosom. "Oh, God!" she wept. "They took her again!"

"Some kinda devil cult? You know what else I seen? That body, or whatever it was over there, it just melted away like a popsicle on a hot sidewalk, and there ain't nary trace of it left. Phew!" Zipporah exhaled explosively. "Buddy Buck was right. The devil's here in Massachusetts, and he's spoiled for a fight."

Gina was struggling to rise again. Zipporah said, in a more gentle tone of voice, "Easy, now. I seen where it was they all went. They're in that big barn up on the hill."

"Hillary."

"Don't you worry. We'll get her back. But we need a fightin' man on our side, a man who standeth four-square and righteous in the sight of the Lord, Amen! Come on, we got to get ourselves back to God's Big Green Machine *this minute,* 'fore those devils take a notion to light out after us. I told you my name; what's yours?"

"Gina."

"Gina, can you answer me one question? Have you been born again?"

"Uh . . . no, I'm Catholic."

Zipporah stood back, jerking her hands away from Gina's body as if suddenly she was too hot to handle.

"Holy cats! A papist. I don't know how Buddy Buck's gonna feel about *that.*"

Gina looked hurt and annoyed. "I don't want to argue religion with anybody. I just want my daughter. I'll go by myself."

"Oh, no, you can't do that! Just have a look up there."

Gina turned her face slowly to the barn on the hill. An aura surrounded it, a festering, simmering blackness. She was so appalled and intimidated that she was ready to give up. Her head ached ferociously.

Zipporah put an arm around her. "Don't know about

you, but my heart's in my throat. Buddy Buck will know what to do. Let's go.''

The two women struggled, Zipporah in the lead, back to the road. On the way Zipporah felt obliged to fill Gina in on her recent history. She seemed to be one of those women who worked faster, moved more purposefully, when her motormouth was going at full RPM.

''I only been with Buddy Buck about the last eight months, but some glorious things done happened since we teamed up to bring the good news of the gospel to those folks who are perishin' everywhere for lack of Jesus. He preaches, and I sing. Anyway, Buddy Buck's cousin Bardahl Tillman from Opelika crashed his stock car at the Firecracker 400 trials and needed a couple major operations, which just about put him out of the racin' business for good. He had only two payments to go on the Peterbilt and Joyzell, that's Bardahl's wife, didn't have no use for it; the truck was just a eyesore standin' day and night in the driveway of that nice subdivision where they live, and a couple of the neighbors already done smarted off to her about it. So one night Buddy Buck had this inspiration while we was waitin' to go on at the Evangelistic All-Stars Prayer-a-thon and Miracle Revival Picnic. Well, he just turned to me in his new seersucker suit and I seen this expression come over his face like the crack a dawn; it is some kind of a eerie sight when you know somebody standin' next to you has been touched by the hand of God. He said, 'Zipporah, God wants me to go forth in that old Peterbilt of Bardahl's and preach from coast to coast, bustin' the devil ever mile of the way.' After we was done rejoicin', well it occurred to me to ask him: Buddy Buck, where you gonna get that kind a money, because you know Joyzell is tighter'n the skin on a grape. He said, beamish-like, 'God's gonna point a benefactor our way.' And you know? Somethin' like that did happen. Two weeks later Buddy Buck's uncle, Clemson Hobbie—those are the Georgia Hobbies I'm talkin' about, not the ones from Muscle Shoals—choked on a gob of chicken-fried steak he was eatin' on his regular Friday night out at the L and N café, and as luck would have it not one of the other customers knew beans about the Heimlich maneuver. So he died, poor old soul. Never owned a decent pair a coveralls in his life, and *smell?* There are those folks, you know, that's got all the money in the world, but can't be bothered to spend a nickel on deodorant or clean socks. Clemson was one of them, but our blessed Lord in His wisdom seen to it that Clemson had a up-to-date ironclad will, and Buddy Buck got six thousand dollars out of the tragedy. Just enough to pay off the loan company on the Peterbilt and fit it out for the Crusade. Buddy Buck signed a contract to pay Joyzell another three hundred a month for sixteen months to own the rig free and clear. He ain't missed a payment yet, but there's 'nother one due next Thursday and right now I don't know where we're gonna get the money. This your car? The Cutlass? I am *so* out of breath. Come on, gotta keep movin', you want me to drive?''

Gina nodded and handed over the car keys, sank hollow-eyed and blank of face into the front seat.

"No room to turn around, I'll just back on up to the churchyard. It's a small miracle I come along when I did. But I been cooped up the livelong day in that stuffy trailer, and I just had to get me a breath a clean air. Besides, I heard the explosion, and when I got down the road a little ways I saw that other car burnin' up, and that crowd a evil-lookin' people on the hill.''

Zipporah, looking back over one shoulder, zoomed the Cutlass recklessly uphill and through blind turns. Gina held her face in her hands.

"It's kinda lonely on the road with Buddy Buck. Shoot, I come from a big family and I'm used to havin' whole lots a company. When I was sixteen I joined up with two of my sisters, Moxie Ann and Zelda Fem Honeycutt, and we did a country music act. Like the Mandrell sisters? Called ourselves 'The Honeycats.' Ain't that *good?* But you know we just got farted on by all the bigshot record producers in Nashville. And talk about *horny.* It's all they got on their minds up there. I don't mind tellin' you I have strayed off the straight'n narrow a couple times in my life, it's all a part a growin' up, I guess; but I am not *about* to go down on a man I only just met just because he's got him a little ole recordin' studio and a slick haircut and knows Merle Haggard to say hello to. Here we are.''

Zipporah began to lean on the horn as she backed through

the gates toward the Peterbilt tractor and the rig behind it. She jammed on the brakes and jumped out, waving her hands frantically.

"Budddddyyyy Buccckkkkk!"

He came out from behind the trailer, bowlegged in faded Levi's jeans, wiping his hands on a piece of mechanic's wastepaper. The lanky black man with the Welder's mask perched horizontally atop his head was behind him.

"What are you carryin' on about, sugar?"

"This here is Gina, and her only daughter was snatched by Satan and his minions! Just down the road there! I seen it all myself. It wasn't ten minutes ago! We got to do somethin' fast!"

"Hold on." Buddy Buck's eyes shifted from one face to another, and his lips crimped in a skeptical smile. "Satan? Did I hear you right?"

"Buddy Buck, I swear! There's a whole nest of 'em holed up in a barn, and then there's flocks a dirty-lookin' birds in the trees all around. I guess they're birds, but I never got close enough to take a good look at 'em. I did see when they got hold of Gina's innocent daughter, and God only knows what they are plannin' to do with her."

Buddy Buck, looking into Zipporah's truthful eyes, began to turn a sickly pea-soup color. He licked his lips and hunched his shoulders, and the ball of wastepaper fell at his feet. He smacked his hands together, fist into palm.

"Satan, huh? You don't say. Well well. So it's him. I might a known he'd come up with somethin' to try to block the start of the First Annual Interstate Crusade." Buddy Buck's eyes all but disappeared into his head. He panted grandly for breath, then threw back his head and mop of peroxided hair and shouted, "Gonna let the devil stop me, Lord? Can't let him stop me now, can we?"

Zipporah turned to Gina and put a hand on her shoulder. She said in a calm but thrilled voice, "There he goes. And when he gets worked up like this, he's a powerhouse."

"But what are we going to *do*?"

"Shh, let him talk it out with God first off."

Buddy Buck's knees were shaking. He pounded on his muscular chest, then threw his hands imploringly toward heaven. His lips trembled; he muttered something in a low, unintelligible voice, and burst out: "M'hubla mempsa shabeth. O sho lo wolla coshra dullabublum!"

"It's the Unknown Tongue!" Zipporah exulted. She began to bob and weave, pawing the air with fierce little fists. "Boy, we're gonna get some action now! *Go*, Buddy Buck!"

"Sholum boshra aketh. Wassakallah settai condai!"

Buddy Buck's knees gave way and he fell right down on the ice skin of the parking lot, flivvering and quivering. Then he was absolutely still for a few moments; the wind stirred his hair to the brownish roots, his fingernails looked purple. Suddenly his back arched; he leaped to his feet and, crouching, his eyes burning with zeal, turned three hundred sixty degrees before straightening, his chest swelling up, hands planted contemptuously on his hips. He began to strut, dangerously, his eyes staring off into space. He looked, at that moment, like the warrior he claimed to be.

"Sedalia," he said, "reckon God's Big Green Machine is ready to roll?"

"She's *ready to roll!*"

"Everybody in the truck! Sedalia, you work the light board!"

"YAHOOO!"

Zipporah grabbed the dumbfounded Gina by the sleeve of her jacket and pulled her toward the cab of the Peterbilt. Gina took a good look at the truck and the green-painted trailer rig for the first time. There was a rack of three loudspeakers mounted on the roof of the cab, and the trailer body was studded with numerous shallow cabinets, some only inches deep, of varying sizes. In the center of the trailer on the left side there were two big doors.

"What does this thing do?" Gina asked, as Zipporah stuffed her into the cab.

Buddy Buck settled down behind the wheel, reached for a headset suspended on a hook above his head, and put it on. Zipporah did the same. There were two big reel-to-reel tape recorders on a shelf in the compartment behind them. Zipporah began to check them out. The tape recorders were connected to the speakers mounted on the roof of the cab above their heads. She picked up a hand microphone and sang softly into it; her voice reverberated from the

front wall of the church. "This little light gonna shine. . . ."
The truck's engine came to life with a rackety roar.

Gina thought they were both crazed, and groaned in
despair.

Buddy Buck put the truck in gear and dropped a hand
briefly onto Gina's left knee. "You just leave everythin' to
us. We'll get your little girl back in a jiffy. What did you
say her name was, now?"

"H-Hillary."

"Here we go!"

Whatever else Buddy Buck Mayhew might have been,
he was a good driver. He jockeyed the rig expertly through
a not very wide gate and turned onto the road—which was
scarcely wider than the body of the truck itself—without
first having to stop and then inch his way cautiously
forward.

"How far's this barn you're talkin' about?" he inquired
of Zipporah.

"Maybe a mile on down the road. You'll see a burned-up
Toyota automobile first."

"Play 'Onward, Christian Soldiers,' " he said.

"Comin' right up. You fixin' to hit 'em with everythin'
we got right off the bat?"

"We'll see what it takes, what it takes," the preacher
muttered. "Get ready with my 'Return to Parchman Prison
Revival Hour' sermon."

"I don't recall which one that is."

"You know, where I talk about the devil and his legions
like they was a plague a cockroaches. 'There's only *one
thing* that's better than Raid and Real-Kill and Roach-
Prufe put together, and that's the Word-a-God!' " He said
in an aside to Gina, as she was nearly jolted into his lap by
the potholes in the road, "Jimmy Swaggart himself was so
taken with that sermon when he heard about it, he wrote
and asked me for a copy. I wasn't flattered *too* much."

"Who is—" Gina started to say, but they hit another
bump so hard her teeth almost struck sparks. She didn't try
to say anything else, just stared through the windshield
looking for the barn.

"Sometimes I wish I'd been born with a extra pair of
hands," Zipporah said, mildly complaining. She was very
busy. She had cued up "Onward, Christian Soldiers" on

one of the tape recorders while simultaneously searching through a rack of taped and boxed sermons for the one Buddy Buck had requested. "Can't make out my own writin' sometimes. . . . Here it is."

"Sedalia," the preacher said into his headset microphone, speaking to the black man in the trailer, "you copy me?"

"I copy you, Buddy Buck." His voice was clear in the cab over a small dash-mounted speaker.

"Let's light up. Display number one, number two."

"You got it."

Twinkling lights, like those used to decorate miniature Christmas trees, came on all over the trailer. They spelled out, fore and aft, BUDDY BUCK MAYHEW and GOD'S WARRIOR ON WHEELS.

"I ain't got my own name in lights yet," Zipporah confided, "but I'm gonna have. That'll be my next birthday present."

"Onwardddd Chris-chun So-hol-jurs, marching as to warrrr. . ."

"That's me," Zipporah said. "Me and the New Damascus Consolidated High School marchin' band." She shivered and smiled shyly. "Always gives me ducky bumps when I hear myself sing."

"The car's not there!"

Zipporah glanced out the side window of the cab. "Sure ain't," she said, as if the absence of the Toyota hulk was nothing extraordinary. "And all the tracks we made through the snow, they're gone too. Now look up there, Buddy Buck: you see that barn sittin' on the drop edge of yonder? Looks all peaceful around it now, but a few minutes ago the black fires of hell was ashootin' out everywhere."

"My God, my God, they've all gone! Hillary's gone too!"

"I ain't so sure," Zipporah said quietly, intent on the barn. "You know, Gina, I was the seventh child in my family, and like they say, oft times it's the seventh got special powers. I don't claim to go around seein' the supernatural all the time, but just the same I do get *feelings*. What I feel now is that they are all layin' low waitin' for us to get frustrated and just go away. Because you see, your daughter ain't one of them yet, not by a long shot. To be one of them she's got to surrender her faith and want to be in league with the devil. She may be, like, susceptible to certain influences, but I can't believe you raised that sort of a child. So then they got to work really hard on her, do a job of brainwashing, and—*ohhhhhh,* Buddy Buck, I am gettin' kind of a crawly feelin' now, like hate rainin' down on my skin the closer we come. You feel any of that, honey?''

"Yeah," he said, shifting down to compound low and gripping the steering wheel tightly. "I feel a whole lot of resistance to God's Big Green Machine."

"Don't let it stop us."

"Huh. I'm gonna bag me a whole mess of devils before this day is done. Key up the cockroach sermon, Zipporah, and keep playin' the hymn too."

"Right."

They had reached a rusted pipe-and-wire gate, hinged on one side to a thick wooden post partly buried in snow. On the other side of the gate was a discernible passage—it couldn't be called a road—through trees to the barn, only the roof of which could be seen from where they were.

"Sedalia," the preacher said into the headset microphone, "ready with display number eight, *Washed in the Blood.*"

"We gonna have everything on full power at once; I don't know if the genny can handle it."

"It'll hold up."

"What're you gonna do about the gate?" Zipporah said.

"Ride right over it. Let's go."

"Wonder where all them birds went to. Well, they wasn't real birds, I guess. Gina, you just hang on and be ready for anythin' to happen, 'cause it probably will."

The bumper of the Peterbilt nudged up against the wide gate. It looked flimsy, but when Buddy Buck pushed his foot down on the accelerator the gate stood firm: the truck couldn't move.

"FRIENDS, YOU KNOW WHAT SATAN IS? SATAN AIN'T NOTHIN' BUT A COCKROACH IN THE KITCHEN OF GOD, STEALIN' THE *CRUMBS* OF THE ALMIGHTY IN THE EVERLASTIN' DARK TO WHICH HE HAS BEEN CONFINED. THAT'S RIGHT, I SAID *CONFINED*, BECAUSE ALTHOUGH SATAN AND

ALL HIS DEVILS THINK THEY ARE SO IMPOR-
TANT, MUCKY-MUCKS IN THE COSMIC SCHEME
OF THINGS, WELL, I WANT YOU HERE TONIGHT
TO REALIZE ONE THING: ALL THE TROUBLE THAT
THEY HAVE CAUSED SINCE THE *DAWN* OF RE-
CORDED *HISTORY* IS NOT EQUAL TO THE *GOOD*
THAT EVEN ONE BORN-AGAIN BELIEVER CAN DO
WHEN HE SETS HIS MIND TO IT. AMEN!''

"Jimmy asked for a autographed picture of me in my
suit of lights too," Buddy Buck said, gritting his teeth
then as the front end of the Peterbilt continued to labor
against the impregnable fence. "Sedalia, give us number
twelve."

"Number *twelve?*"

"Do it!"

"Here go."

"Zipporah? 'How Great Thou Art.' ''

"Comin' right up!"

The preacher began blasting away with a siren. There
was a whistle of skyrockets and mortars, crumpling explo-
sions overhead, lush falling blossoms of light over the
barnlot, which was tinted in green and rose and amber. At
the same time two side panels on the trailer opened; one
depicted the Last Supper, stunningly painted in a full range
of Day-Glo colors on black velvet. The other showed, in
rippling neon, a pair of praying hands and the legend I AM
THE WAY.

Buddy Buck Mayhew pushed the accelerator of the
Peterbilt to the floor. The fence flew apart and they roared
toward the barn. Instantly they were greeted by *Sturm und
Drang;* by chaos. A black storm swept over them, debris
thudded against the cab and the trailer, the windshield was
starred in a dozen places by small stones. A smell arose
that turned everyone's stomach.

From the trailer Sedalia complained, "I can't draw breath
back here!"

"Hang on, we'll be through this in a second!"

And, miraculously, they were—only to be confronted
by a horror of such magnitude that Buddy Buck came to a
precarious panic stop, almost causing the trailer to tip
over.

"What is *that?*" Gina gasped.

The barn lay another two hundred yards from them. But between the truck and the barn there was something in the way, a barrier like a suspended tidal wave twelve to fifteen feet high, trembling with latent power. The wave was composed entirely of flesh—living human beings twisted and tumbled agonizingly together. In this press of humanity was everyone the three of them had known and loved in their lifetimes: Gina picked out the faces of her boys, Dean and Charley-chuck, her husband Conor. Buddy Buck saw his mother and father and a host of his kin; his second, fourth, and fifth wives. Zipporah recognized her sisters Moxie Ann and Zelda Fern, her brothers, the lovers whom she had cherished from the age of fifteen. All cried out tormentedly to them: *Stop. Go back. Go away.*

Tears streamed down the preacher's face. The sight was so ghastly, and so heartrending. "I can't drive through *that*," he told them huskily.

"Buddy Buck, you got to! Because it's a lie, a trick! Can't you see? There ain't nobody real in that heap of people."

But Buddy Buck had shifted into reverse.

"I tell you I can't do it!" he blubbered. "Mama's there. And little Tommy, rest his beautiful soul!"

"Now listen to me, darlin'. It's time to use Display Number 22. It's the only thing that's gonna work anymore."

"Number 22? That's for the big finale of our crusade up on top of Lookout Mountain! And we ain't even tested it one time. Sedalia says it could melt the back end right out of this cab, maybe touch off the fuel tanks. God knows what the heat would do to all of us."

"Just keep backin' her on up, and take a good run at that—that—whatever it is."

The pleading shrieks from the victims making up the human wave before them rose to a sickening crescendo.

"That's my daddy's voice! Hear him? *How can I drive straight through my own daddy's flesh and bones?*"

"You ain't gonna hit nothin'. That's the truth I'm tellin' you." When he didn't respond, Zipporah took over. "Sedalia, you copy me? I'm gonna count down now from ten to zero, and when you hear *zero* I want you to fire off Display 22." To the preacher she said, "Buddy Buck, if you ever hope for me to be lucky Wife Number Seven, you better stand on it and I mean *right now!* Bust that devil where it hurts!''

With a yowl of pain the preacher shifted gears, and the big truck rumbled forward over the frozen ground. He saw eyes and ears and tongues and frantically waggling fingers and shut his own eyes tightly.

"Seven . . . six . . . five," Zipporah counted, as they hurtled toward the human wave in their path. "Don't mess up now."

A hatch on top of the trailer toward the front slid back. A large cross appeared, rising like a periscope from the conning tower of a submarine.

"Three . . . two . . . one . . ."

"Mama!" Charley-chuck screamed at Gina, "make him stop! *You'll kill us!*"

He was so cunningly real, every detail of his face clearly rendered down to the precious little mole near his right eye, that Gina cringed in agony and bit her tongue. She threw her arms up around her head.

"ZERO!" Zipporah clapped her hands over her own eyes.

For an instant the sun seemed to shine upon the barnlot with a midsummer fierceness as the large cross atop the trailer was touched off. A total of sixty-four small bulbs outlined the cross. Each bulb cost six dollars and fifty cents and fired 25,000 lumens for one scant second before burning out. There had never been anything quite like the power of this cross seen on earth. A single bulb was enough to blind anyone exposed to it for several minutes. Sixty-four of them obliterated the barrier facing the truck, scoured the barnlot, reached into the barn itself with thousands of brilliant needles. A number of shadowy figures gathered there vanished instantly into perdition.

"Stop, Buddy Buck, we'll crash up 'longside the barn!"

The preacher opened his eyes and applied the brakes at the same time. The truck slid a hundred and fifty feet and came to an unsteady sideways stop near the stone front wall.

They looked all around them in blessed silence. Only the myriad windshield cracks remained as testimony to the trials they had suffered.

"I feel. . . I feel a sense of *peace,* y'all! I think they must be all gone from this place."

"We did it! We did it!" Buddy Buck crowed.

"But we don't have Hillary! She must be in the barn! Let me out!"

"*Wait*," Zipporah cautioned Gina, and frowned.

"What's wrong *now?*"

"I don't know. I can't be sure. Just sit tight, hear?"

"Zipporah, that barn door's opening up," Buddy Buck said.

"Can I get out of this trailer now?" Sedalia inquired a bit peevishly.

"Stay put," the preacher told him. "It may not be over yet."

They saw the front end of an old black Cadillac emerging, with unpleasant slowness, from the dark interior of the barn. The broad curved windshield was dirty and they couldn't see anyone behind the wheel. Gina put a hand on the butt of the Colt Python in her pocket, and held her breath.

The Cadillac, Stegosaurus of pleasure machines, turned creepingly toward them. As it rolled along Buddy Buck put the Peterbilt into reverse, and backed up slowly.

"You gonna run over it?"

"I ain't gonna let it run over *me*," he said, almost whimsically.

But then they saw that the Cadillac was creating its own junkyard as, piece by piece, it fell apart, the tires unspooling in ragged streamers of rubber, the body taking on a rusty hue until the metal was like see-through lace. The car ended up no more than fifty feet outside the barn in an untidy heap of rubber, glass, plastic, pitted chrome, cast iron, metal oxide, and little steaming puddles of vital fluids.

And in the midst of this wreckage, stretched out on a dilapidated seat cushion in her Blessed Sacrament School jumper, Hillary Devon lay in oblivious repose, face to the sky. Even from where she was sitting, Gina could see, as her throat clogged from gratitude, that the possessive handprint had vanished from her daughter's forehead. All was well, for now.

"Thank you, Lord," Zipporah Honeycutt said humbly beside her; and all three bowed their heads.

66

When Conor Devon drove up to his house, at four thirty in the afternoon, with Father James Merlo beside him in the Lincoln, there was a police car parked at the base of his driveway, blocking it. He pulled up in front of the cruiser and they got out, to be met by two cops. Conor, panicky, glanced at the house. Gina's station wagon wasn't in the driveway. There were no lights on in the house, although it was swiftly growing dark.

"What's up?" Conor said to the older of the two policemen, a man with short gray hair and worry wrinkles.

"Are you Mr. Devon?"

"Yes. Has something happened?"

"Sir, I'll ask the questions if you don't mind. Have you seen your wife this afternoon?"

"No, I haven't. I've been at Logan Airport waiting for Father Merlo's flight to land. Now will you please tell me—"

"Mr. Devon, it appears that your wife may be in some serious trouble." He glanced at a page of a notebook in one hand. "She's accused of taking a car belonging to Louise D. Briggens of 984 Judson Lane, Joshua, at gunpoint, from the parking lot of the Grand Union in the Watkins Mill Shopping Center at approximately twelve forty-five this afternoon. If you have any information regarding the whereabouts—"

"At gunpoint? *Gina?* What the hell is this all about? Where are my kids?"

"I wouldn't know anything about your children, Mr. Devon. There's also an unverified report of a shooting that took place in the same area at approximately the same time; a woman answering your wife's description allegedly fired a shot into a blue Toyota waiting for a light change at—"

"This is crazy. You're not talking about *my* wife."

355

''Yes, sir, Mrs. Briggens positively identified her, said she knows her from the school your children attend, they're on the PTA board together.''

Conor just shook his head in frustration and denial. For several seconds there was an uneasy silence, punctuated by the low tones of the dispatcher on the police radio.

''Does your wife own a Colt Python .357 magnum revolver?''

Conor's attention was focused on something else: a hymn, distant against the wind.

''He is trampling out the vintage where the grapes of wrath are stored. . . .''

Three voices, amplified, singing a capella. The sound of it growing stronger. Conor and Merlo looked around, puzzled, for the source of the singing. Far down the street they saw a big Peterbilt truck, lights blazing in the dusk like a traveling carnival.

''Glory, glory, hallelujah. . . .''

Conor turned to face the oncoming truck. Its air horn was hooting madly, disturbing the peace of Revere Park, bringing neighbors to their windows and front porches.

''Who is Buddy Buck Mayhew?'' Merlo said wonderingly. ''Another wrestler?''

''Never heard of him. But whatever he does, he's got a hell of a gimmick.''

''Conor! Conor!''

Gina was leaning out the window, waving. Conor stared in disbelief for a couple of moments, then ran down the street toward God's Big Green Machine. Behind it came the Olds Cutlass which Gina had ''borrowed'' from Louise Briggens with Zipporah Honeycutt at the wheel.

As soon as the little procession had stopped in the middle of the block Gina scrambled down from the cab of the Peterbilt and jumped into Conor's arms, kissing him wildly. Conor had a glimpse of Buddy Buck, all smiles, and beside him, a wan-looking but happy Hillary Devon, wrapped in a blanket. Hillary waved to her father. The police car came lurching down the street, siren burping.

''Oh-oh, the cops,'' Gina said, vaguely contrite.

''What the hell have you been *doing?* They want you for attempted murder and car theft!''

''They can't hang anything on me,'' Gina said toughly;

then, downcast, swallowing hard and blinking back tears: "I guess I do have some explaining to do. Conor, would you mind if we took everybody out to Pizza Hut tonight? There's company for dinner, and I'm just too tired to cook."

67

When Merlo heard a sketchy account of what had happened to Hillary over the past few weeks, he made immediate arrangements for her safekeeping in a convent twenty miles away in rural New Hampshire, where she could be protected day and night from future, possibly even stronger, attacks. Gina pointed out that she hadn't been very safe in the sanctuary of Blessed Sacrament, supposedly holy ground and invulnerable to penetration by an agent of the devil.

"Holy ground is not in itself a shield against evil; nor is the sign of the cross, as Conor found out. Mystic power has always been associated with the cross, and there is both virtue and good in that. But against a devil like Zarach', more concentrated power is needed. Constant, directed prayer will create a web of white light that will surround Hillary for as long as necessary. The Sisters of Mysala have had centuries of experience in neutralizing evil, I can tell you that. Hillary will be safe now."

"A *convent?*" Hillary said, thoroughly outraged.

"It's not much different from boarding school," Merlo explained.

"MOTHER!"

"Hillary," Gina said, gritting her teeth, "did you enjoy what almost happened to you today? Because I damn well didn't enjoy it. And we're all very fortunate to be alive."

Gina's problems with the law had lasted only a little longer than her argument with her daughter. Conor got on the phone immediately to Louise Briggens, who came, looked her car over, heard Gina's account of Hillary's ordeal, and decided not to press charges. Gina, Buddy

Buck Mayhew, and Zipporah were interrogated for an hour and a half at police headquarters. They had rehearsed a story carefully, leaving out any reference to the supernatural, which would only have confused and probably antagonized the investigating officers. Buddy Buck said that he had seen Gina in frantic pursuit of the Toyota and had joined in the chase, eventually forcing the blue car off the road. Confronted by superior numbers, "Richards" had fled on foot, leaving Hillary unharmed but groggy in the back seat. The appearance and subsequent disappearance of "Richards" from the church with Hillary was vouched for by Father Toomey. The cops couldn't find a trace of background for the supposed physician. Nor could they find the blue Toyota. Descriptions of suspect and vehicle went into the computers at the National Crime Information Center in Washington. Gina was relieved of her Colt Python revolver and her carry permit was suspended, subject to review. She was not charged with violating any statutes.

At two-thirty in the morning, with everyone fed and accommodated for the night (Dean and Charley-chuck, having found no one at home upon their arrival from school, had gone directly to a neighbor's home, a contingency Gina had worked out long ago, and they were rather amazed by all the excitement and the novelty of God's Big Green Machine), Gina rose from the side of her snoring husband, with whom she had made vigorous love, walked into the bathroom, sat on the john, one bare foot overlapping the other, pressed a folded bath towel against her face, and had hysterics for a quarter of an hour. Then, at long last, she, too, was able to sleep.

PART THREE

Sundial

68

The fishing in the rich seabeds of the Fuerteventura Channel had been good for many months; so good in fact that Francisco Aponte Olaya, captain and part owner of the seiner *San Patricio* with two of his brothers, had accumulated enough money to replace a no longer repairable pump that had caused considerable listing their last few trips out, and the portside dredger, also a recent source of problems. This rare opportunity coincided with the funeral of a cousin in Tenerife, where the new machinery was to be obtained and installed. On the Tuesday after *santa semana* Olaya took his entire family with him from Heraclio, northernmost of the far-flung Canary Islands that lay off the coast of Saharan Africa. It was the first time the two youngest of the six children had been away from their home, a week-long event of almost unbearable excitement for all of them. Once the obligation of the funeral was out of the way they were free to enjoy themselves at the post-Lenten festivities that enlivened the port city, which was blessed with a bumper crop of European tourists—and not a few Americans, among them one of the biggest men Olaya had ever seen.

His name, he said, was Conor Devon, which the captain had a lot of trouble pronouncing. The bearded man was sweating freely despite the cool harbor breezes. He had with him a pair of French students, slim girls in singlets and sandals who spoke some English and good Spanish and who acted as interpreters for him. He had arrived that morning after a very long flight from a place called Massachusetts. He was in a great hurry to get to Heraclio and could not think of waiting for the twice-weekly deHaviland that flew to the little landing strip outside Puerto Arroyo, the largest of Heraclio's few towns. He was willing to pay the equivalent of two hundred dollars if Olaya would be willing to shorten his family's holiday and return at once.

The captain considered the offer only briefly. The installations had been completed aboard the *San Patricio*, they had been already four days in Tenerife, sleeping in the cramped crew quarters of the fo'c'sle, and so much togetherness had him testy at times. It was nearly a full day's run by sea to Heraclio, and he thought it sensible to conclude their travels while the weather was stable. If they left within the hour they would raise Puerto Arroyo before midnight. The stranger, despite his size and red beard, seemed mild enough, a little dazed by his long transit from the United States. Already he was the ripe, boiled shade of a freckled deep-sea lobster from his limited exposure to the tropical sun. His passport seemed legitimate. And he willingly parted with half of the agreed-upon tariff in advance. Just that much money more than covered Olaya's expense of maintaining his family for most of the week in Tenerife. The appearance of *el rojo senōr* at such a propitious time seemed providential to Olaya. Why his passenger wanted to reach Heraclio so quickly was not his business. Perhaps he was just another tourist with limited time who had a fondness for out-of-the-way places and had heard of the strange splendors of Heraclio. Olaya invited the American aboard and sent his oldest son Socorro to round up the other family members in the quayside bazaars.

69

A worsening pitch and roll awakened Conor from his nap in the topmost bunk at the rear of the fo'c'sle when the *San Patricio* was two hours at sea, on a northeasterly course. He felt the thrumming of the diesel engine and smelled something cooking in the little galley. The fo'c'sle was starkly lit by a swinging light bulb which illuminated in turn the faces of children grouped around a bare knife-scarred table that had been fastened to the deck. Four of them were eating slices of melon that gave them big orange clownmouths, or gnawing on strips of dried shark. A towheaded boy almost as fair as a Swede but with enchantingly elliptical olive-colored eyes was playing a curious-looking musical instrument that produced winsome, burbling notes not unlike the singing of a treeful of wild canaries. The music of the water flute was so delicately beautiful and plaintive it stirred the hairs on the back of Conor's neck.

Conor had to slip off the bunk sideways so as not to bang his forehead on the low ceiling. A woman in a brown dress backed out of the galley carrying baskets of crisp brown fish fillets and hot bread basted with a tomato sauce. She placed the food on the table and smiled at him.

"*Como usted,*" she said. She pointed to a place on the portside bench for him. Two of the kids scooted closer together to give him ample room, and studied him dubiously, as if he were a poorly trained bear who had been set loose among them. The air was close below deck with the fo'c'sle hatch closed, and the bucking of the *San Patricio* through quickening seas didn't agree with him. He was no sailor. He rubbed his stomach to indicate a slight indisposition. One of the children pointed to the head, thinking he wanted to relieve himself. It didn't seem like a bad idea. Conor could barely fit himself inside and close the door. He heard giggles, and the mother spoke sharply to remind them all of their manners.

When he came out of the head Socorro was waiting for him, bolting a sandwich he had made from the bread and the fish. He was one of two children who were blond and tall, after their mother, a beauty except for snaggled teeth. He was also solemn and seemed a little cross, in the manner of children who are a puzzle to themselves. Already he had the hands and wrists of a fisherman, but his deep-set eyes thought and dreamed of more than salt and homely deeps.

"My father," he said between mouthfuls, "says you will be more comfortable in the wheelhouse. There is more room."

"Thank you," Conor said, surprised to hear such good English from the boy.

He followed Socorro through the hatch topside, squeezing his shoulders together in order to make it, and was surprised again, intimidated by the sudden absence of land and the sight of so much water, the dark green vastness of an ocean running now to eight-foot swells and beginning to smash heavily over the lifting bow of what had seemed to be a very substantial boat when it was snuggled in against the stone quay of the calm harbor of Tenerife. Seventy-five feet bow to stern, with perhaps an eighteen-foot beam, it carried two big steel mesh seiners, each of which when loaded had the weight of a Brink's truck. All of this now felt frail and shaky to Conor, a bathtub toy at the mercy of a wind rising and beginning to wail. The sky was a sickly yellow, with streamers of inky clouds running before the wind. Spray lashed Conor, drenching his beard, and he felt the deck shudder beneath his feet as they dashed to the wheelhouse.

"How far do we have to go?" Conor said, as Francisco Aponte Olaya turned from the wheel with a little nod of welcome. Socorro had brought his father a sandwich; he turned the wheel over to the boy and braced himself serenely in a corner while he ate.

"Five hours, perhaps five and a half in such seas," Socorro answered.

"Is it a storm?"

"This? Not yet. If we're fortunate—" he shrugged.

Olaya smiled, not understanding Conor's words but assuming, from the look on his face, that he was concerned about heavy weather. He came forward and with an outstretched hand proudly indicated the modern navigational and radio equipment aboard. Then he took a ragged cheroot of black tobacco from a pocket of his denim shirt and lit up. The odor of it didn't help Conor's stomach.

To take his mind off his discomfort he asked Socorro, "Where did you learn to speak English?"

"School."

"On Heraclio?"

"Yes. The Sundial school. I went there for six years, until a few months ago, when my father said it was time for me to fish every day with him." The boy's lips pressed together in dissatisfaction. Olaya looked at him and smiled and gave him a pat on the back. He asked for a course correction in Spanish.

"*Buen pescador,*" he said to Conor of his son.

"Is the school a part of the Sundial community?" Conor asked Socorro.

"Yes. They have many living there who speak English. I liked the school. But my father believes I will get too many ideas from them."

"Do you know Edith Leighton?"

The boy pondered the name, and shook his head. "No. She was not one of my teachers."

"I've come all this way to see her. I hope she'll be willing to see me."

A particularly big wave, higher than the top of the wheelhouse, rolled them to starboard. Socorro spun the pilot's wheel, and the *San Patricio* labored up out of the foaming sea. Conor swallowed hard and felt his heart running riot. Five more hours of this. Maybe he should have waited for the next plane, or tried to charter one.

"There is no problem," Socorro said, returning to their conversation. "The community accepts visitors. Except it is difficult to find Sundial unless you go with someone who knows the way."

"Could you take me?"

"I don't know. Maybe."

Socorro peered, frowning, at the ship's barometer, and summoned his father. They conversed in Spanish. It was apparent they had not anticipated, or been warned, of a sizable blow. They were worried. *"Viento de diablo,"* the father muttered. The wind shrieked in reply. To Conor it seemed as if every timber and plank in the *San Patricio* was creaking, and the seas had begun to batter them ferociously. The sky outside darkened as the minutes dragged on. He was sweaty and felt light-headed. He needed air. He went to the door of the wheelhouse.

"Be careful!" Socorro said.

"I just—you know—"

Conor tottered outside, and tottered back helplessly as the bow reared up toward the threatening sky, now laced with shards of greenish lightning. He was terrified. Before he could make it to the railing he had puked all over himself. His unseaworthy legs wouldn't hold him up anymore, and he rolled on the deck as a wave poured over him. He glimpsed the faces of the Olayas within the green glow of the wheelhouse as the deck drained rapidly through scupper holes. Then he was being lifted, prostrate and trembling, along with the deck, up, up toward a bulging

dark horizon shedding spray like a firehose. The bow came
down with a terrific impact, and above him he saw the
mailed fist of the new seining purse shuddering from the
port boom arm. He was half drowned and desperately ill.
The sky flared blindingly. The wind had become a gale
and the *San Patricio* heeled to starboard: the seining purse
dangled over his head.

Conor, looking at open water, saw it as a graveyard; he
was spilling into the sea but managed to seize a winch
cable. He hung suspended for a long moment before he
was slammed down stunningly to the deck, covered once
again with a rushing wave, tumbled back to port. It seemed
to go on for a very long time, with no chance to get to his
feet and run for cover. He heard several loud cracking
sounds, like gunshots, and assumed the boat was beginning to come apart from the pounding it was taking. And
when he looked up again through burning eyes he saw the
boom arm give way, the steely mass of the seining purse
dropping down. Even though it was empty it weighed
more than enough to splatter him like a raw egg across the
deck.

He thought: I wasn't meant to get there.

Then he felt hands tugging at him and braced his feet
against the railing, threw himself backward with all his
remaining strength as the seining purse thundered down to
the deck, missing him by inches. The jagged end of the
boom arm followed, swinging wildly at the end of a single
cable. It passed above his head and Conor heard a scream.

He looked around to see Socorro Olaya, kneeling behind
him, just as the wooden arm, with splinters more than a
foot long, sawed through the boy's face and neck and
dashed his head overboard in a pink and billowing spray.

70

It wasn't the biggest news of the day, which happened to be April first, perhaps an unfortunate bit of timing on Adam's part; it competed for attention with genocide in a Latin American republic, the ill health of the Kremlin's leader, the death of a beloved country music star in a bus accident, and a drug bust involving a minor child of a prominent Washington political figure. Nonetheless the New York *Daily News* had the story on page 3, with photos, and the headline NO FOOLIN'! DEVIL MADE HIM DO IT! *The New York Times,* as might be expected, gave the story a more sober heading on page A7, which was dominated by a splashy Bloomingdale's fashion ad: DEFENSE TO PLEAD DEMONIC POSSESSION IN VERMONT MURDER TRIAL. The *Boston Globe,* closer to home, put the news on the front page, along with a brief interview with a prosecutor from the district attorney's office; he called the proposed defense a "sham," "meretricious," and "unworthy of the American legal system." The Braxton *Call,* closer still, was cautiously critical, but praised the firm's founder, Adam's grandfather, and his contributions to the law. The story rated from thirty seconds to two and a half minutes on CNN's *Daybreak,* the CBS *Morning News,* the *Today* show on NBC, and *Good Morning, America* on ABC.

Adam's phone at home began ringing at six thirty-four in the morning.

He was already up and shaving; he had been too nervous to do more than doze since midnight. He took no calls. When Lindsay got up at seven, the answering machine had already logged thirteen messages, two of them from presiding judge Nathaniel "Natty" Eames, also, apparently, an early riser. Lindsay watched a portion of the *Today* show with Adam: a brief interview taped on the street

outside his office. The reporter, a blond third-stringer
from the NBC News Department in New York, asked one
of the most intelligent questions he had heard all afternoon.

"Mr. Kurland, what precisely will be required of you to
prove demonic possession in a court of law?"

"Well, I believe it comes down to proving the existence
of an evil, or negative, force that is operative in the world.
The admission of psychic, as opposed to physical, evidence."

"A case which theologians have been making, or trying
to make, for hundreds of years."

"Precisely. The Catholic Church is well aware of this
force, which is as old as human thought and motivation—
and implacably opposed to the natural order of things, the
laws of God."

"How much help would the Church be able to give you
in court?"

"Expert testimony."

"One more question, please, Mr. Kurland. Are you a
Catholic?"

"No, I am not."

Adam used the remote control handset to change channels. He got Porky Pig in an old Warner Bros. cartoon
stuttering "Uh-b-b-b-b-uh, th-that's all, folks."

They both laughed. Lindsay kissed him on the cheek.
"That's for the bravest man I've ever met."

"Or the dumbest."

The phone rang again.

"Better start taking calls, Linds."

She answered. She didn't get a chance to say another
word for approximately half a minute. She rubbed at her
ear as if it were scorching and turned the receiver over to
Adam, who didn't have to be told with whom he was
about to speak.

"I just want you to know I think you're a disgrace to the
memory of two men I hold in the highest esteem: your
father and your grandfather."

"I'm sorry you feel that way, Your Honor."

"Be in my chambers at ten o'clock sharp."

"Yes, sir."

Adam held the receiver against his chest for a few

moments, his head bowed. Lindsay leaned sympathetically against him.

"I wonder how Conor's making out?" he said. "If he doesn't come through for us, I might as well pull down the old shingle."

71

For Conor, the sun that day had risen in hell.

After the late arrival of the storm-wracked *San Patricio*, with all aboard in a state of misery and mourning, and the inquiry by Heracliotian authorities into the tragic accident that had taken the life of Socorro Olaya, Conor had fallen exhaustedly asleep in his room in the Pensión del Papagayo, a nearly emptied bottle of plum brandy clutched against his chest. He was awakened by the braying of burros, an unidentifiable but hair-raising roar, metallic tinkling as some belled goats were herded down the narrow street beneath his windows, cheerful voices, church bells; by simmering light that came into the room through a gap in the shutters. The day was already hot.

He got out of the low bed where he had lain with his knees up and almost immediately emptied his lurching stomach into a large enameled basin on a wash stand. The remorse, the pity he felt for the bereaved family, remained like a bitter nugget. He condemned himself for the boy's death. Only superb seamanship on the part of Olaya and a boat that had proved itself through many bad gales had saved the rest of them. He wiped his weeping eyes, pushed wide the shutters on windows that faced north and east, and had his first good look at the island of Heraclio.

He saw a stunned and hazy landscape dominated in the distance by cinder cones and dormant volcanoes, all of it treeless, pocked with craters, black and dark brown and naked as elephant hide. The small city of Puerto Arroyo lay between this wasteland and the sea, which was a steel sheet burning incandescently by solar torch on the horizon,

as if the vault of the world were being rudely opened.
There were no clouds. It looked as if the land had never
tasted a drop of rain.

Conor dressed and had weak coffee with a roll at an
outdoor café on the pleasant main boulevard of Puerto
Arroyo, which ran parallel to the long harbor, with a strip
of park between the quay and the street. The park contained the only trees and flowering shrubs he saw growing
anywhere. Its walkways served as a marketplace on this
particular day, and the assembled stalls were heaped with
fruits and vegetables of astonishing variety and dimension.
He wondered where and how they were grown.

It was Friday, and the town had filled up early. Buses
from other parts of the island arrived at a depot near the
desalinization plant at the south end of the harbor. Conor
carried his single piece of luggage to the depot and tried to
find someone who could understand him.

An elderly gentleman wearing a pair of khaki shorts and
no other clothing had brought his very young Heracliotian
wife to the depot on the back of a grimy Vespa; he heard
Conor attempting to communicate by phrasebook with smiling but uncomprehending natives and sauntered over. He
was all bones beneath a deep tan. He had a white goatee
and sharp little eyes, the unplaceable accent of the European polyglot.

"Is it Sundial you want? Yes, I know where they are.
On the other side of Heraclio, on the western skirt of
Montaña del Fuego. The mountain of fire. Largest of the
volcanoes that nearly blew this island off the face of the
earth two hundred and fifty years ago. I believe there is a
bus to La Loma in a short while; let me have a peek at the
schedule, *amorita* . . . yes, here it is. La Loma. Departs
nine fifteen. Once you reach the village you will have
another five miles to go. Sundial community is on a ridge
overlooking the lagoon at Playa Cascajo. Do you know
someone who is living in the community?"

"No."

"Do not count on much of a welcome, then. They're
odd ducks. Keep very much to themselves. Lead busy,
active lives, which I am certainly in favor of. They are
devout, but it is hard to say exactly what religion or
philosophy they are devoted to. They certainly waste none

of their energies proselytizing, although I have never heard of them turning away anyone who wished to settle there, as long as he adhered to whatever standards they have set for themselves. Can't see it, myself. The reclusive life. Retirement villages. That sort of thing. Think young. Act young. Stay young. That is my philosophy.'' He put an arm around his wife, who was delectable, perhaps not fully grown but highly pregnant. To Conor she didn't look much older than Hillary.

"Can I walk from the village to Sundial?"

"I would not advise it. Incredibly windy, most days. And if you stray off the footpaths, well, the unwary have been known to crunch right through the skin of the lava on Montaña del Fuego. Barely two feet below the surface it is still seven hundred degrees Fahrenheit. You will want to inquire locally for transport. Ah, I believe the blue and orange bus there is the one for La Loma. Safe journey.''

Conor had little company on the trip west; a couple of islanders who looked as if they worked the fishing boats, and three German tourists, meaty and pink and somewhat baleful behind severely dark glasses. They carried a fortune in camera equipment and ate sausage for breakfast from a hamper. Conor, feeling desperately homesick, dozed, and mistook the jolting of the bus for the swells of the sea. He saw the troubled eyes of Socorro Olaya at the wheel of his father's boat, steering himself toward death. The tearful face of his own daughter came through with the clarity of a vision; she was calling to him from behind the gates of the convent of the Sisters of Mysala. *Help me, Daddy.* He remembered her taut look of despair as she had turned away from him. Indefinite confinement. Like a prison to Hillary. But what else could he do? Their lives fragmented now, Gina sick with worry. His last chance to help Rich was a woman he had never seen before. But she had already replied to Father Merlo's inquiry. Gentle finality. *Regret that I am unable to help you at this time.* "How can I take no for an answer?" Conor had asked Merlo. "Rich will die. . . . Maybe we are all lost.''

The bus had stopped at a village that was no more than a crossroads, a gleam of white Mediterranean-style buildings set against the dry reds and browns of the lava fields of Montaña del Fuego, which was a series of volcanic peaks

1,500 to 2,000 feet high. The sky was so deep a blue it shaded to purple around the shoulders of the mountain. There was a steady northeast wind, and grit pattered against the windows on one side of the bus.

Everybody got off except Conor. The driver had left the motor running, the air conditioning on. Camels were kneeling beside the road. They roared in protest, like lions, at the sight of the Germans, whom they were to transport up the basalt-strewn slopes of the mountain. A boy climbed aboard and tried to sell Conor cigarettes, fruit juice, figs. Conor shook his head and waited tiredly, eyes closing, for the idling, wind-buffeted bus to continue on to La Loma. The camels, never sweet-tempered beasts, were acting very badly today. One of them had run away. The others roared incessantly.

There was a corresponding roar, more distant, subterranean; and then a cracking sound, like a giant walnut shell fragmenting under pressure. The bus was severely jarred and settled a couple of feet. Then it began to tilt forward alarmingly.

Conor scrambled from his seat, banging his head on the overhead rack, as a boil of dust and heat enveloped the front of the bus. The steep tilting continued, until the bus was on its blunt nose at an angle of forty degrees. Conor felt it sliding slowly downward as the heat worsened. He heard shouts and screams of warning outside. He grabbed his valise from the floor and pulled back a window, hurled the valise into someone's hands. But the window space was too small for him to squeeze through. He knew he had very little time to find a way out.

Only the emergency door in the rear remained above ground; the bus continued to slide into the earth, its descent accompanied by more cracking, groaning, popping sounds, as if an acre of bottles and clay tiles were being pulverized by some infernal machine. Conor climbed up the steep aisle, using the backs of seats for handholds. The dust and fumes swirling into the bus had begun to suffocate him. The heat was terrible. Choking, he grabbed the release bar of the emergency door and tried to pry it up. The bar resisted him. He bent it almost double in a ferocious display of strength and kicked the door out. He jumped.

The bus fell away from him into the gusty pit. His shirt and hair were smoldering from numerous little biting cinders. Someone threw a blanket smelling oppressively of camels over him as he rolled on the ground. Helping hands pulled him to his feet and he ran, stumbling, away from the place where the bus had disappeared into the earth. When he looked back he saw nothing but a cloud of ashes and smoke rising from the hole in the road. The entire town had turned out to marvel at the sight. Conor, bent over, coughed uncontrollably.

"Have a drink of this," a woman said calmly in his ear. "Sounds as if you need it, my dear."

He accepted the bottle of wine without looking at its donor, and drank deep. The wine stung his lips and tongue and washed the dust from his parched throat. He gradually stopped coughing.

"You had a narrow escape. I suppose that bus has parked in that very spot day in and day out for a number of years without mishap. Suddenly a lava tube no one knew was there gives way. Well, that's the nature of this island. I presume no one else was aboard."

"No," Conor said. "Nobody got killed this time." He handed the bottle back and thanked her. She was a small Englishwoman, ruddy, wrinkled, with short gray hair ascatter in the wind, a fine appraising eye, and a stubborn mouth; she looked as if she could be temperamental.

"This time?"

He shrugged; he didn't feel like trying to explain to a stranger. The boy who had wanted to sell him refreshments aboard the bus moments before the ground opened appeared lugging Conor's valise in two hands. Conor gave him money. His face was smarting; he touched it carefully. Blisters.

"Those should be attended to," the woman said. "There's always a danger of infection."

"Yeah," Conor said indifferently. He had been hurt worse at backyard barbecues. "Well, now there's no bus," he said, looking around. "And I have to get to La Loma." He was more annoyed than shaken by his second close shave in twenty-four hours. "I don't suppose I'll find a taxi in this place."

"I think not. I seldom come this way myself. Only

when *la Duquesa* is not feeling up to par. The local vet is very good with camels, particularly a camel with a toothache. There *is* a taxi in La Loma, which may come this far to fetch you or may not, depending on the whim of its owner. But if you're up to it, I can provide you with transportation, as I'm going that way myself.''

From a woven basket at her feet she took a straw hat with a deep brim and a black hatband. She tied it on her head with a bow under the chin. The hat shaded all of her face.

''You mean ride a camel?''

''It takes some getting used to, but the Duchess is very dependable, particularly where there are no roads to speak of.''

''Well, thanks. I—uh . . . why not. Can your camel carry someone my size?''

''If she chooses. You must pass inspection. But her toothache is much better, and she realizes she owes me a favor. Follow me.''

''By the way, thanks for the wine.'' He looked for the label. There wasn't one. The woman smiled acerbically as Conor gave the bottle back to her.

''I am my own vintner. A labor of love. A good bottle of wine is always useful for barter. I carry several with me on town days.''

''You grow grapes in a place like this?''

''This godforsaken pile of cinders?'' Her mouth held amusement like a bird holds a tidbit. ''Yes, we grow grapes, and very successfully. A single one of my vines will often yield more than a hundred pounds of grapes. Where I am living we grow all of our own food; much more, really, than we can consume.''

''Where do you live?''

''In a small community overlooking Playa Cascajo.'' She gestured vaguely to the west.

''Do you mean Sundial?''

''Yes.''

''Do you know Edith Leighton?''

The woman walked on a few paces without replying, and Conor assumed she hadn't heard him because of the incessant wind, which had become a kind of phantom companion, too close for comfort, mindless, a giant who tried to be playful, and spoke in a numbing monotone. Then she turned suddenly, bringing him up short, and lifted her gaze to him from under the brim of her hat.

"I've been on rather good terms with her for some sixty-eight years now."

"You're—"

"Yes. But who on earth are you, my dear?"

"Conor Devon."

"Devon?" She said it a second time, to herself, before signaling recognition. "Oh, I see. Rather unfair of you to show up like this." She set her basket aside and reached down with both hands to bat dust from her long skirt of *azul de añil*. "I must tell you I have no intention of reversing the decision which I relayed to Father Merlo." She looked up then, noted his disappointment with a defensive tightening of her own lips, and turned her black eyes from his face to the jagged hole in the roadway which had swallowed the bus. The hole was still fuming.

"Since you *are* here," she said, after turning the matter over in her mind for a few moments longer, "I suppose I should take you in hand for the remainder of your stay. Otherwise I suspect you have virtually no chance of leaving Heraclio alive."

72

Judge Natty Eames was a little man of threescore and ten; he had bristling gray hair, a flat nose, a smile aggressively filled with little sharp teeth, and the sometimes rabidly hostile eyes of a Pekingese dog. Like any other man, he was not tolerant of those who tried to cross him, particularly ambitious young trial lawyers. His courtroom was sanctified ground. In it he was God Almighty.

He said to Adam, seven withering seconds after Adam had walked into the judge's chambers, "Where do you get off thinking you can turn my courtroom into a freak show?"

"That certainly was not my intention, Your Honor, when I—"

"Just sit down and listen."

"Sir, with all due respect, I'm fully convinced my client is—"

"Sit down!"

Adam sat.

"I have a certain amount of influence in this state where you happen to practice law. I assume you want to continue to practice, and that this notice of 'demonic possession' you've filed is not some form of suicidal bloodletting you've decided to carry on in public. If it is your wish to pursue the practice of criminal law in Vermont, I advise you to take a little time, say forty-eight hours, to think over what you've done, at the end of which time you may withdraw your notice and file another which the court will find more acceptable, and I won't say any more about your faulty judgment and questionable behavior to date. Don't waste your time fiddling around with any notion of a change of venue or a preempt. I feel that I speak for all of my fellow jurists in expressing my contempt for this travesty. While you are mulling over good advice and hopefully coming to your senses, you're restrained from discussing any aspect of this case with the press. Good morning to you, Counselor."

73

There was no art to riding a camel; it was, Conor found, a matter of sheer staying power. He rode in one of two wood and canvas chairs with adjustable footrests, that were suspended from either side of *la Duquesa's* considerable hump. Edith Leighton occupied the other chair. Conor's size put his legs easily within reach of great grinding teeth, and *la Duquesa* had found him an unaccustomed heavy burden. Edith kept the camel's attention properly fixed on the meandering track they followed westward from La Loma with an occasional stinging flick of the whip she held in one hand. In response the Duchess roared in a spine-tingling way, but she made no attempt to gnaw off one of Conor's feet.

The land they passed through was black with cinders and lush with crops that grew on both sides of the track as far as Conor could see.

"There is some rainfall here," Edith said to him above the moaning of the trade winds. "But only about five inches a year. Not enough for the growth of vegetation which, as in Hawaii, would help break down the quantities of lava into a rich loam. The island is a desert. But what seems harsh can be a blessing. Farmers learned long ago that the loose volcanic cinders have their value agricultur-ally. The *lapilli* form a blanket which soaks up the winter rain and the dew that falls every night, and prevents this trapped moisture from evaporating. Not a drop is wasted, and during the rainless months much can be accomplished even with this small amount of water."

Conor looked at a slope pocked, like a section of golf ball painted black, with precisely formed craters, each about ten feet in diameter and three feet deep; each had its little curved wall of black stone to windward. In the craters were vivid green vines, clusters of grapes.

"The craters," she said, "protect the vines from the wind, which would uproot them. But we have uses for the wind as well."

They traveled down through a wild and uninhabited area of crags and volcanic arroyos, where the land fumed hotly around pieces of basaltic lava as colorful as Gypsy beads. The odor of sulfur was a surprising tonic for Conor's hangover, made worse the last few miles by the jouncing ride in the cramped seat. The sea came into view on their left and soon they were going north at the edge of a cliff so barren not even lichens grew there. Below lay windmills and the drying beds of a salt works. Edith explained how the windmills pumped sea water over the beds, where the sun evaporated the shallow water and left deposits of salt, much of it used by the island's fishermen to preserve their catches for export.

"On the other Canary islands flowers grow in tropical profusion, and flowers are used in their celebrations. What we have the most of is cinders and salt. So the salt is colored and made into elaborate paintings for the feast of Corpus Christi and other religious observances. It's a fascinating culture. The fortitude required to get to know it is well rewarded. The original inhabitants, called Guanche, were tall, fair, Stone Age people, but socially well-organized in spite of their primitive status. It took the Spaniards nearly a hundred years to conquer and assimilate the Guanches. Genetically you still see signs of them, quite lovely blond children with penetrating blue eyes. I suppose the strangest thing of all for an island people is the fact that the Guanches had no boats.''

"Where did they come from?''

"Atlantis, I'm sure. These islands were once the easternmost part of the continent of Atlantis, a civilization which flourished, as you may have heard, some twenty-five thousand years ago, when the coasts of Africa and America were in the sea.''

Conor smiled skeptically. The track they were following began to wind down precipitously toward a lagoon of many shades of green, all of them balm for the eyes. He saw bathers on an arc of black beach, small boats and wind-surfers. Behind the beach, at a distance of about a hundred yards, was a reddish cliff like a petrified comber of the sea. Atop the cliff stood the sugar-cube houses, trimmed in cool colors, and the windmills of the Sundial community. The houses and Roman-style pavilions were surrounded by gardens, a few palm trees, and groves of citrus and fig trees planted in great bowls beneath the level of the wind.

The community occupied all of the dark cliff plateau between the eye of the lagoon and the bloody snout of the central volcano of the mountain of fire that loomed in the background. The side of the volcano was broken in places into deep crevasses, studded with the ugly red teats of spatter cones, stained with the yellow spots of sulfur deposits. It was, Conor thought, a bizarre place to choose to live: hell at the back door, demiparadise in front. Yet no one was here who didn't want to be. He knew from Merlo that Edith Leighton had been one of England's most distinguished barristers—a QC, or member of the Queen's Counsel, the juggernauts of the British legal system, called in for only the most important cases. She could have afforded to live anywhere, in distinguished company. But she seemed to relish the peasant clothing of this virtually unknown island, everyday toil in her garden, the company of a balky and complaining camel. Well, *la Duquesa* saved on gas, which was probably scarce here. Conor saw a few rugged four-wheel drive vehicles parked along the unpaved lanes of the community, and more camels in pens.

Edith flicked the Duchess with the whip to coax her off the track as an old Land-Rover, nearly stripped of paint by the grit-laden winds, came grinding up from below. The mailman behind the wheel grinned and waved to Edith.

"How many residents are there?" Conor asked her.

"The number fluctuates. Perhaps five hundred, not counting the students who board during the week. Many of us are still active in the Work, and come and go constantly; others never leave. I detest driving and seldom go even as far as La Loma these days, because of the obvious difficulties in getting there. Perhaps you wouldn't mind walking the last half mile, it's a troubling descent for *la Duquesa* from this point on."

Presently they reached the community and passed low open buildings on the cliff's edge, through which the sea was visible. Conor heard the voices of children, saw them sitting in small groups around their tutors. Beyond the school was a large plaza, covered with a mosaic of salt paintings framed by low rock walls. A huge pelican in one of the paintings had bitten its own snowy breast and was bleeding into a golden chalice. In the midst of the plaza was a great bronze object perhaps twelve feet in diameter, elevated on a pedestal of rough-hewn granite blocks. It was a very old sundial, meticulously maintained, and looked as if it weighed a couple of tons. The paintings and the sundial combined in a motif that was religious, but not recognizably denominational.

"Religion?" Edith said, when he inquired. "We have God here, but not God the son; no 'religion' with its do's and don't's, it's dependency-inducing rituals of blood and emotional purgings, its priestly hierarchies. The leadership of our convocation rotates among us. Out there"—she indicated the world beyond the cliff with a sweeping hand—"is Satan. He is enough for us to fear, and respect.

And oppose, wherever we encounter him. This has been the only purpose of our society since it was founded nearly two thousand years ago. The truth of the human condition is quite simply expressed. There is good in the world, and there is evil. The struggle between the two forces has not let up for even one moment throughout history. What we try to do is to heighten the influence of good, not through rituals and dehumanizing mumbo-jumbo, but through the power of prayer and psychic intervention, which is all one and the same anyway.''

"How did you get a sundial that size down the mountain?''

"It was not brought here, not by human hands. During the great eruptions, earthquakes, and tidal waves of 1730 to '36, the sundial was cast up from the sea and came to rest, on its side, just where you see it now. It remained in that position for another two hundred years. Those few people who saw it during that time had no idea of what it was. Meanwhile certain evolutionary changes in the vibrational patterns of our little square mile of earth were completed, and individuals within our society whose vibrations corresponded with the enhanced frequency here were attracted—''

"Vibrational patterns? I don't know what you—''

"Oh, I haven't time to explain anything now,'' she said impatiently, almost rudely. "I want to get home. You have too much of Outside Earth clinging to you as it is, and it's causing all kinds of interference. I get an uncomfortable buzzing at the temples when I'm too close to you. Let's go.''

Her house was near the cliff's edge, and had two calcimined cement walls around it, one higher than the other. Between the two walls orange and lemon trees, undisturbed by the whipsawing wind, were fragrantly in bloom. In Edith's cinder garden he saw tomato plants, lentils, peppers, even a watermelon patch. The fruits and vegetables were outsized; they didn't look real. She paused to pick a tomato larger than Conor's fist that was drooping almost to the ground by the path to the door. Then, after tethering *la Duquesa* and providing her with a lunch that included prickly-pear cactus and watermelon rind, Edith took Conor inside.

The doorway was low, he had to stoop slightly. He found the interior of the house similarly snug. There were ceiling fans. A windmill he had seen at one side of the house provided what little electricity was required, and running water. The cleverly baffled veranda that seemed to overhang the spectacular lagoon tamed the stiff trade winds to cool breezes, and woven sunscreens filtered the afternoon glare. They went straight through the house to this wide and deep veranda; Conor noticed in passing the excellent paintings on every wall.

There were two people on the veranda. A man about Edith's age, a girl who looked to be in her early twenties. He was sitting to one side of a large round table facing the sea; the girl was constructing a salt painting in a shallow wood box. Some thirty wide-mouthed bottles of colored salt were on the table. The man didn't look around at Edith's bustling return, but the girl, who had been leaning over the table with one knee on a stool, straightened and smiled, brushing grains of green and ochre salt off the backs of her slim hands. She was nearly six feet tall.

"Hello, Philip," Edith said to her husband. "Bit delayed; I'm sorry." She looked at the untouched lunch on the tray beside him. The girl shrugged soberly. "Well, there was some excitement on the road," Edith continued. "Lava tube collapsed, and the La Loma bus was swallowed whole. This gentleman managed to arrange his escape in the nick of time. He was the sole passenger, fortunately. Conor, wasn't it? Yes. Conor Devon, from the U.S. My husband, Philip Leighton."

Leighton's hands remained folded in his lap. He nodded and smiled but didn't look at Conor. And he said nothing. After a moment the smile faded. He had the eyes of a wayfarer locked into some permanent contemplation of unachievable horizons.

"He talked to me for a minute or two this morning," the girl volunteered. "He had some very helpful things to say about my painting. Oh, yes, and he moved his bowels."

"My husband," Edith Leighton said, looking at Conor, "has Alzheimer's disease."

"I don't think I've ever heard of it."

"Not too many years ago Alzheimer's went virtually undiagnosed; its symptoms were mistaken for a host of

other conditions. Now it's become recognized as a rather
pervasive killer: an irreversible form of premature senility.
I find this particularly sad because Philip is an artist, and
had been doing some of his finest work when I noticed he
was—slowing down, talking less, indulging in some erratic behavior that alarmed me." Her husband nodded
gently. "He knows about his condition, and during those
moments of lucidity which he still has, we discuss what
the effects ultimately will be. He accepts the prognosis,
but then he's not really capable of feeling much emotion
anymore. And he can't look after himself. Someone must
be with him all the time."

"I see. I'm very sorry, I didn't have any idea—"

"Quite all right," Philip Leighton said unexpectedly,
with an eager smile. The two women looked expectantly at
him. A small frown creased his forehead. "I must call the
gallery before it closes; remind me again after tea, darling."

"Yes, of course I will. I do wish you had eaten more of
your lunch."

No response; he had lapsed back into his dignified
silence, and Conor felt his own spirits sinking into the pool
of oblivion in which Philip Leighton spent most of his
days.

Edith chose that moment to say, regretfully, "Now you
understand why I cannot consider leaving. But I admit I
was intrigued by the dilemma posed by the possession of
your brother. If you wouldn't think it unkind of me, I
would like to know more. Perhaps we can think of something to do. Oh, this has been dreadful of me! I would like
for you to meet Sigrid Torgeson, without whom I assure
you I would be quite at a loss these days."

Conor had been sneaking glances at Sigrid at every
opportunity. She might not have been the most beautiful
woman he'd ever seen, but looking at her made it impossible for him to remember even the face of his own wife.
There was simply nothing wrong with Sigrid, not in the
cut of her pale hair, the spacing of her lively eyes, the line
of her chin, the dimensions of each dimple that glowed
with white heat in her tanned cheeks when she smiled. Her
body, which was minimally covered—halter top, denim
shorts—also revealed no flaws, only abundance at every
curve and youthful swell of flesh. Maybe, he thought,

knowing he was holding her outstretched hand too long, maybe Sigrid had calluses on the bottoms of her bare feet. She *must* have calluses there. But when he looked down, foolishly, at those desirable feet he saw that even her dusty toes were straight and well-spread, as if she'd never worn shoes. He was so smitten he couldn't utter a sound.

"I have heard about your brother," Sigrid said. "I know the hell he is suffering, and I pray he will be delivered soon."

Conor said wearily, "I was with him a couple of times when—I just don't think any of us can appreciate what it's like for Rich. I don't even know if my brother still exists."

"Oh, yes. He does. And he's terrified, all the time. I know. I was possessed, when I was sixteen years old. It went on for more than three months. I remember nothing of the exorcism, of course. But I know I nearly lost my life."

"Possessed? By the—"

"Yes. I have photographs. It would serve no purpose to show them to you, except to turn your stomach, and I know you have had enough of that already."

Conor smiled, patronizingly, not half believing her. "You seem to have come through okay."

"Mostly okay," she said. "But with a reminder that none of us are ever as beautiful as we wish to be, or as ugly as we fear we really are."

She turned her back on Conor then. It looked as if she had spent her three months of demonic possession on a bed of nails in a torture chamber. The scars, little shallow nicks from the nape of her neck to the waistband of her shorts, were beyond counting. Her back resembled a piece of pumice. It was the faded heliotrope shade of a blotted birthmark.

Conor found himself holding his breath, suffocating in this tragedy of her marred youth and comeliness. He felt, sickeningly, cheated. He felt lust for her that made his head swim.

Sigrid turned back to him complacently, as if she had anticipated some of his emotions before she recognized them.

"But—why don't you—"

"Do something? Plastic surgery would be a long and

painful process. And you see, the scars really don't matter to me in the way you think. They are my scars of war, and I want to remember that the war against Satan is not just a matter for *my* lifetime, but for all time. I don't ever want to feel that I would rather not be involved.''

74

The prisoner was taking good care of his body, spending about forty minutes every other day working out, alone, in the cramped recreational room of the jail, where the leisure-time facilities consisted of one soiled deck of forty-eight playing cards, a black and white TV set on which the picture of the single channel it was capable of receiving appeared in undulating smeary images like a film of oil on the surface of slowly moving water, and coverless back numbers of magazines on the order of *Yankee* and *The Rotarian*.

While he exercised he was guarded by two jailers, one of whom carried a short-barreled shotgun, the High-Standard M-10 model, the low-powered shells of which were loaded with flechettes instead of shot. Flechettes were pieces of brass rod that tore flesh to tatters but had little ricocheting capability, which was desirable if it became necessary to fire the shotgun in an area enclosed by concrete walls. The prisoner customarily filled the forty minutes with situps, pushups, and jogging in place. He seldom paused to rest. When he rested he never spoke or acknowledged the presence of his jailers.

But Duke Fridley felt that, one of these days, the prisoner was going to get out of line again. And Duke was ready for him. Duke was the one with the shotgun, and he had about as much use for the prisoner as he did a maggot in a piece of filet mignon. Duke was just aching for him to try something. For his part he had made attempts to antagonize the prisoner, resorting to verbal abuse, only to be ignored. Most days he had to be content just to let the prisoner finish his routines and then herd him back to his cell.

On this particular day, however, Duke was nursing at the teat of a swollen grudge against his ex-wife, who had taken all the child support money he'd been so faithful about paying and blown it all on her boyfriend; there wasn't a dime of it left to get the kids' teeth fixed. At the same time Duke was working on a fantasy of how he would handle it if the prisoner suddenly bolted up from his current set of pushups and tried to take the gun away from him. BA-ROOM! BA-ROOOMMMMM! Two quick shots, he'd be wearing his ears inside out and whistling through his swallow-pipe. Save the county a whole lot of time and money. So come on, you asshole. You piece of dogshit. Let's see you get tricky. Just look at me the wrong way once.

"Time," said the other jailer, whose name was Parker. He looked up from his wristwatch and yawned. The prisoner kept right on pumping away, on his fingertips, as if he hadn't heard Parker. See about *that*. Duke walked up behind the prisoner and kicked him hard in the tail, sent him sprawling.

"Hey, Duke," Parker said mildly. "What's that about, man?"

"This fucker thinks he can do what he wants, when he wants to do it. That ain't the way it works around here. The man said *time*, Devon. Means you stop what you're doing, get up right then, and hold out your arms for the straitjacket. Got that?"

The prisoner looked up at Duke. There was no anger in his face that Duke could respond to with another admonishing kick, scarcely any expression at all.

Duke did see, or thought he saw, little reddish points of light the size of chiggers in the prisoner's eyes. Duke felt a wave of heat inside his head that left him so lazy-minded he no longer had control of his own body.

To his surprise control was reestablished for him. He felt himself turned and walked to the farthest wall in the rec room, where he was made to stand as close to attention as he could, with the muzzle of the shotgun in his right hand, which he held by the pistol grip with his finger on the trigger, snugged up into his left armpit.

"Duke, what the hell are you *doing?*" Parker yelled.

The prisoner, down on one knee, studied Duke keenly, raising a slow hand to his forehead to wipe away the perspiration there.

"I don't *know* what I'm doing!" Duke squealed. "I mean I can't help myself! Stay away from me, Parker. Don't touch me or the gun—Jesus. It's gonna go *off*, Parker. Those flechettes'll blow my goddam arm to bits! Help. Help. Oh shit *help* me man the trigger gonna blow my own arm no noooooo!"

The prisoner lowered his head momentarily, unperturbed by Duke's terror.

The shotgun didn't fire. But the loss of his arm would have been a joy compared to the horror of the visions that swept through Duke's mind for the next few moments.

He saw his world, the few square miles of rural Vermont through which he swaggered, got drunk, chased random tail, and took his children to the movies on Sunday afternoons, as a permanently darkened and forbidding place filled with remnants of humanity who pursued each other through ruins and tore at living flesh to cram into their mouths. Duke's head lolled stuporously; his eyes were glazed. His right arm jerked out and the shotgun was flung from his hand. The prisoner rose up and caught it deftly before it could hit the floor.

Duke fell to his knees, moaning softly. Parker backed away from the prisoner, not daring to reach for his pistol.

The prisoner gestured for him not to move, and Parker obediently froze, except for the false teeth that were clicking in his mouth.

The prisoner walked over to Duke, who shrank back a little in craven anticipation of the postponed bloodbath.

"You dropped this, Duke," the prisoner said, and handed down the shotgun to him.

Duke took it, shaking, knowing more about the prisoner than he had ever wanted to know. He could summon no belligerence, no desire to fall upon the prisoner and pound him senseless with his baton.

Because it was clear to Duke that the prisoner was in control of *them*, his jailers; not the other way around. He could leave any time he wanted to, and nobody—*nothing*—could stop him.

But he didn't want to leave. For some reason that Duke only vaguely associated with the vision that had crumbled the delusions which enabled him to keep the shoddy engine of his life in motion, the prisoner was content to remain right where he was. Duke licked his lips and tasted the sour knowledge of what a powerless and mediocre little shit he really was.

As soon as Steve, the head jailer, heard Parker's report, he called Duke into his office.

"Duke, you're through. I don't want you around here anymore."

Duke tried to smirk, but it wasn't much of an effort. He was sinking fast into a morass of hopelessness from which he hadn't the resources to extricate himself. He said truthfully, "I wouldn't come around this goddam jail again in a M-60 tank."

75

Conor talked for a long time in Edith Leighton's home by the sea, until his voice had coarsened to a rasp and the woven shades needed to be lowered all the way against the blinding sun. The veranda contained an aging light the color of whiskey in which their faces were deeply shadowed. She had asked for his permission to tape-record everything. He told them all he knew or suspected of how Rich had become entrapped, then possessed, by Zarach' Bal-Tagh. He spoke of the terrifying manifestations which he had seen for himself. Of the dead or missing witnesses who had seen Rich, or Zarach', kill Karyn Vale, too many other sudden or unexplained deaths to be written off as coincidence. Of Adam Kurland's crucial decision to plead demonic possession, although he was aware of the disastrous effect this decision could have on his career. Of the demonic attacks on Hillary and, possibly, himself. Of his own short life as a priest, the feelings of guilt that persisted years after his renouncing of vows. Of his love for his family, his fears for their safety. Of the more specific fear that despite his best efforts nothing could be done now to save Rich.

"There is only one way to save him," Edith said, "and that is to have a trial. Make no mistake: a trial will be a very dangerous business. For one thing, the enormous publicity generated by the trial might very well cause widespread terror and dread in the majority of human beings who are mentally and emotionally unequipped to deal with the idea, the threat to their souls posed by the Legion. One undesirable effect might be the death of religious belief. Another, a paralysis of will, resulting in one's inability to believe in oneself, in the sanctity of human life, which would leave one quite unable to cope with negative forces. That would be an even greater tragedy. The human will is our most precious resource."

"Maybe—if there was some way to control all the publicity—"

Edith scoffed gently. "My dear, the simplest way to establish the existence of Zarach' in court is to reveal him. Can you imagine what that would be like? You've had some experience with the Son of the Endless Night already. Let me assure you that he is capable of a circus of terror far exceeding what he thus far has demonstrated. But a verdict exonerating your brother may not necessarily save him. Not only must your brother be exonerated, but Zarach' must be banished from this earth as well. There are only two ways Zarach' may lose his hold on Richard. Through death, or through the intervention of a powerful positive force. If Zarach' is to be revealed, then there must exist the means to control him. That's the rub."

"What you're saying is, my brother's life isn't worth the consequences of a trial."

"*Have* I said that? I have not. I've pointed out that the undertaking is not for amateurs, however well-meaning your Mr. Kurland may be."

"And you can't help."

"All of us at Sundial can form a circle of psychic light around Richard, and pray for his deliverance. This could be of considerable value. As for my own contribution, even if I were able to leave my husband at this time, it has been several years since I was in a courtroom. My skills, I'm afraid, have been blunted through disuse.''

Sigrid shook her head disbelievingly, but said nothing. Edith put a hand on Conor's arm.

''Well, I think we've all gone round and round this dilemma long enough for one day. You look exhausted. It's time to eat and then to rest. I have a meeting to attend tonight. Perhaps in the morning after you've had your sleep Sigrid would be willing to show you more of our community.''

76

''Martin, you haven't dressed yet.''

Louise Vale had discovered, without having to guess, where her husband had disappeared to. Karyn's room. He had lighted a single small crystal lamp and opened the windows that overlooked the sound. A chill April breeze danced the curtains. Through the budding branches of the oak the evening star flashed like a solitaire. He was sitting on the edge of the four-poster bed with the pink puff quilt, looking out. A drink in one hand.

''I don't think I want to go tonight.''

''Not go to Bill's birthday party? He's your partner. And this is a very important milestone in his life. He'd never understand if you weren't there.''

In a voice thickened by a syrup of grief in the throat Vale said, ''Doesn't anyone realize how much I loved her, and wanted life to be good for her?''

''Oh, Martin. Of course. Everyone does.'' She yearned to sit beside him, but it seemed a violation of the intimacy he was trying, in this room, to reestablish with his dead daughter. ''What's wrong, Martin? Is it the trial that has you down like this? The trial won't start for another six weeks. You can't let it obsess you—you'll just destroy yourself.''

''Something's going to go wrong. I feel it. Devon will get off. He won't be punished the way he should be.''

"It's that demonic possession nonsense that has you upset. Tommie said not to give it a thought. The plea won't be allowed."

"Tommie's a good man. But he's tied in with a rural prosecutor who doesn't have the experience to try a case like this. There are just too many loopholes that boy can slip through, and be free in a year or two."

Vale turned his face slowly toward his wife. Around the eyes, where he'd always been liverish when stress went unbalanced by sufficient sleep and exercise, he was now black as a panda. The tan he had sported in January had faded to yellow in the vertical creases of his face. He hadn't been going to the athletic club; forty laps in the pool, twenty minutes on the Nautilus. His appetite was poor.

He said, "I would give anything—even my life—to see that it doesn't happen."

She spoke sharply, from fear. "You must stop this. We've all been suffering. The law can't be as cruel and indifferent as you think. Listen to Tommie. Now, we're expected for dinner, and I won't make excuses."

An eighteenth-century clock on a French commode whirred and began, delicately, to chime. Time hurried through the neat room like quicksilver bullets, which were stolen by the dark at the windows. Martin Vale held out a hand as if pleading for the clock to stop, to reverse itself. The hand was pierced, invisibly; he held it to his mouth, his eyes spilled over. Silence. Karyn, unblemished, looked down at him from a portrait on the wall, blissfully forbidding. Remember. Remember.

77

The cave into which Sigrid Torgeson and Conor descended was well lighted and some eighty feet high. Unlike caves formed slowly in limestone by the action of subterranean waters, this one had been created in a dramatic fury by a river of lava poured down from the heights of the Montaña del Fuego. The jagged basalt walls were shades of gray and red, the stalactites long lances of solidified lava.

"After the eruption," Sigrid explained, "the lava cooled and hardened quickly on the surface, forming a tube through which more lava continued to flow. In places there are tubes on top of tubes, galleries much larger than this one. Not all of the caves have been explored."

"Where are we going?"

"A little way toward the sea, to a favorite spot of mine. The vibrations are particularly right for me by the Lago de Ilusión."

"The what?"

"You'll see. I wouldn't want to spoil it for you. This way."

Today Sigrid was wearing shoes, stout hiking boots. So was he. She cautioned him about where he put his hands. The ledges could be as sharp as razors.

"I don't understand all this about 'vibrations,' " Conor said.

"Is matter solid?"

"Well—not really. All matter is composed of molecules."

"And there is space between each molecule, no?"

"I wasn't much of a whiz at physics."

"The amount of space between molecules determines density. Air, water, flesh, stone, all have a different density decided both by the arrangement of molecules and their speed relative to one another. Nothing is motionless in nature, ever. Frequency of motion equals vibration. Vibration determines what our senses perceive: in other words, the dimension we inhabit now, the third dimension."

"Is there a fourth dimension?"

"Oh, heavens, yes; *hundreds* of dimensions. But most of them are found well beyond the plane of earth." She had to laugh, but she seemed a trifle apprehensive in the frail light of the cavern. "What a terrible look you have on your face! Have I offended you?"

"What? Oh, no—I get that way when I'm—trying to swallow something that just won't go down."

"Let me say a little more about vibrations. Remember, you asked. Vibrations can be harmonious or disharmonious. Tell me, have you ever met someone to whom you took an instant dislike, or spent time in a place you could hardly wait to be away from?''

"Sure.''

"That was a matter of your vibrations clashing with those of the other person or with the vibrations of the locality. Our own vibrations are harmonized by the mind, and when the mind is not in control then our vibrations fall more and more out of sympathy with those of nature. The consequences, over a long period of time, can be drastic.''

Sigrid was wearing a long-sleeved shirt today; it was cool in the cave through which they were walking. They each carried a staff to help them negotiate the jumbled floor. Conor thought of the scars on her back and said, "How were you possessed?''

"Oh, it happened when I was young and, not stupid, but gullible. Also I had the susceptibility that attracted the wrong spirits, once they had their opportunity to appeal to me. A Ouija board was the catalyst; do you know Ouija boards?''

Conor nodded.

"They are not the innocent toys most people seem to think. A Ouija board is a channel of communication through which unknown spirits may associate with the living. And there are cosmic laws of attraction or invitation the spirits are obliged to obey.

"My friends and I, through the use of our Ouija board, made contact with a spirit that pretended to be positive, angelic, in order to gain our confidence. Well, my friends soon became tired of the game, but I continued with the board, maintaining contact with the spirit for many months—and at night, when I was supposed to be asleep. That is the *worst* time to have any traffic with spirits. This demon was a real flatterer, and I became captivated by him, his little predictions of the future that always came true. It wasn't enough I had become so dependent on his nightly messages; I had to ask to *see* him. That's all it took. I became infested, not with just one demon but many.''

"Why do you stay here, Sigrid?''

"To do what good I can in return for the charismatic help Sundial gave me. Because of the vibrations here that exclude any possibility of evil influence. Haven't you felt it by now, the difference?''

"I don't know. I slept better last night than I have in weeks, and I didn't need four drinks to get to sleep in the first place. I didn't even want a drink."

"It would take a few days longer—who knows—before you felt so completely at home here you might never want to leave."

"But I have to leave. My brother's going to die."

She ducked her head as if chastised and went along silently for a while. Soon they had to climb a heap of rubble that blocked the floor of the rugged cylinder they had been walking through. Atop the rubble pile Conor found himself looking down into an abyss, as well lighted as the walls of the cave around them.

"This is as far as we go? How deep is that hole?"

Sigrid handed him a piece of basalt. "Toss this in, and count the seconds until you hear it hit the bottom. More physics."

Conor threw the rock, but it had scarcely left his hand when the abyss tremblingly vanished before his eyes, like a mirage. He heard a small splash as the rock hit water, the black surface of a pool that had been so immaculately still it had mirrored without flaw the roof and walls of the cavern they were in.

"Only four inches deep," she said. "We can walk across it easily, and go down to the tidal pools from here. There you will see very interesting sea creatures, the like of which you will not find anywhere else in the world. Then it is just a short way to the beach, where we can swim."

"All right." But Conor was reluctant to leave the cavern so soon—the cool, the blessed windlessness—and return to surface things. Here, in solitude, he could be intimate with a woman he had come to adore on terms that satisfied the heart but did not involve sex.

She sensed his need to linger and, loosening the straps of her small carryall, sat down with her elbows on her knees and smiled up at him. He sat, too, more gingerly, not finding a lump of rock that suited his contours.

"Sigrid, what do you think she's going to do?"

"Edith? Well, I don't know what to say. You would have to know her for a long time to realize how deeply disturbed she is by the plight of your brother. Don't think for a moment she has lost her taste for confrontation, or her hatred of the evil which Zarach' represents.''

"But her husband is dying."

"Yes. As I understand it, the disease will eventually shut down his senses one by one; then he will simply forget how to breathe. They have been married forty years. Think of all they must have shared in their love for each other, the good things that life returned to them: the art, the music, the books.'' Sigrid gestured toward the pool, the surface of which was motionless again. "What she has left is an illusion, which is only complete when at rare times he is stimulated in some unknown way to speak as if he had never been afflicted. Then Edith is happy, and grateful for those moments that still remain of the marvelous life she enjoyed with him. But the day will soon come when the rock falls, the water trembles; then no matter how long she waits, the illusion will not reappear. He will not speak again. He will live on for a while, but he will have left her forever.''

78

Judge Natty Eames found the second weekend in April— "mud season" in southern Vermont—too cold for a backyard barbecue, but it was the sixth wedding anniversary of his daughter Olivia, and for the past year and a half he'd been so busy that he and his wife had not had many opportunities to visit the grandchildren, of whom there were two. Natty and Violet (everybody had called her "Buff" as long as she could remember) deliberately drove over to Dorset early, arriving a little after one o'clock. More than a hint of forsythia was showing along the gravel driveway; long gilded tassels of willow hung down at the edge of the pond, where the last ice of winter lay submerged in shallow thinning platelets.

The house had been little more than a drafty cottage when the kids had started out, but Greg was an architect and he'd done a job on the original that Buff claimed put it in the *House and Garden* class. He'd also cleaned out the choked slow-running stream and dammed it, creating the broad reflecting pond that looked so beautiful at the height of spring and again during the fall foliage season. Natty's grandchildren were not allowed to play anywhere near the pond, which lay almost at the front door; their fenced play area was well to the back of the house in a birch grove. Greg had gone all out here. There were sturdy places to climb and crawl and jump and (pretend) to hide; sandboxes, swings, and slides.

Greg and Olivia were genuinely excited by their anniversary gift, a ruby glass punch bowl Buff had unearthed in an out-of-the-way antique shop near Chester Depot. Buff wouldn't even tell Natty what she'd paid for it, but she knew her antiques better than most of the shyster dealers around, and she could strike a hard bargain.

Buff pitched in to give Olivia a hand before the rest of their company showed up. Little Thaddeus, who was three and a half, and Tussy, just turned five, vied for their grandfather's attention. He took them along to the play yard and put them on swings, where he alternated pushing each child. Tad was barely past the timid stage, gripping the chains tightly, not sure he wanted to match Tussy's cries for "higher, Nattypop!"

As he played with the two children Natty Eames found himself thinking about the Devon case. He knew he had acted rightly when he put that smart aleck defense attorney in his place. All the publicity would fizzle for young Kurland now; come Monday he'd have a lot of egg to wipe off his face. Only Natty stood to gain, by showing everyone that this trial was going to be conducted *his* way.

"Higher, Nattypop!"

The wind had sharpened, and Natty trembled in his treasured plaid mackinaw, which had been around for so long Buff jokingly told everybody Natty had named the mackinaw in his will. He glanced over one shoulder at Trent's orchard, the northern boundary of Greg and Olivia's property, and the crest of the hill beyond. The temperature had been in the low forties but seemed to be plummeting; the barbecue might have to be moved indoors.

"Can I get down now?" Tad said. He had to say it twice before Natty heard him.

"Yes, all right." Natty brought the boy's swing to a sudden stop by grasping both of the chains above Tad's little fists. Tussy continued gleefully to soar, her toes pointed toward the blank treetops. Birds flew away from those trees in a ragged line, a signature of wings in the sky, writing off the hour of false spring they had enjoyed.

So cold, Natty thought; maybe we'd all better go in. He turned his head to follow little Tad's progress to the largest of the wooden slides Greg had built.

"Watch me, Nattypop!"

"Be careful."

Natty laughed, and then his teeth chattered. The wind was coming straight down off the hill almost strong enough to blow Tussy out of her seat as she blithely pumped herself up until at the peak of her rise she was horizontal to the ground. The chain of the swing he was holding trembled from the force she exerted on the framework.

"Tussy, you'll fall out of there." He was getting the sniffles; with his other hand he searched a deep pocket for his handkerchief.

"No won't! Love you, Nattypop!"

"I love you, too, Tussy." Tad was swooping down the slide, shouting. Natty laughed again, but the laughter turned abruptly to ice in his throat. The chain he was holding with his right hand had twisted, inexplicably, and was tightly wound around his wrist.

What the devil? Natty thought.

The seat of the swing jumped up several inches and the other chain formed a loop. He'd had no time to think of how to free himself and now the other chain came down swiftly over his head, rasping coldly against his stuck-out ears, and grabbed him around the neck just below the jawline.

Then the swing began to move, jerking the little judge off his feet, dragging him in his galoshes helplessly to and fro while his face turned the color of blackberry wine. He was conscious for only about another six seconds, just long enough to hear Tussy's first terrified scream as she swung by him twice, three times before she had the wits to dig in her heels and bring herself to a stop. His neck was sadly twisted, but his eyes were open. He smiled at Tussy. The smile filled with fresh blood. She ran to the house.

79

"We'll rest here a few minutes, Philip," Edith Leighton said to her husband. She had detected a slight wheeze, a reluctance to lift his heels from the cindery path as they walked.

He smiled in agreement, responding to the gentle pressure of her fingers on the inside of his elbow. They'd followed the edge of the two-hundred-foot cliff for a quarter of an hour that she had filled with conversation: about music, about a retrospective of Philip's paintings that his long-time London gallery had in the works, about a new biography of Leopold Mozart she had received in the mail and was eager to dip into. Every day she saw to it that her husband took at least a half hour of mild exercise. Sometimes Sigrid accompanied him to the beach, but those outings worried Edith. Philip was an excellent swimmer and she feared that he suddenly might decide to head for open water, where unpredictable strong currents could pull him in less than a minute well out to sea; there would be no way to catch up to him before he became exhausted and drowned.

They sat together on a plaza bench beneath the wide overhanging roof of one of the school pavilions. Shady here, the wind not so obstreperous. The children had gone to their homes for the weekend.

Edith had brought along a folio of recent drawings by a protégé of Philip's in years gone by; the young man was now gaining important recognition in Italy and America. She turned the loose drawings over slowly. Beside her Philip looked down at them, nodding. Then he raised his head to gaze out to sea, at a palette of thick massy whites and starry cobalt. His hair riffled around his ears.

"I don't remember the name of the young man we've been spending so much time with," he said apologetically.

It was, she thought, a little like having the radio on all the time, not knowing when you're going to have reception because of a favorable change in atmospheric conditions.

"His name is Conor Devon."

"Oh, yes." He didn't speak again for a sun-filled block of time, during which she smoothed feathers of dormant gray and looked into an ear wishing, whimsically, to be moth-sized, hurled through convoluted channels to his spacious and perplexing mind, there to be ignited in a blaze of the richness she was certain still existed.

Then Philip said, "It sounds very important to me, Edith."

"What does?"

"The demonic possession trial. Zarach' Bal-Tagh is involved."

"Yes, I'm sorry to say."

"Is it because of me you won't go?"

"Of course I don't want to leave you. Also I fear I no longer have the strength."

"Strength is often a matter of conviction, and of faith. Have you lost your faith?"

"No."

She watched his face. He was smiling slightly. That faint touch of radiance, the clarified brow. But she couldn't tell what he was thinking, or if he was thinking at all.

"What does the council say?" he asked her.

"I'm not yet prepared to bring the matter before the council."

"But you intend to."

"Yes. And then—"

"I think we ought to be guided—as we always have—by the will of the majority." He turned then, and looked into Edith's eyes. His hand grasped hers, reassuringly. She mulled the *we*. "You know that I'll be all right here. Sigrid is very protective. I am very fortunate."

And that was all. Philip continued to gaze at her, the rust-flecked familiar gray eyes without flaw but also lacking alertness, his too-placid demeanor suspect: she sensed he had turned a corner, into another long blank alley. The grip he had on her hand loosened. Edith bowed her head,

then looked at the sea, finding distances threatening; she
had too long ago carefully steered her life inward. To
travel so far, to pit herself once more against the force she
loathed—her lips trembled at the thought. There was fear,
which was realistic. And a stealthy stiffening of the
backbone.

Perhaps, she thought.

80

There were fourteen criminal court justices in the Southern
Judicial District of Vermont. Following the shocking death
of Natty Eames, the case of *Vermont* v. *Devon* rotated to
the youngest of these judges, Knox Winford, who was
thirty-four years old.

In the five years since he'd become a judge, Knox had
proved himself to be a young man of probity as well as
ambition. Everybody knew that Knox was pretty well
marking time waiting for the senior senator from the Green
Mountain State to keel over after eight terms in Washington, so that he could run for the vacated office. But he was
not lazy. He continued to be a good student of the law and
was known for his sensitivity to constitutional rights. He
wasn't immune to cronyism, but he chose the right cro-
nies. He had not yet been corrupted by expediency. For
one thing, he didn't need the money. His paternal grandmother had sold maple syrup and wooden salad bowls to
tourists and made enough in her four outlets to put together
a solid trust fund for Knox, the apple of her eye. His
wife's family was well-to-do, and ambitious for him.

Knox had known, even before his friend Adam Kurland
threw the curve ball labeled Notice of Defense of Demonic
Possession at Judge Natty, that the Devon case was going
to be a huge mess. He was glad he didn't have to sit.

When the case fell to him, he had numerous options. He
could have excused himself without citing any very compelling reason. He could have postponed the trial on tech-

nicalities until it was time for him to resign and run for the
Senate. He could have called Adam in and given him the
same treatment, more or less, which the lawyer had gotten
from Natty Eames. He could have applied more subtle and
indirect pressures that would have resulted in a summary
invitation for Adam to appear before the Ethics Committee
of the State Bar Association. But Knox Winford had a
couple of traits that eventually would weigh for and against
him as a legislator. He was curious, and felt that law was a
process, not Holy Writ; and he was not abusive of the
power that he held.

So he met informally with Adam to talk it over, Cokes
and burgers in his chambers, and this time Adam went
prepared to justify his proposed defense. He took with him
both tapes recorded during the manifestations of Zarach'
Bal-Tagh. He took depositions from Father James Merlo,
Conor, and Lindsay.

It was a long session. Knox was impressed by Adam's
sincerity and didn't think that he was having a nervous
breakdown. The tapes, however, failed to make much of
an impression on the judge: he was familiar with criminal-
court actions in other states that had involved cases of
multiple personality. He was nearly ready to offer Adam a
deal that would get everybody off the hook and the trial
smoothly behind them. But he postponed his decision for
two days and went around to the jail to see the prisoner for
himself.

First he talked to Steve, the head jailer with the flamboyant copper-colored mustache. Steve said, "Tell you
this much, Your Honor, he's not like any psycho we've
ever had in here."

"What do you mean?"

"He's had us all spooked, at one time or another. I had
to fire one of my boys the other day, good boy too; he just
couldn't bear up under the strain anymore. Prisoner got the
drop on him. That doesn't happen in *my* jail."

"How does he behave? Is he difficult to handle?"

"Not since a couple months ago, when he demolished
the interview room. Harbison doubled up on his tranquilizers and that quieted him. Considerably. But now he's *too*
quiet."

Steve took a few moments pondering the best way to express his dissatisfaction and uneasiness with this lull.

"Your Honor, I do some hunting for grizzly. That does take a certain amount of balls, you'll have to admit. Been almost face to face with them, no dogs, just a goddam big hunk of hair and fangs and claws like a leaf rake, when you see a grizzly reared up no farther away than I am from you, I mean you *tremble*. You feel all of a sudden like what you've got in your rifle is jellybeans. I'll tell you what. I'd rather be out in the woods right now facing down a grizzly bear than sitting here knowing he's downstairs—and *he's* behind bars. So do you want me to get him up here, Your Honor?"

"That's not necessary. I'll see him in his cell."

Steve smiled in relief. "I was hoping you'd say that."

The lights of the cell, recessed, inaccessible without a ladder, shone brightly. The walls and the floor had been padded with slabs of polyurethane packaged in a tough fabric which fingernails and teeth couldn't shred. The toilet was lidless. The bunk bed bolted to one wall had neither sheets nor a blanket, only a thin mattress of foam rubber covered with the same material as the walls. The prisoner lay on his bunk reading. When he heard the scrape of shoes on the concrete floor outside his cell, he lowered the book, which was *The Psychopathic God,* a study of Hitler, and shaded his eyes with one hand to look out at Knox Winford and the jailer behind him.

The prisoner said nothing, and Knox didn't speak right away either. He couldn't understand what Steve had been trying to tell him. The prisoner was of average size. He'd been given a jailhouse haircut which wasn't flattering, and he was so pale the hollows of his cheeks looked translucent in that downpour of light, but there was nothing overtly menacing about him. Still, you could never judge a mental patient on appearances. They were cunning and could demonstrate terrifying violence, immense strength. So you took extra precautions.

Knox continued to stare at the prisoner, mildly fascinated but by what aspect of the man he couldn't explain to himself. The prisoner seemed to return the stare, but his eyes were nearly invisible beneath the ledge of the hand he held against his brows.

"I'm Knox Winford," the judge said.

"How's Bonnie?" the prisoner said.

Now, it was conceivable that at some point the prisoner might have heard some jailhouse talk about him, but it was very nearly beyond belief that he would know that Bonnie was Knox Winford's wife. And there was something about the way he had spoken Bonnie's name that detonated little flash points of apprehension all over the judge's skin.

It was all they said to each other. After a few moments the prisoner turned on his side on the bunk and went back to his reading.

That night Knox worked in his study at home trying to write an opinion disallowing the plea of demonic possession. He made several attempts and tore them all up. By then the hour was late and his mind, usually clear and rational no matter how hard he'd been working, felt like a dead tooth. In the kitchen he poured himself a beer and wandered back to the front of the house, which had a deep roofed porch on two sides. He heard the creaking of the porch swing that was suspended on chains from eyebolts in the ceiling. It was rhythmic. Sometimes it could be the wind, but tonight he sensed it wasn't. He had a visitor.

Knox went to the windows of the parlor and leaned over the window seat intending to raise the shade, but he couldn't do it. He froze. There was a thick mass of terror in his throat, which he was unable to swallow. He backed away from the windows and switched off the lights in the parlor and the hall. He returned to the parlor and stood gazing at the shadow of the moving glider on the shades, cast by the streetlight at the northeast corner of his property. There was a figure of a man in the glider. Unmistakable. Knox went softly back into the center hall and opened a closet, took down his loaded shotgun from the brackets above the inside of the door where childish hands couldn't reach, and went outside to the porch.

He found the glider empty and now motionless despite the zephyr playing around the corners of the porch. He took a tour of his still-mushy yard with the shotgun in both hands. The tall trees, two weeks away from coming into leaf, lobbed spidery shadows across the moonlit lawn. He surprised the Hubbards' cat with the wing of a thrush in its mouth, but no other intruders.

In bed he tossed and turned, ultimately waking up Bonnie, who complained.

"Bonnie, when was the last time you were down at the courthouse in Chadbury?"

"Months, I guess. A year. Why?"

"No reason. I think I'd like to have Daddy Perce for dinner Friday week."

"Fine. There's no way I'll have the time to drive all the way up to Ripton to get him."

"I'll do it."

"If you're not sleepy," she said, touching the nape of his neck with a gently flicking finger, "would you mind bringing me a glass of milk and, uh, my diaphragm?"

81

Knox Winford's surviving grandfather, on his mother's side, was seventy-seven. He lived by himself in a log cabin alongside a rushing clear stream in a thinly populated area of the state near Breadloaf Mountain. He had had laser surgery three times for macular degeneration, and the last time the surgery hadn't been too successful. He still had enough vision left to look after himself on his sparse acres, and go fishing. His second sight remained impressively sharp. He was a clairvoyant.

Driving down from Ripton, Knox said to his grandfather, "I want to make a detour over Chadbury way. There's somebody I'd like you to see."

"All right," Daddy Perce said. "Leave time for me to pick up a little something for the kids."

"They're spoiled enough already."

At the Chadbury jail Knox took his grandfather downstairs to the isolation cell. The prisoner was lying on his bunk. He opened his eyes at the approach of Daddy Perce. A smile formed.

Perce stood in front of the bars for a long minute, his

eyes narrowed, his Adam's apple jumping. He said to Knox, "It would help to tone those lights down some."

The wattage was lowered until there was very little light at all. The prisoner laughed once; Knox began to feel a numbness along one side of his tongue. He was impatient, even anxious to get out of there.

Finally Perce said, "I've seen all there is to see," and Knox took him upstairs.

When they were in the car and driving toward Braxton, with Daddy Perce enjoying his midafternoon treat, a chocolate sundae from Dairy Queen, Knox asked him, "What did you see in that cell?"

"A black aura. Black flames shooting out from his body, six feet in every direction."

"Have you ever seen anything like that before?"

"No. Not around a living human being."

"What does it mean?"

"It means there's two spirits in one body. A human spirit—but he was so faint I could barely make him out—and an inhuman spirit."

"Oh, dandy," Knox muttered, and drove several more miles while his grandfather placidly cleaned out the sundae cup, going round and round with his little finger until the inside of the cup shone. He would find a use for the cup; he seldom discarded anything that came into his possession. Knox said complainingly, "You know I never have believed in most of that stuff, Daddy Perce." The old man was respectfully silent, his baby blue eyes merely glints in pods of wrinkles. But a mild charge of amusement fluttered his lips. "I do accept auras, which can be photographed, and I accept that auras can tell you a lot about how a person is feeling. Life after death—well, I accept that too. But evil spirits; ghosts; seeing is believing."

"All you're saying is that there are things on this earth, or off it, that you weren't meant to be bothered with. At least until now. What is that boy in jail for?"

"Murder. He killed his girl friend. The facts are not in dispute."

"Are you sitting?"

"I don't know yet if I will. The defense is pleading demonic possession—or trying to."

"For those able to see, the existence of spirits of all

kinds is obvious. For those without the sight—well, undoubtedly there are reasons why they shouldn't have such knowledge. Does that help you to reach a decision about your duty?"

"No."

When they arrived at the house Perce, without looking up, became obviously tense. Then, not getting out of the car, he stared at the porch until Knox became uncomfortable.

"Well, is something the matter?"

The old man didn't answer. He opened the car door and, after stepping out, stretched himself carefully. The sun was on his face. They'd had three warm days, the month of May was around the corner, the earth was free of frost, and the azaleas were about to riot. Perce went slowly up to the porch and walked up and down in his boondockers, paying particular attention to the glider.

"Knox, you've had a visitor," he said finally.

"Last night I thought somebody—"

Perce motioned gently for him to be quiet. His eyes were wizened in thought. "He was here, all right. Leaves a powerful taint, like an animal in heat."

"Who was here? You mean—? Oh, now, Perce—"

"I wish he hadn't been. I don't like it. No, not at all."

Bonnie came outside then to greet Perce and make over the bouquet of pert jonquils they had stopped for at Durwood Brothers' Nursery. There was no further talk of spirits. Daddy Perce's somber mood improved when the children arrived boisterously from school a few minutes later.

But Bonnie said to Knox in the kitchen, "He seems so preoccupied. Not himself. Has he been sick?"

"It was a long winter, Bonnie. And Daddy Perce isn't getting any younger."

The pat answer he had supplied for his wife also served to reduce Knox Winford's lingering uneasiness about his grandfather's hushed revelation on the porch. He now regretted having taken the old man to the Chadbury jail; what had he been trying to prove to himself? That there was definable evil in Richard Devon that atavistically affected everyone who came near him? Or that the evil was more than just the product of a thoroughly rancid human personality—in which case Adam Kurland's defense merited serious consideration. Since he didn't want to believe that, he now tried to rationalize Perce's reaction. There was just that little suspicious touch of senility about the old man these days; and the atmosphere of the jail undoubtedly had depressed him. So he had subconsciously translated his depressed emotions into terms he understood best, blaming them on auras, omens, and presentiments of the supernatural.

After dinner Knox was tied up with a long phone call; Perce helped Bonnie with the dishes. He was full of anecdotes about Robert Frost, who had been a neighbor. Bonnie was about to get down to serious work on her master's thesis and trying to find something to say about the poet that hadn't been covered already. When the judge emerged from his study Bonnie was at the kitchen table scribbling notes and the kids were in front of the television in the parlor; Perce was missing.

Knox checked the bathrooms first and then went outside. The old man wasn't on the porch either. Maybe he had decided to go for a walk. Knox strolled around to the deep side yard and stopped there, listening. He thought he had heard a sound, a congested panicked grunting, as if blows were being struck somewhere. He followed a path through a long-untended grape arbor with its trellises and barren fragments of clinging vines to the latticework jewelbox of the gazebo. He heard the mysterious grunting again, and hurried.

Inside the gazebo he found his grandfather sprawled on the floor, his legs moving sluggishly. Despite his years and slowly failing eyesight Daddy Perce had retained much of his physical vigor, and the dignity that went with it. Now he looked shockingly incompetent.

"Perce, what happened?"

"He was here." The old man's eyes, so often a misty blue, had filled with whiteness, the cataracts of wretched insight. He was besotted with phantoms again.

"What?"

"Now I know why."

"Perce, listen, it was wrong of me to—"

His grandfather's hands seized him; hard knuckles hurt Knox Winford's skinny chest. "He's *chosen* you. That's why you have to do it."

"Do what? Are you talking about the Devon case?"

Knox helped Perce to sit up, and pried his hands from the lapels of the corduroy jacket Knox was wearing. "I've already made up my mind to—"

"But you must preside at his trial. It's what he wants of you. If you don't, he'll come back here, night after night. You don't realize what he can do to you, Knox. He'll make your house unfit to live in. He'll terrorize Bonnie, and the little ones. He'll make all of your lives—hell on earth."

"Perce, stop it!"

The old man wept for his grandson; his eyes, refreshed, became their normal color. "There's nothing else you can do. Give him the trial, and he'll leave you alone."

"*Who*? Who are you talking about? Not Richard Devon."

"No." Something came across from Perce then, from the depths of his psychic ordeal. It fastened chillingly on the side of Knox Winford's throat, a soulless presence, immaculately lethal, like a crystal spider. "His name is Zarach'."

Knox sat back suddenly, crumpling as if all the breath had disappeared from his body. He had heard the name before, had asked Adam Kurland how it was pronounced. But his grandfather knew nothing about Knox's recent meeting with the lawyer, could not have heard the tape recordings of the supposed manifestations or read the depositions that were locked up in the judge's files. Therefore he could not know the name *Zarach'*.

But Perce did. He said it again.

The answers Knox had for this phenomenon were all illogical and absurd.

The truth, when he finally settled for it, was devastating in all of its implications.

82

Shortly after Knox Winford's historic decision to allow the defense in the case of *Vermont* v. *Devon* to plead demonic possession, Tommie Harkrider was chauffeured up to Vermont to see Gary Cleves.

The famous criminal lawyer spent a full day with the prosecutor, honing him as if Gary were a dull razor he had picked up in a thrift shop. Afterwards Gary and Tommie were ready to meet the press.

All the lights made Gary's hands shake; Tommie basked contentedly in their glow, looking for old friends among the ranks of reporters and TV news correspondents. Gary read the prepared statement in a voice that occasionally became too high-pitched. Tommie tried not to wince.

"While I feel that the decision to admit a plea of not guilty by reason of demonic possession sets a dangerous precedent in the annals of American criminal law, I do not intend to challenge this decision by seeking a reversal of the ruling from a higher court. Such an action would result in undesirable delays in bringing the case before a jury. I am confident that we have the evidence to prove that this so-called case of possession is in reality a classic example of multiple personality behavior, which is not, under the laws of this state, regarded as a psychotic condition. We will then prove, beyond all reasonable doubt, that Richard Devon is guilty as charged of murder in the first degree, and I am confident that the jury will return the appropriate verdict."

83

"What? What was that you said, Linds?" Adam Kurland spoke across a table heaped with papers and lawbooks, cupping one ear with his hand, like an old codger. "I'm still a leetle deef from the sound of Gary's Big Gun going off."

"I said, wouldn't it be interesting if we could persuade Zarach' to pay Gary a little visit some dark and windy night?" Then she covered her mouth with her hand. "Ooops. Maybe that's not so funny after all."

The phone rang. "There it goes again. Let's see, that was twenty-three full seconds of blessed silence that time. Shall we try for our one hundredth crank call of the day?"

"Let the machine get it," Adam advised.

"I think we should put a new tape on. 'Dear Sir or Madam: please excuse us for not taking your irate, demeaning, possibly actionable call at this time. If you choose to leave a message at the sound of the raspberry, prithee, try to refrain from using such terms as "commie," "godless," and "motherfucker." Your cooperation is appreciated. While waiting to deliver the message that is bound to gladden our hearts and rekindle our faith in human nature, may we suggest you pacify yourself by bending over, placing your head in your asshole, and breathing deeply. Thank you so very, very much.' "

84

The prisoner waited.

Silently, in the rank, dirty, unfurnished basement room of the Haden County Courthouse. He was in his strait-jacket. There were three guards in the room with him, all well armed. They did not stand anywhere near the prisoner.

They had only been waiting there for a few minutes, but the three men were delighted to hear the knock on the metal door. One of them hastened, keys jangling at his belt, to open it.

Father James Merlo, in vestments, and Adam Kurland entered the room.

The prisoner raised his head slightly and looked at the priest with the ashen hair. At this altered angle the distortion of the prisoner's face, as if viewed through a prism, was almost sly. Something began to occlude the pupils of his eyes like the bloom on bread. His upper lip lifted until his canine teeth were fully exposed. Merlo returned his stare.

Kurland nodded to the guards and they filed out.

The door remained open.

The prisoner was distracted by this flagrant openness, as if it were an invitation to mischief. Or, symbolically, as if it indicated a lowering of his status. His attention shifted completely from Merlo to something, or someone, intruding at the edge of his preternatural consciousness. He made a sound like a drop of water sizzling on a very hot skillet and drew back slightly, until he was against the far wall. Fascinated, he eyed the doorway.

Edith Leighton walked in.

The sibilant, scalded sound continued. She was wearing a dark gray suit almost clerical in its severity. She carried a gleaming black Hermes briefcase. On a chain around her neck was a miniature gold sundial.

The door was closed, and locked from the outside.

"EDITHHHHHHHHHH."

He spat at her like a hiccuping gargoyle with bound wings, eyes protruding greenishly; snaky ribbons of saliva flew through the air and were transformed into a substance that looked like spider's silk but had the strength of steel. They formed a net around her head and shoulders. She never took her eyes from his face, and when she pulled at the net the blister-bright skeins dissolved in her hands.

The prisoner then underwent a number of contortions designed to free him from the straitjacket, which went flying. Noxious odors filled the room and Adam quickly pressed a handkerchief soaked in a solution of holy water to his nose. The priest and the former Queen's Counsel bore this olfactory attack stoically. Merlo had taken a couple of steps to close ranks with her; he wore a crucifix of silver and ebony that hung to the waist of his snugly fitted soutane.

The prisoner, still twisted from his efforts to be rid of the straitjacket, began to slide on his back up the basement wall, writhing and hissing. His nose seemed to disappear. His tongue, divided, flickered from his mouth like streaks of lightning. His eyes were so cloudy they were like pustular pits, sore spots of hate.

Edith watched this display with a pulse visible in the side of her throat but no emotion showing in her narrowed eyes.

"Yes," Edith said. "The Serpent. It's an old fear, never quite subdued. But I assure you, Zarach', you will not win with tactics like this."

The prisoner continued to writhe along the wall, now

going sideways about three feet off the floor. The single light in the room had dimmed to amber.

Edith walked slowly toward the prisoner, who froze in place. Only his head, his abominable tongue moved.

"Edith," Merlo said warningly.

"It's all right," she assured him, not looking around. She studied the prisoner with an intensity that seemed to bring heat to her eyes, a glow of purity from which he cringed and hissed deafeningly.

Then he jumped off the wall, landing at her feet. His mouth opened wider, the jaws cracking from strain. Instead of a tongue a second head appeared, the head of a snake. The prisoner's body was rigid, the heart of him outlined stressfully against the naked chest wall.

The Serpent spoke.

"OPPOSE ME—AND I WILL TAKE HIS WRETCHED LIFE."

Edith continued to gaze penetratingly at the two-headed creature, one head scaly and luminous, the other distended and darkened by blood.

"I think not. He was not so easy to come by in the first place."

The body leaped from the floor and clung to a large rusty pipe overhead, hanging down toward her, the head in the mouth gliding to within inches of her face. She wouldn't flinch.

Edith and Merlo said together, "Richard's soul is of God, not of you!"

The Serpent responded with scornful obscenities.

"You are commanded by the Lord!"

More obscenity.

"Your powers are weak compared to His!"

"I WILL KILL YOU BOTH!"

"Obey the commands of God, Son of the Endless Night!"

The Serpent hissed, but futilely.

"Release Richard Devon, and leave him in peace!"

Instantly the Serpent's head exploded like flame from the mouth of a cannon and the body of the prisoner came crashing limply to the floor. Merlo rolled him over, with difficulty. He was rigid, out cold. After a few moments he began to breathe, and the color of life returned to his waxen flesh, slow-stealing warmth. His eyelids fluttered.

He looked up at the faces of the priest and the retired Queen's Counsel.

Richard Devon began to sob in terror and pain, as if he were still half stranded in a nightmare.

"Help me—help me!"

Edith kneeled and placed a spread hand lightly on his breastbone. Her eyes closed for several moments; she trembled. The heartshocks diminished.

"Help is here, Richard. But you also have to help yourself."

"I killed her. I killed Karyn. I deserve to die for what I did!"

Edith Leighton remained kneeling for several minutes longer, her right hand still on his chest, the other at his right wrist. His violated body found ease. Edith rose, a little staggered, a little grayer, as if she'd tired herself badly, draining a sink of pollution; her hands hung at her sides. There was a small frown on her face.

"There are worse crimes than murder," she said. "Murder was only the beginning."

85

Gary Cleves was on the telephone to Tommie Harkrider as soon as he had been told about the addition to the defense team. "Do you know who she is?"

Tommie chewed on an unlit cigar. "The name is familiar; I'll have to inquire of some of my barrister friends in London."

In forty-eight hours he had a full report on the former Queen's Counsel. After he'd heard all there was to tell of Edith Leighton, a certain bleakness set in. Gary Cleves against Adam Kurland in a courtroom was one thing. But when Gary stooped to seize the gauntlet and that battle-tough warhorse from the Old Bailey came cantering in, he would be trampled before he knew what hit him.

Tommie already was an appointee to the Haden County state's attorney's staff (of five) at no pay; ideally he knew he should be matched against Edith Leighton. But he knew also that Gary Cleves would never accept the implied insult to his competence. Gary was competent, all right: at assembling the facts and nailing them down for the jury like so many planks in a bridge. But this trial apparently would span some murky and uncharted waters before it was concluded. The jury would be asked to respond to matters that were purely theoretical, and the lawyer wasn't thinking only of psychiatric testimony. The ability to choose a jury that would be charged with reaching a momentous verdict, and directing it toward the *right* verdict, required the talents of (Tommie slighted humility in favor of the plain truth) a courtroom genius. Darrow. Nizer. Harkrider. And Tommie wanted it. His blood was surging. He would teach them all a lesson, while banishing the specter of demonic possession pleas from further trials. He was sincerely worried about what might happen to the already abused and overworked system of criminal justice in the United States if he *didn't* win in Vermont.

Gary, he felt, could be made to relinquish his chief prosecutor's role only if, somehow, he were overwhelmed by public appeal and sentiment in favor of his colleague Tommie. If, pretrial, his confidence was shaken to the point where he realized he didn't stand a chance of winning. It was monkeyshines time in Dayton, Tennessee, all over again; unfortunately just seven weeks remained before the scheduled start of the trial.

But Thomas Horatio Harkrider, friend and confidant of presidents, statesmen, and media kings, could call in favors; he was adept at exploiting those exploiters who created or enhanced popular opinion in this country.

A cover story in *Time* magazine might be an excellent way to start, Tommie thought; and he reached for his telephone.

86

Richard Devon sent word that he wanted to meet with his brother. They had had no contact with each other for more than five weeks.

The request made Conor unreasonably nervous. He talked it over with Gina but not with Adam Kurland or Edith Leighton. Gina said that he should go, as long as the jailers took pains to see that nothing potentially tragic could happen to Conor.

"And I'll be praying while you're there," she told him.

At the Haden County jail the ground rules were explained to Conor. Rich could not be removed from his cell. Conor must talk to him through the bars, and maintain an arm's-length distance from the prisoner at all times. He had ten minutes.

Rich was sitting on the edge of his bunk when the guards escorted Conor down the cellblock corridor. The guards withdrew to one end of the corridor and stood there, eyes on Conor.

"Hello, Conor," Rich said, not moving or looking up.

"You wanted to see me, kid?"

"Yeah."

"Tell me one thing. Are you alone in there?"

"It's me, Conor. It's really me." He showed his face to his brother then. And Conor felt a surge of happiness, looking into the younger man's eyes.

Rich's face trembled with emotion, pinched tight at the eyes and then at the corners of his mouth.

"Oh, Conor. I'm a dead man."

"No!"

"I want you to believe this. I don't know why it happened. I only wanted to help Polly. Well, it's done. And here I am. I miss you. I miss Gina and the kids. There's only one thing I want anymore. Maybe I'm asking too much."

"Tell me."

"I want your forgiveness!" And Rich began to sob, tearing at his hair in remorse, beating his naked heels on the concrete floor, rolling from one side of the bunk to the other.

Conor gripped the cell bars and was warned away by one of the guards watching him. He backed off, his own eyes streaming.

"Rich, you've got to hang on. We'll get you out of this."

"Oh, no. You can't. Because—you don't know him. I hope nobody else on this earth ever knows what he's like."

"Hang on, kid, hang on," Conor mumbled, chewing his beard.

"Forgive me, forgive me."

"I forgive you. I know God does too."

Nothing else passed between them. Conor stood staring at his anguished brother until one of the guards called time on him and he was compelled to walk away.

After what had amounted to a reunion with Rich at the jail, Conor went straight to Edith Leighton with tears of jubilation on his cheeks.

"He's not possessed anymore!"

Edith sat him down in her office at Kurland Bates Harpold and spent a quarter of an hour soberly trying to explain that this wasn't the case.

"Zarach' has simply retreated for a little while. There should be frequent periods of, let us say, remission, as we approach the trial. But Zarach' has not given up his hold on your brother. As long as this demonic entity is unbound, unexorcised, the protocol of possession must be observed. Zarach' is a monster of indescribable proportions; he is also a wily strategist, and we have begun the final phase of his hoped-for conquest."

"But—when I'm talking to Rich—the Rich I know—where is Zarach'?"

"With the two of you. Waiting. Perhaps testing you in ways you may not be aware of, looking for weaknesses to exploit. Think of a hurricane, swilling thermally on its own energy. Think of Zarach' as a primal force, but more devastating than anything wrought by nature: when conditions are right for him, Zarach' may easily possess a thousand souls in the blink of an eye. He will wait, because time as we know it is meaningless to him. He has all the time he needs or wants. But we have only a little time in which to stop him, in circumstances he will dictate.''

"Do you mean the trial?"

Edith nodded. "Zarach' wants Richard to take the stand. And this your brother must do, or we have no case. Only Richard can tell us of the events that led up to the murder: his involvement with Polly Windross and the others of that unholy coven who drew him in so skillfully. This is the bargain Zarach' has struck with me. I may have Richard, but only if I can control *him*."

"Can you control Zarach'?"

"God only knows," Edith replied calmly.

87

Edith turned down two invitations to have dinner with Tommie Harkrider, pleading overwork, and accepted a third only when he showed up at her office with an armload of flowers, loosing salvos of extravagant charm. They were chauffeured to a French restaurant in a woodland setting rosy with dogwood and wild rhododendron in bloom, and had their candlelight meal on a porch that overlooked a gorge through which a millrace tumbled.

He was curious about the little sundial which she wore ornamentally; Edith explained its significance.

"The sundial is both light and shadow; it is cosmic, it is temporal; it is eternity, or the freedom from time; it is mortality, or the conquest of time. Our origins are Gnostic, dualist in nature, partaking of the cults of both Sol Invictus and the Essenes; a society that began in Alexandria in the first century A.D. and survived the tyrannies of Bishop Clement and the Council of Nicea."

"A highly mystical society, I presume."

"Mysticism is a thoroughly impractical state; it tends to

enslave the mind. Unlike the Masons, the Prieuré de Sion, or the Rose-Croix, we have a minimum of doctrines, no secrets to veil in metaphor. We have no vested interests, moral or political, and no member has ever aspired to kingship. We believe that the will of God is the supreme power of the universe, and the will of man is the supreme power on earth. Yet there is a force bound by law to continually attempt to subvert that will. The results throughout history have been epic and obscene. Masada. Languedoc. Byzantium. Is there a territory of this earth that has gone unravaged in its time? We believe, as did the Egyptians before Christ, in the positive power of the cross as a force of, and arising from, nature. Our sole ritual, if you want to call it that, is the ongoing work of prayer, which reinforces this power through community effort. I represent, shall we say, a focal point of that belief, and its underlying spirit.''

"Plus, you happen to be a damned good trial lawyer.'' He twinkled. "I was told to watch out for you, Edith.''

"I thought Mr. Gary Cleves was to be the prosecutor.''

"Oh, he is. He will be. I've been working closely with the boy, and I like him. I have a lot of confidence in Gary.''

"But more confidence in yourself. Quite naturally.''

"That goes without saying. Experience is what really counts. The two of us, we've been around practically forever.''

Edith said, pretending to be miffed, "I rather feel I should be on some sort of life-support system.''

Tommie laughed. "Well, speaking of knighthood, and societies and all that, it must have been one hell of a chivalric impulse that brought you this far. I do understand it a little better, now that we've had this chance to talk. But I can tell you, the quest is hopeless.'' He shook his large uncombed head, a display of magisterial severity. "Hopeless, Edith.''

"Why?''

"There is no way that boy is going to be acquitted by a jury, no matter what the plea. The people in this country are plain sick of rapes of justice.''

Edith separated a small oyster from her seafood crepe, and cut it neatly in half with the side of her fork.

"Acquittal," she said, "may be the least important resolution of this trial."

88

Eleven days before the start of the trial, two events of significance took place. *Time* magazine appeared with a profile of Tommie Harkrider, which also included a lengthy indictment of the criminal court system in the United States, most of it from Tommie's viewpoint. The upcoming case of *Vermont* v. *Devon* received a page and a half of coverage.

And Gary Cleves, thinking to apprehend a prowler which turned out to be a raccoon, accidentally shot himself in the left foot with his Police Special.

He read the account of his misadventure in the local papers along with the *Time* spread on Harkrider while lying in a hospital bed after surgery to repair his foot. He was mentioned once, in the eight pages of profile in *Time* as "the able young prosecutor of Haden County." He was pictured on the front page of the Braxton *Call* (an old news photo) as looking somewhat dimwitted. His confidence, which had been slowly eroding since the appearance of Edith Leighton for the defense, now reached a crisis point of nonsupport. He would be out of the hospital in a couple of days but on crutches for five weeks, which would severely limit his mobility in a courtroom. It was clear that if he made any serious mistakes in his handling of *Vermont* v. *Devon,* then what *Time* and now the TV networks were hyping as the "most important and most closely watched trial of the century" would be lost. And it would be nobody's fault but his.

But how could he lose?

But if he did . . .

The gunshot foot developed an infection, which kept

him in the hospital for another four days, with plenty of time to brood alone. His wife and a couple of aides came faithfully, so he was able to keep up with pretrial preparations, which were going smoothly. Tommie Harkrider had brought nine members of his staff to Vermont three weeks previously to assist the prosecutor, and by now they were doing almost all the work. Tommie had commissioned a telephone survey and learned that sixty-six percent of the people interviewed thought that Richard Devon was guilty of murder, and scoffed at the idea of supernatural intervention. He had hired, at a cost of sixteen hundred dollars a day, two professional "jury pickers" to interview prospective jurors. Gary's staff, all of whom were more than a little in awe of the high-powered talent that had moved in on them, had no complaints that would not have made them sound foolish and provincial. It was, after all, a very big case. Gary was informed that 337 representatives of the world's press had applied for credentials to the trial; the courtroom could accommodate only 150 spectators. Knox Winford had rejected live TV coverage for the trial, and banned still photographers.

Gary finally got out of the hospital, hobbling on crutches, and discovered that a media carnival had come trooping into town. Mobile television units were everywhere. He was interviewed on the steps of the hospital, outside his office, and in front of his home. His wife had already been interviewed twice, and had asked him if she could buy a couple of new dresses for the trial. Gary sat down with Tommie and tried to figure out what was going on, but he felt hopelessly left behind. His foot hurt and his nerves were frayed. He had slept badly in the hospital and had trouble keeping his eyes open, his mind focused.

"Won't all this pretrial publicity make it difficult to choose a jury?" he asked Tommie.

"In this instance I believe it will work in our favor. Awareness doesn't necessarily signify predjudice. I want every jury-eligible man and woman in the county *aware* of the *great* significance of this trial even before the voir dire."

That night Gary didn't sleep at all, and in the morning he arose to find that he had lost his voice.

His doctors, including a throat specialist, could find

nothing organically wrong with his larynx. The condition was blamed on a side effect of the painkillers and antibiotic treatment he'd received for his foot. His voice might return in a day or two. Or it might take much longer.

"Gary," Tommie said, "don't worry. You've done a hell of a job on this case, your entire team has been incredible. I feel privileged to have this opportunity to carry the standard for you in court until you're well enough to handle it yourself. You're a fine young fella, and we'll win this one together."

Tommie was certain that Gary's problem was purely psychological, and one of the psychiatrists he had hired to examine the accused confirmed his hunch.

"Gary's self-image has been maintained by his success as a county prosecutor in what is essentially a rural area, where the cases he has prosecuted have not been particularly complex or demanding. He has serviced a mild paranoia by further refining his image in terms of the gun-toting, straight-shooting law and order figure, an aggressive champion of truth and justice. His childhood hero may well have been the Lone Ranger. Appear in the nick of time; do good for the world; vanish mysteriously into the comforting, shadowy realm of the psyche. The attention he has lately received has been like a very strong searchlight focused on that psyche. He finds it painful, potentially disastrous. It aggravates basic fears of incompetence and persecution by a belligerent and intimidating authority figure collectively known as the press. In the case of *Vermont* v. *Devon* Gary was handed a sword the equivalent of Excalibur: should he wield it with heroic vigor, he might then ascend to godlike heights. But Gary knows in his heart he is no hero. Symbolically he dropped the sword on himself by shooting off two toes of his left foot. By standing mute, abdicating all responsibility while maintaining an image of responsibility in the courtroom, he will have ample time to repair the psychological damage. The toes, of course, he can get along without, and a slight limp is often thought to be romantic."

Tommie decided that this particular shrink just might be worth what they were paying him.

89

The courtroom was high and narrow, with a vaulted, not a flat, ceiling of yellowed plaster, from which hung on brass chains a single row of large white chamberpot lighting fixtures; these did an inadequate job, on short sunless winter afternoons or rainy summer days, of illuminating the corners of the oblong room, because all the wood was solid, dark oak: doors and window frames and tiered rows of benches with high backs, wainscoting on the four walls, the jury box, the judge's three-sided bench with its carved intaglios of leaves and the scales of justice. There were drapes at the windows, worn brown velvet that gave off a must like old gloves in the back of a drawer.

The focal point of the courtroom was a small square of unglazed, sand-colored marble. Like an Elizabethan stage it was nearly surrounded by seats for the jury, for spectators; even when empty it was fascinating to observe because it promised drama. Not the clever artifice of the theater but the often excruciating drama of the boxing ring, the bear pit, the slow-moving tumbrel. To her surprise, after walking in and glancing around once, Edith felt very much at home here, in this courtroom in Chadbury, Vermont.

The selection of the jury began on the fourth day of June. It rained, not heavily, but consistently, all day. The courtroom, the largest available in the district courthouse, had big-bladed ceiling fans, but as the day wore on, the air began to feel humid and soggy. There were too many people inside, packed too closely together on the hard wooden benches in the room. Prospective jurors, 130 of them, took up most of the available space. Twenty-five places had been reserved for members of the press.

The prosecution had asked Judge Knox Winford that the prisoner be restrained in the courtroom because of his episodes of violent behavior. Winford had ruled against them but had requested additional security both in the courtroom and outside, because of numerous crank calls from self-appointed instruments of a vengeful God who proposed to kill Rich. He sat at the defense's table unmanacled, wearing a blue suit with a Yale blue-and-white striped tie. With him were Adam Kurland, Edith Leighton, Lindsay Potter, and the psychologist Maggie Renquist. For the next few days Lindsay and the psychologist would keep their eyes on all the prospective jurors as each was questioned, noting subtle reactions that might be grounds for dismissal by the defense.

At the prosecutor's table on the right side of the courtroom facing the bench, special prosecutor Thomas Horatio Harkrider presided over a team that included the voiceless Gary Cleves, who had a stack of yellow legal pads and a dozen sharp pencils with him; Jean Landetta, an associate of Tommie's who also was an experienced trial lawyer, and the two jury pickers.

Conor Devon sat uncomfortably on the defense's side of the courtroom in the second row behind the press, on the aisle so that he could leave freely to visit the men's room.

Judge Winford read from the bench the charge of first-degree murder to the prospective jurors; Richard Devon sat with his hands clasped on the table in front of him, his head slightly bowed throughout. Nearly all the men and women in the courtroom looked at him with observable emotions ranging from curiosity to uneasiness.

Edith Leighton rose to address her preliminary remarks to the prospective jurors.

"You have been informed," she said, "that a murder was committed.

"We do not deny it.

"A beautiful young girl, beloved of her parents, and many friends, was slain.

"Richard Devon, who perhaps loved her more than anyone, sits here stricken by grief, by guilt.

"Did Karyn Vale die by his hand?

"She did.

"Was the heart and soul of Richard Devon involved in the assault on the girl he wished to marry?

"We say it was not.

"The savagery that resulted in the death of this innocent

victim came from a force of incalculable brutality and evil that has existed since the fall of the angels. A force that possessed him totally on the night of the murder, making him incapable of coherent thought and action—''

There was a commotion in the ranks of the prospective jurors. A stout young woman wearing a seedy trench coat and round steel-rimmed glasses stood up with a Bible in her hand and began to flog the air with a judgmental forefinger.

''I can't listen to any more of this!'' she shouted, perspiration pouring down her face. ''For the commandment sayeth, 'Thou shalt not kill!' '' Her voice rose and fell hysterically. ''If devils possess thee, then it is *Jesus* who shall cast out the devils! Give yourself to Jesus, Richard Devon, and thou shalt be *saved*!''

Rich had risen from his seat at the defense's table; he was looking around at the woman. A tremor ran through him.

Knox Winford hammered with his gavel. The first day, and things already were going haywire. ''Bailiffs!''

The young woman dropped her Bible and tore open her trench coat. She was naked underneath. She had singled out Rich and now she cried, ''Hallelu-jah! We will go to Jesus together!'' She tried to climb over the row of unexamined jurors in front of her to get to the defense's table. Various bailiffs, including a woman, intercepted her.

Lindsay said with a wry smile to Adam, ''That's one challenge we won't have to use.''

''Take *me*, Satan!'' the woman exhorted, having forgotten all about Jesus. ''Let Richard go!'' Then she subsided suddenly, almost blissfully, panting and groaning in the grip of the bailiffs.

''I think the poor thing just had her first orgasm,'' Maggie Renquist observed.

Rich sat down slowly, and for a few moments his face was thick with depression. Then, as Lindsay looked his way, his expression changed. His edged smile was like a signature of dark mirth to the outpouring of the erstwhile salvationist. Lindsay felt a bolt of horror twist her shoulders as Rich reached down and fondled an instant erection; she sensed that something had flown from him to the oblivious, deluded woman, a terrifying spirit eager to claim the sacrifice. She pressed a hand against her mouth and thought she was going to faint.

As the young woman was wrapped in her trench coat and hustled out of the courtroom, Adam got a good look at her dowdy behind and cellulite-loaded thighs. "Even Zarach' must have some standards," he said. But his stomach was jumping from all the excitement; he was concerned about the dismal impression the woman had made on the other veniremen, who now would be disposed to look upon the matter of demonic possession as a bizarre comedy indulged in by retardates and sexually repressed zealots. How the hell had fatso survived the initial screening of eligibles so she could wind up in court doing her act? He shook his head. Even skilled jury pickers could blow one occasionally.

Rich's head was bowed contemplatively. Lindsay looked as if she had been hit by a bad menstrual cramp; her lips were bloodless. Edith walked by them all, maintaining her composure. She looked at Rich and then at Maggie, who was still grinning. Edith rapped her knuckles on the table in front of the psychologist and said, "We must not be amused." Then she paced for another five minutes until Knox Winford had succeeded in restoring order in the courtroom. When the mood was more to her liking, Edith resumed.

"It is a formidable task that faces you as jurors. You will hear from Richard himself the terrible story of how he was made a prisoner in his own body, and of the perpetual nightmare he has endured since."

Tommie Harkrider sat up a little straighter at this assertion and almost smiled for a moment as Edith, aware of the movement, flicked her eyes to him. Then she said, addressing the courtroom again, "We will prove to you that Richard Devon is as much a helpless victim of a murderous act as was his beloved Karyn. You will hear testimony from others, similarly possessed but more fortunate than Richard, in that they were not compelled to commit despicable crimes against other human beings. You will be asked to view photographs of individuals possessed by demonic spirits undergoing the tortures of exorcism. It is not a pretty picture we will paint for you; but every word is truth. The truth of the deadly war between the light of God and the darkness of Satan, which is everywhere upon the earth at this very moment, and which must engage us all in the service of the light if mankind is to persevere."

Tommie Harkrider was as ramshackle as ever as he stepped nippingly around the small arena formed by the judge's bench and witness stand, the now-empty jury box, and the tables for prosecution and defense. The knot of his unfashionable black knit tie was askew, one shirt cuff was decidedly frayed, his suit shone at the elbows and the seat of the pants. But his voice was his image: it clothed him in the radiant robes of an angel, an angel of might, of thundering omniscience and truth. He was an old-fashioned orator with the gift of inspiring each member of a large audience to believe that he and he alone was being addressed, the confidant of Tommie Harkrider.

Tommie said, not too sorrowfully, "We have already had a demonstration of what disordered minds and emotions may lead one to do. The poor woman is to be pitied, not censured; but you must think now about the impulses that led her to commit this act of public lewdness. And think also of how much more the *truly* disturbed mind is capable of conceiving, plotting, carrying out, all in the name of truth, or justice. Or love. Or . . . *revenge* for unrequited love.

"The prosecution is prepared to refute with *scientific,* psychiatric testimony any so-called 'evidence' of demonic possession, a purely theological concept which we submit has no basis in observable fact. We will prove, rather, that Richard Devon, far from being 'possessed' "—Tommie made quibbling quotation marks in the air with his fingers—"by 'demonic influences,' whatever they are, is in actuality so stricken by guilt that he must *repress* that guilt—must erase all thought of the murder from his conscious mind—by providing a surrogate to take the blame, a surrogate who does not in fact exist, and has never existed.

"Ladies and gentlemen, there will be only two points pertinent to the outcome of this trial. It may well be that *all* murderers are deranged at the moment they commit their crime, an irrational and antisocial act. Perhaps they are figuratively 'possessed' by emotional demons of their own devise—jealousy, passion, hatred. The fact remains that if there is such a crime as murder, and the statutes of the great state of Vermont so affirm, then Richard Devon is either guilty or not guilty under those statutes. His state of mind, and his emotional condition at the time of the murder, are not relevant.''

90

After several more hours, during which the defense and the prosecution could not agree on the selection of the first juror, Winford adjourned the proceedings.

Conor came as close to Rich as he was allowed and said, "It's going to be okay, you'll see."

"You *don't* see," Rich replied, downcast, and was led away.

Conor, desperate for something to be hopeful about, said to Edith, "How do you think we did?"

"I've had better days," Edith replied tartly. "But we have far to go. And now for tea."

91

It took them twelve days to impanel the jury.

Choosing a jury through the method of interrogation and challenge was almost unknown in England, where jurors are seated by lottery. And Queen's Counsels limit their activities to arguing cases prepared for them in full by junior barristers. Edith had been grateful for Adam's unselfish cooperation in assuming most of the pretrial workload, and was now benefiting from his experience at sizing up and questioning candidates for the panel.

The prosecution and the defense each had twenty challenges. Potential jurors could also be dismissed without a challenge on grounds such as age. For Tommie Harkrider the process of interrogation and acceptance was more exacting, and excruciating, than it was for Edith and Adam. Under different circumstances Tommie would have welcomed jurors with deep religious convictions, for whom the act of killing was anathema. But the deeply religious also tended to believe in the existence of the devil; whether they also believed human beings could be possessed by him was another matter, but Tommie had no intention of handing counsel for the defense a built-in advantage. Catholics, even lapsed Catholics, were out, along with Bible Fundamentalists and Orthodox Jews. Middle-of-the-road Presbyterians and Congregationalists were okay, and Unitarians, better still. He knew he had no chance to get either an agnostic or an atheist by the defense, and didn't try very hard. He hesitated the longest over an accountant who was also a Christian Scientist; he finally dismissed her.

Tommie wasn't keen on dreamers, dropouts, or professional students. Artists were a difficult lot to judge. He took one who had owned his own gallery for twenty years, rejected one who sold his work out of a hand-decorated van at flea markets. His preference was for solid, older, well-educated or self-made individuals who had never smoked pot or dropped acid (he certainly didn't need someone harboring a secret mystical experience) and who would have the stamina to follow often-complicated lines of psychiatric reasoning and opinion while keeping a clear head. He preferred jurors with previous jury experience. He preferred women to men. Color didn't matter, but Haden County had very nearly an all-white population.

Edith's needs were simpler. She did not want a juror who had a female relative who had ever been in physical jeopardy, a mugging or rape victim. She sought a quality of open-mindedness, jurors with spirit who would not easily be bullied. Tommie could be a bit of a bully when it suited his tactics; so, she knew, could Zarach', which worried her more.

The first juror selected was Mary Adelaide Hotchkiss, age thirty-six, resident of Coldwater, mother of three. All boys. She was a Methodist and had taught Sunday school. She wasn't sure she accepted everything in the Bible as historical fact, but appreciated the "moral lessons to be learned from the parables." She was civic-minded and a conservationist. She had served on juries before, but this was her first murder trial. She had a graceful neck and a nice smile, wore glasses to correct astigmatism. Tommie liked her because she had graduated summa cum laude in psychology from Temple University. Edith liked her because her hobby was whitewater kayaking. As the first juror named, Mary Adelaide became forelady.

The last juror whom the adversaries agreed upon was Walter Durrah, sixty-eight, of Glendinning. He neither smoked nor drank. He was a lifelong Republican and a former selectman. He did not like to be called Wally, or even Walt. He and his wife raised thoroughbred Irish setters. He had won a number of fly-fishing trophies. He read the Bible, which he considered "literature," but didn't go to church. Among other jobs he had worked for a year as an attendant at the state mental institution. He recalled the experience as "fascinating." Edith was suspicious of his attitude toward "mental defectives," as he called them; there was more than a hint of condescension, a deep-rooted belief that most of the incarcerated were fakers and malingerers. Walter Durrah had never been sick a day in his life, seldom knew fear, and thought that most people tended to "pamper themselves." But Edith was down to one challenge. Walter Durrah was borderline, a risk, but the next candidate might prove to be totally unacceptable. So she let the dog breeder pass, and the jury was complete. Both lawyers turned their attention to the main event.

92

Shortly after dawn on the twenty-first of June, the summer solstice, nearly a thousand people were in front of the district courthouse and on the green hoping to be chosen by lot to attend the trial. There were thunderheads to the north, a smell of rain was in the air, but the sun rose higher and the rain passed Chadbury by, leaving the air sultry.

Conor Devon entered the courthouse by a rear door and took his seat early; a few minutes before ten Martin and Louise Vale were escorted into the courtroom by Tommie Harkrider. Martin Vale glanced at Conor; he realized who he was but didn't speak. He had been sailing on the weekend and was windburned, but still looked haggard. His wife wore a hat with a veil, maintaining an attitude of mourning. She kept fingering a pulse in her throat, trying to quell it. She stared straight ahead, at the flags of the nation and the state behind the bench.

The spectators who had won seats were let in as soon as the press had filled up the first row. At ten minutes after ten Knox Winford took his seat on the bench and nodded to the court clerk, who opened the proceedings.

"The people are ready, Your Honor," Tommie Harkrider said for Gary Cleves. Gary's voice had begun to come back, but he was able to communicate only in a ragged whisper. Gary, seated beside Tommie, nodded.

"The defense is ready, Your Honor," Adam Kurland said on behalf of Richard Devon, who wore the same blue suit he'd had on throughout the selection of the jury. He seemed a little dazed by the sunlight slanting down on him from a window above the juror's box, and Lindsay asked a bailiff to change the angle of the blinds.

Knox Winford cleared his throat and addressed himself to the jury. "Out of some four hundred candidates it has fallen to you, ladies and gentlemen, to return a verdict which may well have consequences reaching far beyond the confines of this courtroom. It is not only desirable but essential that you hold yourself aloof from all considerations of pity and sympathy, forget what prejudices you may now hold, maintain your good judgment no matter how long this trial continues, and base your verdict solely on what your common sense tells you is valid. The issue is simply stated: Is Richard Devon guilty as charged of murder in the first degree? The way to a resolution of that issue may lie through as-yet uncharted territory. My responsibility is to you, the members of the jury. Our standard at all times shall be clear reasoning."

After a few moments Tommie Harkrider rose and walked gimpily to the lectern in front of the jury box to begin his opening statement, which would take one and three-quarter hours.

"May it please the court . . ."

He spoke without notes. He had long since committed to memory details of Richard Devon's life that even Conor didn't know. This preparedness represented several hundred hours of work by Tommie's team of investigators.

He skillfully drew a psychological portrait of Rich as a street kid, undersized and aggressive in his youth, sometimes hotheaded and impulsive, always argumentative, capable of an occasional violent outburst. He talked about Rich's brushes with the law, and the harsh discipline handed out to him by Conor, who was also a priest and a sometimes fearsome authority figure to the nearly orphaned boy. Tommie dwelled on the fact that although Rich had a conventional Catholic upbringing, he was both attracted to and repelled by his religion, particularly susceptible to nightmares inspired by fears of a hell presided over by devils, a place of everlasting torment. By the time he entered Yale, Rich had fallen away from the Church. Outgrown it. But had he—asked Tommie—been simultaneously released from the psychological chains that bound him, his sense of guilt at having forsaken the faith of his childhood?

At this point Tommie introduced Karyn, and for fifteen minutes he eulogized her with such sweetness and fidelity and deep sense of loss that it was as if he had known her more intimately than her own parents, or the last of her lovers. Louise Vale sat sobbing quietly in her seat. At one point Rich put his hands over his face, gropingly, as if he sought to identify himself through a mask not of his making, then let his hands drop hopelessly into his lap and bowed his head. Tommie spared no details of the love affair between Rich and Karyn: the laughter, the magic, the quarrels. For, as Tommie solemnly pointed out, inevitably there were quarrels. They came from "two different worlds." Rich from the "mean streets of south Boston," Karyn from the "graceful lawns and vistas" of wealthy Rye, New York. Even as intimacy deepened (as Tommie would have it) the distance between them was magnified.

Karyn had had other lovers before Rich. He knew this. But how well had he accepted this fact?

Tommie shook his head somberly and looked at each of the twelve jurors in turn. They were raptly attentive. Not well at all, he said, and turned for a moment, directing their attention to the defendant.

Rich looked at the jurors and then away, seemingly unable to meet anyone's eyes.

Tommie shook his head again, and launched into an account of the ill-fated hours of the January ski vacation that had culminated in the brutal murder. He told the jurors about their public set-to near the lift return at Hermitage Mountain, witnessed by scores of people, including friends of the deceased. Karyn had already expressed misgivings about the relationship to her mother, and then she confided her desire to break completely with Rich to an old flame, Trux Landall.

"A *complete* break," Tommie said, and paused to let that sink in with the jury. "Karyn didn't want to see Rich anymore. And when he found out—"

He then proceeded to give as chilling a blow-by-blow account of the murder as anyone could dread to hear.

Louise Vale had to be helped from the courtroom by her husband.

Two of the jurors broke down in tears.

The others stared at the defendant with expressions ranging from sullen loathing to naked hate.

Tommie wiped his own eyes with a handkerchief, looked at the bench, gestured like a broken man to Edith Leighton, and sat down to collect himself.

Edith rose slowly from the defense table and walked toward the lectern. She might have had tougher acts to follow, but she couldn't remember when.

She was far too wise to attempt to go against the mood which Tommie in all of his dramatic eloquence had orchestrated. She decided on the instant to go with it instead.

A few scattered coughs in the courtroom; the sounds of charcoal and chalk on sketchpads as the artists along the press row worked at their impressions of the principals of the trial. Edith kept her voice low, so that the jurors would be securely drawn to her as they strained to hear.

"A murder is committed. Terrifying in its irrationality,

the almost passionless repetition of blow after blow after blow; murder inhuman, even bestial, in the scope of its violence. And there were five witnesses to this seemingly endless, robotlike assault on a human life. Five young people who watched helplessly while Karyn Vale was bludgeoned to death. We have their statements but unfortunately we don't have *them*, because of the five only one is alive today, scarcely five months after Karyn Vale herself was laid to rest. The survivor, Warren Hasper, is attending school in Europe and has refused to return to this country to testify as to what he saw because he has admitted he is afraid he may not live long enough to take the stand.

"*Afraid!*

"But of what?

"That is a question we must answer.

"Four grotesque, unexplainable deaths of vibrant, healthy young people in such a short period of time cannot be lightly passed off as 'coincidence.' Nor can the disappearance of trooper Norm Granger of the Vermont State Police, one of two policemen who were the first to reach the scene of the murder. Nor can the death by suicide of his twenty-six-year-old partner, Peter Raff, who died the night trooper Granger disappeared.

"Before this trial is over, you will know that his disappearance, the strange deaths, are directly related to the death of Karyn Vale; and you will know why. You will know that the motive for Karyn's death is *not* the motive so exhaustively suggested by the prosecution. You will know the full, horrifying story of what happened to Richard Devon from the moment he arrived in Chadbury on the night of January eighteenth.

" 'A person is guilty of murder in the first degree when with intent to cause the death of another, he causes the death of such person.' "

Edith indulged in a long and searching pause. But she had them.

" 'Intent to cause,' " she repeated. "I urge you to ponder the meaning of that phrase.

"Ladies and gentlemen of the jury, when all of the evidence has been presented to you, I am confident that you will know that Richard Devon not only lacked the intent, but in fact *did not* kill the girl he loved."

93

"Well," Tommie said to his colleague Jean Landetta, over Drambuie in the cocktail lounge of the inn where they were staying, "she throws a pretty good block, does Edith. I wouldn't exactly say she won the jury back after I got through with them. But she sure as hell has them curious, and maybe a little on edge."

"I still wish we had the last of those kids who saw the murder being committed," Jean said.

"We won't need Warren Hasper. We've got Trux Landall and plenty of other witnesses who will testify that Devon was acting like an animal before and after he killed the girl."

"Do you think Edith will put him on the stand?"

"She practically promised to do that today. She has to. Her bucket won't hold water without him. But it's the old double-bind effect. No matter what kind of tale he chooses to tell, he won't have a shred of credibility left when I'm finished with him."

94

Trux Landall was the first witness called by the state the next day.

In contrast to Rich, who looked jail-puffy around the eyes and fidgeted as if demoralized at the defense table while Trux took the stand, the Harvard Law student cut an impressive figure. His French blazer and tie were impeccable. He'd just returned from a few days' loafing in Virgin

Gorda, and his eyes, enhanced by a deepwater tan, gleamed in his good-looking face.

"Mr. Landall," Tommie asked him, "when did you first meet Karyn Vale?"

Tommie, like any good trial lawyer, never asked a question in court unless he already knew the answer. He led the witness through an account of his romance with Karyn and their subsequent parting.

"And the next time you saw Karyn was at Hermitage Mountain on the morning of January nineteenth?"

"Yes, sir, that is correct."

"Were you introduced to the defendant, Richard Devon, at that time?"

Trux glanced to where Rich sat, eyes down. Rich was tearing thin little strips of yellow paper from a legal pad. "Yes, I was."

"What was your first impression of the defendant?"

"He didn't have much to say. Not shy. Just—aloof, like he didn't want anything to do with us."

"Was Karyn happy to see you?"

"Yes, sir, I had that impression."

"How long did you talk to Karyn?"

"Only a few minutes. Then I went with my friends to the lift."

"Did you make a firm date to join Karyn and Rich at a later time?"

"No. It was just sort of, we'll get together while we're up here. That sort of thing."

"Can you tell me what happened while you were waiting in line with your friends for the chair lift?"

"Karyn and, uh, Rich got into an argument. They were pretty loud. She was crying."

"Do you know what they were fighting about?"

"Objection, Your Honor," Edith said. "The witness has said that Richard and Karyn were *arguing*. May we continue with that usage?"

"Sustained," Knox Winford said.

"Do you know what they were arguing about?" Tommie amended.

"All I heard her say was 'You better just forget about me.' "

"Did they reconcile their differences while you were observing them?"

"No, sir. Karyn got her skis and poles from the corral and skied off to the T-bar."

"And did you see Karyn again that day?"

"Yes, sir. A group of us got together at the Frog Prince restaurant. That's in Londonderry."

"Was the defendant with her?"

"No, she was with a couple of girls."

"Did she seem upset that Rich wasn't there?"

"No. She had a good time. She was expecting him, but he just never showed up."

"What happened after dinner was over?"

"We all, uh, went back to the Davos Chalet Lodge. I went upstairs with Karyn, but Rich wasn't in their room. I asked her if they were having problems, and she said, 'Everybody has problems.' We talked for a while, and then I left."

"Did you kiss her good night?"

"Yes. I did. In the hall outside."

"There was no impropriety?"

"It was just a friendly good-night kiss. Anyone could have seen us, it didn't matter."

"But it was Rich who saw you?"

"Yes."

"And how did he react? With reasonable behavior, or—"

"Your Honor, I shall object to that," Edith said.

"Sustained."

"How did he react, Mr. Landall?"

"He didn't say a word. He just glared at me, and came at me. Swinging."

"He was violent? He assaulted you?"

"He tried to kick me in the groin."

"How did you react?"

"I didn't want any part of a fight; it wasn't worth it. I said, 'Take it easy, guy,' but he just kept coming at me. Karyn pleaded with him to stop. After he landed a couple of punches—he got me on the elbow, and the shoulder, and also he kneed me in the thigh—I figured I'd better do something to stop it."

"When did you make that decision?"

"Well, Karyn grabbed hold of Rich trying to stop him, and he shoved her out of the way. I thought he was going to throw a punch at her—"

"Object to speculation on the part of the witness. We are concerned with what actually did happen, not what might have happened."

"In your opinion, the defendant was out of control—"

"Objection, Your Honor!"

Tommie wheeled on Edith and snapped, "The opinion of the witness, who was brutally under attack, is perfectly valid at this point."

"Overruled. I'll allow it." Winford told them.

"You found yourself taking a beating from the defendant, and were forced to fight back in order to avoid serious injury?" Tommie asked Trux.

"That's correct, sir. I hit him. Just once. A short jab below the breastbone. He folded up."

"What was Karyn's reaction?"

"She was upset. And mad."

"Mad at the defendant?"

"Yes. I apologized for hitting him. And she said, 'He's impossible when he gets like this.' "

"Was the defendant able to talk? Did he say anything to you, or to Karyn?"

"A lot of obscenity. I don't know if I should repeat it verbatim. He accused Karyn and me of—getting it on."

"Having sex together?"

"Yes, sir."

"In fact, you did not have sexual relations with Karyn that night?"

"No, I didn't."

"Did the defendant say anything else before you left?"

"Yes. He said, 'I'll get you for this.' "

"To whom did the defendant say 'I'll get you for this'?"

"He said it to Karyn."

Tommie paused and strolled to the jury box, looking at each of their faces like a beneficent old uncle. He was terribly fond of them all, and let them know it. And he was becoming intimately familiar with every detail of their faces, their unconscious idiosyncrasies as they listened to the proceedings. With his back still to the witness stand, Tommie began his next line of questioning.

"When was the last time you saw Karyn Vale alive?" he asked.

Trux described his encounter with Karyn in the tavern of the Davos Chalet Lodge, and their subsequent midnight walk through the snow. He told of her decision to break off with Rich, and her feeling of relief at finally being able to make this decision.

"I walked her back to the lobby of the hotel and said good night. Some of the kids were leaving just then and I got a lift down to the lodge were I was staying."

Trux's voice became strained. He paused for a long time, sniffing, his coppery brightness scuffed and dimmed by tragedy relived, his composure cracking.

"Next morning one of the guys I was bunking with shook me awake. 'My God,' he said, 'my God, Trux. Get up. Karyn's been murdered.' And that's the first . . ."

Trux sobbed and put a hand over his mouth. He looked at the defense table.

Rich's head was up. His eyes were on the witness. They expressed a chilling contempt. Edith, seated at the end of the table, did not have to look at Rich to be aware of the evil of Zarach'; it attacked her like a migraine. She was all but blinded.

"No further questions," Tommie said.

Edith, her eyelids fluttering, slumped against Adam.

"Your Honor, may we have a recess at this time?" Adam requested.

Rich turned his attention from the witness stand to the jurors. Smiling. All twelve jurors were appalled and angered by this show of heartlessness.

"Stop it," Edith murmured. She pressed a hand against the top of her forehead, thumb and forefinger on her temples.

"We will have a fifteen-minute recess," Judge Winford announced from the bench. To Edith he said, "Shall I call a doctor for you, Counselor?"

Edith, with a great effort, straightened in her chair and opened her eyes. She looked momentarily confused, and further confused herself by saying "Thank you, my Lord—I mean, Your Honor. I'll be all right. Just some water."

Tommie, looking on with a pucker of concern, said

quietly to Jean Landetta, ''She'll never make it through the trial.''

The defendant went back to compiling thin strips of paper from the legal pad he'd been destroying. His ardor had dwindled; he showed no interest in Edith's distress. Except for his attention to his strips of paper he seemed close to oblivion.

95

When they reconvened, Edith approached the witness stand with her customary briskness. The milky cast of pain had disappeared from her eyes. She took several seconds to look over the jury, particularly the young woman in the first seat of the second row, behind the forelady.

Angela Gunther was an unmarried dental technician. At twenty-four, she was the youngest of the jurors, and, Edith thought, the most impressionable. It was Angie's first trial. She was excited about it, and very determined to do a good job. So far life had treated her very well. She had a supportive and affectionate family. She ''loved people.'' By her own admission she'd had ''loads of boyfriends,'' but ''nothing too serious so far.'' She had yet to face a major problem or tragedy in her life. She usually skipped the front page of the daily paper if the news looked ''real depressing'' and concentrated on the advice and social columns.

Angie was one of Tommie Harkrider's favorite jurors, a fact he'd already made apparent by the attention he gave her, but Edith felt that the sharp-eyed barrister had fundamentally misjudged the direction which this good-hearted and uncomplicated girl's sympathies would take. Edith's instinct told her that Angie was still finding it impossible to comprehend how one human being could so wantonly and viciously take the life of another. Nobody *she* had ever known could do a thing like that. Eventually she would welcome, and stubbornly support, the explanation Edith had to offer.

Right now Edith wanted to reinforce Angie's subconscious bias, and see if she could cast a slight shadow of doubt across the minds of those jurors who were already convinced that Rich was guilty.

"Mr. Landall, when you were awakened in the morning following the death of Karyn Vale, can you tell us what it was you said to your friends once you had been apprised of the shocking details?"

Trux hesitated, thinking, biting his lower lip. "I—I said, 'Only a monster could do something like that.' "

"A *monster*. Thank you, sir. That will be all."

96

Tommie made sure the jury was aware of every gruesome detail of the murder by calling the county coroner, who came with multiple copies of the autopsy photos to hand out. Edith raised no objection. The recess that followed was much lengthier than the one she had needed during the morning's session.

After the coroner, police surgeon Arthur Harbison took the stand.

"Dr. Harbison," Tommie asked, "how long have you been a police surgeon?"

"For twenty-one years."

"When did you first examine the accused, Richard Devon?"

"At approximately three fifteen A.M. on the morning of January twenty-first of this year."

"What was his physical condition at that time?"

"His pulse was rapid, more than a hundred and twenty beats per minute. The pupils of his eyes were fixed and dilated; his skin was cold and clammy to the touch."

"In other words, he was in a state of shock."

"That is correct." All witnesses, no matter how many trials they have been through, exhibit nervous mannerisms.

Harbison had a mild sty on his left eye, and was continually pulling off his glasses to nudge it with a fingertip.

"Was he physically injured?"

"No, sir."

"Was he able to speak?"

"Yes, he was. But his speech was rambling, disconnected, more often than not inappropriate to the situation."

"Did he know who he was?"

"Yes."

"Did he know where he was?"

"Yes, he knew he was at the police station."

"Did he know *why* he was there?"

"I do not believe he did, not at that time. No, sir."

"Why is that, Dr. Harbison?"

"His lack of cognizance of recent events is all part of the normal emotional reaction to a shocking and highly stressful event. A serious accident, a sudden death, any sort of unexpected and overwhelming tragedy."

"Have you observed this partial or total lack of coherence before, in other victims of shock?"

"Hundreds of times."

"Richard Devon, then, was in a state of shock, which is understandable, considering what he had just done, but he was not, in your opinion, mentally deranged?"

"Objection, Your Honor! The witness is a medical doctor, not a psychiatrist. Symptoms of shock could easily mask other symptoms which would not be evident until long after the precipitating event."

"Objection sustained."

"I believe," Tommie said, unruffled, "that all medical doctors, as well as many laymen, are familiar with the term temporary amnesia, is that not so, Doctor?"

"It is certainly familiar to me."

"Is temporary amnesia a form of mental illness?"

"Not to my knowledge, no. It is a condition directly related to shock trauma and usually disappears in a matter of hours, or days at the most."

"In your expert opinion, was Richard Devon suffering from temporary amnesia when you first saw him?"

"Yes."

"Thank you, Dr. Harbison. I have no further questions."

"No questions, Your Honor," Edith said.

97

At dinner that night at Morecambe's with Rich's lawyers, Conor asked Edith why she had limited her cross-examination of the witnesses so far to the one question she had asked Trux Landall—whose answer, Conor felt, had been even more damaging to Rich's cause.

"There is no way I can refute the basic facts which the prosecution has thus far presented. There was a murder, and it was a gruesome affair. What I want the jurors to keep in mind is the gross inhumanity, the monstrousness of the act. Only a monster could have done it. But that monster is Zarach', not Richard. And I will have the opportunity to prove it before long."

"Where do you think Tommie is going from here?"

"He must now attempt to establish that Rich was sane when Karyn was murdered, that your brother, quite in keeping with his psychoanalytical profile, reacted to her desire to end the relationship in a paroxysm of jealousy and rage. Tommie will also, if he is clever—and I cannot fault him there—do everything he can, through psychiatric testimony, to destroy our credibility even before we have had the opportunity to present our case to the jurors."

"Edith, you haven't touched your salad," Lindsay said. "As a matter of fact, I haven't seen you take a bite for three days. I'm worried about you."

"I'm not ill, my dear. I'm not taking any food as a matter of choice, and necessity. I must fast at this time, to be prepared, to keep all of my channels of perception open, and clear."

"You almost fainted this morning," Adam said.

"I was taken quite by surprise," Edith admitted.

"By Zarach'?" Conor asked her.

"Yes. But it shan't happen again."

98

The prosecution was able to conclude its case in only three and a half days. The last witness Tommie Harkrider called, one of three psychiatrists who had examined Rich and spent a total of twenty-seven hours taking detailed case histories, was Dr. Lewis Shea, director of forensic psychiatry at the Columbia-Presbyterian Medical Center in New York City.

Dr. Shea was an affable man with a high forehead, squirrel teeth, and the wiry toughness of a dedicated jogger. He had testified at numerous criminal trials in the East. He had written half a dozen books and was a recognized authority on a specialized subject, the minds of murderers.

"In your expert opinion, sir," Tommie said, after he had spent considerable time impressing the jurors with his witness's qualifications, "was Richard Devon suffering from any form of mental illness at the time he killed Karyn Vale?"

"No, he was not."

"Is he mentally ill at this time?"

"No, sir."

Rich, who was busily weaving a basket from his many strips of legal-pad paper, took time to glance at the eminent psychiatrist.

"At no time during your interviews with Richard Devon, which took up a total of nine and a half hours over a four-week period, did you observe any evidence of psychotic behavior on his part?"

"Mr. Devon is not psychotic."

"I see. Did he at no time mention to you an entity, whom he referred to as 'Zarach' "—Tommie took the time to spell the name for the jury—"and who he claimed was living in his body with him?"

"Oh, yes," Shea said calmly. "I heard quite a bit about Zarach'."

"*Did* you?" Tommie turned away from the witness stand, looking as if he could barely contain his astonishment. "Well, Doctor. Pardon me for being confused, but if I spent considerable time talking to somebody who advised me, out of the blue, that he wasn't just who I thought he was, that he had another, totally different *personality* living inside his body with him, well then, I don't claim to be well schooled in the fundamentals of psychology, Doctor, but I'd sure think that guy was *whacko*." Tommie made bird-twittering sounds and circled a finger in the air while rolling his eyes at the same time. The courtroom erupted in laughter.

"Order!" said Judge Winford, and he frowned at Tommie, who smiled slyly as he returned to the witness stand.

Dr. Shea also was smiling. Tommie looked long and hard at him.

"You mean he wouldn't necessarily *be* whacko, Doctor?"

"Not at all, sir."

"Well, then, is there some kind of psychiatric terminology that we can all understand that would account for this—this rather *strange* belief?"

"It is most frequently known, in lay terms, as denial. To be more specific, a guilty-reactive mechanism."

"Thank you, thank you, Dr. Shea. No, I'm not through with you yet. I just want to analyze what you've told me, see if we can break it down into terms that a layman like myself can understand without boiling his brains. Okay, so we have this guilty-reactive mechanism—"

Edith said, "Your Honor, is the prosecution going to address a question to the witness, or will this become a monologue?"

"Please address yourself to the witness, Mr. Harkrider," Winford directed.

"I intend to, I intend to. My apologies, Your Honor. Now, Dr. Shea, you have observed this guilty-reactive mechanism at work in the defendant?"

"Yes, sir."

"What he has to feel guilty about is, of course, the murder of Karyn Vale."

"Yes, sir."

"Objection, Your Honor. The prosecutor is leading the witness."

"Sustained. The witness's reply will be stricken from the record."

"Tell me, Dr. Shea, during your long hours of interviewing the defendant, did you discuss the murder with him?"

"I made several attempts to do so."

"He wouldn't talk about it?"

"No. He was evasive at first. But I could see that any mention of the girl, and the murder, placed him under tremendous tension. It was only later during our sessions, when I persisted in referring to the murder, that he blamed Zarach'."

"Exactly how did the defendant put it, Doctor?"

"He finally said to me, still under tension, 'No, no. I didn't want to. It was Zarach'. He wanted her to die. He made me do it.' "

" *'He made me do it,'* " Tommie repeated slowly, and glanced at the jurors. "Did the defendant tell you anything about this Zarach' who was suddenly giving the orders?"

"Yes. He referred to Zarach' as an inhuman spirit, one of the fallen angels."

"A devil?"

"That is theologically correct, yes."

"Did he tell you how he came to be possessed by this devil?"

"No, he didn't."

"Do you have any ideas as to where this so-called Zarach' might have come from, Dr. Shea?"

"Yes. Richard had a strict Catholic upbringing. He was both obedient to and in terror of the Church, the priests and nuns who taught him. Our youthful fears can be sublimated, but we never outgrow them. Nowadays Catholicism places less emphasis on hell and the devil than it once did, but I'm Catholic myself and I can tell you that some of the older sisters could frighten the wits out of impressionable children with their stories of sinners flogged across the fiery coals of hell, of souls seized by the devil because they skipped Mass one Sunday. Richard was certainly impressed by all of this, and he never got over his feelings of guilt when he fell away from the Church shortly after he entered Yale. The 'Zarach' ' that exists in Richard's mind now is a specter recalled from childhood. Perhaps in reading the Bible he ran across the name—''

"What you are trying to tell us—just to keep this a little shorter, Doctor—is that the defendant, Richard Devon, is blaming the murder on a quasi-religious or mythological being?"

"Because he simply cannot come to terms with the enormity of the crime he committed. All of us have various techniques for avoidance or evasion of the unpleasant things of life, the unthinkable; we rationalize our little fears and our minor transgressions so we can continue to live on good terms with ourselves. But Richard was so overloaded with guilt following the slaying that all of the mind's usual means of coping were inadequate. So that he wouldn't be driven to madness or suicide, a new pathemic channel was opened, through which appeared Zarach'—the archetypal blame-taker. Omnipotent, powerful, evil. Only Zarach' could handle the input of guilt and grief that was suffocating Richard."

"But his belief in the existence of this devil does not mean that Richard Devon is mentally ill?"

"Such a belief is purely neurotic in origin and function. Rich is using this imagined possession as a guilt-blocker in much the same way as a dentist uses lidocaine to deaden the nerve impulses in a tooth."

"And there is no way this Zarach' could have been around *before* the defendant killed Karyn Vale?"

"Only as an archetype buried deeply in the Jungian unconscious." Dr. Shea smiled. "But in that sense, we *all* have our Zarach's."

"Thank you very much, Doctor. Your Honor, I have no further questions."

At first it seemed as if Edith didn't care to cross-examine Dr. Shea; she closed a folder in front of her that contained a number of copies of reports and documents and fiddled indecisively with her reading glasses before rising and, perhaps reluctantly, approaching the witness stand. She smiled tentatively at the psychiatrist.

"Dr. Shea, is there any limit to the varieties of neurotic behavior you've observed in your professional career?"

"None so far. Every day brings a new surprise."

"And how many categories of mental disorders are there?"

"Oh, dozens."

"Every day brings a new surprise?"

"No, that's not true of pathological behavior. It's safe to say we've seen everything there is to see."

"All pathological behavior is classifiable by type, is that correct?"

"Yes, I'd say so."

"Would you also say that, from a psychiatric viewpoint, there is no such thing as motiveless behavior?"

"Yes, that's an accurate statement."

"I was merely asking a question; but you've answered it very assuredly. Do you still practice your religion, Doctor?"

The abrupt change in the line of questioning flustered him slightly. "Oh, yes."

"You're basically in agreement with the major doctrines of your faith?"

"If I wasn't, I couldn't call myself a Catholic."

"You accept the virgin birth, the veneration of Mary, the resurrection of the body, the confession of your sins, and the sacrament of reconciliation?"

"Yes," the doctor said, a trifle impatiently.

"Do you believe, as your Church does, in the existence of the devil?"

"As—metaphor; I can't seriously—"

"Your Honor," Tommie Harkrider said, "I don't know where we're going with this line of questioning."

"Allow me to complete it and we'll all find out," Edith retorted.

"Do you have an objection, Mr. Harkrider?" the judge asked him.

Tommie hesitated, then sat down with a little exasperated shake of his head. "No, sir."

"As a Catholic psychiatrist, Dr. Shea, have you had cases referred to you by your archdiocese, cases involving prominent laymen or members of the hierarchy itself?"

"Occasionally. Priests have emotional problems like anyone else."

"And nuns. Nuns also have emotional problems?"

"Certainly."

"Have you ever examined a nun whose symptoms were

so baffling and so persistent that you found yourself unable either to categorize her presumed psychosis or treat her successfully?''

Lewis Shea looked amazed. ''There—was such a case, yes.''

''And what, ultimately, was your conclusion?''

''I concluded that it was—a matter for the Church.''

''And not for psychiatry? Why not?''

''After thoroughly investigating her condition, I felt its origins were so deeply rooted in—in religious mania, that she could only benefit from—certain prescribed rites of the Church.''

''Which rites?''

''The—*Rituale Romanum*.''

''In English?''

''The Roman Ritual—the rites of exorcism.''

''Did you, in fact, believe that psychiatry was of no use in her case because she was possessed by the devil or demons from hell?''

''I never believed any such thing! As I've said, in stubborn cases of religious mania manifested as psychotic behavior, I've found that religion itself, properly administered, is the best healer.''

''Hair of the dog?'' Edith suggested, with a lean smile. ''Thank you, Dr. Shea. This has been very illuminating. No more questions.''

Tommie Harkrider decided that Edith had not done much damage to the psychiatrist's firm position that Richard Devon was not mentally ill. He passed up the redirect and said portentously, ''Your Honor, the state rests.''

99

As it was ten minutes to two in the afternoon, Edith requested a recess until the following day, preferring to give the members of the jury a chance to think about her line of defense, which she had just previewed for them.

"How did you know Shea had seen a case of demonic possession in his practice?" Adam asked the former Queen's Counsel after they had left the courthouse and run the gauntlet of photographers and TV news correspondents waiting on the lawn.

"But I had no such information," Edith replied blithely. "I went fishing."

Lindsay nearly steered the car into a rock wall by the side of the road.

"Edith," she scolded. Edith attempted but couldn't manage a contrite look.

"One must sometimes trust one's instincts, and seize the moment. It was rational to assume that Dr. Shea, a devout Catholic who had practiced his profession for some twenty-one years, had many times been asked to treat disturbed individuals within the Church. He practices in one of the largest dioceses on earth. The incidence of priests and nuns afflicted with *feelings* of persecution by the devil is higher than you might expect. There have been rare, authenticated cases of possession as well. Cloisters and monasteries are hotbeds of neuroses. The veil and the cloth do not disguise the fact that they are all human beings. Remember this: God permits the existence of the shadow in order that it may intensify the purity of the light. He has created both; they are inseparable. Each is necessary, and each is incomprehensible without the other. But to live with a knowledge of the shadow so close, so everlastingly close, can become a test of will that, unfortunately, results in casualties of the mind and spirit."

100

During the selection of the jury and through the first days of the trial small groups of religious people had peaceably gathered on the spacious Chadbury village green opposite the district courthouse. They represented long-established churches with millions of members, and churches that consisted of a few rows of folding chairs in the basement recreation room of their founders. They all wanted to see Richard Devon go to jail forever. For the most part they kept silent vigils, read their Bibles, lighted candles toward nightfall, unfurled banners which revealed Christ bleeding for our sins, and wore placards with biblical quotations badly printed on them. They were not allowed to display anything that might be interpreted as an attempt to persuade the hearts and minds of the jury, like one confiscated poster that had proclaimed RICHARD DEVON WILL BRING US HELL ON EARTH. All but official traffic was banned in in front of and behind the courthouse, to lessen the danger that someone might actually attempt to carry out one of the numerous daily threats to car-bomb the proceedings. Police Chief Jim Melka had established a bullpen for the many representatives of the media who couldn't get into the courtroom, which restricted their activities most of the time. He was enforcing, in cooperation with Captain Moorman of the state police, a temporary ordinance prohibiting more than four people at a time from gathering on the streets of Chadbury from sunset to sunrise. Moorman had asked for additional troopers and police cars from other parts of the state, and these were prominently displayed at every intersection and on the several roads leading into town. Rottweilers and Dobermans were paraded on short leashes.

All of this latent power on view didn't discourage nineteen members of the Church of Satan the Revealed Messiah from trying to set up shop on the green the morning the defense was to begin presenting its case.

Their leader, Lord Mongo, provided just that dash of eccentricity and flamboyant menace the press had been needing for an exaggerated but colorful illustration of the dark side of the trial in progress. Mongo was six and a half feet tall, of indeterminate age, very thin, with a shaved head and a long waxed beard, the sharp point of which ended at his breastbone, on which was tattooed a circle containing an emblem of the devil. Naked to the waist, he wore black silk pants and black patent leather boots and a cape that was decorated with talismans of evil. One of his necklaces was composed of tiny replicas of human skulls. On his long fingers he wore a number of gold rings with moody-looking stones in them. His fingernails were long and painted jet black. He had the numbers 666 branded on each cheekbone. He smelled as if he had gone unwashed for at least a couple of weeks.

Mongo's dark eyes had a baleful glow reflected in dozens of camera lenses pointed his way.

"We are here to support our brother in darkness, so unjustly accused."

"Do you mean Richard Devon?"

Mongo bowed in a sinister way, his eyes half closing. "Richard," he confirmed, as if it was necessary. "Beloved of our Most Holy Prince."

Someone shouted, "What do you mean, unjustly accused? Do you have evidence that Richard Devon didn't murder Karyn Vale?"

Mongo raised his head and glared, but was pacified by the constant whirring of motor-driven camera shutters.

"She was *not* murdered. The girl was a most willing and joyous sacrifice to him we serve, the coming messiah, our master Satan."

It was as far as he got; the state police converged from all directions before a group of outraged Seventh Day Adventists nearby began to throw the clods of flowerbed dirt they had been picking up. Sirens. Dogs. Screams. There was a melee, gleefully filmed by the cameramen present, but it was bloodless. The smirking and satisfied satanists had no desire for violence. They were driven safely away in police vans, but not before the members of the jury had passed by on their way into the courthouse.

Before the defense called its first witness Judge Winford felt obliged to instruct the jury to ignore what they may have seen, and the coverage that would be all over the television news programs that night. He did not make a particularly strong impression on them.

"Just what we needed to start off our day," Adam said unhappily at the defense table.

"Never mind," Edith told him. "They were poseurs, lunatic cultists, and any intelligent person could see that. They know less of the true nature of evil than children who play with matches know of hellfire."

Edith inclined her head to look past Adam and Lindsay

at Richard, who sat at the far end of the table. He was instantly aware of her scrutiny, but didn't look around.

"And how are you this morning?" Edith said. His reply was the faintest of smiles. Lately she had sensed that there was less of Rich in the courtroom, and more of Zarach'; she felt a sharpness at the breastbone and then at the nape of her neck, a probing that had her on guard.

And will you let him speak? she wondered. What Rich would have to say was the key to her successful defense; quite possibly, it would mean her downfall as well.

"Anything wrong, Edith?" Lindsay asked.

Edith smiled and shook her head slightly, wishing she could reveal to her cocounsel what she knew was about to take place, with the introduction of her first witness.

My dear Lindsay. There are two prime antagonistic forces at work in this courtroom, representing right and wrong, the great dual law: the duad. *It is the secret of life; to reveal that secret, which is embodied in the myth of the tree of knowledge in Genesis, means death. And only in death may these supreme forces be finally reconciled.*

She looked, as she so often did, at the faces of the jurors, the twelve. *Twelve.* Another ritual number. The twelve primal fears of man, she thought idly. The fears of water, fire, air, earth, and on to the most agonizing fear of all: of death and punishment, the rejection by God. The soul lost forever. Each face suddenly had new meaning for her, because now she sensed where the full force of Zarach's attack was going to go. In the fourth seat of the first row was Ivan Mandelko, a small bearded man, intense and earnest, who owned a nursery business. He was the émigré son of a Russian who had died during the Stalinist purges. Would Zarach' go first to Ivan, or would he choose—

"Is the defense ready to proceed?"

Edith rose and stepped out from behind the table. "Thank you, Your Honor. We are ready."

"You may call your first witness."

"The defense calls Conor Devon."

101

Edith spent a great deal of time that morning, through her questions and his answers, giving the members of the jury full knowledge of the man who was going to spend most of the rest of the day testifying; his initial testimony was extremely important. When she was fully satisfied that the jurors had accepted Conor as a man of strict conscience and honesty, she began the substantive questioning.

"Mr. Devon, will you tell us when you first learned that your brother Richard had been arrested for the murder of Karyn Vale?"

From there she led him, slowly, to an account of his first meeting with Rich at the county jail, his shock and feelings of terror. Conor's tears flowed freely and he shuddered as he recalled Rich's words.

"He said, 'You're a priest, Conor. You can help me, can't you? Get him out of me! Before he makes me do . . . something terrible again.' "

At the defense table Rich scuffed his shoes together and wetted his lips, giving his brother swift, darting looks, as if he himself doubted what Conor was relating.

"Can you tell us if the police have ever interrogated any of the people Rich named during your conversation with him?"

"No, they have not."

"Why not?"

"Because—Henry Windross was killed by a train a few days later. Polly Windross disappeared. And—no trace has ever been found of Inez Cordway."

"Did you believe your brother when he insisted he had been possessed by a demon?"

"No, I did not."

"Why not, sir?"

"I didn't really believe—that kind of thing could happen."

"You did not believe in the possibility of the devil or demons possessing another human being?"

452

"In seminary I took an elective course in demonology, but I—I suppose I never wanted to think too deeply about it."

"Subsequently you became a priest. Did you ever see a case of demonic possession?"

"No, and I never met a priest who had either. It just wasn't something we talked about."

"What happened, sir, to change your belief?"

Conor described his brother's persistently bizarre behavior during subsequent meetings, his own nagging doubts that had led him to consult Monsignor Garen and, finally, the shelves of the Boston Public Library. Which inspired his experiment with the gold cross in the interview room not far away from where the court was in session. He told that story calmly, and in great detail. Lindsay Potter rubbed her forehead where a hairline scar remained from the cut she had received.

"If it please the court," Edith said, "I would like to have Mr. Devon step down and approach the jury box so that the jurors may see for themselves the scars which were caused by the melting of the gold cross which he had in his hand on the morning in question."

Judge Winford granted permission and Conor passed self-consciously with Edith at his side the length of the box, holding out his left hand, palm up. Tommy Harkrider sat with his arms folded studying Conor closely; Gary Cleves scribbled a note on his yellow legal pad, which he pushed toward Tommie. The note said, "Feb.—radiator on"; Gary then pulled a three-dimensional sketch of the interview room from a folder. But Tommie already knew what his rebuttal would be. Nothing Conor had said so far bothered him in the slightest. At this point in the trial Tommie's comfort level was very high.

As she was returning to the witness stand with Conor, Edith glanced at the forelady of the jury, Mary Adelaide Hotchkiss, who seemed less bright-eyed and attentive than she usually was. She had a hand at the base of her throat, massaging gently. Her eyes were not on Conor.

She was staring at Rich. The look on her face could only be described as haunted.

Edith stopped squarely in Mary Adelaide's line of sight and turned toward the defense table. *So you've begun. But it is Richard Devon who I will put on the witness stand. And not Zarach' Bal-Tagh. You will not be allowed to terrorize these people.*

The defendant turned his head aside, blinking, looking a little bored.

102

It was close to four thirty by the time Conor had completed his second, harrowing account of manifestation which he had witnessed in the company of Adam and Father Merlo in the basement room of the courthouse. His long testimony, Edith realized, had been too heavy a dose for the jurors to swallow; the dose had very nearly turned into a doze despite their best efforts to be alert. She was tired herself, and inclined to be irritable. Few of the jurors would sleep well tonight, weighted as they were with too much difficult information, with skepticism and the anxiety to be, above all, reasonable. Thus in the morning they would all look hopefully to Tommie Harkrider to establish for them in his cross-examination that Conor—a demonstrably *good* man, a former priest—had suffered deeply on behalf of his brother, and in his suffering had, innocently enough, deluded himself.

Edith had worked hard, she could not have done a better job of presenting Conor to the jury. But she had decisively lost the day.

103

Mary Adelaide Hotchkiss was one juror who did not give much thought to what Conor had been telling them. For most of the day she had not listened very closely, although she tried to maintain an appearance of alertness; it had been an ordeal for her. And that night she couldn't close her eyes for long as she tried to make herself comfortable on the lumpy bed in her room at the inn where the jury was sequestered. She was too engrossed in reliving the horror of having been a spectator at her own death.

For relaxation Mary Adelaide and her husband Andy liked to shoot whitewater rapids in small rubber rafts or narrow, fragile boats called kayaks in which there was room, barely, for one person. They belonged to a club that made weekend trips in the spring to nearby rivers swollen by the waters of melting snow.

In her vision, or whatever it was she had suddenly switched on to in the courtroom, she had seen herself clearly, wearing her prescription goggles and paddling furiously as her kayak leaped and skimmed through a shallow twisting gorge, spray dashing high above her head, wet black rocks looming all around. In this place she had split seconds to make hairsbreadth calculations, but what it came down to was instinct and experience, with a sizable luck factor involved. And her luck simply had run out. Her kayak, tossed end over end like a matchstick, had become wedged between two boulders by the pressure of the water pouring through a bottleneck, and she was trapped, upside down, in four feet of water. All of this she had perceived in a flash as she sat in the courtroom looking at the defendant, who had looked back at her for a few seconds. And more: she could feel her scalded throat open, the impact of cold water rushing into her lungs.

Hours later she wept, and thereafter was successful in blocking out the specific, oppressive sensations of death by drowning. She knew very well she didn't ever have to take that kayak down from its rack in the garage if she didn't choose to do so. And she *wanted* to live. But something dreary diluted this conviction, a thinness of spirit resulted. There was no responsive joy at the thought of her children. Because something had been stolen from her in the courtroom: it was a theft of light, a little of the light from one soul. Mary Adelaide didn't even know she was missing it, this too-small-to-measure portion of the larger light that had always served to keep the unimaginable, the hunters of the Endless Night, at bay. But because it wasn't there any longer the dark was just a little closer, a little more threatening than it had been before.

104

"Now, Mr. Devon, when you thought you saw—"

"Objection, Your Honor! Mr. Devon has described faithfully to us what in fact he *did* see take place in the interview room on the morning of February fourth, and I object to the prosecution's attempt to cast doubt on the accuracy of his perceptions, or his memory."

"Sustained."

"Mr. Devon, when you saw what appeared to be—"

"I *object,* Your Honor!"

The wrangling over Tommie Harkrider's cross-examination became so heated that Judge Winford called both barristers to the side bar to try to straighten out their fundamental disagreement before any more bad blood could taint the proceedings.

"Your Honor," Tommie said, his cheeks flushed to the whites of his eyes, "I'm not sure of just how it's done in the Old Bailey, but I do know in an American court of law I have every right to contest the accuracy of the witness's memory, particularly in light of recent research that has cast considerable doubt on whether a man's memory has any more permanence than a baby tooth. It is a well-known fact that in a stressful situation eyewitness accounts of an event can and do differ widely—that a witness's 'memory' of such an event may consist of facts from unrelated experiences, of totally fictional material provided by the unconscious mind to fill gaps in the story, and of conscious lies. What I'm looking for are obvious contradictions that I have reason to believe will invalidate a large part of Mr. Devon's testimony."

"Okay," Winford said. "If you have reason to believe

there are contradictions, then you may establish them, but through the witness's conflicting testimony and not by implying there *is* a conflict even before you ask the question.''

"None of these 'well-known facts' regarding memory that Mr. Harkrider has referred to have been established in this courtroom by expert testimony, and it would not please me to have him try to establish them at the expense of Mr. Devon.''

"Oh, I don't need to do that, Edith. The witness is my expert on the fallibility of memory, and he's about to demonstrate it very conclusively.''

Edith smiled dubiously; the look on Tommie's face was that of an old alley cat with bird feathers leaking down his chin.

The prosecutor labored at Conor for more than three hours. Conor proved equal to the demands Tommie made on him, tripping up only in his inability to remember just where the radiator was located in the interview room. It was beneath the window, and not on the opposite wall where he had placed it. He was also forced to admit that at some time during the confusion and turmoil in the room his burned hand might have come in contact with an exposed—and scalding—pipe near floor level. But he still insisted the partly melted cross, which the jury had viewed the day before, had caused his injuries.

When Conor was finally allowed to stand down, most of the jurors looked at him in sympathy, and perhaps with respect. No one at the defense table detected any hostility, but Lindsay leaned toward Edith and said, "Mr. Aughtman doesn't look so good, Edith.''

Edith glanced at the juror in question and immediately asked permission to approach the bench. She called Winford's attention to Gerald Aughtman, who sat in the third seat of the second row. He was a forty-year-old car salesman from Cheswick whose only serious flaw as a juror had been his abominable taste in neckties. He looked pale and uncomfortable and had been rubbing the back of his neck. Winford immediately declared a fifteen-minute recess.

"I'm fine," Aughtman told the judge. "Just—something came over me, I don't know what.'' He smiled, and looked like a man who is smiling to deny an urge to scream instead. Winford let him lie down for a few minutes in chambers.

Edith strolled around the emptied courtroom as if her mind was on her next witness, but she was concentrating on Rich. He had remained seated at the defense table. He was drinking a Coke from a paper cup. A bailiff stood nearby, keeping an eye on him. Rich was aware of the attention from Edith, but he didn't acknowledge her. He had quite a collection of tidy little baskets woven from strips of yellow paper on the table in front of him.

A basket for a soul, she thought. The looks on the faces of two of the jurors that morning—Mary Adelaide Hotchkiss and now Gerald Aughtman—had convinced her beyond a doubt. Zarach' was preparing a conduit through which all of hell would flow into the courtroom before long. It was a direct challenge to her and the power she represented.

She touched the small sundial she wore just below the notch of her throat and bowed her head for a moment. She heard, in the back of her mind, a snarl like that of a maddened wolf. The defendant put his Coke aside and reached for a fresh pad of legal paper. He began deliberately to turn its pages into more neat strips.

105

After his brief rest in the judge's chambers Mr. Aughtman was able to resume his duties, but he was still shaken, unable to forget an extraordinarily clear vision of being slowly sucked into a whirlpool of hot, choking desert sand. Asthmatic as a child, he had always been in terror of not being able to breathe. He jogged almost every day to improve his lung capacity, and was an ardent nonsmoker. When he returned to his seat in the jury box and looked quickly at the defendant, he felt his throat tighten and his lungs compress into chunks of hot coals; thereafter he avoided looking anywhere but at the witness stand. He tried to shut the trial out of his mind, concentrating instead on his lengthy client list—over three hundred names, addresses, and telephone numbers filed neatly in memory—and the sales of the new models he hoped to make in the first quarter. But he just couldn't feel the old enthusiasm, the anticipation. Maybe the new models were lemons. Maybe the uptrend in sales wasn't going to continue. Maybe he wouldn't be able to keep up his alimony payments to Hilda. Maybe, just maybe, life didn't mean a hell of a lot anymore.

The defense called Father James Merlo.

Edith had an outstanding witness in Merlo. He was testifying with the full approval of his superiors in the Vatican, testimony in itself of how seriously they regarded this trial.

"Father Merlo, you are an exorcist for the Catholic Church, is that correct?"

"Yes, it is."

"And what does it mean to be an exorcist, to 'exorcise'?"

"By the use of certain ritual words, phrases, and ceremonies, to bind the devil and evil spirits to strict obedience to the will of God."

"When one hears of the rites of exorcism, of an exorcism that has been performed, it seems as if there is always a Roman Catholic priest involved. Is exorcism a phenomenon relating only to Catholics and their Church?"

"No. Exorcism, and the trade of the exorcist, has existed probably since man first became aware of the influence of evil spirits. There were exorcists in ancient Greece and they are referred to in both the Old and the New Testament, among other references Acts 19. Solomon was an exorcist. All major religions today practice exorcism in one form or another."

"How many exorcisms have you participated in, Father Merlo?"

"More than a hundred."

"In all cases demonic possession or infestation was involved?"

"Yes."

"Could you explain to us, please, just what is meant by 'demonic possession'?"

Merlo explained with care the circumstances through

which the demonic spirits were licensed and, in most cases, obligated to plague human beings.

"Is there any such thing as a 'typical' case of possession?"

"Whenever a devil or a demon has established dominion over a human soul, his presence is announced by physical disturbances within the environment of the individual who is possessed. These include foul odors, loud noises, destructive activity, inexplicable and frightening occurrences that symbolize the presence of evil. Animals behave erratically in the presence of the possessed; they run away. Entire houses have been torn to pieces by the actions of the possessor. There can be gross deformities of the body, but not always. However there is a look of depravity, a maniacal intensity in the eyes that, once seen, isn't easily forgotten. The possessed can, and does, demonstrate incredible strength. Once the rites of exorcism have begun, some or all of these phenomena may recur, so repetitively and with such violence that the body of the possessed may be distorted almost beyond recognition."

"Thank you, Father Merlo. Will you tell us now, please, what you observed when you met the defendant, Richard Devon, for the first time on the morning of February twenty-third?"

Merlo told them, leaving out no detail, however repugnant. He substituted "excrement" for "shit," but otherwise he made no effort to spare anyone's sensibilities.

Although the priest was doing the talking, Richard Devon was, again, the center of attention in the courtroom. He looked introspective and a little glum. He met no one's eyes, but there was nothing abnormal about his own eyes, no unholy light shining redly from the pupils. He didn't rave, fart, belch, or drool. It simply wasn't possible to relate him to the horrors Merlo recited.

Edith seemed blissfully unaware of this.

"In your expert opinion, Father Merlo, was all of the phenomena that you, Mr. Conor Devon, and Mr. Kurland observed an indication of demonic possession?"

"A very clear indication, yes."

"Did this demon or devil identify himself to you when called upon to do so?"

"Yes. He said, 'I am Zarach' Bal-Tagh.' The name means Son of the Endless Night in a dialect of Hittite, which is the oldest recorded Indo-European language. The Hittite people had a civilization that rivaled Egypt and the most powerful kingdoms of Mesopotamia in the fourteenth and thirteenth centuries before Christ. So you can see that conflict between man and demons goes far back into history.''

"In your experience as an exorcist, had you ever encountered this particular devil named Zarach'?''

"No. The number of inhuman spirits is close to infinite. And not all of them have names.''

"But you had heard of Zarach' Bal-Tagh?''

Tommie Harkrider shifted restlessly in his chair at the prosecution's table and said in a voice so low only Gary Cleves could hear, "Oh, baloney. Baloney, baloney, baloney. That's a translation from the modern vernacular of trial lawyers, and it means 'Don't shit me.' ''

"Yes,'' Merlo said, in response to Edith's question. "The Church has known about him for more than ten centuries.''

Tommie was so eager to begin his cross-examination of the priest that he almost bounded up to the stand when Edith was finished.

"Father Merlo, did the jail guards who brought the accused to the basement room of the courthouse remain in the room long enough to witness any of the phenomena you've described to us?''

"No, sir, they were waiting outside.''

"Do you happen to know how far outside? Did they go down the corridor to have a smoke?''

"I believe they waited just outside the door.''

"And when you spoke to the, ah, this Zarach', in what tone of voice did you address him? A normal, conversational tone?''

"No, I spoke more firmly than that.''

"And more loudly? LOUDER THAN I'M SPEAKING TO YOU NOW?''

"A little louder, perhaps.''

"Would you speak to us now in the same tone of voice you used when speaking to Zarach'? Would you mind repeating exactly what you said to him?''

"I'm sorry; I can't do that.''

"Do you mean you don't remember just what it was you said?''

"What I mean is, the words I spoke at the time were part of a religious ritual which I am bound by the regulations of my office not to repeat without observing all forms of the ritual. There could be some harm in it."

"All right, Father Merlo. Now tell me, did you get an answer out of Mr. Zarach'—"

"Objection, Your Honor. The reference is plainly sarcastic and unnecessary."

"Sustained. Mr. Harkrider—"

"Yes, sir. All right, Your Honor. We'll just call him, or it—if I may be so presumptuous as to assume inhuman spirits are not classifiable by gender—Zarach'. The question is this, Father Merlo: did Zarach' reply to your request to identify himself promptly, or did you have to hassle him to get that information?"

Merlo smiled. "I had to hassle him."

"Was he giving you an argument, calling you names?"

"Yes, he was."

"Things got pretty lively in there, and you had to really get tough with him, shout him down I presume?"

"I wasn't quite shouting."

"And when he answered you, how did he sound?" Tommie dropped his voice to a whisper. "Like this?"

"He was much more forceful."

"WELL THEN DID HE BELLOW LIKE THIS, SO YOU COULD HEAR HIM ACROSS THE CHADBURY GREEN?"

"Something like that."

Tommie dropped his voice to a more reasonable level. "And while this argument was going on, there was a whole lot else going on at the same time. That room must have looked and smelled terrible. There were, we are told, dungheaps on the floor. I hope I'm saying it with sufficient delicacy, but I think we all know what I mean. Would you say you were engaged at that point in an all-out struggle, a contest of wills with Zarach'?"

"Yes."

"And you won?"

"I was able to control the manifestation."

"Through the power of your ritual?"

"Yes."

"Did you, in fact, exorcise the demon of Zarach' from the body of Richard Devon?"

"I made no attempt to do that."

"*What*?" Tommie said, astounded. He turned and gazed in dismay at the defendant before slowly giving the priest his attention again. "Father Merlo . . . you mean to say that when you finally finished with your—your epic encounter in that basement room, and the door was opened and the guards came in to take the prisoner back to his cell, Richard Devon"—Tommie pitched his voice to a theatrical whisper—"still had the devil in him?"

"No aspect of the possession had been altered."

"Why, those poor guards must have taken one look and run away in terror! Screaming! Overcome by the stenches of evil and corruption, by the gross disfigurement of Mr. Devon's body! Is that in fact what happened?"

"No, sir. By the time they came in, all of the fecal matter and other organic substances produced during the manifestation had dematerialized."

"Do you mean *vanished*? Into thin air?"

"Vanished is correct. This is quite common. As I was saying, Mr. Devon was lying unconscious on the floor, without his straitjacket. The physical distortions, particularly of his facial features, were no longer evident."

"What you are telling me, Father Merlo, is that everything occurring in that room went unobserved and unremarked by the guards, despite the fact that they were just outside while all the bellowing and caterwauling was going on; that the whole remarkable series of events seems to have been presented strictly for the benefit of, shall we say, those initiated into the mysteries of 'demonic possession': or in other words, true believers?"

Merlo said wryly, "I doubt if you could have counted Mr. Kurland among the true believers at that time; but you'll have to ask him."

"I don't want to ask Mr. Kurland anything." Harkrider turned from the witness stand to the bench. "Your Honor, if it please the court, may we have the defendant rise and stand for a few moments, just where he is, so we can all see him better?"

Knox Winford considered the request and glanced at Edith, who said nothing. "The defendant will please rise."

Lindsay Potter had to speak to Richard before he stirred himself and, reluctantly, stood up. One of his meticulously constructed paper baskets—he had made several of them so far—fell off the table to his feet. He made a motion as if to retrieve it and then straightened self-consciously, hands at his sides, avoiding eye contact with anyone, his stance that of the shunned.

"Thank you, Your Honor." Tommie again approached the witness.

"Father Merlo, if you were unable to exorcise Zarach' from the body of Richard Devon on the day in question, *which was nearly four months ago,* what then do you think has become of Zarach'? Did he leave voluntarily?"

"No. Once an inhuman spirit is in possession of a human being, he will never leave until, through the intervention and authority of an exorcist, he is compelled to do so."

"Then—then what you are telling us is that the defendant, the very same Richard Devon who is standing there—is still possessed by this demonic spirit?"

"That is my belief, yes."

"Have you personally, in all your wide experience as an exorcist, seen a case where the possessing devil, once he was in charge, just seemed to get bored with it all and departed without a word or a sign to anyone?"

"No. I have not."

"But, Father: what about all these gruesome, frightening things we're supposed to see? The distorted, brutish features, the inhuman glare of hate in his eyes? I don't see any of those things when I look at the defendant, do you? He appears to have behaved with decorum during this trial. Where is *any trace whatsoever* of this loathsome demon from whom we should all be cowering in fear?"

Merlo had known this was coming from the moment he had taken the stand. He smiled gently and said, "The phenomena you've described are not constants in cases of demonic possession."

Tommie Harkrider waved a hand in Rich's direction. "Father Merlo, if, as we have rather painstakingly established, there are *observable phenomena*—or let's call them laws—peculiar to the condition known as demonic possession, then do these laws not apply in the case of Richard Devon?"

"Zarach' is not your ordinary—"

"Please answer the question: yes or no."

"Yes. The laws apply."

"Then where is Zarach'?"

The priest's eyes changed focus, he flinched slightly as if he were seeing, deeply, something abhorrent, a roaring sewer diverted through the courtroom yet cheating the surface of their dimension; on his high forehead a maroon vein rose and thrashed at the edge of his gray skullcap. Then Merlo flexed his long fingers, effecting control over himself; he gazed above the heads of the spectators and was still.

"I can assure you he's here," Merlo said reluctantly.

"There?" This time Tommie jabbed a finger sharply at the hapless defendant.

"In the courtroom," Merlo amended.

Tommie made a slow full circle on his sore feet in front of the witness stand, looking high and low, mouth open in wonderment.

"But where? Is he up there with Judge Winford? Is he hiding behind the flag of these United States? Is he sitting like a june bug on that windowsill over there? I really wish you'd help me out, Father Merlo—how do you know, for a certainty, that Zarach' is with us today?"

"Through the power of discernment."

"A power which the rest of us, regrettably, are lacking."

"Perhaps not all of us."

Tommie just shook his head wearily and walked toward the defendant. Halfway to Rich he seemed to change his mind about something. He gestured for the defendant to take his seat again, and approached the jury box.

"Just one small sign," he said. "Any indication at all that us lesser mortals can grasp, so that we know the—the *laws of possession* are in force here—is that asking too much?" The prosecutor threw up his hands in despair. "There is a question we all want an answer to," he said, as if he had appointed himself the thirteenth juror. "But it is a question that has no answer; that in truth cannot be answered. Because, Father Merlo, I submit there is not, and *never was,* a creation known as Zarach' Bal-Tagh!"

"Objection, Your Honor!" Edith said peevishly. "We are not into summation here."

"Sustained. Mr. Harkrider, do you have further questions for this witness?"

"No further questions, Your Honor. Thank you."

106

Tommie was determined not to let the next witness for the defense be sworn in. As soon as her name was called, the prosecutor was up, asking for a meeting of counsel with the judge at the side bar.

"Your Honor, I fail to see what connection Sigrid Torgeson has with the case being tried! She was not even in this country at the time of the murder, and she has never met the defendant."

Edith said, "Miss Torgeson's ordeal as a victim of possession is well documented. We require her testimony as further validation of the phenomenon of demonic possession."

"The issue here is whether or not Richard Devon was demonically possessed when he committed the murder! Nothing Miss Torgeson may have to say could possibly be considered relevant to that issue, Your Honor. And how many supposed victims of possession must we listen to while counsel for the defense continues to stall in her attempt to avoid putting her key witness on the stand? Miss Torgeson may look terrific on the seven o'clock news, but it's only the testimony of Richard Devon that matters now. I respectfully request a ruling on this, Your Honor."

It was already a little after four in the afternoon. Winford said, "Since it's getting late in the day I think we'll adjourn, and I'll have a ruling on Sigrid Torgeson in the morning. Mr. Harkrider, you may enter your motion for dismissal of this witness for the record."

107

Edith had continued to fast and meditate; she was getting by on four hours of sleep a night but didn't seem to be any the worse for it. Having Sigrid there, however briefly, and having a full report on Philip's condition—which had not worsened appreciably—gave her strength.

Although she was taking only fruit and vegetable juices, Edith didn't find it objectionable to accompany others to dinner.

"Do you think she'll be allowed to testify?" Conor asked Edith as he cut into a rare T-bone steak. Sigrid, not a meat eater, was making a salad for herself and attracting nearly as much attention as a film star in the restaurant.

"There is almost no chance of that. Tommie was quite correct in his objection; I would have done the same in his place."

"Seems like she made a long trip over for nothing," Conor said, glancing up as Sigrid made her way back to their table with her salad.

"Not at all; I needed her here at this time." She smiled at Sigrid as the girl sat down.

"What other witnesses can you call?" Sigrid asked.

"Maggie Renquist; Lindsay Potter. Perhaps Benny Childs, to testify as to Rich's sudden interest in demonology just before the murder occurred. None of their testimony will be of great help, but it will use up time; a day and a half, perhaps two days."

"What are you waiting for?" Conor asked Edith, looking at a piece of steak on the end of his fork. Sigrid looked at it, too, with faint disapproval. Conor put his fork down; his appetite wasn't what he had thought it would be.

"She's waiting for another juror to go down," Sigrid offered, with a glance at Edith.

"I don't understand."

"Zarach' has placed two of the jurors under psychic

467

attack; there will be others," Edith said. "But one more will be enough for our purposes."

"What purpose? What are you going to do?"

"Three jurors are needed to complete the *tetrad*," Sigrid explained.

"What is that?"

"The tetrad is the Trinity, plus one to make four, because unity is required to explain the doctrine of the Trinity, which is three persons in God."

"I know what the Trinity signifies, but—"

"Four is also the perfect number; it is the source of all numerical combinations. In nearly all the ancient languages the name of God had four letters. According to the lore of the cabalists, the personification of evil was God spelled backwards, meaning that evil is merely the shadow or reflection of good. Goodness loses its meaning if there is no opposite in nature. Are you still confused?"

"I don't know what the tetrad has to do with Rich being guilty or innocent."

"The tetrad," Edith told him, "may be the only way in which his guiltlessness can be revealed. But for the purity of the light of the tetrad to prevail, the shadow must first be seen. I wonder how many of us are prepared to survive that experience."

"What if you don't put him on the stand, Edith?" Conor said, after a long silence.

"Then the trial has been for nothing. And Zarach' will own his soul. Permanently."

108

Conor said on the phone to Gina that night, "So Rich has to take the stand. It's just about our last hope of convincing the jury."

"When will that be?"

"Probably the day after tomorrow."

"I'm coming," she said.

"Gina—I don't know; maybe that's not such a good idea. I'm afraid—"

"Afraid of what? Conor, he needs all of us now. All of our support and prayers. I'm going to be there."

109

"Martin," Tommie Harkrider said to his former client Martin Vale, after watching him finish off a fourth vodka and tonic in just under three minutes, "I'm going to throw caution to the winds at this point and predict the outcome of a trial, which is something I *never* do. The fact is, I just don't see how we can lose."

"How much time will he serve?" Martin Vale mumbled. "How many years for the years my daughter had coming to her? Is that a prediction you'd care to make?"

Tommie reached out and put a hand on the smaller man's shoulder. "I just don't know. But I can tell you we'll be asking the maximum."

"Whatever he gets, it won't be enough."

"Martin, as a sympathetic friend, I'd urge you to spare yourself and Louise by skipping the rest of the trial. I see you sitting there, day after day, and I know how it's eating you up."

Martin Vale's chin bunched and there were tears in his eyes. "Eating me up," he acknowledged. He licked a last drop from the inside rim of his glass. Tommie tightened his grip a little on Martin's shoulder. It was past midnight. They were sitting on the screened porch of the luxurious summer home which the Vales had rented for the duration of the trial. Ceiling fans with varnished wooden paddles cooled the air around them. Moths prostrated themselves on screenwire, magnetized by distant lamplight.

"Why don't you go on up and try to get some sleep?" Tommie advised. "I'll let myself out."

But long after he had gone Martin Vale continued to sit on the porch, moping on wicker, down to one lamp, down to an ounce of vodka in the bottle he had opened a few hours ago.

There were creatures in the dark, nightsingers. The track of the moon lay fernlike on the surface of the nearby lake. The moths on the screen in front of him had rearranged themselves subtly into an image that at first was as dim and shadowy as the face of Christ on the shroud of Turin. The last ounce of vodka, taken neat, helped to clarify what he was seeing. Karyn, pale but full-blown. The moon shining through her silent form except where the two dark ellipses of her eyes gazed steadfastly into his heart. Those eyes judged him. As a father. As a man.

The little Smith and Wesson Bodyguard Airweight revolver which Martin Vale held in his right hand weighed only fourteen and a half ounces. When loaded with the five .38 Special cartridges which he held in his left hand, it would weigh a little more.

He loaded it, and put out the last light. The image of Karyn on the screen faded gradually to a bearable distance from his mind. He fell asleep on the porch, the revolver in his hand.

110

As she had said she would do, Edith stalled for time. Sigrid was on her way back to Heraclio. Until she got there, Edith knew she couldn't put Rich on the stand.

Tommie lost his temper twice over the time she was taking to question Benny Childs on matters of theology that seemed to have been of interest to the defendant before the murder. Tommie argued with Winford, and he argued with Edith.

"All I want to know, and a simple yes or no will do, is: do you intend to call Richard Devon?" When Edith wouldn't answer him he appealed to the judge. "Because I fail to understand, Your Honor, how the information gleaned thus far from the memory of Mr. Childs has been worth three hours of our time."

Tommie lost his argument and was forced to sit through another forty-five minutes of Edith's painstaking interrogation of the witness before she turned Benny Childs over to him. By then it was four thirty-five in the afternoon; there was an air of torpor in the courtroom.

"No questions!" Tommie snapped.

The trial was adjourned for the day.

111

At noon on the following day on the island of Heraclio nearly two hundred people, Sigrid among them, gathered in the plaza around the bronze sundial. At that moment of the day when there was not a trace of a shadow on the face of the sundial, the members of the society linked hands and began the prayers that would continue until the rim of the setting sun was extinguished on the horizon nine hours later.

It was eight o'clock in the morning in Chadbury, Vermont.

112

At six minutes after ten Edith Leighton announced to the court, "The defense calls Richard Devon."

The soporific dullness of the day before had been replaced by a tension that was almost morbid. Edith reacted to this negative charge by shielding herself with a psychic white light. She continued her close appraisal of Rich, begun the moment the bailiffs escorted him into the courtroom through a side door. He looked, more than ever, shackled by chains of guilt as he slumped into his chair at the end of the defense's table. The movements of his hands were tentative; he looked weak around the mouth, his face half wakened, with an unlit pallor despite the flow of sun through the windows. Edith was as fully absorbed as with an immense work of art that was simultaneously an allegory and a conundrum; she might have been studying a medieval tapestry into which one had to delve, to penetrate beyond thick interweavings and layers of meaning to an elusive image of God or His nemesis. There were no clues, yet, as to which personality she would encounter on the witness stand: the hell-bound youth, or the consummate, Infernal Trickster.

What she must do was done; she would not consider the possibility of failure.

From her seat beside her husband in the second row of the courtroom, Gina Devon leaned forward to get a better look at Rich in those moments of silence before he rose from the table to walk to the witness stand. She had to look away quickly, afraid she would cry. She pressed closer to Conor.

"What is that in your hand?" Judge Winford asked from the bench, before the defendant reached the witness stand.

Rich stopped as if he were about to stumble and looked confused; he stared up at the judge.

"I don't—did you say—?"

"I said, you're carrying something in your right hand. Would you tell us what it is?"

Rich lifted his hand. From it dangled little baskets of yellow paper, a chain of them. There were twelve in all.

"These are"—Rich's voice was very low-pitched—"baskets I've been making." They could barely hear him in the jury box ten feet away; behind him, in the spectator's seats, he wasn't audible at all. His lack of volume provoked a stir.

Edith, coming up behind Rich, said, "Why don't I take those? You won't need them while you're testifying."

Rich nodded, holding out the little baskets to her and for a moment she saw far down into his eyes. She felt the drag of those depths despite her shield: the attraction of two small, almost microscopic pips of red.

There you are.

"You keep them; I made them for you," Rich asserted. He smiled, and the two of them were joined by some arc of the sinister, brighter than the day around them. But of the others in the courtroom, only Father James Merlo was aware of it.

Edith looked into one of the linked baskets. It appeared to contain, in fine miniature, the writhing form of the juror named Ivan Mandelko. He was naked and cruelly blemished. His eyes had been put out; their sockets steamed as if the white-tipped irons had only that instant been withdrawn. In places his skin and flesh hung in strips and tatters from his bones. His genitals had been turned to charred stubs by those same hot irons.

She was just able to suppress an outcry. She looked up and into the eyes of Ivan Mandelko in the jury box. He was dropsical from shock. She couldn't make contact with him.

Edith felt all the baskets sagging slightly in her hand, as if from added weight. She realized what she would see if she looked into any more of them. She did not look. She carried the baskets to the defense table and placed a heavy lawbook on top of them. Then she walked slowly back to the witness stand, a matter of a few steps but a road of infinite hardship to travel against the red fury that was streaming at her from the pupils of the defendant's eyes, an assault against her own light, the strength of her resolve.

And as quickly as it had begun, the onslaught ended. The possessor, confident of his gamesmanship, dealt Rich back to her like a dog-eared trump and withdrew a little distance from the proceedings. Rich sat twisting his hands, his head bowed. He mumbled at the swearing-in, and had to be asked repeatedly to sit closer to the microphone.

Then it was Edith's turn.

"Mr. Devon, will you please tell us when you first met Polly Windross?"

Silence. Rich held his throat and breathed harshly, and Edith wondered, bleakly, if he was going to be allowed to speak at all.

"Mr. Devon, are you all right?" Judge Winford asked from the bench.

Rich continued to massage his throat. He nodded slightly.

Edith said calmly, "Allow me to repeat the question. When did you first meet Polly Windross?"

"It—it was—August—a year ago."

"Are you finding it difficult to speak to me, Mr. Devon?"

"Yes."

"I'm only here to help you. And you *will* be helped. But as I told you in the beginning, you must help yourself too."

Tommie Harkrider slapped a hand on the prosecutor's table and said, "Objection, Your Honor. What is this all about? Can the witness testify, or can't he?"

"I c-c-can testify," Rich got out, twisting and turning his head as if to dislodge an obstruction from his throat. Whatever it was, he swallowed it and was momentarily still.

"Was Karyn Vale with you when you met Polly Windross last year?"

"Yes . . . she was."

"Just take your time," Edith advised. "We have all the time you need, Richard."

With halting slowness, guided by her questions, Rich established the relationship he'd had with Polly. Edith brought him forward in time then, to January, the message left on his answering machine. This tape was introduced as evidence, and the jurors heard the voice of Polly Windross.

"Could call you if I ever needed . . ."

". . . hurting me, I'm afraid . . ."

". . . somebody doesn't stop . . ."

". . . you're the only one . . ."

". . . can trust you . . ."

". . . can trust you . . ."

". . . please come . . ."

Rich's expression, at her first words, underwent many rapid shadings, changes flashing one through another like tinted glass balls in a juggler's deceptively lazy hands: anxiety, fear, anger, pity, mourning. Finally overcome, he listened, unbreathing, with a lowered face that slowly darkened as if he were suffocating. Only the end of the tape relieved him.

"Mr. Devon," Edith said, "is there any doubt that the voice you've just heard is the voice of Polly Windross?"

"No. That's—that was Polly."

"When you arrived with Karyn at the Post Road Inn on the evening of January the eighteenth, were you able to get in touch with Polly right away?"

"I—uh—touched her—so she was real." He began to nod, brows knitted, concentrating on the perplexing matter of Polly until Edith said quickly, "Did you understand my question? Can you—"

"What's real, and what isn't real. That's the crucial question, right? The sad news is, what's real one minute isn't real the next. It depends on the degree of apprehension. Synchronicity is involved, and—and—the light has to be right, among other things—"

"Richard—"

"Well! To answer your question, Polly . . . was . . . *real,* that's as true as I can tell you." He looked up at his counsel, waiting for her to acknowledge his sincerity.

Edith smiled comfortingly. "All right, Richard. Now let's go back. Will you please tell us what happened when upon your arrival you inquired after Polly?"

She was expecting almost anything, but after Rich thought for a few moments, he answered the question in a straightforward manner, with no hint of ellipsis or a gimcracked mind. Prompted by Edith, his voice growing stronger, more confident in his memory, Rich explained all his difficulties in discovering the girl's whereabouts. He told of his climb over the icy roof, his shock at discovering that Polly had been physically abused. Then came the most profound shock of all: when he returned with the police, there was no trace of her in room 331.

With that revelation Rich's spirits sagged, his voice thinned, he lost heart. It was twelve thirty, he'd spent a grueling two hours on the stand with more to come. Judge Winford called a recess for lunch. The defendant was taken away, drank two cups of black coffee but ate nothing, and napped in his cell, breathing through his mouth, the landscape of his upturned face constantly illuminated by bolts and twitches of dream lightning.

The trial resumed at one thirty. By three o'clock the jury had heard every harrowing detail of the dinner party at the Courdewaye house in Ripington Four Corners, and the rite of possession that followed. Rich was laboring by then, his voice nearly gone. Conor, in a sweat bath of sympathy that ruined the shirt he was wearing, chewed his lips raw.

Before her last questions Edith turned and with a glance at the courtroom clock knew that the sun had begun to set in Heraclio, three thousand six hundred miles away, off the coast of Africa. The prayers of the members of the society would be continuing around the sundial.

Nonetheless she felt a need to hurry, to conclude.

"Do you remember leaving the Courdewaye house and driving back to the Davos Chalet Lodge?"

Rich writhed slowly, his gaze wandering. "No, I don't remember."

"Do you remember taking a tire iron from the boot of your car and going in search of Karyn?"

He cried out unintelligibly, but shook his head.

"And do you remember striking her with the tire iron?"

"It wasn't me! I know everybody says I killed her, but it wasn't me!"

Edith asked no more questions. Rich slumped on the witness stand, his head in his hands, groaning almost inaudibly. She looked again at the courtroom clock. It was now three twenty. Tommie Harkrider had risen to begin his cross-examination.

Edith said quickly, "Your Honor, I don't believe the witness is capable of answering many more questions today. I move that we adjourn until the morning, when—"

"Oh, now, wait just a minute!" Tommie protested.

"It *is* getting late in the afternoon, Mr. Harkrider," Judge Winford reminded him.

"But not that late, Your Honor. Now, I don't intend to be longwinded. In fact I can promise"—Tommie also turned and glanced at the clock—"that we'll all be out of here by four fifteen at the latest."

Winford considered this proposal, then looked down at the witness stand.

"Mr. Devon," he said, "I'll leave this up to you. If you're not feeling well enough to continue at this time, we'll adjourn."

Edith waited, gazing at Rich's bowed head, her agitation well concealed. Then the defendant raised his head slowly and looked right at her, and Edith swallowed a nugget of gall, seeing in his eyes the red of sunset, the coming of Endless Night.

"I'll go on," he said, smiling gamely. "Could I just have a drink of water, please?"

Water was brought to him in a glass. He sipped slowly.

More time passed. Tommie was pacing. Edith fingered the small sundial at her throat, and studied the jurors; she paid particular attention to the forelady, Mary Adelaide Hotchkiss, the émigré Mandelko, and Mr. Aughtman, the car dealer with the awful neckties.

"Mr. Devon," Tommie said, "we have heard you describe the evil spirit which ostensibly has possessed you as being a pretty little girl in white stockings, and as some kind of prehistoric-looking winged creature as big as a Cessna 150. And then again as an inhuman spirit who goes by the name of Zarach' Bal-Tagh, whom you haven't said much about: but given that you have been in rather close association with the spirit for the last several months, you must have a very good idea of what he looks like; so would you mind describing him to us?"

"He looks like me," Rich said.

"Does he!"

"Or you. Or"—he searched the rows of spectators—"Gina. Or anybody he wants to look like. Or nothing and nobody."

"What you are trying to say is, he doesn't have a face of his own?

"I didn't say that."

"Let me tell you, sir, I don't appreciate your playing games with me, and I'm sure I can speak for all of us in this courtroom when I say—"

"Objection, Your Honor!"

"Mr. Harkrider—"

"Oh, all right," Tommie said angrily. "Now, Mr. Devon, does this Zarach', who you say possesses you and controls your every thought and action, who presumably has intended for you to answer as you've been answering, does he talk to you?"

"Talk?"

"Talk, yes, *converse,* tell you what he wants you to do at a given time?"

"No. He doesn't have to."

"Well, then, what is it, this controlling mechanism, some kind of thought process? Telepathy? I don't understand it at all. Can you possibly enlighten me?"

"I am he and he is me."

"Is that supposed to imply a symbiotic relationship?"

"No."

"So you want it both ways, is that it? When you don't care to be held accountable for your actions, Zarach' is to blame?"

"Zarach' is not blamable. There is no concept of guilt."

"There is no guilt in the murder of an innocent girl?"

"Only Richard feels guilt."

"Only Richard—" Tommie stopped his pacing and stared at the defendant. "Am I talking to Richard now?"

"Yes."

"And who else am I talking to?"

Silence.

"The witness is directed to answer the question."

"Your Honor, objection!"

Tommie went on, as if no one else had spoken, "Is it possible that I'm talking to the almighty Zarach' we've heard so much about?"

"Tommie, stop!" Edith said chillingly.

The defendant turned his head slowly, vaingloriously, toward her.

"Edithhhhh." It was a dry sound, with faint rustlings of malevolence as of ancient silk stirring in a newly opened tomb.

Seeking to regain the defendant's attention, Tommie Harkrider pressed closer to the witness stand and said in a loud hectoring voice, "Well, I want to talk to you, Zarach'. Because I want to hear the *truth*, and I know damn well I'm not going to hear it from Richard Devon!"

Gavel. "Mr. Harkrider—"

"Edith," said the defendant, growing as giddy as ribtickling Death, "the sun has set. The time is *now*."

"Get away from him, Tommie!" There was a note of despair in her ultimate warning.

Harkrider turned quickly, glaring, offended by her interruption, then thrust his face to within inches of the defendant's. He was like a beast sniffing excitedly the blood pumping from a torn jugular.

"Come out, come out!" he said challengingly. "Come out and talk to me, *Zarach' Bal-Tagh*!"

Tommie stood on his toes, trembling from the force of his righteous contempt, both hands clutching the railing of the witness stand. The defendant was aloof. He had raised his eyes to the courtroom clock. It was three fifty-one in the afternoon. A slight tremor went through him.

And if Tommie Harkrider, or anyone else, could have looked directly into his eyes at that moment, they would have seen the beginnings of a stormy eclipse.

113

In Heraclio, the plaza was now deserted, except for Sigrid Torgeson.

The burnished bronze sundial gleamed in the last rays of the setting sun.

Seabirds wheeled raucously overhead.

There was no wind, but the force issuing from the sundial peeled Sigrid's blond hair back from her temples. Her body, minimally clad in a singlet, was outlined in an aura of scintillating, foaming white light.

114

The clock in the courtroom in Chadbury stopped.

Edith, braced for a taxing denouement, bowed her head.

The courtroom was plunged into hell.

115

At approximately three-fifty that afternoon, the twenty-ninth day of June in Chadbury, Vermont, a plague of insects appeared from out of a fair sky and poured, like ruby red wine from a transparent vessel, onto the courthouse, the small lawn in front and the locust trees that grew there. They covered the sidewalk, the street, and part of the village green. They were a little like horseflies and a little like grasshoppers. From a single thick stream they separated into millions of individuals. They had a high, honed, whining sound in concert that tended to give pain to the eardrums. Dogs, cats, and even birds fled the vicinity.

The insects seemed to prefer crawling to flying. They crawled over everything, not voraciously but with a blanketing, stifling effect, obscuring the outline of the three-story courthouse, covering all the windows, burying the roof inches-deep, and the clock tower. The clock soon stopped, its works gummed by a mass of insects. The sun shining through rosy wings cast a pall over the area. No one was able to go in or out of the courthouse without literally taking a bath in insects. The red bugs didn't bite, but they disintegrated all too easily, giving off a noxious odor and searing human skin with their vital fluids. After a few painful welts had been raised, people kept their distance. It got late.

Entomologists and pest-control experts were sent for. The insects willingly died at the first whiff of toxic chemicals, but the odors of their dying drifting on the evening breeze threatened to make much of the surrounding area uninhabitable. And when the insects died, there seemed to be even more to take their places. Tens of millions of people saw live coverage of the eradication attempts on television, and close-ups of the unidentified insects. Within the hour a number of amateur and professional authorities on prehistoric fossils had concluded that the last-known specimens of this now-abundant insect dated from the late Jurassic period, an epoch one hundred sixty million years distant.

Meanwhile no communication had been possible with anyone inside the courthouse. Telephone lines were dead. There was a great deal of concern. The fire department tried to open a path to the front doors with a high-pressure hose. The insects loved water. They reconverged almost as soon as they were washed aside. Men in awesome white suits, hoods, and boots waded toward the doors but became so covered with insects they couldn't see where they were going; they slipped and fell on smashed bodies as thick as cranberry sauce.

Not a few people, relating the phenomenon of the insects to the trial going on inside the courthouse, gathered spontaneously at dusk a block away. They prayed for divine intervention but were soon acrawl with vivacious, glittering red insects and fled in terror.

It was eight fifteen P.M. For more than four hours no one had emerged, not a sound had been heard from inside the courthouse.

116

In the courtroom to which Zarach' Bal-Tagh had been summoned, time had no meaning at all.

At the instant the clock stopped, the light of day, occult in its mathematics, reversed itself, spiraling in toward the center of the feverish eclipse.

The light changed swiftly; in the disorienting deepness of vermilion, faces glowed like pink ingots. A magnetic disturbance combed through each of them, huge as a stellar tide.

At each window tiny wings oscillated. Their room had become a nest, and they were food for the nest.

On the witness stand the defendant rose, and lowered his gaze to the captive spectators. To the jury of those who were no longer his peers. The radiance of his eyes painted the room with magenta shadows.

To each of them he gave clairvoyance; and from all but a few, he took reason.

They found themselves removed to the far edge of the universe, their little seething nest suspended over a void terrifying in its immensity, scorching in its blackness. Here the soul of a man had no more hope of survival than a drop of water in a desert, and they screamed telepathically in fright.

The defendant smiled at this tribute to the effectiveness of his initial exercise. Then his magic became harsher.

Those who tried to escape from their seats, to trample

others mindlessly and batter themselves against unyielding walls and doors, found themselves immobilized by various ingenious means.

Tommie Harkrider had taken only two steps before he felt a biting pain in his left ankle. He looked down and saw that he had stepped into a trap of sorts: the gaping jaws of a human skull. Strong teeth bit him to the bone.

At the prosecutor's table Gary Cleves could move his hands and feet, but not his head. His bearded chin was pressed against the top of the table and his extended tongue was impaled on a wooden stake. As he struggled to free himself the stake grew like a tree from the roots of his tongue; his body rotted to feed it. And in the branches of the tree that swelled above him deformed shapes stirred and spread their wings.

Opposite him Edith Leighton sat with her head bowed, almost on her chest. Alone in the ruddiness, the blood-splashed gloom that had turned other faces to anguished masks drawn in shadows, she glowed like a lantern. There were fierce pulses in the otherwise dormant flesh of her body. She was impervious to the horrors now visiting them, the withering vanity of the master of the revels, their oppressor. Her eyes were narrowed, but in them were steady depths. Inwardly she was a coldly burning skein of nerves, a puzzlebox of impulse, a psychic transmitter.

Louise Vale, the bereaved mother of Karyn, found herself on her back with her knees up, her belly a heaving mountain as she gave birth—to dribbling packs of rodents, which upon entrance into the air, began voraciously to pierce her thrombosed veins for nourishment.

The eyes of the oppressor touched them all in turn; his lurid alchemy raged in the secret mind.

Some were toughened by the assault: their minds held fast. Father James Merlo, acclimated to horrors, prayed steadfastly in support of Edith Leighton, prayed for a turning of the black torrent.

And still they had seen nothing of the oppressor's full power. They had yet to look into the face of Zarach' Bal-Tagh.

Gina Devon, her mind too still, like a glassy pond beneath the threat of a runaway moon, sought the strength of her husband. Turning to Conor, she found he had divided at the waist into two warring wolves, yellow-eyed: they snapped and slavered in each other's faces.

Lindsay Potter, violated once again by the crack of doom, embraced her pain and shuddered in orgasms that rubbed her raw; with nerves unbraided and flesh falling from her bones like drops of dark rain she sorrowed for a more powerful, truly consuming love.

WHO SEEKS ME? went the whisper around their minds.

Edith felt the stirrings, the craving for deliverance in the three jurors whom she also coveted: Mary Adelaide Hotchkiss, Ivan Mandelko, and Gerald Aughtman. She felt the confusion of their naked souls; she fought the further encroachment of Zarach' Bal-Tagh, who lied like the Serpent, flattered with a winkless eye. Her features all but disappeared in the scintillation from the sundial on her breast.

Her own power gave the oppressor pause. But then, enriched by the violence around him, by primal fear and blood, he descended from the witness stand. And with each princely step, he stood taller.

Tommie Harkrider fell shuddering at the feet of the oppressor, who looked past him at Edith. Edith's own eyes waxed distantly behind the helm of white light that protected her.

He knew she could not, by herself, stop his transformation, his tumultuous growth.

With a beautifully disarming gesture, Zarach' Bal-Tagh revealed himself.

In the language they had all been given to understand— and speak—they heard him: the seductive lyre of his palate, the gracious, singing tongue.

His looks were a match for his voice: in the midst of red chaos, anarchy of the senses, self-torture, shone the redeemer's golden eyes, a brazzle in their ashen bones.

"I AM ZARACH'," he advised them.

"ONLY I CAN SAVE YOU."

"Yes, save us! Zarach'! Zarach'! Save us!" Threatened, groveling, they begged for a glint of his compassion.

Edith groaned, as if she lay in drugged sleep.

"WHO AM I?" Zarach' demanded.

"You are Lord!" they answered, forgetting pain, obsessed by his beauty.

He nodded devotedly. Eight feet tall, robed like the phoenix, he spread his arms to embrace them.

"No!" Edith shouted, in the only language they now understood. Almost no one heard her.

"THEN YOU SHALL BE SAVED," Zarach' said. "AND ALL OF YOUR KIN."

"All! All!"

"AND ALL OF THE PEOPLE OF THE EARTH WHO COME TO ME, AND PLEDGE THEMSELVES TO ME, THEY TOO SHALL BE MY CHILDREN."

"We will all come to you, Lord! We will follow you!"

"He is no messiah," Edith warned. "He is worse than death. He is the Endless Night!"

But they had suffered too much; they believed the lies of Zarach'. Many of them rejoiced in the dysangel's undeniable majesty: the caves of light at his temples, cheeks of milk and blood, mercy in the offered palm. His strong body attracting them as sky attracts the bird.

Even as he seduced the others Edith felt the boldness of Zarach' swelling like a storm-driven sea, rounding on the light of the sundial which she had so zealously conserved; the breadth and blackness of the wave approaching her scared her to the marrow. In this winding-sheet of salt rose heavy, mouthing things, to swallow the light from her breast—and then her powerless, emptied bones.

Strength, she murmured to herself, now sightless within the storm breaking around her head, wearied by the outcries of the nearly maddened souls she must somehow turn away from Zarach'.

Edith's hands were raised to her breasts, fingers pointing outward. The sundial glowed within her hands like a star exploding into thought.

Engrossed, she nursed it to a white noon of volatility. Then, refreshed, Edith hurled the equation of the light into the jury box, into the shadowed minds of Hotchkiss, Mandelko, Aughtman.

At the first tentative bonding of the tetrad, before its power could be released, Zarach' Bal-Tagh's siren song ended and he flew into a frenzy of hate. With the full resources of the demon-sorcerer he struck at them all. New horrors abounded in the courtroom.

In a dreary winter landscape Martin Vale sat sobbing,

surrounded by the truncated flesh of his daughter. He sorted through feet and hands and tresses trying to put her together again while nearby, crouching, Richard Devon with eyes lividly mad was eating the heart he held in streaming hands. Dark rays fell from the sun like petals from a blackened rose.

"WHO SEEKS ME?" Zarach' demanded.

"Zarach'!" they began again, wailing.

In the hands of Judge Knox Winford were the faces of his children, their throats swelling up from the cruel tendons of his wrists, eyes of fancy blue. He began sadly to applaud, ignoring their screams and then the sharp bone-crack, bringing his hands together again and again until the faces became squashed, mixed, unrecognizable.

The population of the courtroom doubled in an instant, became crowded with breath. There were ant forms, and fan-shaped serpents, and slinking noisome beasts of no known species. There were jaded ladies with the stingers of scorpions curled over their shoulders and perplexing eyes faithless as gold. A mob of youths fair-faced but grossly furred at the hips and wobbling on claws. Great cats, all ebony and ire, with the slowly stirring wings of jackdaws. Old demons in rouge and silk, the long nails of their hands whispering like rapiers for the unguarded soul. Late of this earth, they were the scarred, the treacherous, the corrupt. They contributed to the tumult until the thin, pure light of the cross of the tetrad shone through the bloodred murk.

The lesser demons panicked easily at the sight of the living cross that lay from the point of Edith's breastbone across the courtroom to the jury box. They went whining and howling and tumbling head over heels back to the Endless Night. They went empty-handed while Zarach' fulminated; he dwelled on Edith alone, source of his misery and potential defeat. His eye a weight of toppling stone, his countenance like the volcano towering over the sundial of Heraclio.

Bound by the law of the light, her energy committed, Edith trembled, clinging to her life as weightlessly as a damp leaf on a windowpane.

IT IS YOU WHO SEEKS ME, EDITH.

She had tried to prepare herself for pain, for the torment

of having her mind pressed and pressed again until it leaked drop by inky drop down the sheer white bone of her forehead. She had not been prepared for such outrageous confidence.

I do not.

Her anger at Zarach' nearly exhausted her; she had never felt this frail.

He drew closer, as close to the light as he dared; peering in, like a giant at a keyhole. Her eyelids fluttered, her pupils darkened with his handsome head.

WE SHALL SEE.

And when he withdrew to a more bearable distance he did so with a shrug. In the next instant with a snap of his fingers he shed his plumed but smoldering resurrection robe, stood naked as glass to her enchanted eye, a tower of mirrors, bright prisms of magic in which she saw (closing her eyes but seeing through the lids) what she most feared to see:

Herself.

No!

But there was a shaking in the air, in the chill and deathwatch mirrors: her veins were ripped from her flesh and writhed round the light like strangler fig.

The power of the tetrad began to wane; the light was dying.

In the many-mirrored, enslaving body of the demon Edith sank slowly to those depths where sorrow goes.

I must not fail.

Another flicker of his magic; Zarach' showed her the twin side of her nature, with every weakness, every flaw magnified into evil.

WE WILL WORK SO WELL TOGETHER, EDITH.

So little of the light left; his shadow falling swift and fatally.

It was the will of God that the shadow exist. And Zarach' was a part of God; powerful, yes, but imperfect. He could torment them, make them suffer. But in their suffering they were redeemed. This was the power they had over Zarach', and even as she weakened and prepared herself to lie down in the grave of his illusion, there was a last exultant flaring of Edith Leighton's spirit.

Edith reached for the sundial on the chain around her withered neck, and found the strength to snap the chain.

Turning, she hurled the little sundial toward the smoking red-eyed mirrors of the demon-magician.

In midflight the sundial began to glow again; to speed. It struck the body of Zarach' with the force and luminosity of a comet. Light erupted piercingly, intensified by every shattered facet; spears of light shot everywhere through the courtroom as the whirling, white-hot sundial penetrated more walls of cascading glass. Zarach' turned, falling to pieces, roaring like a tornado as glass streamed inward toward a distant spot of darkness, following the flight of the sundial. The courtroom was afire like a tropic noon, but heatlessly. Only the spot of darkness persisted, entry to the Endless Night, a whirlpool of stygian blackness terrible to contemplate.

Give him back to us, Edith prayed. *Give him up. Now.*

From out of the sink of darkness something came flying, almost too small at first to be grasped by the eye; then Edith realized it was a human body, small but perfectly formed, tumbling into the light. Just before it hit the floor it became the size of a man.

Richard Devon lay sprawled on his face, twitching, dazed, but with a cry for breath. In that instant the dark entry shrank to the size of a pinpoint; with a last stupefying shriek from an inhuman throat it closed altogether.

In Rich's outstretched hand was the sundial. Its light continued to flow over them like a warm and nourishing sea. Balm for the eyes, for the mind. No one stirred. Not one of them had the power to speak, or even to think very clearly: but there was no need for thought. They all had the same insatiable need, to bathe in the purifying light, and be cleansed.

117

In Heraclio several members of the Sundial community carried Sigrid gently from the plaza and put her to bed. She was trembling uncontrollably, and the muscle spasms continued for a while. Three of the women took turns rubbing her down. Part of the time she was conscious. She babbled happily, the way a new mother still under the influence of anesthesia will babble about the baby to whom she has given birth but hasn't yet seen. When Sigrid finally fell asleep, she would sleep for twenty hours straight.

118

Shortly before eleven o'clock that night in Chadbury, those observers still keeping watch on the courthouse witnessed the abrupt disappearance of the insects. The formless mass became cone-shaped, as if it was under the influence of an attractive force stronger than the gravitational field of earth. Then the head of the cone burst like a lanced boil and insects poured into the sky, staining the moon red. Swiftly this stain shrank in size, resembling a large spot in a blood orange. The spot continued to diminish until it was a pinpoint and could barely be seen by the naked eye.

Around the courthouse there were no reminders of the visitation; not so much as a single frayed wing remained on the windows or the lawn.

At the west end of the Chadbury green, where access to the green was blocked by a line of state police vehicles, Captain Moorman stood beside Police Chief Jim Melka; both men studied the entrance to the courthouse with binoculars.

"There's not one damn bug left," Melka muttered.

Moorman lowered his glasses and snapped at a subordinate, "Jim and I are going in. Keep everyone else *back*."

They drove the two short blocks to the courthouse in Moorman's car and lurched up the sloping lawn to the steps. As they got out of the car a courthouse door opened and a stout middle-aged woman carrying an attaché case stepped outside. She stiffened and looked around in shock, glanced at her wristwatch, shook it, held it to her ear. She drew back anxiously when the two policemen ran up the steps toward her. Her lips trembled as she tried to smile.

"How could it be dark already?" she said to Melka. Her voice squeaked.

"What's going on in there?" Moorman demanded. The woman looked oddly at him, frowning, as if she had found his tone accusatory.

"What? I'm sure I don't know what you mean. I just came down from the recorder's office—I couldn't have been there more than fifteen or twenty—" She gazed in fright at the black sky. "It can't be *so late.*"

From somewhere in the courthouse there was a gunshot, followed by a piercing scream.

The woman jumped and began, incoherently, to wail.

Moorman ignored her and looked at Melka. He knew in his bones where the shot had come from.

"Upstairs," he said. "Main court. Hurry."

119

On the threshold of consciousness Richard Devon moved slowly, his cheek dragging on the worn marble floor of the courtroom, his hands clenching and unclenching. Edith Leighton's sundial had fallen from his fingertips. With most of its energy dissipated, the sundial retained only a faint, warm, slightly animated aura.

The intensity of the light it had brought to the courtroom had dimmed to a shadowless summery twilight in which the figures of men and women stirred. All around him Rich heard them sighing, weeping quietly, rejoicing in whispers. He felt a sense of community to which he did not belong.

He felt something else: where an ugly growth had taken root in the conscious mind, a twisted dark mandrake crowding him to the outer edge of sanity, permitting him to exist only as an observer of his soulless life, there was now a contracting void. Yet he felt a remnant of a tidal pull, excruciating, twisting his bones; he smelled a scorched blackness, as if there was a blot in the comfortable twilight, like the head of a just-extinguished match. His nostrils were clogged with the odor. His hands, unbound, moved more frantically, fingers scrabbling for life, for safety. The marble was too smooth, too hard; he found no handholds. His eyelids fluttered. Blood surged. Adrenaline hit him like a round of chilled brandy, enlarging his perceptions, his panic and pain. He cried out deliriously.

120

Conor had his arms around his wife. He trembled windily, a spent and battered man, but felt himself on a sharp edge of exultation: the self-inflicted wounds of years, erupting all at once, now were clean from the fire and would heal; he would be stronger than before this reckoning. Half blinded by tears, Gina ran a hand over his face, her lingering fear of wolves vanishing as her fingertips were charged with the familiar rough tangle of his beard: she kissed him.

"You're all right. You're *you*. God be praised."

"God be praised," he repeated in a confident voice. Then he turned his head, straining, trying to distinguish one small cry in the babble around them.

"Listen. Wasn't that Rich? He needs help. Come on."

121

But Edith was the first to reach him.

With a slow hand she retrieved the sundial from the floor. Her face, in the steadfast light—an eternal amber enclosing them all like remnants, like ghostly husks—looked as worn and tightly shrouded as a mummy's. The bravery extinguished now. The lean flesh chilly and rendered close to the bone. The eyeways dark entries, sunken passages. She had given nearly all she had.

His eyes, open, asked for more. Pleaded.

"No, Richard. Stand on your own feet now. There's nothing else I can do for you."

He staggered getting up, nearly pitched head first to the marble floor. Then he straightened. He was steadier as his brother closed in, followed by Gina and Adam Kurland.

"Am I going to die, Conor?" Rich sobbed.

"No, kid. It'll be all right now."

Edith bowed her head slightly and walked away to lean against the defense table as, slowly, Rich was surrounded by others, including several members of the jury. Some, like Lindsay, who would have been afraid to touch or even speak to him before, now offered encouragement. Rich, unheeding, continued to weep.

No one paid attention to Martin Vale, no one was aware of the gun in his hand until Knox Winford, from the bench, shouted a warning.

By then the two-inch barrel of the revolver was nearly against Rich's forehead.

"Nothing's changed," Vale screamed. "She's still dead, isn't she? Don't any of you see? *Nothing's changed!*"

Rich clenched his teeth, now feeling the weight of the muzzle a half inch above his left eyebrow. It tilted his head back sharply. His eyes were fixed on air. Martin Vale was no more than a shadow to him, a cloud of hatred at the lower limit of his vision.

Rich felt, behind him, Conor's bulk, his brother's large hand stealthily loosening its grip on his upper arm.

"Don't, Conor," Rich said. The strong, violent pulse in his temple seemed to dare a bullet. But in the threat of death there was an ardor he welcomed, a clarifying force. *Stand on your own feet, Richard.* To Martin Vale he said, "If nothing's changed, then you have to kill me."

His charge, his admonition to Vale, had no immediate effect. They remained poised against each other in an atmosphere dense as a thunderstorm. The fatal shot was withheld. Yet Vale, stunned by the inevitability of his action, seemed to have no mind other than what was contained in his outstretched hand, no desire except to be rid of the lethal poison that slowly had been wrung from his body during the trial and was now concentrated like a boil on the tip of his tongue.

"Martin," his wife said behind him, her voice so slight and familiar it caused no change in his expressionless face, no ripple in the steel of his concentration, "it could have been a truck without brakes running a red light. It could have been her boat tipping over on the sound. It could have been a blood clot when she had her tonsils out, or a careless surgeon or too much anesthetic. Or a fall down a flight of stairs. A snake. A disease. A rapist. A fire."

Now her voice trembled; so did the hand that held the revolver at Rich's bloodless forehead. Louise came closer. She touched calmingly the nape of her husband's neck. Her face, half hidden by his large, motionless, totem head, had, in her sincerity and anguish, a kindled look, the glow of the salvationist.

"She was simply—taken from us. Now we know why. The truth is more terrible than anything we thought—but at least we know the truth. Martin—will you listen? Please. Come and sit down. I don't know if we're ever going to feel any better. But it'll be over."

Vale shuddered, and it became a small seizure. No one else moved; they had all dried up from fear. They watched him. Vale's mouth opened in a kind of grin. Death grinned at Richard Devon and withdrew.

Vale's hand fell away from Rich's forehead in a slow outward arc which Conor deftly intercepted, at the same time yanking Rich to one side and out of danger. As he snatched the revolver from Vale's unresisting hand, it fired. The bullet, traveling upward, shattered one of the chamberpot light fixtures near the judge's bench; fragments showered down as the fixture sparked. A woman screamed, but no one was cut by the pelting glass.

"Bailiff," Judge Winford called out, "put some lights on in here!"

After fifteen or twenty seconds the lights sprang on in the courtroom.

Caught in the sudden brilliance, expelled from the borderline of unreality between the Endless Night and the world in which they must resume their appointed places, most of them flinched or cringed; others shielded their eyes and bowed their heads.

Captain Moorman and Chief Melka came running into the courtroom with drawn guns. As soon as he saw them, Conor slipped the Airweight revolver he had taken from Martin Vale into a pocket of his jacket. Vale, in his wife's embrace, still shuddered, the broad white wings of his hair slumped over his ears. With the wick of his passion snuffed, there was no life at all in his eyes. She led him as easily as her own shadow to the rows of seats, sat with her mouth to his ear, consoling, stroking, loving him.

"Your Honor—" Melka began.

"What's the meaning of this?"

Moorman said, "We heard a shot and—"

Winford looked up from rubbing his temples and said, "You mean the light fixture? It exploded. No harm done. Bailiff, will you please get a broom and sweep up that glass?"

"Yes, Your Honor," said the perplexed bailiff.

"Gentlemen," Winford said to the policemen, not concealing his irritation, "you're in a court of law. Put those guns away. You've disrupted proceedings."

"Disrupted?" Melka said incredulously, looking around while trying to holster his gun. Only a few people were in their seats. Most of them looked as if they'd just walked away from a plane crash. Several jurors were standing near the defendant on the floor. There was a livid round spot on the defendant's forehead that looked as if it had been made by the muzzle of a revolver. Conor Devon had one hand on his brother, as if he were holding him up. Tommie Harkrider was leaning against the prosecution's table with one hand, and the other hand was pressed against his chest. He was the color of day-old hollandaise. "Your Honor," Melka continued, "do you realize what time it is? And court is still in session? Don't you know what's been happening outside?"

Winford pounded his gavel hard. "Yes, this court is still in session! It will remain in session until this time next week if need be, and in the meantime we can do without further interruptions. Do I make myself clear?"

There was a mild stirring in the courtroom; all of them, including the defendant, turned to look at Knox Winford.

Then, spontaneously, applause began.

Winford looked enlightened, and rewarded. He let the applause run for a few seconds. Then he nodded, smiled briefly, and gaveled for order.

"All right, I want everyone back in their seats. Will the defendant please take the stand?"

Rich seemed too dazed to move. Conor, after another look at the judge, guided his brother by the elbow.

Tommie Harkrider brushed past them on his way to the bench. He didn't move quickly. His complexion was still poor. He opened and closed his mouth several times, as if to get his wind up as he stared at the judge.

Knox Winford leaned over the bench toward him.

"I couldn't quite make out what you said, Mr. Harkrider."

"I said—" Tommie sputtered. Then he caught fire. "SAID JUST WHAT THE HELL IS GOING ON HERE?"

"A trial is going on, Mr. Harkrider. And if you ever address me in that tone of voice again, you'll be held in contempt. Please proceed."

"Proceed? With what? This is a mistrial! I demand that you declare a mistrial! We were all—we've all been under— what happened here was—hallucination! Yes! Some kind of—of mass hypnosis, by God!"

Where she sat with her head lowered, Edith's lips moved. "Not by God, sir," she murmured. No one heard her. But the sound of her own voice, the wan attempt at humor, stimulated her. She straightened and looked at Tommie Harkrider.

"Look at them!" Tommie waved his hands at the jurors. "You saw them! Congratulating this murderer like he was some kind of hero!"

"That's not fair," Mary Adelaide Hotchkiss shot back.

"Mr. Harkrider, a last warning," Winford said, his gavel poised.

Thomas Horatio Harkrider took a step away from the bench and rocked on his tender feet. His lips quivered. He struck his thighs with his fists. He said, in a controlled voice, "There has been a theft of reason in this courtroom; I will not stand for a rape of justice as well. How the—the display we were made to suffer was achieved I don't know, but I will not, even at the risk of being held in contempt, continue to be a party to—"

"Mr. Harkrider—"

"I am, sir, a believer in the sanctity of the courtroom,

the majesty of the law. I will stake my life on my—my reputation, my veracity, my dedication, my *love,* sir, my love for the legal profession.'' And suddenly Tommie had no more control. His face sagged and he gushed tears. Twitching and turning, he looked up at the judge like a hurt and indignant child.

Winford sank back wearily in his leather chair.

''Mr. Harkrider.''

''I'm—sorry, Your Honor.''

''We are going to continue. Try to calm yourself. You and your colleagues for the state may file whatever motions you feel are called for upon the conclusion of this trial. But let me say a few words. I think my ability to reason, to separate fantasy from reality, is as good as the next man's. I haven't been drunk since I was seventeen years old. I've never taken a drug stronger than aspirin. Nor have I been treated by a psychiatrist for mental difficulties. I sleep well at night and I don't have nightmares and I've never claimed to have much of an imagination.

''There are two things of which I am certain: if I were in a war, I would damn well know when I was being shot at. And if I were in hell, I'd know the devil when I saw him.''

Winford paused for a long time, as if his voice had given out. When he spoke again it was in such a low tone the microphone mounted on his bench barely amplified his words enough to carry through the courtroom.

''Well, today I saw him. Therefore by simple logic I'd have to say that for a little while I was in hell. We all were. Some of us eventually will deny that, and some will try to forget it. Every one of us will deal, in his own time and his own way, with what he saw and experienced. In the meantime—we have a duty to perform. My head aches and I want very much to go home. So let us get on with it.''

Judge Winford looked at Edith.

''Mrs. Leighton, are you able to proceed for the defense?''

''Yes, Your Honor.''

''He is still your witness, Mr. Harkrider.''

Rich turned his face to the prosecutor. He could not have looked more terrified or drained of hope than if he had been on the chopping block. His teeth chattered and came together.

Tommie studied him in confusion and despair. He seemed about to speak. His shoulders lifted and fell.

"Mr. Harkrider, do you have further questions for this witness?"

Tommie shook his head, turned quickly, and walked back to the prosecution's table, where he slumped down beside Gary Cleves. Gary looked at him, and then away.

"Mrs. Leighton?" Winford inquired. "Would you care to redirect?"

Edith rose, very slowly, gripping the edge of the table with both hands.

"No, Your Honor," she said. "The defense rests."

122

As part of her summation to the jury, Edith Leighton said, "I have no doubt in my heart that you will find Richard Devon not guilty by reason of demonic possession. But there are questions that must be answered, tonight, by all of us—although the hour is late, and we are all very tired.

"As long as there are evil men who pass from this earth and live in the Endless Night, there will be the likelihood of evil revisited on human beings. Is there a remedy for this evil?

"The possibility for sin and error is consistent with, and inseparable from, life itself. More force of character, more power for good, is displayed by the sinner who ultimately redeems himself than by the meekly obedient. Therein lies our greatest glory, and a clear and present danger. Such power is the most precious thing we know in life: the determination to be masters of ourselves. With it, we are a force that defeats the darkness.

"Without it, we are doomed.

"Richard has suffered from the murder of Karyn Vale; through your power he will gradually be restored, and relieved of this crippling guilt.

"Through your verdict on his life he will achieve life, and the opportunity to make himself whole again."

EPILOGUE

Heraclio

The trial of Richard Devon ended shortly after midnight on the first of July. After deliberating for no more than twenty minutes, the jury returned a verdict of not guilty by reason of demonic possession.

Events that had taken place on the final day of the trial—the infestation of primordial insects, the apparent suspension of time within the courthouse—already had caused a morbid sensation, which was intensified upon release of news of the verdict.

The news itself was fashioned by the twenty-five journalists who had attended the trial from the beginning, and who were present on that marathon last day. They reported for the TV cameras or filed with their respective newspapers and services stories that were factual as far as they went, as similar in tone and content as if they had reached a communal decision on what to say and how to say it. None of them referred to Zarach' Bal-Tagh's appearance in the courtroom. Each journalist depended for his living on his objectivity, judgment, sobriety, and obedience to the facts. Each of them knew very well what he had seen. But to experience Zarach' was one thing. To describe him was another.

The human mind is very well equipped to deal with irrationalities and to tidy up the inconsistencies which everyday living presents. And human behavior, even on a mundane level, is more often than not inexplicable, perverse, and even bizarre; behavior dictated by the intricacies of surviving in a world in which there is too much competition among the would-be survivors, too many demands and not enough rewards, and too much news of all kinds, much of it morbid, oppressive, or fear-provoking. The nursery school teachers running a kiddie porn ring. The respected obstetrician with a collection of more than a thousand human fetuses in a trunk in his basement. The necrophiliacs in a California mortuary. The fullmoon snipers. The cow-pasture ritualists. The sadist tinkering with packaged headache remedies in drugstores. The religious paragon sacrificing children in an endless desert war.

Just as there was no beginning or end to the horrors of Zarach', there was no way to deal adequately with his manifestation in words. A few of the journalists, secretly, tried. And tore up what they had written. After Chadbury not many of the journalists remained in the profession. Not unexpectedly, they found they had reached a junction in their lives where simpler pursuits, a less detached involvement with human beings, would be good for their souls. And eventually they achieved peace of mind.

The other spectators and participants were reticent in response to endless questions about the last day of the trial. There was no way to say what they felt. But their silence was not hysterical, it was meditative.

Thomas Horatio Harkrider went back to New York, and issued dire prophecies about the turmoil that would ensue in the criminal courts of America if *Vermont* v. *Devon* was not overturned by the state supreme court. But Gary Cleves failed to file the appropriate motions; ten days after the verdict in district court, he abruptly resigned as state's attorney for Haden County. He went into private practice and prospered. In the year that followed, five pleas of demonic possession in capital cases were entered in five different states; in each case the jury rejected the plea and found the defendants guilty as charged. The plea of demonic possession did not become the rage that Tommie Harkrider had predicted. He died, peacefully and in his sleep, of a cardiac event, almost one year to the day he had risen to address the prospective jurors in the Chadbury courthouse.

Conor and Gina went home, stopping en route to retrieve their daughter from the convent in New Hampshire. Conor cut back on his drinking and returned to the wrestling ring. A knee injury ended that career a few months later. Gina moved her boutique to the new mall in Lowell, a move that coincided with an upswing in the country's economic cycle. Things went well for her. She supported the family until Conor wrapped up his Ph.D. in comparative literature and began teaching at a small college near Joshua.

Adam and Lindsay were married four days before Christmas in the Catholic church in Braxton. Even before the trial Lindsay had begun attending Mass again, and her experience with Zarach' Bal-Tagh was just the impetus needed to bond her strongly to her faith. Her wedding present to Adam was a solid gold sundial on a chain with the dates of the trial engraved on the back. His present to her was a full partnership in the firm of Kurland Bates Harpold and Potter.

Father James Merlo was invited to the wedding, but by then he was involved in a case of possession in a remote mission village in the highlands of Cameroon and couldn't make it.

The principal in the trial might well have become the object of as much speculative publicity as any luminary of the twentieth century. Because there were far more questions about Richard Devon than there were answers. But sixteen hours after he was acquitted, Richard Devon, accompanied by his brother and two of his lawyers, eluded packs of investigative reporters and disappeared.

And Edith, declining to give interviews, returned to Heraclio after a brief stopover in London.

When she heard the Land-Rover pull up outside the double walls that surrounded the house, Sigrid Torgeson got up from the mat on the floor of the veranda where she had been meditating and said to the man sitting silently nearby, "Edith's here." She saw a rearrangement of the facial muscles that, not too long ago, might have resulted in a smile; but again, the afternoon shadows were tricky, and maybe she'd only fooled herself into thinking that Philip had reacted. She slipped into her sandals and went out to open the gates.

Edith had gotten out of the Land-Rover and was pulling her luggage from the back. She moved jerkily and impatiently. In the blaze of sun her face looked blanched, except for the hard butternuts of her eyes. Her brows needed plucking. There was a heavy squiggle of a vein at one sunken temple, and wispy commas of gray hair were sticking to her forehead. She was so pale and thin that

Sigrid was alarmed. But even as Sigrid watched, the skin of Edith's face was beginning to lose its deathly grayness, as if in these first moments of homecoming she had begun to cast off veils.

Sigrid gave Edith a hearty welcoming kiss and tried to take the luggage from her. Edith shook her head curtly, then shrugged and with a backward nod indicated the young man behind the wheel of the Rover, who was gazing vacantly through the dusty windshield. He had driven them all the way from the airfield at Los Arroyos. Now he just sat there, looking from the ugly blistered flank of the Mountain of Fire to the cool green lagoon at the base of the cliff. And back again.

"How is he?" Sigrid said to Edith in a low voice.

"In that miserable transition state; he is gradually losing his self-loathing and self-pity but isn't quite ready to accept himself as a useful human being. He is convinced that because Karyn's life has ended, his own can have no value. The usual nonsense that I'm too old and impatient to deal with."

"I'm not. But what do I say to him?"

Edith, with a quizzical little smile, stared up at her for a few moments. "It will amaze me if you have to say much of anything." And she went into the house, calling cheerily to her husband.

Sigrid looked around thoughtfully at Rich, who hadn't yet taken notice of her. After a few moments of standing there edgily she walked up to the Land-Rover and intruded on his view, the cool shadow of her head eclipsing his heated face. He looked startled. Her blue eyes were wide and tranquil, but there was a hint of confrontation in her gaze.

"I'm Sigrid. Welcome to Sundial."

He nodded and licked his drying lips. There was a pained cleft between his eyes. He resumed staring up at the mountain, as if he had taken flight only to find himself in an airy prison.

She knew, oh how well she knew, what he must be feeling. Sigrid had not murdered anyone during her own captivity, but for a year after being exorcised she had felt so abused and defiled it was difficult to look anyone in the eye. Time and this place, the fellowship of the Sundial, had healed her. Richard would come around, she was confident. He had to. Because they needed him badly.

"I'm sure it's all right if you sit there the rest of the day. But aren't you tired? Wouldn't you like to come in?"

He stirred and flinched as the changed angle of his face brought the sun to his eyes like the point of a spear. He looked around for shade; for a blade of grass.

"I've never—seen anything like this," he said, his tone dismayed. "I don't know what to think."

"Who can tell?" Sigrid said. She put a hand on his right forearm, which was rocklike: he still had a tight grip on the steering wheel. She leaned closer to him. The wind lifted her blond hair, and it fluttered across his sunburnt cheek, softly enclosed his throat. Again she caught his eye; this time held it. His expression didn't change, but his lips parted slightly. She detected a quickened breath and, beneath the skin, the one vital impulse beyond the will of any man to control—the longing, the need for another human being.

She nodded, just a little, and smiled at him.

"Maybe it's home, Richard," Sigrid said.

SPECIAL PREVIEW

Here is a sizzling scene from SHATTER,
the next exciting TOR novel
from John Farris,
coming in June

. . . Anneliese was using the toilet when they came in.
Two or three men. She had only a startled glimpse before
all lights but one went out and she was snatched up with
her pantyhose below her knees. A gloved hand sealed her
mouth before she could scream. They were wearing black
stocking masks.

She tried to bite and tried to claw, humiliated by her
nakedness. Her legs were neatly bound together by the
mobbed pantyhose. The skirt had fallen off. They handled
her firmly, without roughness, and immediately she sensed
it wasn't going to be rape. What then, murder? Only the
ceiling light in the shower had been left on; it provided
faint illumination through the opaque glass. But there was
enough light to reveal all of the thin pointed blade in the
hand of one of the men. Her insides felt like cold rusted
machinery. Her neck, which had been twisted as she struggled, ached. She felt an involuntary dribble of urine.

Three of them for sure. The third man, the one with the
knife, had picked up the expensive borrowed skirt. His
knife was like a razor. Quickly he made strips of the
cambric before her eyes. Then the other two, holding her
arms behind her back, still gagging her, offered her up to
the knife wielder like a sacrificial virgin.

He was careful as he slashed the *blouson* to rags, not
drawing even a drop of blood. But by then Anneliese had
stopped struggling. Her head was dizzy with horror, her
vision blurring.

They jammed one of the cotton gloves in her mouth,
dropped her on the pile carpet. For a few moments the one
with the knife held her head up by the hair. Anneliese's
face was inches from the flat, stocking-black face. She
could see the glint of eyes, the mashed-down nose. Her
hands and feet were cold. She had the highly stressed,
roller-coaster feeling that comes just before fainting.

But there was something else, a faint odor of yesterday's perfume, and she realized that it wasn't a man who held her after all.

"We won't forget you, Anneliese."

Words in a windy tunnel. She was released. She didn't feel the soft drub of her head hitting the carpet again. . . .

JOHN FARRIS

"America's premier novelist of terror. When he turns it on, nobody does it better."　　—Stephen King

"Farris is a giant of contemporary psychological horror."
　　—Peter Straub